TIMELINE OF THE PLANET OF THE APES

THE DEFINITIVE CHRONOLOGY

By Rich Handley

For my brother,

Eric Tyner (1981-2001),

and my father,

Vincent Handley (1946-2008),

who never met an ape

they didn't like.

Book layout and design by Paul C. Giachetti

Cover art by Patricio Carbajal

Cover design by Joseph Bongiorno

ISBN-13: 978-0-615-25392-3

Library of Congress Cataloging-in-Publication Data

First Edition: November 2008

10 9 8 7 6 5 4 3 2 1

CONTENTS

THE TIMELINE

APPENDICES

— Acknowledgements —
The Only *Good* Humans...

This book was made possible by the contributions, great and small, of many individuals. My heartfelt thanks go out to the following:

Planet of the Apes creators Dan Abnett, Sam Agro, Gary Chaloner, Lowell Cunningham, Ian Edginton, Roland Mann, Charles Marshall, Tom K. Mason, Doug Moench, Jorge Morhain, Sergio Mulko, Joe O'Brien, Ty Templeton, Sonny Trinidad (and his children, Norman and Cherry), Mike Valerio and John Whitman for sharing information about their unpublished *Apes* work—and, in some cases, the work itself.

My appreciation goes out to James Aquila, Neil Foster, Hunter Goatley, Graham Hill, Bill Hollweg, Chris Lawless, Alan Maxwell, Valerie Parish, Greg Plonowski, Alex Ruiz, Glen Sheetz, Chris Shields, Michael Whitty and others who have kept the simian spirit alive. Kudos also to Dave Ballard, Dean Preston and John Roche of *Simian Scrolls* (to learn more about this informative *Planet of the Apes* publication, e-mail john@johnroche6.wanadoo.co.uk) and Terry Hoknes of *Ape Chronicles* (planetoftheapesfanclub.com). Thanks also to Dave, Dean and James for expertly proofing the manuscript (blame them if you find any errors), and to Brian "Doc" O'Neill of Sci-Fi Storm (scifistorm.org) for transcribing the Blu-Ray set's new ANSA footage.

This book would never have been completed without the design and layout expertise of Paul C. Giachetti. Also vital to this work's creation was illustrator Patricio Carbajal, whose stunning artwork graces the cover. Thanks also to Joseph Bongiorno for his initial cover layouts; Tim Parati for his generous scanning help; Mark Terlino for font assistance; Michael Andrews for his eagle eyes; Dario Sciola, Malcolm Burbridge, Wayne Lawton and Tri-ring for help procuring rarities; and Edward Gross for inspiring me to write this book.

Finally, special thanks to my parents and siblings for being so supportive—and, most importantly, to my wife Jill and our children, Emily and Joshua, for waiting patiently like good little monkeys while I completed the manuscript.

— FOREWARD —
It's a Madhouse...
and It's All Mom's Fault

Well... my mother and a faceless spinning cameraman, that is.

My fascination with *Planet of the Apes* began in 1977. Like many children in New York, I lived for *The 4:30 Movie*, a daily film showcase airing on ABC's local Channel 7 affiliate at 4:30 (p.m., of course—in those days, the only thing on TV at 4:30 a.m., besides a variety of off-the-air test patterns, was static).

The films were edited, and I watched them on a small black-and-white set with a 13-channel dial, a wire antenna and a second dial for UHF. But that didn't matter—*The 4:30 Movie* introduced me to such classics as *Journey to the Center of the Earth*, *Fantastic Voyage*, Adam West's *Batman*, *The Pink Panther* series, *Westworld* (and its sequel, *Future World*), *The Land That Time Forgot*, *Godzilla*, *Ben-Hur*, *The Omega Man* and *Soylent Green* (apparently, Channel 7 had a Charlton Heston fixation).

But my most vivid memories of *The 4:30 Movie* were of "*Planet of the Apes* Week." Between 1977 and 1981 (when ABC replaced *The 4:30 Movie* with, of all things, *People's Court*), Channel 7 aired the first four *Apes* films—three if an *ABC After School Special* ran on Wednesday—as an annual marathon. (The fifth *Apes* film, *Battle for the Planet of the Apes*, aired during "Sci-Fi Week" since the first film was split into two parts, shown on Monday and Tuesday.) This was before VHS, DVD, DVR and other home-viewing options, so being able to see the *Apes* films, long after they'd left theaters, was a *big deal*.

I had never seen *Planet of the Apes* before, having been born the same year the first film hit theaters. I was hooked, and developed a real passion for the series—as much as any kid just adding a second digit to his age could—but that wasn't why it was so important to me. No, the reason I most looked forward to "*Planet of the Apes* Week" was that it was something my mother and I could do together. It became a tradition. I get my sci-fi addiction from her, and the movies, TV shows and books I'm most into, she usually is as well. So when it came time for Channel 7 to air its annual—mostly complete—*Apes* film festival, my mom and I made sure my homework was done, dinner was in the oven and our bladders were empty (there were far fewer commercials on TV in those days).

As the clock ticked 4:30, we'd relax in front of the set, giddy with anticipation as the familiar *4:30 Movie* logo would come onto the screen. That's where the faceless spinning cameraman comes in. As anyone from New York over age 30 will recall, *The 4:30 Movie* featured an animated camera operator spinning around to aim his lens at the viewers, followed by a sea of yellow "7"s (which I saw as grey at the time) and accompanied by a catchy orchestral theme (check it out on Youtube—you'll be humming it for days). Just as *Star Wars* fans get excited when the Twentieth Century Fox and Lucasfilm logos herald the start of a film in that series, so did this animated cameraman signify the start of "*Planet of the Apes* Week" for the New York television viewing audience of the late 1970s.

In the nearly 30 years since *The 4:30 Movie* and its glorious theme weeks went off the air, my *Apes* mania may have waned a bit as I acquired other interests, started a career, got married and had children…but it's never gone away. I devoured the TV series, then the cartoons, and—ironically, not until I was an adult—the comic books. I even enjoyed Tim Burton's remake to some extent, which led to my joining *Apes* e-fandom and, a few years back, my involvement with a fan project to translate some long-overlooked, Spanish-language *Apes* comics into English (archived at http://potav.kassidyrae.com/simios.html). This culminated in my creation of an online *Planet of the Apes* timeline, The Hasslein Curve, which evolved into the book you now hold.

I still love the *Planet of the Apes* series, and as I turn 40 this year along with those films, my memories of watching their edited *4:30 Movie* versions are a large part of their continued appeal. In fact, my mother and I still have our own little "*Planet of the Apes* Weeks" from time to time, so the 4:30 tradition lives on. I can genuinely say this book would not exist without her. Thanks, Mom… and thank *you*, faceless spinning cameraman.

Rich Handley
August 2008

— INTRODUCTION —
Time-Traveling on a Highway of Infinite Lanes

"A planet where apes evolved from men?!"
—Charlton Heston (as Col. George Taylor)

When Charlton Heston's Taylor summed up the madhouse of a future he'd entered in 1968's *Planet of the Apes*, he wasn't entirely accurate—the apes had not actually *evolved* from man, so much as inherited the Earth in the wake of man's evolutionary and revolutionary downfall. Still, when the film hit theaters, audience members experienced the same thrilling mixture of shock and wonder that gripped Taylor.

Four sequels, two television series, a film remake, a dozen-plus novels and more than 120 comics later, *Planet of the Apes* remains a living, breathing universe as it celebrates its fortieth anniversary this year. Though not quite as mainstream as "the four stars" (*Star Trek*, *Star Wars*, *Stargate* and *Battlestar Galactica*), the *Apes* mythos—created by French novelist Pierre Boulle in his classic *La planète des singes* ("The Monkey Planet"), and crafted for the big screen by Rod Serling, Michael Wilson, Paul Dehn and others—is a four-star saga all its own, with its own share of loyal fans who watch and rewatch, read and re-read, endlessly debating these and other questions:

Which film was the best—and the worst? Was Tim Burton's "re-imagining" a worthy addition, or a disastrous disappointment? Did Taylor intentionally destroy the Earth, or was the bomb's detonation an accident? Was Brent a compelling new character, or just a bland replacement for Taylor? How could the apes have learned to think and speak in so short a span of time? Where and when does each story take place, given the films' contradictory settings? Where do the TV series and cartoons fit into the picture? And what's with the giant brain jars, anyway?

A MATTER OF TIMING

One hotly debated topic involves the fourth dimension—namely, do the films form a circular chronology, with three through five leading to one and two, then back to the last three...or does the final trilogy create an alternate, more optimistic future, canceling out the dismal world seen in the first two? Strong evidence exists to support both stances. Some maintain that Dehn intended to create a circular timeline when he wrote the sequels, with Cornelius and Zira beginning the cycle in Taylor's era, and him ending it in theirs. Others believe Caesar changed everything, citing discrepancies between the past as related in the first three films, and the events actually occurring in the final two. Those favoring a circular timeline dismiss such contradictions as historical inaccuracies in the Sacred Scrolls.

Debated just as fervently is the concept of

canonicity—that is, which stories to consider "real," and which to label as apocryphal. Many fans accept only the classic films, deeming all other incarnations irrelevant. Some accept the TV series and comics in their personal canon, while others embrace the cartoons and Burton's film, though both diverge so wildly from continuity that most consider each to exist in its own separate reality.

This book does not take sides in such disputes, for that would surely be a futile effort, doomed to failure for two reasons: first, fans already have their opinions on the subject, and no amount of timeline-reading would convince anyone otherwise; and second, it doesn't matter anyway, since it's all fiction. Rather than enter the "circular vs. changing" debate, *Timeline of the Planet of the Apes: The Definitive Chronology* merely documents when every event in the mythos occurs in relation to the rest. My goal is to present what happened when, and in which story, enabling readers to decide which elements to accept or discard, according to their own personal preferences.

The result is not a perfect fit, for the saga is a flawed construct. The TV series features dogs a thousand years after the plague. NASA and the U.S. Air Force are shown operating into the 21st century, despite the ape rebellion and nuclear war. The cartoon has Nova going by that name since childhood, long before Taylor first gave her the moniker. Virdon and Burke's spaceship blows up a second time in a little-known comic from Argentina. None of the many time-displaced astronauts know about the ape-controlled future, despite the news coverage of Cornelius' and Zira's arrival in 1973. Both the TV series and Apeslayer saga portray New York as intact and thriving long after it was leveled. Some sources place the final two films in California, even though the first two took place in New York. Attar, from Tim Burton's film remake, is said to be an orphan—and yet he knows his father. And, of course, Boulle's novel contradicts every account that came after it (or, more accurately, *they* contradict *it*).

MONKEYING WITH THE FUTURE

Still, even though continuity is not fluid, I've opted to keep everything on one timeline. Smoothing out the bumps along the way is half the fun, and (as stated) this isn't about judging canonicity, but rather preserving posterity. I've tried to work out the discontinuities, but in cases where that hasn't been possible, I've simply kept the contradictory accounts and commented the heck out of them (at times with tongue planted firmly in cheek).

Other *Apes* timelines, both online and in print, have incorporated only stories their creators have decided can be made to fit together as smoothly as possible (frequently just the classic five films, and sometimes the TV show), ignoring the cartoons, comic books, Burton remake and so forth. And that's fine—such chronologies have a different purpose than this book, in that they are intended to exclude rather than include, in order to fluidly avoid any snags. This volume, on the other hand, is meant to be all-inclusive; it's less concerned with seamless fits, and more with the bigger tapestry. No doubt this will rub some the wrong way, particularly with regard to Burton's "re-imagining" and the animated series, but I can only hope readers can still enjoy the book for what it represents.

A note on the Burton film: Combining his *Planet of the Apes* with the previous films on a single timeline might not be as ludicrous as it sounds. Ty Templeton, author of *Revolution on the Planet of the Apes* and a fan of the film, originally conceived his miniseries as tying all six films together. And writers Ian Edginton and Dan Abnett had hoped to do something similar during their stint on Dark Horse's comic based on Burton's re-imagining.

Though not overly well received by fans or critics, Burton's film *is* an official release based on Boulle's *The Monkey Planet*, and ultimately, I enjoy the challenge of trying to work in the unworkable—what's more, the comics and novels that spun off from that film are quite enjoyable (far more so than the film), and ignoring those works would be a shame. In truth, aside from the movie's framing story, in which Leo Davidson launches his pod through the anomaly and later returns to find an ape-controlled Earth, the entirety of that universe otherwise takes place on another planet, so continuity issues are actually quite minimal (major, perhaps…but minimal).

The thing to remember is that *Planet of the Apes* is a saga replete with time-hopping astronauts, scientists and soldiers—and not just in the films and TV shows, but in many of the comic books as well, including one unpublished comic starring, believe it or not, Thomas Edison. With time travel, there's infinite potential for altered histories and parallel universes. I can only hope those who pick up this book will keep in mind the purpose behind this timeline—namely, to set every event wherever its respective story places it, leaving fans to accept or discount specific tales or aspects of the franchise as they please.

Marvel's android gorillas, and the aforementioned brains in jars? Present. Ape ninjas and the simian Santa Claus? Included. Four different giant apes? Accounted for. Sentient gibbons and mandrills and baboons and bonobos, oh my? All here. Taylor's two daughters? Yep. Breck's *three* first names? Here as well. Three explanations for the plague? Incorporated as one. Apeslayer, Martian apes, Monstrous Rodents, Funky Monkeys and other bizarre characters and creatures? Got 'em all. Three different alien invasions—including a visit from *Alien Nation*'s Tenctonese refugees? Like the old Prego spaghetti-sauce commercial used to say…"it's in there."

And I've even managed to work in details from numerous unpublished tales—comics, novels and cartoons—along the way, thanks to the kind assistance of the creative teams behind such lost gems (see the Title Index on page 253).

MARVELING AT THE PAST

In issue #11 of its 1970s *Planet of the Apes* magazine, Marvel Comics published a timeline by Jim Whitmore detailing the events of each film alongside those of its own comics, and filling in gaps along the way. Despite some factual gaffes and leaps of logic, that timeline stands as a solid basis for dating the mythos.

As such, I have used that timeline as the backbone for my own chronology, fixing Marvel's snafus along the way and adding many stories that hadn't yet existed—and, hopefully, not creating any new errors in the process. Dayton Ward also based his *Apes* timeline—published in Paul A. Woods' *The Planet of the Apes Chronicles*—on Whitmore's, adding several tales from Adventure Comics to the mix.

Both Whitmore's and Ward's chronologies adhere to a circular timeline, as does another packaged with the *Planet of the Apes* Widescreen 35th Anniversary Edition DVD, whereas a chronology included with the 40th Anniversary Collection Blu-Ray set employs alternate histories. For the purpose of this book, I've referenced all four timelining efforts.

In addition, I've worked out birth years for many characters from the films and TV shows. When specific dates are impossible to pin down, I've established spans of time in which they likely occurred. In determining the characters' birth years, I've adhered to any ages specified in print or dialog. For the rest, I've followed a simple formula: subtracting the actor's age when the film or episode was produced from the year in which that tale takes place.

CHANGING LANES
AND CURVING TIME

In *Escape from the Planet of the Apes*, Dr. Otto Hasslein explains time as a highway of infinite lanes, each stretching from the past to the future. One can alter the future, Hasslein postulates, by changing lanes. (The orangutan philosopher Virgil later proposes the same theory in *Battle for the Planet of the Apes*—an irony, given Hasslein's efforts to prevent the apes from dominating mankind in the first place.) In *Beneath the Planet of the Apes*, Brent describes the time-warp through which his spaceship has passed as a Hasslein Curve, named for Dr. Hasslein's theories of infinite regression, which Taylor's crew proved correct in the first film.

Every time someone crosses the time barrier—the Hasslein Curve—in either direction, it's possible for history to become modified. If so, given the astounding number of time-trips in this mythos (see "A Brief History of Time Travel" on page 245) this renders the whole "circular vs. changing" debate a far more complex question, for instead of two or three histories, we now have the potential for many more—infinitely more, in fact—which could explain the number of Ziras, Corneliuses, Zaiuses, Novas, Urkos and Brents in the various incarnations.

Planet of the Apes history could very well be neither a circular loop nor an "A or B" set of divergent highway lanes, but rather a Möbius strip embedded in an Escher landscape twisted up in a pretzel and tied up in a sailor's knot, continuously looping back upon itself, readjusting with each successive time-trip and enabling all of the various contradictory incarnations to occur on the same continuous, ever-changing loop. Sorting out one timeline from the next thus becomes virtually impossible.

A further note: I've opted to leave fan fiction off of the timeline. There are some excellent fanfics out there, such as Mike McColm's "Return to Yesterday" and the audio adventure *Values*, by Dave Ballard, both of which offer possible fates for the TV series characters. Then there's *Beware the Beast*, by Ballard and Neil Foster, which tells the story of Gideon, an ape hunter who goes from predator to prey when a human tribe fights back, chasing him to the crash site of a certain spacecraft from the second film. These and several other fan stories are better written and illustrated than some of the licensed tie-ins, and would certainly be worthy of official publication.

Unfortunately, there's just no way to be all-inclusive with fan-based tales, and quality control is never a given with such stories anyway. That said, I urge readers to check out these particular pieces—*Beware the Beast* at Hunter's *Planet of the Apes* Archive (http://pota.goatley.com); and "Return to Yesterday," *Values* and other fine tales at Kassidy Rae's *Planet of the Apes*: The Television Series site (http://potatv.kassidyrae.com, which also offers access to *Simian Scrolls*, a fan magazine produced by Ballard, John Roche and others). Kassidy and Hunter have archived a combined treasure trove of forgotten *Apes* gems on their sites, so check them out.

And for those new to the *Planet of the Apes* saga, a Viewing/Reading Order timeline is available on page 241.

Okay, the ground rules have been set and the timeline awaits. Sit back, grab a banana and chug some grape juice-plus…it's time to go ape.

— Abbreviation Key —

Listed below each timeline entry is the title of the work from which it was derived, followed by a three-letter abbreviation in parenthesis, indicating the publisher or studio that produced that work, and the medium in which it was presented. For readers' convenience, a handy quick-glance version is provided throughout the timeline. Here is a key to those abbreviations.

PUBLISHER / STUDIO

AB .... ABC-TV
AC .... Adventure / Malibu Comics
AW .... Award Books
BB .... Ballantine Books
BN .... Bantam Books
BW .... Brown Watson Books
CB .... CBS-TV
CV .... Chad Valley Sliderama
DH .... Dark Horse Comics
ET .... Editorial Mo.Pa.Sa.
FX .... 20th Century Fox
GK .... Gold Key / Western Comics
HE .... HarperEntertainment Books
HM .... Harry K. McWilliams Assoc.
MC .... Marvel Comics
MR .... Mr. Comics / Metallic Rose
NB .... NBC-TV
PR .... Power Records
SB .... Signet Books
TP .... Topps
UB .... Ubisoft

MEDIUM

a .... animated series
b .... book-and-record set
c .... comic book or strip
d .... trading card
e .... e-comic
f .... theatrical film
k .... storybook
m .... magazine article
n .... novel or novelization
p .... promotional newspaper
r .... recorded audio fiction
s .... short story
t .... television series
u .... unfilmed script or story
v .... video game
x .... Blu-Ray exclusive
y .... young adult novel

TIMELINE OF THE PLANET OF THE APES

THE DEFINITIVE CHRONOLOGY

Part 1: Prehistory of the Apes (before 1972)

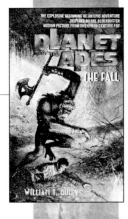

c. 1 BILLION B.C.

◆ Comets bombard Ashlar, a planet far from Earth, causing great pain to the dominant lifeform there—the Great Nest, a species of brachiopods controlled by a primitive insectile hive-mind known as the Core. This leaves the planet covered in massive craters that, over time, form mountainous valleys.

Planet of the Apes: The Fall, Chapter 3 (HE-n)

NOTE: This planet will, a billion years hence, be the site of Semos' uprising, as revealed in Tim Burton's Planet of the Apes *"re-imagining." The name Ashlar appears in William Broyles' initial script.*

c. 1445 B.C.

◆ Moses writes *Genesis*, the first book of *The Holy Bible*, espousing the Judeo-Christian belief that God created man in his own image. According to the *Bible*, man was chosen by God to rule over all other species on Earth, and will remain God's favored species until the End of Days.

Real Life

NOTE: This and other "Real Life" entries are included to set an ironic stage for the future, in which both religious and scientific dogma will ultimately turn on their ends. By amusing coincidence, one of Charlton Heston's most famous movie roles was as Moses in The Ten Commandments.

1859

◆ English naturalist Charles Darwin publishes *The Origin of Species*, presenting his theory of evolution. The fifth edition adds the phrase "survival of the fittest," purporting that those species most able to adapt will emerge as dominant. A radical change from contemporary thought, his ideas are met with skepticism.

Real Life

1871

◆ Darwin publishes *The Descent of Man*, making explicit connections between man and ape, and claiming man evolved from a lower order of animal to one capable of self-conscious thought. He sees man's mind as the accidental outcome of random variations over time, his achievements dependent on the evolution of articulate language. As with *The Origin of Species*, this volume is criticized by the religious, who accuse Darwin of robbing mankind of its special place in the universe, and of denying God's existence.

Real Life

SHORTLY AFTER 1871

◆ Dr. Foucault, proprietor of Foucault's Institute for Mental Incurables, experiments on patients, hoping to denounce Darwinism, confirm Biblical creationism and prove man did not evolve from apes. He and his assistant Dugan build a time machine and send patient Sebastian Thorne to the year 2142, intending to retrieve him after he's studied the future. Ironically, that future is ape-controlled—instead of retrieving Thorne, the machine brings back a gorilla warrior named Col. Urchak.

Urchak's Folly #4: "Chapter Four—The War" (AC-c)

NOTE: With this story, Gary Chaloner pays homage to Edgar Rice Burroughs' Tarzan series. The novel Tarzan Alive, *by Philip Jose Farmer, establishes the apeman's birth in 1888; lost in the jungle as an infant, Tarzan is raised by the maternal Kala, a member of a tribe of hybrid apes, led by the ferocious Kerchak, that possess the power of speech. According to Chaloner, the similarity of the names Urchak and Kerchak is intentional.*

◆ Foucault and Dugan subdue the speaking gorilla and submit him to a number of cruel experiments.

E-mail from Author Gary Chaloner

NOTE: Chaloner offers this glimpse at Urchak's fate in the Victorian past. How history is affected by the presence of a sentient, speaking ape 100 years before the arrival of Cornelius and Zira is unclear, though it appears not to have had much of an effect.

◆ Upon his death, Urchak is stuffed and mounted in a glass exhibit case in the Victorian institute.

Urchak's Folly #4: "Chapter Four—The War" (AC-c)

BETWEEN 1877 AND 1931

◆ Thomas Alva Edison builds a time machine and travels to the year 3085, where he encounters astronauts Alan Virdon and Peter Burke and their chimpanzee companion, Galen. The machine eventually brings Edison home again, stranding the others in the future.

El Planeta de Los Simios: "Encounter with Edison" (ET-c, unpublished)

NOTE: Slated for release in Argentina, this comic was never published due to the title's cancellation. Edison's launch must occur between 1877 (when he began inventing) and 1931 (the year of his death). Details were provided by author Jorge Claudio Morhain.

LATE 1910s OR EARLY 1920s

◆ Future ANSA astronaut George Taylor is born, presumably in or near Fort Wayne, Ind.

Planet of the Apes (FX-f)

NOTE: Taylor's birth year is based on his 1941 West Point graduation, as revealed in A Public Service Announcement From ANSA, *a short film included in the Blu-Ray release (an early-draft script gives his age in 1972 as 35—Charlton Heston's age at the time—but the ANSA film's dating would make him about 50). Since he attended school in Fort Wayne, it's likely he was born there. In Pierre Boulle's novel* The Monkey Planet, *Taylor's name is Ulysse Mérou; in early script drafts, it is John "Johnny" Thomas.*

1922

◆ Future circus owner Armando, last name unknown, is born to parents of Hispanic origin.

Escape from the Planet of the Apes (FX-f)

NOTE: Since Armando's age is unknown, I have based this figure on actor Ricardo Montalban's age (51) when the film (set in 1973) was produced.

c. 1920s

◆ Future ANSA astronaut George Taylor attends Jefferson Public School in Fort Wayne, Ind.

Planet of the Apes (FX-f)

1932

◆ Future scientist Lewis Dixon is born, presumably in or near Los Angeles, Calif.

Escape from the Planet of the Apes (FX-f)

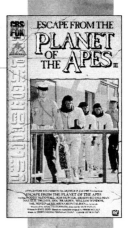

NOTE: Since Dixon's age is unknown, I have based this figure on actor Bradford Dillman's age (41) when the film (set in 1973) was produced. Since Dixon is said to have spent his youth in Los Angeles, it's likely (though not certain) he was born there.

1934

◆ Future ANSA astronaut Donovan "Skipper" Maddox is born.

Planet of the Apes 40ᵗʰ Anniversary Collection: A Public Service Announcement From ANSA (FX-x)

NOTE: "Skipper" (as he is known in Beneath the Planet of the Apes*) remained unnamed until this short film, included in the Blu-Ray release, christened him Donovan. His uniform patch bears the name "Maddox" onscreen, however, and a timeline packaged with this collection uses that name. To reconcile the discrepancy, I assume his full name to be Donovan Maddox. The ANSA film reveals him to have been 38 in 1972, establishing a 1934 birth year, though actor Tod Andrews was 56 when* Beneath *was produced.*

EARLY TO MID 1930s

◆ Future astronaut Bill Hudson's boyhood swimming instructor is born.

Return to the Planet of the Apes episode #5: "Lagoon of Peril" (BB-n)

NOTE: This placement is approximate, based on information in the novelization.

MID TO LATE 1930s

◆ Dr. Otto Victor Hasslein—future science advisor to the president of the United States—is born.

Escape from the Planet of the Apes (FX-f)

NOTE: Hasslein's exact age is unknown. Actor Eric Braeden was 30 years old when the film (set in 1973) was produced, implying a 1943 birth year. Since the novelization reveals the scientist to have a 14-year-old son in 1973, however, I have pushed his birth back to the late 1930s. Hasslein is named Otto onscreen in Escape from the Planet of the Apes, *but Victor in the film's novelization; to reconcile the discrepancy, I have combined the two.*

1937

◆ Future ANSA astronaut Thomas Dodge is born.

Planet of the Apes 40ᵗʰ Anniversary Collection: A Public Service Announcement From ANSA (FX-x)

NOTE: The Planet of the Apes *script notes Dodge to be around 30 years old in 1972, but the ANSA film specifies 35, establishing a 1937 birth year. The ANSA film also provides his first name. A 1974 coloring book misspells his last name as "Hodge."*

1938

◆ Future ANSA astronaut John Christopher Brent is born, presumably in or near New York City.

Beneath the Planet of the Apes (FX-f)

NOTE: Brent's full name appears in the film's script, and in Marvel's comic adaptation. His age is cited as 26 in an early-draft script, but A Public Service Announcement From ANSA establishes him as being 34 in 1972, setting his birth in 1938 (actor James Franciscus was 36 when the film was produced).

1939

◆ Future ANSA astronaut Maryann Stewart is born.

Planet of the Apes 40ᵗʰ Anniversary Collection: A Public Service Announcement From ANSA (FX-x)

NOTE: Stewart's first name and age (33 in 1972) remained unknown until this short film, included in the Blu-Ray release. In early drafts of the Planet of the Apes script, Stewart was a male astronaut named Blake.

c. LATE 1930s TO EARLY 1940s

◆ Future ANSA astronaut John Landon is born.

Planet of the Apes (FX-f)

NOTE: Landon's first name appears in Marvel's and Power Records' comic adaptations. His age is unspecified (just that he was 25 when chosen for the Liberty 1 mission), and actor Robert Gunner's age is unknown; this placement is based on his onscreen appearance as a man in his 30s. In early drafts of the film's script, Landon was known as Paul LeFever.

◆ Future scientist Lewis Dixon spends his youth playing in an abandoned oil tanker off the coast of Los Angeles, in which, some 30 years later, he'll eventually hide two talking apes.

Escape from the Planet of the Apes (FX-f)

1941

◆ George Taylor graduates from West Point and becomes an ace World War II fighter pilot.

Planet of the Apes 40ᵗʰ Anniversary Collection: A Public Service Announcement From ANSA (FX-x)

1942

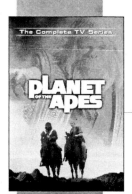

◆ Future ANSA astronaut Alan J. Virdon is born.

Planet of the Apes episode #1: "Escape from Tomorrow" (CB-t)

NOTE: Since Virdon's age is unknown, I have based this figure on actor Ron Harper's age (38) when the TV series was produced, given a date of 1980 for the time-warp. Virdon's middle initial appears in an unused episode script, entitled "A Fallen God."

◆ As a child, Virdon grows up in Jackson County, spending his youth working on farms.

Planet of the Apes episode #4: "The Good Seeds" (CB-t)

NOTE: Which particular Jackson County is unspecified, but since there is such a county in Texas, where Virdon will later own a farm, that's a likely candidate. This would indicate Virdon hails from one of the county's three main cities (Edna, Ganado or La Ward), or from one of its smaller communities (such as Lolita or Vanderbilt).

◆ Future scientist Stephanie "Stevie" Branton is born.

Escape from the Planet of the Apes (FX-f)

NOTE: *Since Branton's age is unknown, I have based this figure on actress Natalie Trundy's age (31) when the film (set in 1973) was produced.*

c. 1940s

◆ As a child, future astronaut John Christopher Brent loses his parents. His grandmother thus brings him up in her home near New York City's Queensboro Plaza subway station.

Beneath the Planet of the Apes (FX-f)

NOTE: *Brent's parents' deaths, and his being raised by his grandmother, are mentioned in an early-draft script of the second film, entitled* Planet of the Apes Revisited.

◆ As a boy, Otto Hasslein reads stories about computers taking over the world and making mankind useless. Taking the threat seriously, he focuses his academic attention on science—and, later, on computers.

Escape from the Planet of the Apes (AW-n)

NOTE: *This information appears in the novelization, and may have been an homage to Eric Braeden's lead role in* Collossus: The Forbin Project.

1948

◆ Future governor Arnold Jason Breck is born.

Conquest of the Planet of the Apes (FX-f)

NOTE: *It's unclear as to which U.S. state Breck governs. The* Conquest *novelization implies California, and both Marvel's timeline and* Revolution on the Planet of the Apes *concur. Script treatments for* Conquest *and* Battle for the Planet of the Apes, *however, place both films on the East Coast, setting the stage for* Beneath the Planet of the Apes. *Dayton Ward's timeline, published in* The Planet of the Apes Chronicles, *concurs with the eastern placement. The novelization cites Breck's age as 33 in 1991, but that would not jibe with his having helped create the Alpha-Omega Bomb in the 1960s. As such, I have instead based Breck's age on actor Don Murray's age (43) when the film was made. The novelization names him Jason, but* Revolution #1 *calls him Arnold; I have, therefore, combined them to reconcile the discrepancy (an early-draft script names him Harvey Breck III, but the character is very different in that script, so I am discarding that alternative).*

◆ Arthur Vernon Kolp, future governor of New York City's mutant population, is born.

Conquest of the Planet of the Apes (FX-f)

NOTE: *Since Kolp's age is unknown, I have based this figure on actor Severn Darden's age (43) when the film (set in 1991) was produced. An early-draft script names him Arthur, but* Revolution on the Planet of the Apes #4 *calls him Vernon. To reconcile this discrepancy, I have combined the two.*

1949

◆ Alan J. Virdon, age seven, learns to ride a horse. Eventually, the youth becomes a champion rider, able to calm wild horses in seconds.

Planet of the Apes episode #9: "The Horse Race" (CB-t)

NOTE: *This assumes a birth year of 1942.*

LATE 1940s OR EARLY 1950s

◆ Future NASA astronauts Bill Hudson, Jeff Allen and Judy Franklin are born.

Return to the Planet of the Apes episode #1: "Flames of Doom" (NB-a)

NOTE: Each astronaut's birth year is unknown. This estimate is based on the assumption they're all in their mid 20s or early 30s at the time of the 1976 mission launch.

◆ As a young child, Jeff Allen often wishes he could cut down trees and yell "Timber!"

Return to the Planet of the Apes episode #9: "Trail to the Unknown" (BB-n)

NOTE: This is revealed in the novelization.

c. 1950 to 1953

Future astronaut George Taylor serves as an ace fighter pilot during the Korean War.

Planet of the Apes 40ᵗʰ Anniversary Collection: A Public Service Announcement From ANSA (FX-x)

1951

◆ Future ANSA astronaut Peter J. Burke is born, presumably in or near Jersey City, N.J.

Planet of the Apes episode #1: "Escape from Tomorrow" (CB-t)

NOTE: Since Burke's age is unrevealed, I have based this figure on actor James Naughton's age (29) when the TV series was produced, given a date of 1980 for the time-warp. Since Burke is said to have spent his youth in Jersey City, it's likely (though not certain) he was born there. In early-draft scripts, Burke is named Ed Rowak and Stan Kovak. His middle initial is revealed in "The Interrogation."

◆ Malcolm MacDonald, future assistant to Governor Arnold Jason Breck, is born.

Conquest of the Planet of the Apes (FX-f)

NOTE: Since MacDonald's age is unknown, I have based this figure on actor Hari Rhodes' age (40) when the film (set in 1991) was produced. His first name is established in Revolution on the Planet of the Apes *issue #4.*

EARLY TO MID 1950s

◆ Future astronaut Bill Hudson, age 7, learns to swim with the help of a beautiful 19-year-old lifeguard. Though just a child, he develops quite a crush on her.

Return to the Planet of the Apes episode #5: "Lagoon of Peril" (BB-n)

NOTE: This is revealed in the novelization.

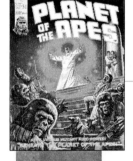

◆ Frankie Peters, a bully in Derek Zane's neighborhood, delights in torturing and shooting squirrels.

Planet of the Apes #10: "Kingdom on an Island of the Apes—The City" (MC-c)

1954

◆ Tommy Billings, a future orderly for the U.S. Navy, is born.

Escape from the Planet of the Apes (AW-n)

NOTE: This information appears in the film's novelization.

1955

◆ Mandemus, an orangutan and future Keeper of Ape City's armory, is born.

Battle for the Planet of the Apes (FX-f)

NOTE: Since Mandemus' age is unknown, I have based this figure on actor Lew Ayres'
age (65) when the film (set in 2020) was produced.

1959

◆ Dr. Otto Victor Hasslein and his wife celebrate the birth of their first baby. Unfortunately, the child is born with Down Syndrome.

Escape from the Planet of the Apes (AW-n)

◆ Lisa, a chimpanzee and future wife to Caesar, the First Lawgiver of Ape City, is born.

Conquest of the Planet of the Apes (FX-f)

NOTE: Since Lisa's age is unknown, I have based this figure on actress Natalie
Trundy's age (32) when the film (set in 1991) was produced.

LATE 1950s OR EARLY 1960s

◆ Alan Virdon passes his Electronics Lab One course despite accidentally sitting on an awl during class.

Planet of the Apes: "Hostage" (CB-u)

NOTE: This script was never filmed. It is unclear if Virdon is relating an event from
high school or college, so it's difficult to be more specific in dating this event.

◆ Halfway through college, George Taylor decides to take up astronautical engineering.

Planet of the Apes (FX-f)

NOTE: This information appears in the film's script.

c. 1950s TO 1960s

◆ As a child, Peter J. Burke attends P.S. 103 in Jersey City, N.J.

Planet of the Apes episode #7: "The Surgeon" (CB-t)

◆ Never able to see the stars at night, Burke longs one day to be out among them.

Planet of the Apes episode #1: "Escape from Tomorrow" (CB-t)

◆ Burke's mother often tells him the Biblical story of Isaac and his twin sons, Jacob and Esau, hoping to instill in him the importance of avoiding deception.

Planet of the Apes episode #8: "The Deception" (CB-t)

◆ Burke's father, meanwhile, frequently tries to teach him an important lesson by asking, "Son, when the going gets tough, and the tough get going, what will *you* do?"

Planet of the Apes episode #8: "The Deception" (AW-n)

NOTE: This is revealed in the novelization.

◆ Otto Victor Hasslein specializes in solid-state physics, earning a reputation as an expert in the field.

Escape from the Planet of the Apes (AW-n)

NOTE: This information appears in the film's novelization.

PUBLISHER / STUDIO
AB . . . . ABC-TV
AC . . . .Adventure / Malibu Comics
AW . . . . Award Books
BB . . . . .Ballantine Books
BN . . . . Bantam Books
BW . . . . Brown Watson Books
CB . . . . CBS-TV
CV . . . . Chad Valley Sliderama
DH . . . . .Dark Horse Comics
ET . . . . Editorial Mo.Pa.Sa.
FX . . . . 20th Century Fox
GK . . . .Gold Key / Western Comics
HE . . . HarperEntertainment Books
HM . . Harry K. McWilliams Assoc.
MC . . . . Marvel Comics
MR . . . Mr. Comics / Metallic Rose
NB . . . . NBC-TV
PR . . . . .Power Records
SB . . . . Signet Books
TP . . . . .Topps
UB . . . . .Ubisoft

MEDIUM
a . . . . animated series
b . . . . .book-and-record set
c . . . . .comic book or strip
d . . . . trading card
e . . . . e-comic
f . . . . .theatrical film
k . . . . .storybook
m . . . . .magazine article
n . . . . .novel or novelization
p . . . . promotional newspaper
r . . . . .recorded audio fiction
s . . . . short story
t . . . . television series
u . . . . .unfilmed script or story
v . . . . video game
x . . . . .Blu-Ray exclusive
y . . . . .young adult novel

◆ Burke is one of three children, with two sisters. His family also has a dog, though young Pete decides he would prefer two dogs and one sister.

Planet of the Apes: "Hostage" (CB-u)

NOTE: This episode was never filmed, but the script is available online at Hunter's Planet of the Apes Archive.

1962

◆ The U.S. government establishes the American National Space Administration (ANSA), dubbed the greatest conglomerate of scientific vision and knowledge in history, and chaired by Dr. Otto Hasslein. The first candidate of the organization's elite astronaut corps is veteran pilot Col. George Taylor.

Planet of the Apes 40ᵗʰ Anniversary Collection: A Public Service Announcement From ANSA (FX-x)

1962 TO 1972

◆ ANSA launches the first manned spacecraft into Earth orbit, then lands men on the moon and Mars. Exploration of neighboring planets follows, with photon propulsion and near-light-speed travel enabling Hasslein's team to target distant galaxies and nebulae. Thus, is born Project Liberty—an attempt to send a manned spaceflight to the Centaurus constellation, four light-years distant.

Planet of the Apes 40ᵗʰ Anniversary Collection: A Public Service Announcement From ANSA (FX-x)

NOTE: Although NASA exists in the Apes mythos, it is apparently ANSA that achieves these milestones. Adventure Comics' issue #15 sets the first Mars mission in 1991.

BEFORE 1966

◆ Astronaut George Taylor enjoys a number of romances with women, none of which last long—as he describes it, "lots of love-making, but no love."

Planet of the Apes (FX-f)

◆ Taylor eventually marries and starts a family, though the marriage is a bitter one.

Ape City #2: "See No Evil, Hear No Evil, Speak No Evil" (AC-c)

NOTE: The name of Taylor's wife has yet to be revealed.

◆ Though she loves him, Taylor's wife sees him as a "magnificent bastard"—a tough man who doesn't suffer "wusses" or "wimps."

Revolution on the Planet of the Apes #4: "Paternal Instinct" (MR-c)

◆ Eventually, Taylor's wife begins drinking heavily to deal with their marital issues.

Ape City #2: "See No Evil, Hear No Evil, Speak No Evil" (AC-c)

1966

◆ Jo Taylor, elder daughter of ANSA astronaut George Taylor, is born.

Ape City #2: "See No Evil, Hear No Evil, Speak No Evil" (AC-c)

◆ The Down Syndrome child of Dr. Otto Hasslein ceases progressing mentally at age seven. Hasslein and his wife raise the boy with love, hoping science will one day find a cure, but it never does.

Escape from the Planet of the Apes (AW-n)

◆ Alan J. Virdon and his wife Sally have a daughter, who grows up on their farm in Houston, Texas.

Planet of the Apes episode #12: "The Cure" (AW-n)

NOTE: The daughter, mentioned in the script and novelization, is said to have been 14 when Virdon vanished in 1980. The Houston farm is established in the Planet of the Apes Initial Concept Pages. *Sally is named in "The Surgeon."*

◆ Armando purchases a female chimpanzee named Heloise, intending someday to open a circus.

Escape from the Planet of the Apes (FX-f)

◆ Determined to work in the entertainment industry, Armando drops his last name, legally registering himself under the stage-name "Señor Armando."

Conquest of the Planet of the Apes (AW-n)

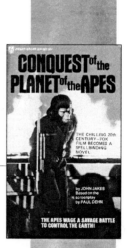

MID TO LATE 1960s

◆ Karen Carroll, future reporter for *People News Monthly*, is born.

Revolution on the Planet of the Apes #2: "People News" (MR-c)

NOTE: This story's script reveals Carroll's first name and says she is in her 20s in 1992.

◆ Future ANSA astronaut Thomas Dodge, while working as an organic chemistry professor at the University of Maryland, Annapolis, dreams of discovering intelligent life on another world.

Planet of the Apes 40th Anniversary Collection: A Public Service Announcement From ANSA (FX-x)

◆ At age 25, ANSA astronaut trainee John Landon graduates at the top of his class.

Planet of the Apes (FX-f)

◆ Landon distinguishes himself as a navigator on ANSA's Juno Mars mission. Lt. Maryann Stewart, an astronaut and biological researcher, also serves on the Juno team, as well as in ANSA's Apollo program.

Planet of the Apes 40th Anniversary Collection: A Public Service Announcement From ANSA (FX-x)

c. LATE 1960s

◆ Future astronaut Peter J. Burke pitches a no-hitter game of baseball while still in high school.

Planet of the Apes episode #14: "Up Above the World So High" (CB-t)

NOTE: This placement is based on a birth year of 1951, placing his high school years in the late 1960s.

◆ Dr. Otto Victor Hasslein theorizes the existence of a space-time tangent as a means of interstellar travel involving time, dimensional matrices and infinite regression. Due to the relativistic nature of time, the scientist postulates that mankind should be able to travel great distances in space at super-fast speeds, with time passing much more slowly than normal aboard ship. Determined to prove his theory, he drives congressional funding into the development of an experimental spacedrive.

Revolution on the Planet of the Apes #3: "Hasslein's Notes" (MR-c)

◆ Hasslein's theories depict the space-time continuum as a series of eight interlocking Möbius strips, made up of "curved time" and "alternative time-tracks."

Planet of the Apes: "Journey to the Planet of the Apes" (MC-c, unpublished)

NOTE: This tale—originally titled "Return to the Planet of the Apes" but renamed so as not to conflict with the cartoon—was never released due to the Marvel series' cancellation. The above details were provided by author Doug Moench.

PUBLISHER / STUDIO
AB .... ABC-TV
AC .....Adventure / Malibu Comics
AW .... Award Books
BB ....Ballantine Books
BN .... Bantam Books
BW .... Brown Watson Books
CB .... CBS-TV
CV ..... Chad Valley Sliderama
DH ....Dark Horse Comics
ET .... Editorial Mo.Pa.Sa.
FX .... 20th Century Fox
GK ....Gold Key / Western Comics
HE ... HarperEntertainment Books
HM .. Harry K. McWilliams Assoc.
MC .... Marvel Comics
MR ... Mr. Comics / Metallic Rose
NB .... NBC-TV
PR ....Power Records
SB .... Signet Books
TP .... Topps
UB .... Ubisoft

MEDIUM
a .... animated series
b ....book-and-record set
c ....comic book or strip
d .... trading card
e .... e-comic
f ....theatrical film
k .... storybook
m .... magazine article
n ....novel or novelization
p .... promotional newspaper
r ....recorded audio fiction
s .... short story
t .... television series
u ....unfilmed script or story
v .... video game
x ....Blu-Ray exclusive
y ....young adult novel

◆ To protect the United States from all possible enemies, the U.S. military designs the Alpha-Omega Bomb, a cobalt-encased atomic missile (or "doomsday bomb") able to decimate the planet. The weapon's name comes from *The Bible*'s *Revelations* 22:13: "I am the Alpha and the Omega, the First and the Last, the Beginning and the End." Only those with top security clearance—such as ANSA astronaut George Taylor—know of the project's existence.

Beneath the Planet of the Apes (FX-f)

NOTE: This event is undated. However, since Taylor knows of the project, it must have originated before the Liberty 1*'s 1972 launch.*

◆ The Alpha-Omega Bomb, code-named "Project Churchdoor," is deemed top-secret, overseen by future governor Arnold Jason Breck, a cruel young man aspiring to great power.

Revolution on the Planet of the Apes #1: "Part One: The End of the World" (MR-c)

NOTE: Given actor Don Murray's age (43) when the film (set in 1991) was produced, that would make Breck around 20 years old when Project Churchdoor was created.

◆ Having conceived and commissioned Project Churchdoor, Breck oversees the black budget to fund it.

Revolution on the Planet of the Apes #5: "Part Five: Weapon of Choice" (MR-c)

◆ To make sure the missile never falls into the wrong hands, Breck develops the Inferno Protocol, a mass-destruction plan for use only as a last resort.

Revolution on the Planet of the Apes #3: "Part Three: Intelligent Design" (MR-c)

◆ At least two Alpha-Omega devices are produced: a prototype and a larger, next-generation model.

Online Posting from Ty Templeton

NOTE: Templeton offered this tidbit on the POTA Yahoo Group regarding the bomb in Revolution on the Planet of the Apes, *which was smaller than that seen on film. A third A-O Bomb may also have been created; while conceiving* Revolution, *Templeton planted seeds for a future storyline following up on the idea that Earth had no moon in the first film. The author says he conceived the destruction as occurring a century or so after* Conquest of the Planet of the Apes, *and that his notes included the detonation of a doomsday bomb on a lunar colony. In the novelization of* Beneath the Planet of the Apes, *Taylor says only one was built, but he might not have been aware of the others.*

1967 OR 1968

◆ On his farm in Houston, Texas, Alan J. Virdon watches veterinarians work so he can learn birthing and other medical techniques, such as helping a cow in labor whose calf has turned around in the womb.

Planet of the Apes episode #4: "The Good Seeds" (CB-t)

◆ Chris Virdon, son of Alan and Sally Virdon, is born.

Planet of the Apes Concept Guide (CB-t)

NOTE: Chris' age is unspecified, but Virdon is strongly reminded of him upon meeting Kraik (said to be age 12 or 13 in the script), so it's safe to assume that was Chris' approximate age when Virdon vanished in 1980.

◆ Tammy Taylor, youngest daughter of ANSA astronaut George Taylor, is born.

Revolution on the Planet of the Apes #4: "Paternal Instinct" (MR-c)

NOTE: When Sam Agro penned this story, neither he nor Ty Templeton were aware Adventure Comics*' Ape City miniseries had established the existence of a daughter for Taylor, named Jo. Since neither is said to be an only child, and since their ages and names differ, I have accepted both accounts, making Jo and Tammy sisters.*

1967 TO 1972

◆ During a five-year series of exhaustive tests and prototypes of Project Liberty, Otto Hasslein theorizes that as a spacecraft approaches the speed of light, time will dilate. Thus, during a proposed 18-month voyage, the astronauts would age only that amount, though 2,000 years would pass on Earth. ANSA's Life Science group creates a means for chemically inducing human hibernation, so astronauts aboard such a craft can enter suspended animation, inside hermetically sealed pods.

Planet of the Apes 40th Anniversary Collection: A Public Service Announcement From ANSA (FX-x)

1968

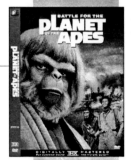

◆ Mendez (first name unknown), future founder of the mutant House of Mendez, is born.

Battle for the Planet of the Apes (FX-f)

NOTE: Since Mendez's age is unknown, I have based this figure on actor Paul Stevens' age (52) when the film (set in 2020) was produced.

c. 1960s OR 1970s

◆ A criminally insane child, age seven, kills his entire family—and nearly himself—in a fire. In later years, he will be known only as Scab.

Ape City #2: "See No Evil, Hear No Evil, Speak No Evil" (AC-c)

NOTE: The incident is undated, but I assume he was in his 20s or 30s in 1990.

LATE 1960s TO EARLY 1970s

◆ As Chris Virdon grows up, his father teaches him all he knows about farming—particularly the importance of planting the best seeds to ensure the health of the following year's crop.

Planet of the Apes episode #4: "The Good Seeds" (CB-t)

c. 1970

◆ Bruce "Mac" MacDonald, brother of Malcolm MacDonald and future advisor to Caesar, is born.

Battle for the Planet of the Apes (FX-f)

NOTE: Bruce's first name appears in Marvel's adaptation, while Revolution on the Planet of the Apes #4 names Malcolm. Bruce is said to have supervised Ape Management's archives before the war of 1992, but actor Austin Stoker was 30 years old when the film (set in 2020) was made, which would make Bruce an infant. Clearly, then, the character must be at least 20 years older than the actor, despite his youthful appearance.

1971

◆ The ANSA space shuttle *Liberty 1*—the culmination of Hasslein's work on Project Liberty—is prepared for its historic launch.

Planet of the Apes 40th Anniversary Collection: A Public Service Announcement From ANSA (FX-x)

NOTE: Taylor's ship had been known as Icarus—*a name coined by fan Larry Evans in 1972, and later legitimized by toy model companies, as well as in* Revolution on the Planet of the Apes—*before this short film, included in the Blu-Ray release, established the name* Liberty 1. *The shuttle is named* Air Force One *in a test set of Topps collectible cards, and* Immigrant One *in an early-draft Planet of the Apes script.*

◆ A program is created to test both the spacedrive and Hasslein's space-time tangent theory. This program is dubbed the Interstellar Exploration Program (IEP).

Ape City #2: "See No Evil, Hear No Evil, Speak No Evil" (AC-c)

◆ The U.S. president chooses Col. George Taylor to head the *Liberty 1* mission.

Escape from the Planet of the Apes (AW-n)

◆ Taylor, a bitter man with a history of running away from those who love him, accepts the mission, abandoning his family in the process.

Ape City #2: "See No Evil, Hear No Evil, Speak No Evil" (AC-c)

◆ Asked why he would leave behind the world he knows to explore the vastness of deep space, Taylor—tired of man's cruelty to his fellow humans—replies, "For the promise of a better world."

Planet of the Apes 40ᵗʰ Anniversary Collection: A Public Service Announcement From ANSA (FX-x)

◆ Taylor's daughter Jo is five years old at the time.

Ape City #2: "See No Evil, Hear No Evil, Speak No Evil" (AC-c)

◆ Jo's younger sister, Tammy, is four.

Revolution on the Planet of the Apes #4: "Paternal Instinct" (MR-c)

◆ Lt. John Landon is nominated to join the *Liberty 1* crew as navigator. Eager for fame and immortality (and unable to turn it down without looking bad), ANSA's "golden boy" accepts the posting. Lt. Thomas Dodge, age 35, signs up as well, relishing the opportunity to learn something new. A fourth astronaut, Lt. Maryann Stewart, age 33, also joins the team.

Planet of the Apes (FX-f)

> NOTE: Landon's first name is revealed in Marvel's adaptation. Dodge's rank appears in the Escape from the Planet of the Apes *novelization; his first name, as well as Stewart's rank and first name, come from* A Public Service Announcement From ANSA.

◆ In accepting the mission, Landon leaves behind a wife who admires his sacrifice, and an infant son, Mike. Dodge serves as head science officer, while Stewart is a biological researcher. Two first alternates round out the crew: John Christopher Brent, age 34, and Col. Donovan "Skipper" Maddox, 38.

Planet of the Apes 40ᵗʰ Anniversary Collection: A Public Service Announcement From ANSA (FX-x)

> NOTE: "Skipper" (as he is known in Beneath the Planet of the Apes) remained unnamed until this short film, included in the Blu-Ray release, christened him Donovan. His uniform patch bears the name "Maddox" onscreen, however, and a timeline packaged with this collection uses that name. I thus assume his full name to be Donovan Maddox.

◆ Derek Zane, an inventor and dreamer, becomes fascinated with George Taylor, the *Liberty 1* mission and Dr. Otto Hasslein's theories concerning time, dimensional matrices and infinite regression.

Planet of the Apes #9: "Kingdom on an Island of the Apes—The Trip" (MC-c)

◆ Hasslein visits the L.A. Zoo as part of an advisory board reviewing grant applications. His wife and two of their children accompany him. Staff veterinarian Stephanie Branton finds him pleasant but cold.

Escape from the Planet of the Apes (AW-n)

BEFORE 1972

◆ George Taylor befriends Dr. Lewis Dixon, an animal psychologist at UCLA.

Escape from the Planet of the Apes (AW-n)

Part 2: Genesis of the Lawgiver (1972 to 1973)

BETWEEN 1971 AND 1973

◆ The family of Major Gen. Raymond Hamilton (an officer of the U.S. Strategic Air Command) suffers the thefts of three ten-speed bicycles over a two-year period.

Escape from the Planet of the Apes (AW-n)

NOTE: This information appears in the film's novelization.

FEBRUARY 1972

◆ The *Liberty 1* launches from Cape Kennedy, bound for the Centaurus constellation. Upon arrival, its crew intend to build a human colony, with Stewart serving as the metaphorical "Eve" to their "Adams." Due to the distance involved and the mission's nature, the trip is designed to be one-way, with four suspended-animation capsules carrying them asleep for the majority of the voyage. ●

Planet of the Apes (FX-f)

NOTE: The February setting is from Marvel's chronology (a timeline packaged with the Planet of the Apes *40th Anniversary Collection indicates January). A Public Service Announcement From ANSA, a short film from that same box set, notes the ship's Centaurus destination.*

◆ With the *Liberty 1* crew traveling in suspended animation, the ship contains only limited supplies—not enough, even, to sustain the four astronauts for a year.

Escape from the Planet of the Apes (AW-n)

NOTE: This information appears in the film's novelization.

◆ George Taylor's wife and daughter Jo watch the launch on television. Jo is sad to see him go, her mother succumbing to alcoholism to deal with the abandonment.

Ape City #2: "See No Evil, Hear No Evil, Speak No Evil" (AC-c)

NOTE: The whereabouts of daughter Tammy (seen in Revolution on the Planet of the Apes #4) *is unknown.*

◆ Taylor also leaves behind a pet puppy that often licked his hand but never barked.

Planet of the Apes (MC-c)

NOTE: This information comes from Marvel's comic adaptation of the film.

◆ Following *Liberty 1*'s launch, Otto Hasslein sits alone at his desk one evening, affected by the sadness of the astronauts' sacrifice and the thrill of discovery. An amateur poet, he jots the following words on an envelope, which become a motto and a prayer for the Liberty Project's explorers: "To the distant reaches, climb / Far beyond space / Far beyond time." ANSA records, on a reel of 16-millimeter film, a public service announcement outlining the Liberty Project and honoring the crew of the *Liberty 1*.

Planet of the Apes 40th Anniversary Collection: A Public Service Announcement From ANSA (FX-x)

◆ *Liberty 1* passes through a fold in space—what will later be called a "Hasslein Curve" in honor of Dr. Otto Hasslein—and is propelled to the year 3978, where it crashes off the coast of Long Island. Hasslein's theory is proven true, but no one in his era knows it.

Planet of the Apes (FX-f)

◆ Unable to reach Taylor, ANSA realizes something has gone wrong and prepares a second ship to follow *Liberty 1*'s trajectory, determine what happened to its crew and mount a rescue.

Beneath the Planet of the Apes (FX-f)

NOTE: Why ANSA would do this is a mystery, given that Liberty 1*'s journey was intended to be one-way—a time warp was fully expected, as would be loss of contact. Sending another ship would just mean losing another crew.*

JULY 14, 1972

◆ Astronaut George Taylor records his final message to ANSA before joining his crewmates in suspended animation. Although 700 years have passed on Earth, only six months have passed aboard ship due to time dilation—*Liberty 1*'s time chronometer reads July 14, 1972, while on Earth the date is March 23, 2673.

Planet of the Apes (FX-f)

◆ ANSA, however, never receives any of Taylor's messages.

Beneath the Planet of the Apes (FX-f)

JULY 1972 TO EARLY 1974

◆ Derek Zane, an inventor and dreamer fascinated with Taylor's mission, correctly discerns that the *Liberty 1* crew has vanished into a time warp. Zane sets out to construct a time machine and prove his theory correct, but no one—not even his girlfriend Michelle—believes him.

Planet of the Apes #9: "Kingdom on an Island of the Apes—The Trip" (MC-c)

◆ Zane's invention, the Time Displacement Module, is based on Dr. Otto Hasslein's theories involving dimensional matrices, infinite regression, curved time and alternative time-tracks.

Planet of the Apes: "Journey to the Planet of the Apes" (MC-c, unpublished)

NOTE: This tale—originally titled "Return to the Planet of the Apes" but renamed, presumably, so as not to conflict with the cartoon series—was never released due to Marvel's decision to stop publishing Planet of the Apes *comics as of issue #29, in response to increased licensing fees. The above details come from a story outline and dialog breakdown provided by author Doug Moench.*

NOVEMBER 1972

◆ ANSA launches a second ship to find *Liberty 1*. Its crew includes commander Donovan "Skipper" Maddox and ship's medic John Christopher Brent. This ship slips through the same Hasslein Curve and is thrown forward in time as well. Maddox leaves behind a wife and two daughters.

Beneath the Planet of the Apes (FX-f)

NOTE: The November setting is established on the timeline in Marvel's issue 11. Brent's status as ship's medic comes from Marvel's comic adaptation.

◆ To avoid public curiosity, the U.S. government issues a press release claiming Taylor's and Brent's ships both disintegrated in orbit.

Escape from the Planet of the Apes (FX-f)

◆ The *Liberty 1* is officially listed as destroyed, its crew honored with a full state funeral.

Revolution on the Planet of the Apes #1: Timeline (MR-c)

NOTE: Presumably, the same is true for Brent and Maddox, who were also lost.

AFTER 1972

◆ The USNSA, determined to find Taylor, also sends a ship to locate him, this time commanded by an astronaut named Ben. As with Taylor's ship, Ben's vanishes in a time-warp.

Planet of the Apes (UB-v)

NOTE: This video game is not easily added to a timeline—after all, since game sessions are different every time, which specific session "happened?" What's more, it's unclear how the USNSA relates to either NASA or ANSA. Thus, I am only including the game's premise, not the specifics of gameplay.

1972 TO 1990s

◆ George Taylor's wife tells their daughter Tammy that her father was a tough man, a "magnificent bastard" who hated "wusses" and "wimps." Tammy grows up both hating and emulating the man, vowing never to show those qualities and determined to be just like the father she never knew.

Revolution on the Planet of the Apes #4: "Paternal Instinct" (MR-c)

◆ Jo Taylor, on the other hand, follows in her father's footsteps to become an astronaut.

Ape City #2: "See No Evil, Hear No Evil, Speak No Evil" (AC-c)

BEFORE 1973

◆ Stay-DriEST deodorant hits the market.

Escape from the Planet of the Apes (AW-n)

NOTE: This is revealed in the film's novelization.

◆ Dr. Radak Hartley, chairman of Harvard's zoology department, wins a Nobel Prize.

Escape from the Planet of the Apes (FX-f)

◆ The U.S. president authorizes the assassination of a Soviet marshall he deems an evil and dangerous man.

Escape from the Planet of the Apes (AW-n)

NOTE: This is revealed in the film's novelization.

1973

◆ Señor Armando establishes Armando's Old-Time Circus.

Conquest of the Planet of the Apes (FX-f)

◆ Aldo, a gorilla and future leader of Ape City's military, is born.

Battle for the Planet of the Apes (FX-f)

NOTE: Since Aldo's age is unknown, I have based this figure on actor Claude Akins' age (47) when the film (set in 2020) was produced.

EARLY 1973

◆ A female gorilla dies at the Los Angeles Zoological Gardens. Its mate, Bobo (a.k.a. "Monstro"), becomes depressed and brooding without her.

Escape from the Planet of the Apes (AW-n)

NOTE: This information appears only in the novelization.

APRIL 1973

◆ NASA astronauts Bill Hudson, Jeff Allen and Judy Franklin enter the U.S. space program.

Return to the Planet of the Apes episode #1: "Flames of Doom" (NB-a)

◆ Hudson enters the program a few days before the others and is named mission commander. The trio form a close bond. Allen's identity as a dark-skinned man makes him sensitive to racial inequality, but their color difference (the others are Caucasian) is never an issue among them.

Return to the Planet of the Apes episode #4: "Tunnel of Fear" (BB-n)

NOTE: This is revealed in the novelization.

◆ A chimpanzee named Heloise, an animal acrobat in Armando's Old-Time Circus, goes into labor. Dr. Lewis Dixon, an animal psychologist at the Los Angeles Zoological Gardens, helps Heloise give birth to a daughter, Salome. The chimp's owner, Señor Armando, is very grateful.

Escape from the Planet of the Apes (FX-f)

◆ Dr. Stephanie "Stevie" Branton, an animal psychologist, is assigned to assist Dr. Lewis Dixon at UCLA. The two fall in love, and Dixon considers marriage after only three weeks.

Escape from the Planet of the Apes (AW-n)

NOTE: The novelization establishes their romance, the fact that they work for UCLA, and that they'd only known each other for three weeks at the time of the film.

APRIL TO MAY 1973

◆ The *Liberty 1*, George Taylor's lost spaceship, suddenly reappears in Earth's atmosphere and falls back to the planet. As the government and military scramble to action, no one recognizes the ship initially.

Escape from the Planet of the Apes (FX-f)

NOTE: The timeline in Revolution on the Planet of the Apes #1 *places these events two years after* Liberty 1's *launch, based on the president's statements on film—however, Marvel's timeline sets the film in April 1973, a year and two months after Taylor's ship was lost. The Ape News, a mock newspaper released to promote the film, bears a date of March 1, 1973, and Marvel's adaptation places it in 1975. A bigger question involves the feasibility of* Liberty 1's *return, given the damage the shuttle suffers upon crashing. For one possible explanation, visit Chris Shields' The Last Flight of the* Icarus *website.*

◆ Western Control, a branch of the U.S. Navy, spots the capsule on radar. Cmdr. W.D. Deyerle of the Destroyer *Spearhead* oversees a rescue operation. Unable to make voice contact, Deyerle gives up hope that anyone aboard could still be alive.

The Ape News (HM-p)

◆ At Offutt Air Force Base in Omaha, Neb., Major Gen. Raymond Hamilton of Strategic Air Command is alerted to the craft's appearance. NORAD's Air Defense locates a bogey approaching re-entry over the North Pole, estimated to come down in San Diego. Worried it might be a Soviet missile, he sounds Emergency War Orders (EWO) and tells March Air Force Base in Riverside to launch B-52s.

Escape from the Planet of the Apes (AW-n)

NOTE: This information appears in the film's novelization.

◆ Deyerle, suspecting the craft may be a U.S. satellite stolen by Russian or Chinese soldiers, activates the Coastal Protection Team and orders *Spearhead* to mount a rescue. Splashdown occurs at 11:50 a.m.

The Ape News (HM-p)

◆ *Liberty 1* lands off California's coast, north of San Clemente. Hamilton cancels EWO, recalls the March AF wing and orders the Miramar Marine Corps Air Station to deploy a rescue team. As troops tow the craft to shore, another chopper delivers Col. Winthrop and Lt. Cmdr. Greg Hartley.

Escape from the Planet of the Apes (FX-f)

NOTE: *In the novelization, Winthrop is named Adm. George "Snapper" Jardin. In Marvel's adaptation, Hartley is named Ralston.*

◆ *Liberty 1* is identified. Gen. Len Brody, White House chief of staff, alerts the president to the return of Taylor's ship. To prevent security leaks, the president orders Brody to keep the story from the press.

Escape from the Planet of the Apes (AW-n)

NOTE: *This information appears in the novelization. The president's name is unknown.*

◆ Soldiers retrieve *Liberty 1*. Three space-suited figures emerge and are escorted to the beach, where they remove their helmets to reveal themselves to be chimps. Hamilton orders the apes moved to a Marine Corps Air Station in El Palomar, arranging for the L.A. Zoological Gardens to take them in secret.

Escape from the Planet of the Apes (FX-f)

◆ At the El Palomar station, the apes are examined by Lt. Cmdr. Gordon Ashmead, USNR.

Escape from the Planet of the Apes (AW-n)

NOTE: *This information appears in the film's novelization.*

◆ Hamilton and Winthrop visit the apes, who wear clothing and use plates and cutlery. Winthrop orders a police escort to the zoo infirmary, where animal keeper Jim "Arthur" Haskins tends to a sick gorilla.

Escape from the Planet of the Apes (FX-f)

NOTE: *In the novelization, Arthur's name is Jim Haskins. To reconcile the discrepancy, I assume "Arthur" to be a nickname. The book names the gorilla Bobo.*

◆ The chimps are Dr. Cornelius, an archeologist; his pregnant wife, Dr. Zira, a veterinarian and animal psychologist; and Dr. Milo, a genius of many sciences. Realizing they've been thrown back in time by Earth's destruction, Milo urges them to keep silent (present apes can't talk) and not to reveal that an ape war will destroy the planet. Lewis Dixon and Stephanie Branton submit Zira to psychological testing, but she grows impatient and speaks. Her agitation affects Bobo, who strangles Milo to death.

Escape from the Planet of the Apes (FX-f)

◆ Milo's corpse is dissected, with particular attention paid to the temporal lobes and speech centers.

Escape from the Planet of the Apes (AW-n)

NOTE: *This occurs in the film's novelization.*

◆ Amazed, Dixon begins a journal detailing the chimps' statements about the future.

Urchak's Folly #3: "Chapter Three — The Savages" (AC-c)

◆ Hasslein convenes a Presidential Commission of Inquiry at the L.A. Federal Building, with the press in attendance. Dr. Radak Hartley, chairman of Harvard's zoology department, heads the commission, along with Col. Winthrop; Congressman Jason Boyd of the House Science and Astronautics Committee; Cardinal MacPherson, a Jesuit Catholic official; and Senator Yancey of the Armed Forces Committee. The apes charm the press, but Hasslein worries about their claims that humans will one day become dumb brutes. When Yancey asks if they know Taylor, Cornelius feigns ignorance.

Escape from the Planet of the Apes (FX-f)

NOTE: *The Ape News identifies two commission members as Gen. Faulkner and Senator Blaine, and also calls Winthrop a senator rather than a soldier.*

PUBLISHER / STUDIO
AB . . . . ABC-TV
AC . . . .Adventure / Malibu Comics
AW . . . . Award Books
BB . . . . .Ballantine Books
BN . . . . Bantam Books
BW . . . . Brown Watson Books
CB . . . . CBS-TV
CV . . . . Chad Valley Sliderama
DH . . . . .Dark Horse Comics
ET . . . . Editorial Mo.Pa.Sa.
FX . . . . 20th Century Fox
GK . . . .Gold Key / Western Comics
HE . . . HarperEntertainment Books
HM . . Harry K. McWilliams Assoc.
MC . . . . Marvel Comics
MR . . . Mr. Comics / Metallic Rose
NB . . . . NBC-TV
PR . . . . .Power Records
SB . . . . Signet Books
TP . . . . Topps
UB . . . . Ubisoft

MEDIUM
a . . . . animated series
b . . . . .book-and-record set
c . . . . .comic book or strip
d . . . . trading card
e . . . . e-comic
f . . . . .theatrical film
k . . . . .storybook
m . . . . .magazine article
n . . . . .novel or novelization
p . . . . promotional newspaper
r . . . . .recorded audio fiction
s . . . . short story
t . . . . television series
u . . . . .unfilmed script or story
v . . . . video game
x . . . . .Blu-Ray exclusive
y . . . . .young adult novel

◆ The chimps are subjected to extensive study by a number of scientists. This includes collecting genetic material from Cornelius and Zira.

Redemption of the Planet of the Apes (AC-c, unpublished)

NOTE: Lowell Cunningham, Men in Black creator and author of Adventure's The Forbidden Zone, proposed this four-issue miniseries to creative director Tom K. Mason as well. However, Cunningham says, the idea was rejected for being similar to the Planet of the Apes film remake then being considered, starring Arnold Schwarzenegger.

◆ As word of the apes' arrival spreads, many voice their opinions as to their origins. Anthropologist Margaret Smee, convinced they are from another planet and may be smarter than humans, presents a scholarly statement on Johnny Carson's *Tonight Show*. Dr. Sprocket, a pediatrician and folk philosopher, is impressed at the quality of their feet—a sign they won't become fascists. And author, social critic and revolutionary Jerry Ruby calls the apes "right on," saying they'll always be welcome in Woodstock.

The Ape News (HM-p)

◆ Hasslein appears on a television news broadcast, *Big News*, to discuss time travel. Reporter Bill Bonds tells him the "apeonauts," as they've been dubbed, have become quite popular.

Escape from the Planet of the Apes (FX-f)

NOTE: Bill Bonds is an actual TV news anchor and reporter, who worked in Los Angeles at the time the film was produced. In the novelization, his character is named Walter.

◆ To make amends for their earlier treatment, the Navy's Admiral Taylor arranges for a wealthy retired admiral friend to transfer the chimps, via a chauffered Mercedes, to better accomodations.

Escape from the Planet of the Apes (AW-n)

NOTE: This information appears in the novelization. It's unknown if the admiral is related to George Taylor.

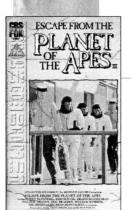

◆ Housed at the Beverly Wilshire Hotel, Zira and Cornelius are happy for a time. Reporters attend a party at the hotel, hoping to hear them speak. Attending journalists include Jeanna Robbins of *Fur and Feather*, Bill Cummings of *Men's Hunting and Outdoors* and Joe Simpson of *Ebony*.

Escape from the Planet of the Apes (FX-f)

◆ At the request of the mayor and the city council, the apes are given a tour of the city. Zira and Cornelius receive keys to the city and a gold-plated banana inscribed with "See California and Go Bananas!"

The Ape News (HM-p)

◆ The commission re-convenes, this time joined by Dr. Raymond Wilson, a naturalist specializing in great apes. Wilson is skeptical, questioning anything that does not jibe with his understanding of modern-day simians. Cornelius tells the commission their two species must learn to get along, and Hasslein agrees.

Escape from the Planet of the Apes (AW-n)

NOTE: This information appears in the film's novelization.

◆ Zira speaks before the Bay Area Women's Club (BAWC), while Cornelius attends a prize fight. Hasslein takes her to the L.A. County Museum of Natural History, where she sees a stuffed ape and faints. Returning her to the hotel, Hasslein plies her with champagne, records her drunken comments and warns the president of Earth's destruction. The commission orders the apes moved to Camp XI, a secret interrogation lab in New Mexico, where Hasslein questions them alongside CIA agents Henry Amalfi and Larry Bates. Cornelius says a plague will eventually wipe out most dogs and cats, so man will take apes as pets and later as servants, but that the apes will become alert to the concept of slavery and rebel. Drugged with sodium pentathol, Zira admits to knowing Taylor, and to practicing comparative anatomy on humans, who will be hunted for sport and dissected for science in her time.

Escape from the Planet of the Apes (FX-f)

> NOTE: *Amalfi and Bates are named in the novelization, working for the NSA rather than the CIA. The film credits list them simply as E-1 and E-2. Camp XI's location is revealed in* The Ape News, *a promotional newspaper distributed to moviegoers during the film's release. The novelization calls it Camp Pendleton.*

◆ The FBY, CID and WPA investigate the apes, as do several congressional and senatorial committees. The public is outraged, saying the couple are friendly visitors deserving of respect and hospitality. Citizens' groups battle over who should look out for them; the American Civilian Liberties Union (ACLU) claims jurisdiction since they landed in the United States, while the ASPCA claims priority since they aren't human. Several minority groups enter the debate as well, claiming the apes represent an obvious minority.

The Ape News (HM-p)

◆ The commission votes to abort Zira's baby and render the apes sterile. Cornelius attacks and inadvertently kills an orderly, Corp. Tommy Billings, for calling the fetus a monkey. The couple sneaks past a security guard named Charlie, stopping when Zira goes into labor. Cornelius finds Branton, and Dixon delivers the child, whom Zira names Milo. Señor Armando offers to hide them for a month and release them in the Florida Everglades, but when Hasslein orders Capt. Osgood to search all city zoos, the circus owner is no longer able to keep them safe. He gives Zira a medal of Saint Francis of Assisi, and she switches babies with Heloise before leaving. Dixon and Branton drive them to the Point Doom oil field so they can hide in a derelict tanker at McKinley & Sons Naval Scrapyard until Dixon can smuggle them back to the circus. In case they're caught, Dixon gives them a gun to kill themselves.

Escape from the Planet of the Apes (FX-f)

> NOTE: *McKinley is named in the Power Records and Marvel comic adaptations, Osgood is named in Marvel's version and Billings is named in the novelization.*

◆ A homeless drunk named Zeke encounters the apes, but Cornelius lets him go, unwilling to hurt another innocent man. Arrested for disorderly conduct, Zeke rambles about talking apes. The police eventually contact Hasslein, who interrogates the wino, then heads for the shipyard.

Escape from the Planet of the Apes (AW-n)

> NOTE: *This scene occurs in the film's novelization.*

◆ Hasslein writes a letter to the president, blaming himself for their predicament. His theory, he writes, has a fatal flaw: The "Hasslein Curve" is really a recursive loop, folding back infinitely upon itself, from the future into the past and back. He suspects Earth's future destruction to be the catalyst, and that *Liberty 1*'s return flight paradoxically enabled the apeonauts' original time journey. Man's biggest threat, Hasslein notes, comes not from the apes but from his own ignorance, and so he must take steps to ensure humans prevail.

Revolution on the Planet of the Apes #3: "Hasslein's Notes" (MR-c)

PUBLISHER / STUDIO

AB . . . . ABC-TV
AC . . . . Adventure / Malibu Comics
AW . . . . Award Books
BB . . . . Ballantine Books
BN . . . . Bantam Books
BW . . . . . . Brown Watson Books
CB . . . . CBS-TV
CV . . . . . Chad Valley Sliderama
DH . . . . Dark Horse Comics
ET . . . . Editorial Mo.Pa.Sa.
FX . . . . 20th Century Fox
GK . . . . .Gold Key / Western Comics
HE . . . HarperEntertainment Books
HM . . Harry K. McWilliams Assoc.
MC . . . . Marvel Comics
MR . . . Mr. Comics / Metallic Rose
NB . . . . NBC-TV
PR . . . . Power Records
SB . . . . Signet Books
TP . . . . Topps
UB . . . . Ubisoft

MEDIUM

a . . . . animated series
b . . . . .book-and-record set
c . . . . .comic book or strip
d . . . . trading card
e . . . . e-comic
f . . . . .theatrical film
k . . . . .storybook
m . . . . .magazine article
n . . . . .novel or novelization
p . . . . promotional newspaper
r . . . . .recorded audio fiction
s . . . . short story
t . . . . television series
u . . . . . . .unfilmed script or story
v . . . . video game
x . . . . Blu-Ray exclusive
y . . . . .young adult novel

◆ The police check Armando's circus but find nothing. Zira sets her bag down at the refinery, which cops discover the following morning. Cornelius seeks a clean spot on the tanker so Zira can nurse two-day-old "Milo." Helicopters and police surround the boat, and Dixon and Branton arrive just as Hasslein shoots Zira and the baby. Cornelius kills Hasslein, then is gunned down by Marine Sgt. Meissner, plummeting to his death. Zira throws the baby chimp into the water, then dies next to her husband's broken body.

Escape from the Planet of the Apes (FX-f)

NOTE: *Revolution on the Planet of the Apes #3 establishes Milo as dying at age two days. Meissner is named in the film's novelization.*

◆ Hasslein Air Force Base, located at Area 51 in Groom Lake, Nevada, is named in the scientist's honor.

Revolution on the Planet of the Apes #1: "Part One: The End of the World" (MR-c)

◆ Lewis Dixon arranges for the ape couple and their child to be buried together. A scientist who proposes they instead be stuffed and exhibited in a museum barely escapes being killed by his own students. Nearby police, touched by the chimps' plight, stand by and do nothing to protect the man.

Escape from the Planet of the Apes (AW-n)

NOTE: *This information appears in the film's novelization. Apparently, the U.S. government opts not to dissect them, which seems a rather unusual oversight given their special nature, and the known fate of mankind.*

c. JUNE 1973

◆ Armando's Old-Time Circus closes up shop in California and heads for Florida. As his staff breaks down the tents, Señor Armando caresses young Milo—still wearing the Saint Francis medal—and tells him he's very intelligent, like his parents. In response, the infant repeatedly utters his first word, "mama."

Escape from the Planet of the Apes (FX-f)

◆ Armando renames Milo "Caesar" to hide his identity as the apeonauts' son.

Planet of the Apes #11: "Outlines of Tomorrow—A Chronology of the Planet of the Apes" (MC-m)

NOTE: *Presumably, he also changes the baby's gender on all records—after all, Heloise delivered a* female *child.*

AFTER JUNE 1973

◆ Armed with foreknowledge of Earth's destruction at Taylor's hands, the U.S. government and military implement Operation: Hasslein. This shadow program is dedicated to developing a time-travel device, then sending an assassin into the future to kill Taylor before he can detonate the Alpha-Omega Bomb.

Manhunt on the Planet of the Apes (AC-c, unpublished)

NOTE: *Mike Valerio, author of Adventure Comics'* Sins of the Father, *proposed this one-shot to creative director Tom K. Mason as well. However, Valerio says, the idea was scrapped for being too similar to* The Terminator, *and for the assassin's being reminiscent of* Alien's *Ellen Ripley, in addition to some plot-logic problems. As he explains, "If you're going to send somebody into the future to kill Taylor, why wait until Taylor arrives, when you could kill him before he ever goes on his mission? Or, if you do have a time machine, why not send that assassin to kill Caesar before he ever leads the revolt? Or to kill Zira before she can give birth to Milo/Caesar?" For that matter, why murder at all—why not just prevent Taylor's mission from launching, thereby preventing the entire cycle from occurring? Then there's the question of how anyone in the past would know it was Taylor who detonated the bomb. It's interesting to note that despite all this, Adventure's* Ape City *miniseries utilized a similar premise.*

EARLY 1970s

◆ While attending Michigan State University, future ANSA astronaut Peter J. Burke plays college football, earning himself a reputation as a great running back.

Planet of the Apes episode #4: "The Good Seeds" (CB-t)

NOTE: This placement is conjectural, based on the usual age of a college student.

◆ During his junior year, Burke makes a particularly unpopular play during a game against Ohio State.

Planet of the Apes episode #2: "The Gladiators" (AW-n)

NOTE: This is revealed in the novelization.

◆ In his senior year, during the final quarter of a game between Michigan and Michigan State, with a score of 14-14, Burke experiences a moment of panic when the punter kicks the ball his way and he notices the other team's linemen running toward him.

Planet of the Apes episode #12: "The Cure" (AW-n)

NOTE: This is revealed in the novelization.

◆ During this period, Dr. Walter Mather, F.A.C.S., of the Hanson Clinic, develops a reputation as one of the greatest surgeons of his era. Pete Burke is familiar with the man's work.

Planet of the Apes episode #7: "The Surgeon" (AW-n)

NOTE: This is revealed in the novelization.

◆ Dr. Mather writes a medical reference book titled *Principles of Surgery*, containing detailed explanations of human anatomy, as well as a variety of advanced surgical techniques.

Planet of the Apes episode #7: "The Surgeon" (CB-t)

1973 TO 1981

◆ Space exploration grows. Unmanned probes soar to the stars and back, thanks to Hasslein's discovery of faster-than-light travel, and manned flights over vast distances become common. Earth's governments grow ever more totalitarian, however, to handle increasing economic, political and energy pressures. All data regarding the lost spaceships, and the future revealed by Zira and Cornelius, is locked away under heavy security clearance, and the "talking chimpanzee" story is publicly denounced as a hoax.

Planet of the Apes #11: "Outlines of Tomorrow—A Chronology of the Planet of the Apes" (MC-m)

NOTE: This partially explains why the astronauts from both the television series and cartoons have no knowledge of the ape-controlled future only a few years later… but not entirely. A lot of people saw the apes, both on TV and at public events, surrounded by government officials and other notable persons—for the masses to then accept the apeonauts as a hoax seems rather far-fetched.

1973 TO 1991

◆ For a time, Señor Armando's circus operates under the name Armando's Marvelous Menagerie Circus.

Revolution on the Planet of the Apes #3: "Little Caesar" (MR-c)

NOTE: This tale was published as a sneak preview in issue #1 of Mr. Comics' Big Max, under the title "Armando's Marvelous Menagerie Circus."

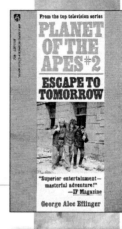

From the top television series
PLANET OF THE APES #2
ESCAPE TO TOMORROW

"Superior entertainment—
masterful adventure!"
—IF Magazine

George Alec Effinger

PUBLISHER / STUDIO

AB . . . . ABC-TV
AC . . . Adventure / Malibu Comics
AW . . . . Award Books
BB . . . . .Ballantine Books
BN . . . . Bantam Books
BW . . . . Brown Watson Books
CB . . . . CBS-TV
CV . . . . Chad Valley Sliderama
DH . . . . .Dark Horse Comics
ET . . . . Editorial Mo.Pa.Sa.
FX . . . . 20th Century Fox
GK . . . .Gold Key / Western Comics
HE . . . HarperEntertainment Books
HM . . Harry K. McWilliams Assoc.
MC . . . . .Marvel Comics
MR . . . Mr. Comics / Metallic Rose
NB . . . . NBC-TV
PR . . . . .Power Records
SB . . . . Signet Books
TP . . . . .Topps
UB . . . . Ubisoft

MEDIUM

a . . . . animated series
b . . . . .book-and-record set
c . . . . .comic book or strip
d . . . . trading card
e . . . . e-comic
f . . . . .theatrical film
k . . . . .storybook
m . . . . .magazine article
n . . . . .novel or novelization
p . . . . promotional newspaper
r . . . . .recorded audio fiction
s . . . . short story
t . . . . television series
u . . . . .unfilmed script or story
v . . . . video game
x . . . . .Blu-Ray exclusive
y . . . . .young adult novel

◆ The show also goes by the name Armando's Sensational Circus for a time.

Escape from the Planet of the Apes (MC-c)

NOTE: This information comes from the Marvel adaptation and the novelization.

◆ Since only Armando knows Caesar's true identity, the chimp must act unintelligent around humans.

Conquest of the Planet of the Apes (FX-f)

◆ Having gestated during time travel, Caesar perceives the past, present and future simultaneously. Thus, as a young ape, he knows he will one day become a revolutionary, and dreams of events he will never witness, such as Taylor's detonation of the Alpha-Omega Bomb. Disturbed, Caesar wonders how hatred could so fully consume a person.

Revolution on the Planet of the Apes #1: "Part One: The End of the World" (MR-c)

◆ Armando's animals, in tune with Caesar's mind, bend easily to his will. If Caesar dreams of them doing tricks, they do so days later, without training. Unsure if he's seeing the future or dreaming it into reality, Caesar finds his abilities frightening, but Armando says it's a gift from God—and since it helps him earn a tidy living, all the better.

Revolution on the Planet of the Apes #3: "Little Caesar" (MR-c)

NOTE: This might not be as far-fetched as it seems. Fox's Preliminary Production Notes for Conquest of the Planet of the Apes *describe Caesar as "a chimpanzee with supernatural powers," and the film hints at such abilities when Caesar communicates non-verbally with other apes. It's possible Zira may have possessed such powers as well, as she somehow communicates to Heloise her intention to switch babies in* Escape from the Planet of the Apes.

◆ At night, young Caesar frequently awakens screaming from his visions. Armando assures the young chimp they're only nightmares, but Caesar realizes his foster-father does not entirely believe that himself.

Revolution on the Planet of the Apes #2: "Caesar's Journal" (MR-c)

◆ Among the circus apes is an orangutan named Mandemus, who acquires the power of speech from being in Caesar's proximity. History will later record other apes (Aldo and Lisa) as the first primitive apes to speak, overlooking Mandemus' achievement.

Empire on the Planet of the Apes (MR-c, unpublished)

NOTE: Ty Templeton, author of Revolution on the Planet of the Apes, *posted this tidbit on the POTA Yahoo Group as a hint at his plans for a proposed follow-up to that comic-book miniseries.*

Part 3: Under Ape Management (1974 to 1990)

EARLY 1974

◆ Derek Zane, an inventor obsessed with rescuing the *Liberty 1* crew, finishes building his time machine. His girlfriend Michelle, however, decides he's lost touch with reality and ends their relationship. Zane flies to Houston, Texas, to meet with Dr. Krigstein, a top-level NASA administrator. He explains his fascination with Hasslein's theories, and his belief that Taylor's crew entered a time warp. Krigstein scoffs at the idea, however, so Zane tests the machine himself and is propelled to the year 3975.

Planet of the Apes #9: "Kingdom on an Island of the Apes—The Trip" (MC-c)

NOTE: Since Marvel's comic adaptation sets the first film in 3975 instead of 3978, it's safe to assume the 3975 placement of this story is meant to imply Zane arrives in the same year as Taylor's crew. I've kept the 3975 setting, however, as his arriving too soon makes his tale that much more tragic. Why Zane would contact NASA, though, instead of ANSA (for whom Taylor worked) is unclear. Dialog in an unpublished Marvel comic entitled "Journey to the Planet of the Apes" sets this tale in early 1974.

◆ Abe (last name unknown), future teacher and advisor to Caesar, is born.

Battle for the Planet of the Apes (FX-f)

NOTE: Since Abe's age is unknown, I have based this figure on actor Noah Keen's age (46) when the film (set in 2020) was produced.

BEFORE 1976

◆ Scientist Dr. Stanton puts forth his controversial "time-thrust" theory that humans can propel themselves into the future if they travel fast enough.

Return to the Planet of the Apes episode #1: "Flames of Doom" (NB-a)

NOTE: How Stanton's theory relates to similar (and already proven) notions theorized by Dr. Otto Hasslein is unclear.

◆ While learning to fly, astronaut Bill Hudson learns that "heroes can't imagine their own death, and that's why they are heroes." He disagrees, however, believing the concept applies to all people, not just to heroes.

Return to the Planet of the Apes episode #9: "Trail to the Unknown" (BB-n)

NOTE: This is revealed in the novelization.

◆ During his NASA training, Hudson learns to will himself asleep whenever and wherever necessary.

Return to the Planet of the Apes episode #4: "Tunnel of Fear" (BB-n)

NOTE: This is revealed in the novelization.

◆ Hudson spends time on a debating team, but fails to perform well.

Return to the Planet of the Apes episode #5: "Lagoon of Peril" (BB-n)

NOTE: This is revealed in the novelization.

◆ At some point before the historic launch of the *Venturer*, Hudson owns a pick-up truck.

      Return to the Planet of the Apes episode #11: "Mission of Mercy" (NB-a)

◆ NASA astronaut Jeff Allen learns about old-time freight trains from magazines belonging to his cousin Benny, who has a passion for trains and maintains an elaborate electric-train layout.

      Return to the Planet of the Apes episode #8: "Screaming Wings" (BB-n)

      NOTE: This is revealed in the novelization.

◆ Allen watches an old black-and-white *Quatermass* film on television, starring Brian Donlevy, and is struck by how much scarier a partially human monster can be than one that is pure creature.

      Return to the Planet of the Apes episode #9: "Trail to the Unknown" (BB-n)

      NOTE: This is revealed in the novelization.

◆ A NASA spaceship makes a forced landing in a small Arab country. A sheik scavenges its computer and sells it to China for 100 million dollars. Accessing its files, the Chinese government learns that the civilian-run program had conducted military reconnaissance in the Far East. This embarrasses the U.S. government, and NASA vows never again to let that happen. Thereafter, all spacecraft computers are equipped with key-operated explosives to keep them from falling into unfriendly or mercenary hands.

      Return to the Planet of the Apes episode #5: "Lagoon of Peril" (BB-n)

      NOTE: This is revealed in the novelization.

◆ Laser technology progresses to the point that handheld lasers become standard equipment aboard NASA spacecraft such as the *Venturer*.

      Return to the Planet of the Apes episode #7: "River of Flames" (NB-a)

◆ NASA astronaut Judy Franklin flies a P-40 World War II fighter plane in an air show.

      Return to the Planet of the Apes episode #8: "Screaming Wings" (NB-a)

1976

◆ Production begins on Ever-Seal butane lighters.

      Return to the Planet of the Apes episode #3: "The Unearthly Prophecy" (BB-n)

      NOTE: This is revealed in the novelization.

AUGUST 6, 1976

◆ Three NASA astronauts—Cmdr. Bill Hudson, Jeff Allen and Judy Franklin—launch from Earth on an interstellar mission aboard the spacecraft *Venturer*.

      Return to the Planet of the Apes episode #1: "Flames of Doom" (NB-a)

      NOTE: The novelization reveals Hudson's rank but sets the launch in 1979.

◆ The *Venturer*'s mission is to test NASA's newest type of spaceship.

      Return to the Planet of the Apes episode #9: "Trail to the Unknown" (BB-n)

      NOTE: This is revealed in the novelization.

◆ Due to the *Venturer*'s advanced speed, time moves more slowly aboard ship than on Earth, proving Dr. Stanton's time-thrust theory. Within minutes, the ship's Earth-time clock reads 2081, though ship-time is 1976. The *Venturer* enters a strange energy distortion and jumps forward to the year 3979. Franklin leaves behind a sister named Lily.

Return to the Planet of the Apes episode #1: "Flames of Doom" (NB-a)

NOTE: Presumably, the Venturer *enters the Hasslein Curve.*

◆ The *Venturer* crew fails to return from its mission and is presumed dead. To honor the astronauts, NASA erects stone busts in New York City in their likenesses.

Return to the Planet of the Apes episode #3: "The Unearthly Prophecy" (NB-a)

NOTE: It's unknown if busts were erected for Taylor's, Brent's and Virdon's crews.

EARLY 1977

◆ Investigating the 1974 disappearance of inventor Derek Zane—who, convinced the *Liberty 1* crew was lost in time, built a time machine to rescue them from the future—NASA's Dr. Krigstein finds scientific papers Zane left behind in his apartment. Among these are plans for a Temporal Displacement Module (time machine), based on Hasslein's theories of dimensional matrices, infinite regression, curved time and alternative time-tracks. Krigstein deems the equations revolutionary, and NASA spends nine months building its own model, *Chronos I*, to mount a rescue.

Planet of the Apes: "Journey to the Planet of the Apes" (MC-c, unpublished)

NOTE: This tale—originally titled "Return to the Planet of the Apes" but renamed so as not to conflict with the cartoon—was never released due to Marvel's decision to stop publishing Apes comics as of issue #29, in response to increased licensing fees. Details of the story come from an outline and dialog breakdown provided by author Doug Moench. The year changes from 1976 to 1977 in the transition from story breakdown to script; I have adhered to the latter date. Despite the events of the third film, NASA seems unaware of the future ape-controlled society.

LATE 1977

◆ NASA calls a top-priority meeting for staff and press and announces the construction of *Chronos I*. Krigstein tells attendees that NASA will soon complete the device, and plans to send a team of astronauts to rescue Zane from the year 3977. Two "tempunauts," Mara Winston and Jackson Brock, are chosen for the mission. Brock, however—who volunteered only so he can profit from knowledge of the future—cares little for Zane's safety.

Planet of the Apes: "Journey to the Planet of the Apes" (MC-c, unpublished)

NOVEMBER 29, 1977

◆ The day before the launch of *Chronos I*, a newspaper headline reads "Time Trip Set for Tomorrow—Tempunauts in Good Spirits, Say NASA."

Planet of the Apes: "Journey to the Planet of the Apes" (MC-c, unpublished)

NOVEMBER 30, 1977

◆ After a briefing with NASA, the tempunauts board *Chronos I* at NASA's Time Research Labs in Long Island, New York, and vanish into the future. Unable to broadcast radio signals through time, the duo are entirely on their own.

Planet of the Apes: "Journey to the Planet of the Apes" (MC-c, unpublished)

DECEMBER 1977 OR LATER

◆ Derek Zane finally returns to his own era, along with Mara and a chimp fugitive named Faron, whom he befriended in the future. However, Zane feels like a misfit in this world he once knew. Missing Lady Andrea (his future wife), Zane builds another time machine so he can return to 40th-century Avedon.

Planet of the Apes: "Beyond the Planet of the Apes" [multiple issues] (MC-c, unpublished)

NOTE: Doug Moench's story breakdown for "Journey to the Planet of the Apes" concludes with notes to artist Val Mayerik and editor John David Warner, detailing future plans to craft a "movie sequel" spanning eight to ten issues involving an ape culture similar to that from Pierre Boulle's novel The Monkey Planet. *Other multi-issue "sequels" would have followed, each starring Zane and friends as the main cast. The first of these would have been "Beyond the Planet of the Apes." Moench's notes do not indicate the mechanism for traveling back in time, but he describes this story arc as "John Chimper of Mars," a reference to Edgar Rice Burroughs' John Carter of Mars novels. Zane's return to 3977, Moench says, would have occurred around issue #60 or so, had the series run that long.*

LATE 1970s

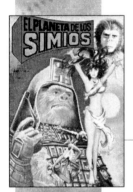

◆ U.S. scientists begin experimenting with solar-powered batteries.

El Planeta de Los Simios #4: "Ultrasonic" (ET-c)

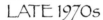

NOTE: This Spanish-language comic was released only in Argentina.

◆ San Francisco outfits its Bay Area Rapid Transit (BART) subway trains with nuclear energy. Subway stations are illuminated with lights powered by solar energy batteries drawing electricity from large solar shields. Other innovations include a "meal in a pill," eaten three times daily in lieu of food—for full vitamin content with no caloric intake; painless organ replacement in a day, developed by CA[3]; disposable clothing, meant to be worn and then washed down the drain; and Cefaloradion's electronic neurological monitor (ENM), a device hooked to the head to provide emotional stability to the distressed.

Planet of the Apes episode #3: "The Trap" (CB-t)

NOTE: Some product details appear onscreen on subway-station posters; others are noted in the episode's script.

◆ NASA produces an experimental spacecraft, 30 feet wide by 8 feet high. A ruthless Nazi-esque criminal named Trang steals the ship and travels with his followers to the year 3085, hoping to subjugate the planet.

Planet of the Apes—4 Exciting New Stories #3: "Battle of Two Worlds" (PR-r)

NOTE: The following entries are undated, but must occur before the astronauts' mission to Alpha Centauri.

◆ Assigned to Edwards Air Force Base as cadets, ANSA astronauts-in-training Alan J. Virdon and Peter J. Burke serve under Major Jennings. His nose is large and crooked, and one of them names a nearby hill "Jennings' Nose" due to its similarity. Jennings never learns who coined the term.

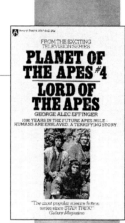

Planet of the Apes episode #11: "The Tyrant" (AW-n)

NOTE: This is revealed in the novelization.

◆ Alan Virdon and Pete Burke are assigned a mission for ANSA. After preflight indoctrination, the duo enjoy a relaxing couple of days at Hanson Point, on the shore of California. Virdon's wife Sally is there, while Burke is accompanied by a redhead named Jan Adams. Burke carves her initials in a beach cave—the only woman ever to inspire such tribute from the ladies' man.

Planet of the Apes episode #8: "The Deception" (AW-n)

NOTE: This is revealed in the episode's novelization. The script erroneously places the astonauts' vacation at Pebble Beach.

◆ Pete Burke meets Verina, a fellow ANSA astronaut-in-training. Though she is younger than he, the two become friends.

Planet of the Apes (Authorised Edition) #3: "From Out of the Sky" (BW-c)

◆ Pete Burke is eventually promoted to the rank of major.

Planet of the Apes episode #10: "The Interrogation" (CB-t)

NOTE: This information appears only in the script of the episode.

◆ Burke considers purchasing a bar in Jersey City, but ultimately opts not to do so.

Planet of the Apes episode #4: "The Good Seeds" (CB-t)

NOTE: The novelization of the episode erroneously places the bar in Galveston.

◆ Burke dates a woman named Susan, enjoying many picnics and romantic moments. Despite her attempts to get him to talk about his past, he keeps his emotional distance, dooming the relationship.

Planet of the Apes episode #10: "The Interrogation" (CB-t)

NOTE: Susan is named Nora in the episode's script. It's unclear whether Burke dated her, however, as he recalls their relationship during an interrogation sequence—the memory may have been entirely manufactured.

◆ During his military training, Pete Burke hates the hours spent running on a treadmill.

Planet of the Apes episode #12: "The Cure" (CB-t)

NOTE: This information appears only in the script of the episode.

◆ Burke is subjected to a mock interrogation. An American officer, Lt. Hal Martin, poses as an enemy agent and tries to make him incriminate his battle group commander, Col. Perry, and company commander, Capt. Logan. Burke resists, providing only his name, rank and serial number.

Planet of the Apes episode #10: "The Interrogation" (CB-t)

NOTE: This scene appears in the script, but not in the final televised episode. It's unclear if this actually occurred, as Burke recalls it during an interrogation. It's possible the memory may have been manufactured by the interrogator.

PUBLISHER / STUDIO
AB . . . . ABC-TV
AC . . . . Adventure / Malibu Comics
AW . . . . Award Books
BB . . . . .Ballantine Books
BN . . . . Bantam Books
BW . . . . Brown Watson Books
CB . . . . CBS-TV
CV . . . . Chad Valley Sliderama
DH . . . . .Dark Horse Comics
ET . . . . Editorial Mo.Pa.Sa.
FX . . . . 20th Century Fox
GK . . . .Gold Key / Western Comics
HE . . . HarperEntertainment Books
HM . . Harry K. McWilliams Assoc.
MC . . . . Marvel Comics
MR . . . Mr. Comics / Metallic Rose
NB . . . . NBC-TV
PR . . . . Power Records
SB . . . . Signet Books
TP . . . . Topps
UB . . . . Ubisoft

MEDIUM
a . . . . animated series
b . . . . .book-and-record set
c . . . . .comic book or strip
d . . . . trading card
e . . . . e-comic
f . . . . .theatrical film
k . . . . .storybook
m . . . . .magazine article
n . . . . .novel or novelization
p . . . . promotional newspaper
r . . . . .recorded audio fiction
s . . . . short story
t . . . . television series
u . . . . .unfilmed script or story
v . . . . video game
x . . . . .Blu-Ray exclusive
y . . . . .young adult novel

◆ Alan Virdon and Peter Burke serve together on a manned mission to Titan. Along the way, they sample banana sundaes supplied by ANSA, which they consider among the worst things they've ever eaten.

Planet of the Apes episode #7: "The Surgeon" (AW-n)

NOTE: This is revealed in the novelization.

◆ Pete Burke learns how to fight melee-style.

Planet of the Apes episode #2: "The Gladiators" (CB-t)

NOTE: Thus begins a long string of abilities demonstrated by Burke and Virdon, many of which would not be part of an astronaut's standard training. It's unknown when they learned to do the following tasks, or the order in which this training occurred, but clearly it all must have been before their mission to Alpha Centauri.

◆ Burke trains in the Japanese art of kendo and learns to fight with knives.

Planeta de Los Simios #7: "The Circus" (ET-c)

◆ Alan Virdon learns how to wrestle alligators in Florida.

Planet of the Apes—4 Exciting New Stories #2: "Dawn of the Tree People" (PR-r)

◆ Both men are trained how to destroy a building with a controlled explosion.

Planet of the Apes (Authorised Edition) #2: "Pit of Doom" (BW-c)

◆ Virdon learns how to erect a fulcrum-and-pulley system capable of lifting heavy objects.

Planet of the Apes episode #3: "The Trap" (CB-t)

◆ The duo also learn how to build a giant water wheel.

El Planeta de Los Simios #6: "The Zombies" (ET-c)

◆ Virdon and Burke are trained in such advanced agricultural methods as windmill power, irrigation, soil-tilling and constructing sturdy fences.

Planet of the Apes episode #4: "The Good Seeds" (CB-t)

◆ Virdon learns how to churn butter from milk.

Planet of the Apes episode #4: "The Good Seeds" (AW-n)

NOTE: This is revealed in the novelization.

◆ The duo learn how to build batteries from scratch.

Planet of the Apes episode #5: "The Legacy" (CB-t)

◆ They also learn how to create compasses from raw materials.

Planet of the Apes episode #4: "The Good Seeds" (CB-t)

◆ Virdon and Burke are trained as expert fishermen—including, apparently, how to kill a shark with a knife. They also learn how to weave nets and construct elaborate rafts by hand, using logs and rope.

Planet of the Apes episode #6: "Tomorrow's Tide" (CB-t)

◆ Burke is trained in advanced human anatomy, including how to perform blood transfusions.

Planet of the Apes episode #7: "The Surgeon" (CB-t)

◆ Burke is also trained to perform artificial respiration.

El Planeta de Los Simios #6: "The Zombies" (ET-c)

◆ Burke and Virdon learn how to recognize the symptoms and causes of malaria, and how to cure the disease using quinine from a cinchona tree.

Planet of the Apes episode #12: "The Cure" (CB-t)

◆ Both men are trained to recognize biological weaponry used in germ warfare, and how to protect themselves in the event of such an outbreak.

Planet of the Apes (Authorised Edition) #2: "Pit of Doom" (BW-c)

◆ They learn to construct gas masks from scratch, using wet cloth and ground charcoal, as well as how to create a tourniquet to stop bleeding.

Planet of the Apes episode #13: "The Tyrant" (CB-t)

◆ The duo also learn how to recognize the effects of wine laced with opium.

El Planeta de Los Simios #6: "The Zombies" (ET-c)

◆ Virdon and Burke learn how to sew garments.

Planet of the Apes episode #11: "The Tyrant" (CB-t)

◆ Virdon also studies wood-carving.

Planet of the Apes episode #5: "The Legacy" (CB-t)

PUBLISHER / STUDIO
AB . . . . ABC-TV
AC . . . Adventure / Malibu Comics
AW . . . . Award Books
BB . . . . Ballantine Books
BN . . . . Bantam Books
BW . . . . Brown Watson Books
CB . . . . CBS-TV
CV . . . . Chad Valley Sliderama
DH . . . . .Dark Horse Comics
ET . . . . Editorial Mo.Pa.Sa.
FX . . . . 20th Century Fox
GK . . . .Gold Key / Western Comics
HE . . . HarperEntertainment Books
HM . . Harry K. McWilliams Assoc.
MC . . . . .Marvel Comics
MR . . . Mr. Comics / Metallic Rose
NB . . . . NBC-TV
PR . . . . Power Records
SB . . . . Signet Books
TP . . . . .Topps
UB . . . . .Ubisoft

MEDIUM
a . . . . animated series
b . . . . .book-and-record set
c . . . . .comic book or strip
d . . . . trading card
e . . . . .e-comic
f . . . . .theatrical film
k . . . . .storybook
m . . . . .magazine article
n . . . . .novel or novelization
p . . . . promotional newspaper
r . . . . .recorded audio fiction
s . . . . short story
t . . . . television series
u . . . . .unfilmed script or story
v . . . . video game
x . . . . .Blu-Ray exclusive
y . . . . .young adult novel

◆ The astronauts learn how to operate a heliograph, a 19th-century device that used a mirror to reflect sunlight for the purpose of communicating information to a distant observer.

Planet of the Apes episode #11: "The Tyrant" (AW-n)

NOTE: This is revealed in the episode's novelization. Heliographs were not much in use after 1935, so it's especially astounding that the astronauts would both know how to operate one.

◆ Burke and Virdon are trained how to operate warplanes, including how to fire rockets.

Planet of the Apes (Authorised Edition) #1: "When the Earth Shakes" (BW-c)

◆ The astronauts learn how to build a hot air balloon, and to channel natural gas from vents in the ground to power such a contraption.

Planet of the Apes (Authorised Edition) #3: "Breakout" (BW-c)

◆ Additionally, the duo learn how to build a hang-glider.

Planet of the Apes episode #14: "Up Above the World So High" (CB-t)

◆ Burke learns how to build a wind generator capable of powering a computer.

Planet of the Apes (Authorised Edition) #2: "From Out of the Past" (BW-s)

◆ They also learn how to ground crystal into a magnifying glass, and to construct a javelin catapult.

Planet of the Apes episode #14: "Up Above the World So High" (CB-t)

NOTE: Mention of the javelin catapult appears in an early outline, according to Simian Scrolls issue #12, but was apparently cut from the final televised episode.

◆ Burke and Virdon learn how to operate movie-theater projection booths, and how to fix generators.

El Planeta de Los Simios #1: "The Wandering Jew" (ET-c)

◆ Virdon learns how to build a goniometric radiometer—a device used to measure the far-field irradiance pattern of a divergent source such as a light-emitting diode (LED), laser diode (LD) or fiber tip—and how to use the instrument to track radio broadcasts.

El Planeta de Los Simios #3: "The Beach of Time" (ET-c)

◆ The *Blue Star*, a missile-equipped USAF spaceship, encounters an electrical storm near Alpha Centauri. Propelled in time to the year 3085, the vessel is presumed lost.

El Planeta de Los Simios #5: "The Star Gods" (ET-c)

NOTE: This Spanish-language comic was released only in Argentina. The Blue Star is said to have been lost two months before the launch of Virdon's and Burke's mission.

◆ Two months later, Virdon, Burke and a third officer nicknamed Jonesy begin a long-range reconnaissance mission to circumnavigate the Belt of Orion and its moons, aboard an ANSA spacecraft called *Probe Six*.

Planet of the Apes episode #1: "Escape from Tomorrow" (CB-t)

NOTE: The ship's name and mission are revealed in the Planet of the Apes Initial Concept Pages. *It's unclear when* Probe Six *launched, but since it reached Alpha Centauri by 1980, it likely left Earth some time in the 1970s.*

AUGUST 19, 1980

◆ *Probe Six* encounters violent radioactive turbulence near Alpha Centauri, causing severe damage and loss of ship control. Jonesy activates an automatic homing device, redirecting the spacecraft back to Earth. The astronauts lose consciousness as the ship is propelled to the year 3085. Virdon leaves behind his wife and children, while Jonesy leaves a wife and child as well.

Planet of the Apes episode #1: "Escape from Tomorrow" (CB-t)

NOTE: The ship's name and mission are revealed in the Planet of the Apes Initial Concept Pages. *The Chad Valley Picture Show filmstrips date the ship's loss and future arrival in 2105 and 3975, respectively, calling the mission "man's first attempt to reach the stars" and attributing the accident to the failure of the ship's automatic drive.*

◆ *Probe Six* is officially recorded as missing.

Planet of the Apes (Authorised Edition) #3: "From Out of the Sky" (BW-c)

NOTE: Probe Six *is not actually mentioned by name in this story.*

◆ When Burke vanishes, his friend and fellow astronaut, Verina, is still in the Space Academy.

Planet of the Apes (Authorised Edition) #3: "From Out of the Sky" (BW-c)

AFTER AUGUST 1980

◆ Pete Burke's friend Verina graduates the Space Academy and is assigned her own ANSA mission, along with two other astronauts. Her ship encounters an anomaly and is propelled forward to the year 3085. Eventually, she manages to return home again.

Planet of the Apes (Authorised Edition) #3: "From Out of the Sky" (BW-c)

NOTE: The anomaly is likely the Hasslein Curve, though this is unstated.

◆ Virdon and Burke finally return to their own era by traversing the Hasslein Curve once more.

Telefilm #1: Back to the Planet of the Apes (AB-t)

NOTE: Ten episodes of the TV series were re-edited into five telefilms, which ABC affiliates aired with newly filmed framing footage starring Roddy McDowall as Galen, speaking to an unseen human time-traveler about his adventures with Burke and Virdon—whom he says returned home. This revelation is the most intriguing aspect of these scenes, though it does create a paradox—if they could warn humanity of the ape-controlled future, why would man still take apes as pets, allowing that future to unfold? These scenes were excluded when the TV series was released on DVD, but can be viewed online at Kassidy Rae's Planet of the Apes: The Television Series *Website.*

BETWEEN 1980 AND 1989

◆ Karl Vasich, future flight officer aboard the USAF *Oberon*, is born.

Planet of the Apes (FX-f)

NOTE: The script identifies Vasich as being in his 40s in 2029 (actor Chris Ellis was 45 when the film was produced). The novel The Fall *misspells his first name as "Carl," but the script spells it "Karl."*

BETWEEN 1980 AND 1992

◆ The United States creates the first laser-powered pistols, flare-mouthed in design.

Planet of the Apes: "Hostage" (CB-u)

NOTE: This script was never filmed. The weapons are said to have been created after Probe Six *vanished, but before the nuclear war. They must differ from the laser gun featured in* Return to the Planet of the Apes, *which was among the* Venturer's *equipment in 1976.*

◆ The California government builds a city powered by a miniature nuclear generator, and filled with impressive skyscrapers containing advanced computer systems.

Planet of the Apes (Authorised Edition) #2: "From Out of the Past" (BW-s)

NOTE: This is said to have happened after Virdon and Burke left for space. Since it's unlikely anyone would have built a city after the nuclear war, its construction must occur between 1980 and 1992.

c. 1980s

◆ Time capsules become a popular craze, as many humans bury items for future generations to uncover.

Planet of the Apes episode #10: "The Interrogation" (CB-t)

◆ A military officer named Moriah shoots her commanding officer and most of her platoon during a backwater battle. Another soldier, known as π [*pi*], sells military secrets to enemy nations. A third, Devon, a technical whiz with a harsh mean streak, blows up a car containing four generals and other officers after failing to progress in rank. The three are convicted and imprisoned for their crimes.

Ape City #2: "See No Evil, Hear No Evil, Speak No Evil" (AC-c)

◆ The Keepers, an alien race brazenly calling themselves the Future Rulers of Earth, attempt to conquer the planet. Their spaceship, the *Psychedrome*, is shot down and crashes into a mountain near South Dakota. The aliens survive, but the *Psychedrome* is embedded deep in the mountain. U.S. government officials ally with the Keepers, who brainwash American dissidents never to question government authority or be unhappy. In return, the military provides weapons of mass destruction. The Keepers and their army of winged monkey-demons pretend to be their allies, all the while waiting for a chance to conquer the planet.

Planet of the Apes #20: "Terror on the Planet of the Apes, Phase 2—Society of the Psychedrome" (MC-c)

NOTE: *This is the first of three attempted alien takeovers of Earth. The others happen circa 2150 and 2200. The event is undated, but presumably occurs in the late 20ᵗʰ century, before the nuclear war.*

LATE 1981

◆ Caesar, age 8½, begins bareback-riding acrobatics with Señor Armando's circus. Across the country, meanwhile, political repression forces small circuses to play to increasingly dwindling audiences. This enables Caesar to avoid dangerous publicity, away from the prying eyes of city governments.

Planet of the Apes #11: "Outlines of Tomorrow—A Chronology of the Planet of the Apes" (MC-m)

NOTE: *Marvel's chronology places this event in 1980, which does not jibe with the films, given his birth in early 1973. Therefore, I have moved it to late 1981.*

1981 TO 1992

◆ At the circus, Caesar leads a chimp acrobat group known as the Soaring Simians. Other performers include Pierre the Mute Mountain and an elephant named Sheba, with Armando as emcee and snake-charmer. Paula Dean, of the Society for the Prevention of Cruelty to Animals (SPCA), accuses Armando of mistreating his animals. He assures her his methods are humane, but when she threatens to call the press, he pulls up stakes and heads for Mexico to protect Caesar. Meanwhile, the chimp's dreams foretell a future of bombs, war, scar-faced masked men and gorilla hunting parties—and everything can talk (horses, cats, dogs, even Pierre). Armando assures him not every dream will come true, but the deaf-mute Pierre—suddenly able to speak—responds that it will.

Revolution on the Planet of the Apes #3: "Little Caesar" (MR-c)

NOTE: *This tale was published as a sneak preview in issue #1 of Mr. Comics'* Big Max, *under the title "Armando's Marvelous Menagerie Circus." Paula Dean is named for* Apes *screenwriter Paul Dehn.*

◆ As more visions come to pass, Caesar realizes he's dreaming the future into being. One particular vision haunts him, in which his grandchildren fight in a global war with humans, destroying the moon in "an orgy of violence and madness." He sees his sons and daughter, far off in his future, one of whom he knows will die by violence. Armando calls the dreams a gift from God, not to be questioned, but still Caesar wonders: If he stops dreaming about the future, will that prevent the sky from catching fire?

Revolution on the Planet of the Apes #4: "Caesar's Journal" (MR-c)

NOTE: *Caesar foresees the death of his first son, Cornelius, as a child. Marvel's timeline in* Planet of the Apes #11 *claims Caesar had no offspring after Cornelius, but the Adventure comics feature a grandson, Alexander. Since Cornelius can't be the father, this implies a sibling. Revolution on the Planet of the Apes backs this up, revealing a daughter and at least one more son in addition to Cornelius.*

1982

◆ The 1982 edition of the *World Book Encyclopedia* includes an entry portraying gorillas as peaceful.

Planet of the Apes #1: "The Monkey Planet—Beneath" (AC-c)

NOTE: Ironically, this is one of the only times the Planet of the Apes *mythos accurately portrays gorillas.*

FEBRUARY 1983

◆ A plague devastates Earth, ravaging the planet in months. Thousands of dogs and cats die, and thousands more are destroyed to prevent further infection. Huge dog bonfires are held, and mankind is left without its favorite pets. The Pet Memorial, a statue of a dog and a cat, is erected not far from the Mall of the Four Muses to commemorate the loss of man's best friends. Humans and most other animals are unaffected by the plague—for a time.

Conquest of the Planet of the Apes (FX-f)

NOTE: Cornelius says the plague lasted weeks, but Armando indicates (in Conquest of the Planet of the Apes) *that it spread for months. Armando's account seems more likely since it occurred in his lifetime, while Cornelius' knowledge comes from ancient records. The year of the plague (1983) is established on the memorial, though the novelization and Marvel's* Conquest *adaptation claim 1982; the February setting is revealed in a timeline packaged with the* Planet of the Apes 40th *Anniversary Collection Blu-Ray set. That chronology establishes two parallel histories for the* Apes *mythos, dating the original timeline's plague at 2050 and the revised version in 1983.*

◆ The plague kills off most wolves as well.

Ape Nation #1: "Plans" (AC-c)

◆ Some cats survive the plague.

Planet of the Apes #24: "The Birth of Apeslayer" (MC-c)

◆ Some dogs survive as well.

Planet of the Apes episode #1: "Escape from Tomorrow" (CB-t)

◆ Humans and all simian species, even the smallest, are thought immune to the virus.

Conquest of the Planet of the Apes (FX-f)

◆ Some suspect the plague to have been brought back to Earth by an unmanned space probe.

Escape from the Planet of the Apes (FX-f)

◆ Others theorize, in whispered tones, that the disease was caused by U.S. government testing gone horribly wrong. No one, however, knows for sure.

Planet of the Apes #19: "Quitting Time" (AC-c)

◆ In actuality, the virus is extraterrestrial in nature, brought to Earth by astronauts ferrying virus-tainted samples from space.

Planet of the Apes 40th Anniversary Collection: Timeline (FX-x)

NOTE: This explanation is supported by Conquest of the Planet of the Apes, *which indicates the public story to be a space-borne virus. Fans have also speculated that the plague could have paradoxically been brought back in time by Zira and Cornelius.*

PUBLISHER / STUDIO

AB	ABC-TV
AC	Adventure / Malibu Comics
AW	Award Books
BB	Ballantine Books
BN	Bantam Books
BW	Brown Watson Books
CB	CBS-TV
CV	Chad Valley Sliderama
DH	Dark Horse Comics
ET	Editorial Mo.Pa.Sa.
FX	20th Century Fox
GK	Gold Key / Western Comics
HE	HarperEntertainment Books
HM	Harry K. McWilliams Assoc.
MC	Marvel Comics
MR	Mr. Comics / Metallic Rose
NB	NBC-TV
PR	Power Records
SB	Signet Books
TP	Topps
UB	Ubisoft

MEDIUM

a	animated series
b	book-and-record set
c	comic book or strip
d	trading card
e	e-comic
f	theatrical film
k	storybook
m	magazine article
n	novel or novelization
p	promotional newspaper
r	recorded audio fiction
s	short story
t	television series
u	unfilmed script or story
v	video game
x	Blu-Ray exclusive
y	young adult novel

LATE 20ᵗʰ CENTURY, BEFORE 1992

◆ Mankind experiments with cybernetic life prolongation. One model is perfected, who lives for two millennia. Forgetting his name, the cyborg calls himself Ahasuerus, after the story of the Wandering Jew.

El Planeta de Los Simios #1: "The Wandering Jew" (ET-c)

NOTE: This Spanish-language comic was released only in Argentina. No date is provided, just that it happened in the late 20ᵗʰ century.

1983 TO 1986

◆ Humanity faces the first repercussions of the plague. Anxious to replace their lost pets, humans turn to small primates, birds, lizards and other creatures. The primates, the most useful and easiest to train, gradually become the most common household animal.

Planet of the Apes #11: "Outlines of Tomorrow—A Chronology of the Planet of the Apes" (MC-m)

◆ Marmosets and Tarsier monkeys are among the first primates taken as pets.

Conquest of the Planet of the Apes (MC-c)

NOTE: This information comes from Marvel's comic adaptation of the film.

◆ Eventually, human pet owners turn to apes. Though not as intelligent as man, apes are said to be 20 times' smarter than cats and dogs, and learn quickly from living in human homes.

Escape from the Planet of the Apes (FX-f)

NOTE: A timeline packaged with the Planet of the Apes *40ᵗʰ Anniversary Collection indicates that by July 1983, apes become the predominantly popular choice for pets. That governments would still allow this, however, knowing mankind's fate, is unfathomable.*

◆ Humans gradually take larger simians as pets. During this generation of primates, the plague's genetic effects first manifest: Their stature increases, as does intelligence in the larger orders.

Planet of the Apes #11: "Outlines of Tomorrow—A Chronology of the Planet of the Apes" (MC-m)

NOTE: This was Marvel's attempt to reconcile the future apes' increased height with that of real-life simians. What it doesn't explain is why no one in 1973—a decade before such effects would surface—seemed to find it odd that the apeonauts were so tall.

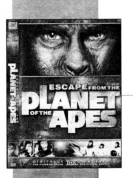

◆ The primitive apes begin to comprehend the languages of their human masters, and quickly evolve from simply performing tricks to rendering services.

Escape from the Planet of the Apes (FX-f)

◆ Thus, rather than pets, humans quickly realize the apes' value as servants and laborers.

Revolution on the Planet of the Apes #1: "Part One: The End of the World" (MR-c)

NOTE: In Escape from the Planet of the Apes, *Cornelius claims it will take two centuries for primitive apes to evolve into servants, but it occurs in just eight years. Some cite this as evidence of an altered timeline, though Cornelius may have read inaccurate scrolls.*

NOVEMBER 1984

◆ Increasing international hostilities cause an upset in the 1984 U.S. presidential election, resulting in a complete regime change. Tensions between superpower countries mount, and worldwide production of devastating nuclear weapons increases rapidly.

Planet of the Apes 40ᵗʰ Anniversary Collection: Timeline (FX-x)

1986

◆ Ape Management is incorporated as a semi-public branch of the government, with the sole task of rudimentarily conditioning apes.

Planet of the Apes #11: "Outlines of Tomorrow—A Chronology of the Planet of the Apes" (MC-m)

◆ Using negative reinforcement, severe punishments and such fear-inducing tactics as fire to scare the simian servants into submission, Ape Management's trainers condition the apes to respond to single-word commands such as "Do."

Conquest of the Planet of the Apes (FX-f)

◆ The Ape Management complex is headquartered in a facility spanning ten city blocks.

Revolution on the Planet of the Apes #1: "Part One: The End of the World" (MR-c)

NOTE: The location of Ape Management is a source of some debate. The Conquest *novelization implies it's in California, and Marvel's timeline and* Revolution on the Planet of the Apes *concur with this placement,* Revolution *specifically setting it in San Diego. Script treatments for* Conquest of the Planet of the Apes *and* Battle for the Planet of the Apes, *however, place both films on the East Coast, setting the stage for* Beneath the Planet of the Apes' *New York setting for the mutant population and the Alpha-Omega Bomb.*

◆ The facility is located two blocks east of 11ᵗʰ Avenue.

Battle for the Planet of the Apes (FX-f)

◆ Ape Management becomes a thriving institution, teaching servant apes to clean houses, carry packages, shine shoes, shop, bus tables, run errands and perform other chores humans once did for themselves. To reward them for their services, humans "pay" obedient apes with raisins and other treats.

Conquest of the Planet of the Apes (FX-f)

◆ Chimps, orangutans and bonobos are primarily trained as domestic servants, while gorillas are mainly used as laborers. Treated far worse than other simians, the gorillas grow to fear and resent humanity.

Empire on the Planet of the Apes (MR-c, unpublished)

NOTE: Details of this proposed sequel to Revolution on the Planet of the Apes *were provided by authors Ty Templeton and Joe O'Brien.*

◆ A book about brainwashing techniques is published, title and author unknown.

Planet of the Apes episode #10: "The Interrogation" (CB-t)

◆ Alma (first name unknown), future mutant and assistant to Governor Arthur Vernon Kolp, is born.

Battle for the Planet of the Apes (FX-f)

NOTE: Since Alma's age is unknown, I have based this figure on actress France Nuyen's age (34) when the film (set in 2020) was produced.

AFTER 1986

◆ An unknown person buries a time capsule for future generations to find. This capsule contains a book about brainwashing, published in 1986.

Planet of the Apes episode #10: "The Interrogation" (CB-t)

MID 1980s

◆ Arthur Bishop Trundy, a power-hungry right-wing opportunist, is named governor.

Revolution on the Planet of the Apes #1: "For Human Rights" (MR-c)

NOTE: It's debatable as to which U.S. state Trundy governs. The story indicates he is the governor of California, and both the Conquest of the Planet of the Apes *novelization and Marvel's timeline would concur with such a placement for* Conquest *and* Battle for the Planet of the Apes. *Script treatments for both films, however, place them on the East Coast, setting the stage for* Beneath the Planet of the Apes' *New York setting for the mutant population and the Alpha-Omega Bomb. Trundy is named after actress Natalie Trundy, who appeared in four of the original* Planet of the Apes *films.*

◆ The U.S. government grows increasingly more authoritarian over a short period of time. A reverse migration from the suburbs into the cities results in large towns devolving into feudal ports surrounded by farmlands known as provinces. With this increase in governmental structure, a slave class develops—namely, the apes.

Planet of the Apes #11: "Outlines of Tomorrow—A Chronology of the Planet of the Apes" (MC-m)

◆ Due to rising levels of pollution, the air in California becomes increasingly unbreathable.

Conquest of the Planet of the Apes (AW-n)

NOTE: This information appears in the film's novelization.

◆ To bring the pollution level in the provinces under control and clean California's air, the U.S. government builds a massive air-purification plant in the Rocky Mountains.

Planet of the Apes #11: "Outlines of Tomorrow—A Chronology of the Planet of the Apes" (MC-m)

◆ The government also constructs a series of huge air-scrubbing plants along a mountain chain a hundred miles east of San Diego.

Conquest of the Planet of the Apes (AW-n)

NOTE: This information appears in the film's novelization.

1987

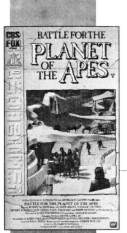

◆ Carson McCormick is hired by Ape Management Publications (AMP) to write instructional pamphlets for human owners, explaining how to handle apes within the home. The more he witnesses at his job, however, the more McCormick grows uncomfortable with ape enslavement, knowing it will one day backfire on humanity.

Planet of the Apes #19: "Quitting Time" (AC-c)

◆ Virgil, an orangutan and future advisor to Caesar, is born.

Battle for the Planet of the Apes (FX-f)

NOTE: Since Virgil's age is unknown, I have based this figure on actor Paul Williams' age (33) when the film (set in 2020) was produced.

◆ Jake, a future human citizen of Ape City during Caesar's reign, is born.

Battle for the Planet of the Apes (FX-f)

NOTE: Since Jake's age is unknown, I have based this figure on actor Michael Stearns' age (33) when the film (set in 2020) was produced.

MID TO LATE 1980s

◆ *Time* magazine publishes a story detailing how apes came to replace dogs and cats as household pets.

Planet of the Apes #15: "Countdown Zero—Part Two" (AC-c)

◆ To ensure that ape supply can meet human demand, the U.S. government begins administering fertility drugs to the simian population.

Planet of the Apes #19: "Quitting Time" (AC-c)

NOTE: These drugs may have had other effects as well, such as stimulating speech centers and minds. It's also possible they were created from the deceased apeonauts' DNA, collected before they were buried.

◆ Eventually, the integration of apes into human society grows so complete that gas stations and other public areas begin providing separate rest rooms for simians.

The Forbidden Zone #1: "Part One—Forbidden Knowledge" (AC-c)

◆ Señor Armando tells Caesar about the circumstances surrounding his birth and his parents' deaths. As he grows older, Caesar's dreams grow clearer and more vivid, revealing faces and places he doesn't know, and he wonders if they are memories passed down by his parents. Seeing how different he is than other apes, Caesar sometimes wishes he couldn't speak, but Armando says he's special—not just because he can speak, but because he can think and reason, and see things in a way other apes cannot.

Revolution on the Planet of the Apes #2: "Caesar's Journal" (MR-c)

NOTE: The exact date is not provided, just that it occurred when Caesar was "older."

◆ As the world's political climate spirals out of control, a group of U.S. scientists, realizing war is imminent, builds secret repository vaults throughout the country, uploading the sum total of human knowledge into large computers, along with a holographic recording to educate future generations. One such repository is hidden in the basement of the Oakland Science Institute, a government think-tank in California.

Planet of the Apes episode #5: "The Legacy" (CB-t)

◆ The U.S. government launches a spaceship containing four astronauts: Taylor, Thomas, LaFever and Bengsten. Lost in a time warp, the ship is propelled forward to the 3070s.

Planet of the Apes episode #1: "Escape from Tomorrow" (CB-t)

NOTE: Little is known about this mission other than a few references in episode #1 of the TV series. The astronauts' names are noted in an early-draft script of the first episode, written by Rod Serling; the names Thomas and LaFever are holdovers from Serling's early-draft script from the first Planet of the Apes *film, in which George Taylor and John Landon are known, respectively, as John Thomas and Paul LaFever. It's unrecorded if this Taylor is related to George Taylor and his daughters, Jo and Tammy.*

◆ Yet another spaceship is lost in a time warp, arriving on Earth some time after 3085, where its crew befriends a chimpanzee named Galen.

Telefilm #1: Back to the Planet of the Apes (AB-t)

NOTE: Ten episodes of the TV series were re-edited to create five telefilms, which ABC affiliates aired with newly filmed framing footage starring Roddy McDowall as Galen. All that is known about these astronauts is that Galen tells them of his adventures with Alan Virdon and Pete Burke.

PUBLISHER / STUDIO
AB . . . . ABC-TV
AC . . . . Adventure / Malibu Comics
AW . . . . Award Books
BB . . . . Ballantine Books
BN . . . . Bantam Books
BW . . . . Brown Watson Books
CB . . . . CBS-TV
CV . . . . Chad Valley Sliderama
DH . . . . Dark Horse Comics
ET . . . . Editorial Mo.Pa.Sa.
FX . . . . 20th Century Fox
GK . . . . Gold Key / Western Comics
HE . . . HarperEntertainment Books
HM . . Harry K. McWilliams Assoc.
MC . . . . Marvel Comics
MR . . . Mr. Comics / Metallic Rose
NB . . . . NBC-TV
PR . . . . Power Records
SB . . . . Signet Books
TP . . . . Topps
UB . . . . Ubisoft

MEDIUM
a . . . . animated series
b . . . . book-and-record set
c . . . . comic book or strip
d . . . . trading card
e . . . . e-comic
f . . . . theatrical film
k . . . . storybook
m . . . . magazine article
n . . . . novel or novelization
p . . . . promotional newspaper
r . . . . recorded audio fiction
s . . . . short story
t . . . . television series
u . . . . unfilmed script or story
v . . . . video game
x . . . . Blu-Ray exclusive
y . . . . young adult novel

LATE 1980s

◆ As the U.S. government grows increasingly oppressive, some businessmen find it difficult to make money. The space program falls out of favor, and the supersonic transport industry shuts down completely. Synthetic alloy companies, meanwhile, only continue turning a profit by selling directly to the government. Hydroponic farming is seen as the future of industry.

Conquest of the Planet of the Apes (AW-n)

> *NOTE: This information comes from the film's novelization. It's interesting to note that although the space program is said to be falling out of favor, several more space missions occur after this period.*

◆ During this period, a strong anti-ape sentiment begins to build, as many humans feel threatened by the ever-growing simian population.

Revolution on the Planet of the Apes #1: "For Human Rights" (MR-c)

BEFORE 1988

◆ The U.S. government faces a string of catastrophes, including a war in Venezuela and a nuclear meltdown in Utah. California endures increased unemployment, a massive earthquake, environmental setbacks and a poor economy.

Revolution on the Planet of the Apes #1: "For Human Rights" (MR-c)

1988

◆ Grace Alexander, a future medical officer aboard the USAF *Oberon*, is born.

Planet of the Apes (FX-f)

> *NOTE: Since Alexander's age is unknown, I have based this figure on actress Anne Ramsay's age (41) when the film (set in 2029) was produced.*

◆ Jo Taylor, daughter of missing ANSA astronaut George Taylor, follows in her father's footsteps by joining the U.S. space program.

Ape City #2: "See No Evil, Hear No Evil, Speak No Evil" (AC-c)

> *NOTE: The events of this story are undated. I have placed the departure of Jo Taylor's mission in 1990, setting her entry in the space program—two years prior—in 1988. However, since her departure year is not set in stone, this date is open to debate.*

◆ Governor Arthur Bishop Trundy capitalizes on anti-ape sentiments by running for the U.S. presidency on a "manifest human superiority" platform, touting the slogan "For Human Rights." At a political rally, Trundy mocks the incumbent president's pro-science stance, warning that some apes are learning Sign Language and will soon demand a right to vote. Radical activist Chris Leung attends the rally, intending to assassinate him for focusing on the ape crisis to the exclusion of all other issues. Sensing his intentions, a gorilla servant named Toby knocks the gun from his hand. Guards shoot Toby, mistaking the ape's actions as a threat, and Leung escapes, leaving Trundy's security chief, Segarini, wondering if the gorilla gave its life to save a human.

Revolution on the Planet of the Apes #1: "For Human Rights" (MR-c)

◆ Arthur Trundy is elected president. Within his first months in office, the *Constitution* is amended to codify the divine superiority of the human race above all other creatures.

Revolution on the Planet of the Apes #1: "Part One: The End of the World" (MR-c)

NOTE: The timeline in Revolution #1 *places the events of* Conquest of the Planet of the Apes *in 1994 rather than 1991, with Trundy becoming president in 1992. Since that doesn't jibe with the movies' chronology, I have moved these events back to 1988 to compensate.*

◆ Arnold Jason Breck, a power-hungry, self-important fascist, succeeds Trundy as governor. Threatened by the rising ape population, Breck makes this issue a priority for his administration. Breck sees apes as a reflection of man's darker, more primal side, his hatred fueled by a desire to extinguish humanity's primitive past.

Conquest of the Planet of the Apes (FX-f)

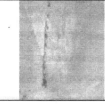

NOTE: The film's novelization gives Breck the first name Jason, but Revolution #1 *calls him Arnold; I have thus combined the two to reconcile the discrepancy.*

◆ A road four blocks to the west of Ape Management's main facility is renamed in Breck's honor.

Battle for the Planet of the Apes (FX-f)

BETWEEN 1988 AND 1992

◆ Trundy names his advisors and cabinet, including Culley Sparks as defense secretary and the wheelchair-bound Dr. Karl Reich as science council advisor.

Revolution on the Planet of the Apes #1: "Part One: The End of the World" (MR-c)

NOTE: It's unclear if Segarini, Trundy's security chief during his governorship, joins him at the White House.

◆ Gen. Norman "Bud" Akins serves as Trundy's chairman of the Joint Chiefs of Staff, while Arthur Vernon Kolp serves as a senior member of his Defense Council.

Revolution on the Planet of the Apes #4: "Part Four: Truth and Consequences" (MR-c)

◆ Trundy's vice president and chief advisor is named Henry (last name unknown).

Planet of the Apes #14: "Terror on the Planet of the Apes, Phase 2 — Up the Nose-Tube to Monkey-Trash" (MC-c)

NOTE: This issue features the corpse of a U.S. president and his chief advisor, Henry, both survivors of the nuclear war. Though the president is unnamed, the events of Revolution on the Planet of the Apes *make it clear he must be Trundy. According to* Revolution *author Ty Templeton, a cut scene from* Revolution #5 *would have established Henry as being Trundy's vice president.*

◆ Trundy assigns Nora Rhodes as media undersecretary of the Pentagon Bureau of Information (PBI). Her job is to put forth misinformation with a truthful spin, to keep the masses ignorant of his actions. Rhodes ends her engagement to Dr. Bryce Evans, a geneticist, before leaving for Washington, D.C.

Revolution on the Planet of the Apes #2: "Part Two: Lines of Communication" (MR-c)

◆ Given the rising ape problem and the recent planetary takeover attempt by the *Psychedrome* aliens, the president enacts Project: Last Ditch, a top-secret plan to assure his enemies' destruction.

Planet of the Apes #20: "Terror on the Planet of the Apes, Phase 2 — Society of the Psychedrome" (MC-c)

◆ In preparing Last Ditch, the government stockpiles missiles, lasers, nuclear warheads and other weapons of mass destruction in a South Dakota silo within the same mountain as the *Psychedrome*. Railway tracks line the subterranean chamber, facilitating weapons movement on a traincar system called a snaker-railer.

⬤ *Planet of the Apes #23: "Terror on the Planet of the Apes, Phase 2—Messiah of Monkey-Demons" (MC-c)*

◆ An underground archives section is added to Ape Management's main facility beneath the corner of Breck and Ackerman, two blocks west of 11th Ave and built to withstand the blast of a 10-megaton atomic bomb. Among the records are sealed tapes of Cornelius and Zira, revealing mankind's fate. This area is supervised by Bruce "Mac" MacDonald, brother of Governor Breck's assistant, Malcolm MacDonald.

Battle for the Planet of the Apes (FX-f)

NOTE: Bruce MacDonald's first name is revealed in Marvel's comic adaptation of the film, while Revolution on the Planet of the Apes #4 *provides Malcolm's first name. Bruce's age is a bit of an issue, as actor Austin Stoker was 30 years old when the film (set in 2020) was made; if Bruce is the same age as the actor, he'd have been born in 1990, making him an infant at this point—clearly, then, the character must be at least 20 years older than the actor who portrayed him, despite his youthful appearance.*

◆ The United States faces a military threat to national security. Trundy sends members of the National Guard to handle it, deploying two-thirds of the Guard overseas, thus leaving the country vulnerable.

Revolution on the Planet of the Apes #2: "Part Two: Lines of Communication" (MR-c)

NOTE: This deployment is likely a comment on the Iraq War and President George W. Bush. Whether either is part of Planet of the Apes *history, however, remains unknown.*

c. 1988 TO 1990

◆ For two years, astronaut Jo Taylor—daughter of the late George Taylor—works her way up the chain of command, seeking answers regarding the sealed records of her father's disappearance. At long last, she meets someone with the necessary computer codes and learns of his (and Earth's) fated demise in 3979.

Ape City #2: "See No Evil, Hear No Evil, Speak No Evil" (AC-c)

NOTE: These events are undated, but must occur between Jo's entrance into the space program, circa 1988, and her mission departure in or around 1990.

1989

◆ Outnumbered by ape workers three to one, humans officially become a U.S. minority.

Revolution on the Planet of the Apes #1: "Part One: The End of the World" (MR-c)

◆ The last of a series of air-scrubbing plants is constructed in California, along a mountain chain 100 miles east of San Diego, at a cost of billions of dollars. In conjunction with stringent laws, the plants begin to make the air in this part of the state breathable again.

Conquest of the Planet of the Apes (AW-n)

NOTE: This information appears in the film's novelization.

1989 TO 1991

◆ President Trundy creates the American News Network (ANN), a cable channel operating out of the Pentagon to spread government-friendly propaganda disguised as news. A national swell of fear surrounding the growing ape population leads to draconian laws intended to contain and control them.

Revolution on the Planet of the Apes #1: "Part One: The End of the World" (MR-c)

◆ Circuses and other older forms of entertainment become increasingly rare.

Conquest of the Planet of the Apes (AW-n)

NOTE: This information appears in the film's novelization.

BEFORE 1990

◆ The U.S. government creates the Vindicator Project, a top-secret operation intended to prevent Earth from becoming the ape-controlled society described by Zira and Cornelius. A specialized flying vehicle, energized by a power crystal, is designed to carry covert operatives into the future and back.

Ape City #1: "Monkey Business" (AC-c)

NOTE: If preventing such a future was so important, one wonders why the U.S. government sanctioned using apes as pets, and then servants, in the first place — it had been forewarned, after all. Presumably, the Vindicators' ship uses technology similar to Derek Zane's Temporal Displacement Module.

1990

◆ Determined to avenge the death of her father (Col. George Taylor), and to alter the future that killed him, astronaut Jo Taylor volunteers for the Vindicator Project. A crew of specialists is selected to join her, four of whom—Scab, Devon, Moriah and π [*pi*]—are convicted killers offered amnesty for undertaking the mission. The sixth team member, MX, is a fellow volunteer.

Ape City #1: "Monkey Business" (AC-c)

NOTE: These events are undated. I have placed the ship's year of departure in 1990 (the year the story was published), allowing Jo ample time to grow to adulthood.

◆ MX, who lives only to fight, thinks he is perpetually involved in World War II. Jo Taylor is unimpressed with any of her teammates.

Ape City #2: "See No Evil, Hear No Evil, Speak No Evil" (AC-c)

◆ The Vindicator Project launches, propelling the team forward in time to the year 2140. Their mission: to kill as many apes as possible, thereby giving humans a fighting chance to regain dominancy.

Ape City #1: "Monkey Business" (AC-c)

BEFORE OCTOBER 1990

◆ Congress passes the Media Act, making it a crime to broadcast unauthorized footage. Meanwhile, the FCC is rolled into the U.S. Department of Homeland Security, making television a lot less interesting.

Revolution on the Planet of the Apes #1: "Part One: The End of the World" (MR-c)

NOTE: Apparently, Homeland Security is established a decade earlier in the Planet of the Apes *universe.*

OCTOBER 1990

◆ Riots break out following a massive earthquake in California, causing the U.S. government to declare martial law. Blaming the commercial media for inciting such violence, President Trundy declares all private broadcasts illegal under the Media Act.

Revolution on the Planet of the Apes #1: "Part One: The End of the World" (MR-c)

NOTE: The timeline in Revolution on the Planet of the Apes #1 *places* Conquest of the Planet of the Apes *six months after Trundy declares martial law. Marvel's timeline in issue #11 places the film in April 1991, setting the martial law declaration in October 1990.*

BETWEEN 1990 AND 1999

◆ Frank Santos, a future technical specialist aboard the USAF *Oberon*, is born.

Planet of the Apes (FX-f)

NOTE: The script identifies Santos as being in his 30s in 2029 (actor Michael Jace was 36 when the film was made).

BEFORE 1991

◆ Heeding the apeonauts' warning regarding Earth's future destruction, mankind launches a colony ship carrying 40 females and 10 males into space in suspended animation, intending to preserve the species on another planet. The ship enters a Hasslein Curve, however, and is propelled to approximately 5000 A.D.

Sky Gods #1 (AC-c, unpublished)

NOTE: Roland Mann, author of Adventure's Blood of the Apes, *proposed this four-issue miniseries (alternately titled "Second Coming") to creative director Tom K. Mason as well. Although Mason greenlit the proposal, it was ultimately scrapped before going to contract, when Malibu opted to scale back its* Planet of the Apes *titles. The proposal does not indicate when the story occurs, though it most likely takes place before Caesar's rebellion in 1991.*

◆ A scientist studying how memory is stored and passed down through generations creates a clone of Cornelius (from genetic material collected during his visit to 1973) and names him Janus. The clone retains Cornelius' memories and tells him of Earth's future destruction. The scientist seeks a way to stop George Taylor from detonating the Alpha-Omega Bomb, but realizes the forces leading to that destruction are already in motion and out of his control. He, therefore, focuses not on altering the future, but rather on creating a plan to ensure the planet survives the bomb's detonation. To that end, he develops an energy device as a defense against the missile, enabling the weapon's destructive power to be shunted into space.

Redemption of the Planet of the Apes (AC-c, unpublished)

NOTE: Lowell Cunningham, Men in Black creator and author of Adventure's The Forbidden Zone, *proposed this four-issue miniseries to creative director Tom K. Mason as well. However, Cunningham says, the idea was rejected for being similar to the* Planet of the Apes *film remake then being considered, starring Arnold Schwarzenegger. This comic would have continued in the era of the first two films. It should be noted that Cornelius could not have known about the Alpha-Omega Bomb, or Taylor's part in detonating it—just that the world melted.*

◆ The World Wide Web and the Internet become a widespread source of news and information.

Revolution on the Planet of the Apes #2: "People News" (MR-c)

NOTE: *In real-world 1991, the Web and the Internet were still in their infancy. As author Ty Templeton confirms on the letters page of* Revolution *issue #3, both developed several years earlier in the* Planet of the Apes *mythos.*

◆ Blogging becomes a common practice for radical activists opposing the oppressive government.

Revolution on the Planet of the Apes #1: "Part One: The End of the World" (MR-c)

NOTE: *Given the decade-early development of the Internet, it's natural that blogging would begin earlier as well.*

◆ A book is published offering futuristic depictions of what New York City might be like in 2503. The book also contains photos of gorillas in cages.

Planet of the Apes episode #1: "Escape from Tomorrow" (CB-t)

NOTE: *The TV series shows New York in fine condition 500 years after being leveled in a nuclear war. I, therefore, assume the book was published pre-war, featuring artistic interpretations of a possible future. Some fans cite the book as evidence the later films altered the timeline, or that the TV show exists in an alternate timeline.*

◆ Notebook-style laptop computers become commonplace.

Revolution on the Planet of the Apes: "The Believer" (MR-c, unpublished)

NOTE: *This tale, intended as a* Revolution *back-up story, was written, penciled and lettered by Sam Agro, but was cut due to concerns over religious overtones. At presstime, it was slated to appear in issue #16 of* Simian Scrolls *magazine, with the author's permission. The use of laptop computers in 1991 jibes with other technological innovations occuring earlier in the* Apes *universe than in the real world.*

◆ Cigarette manufacturers begin making products safer for smokers' health. No longer concerned about dying, some find them less enjoyable.

Conquest of the Planet of the Apes (FX-f)

◆ Ape Management Publications (AMP) writer Carson McCormick attends a simian civil-rights speech at a San Diego university, given by Malcolm MacDonald, assistant to Governor Breck. MacDonald urges mankind to stop treating apes as slaves. Although many agree with him, nothing changes societally.

Planet of the Apes #19: "Quitting Time" (AC-c)

◆ Among those in agreement are the Animal Rights Coalition (ARC), who urge people to stop referring to genetically engineered apes as animals. A group of legislators considers giving limited voting rights to the smartest of all the altered apes.

Planet of the Apes: The Fall, Chapter 2 (HE-n)

NOTE: *Given the political climate under Trundy's administration, it's safe to assume such a measure would have no chance whatsoever of being passed.*

◆ Ape Management passes Article 4, Paragraph 9, making it a punishable crime for any ape to commit an overt act of disobedience.

Conquest of the Planet of the Apes (FX-f)

PUBLISHER / STUDIO

AB . . . . ABC-TV
AC . . . .Adventure / Malibu Comics
AW . . . . Award Books
BB . . . . .Ballantine Books
BN . . . . Bantam Books
BW . . . . Brown Watson Books
CB . . . . CBS-TV
CV . . . . Chad Valley Sliderama
DH . . . . .Dark Horse Comics
ET . . . . Editorial Mo.Pa.Sa.
FX . . . . 20th Century Fox
GK . . . .Gold Key / Western Comics
HE . . . HarperEntertainment Books
HM . . Harry K. McWilliams Assoc.
MC . . . . .Marvel Comics
MR . . . Mr. Comics / Metallic Rose
NB . . . . NBC-TV
PR . . . . .Power Records
SB . . . . Signet Books
TP . . . . .Topps
UB . . . . .Ubisoft

MEDIUM

a . . . . animated series
b . . . . .book-and-record set
c . . . . .comic book or strip
d . . . . trading card
e . . . . e-comic
f . . . . .theatrical film
k . . . . .storybook
m . . . . .magazine article
n . . . . .novel or novelization
p . . . . promotional newspaper
r . . . . .recorded audio fiction
s . . . . short story
t . . . . television series
u . . . . .unfilmed script or story
v . . . . video game
x . . . . .Blu-Ray exclusive
y . . . . .young adult novel

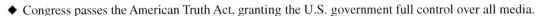

◆ Congress passes the American Truth Act, granting the U.S. government full control over all media.

Revolution on the Planet of the Apes #2: "Part Two: Lines of Communication" (MR-c)

◆ The U.S. government deems it a crime to show disrespect to a state official.

Conquest of the Planet of the Apes (MC-c)

NOTE: This event, mentioned in Marvel's comic adaptation of the film, is undated. I've placed it alongside the passing of the American Truth Act, since it fits well with such a totalitarian motif.

◆ Dr. Karl Reich of the Presidential Science Council, a wheelchair-bound man who keeps a pet monkey on his shoulder, presents controversial theories regarding the potential intelligence of apes. Reich makes many enemies for espousing such beliefs and is deemed paranoid for claiming the child of Cornelius and Zira may have survived.

Revolution on the Planet of the Apes #4: "Part Four: Truth and Consequences" (MR-c)

◆ To prevent mass panic, Nora Rhodes, the Pentagon's undersecretary of media, publicly discredits Reich. This greatly weakens his position as a prominent scientific figure, for which he never forgives her.

Revolution on the Planet of the Apes #1: "Part One: The End of the World" (MR-c)

◆ Astronaut August Anne Burrows suffers a series of emotional scars caused by a bad marriage, the deaths of her parents and growing up in a male-dominated society.

Planet of the Apes #14: "Countdown Zero—Part One" (AC-c)

◆ Karen Carroll, a young reporter for a New York-based tabloid publication, *People News Monthly*, covers a controversial incident in Colorado Springs but is humiliated when her article is retracted.

Revolution on the Planet of the Apes #2: "People News" (MR-c)

NOTE: This tale was previewed online at http://www.mrcomics.ca/freestory.html, but is no longer available at that site. The preview was entitled "People in the News," but the print issue's contents page lists it as "People News." Carroll's first name does not appear in the published comic, but can be found in the script.

◆ Governor Arnold Jason Breck and his wife have a son. She lets the baby pick his own name by pointing to a baby-naming book. Charmed, Breck uses the same practice when naming ape servants.

Conquest of the Planet of the Apes (FX-f)

◆ President Trundy deploys more than half of the National Guard to a crisis overseas, leaving the country without the manpower required to deal with potential domestic threats. To supplement homeland forces, Defense Secretary Culley Sparks implements a pilot program to turn gorillas into combat soldiers.

Revolution on the Planet of the Apes #4: "Part Four: Truth and Consequences" (MR-c)

◆ Sparks enacts his plan at Area 51's Hasslein Air Force Base in Groom Lake, Nevada. There, a scientist named Dr. Constantine genetically experiments on apes, attaching electrodes to their heads to enhance intelligence so they can learn to fly jet planes and perform other advanced tasks.

Revolution on the Planet of the Apes #1: "Part One: The End of the World" (MR-c)

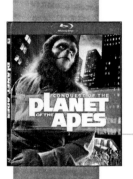

◆ The government also develops the Authenticator, a computerized scanner chair designed to determine the validity of a person's responses to interrogation.

Conquest of the Planet of the Apes (FX-f)

NOTE: The device's invention is undated, but must occur before its use on Armando.

◆ A brand of soft drink known as Cooky Cola is introduced.

The Forbidden Zone #2: "Part Two—Danger Zone" (AC-c)

NOTE: It's impossible to be more specific in dating this and the following entries, but I assume all to have occurred before Caesar's rebellion and the subsequent war.

◆ A children's book is published entitled *A Day at the Zoo*, involving a family's trip to the local zoo. Among the book's photos are shots of free humans gazing at caged apes.

Return to the Planet of the Apes episode #6: "Terror on Ice Mountain" (NB-a)

◆ Author Charles Winraad publishes a reference book entitled *Archaic Genealogy*.

Planet of the Apes #20: "Terror on the Planet of the Apes, Phase 2—Society of the Psychedrome" (MC-c)

◆ The U.S. government builds a network of trans-national transport tubes, designed to facilitate the movement of people and supplies from one coast to the other.

Planet of the Apes #11: "Outlines of Tomorrow—A Chronology of the Planet of the Apes" (MC-m)

◆ The U.S. Army constructs a biological weapons storage bunker in California, containing a number of deadly plagues used in germ warfare.

Planet of the Apes (Authorised Edition) #2: "Pit of Doom" (BW-c)

NOTE: It's unknown if the plague materials were at all responsible for the eventual degeneration of mankind.

◆ Handheld, heat-powered radios come into use.

El Planeta de Los Simios #3: "The Beach of Time" (ET-c)

◆ Also developed are solar-powered portable transceivers.

El Planeta de Los Simios #4: "Ultrasonic" (ET-c)

◆ A bubble-shaped city is built in the United States, its dome strong enough to withstand an atomic bomb.

Planet of the Apes: "Journey to the Planet of the Apes" (MC-c, unpublished)

NOTE: This tale—originally titled "Return to the Planet of the Apes" but renamed, presumably, so as not to conflict with the cartoon series—was never released due to Marvel's decision to stop publishing Planet of the Apes *comics as of issue #29, in response to increased licensing fees. The above details come from a story outline and dialog breakdown provided by author Doug Moench.*

◆ Auditors at the National Archives in Washington, D.C., discover a narrated reel of 16-millimeter film labeled "Project Liberty," recorded by ANSA in 1972 to provide a "public service announcement" regarding the history of its Liberty Project. The Library of Congress, confirming its importance to the U.S. Space Program, preserves the film unaltered, without editorial comment.

Planet of the Apes 40th Anniversary Collection: A Public Service Announcement From ANSA (FX-x)

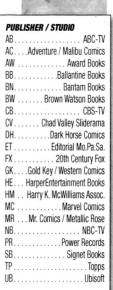

Part 4: The Beast, Man
(1991 to 1992)

1991

◆ Ape Management, now a government-operated monolith, takes on a wider range of responsibilities, training apes for day-to-day life with humans and accelerating the apes' mental development. Those slow to learn are subjected to cruel punishment called "reconditioning," with any resistant apes summarily destroyed.

Planet of the Apes #11: "Outlines of Tomorrow—A Chronology of the Planet of the Apes" (MC-m)

◆ Concerned that the apes might one day rise up against mankind, Governor Breck orders the vicinity near Ape Management and the Archives Section lined with surveillance cameras so as to forestall any ape conspiracies.

Battle for the Planet of the Apes (FX-f)

◆ Three of the six remaining circus troupes in the United States disband, leaving only Armando's Old-Time Circus and two competitors.

Conquest of the Planet of the Apes (AW-n)

NOTE: This information appears in the film's novelization.

◆ Brought back from cancellation, the popular television show *B.J. and the Bear* goes back into production under a new title, *B.J. and the Bear: Reloaded.*

Revolution on the Planet of the Apes #1: "Part One: The End of the World" (MR-c)

◆ Astronauts Capt. James Norvell, August Anne Burrows and Lt. Ken Flip undertake the United States' first manned orbit of Mars. Due to communications equipment malfunction, the team loses contact with Earth for the duration of their 18-month mission.

Planet of the Apes #15: "Countdown Zero—Part Two" (AC-c)

NOTE: Dayton Ward's timeline, published in The Planet of the Apes Chronicles, dates these events circa 1985. A Public Service Announcement From ANSA, a short film included in the Blu-Ray release, sets the first Mars mission in the 1960s.

◆ Eventually, the U.S. space program is shut down completely.

Conquest of the Planet of the Apes (AW-n)

NOTE: It's no wonder the government would finally shut down the space program—the United States has lost a lot of spaceships to time warps and other anomalies. Later stories—the animated series, Tim Burton's "re-imagined" film and the Ubisoft video game, for instance—show the space program still operating after this date, but many consider the canonicity of those stories questionable.

◆ The quickly evolving apes gain awareness of the concept of slavery. Meeting in small groups, they grunt their refusal to obey their masters, thus sowing the seeds of discontent until it's time to act.

Escape from the Planet of the Apes (FX-f)

NOTE: Cornelius tells Hasslein it will take two centuries for primitive apes to recognize their status as slaves. However, the final two films show this to occur at a much more accelerated rate—possibly evidence of an altered timeline, or Cornelius may have been misinformed by inaccurate scrolls.

PUBLISHER / STUDIO
AB . . . . ABC-TV
AC . . . . Adventure / Malibu Comics
AW . . . . Award Books
BB . . . . .Ballantine Books
BN . . . . Bantam Books
BW . . . . . Brown Watson Books
CB . . . . CBS-TV
CV . . . . Chad Valley Sliderama
DH . . . . .Dark Horse Comics
ET . . . . Editorial Mo.Pa.Sa.
FX . . . . 20th Century Fox
GK . . . Gold Key / Western Comics
HE . . . HarperEntertainment Books
HM . . Harry K. McWilliams Assoc.
MC . . . . Marvel Comics
MR . . . Mr. Comics / Metallic Rose
NB . . . . NBC-TV
PR . . . . Power Records
SB . . . . Signet Books
TP . . . . Topps
UB . . . . Ubisoft

MEDIUM
a . . . . animated series
b . . . . .book-and-record set
c . . . . .comic book or strip
d . . . . trading card
e . . . . e-comic
f . . . . .theatrical film
k . . . . storybook
m . . . . .magazine article
n . . . . .novel or novelization
p . . . . promotional newspaper
r . . . . .recorded audio fiction
s . . . . short story
t . . . . television series
u . . . . .unfilmed script or story
v . . . . video game
x . . . . .Blu-Ray exclusive
y . . . . .young adult novel

◆ With simian disobedience rising, Ape Management's reconditioning complex grows overcrowded with rebellious apes. Worried that the animals are awaiting a simian smart enough to lead them in rebellion, Governor Breck—under Article 4, Paragraph 9—orders the creation of the Achilles List, a document naming every ape to commit an overt act of disobedience throughout the previous year.

Conquest of the Planet of the Apes (FX-f)

◆ Businessman Leland Reilly suffers a coronary but survives the attack. Reilly and his wife are among Governor Breck's business associates.

Conquest of the Planet of the Apes (AW-n)

NOTE: This information comes from the novelization of the film.

JULY 1991

◆ With attendance dropping off sharply, Señor Armando takes drastic action to avoid losing his circus: He brings 18-year-old Caesar on a publicity tour to hand out fliers, hoping his star performer might inspire increased interest.

Conquest of the Planet of the Apes (AW-n)

NOTE: This information appears in the film's novelization. The July setting is established in a timeline packaged with the Planet of the Apes *40th Anniversary Collection.* Revolution on the Planet of the Apes *places* Conquest *in San Diego, while* Future News, *a promotional newspaper distributed during its theatrical release, sets it in a city known as Megalopolis, which sports a New York zip code. Dayton Ward's timeline, meanwhile, published in* The Planet of the Apes Chronicles, *sets the film in New York City.*

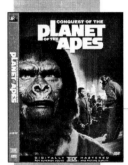

◆ An ape assaults its owner and is killed escaping, its body covered with welts and bruises. When Armando and Caesar arrive via helicopter the next day, they find apes enslaved in a Gestapo-esque shackle of oppression. Armando shows Caesar the Pet Memorial and explains how the slavery evolved. While handing out fliers, Caesar sees a chimp servant named Lisa at Jolly's book store. The chimps transfix on one another as Lisa delivers a note from Mrs. Reilly, requesting *A Young Queen Falls*. Other apes in town sense Caesar's anger and commit acts of rebellion: At an outdoor restaurant, a gorilla waiter called Frank misbehaves until his handler, Mr. Lee, can reign him in; and at Henri's Beauty Salon, a chimp named Zelda grooms Mrs. Reilly's hair instead of cutting it.

Conquest of the Planet of the Apes (FX-f)

NOTE: Marvel's timeline in issue #11 places the film in April 1991 and the war in 1992; Revolution on the Planet of the Apes *has the war happening weeks after the film. Marvel's comic adaptation sets the film in November 1991, enabling the war to occur soon thereafter and still take place in 1992.* Future News, *a mock newspaper released to promote the film, bears a date of May 22, 1992, but I have ignored that date since it does not jibe with other evidence. Marvel's adaptation names the salon Henri's Beauty Salon, while the novelization calls it Mr. Phyllis—Coiffures. The novelization identifies one of the diners as Harry; another is called Charles onscreen. The Marvel adaptation names Mr. Lee. The opening scene, of the ape being killed, appears in Marvel's version, but not in the final cut of the film.*

◆ Carson McCormick senses rebellion in the air as he heads to Ape Management Publications that day. Accepting a circus flier from Armando and Caesar, he smiles, recalling better days. His happiness ends at work, however, when he senses that same change in Stella, his office ape.

Planet of the Apes #19: "Quitting Time" (AC-c)

◆ Human laborers picket Nationwide Ape Employment Inc.'s Civic Center Branch, located in the Mall of the Four Muses. Opposing ape labor practices, the protestors foist signs with such slogans as "Unfair to Waiters," "Slaves Are Scabs" and "Hire Men—Not Animals."

Conquest of the Planet of the Apes (AW-n)

NOTE: The protest is shown on film; the company targeted by the picketers is named in the film's novelization. The book identifies one protestor as Max.

◆ A pair of handlers escorts an ape named Aldo to the Civic Center. The protestors bar the way, causing Aldo to panic. Police beat him down for disobedience until Malcolm MacDonald orders them to stop. When they continue, Caesar yells out "Lousy human bastards!" then runs off. Armando tells the police he said it, not the chimp, then runs after Caesar, urging his foster-son to let him handle the authorities.

Conquest of the Planet of the Apes (FX-f)

NOTE: The film's novelization identifies one of Aldo's handlers as Leo.

◆ Carson McCormick works late when Breck orders pamphlets entitled *Breeding Your Ape* and *Punishing Your Ape*. His secretary, Doris, finds such treatment distasteful. Carson heads home to his wife Ruth and son Michael. Ruth wants a second ape, as they are the only single-ape family in the neighborhood, but Carson is wary, knowing how man has mistreated them.

Planet of the Apes #19: "Quitting Time" (AC-c)

◆ Armando appears before Breck, MacDonald and two members of the State Security Agency (SSA)— Chief Inspector Arthur Vernon Kolp and his assistant, Inspector Hoskyns.

Conquest of the Planet of the Apes (FX-f)

◆ Kolp, Breck's chief security advisor, is also a senior member of President Trundy's Defense Council.

Revolution on the Planet of the Apes #4: "Part Four: Truth and Consequences" (MR-c)

◆ Skeptical of Armando's story, Breck and Kolp hold him in custody as his staff is questioned. Caesar sneaks aboard the S.S. *Pacifica*, a cargo ship owned by Atomic General Lines Inc., and hides in a cage of orangutans from Borneo. Fingerprinted and sent to Conditioning Cage 90, he witnesses apes being beaten and taunted with fire and electricity, while a scientist named Dr. Bowen conditions them to fear the word "no." Caesar is placed in a cage with three other chimps. A kindly handler, Eddie Morris, gives him a banana, which Caesar divides among the others.

Conquest of the Planet of the Apes (FX-f)

NOTE: Marvel names the Pacifica *and Atomic General Lines. Morris' first name appears in that adaptation; his and Bowen's last names can be found in the novelization.*

JULY TO SEPTEMBER 1991

◆ To the humans' amazement, Caesar excels at every task without conditioning. Impressed, Training Control sends him to the Breeding Annex.

Conquest of the Planet of the Apes (FX-f)

NOTE: The July-to-September setting is established in a timeline packaged with the Planet of the Apes *40th Anniversary Collection.*

◆ En route to the annex, Caesar passes a nursery full of ape children and is touched deeply.

Conquest of the Planet of the Apes (MC-c)

NOTE: This scene appears in the Marvel comic adaptation.

PUBLISHER / STUDIO
AB . . . . ABC-TV
AC . . . . Adventure / Malibu Comics
AW . . . . Award Books
BB . . . . Ballantine Books
BN . . . . Bantam Books
BW . . . . Brown Watson Books
CB . . . . CBS-TV
CV . . . . Chad Valley Sliderama
DH . . . . Dark Horse Comics
ET . . . . Editorial Mo.Pa.Sa.
FX . . . . 20th Century Fox
GK . . . Gold Key / Western Comics
HE . . . HarperEntertainment Books
HM . . Harry K. McWilliams Assoc.
MC . . . . Marvel Comics
MR . . . Mr. Comics / Metallic Rose
NB . . . . NBC-TV
PR . . . . Power Records
SB . . . . Signet Books
TP . . . . Topps
UB . . . . Ubisoft

MEDIUM
a . . . . animated series
b . . . . book-and-record set
c . . . . comic book or strip
d . . . . trading card
e . . . . e-comic
f . . . . theatrical film
k . . . . storybook
m . . . . magazine article
n . . . . novel or novelization
p . . . . promotional newspaper
r . . . . recorded audio fiction
s . . . . short story
t . . . . television series
u . . . . unfilmed script or story
v . . . . video game
x . . . . Blu-Ray exclusive
y . . . . young adult novel

◆ By breeding with primitive apes, Caesar introduces his advanced genetic makeup into their gene pool.

Conquest of the Planet of the Apes (FX-f)

NOTE: The ramifications of Caesar breeding with primitive apes is intriguing, as numerous illegitimate children with his advanced bloodline would undoubtedly be created by such unions. To date, no official lore has dealt with this question.

SEPTEMBER 1991

◆ After two weeks in the Annex, Caesar is auctioned to Governor Breck for $1,500. Breck's administrative assistant, Morgan Pine, brings the governor an IQ profile showing ape scores have risen 3 $^{2}/_{3}$ points in four weeks, with ape workloads improving. MacDonald teaches Caesar to mix drinks, which he pretends to do wrong; Morgan suggests reconditioning, but MacDonald protests. Pulling out a book of names, Breck tells Caesar to pick one for himself (he chooses Caesar), then meets with the Defense Council. As MacDonald takes Caesar to work at the Command Post, other apes gaze at him in awe. The chimp is assigned low-priority filing duties, and is surprised to find Lisa working there as well.

Conquest of the Planet of the Apes (FX-f)

NOTE: The two-week figure and Morgan's last name appear in the novelization. The September setting is established in a timeline packaged with the Planet of the Apes *40th Anniversary Collection.*

◆ Caesar overhears snippets of a top-secret project, code-named "Churchdoor." Ordered to deliver classified documents about this project to the security section, he reads them en route and learns about the Alpha-Omega Bomb—a "doomsday bomb" capable of destroying the world.

Revolution on the Planet of the Apes #2: "Caesar's Journal" (MR-c)

◆ Having envisioned such a weapon as a youth, Caesar is horrified to find his dreams again coming true.

Revolution on the Planet of the Apes #5: "Part Five: Weapon of Choice" (MR-c)

◆ Kolp orders the distribution of a new AMP pamphlet, *Punishing Your Ape*. While writing the document, Carson McCormick wonders what would happen if ever the simians revolted. Neither he nor his secretary Doris notice their office ape, Stella, quietly pocketing Carson's letter-opener.

Planet of the Apes #19: "Quitting Time" (AC-c)

◆ Kolp and Hoskyns subject Armando to the Authenticator, a device designed to determine the validity of a person's claims. When asked if he'd heard of Cornelius before their meeting, he realizes he's been exposed and tries to escape. While struggling with a guard, he falls out a high window and dies. In the Command Post, Caesar hears Breck and MacDonald discussing his foster-father's death and cries with grief. Heading outside, he sees a sign for the circus and screams in rage.

Conquest of the Planet of the Apes (FX-f)

OCTOBER 1991

◆ Caesar decides to halt human cruelty toward his kind. Stopping outside the gorilla messengers' quarters, he assures Aldo they'll soon end their masters' hold over them. He then snaps a broom in half, giving a piece to Aldo, who breaks it as well. As he leaves, other gorillas tear the broom to pieces.

Conquest of the Planet of the Apes (MC-c)

NOTE: This scene appears in both the Marvel comic adaptation and the novelization. The October setting is established in a timeline packaged with the Planet of the Apes *40th Anniversary Collection.*

◆ That night, security forces arrest servant apes from widely-scattered households, found gathering in an unused building in the East Sector. The next afternoon, upon seeing Caesar in the Civic Center Plaza, Lisa throws down a book she'd been delivering, entitled *Empress of Love*; a gorilla street-cleaner dumps his trash on the ground; Frank the waiter refuses to light a cigarette; and an ape busboy steals several knives.

Conquest of the Planet of the Apes (FX-f)

NOTE: *The book's title appears in the film's novelization.*

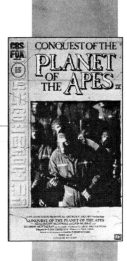

◆ Over lunch, Carson McCormick stops for a shoe-shine, but the rebellious ape worker polishes his sock instead of his shoe. His wife later visits his office, repeating her need for a second house-ape. That night, he dreams of a circus in which ape clowns taunt a human audience.

Planet of the Apes #19: "Quitting Time" (AC-c)

NOTE: Conquest of the Planet of the Apes *shows the shoe-shining incident in a montage of ape disobedience, though McCormick is identified by name only in this comic.*

◆ Caesar instructs Aldo and other messenger gorillas to meet him at a specific janitorial closet each day. Word spreads to other apes, who join them in increasing numbers.

Conquest of the Planet of the Apes (AW-n)

NOTE: *This occurs in the film's novelization.*

◆ At such meetings, Caesar alters shopping lists to include weapons, kerosene and other products. The apes continue staging acts of disobedience, such as setting fire to the restaurant. Furious, Breck disseminates the Achilles List, then orders Malcolm MacDonald to locate the talking ape.

Conquest of the Planet of the Apes (FX-f)

◆ In an effort to recondition Aldo, Ape Management assigns the gorilla to Area 51 in Groom Lake, Nevada. There, his anger at humans worsens when he witnesses first-hand the atrocities to which scientists subject the captive apes.

Revolution on the Planet of the Apes #1: "Part One: The End of the World" (MR-c)

◆ Under the Area 51 project, initiated by Defense Secretary Culley Sparks, gorillas' intelligence is enhanced, enabling them to speak and serve as combat soldiers. Driven by Caesar's unconscious mind—and by his own desire for revenge—Aldo learns all he can, yearning to turn man's weapons against him. In time, Aldo and other Area 51 enhanced gorillas learn to speak like humans.

Revolution on the Planet of the Apes #4: "Part Four: Truth and Consequences" (MR-c)

NOTE: *In a posting at the POTA Yahoo Group,* Revolution *author Ty Templeton explained that the gorillas' speech capability was made possible due to genetic and biological experimentation.*

◆ Ape Management stops accepting apes for reconditioning, or importing new apes into the country, until the crisis passes. Breck orders a new pamphlet from Ape Management Publications—*How to Terminate Your Ape*—which makes Carson McCormick particularly uneasy. Meeting his friend Miles for lunch, he learns that Armando jumped to his death from their building. Moments later, a gorilla nearly kills them both.

Planet of the Apes #19: "Quitting Time" (AC-c)

◆ Ape Management discovers an error in its records—a chimp from Borneo, where none such creatures exist. Kolp realizes it must be Caesar and advises Breck to prove he can speak before killing him. MacDonald helps Caesar escape, but guards recapture him. Dr. Johnny Chamberlain tortures Caesar on a shock table until he begs for mercy. MacDonald cuts the power, and as the guard ramps up the voltage to lethal levels, Caesar fakes his death, then jumps the guard and escapes. He leads Lisa and others in rebellion, storming the plaza outside Training Control. The apes slaughter the handlers inside, freeing others to join them.

Conquest of the Planet of the Apes (FX-f)

NOTE: Chamberlain's first name appears in Marvel's film adaptation, his last name in the novelization.

◆ Caesar warns Eddie Morris to take cover, but the apes beat the handler to death. Caesar regrets that one of the few humans to ever treat his people with kindness should meet so horrible a fate.

Conquest of the Planet of the Apes (AW-n)

NOTE: This scene occurs in the film's novelization.

◆ Caesar gains control of Ape Management. Breck calls a curfew, mobilizing all forces. When a television program airs news of the rebellion, Breck tells MacDonald to order a retraction and claim the talking ape has been executed.

Conquest of the Planet of the Apes (FX-f)

◆ Carson McCormick sees the newscast and calls his wife Ruth, but hears only the laughing growl of his servant ape, Dina. He finds the slain body of his secretary Doris, then meets his own end when the office ape, Stella, stabs him with a letter-opener. As McCormick dies, his last thoughts are of simpler times, and of the circus.

Planet of the Apes #19: "Quitting Time" (AC-c)

NOTE: Presumably, Dina also kills Michael, McCormick's son, though this is unstated.

◆ A scientist finishes building a device to prevent Earth's future destruction by shunting the Alpha-Omega Bomb's energies into space. Fighting his way through the chaos caused by Caesar's rebellion, he hides the device—containing a cryotube holding Janus, a clone of Cornelius—within the Statue of Liberty, to be activated in 3979. Since he knows, from the apeonauts' testimonial, that parts of the statue will survive the impending nuclear war, he hopes his plan to save the Earth from destruction has a high chance of success.

Redemption of the Planet of the Apes (AC-c, unpublished)

NOTE: Lowell Cunningham, Men in Black creator and author of Adventure's The Forbidden Zone, proposed this four-issue miniseries to creative director Tom K. Mason as well. However, Cunningham says, the idea was rejected for being similar to the Planet of the Apes film remake then being considered, starring Arnold Schwarzenegger. This unpublished comic would have continued during the era of the first two films.

◆ As the apes march along Alpha Blvd., soldiers gun down the first wave before the next takes them out. Riot-control units attempt to stop them, but the apes are well-armed and organized. One ape tosses a firebomb, the rest attacking from behind a wall of flame. Many die on both sides, but the apes prevail.

Conquest of the Planet of the Apes (FX-f)

NOTE: Alpha Blvd. is named in the film's novelization.

◆ Some apes involved in storming Ape Management are trapped in the sub-basement with little food or water, cut off from the rest of the rebellion.

Planet of the Apes #2: "The Monkey Planet—Escape" (AC-c)

◆ The apes storm Langlan's Gunsmith Shop, then rush the Command Post with rifles. Killing most humans within, they set fire to the building and make Breck bow before Caesar, who nearly kills him outright but instead orders Breck shackled and dragged outside. Lying bound on the pavement, surrounded by chanting apes, Breck calls out in terror as the simians whip and torture him. ●

Conquest of the Planet of the Apes (FX-f)

NOTE: Langlan's is named in Marvel's comic adaptation.

◆ Caesar orders the Pet Memorial torn down, eliminating a reminder of man's dominion over ape.

Conquest of the Planet of the Apes (AW-n)

NOTE: This information appears in the film's novelization.

◆ MacDonald begs Caesar to avoid violence, which would make the apes no better than their ex-masters, but Caesar is unmoved. Apes on five continents will join them, he proclaims, and he shall lead them from the wasteland of human cities, showing no mercy. The apes stare in awe, raising rifles to execute Breck, until Lisa utters "No!" and Caesar reconsiders. If it is God's will that man be dominated, he declares, it must be with compassion and understanding. As the apes revel in their victory, MacDonald eyes the first King of the Apes, wondering what the future holds for both of their species.

Conquest of the Planet of the Apes (FX-f)

NOTE: In an earlier cut of the film, Caesar did not stay Breck's execution. That original ending, along with other scenes of violence cut from the theatrical release, were restored in an extended-length Blu-Ray release, the Planet of the Apes *40th Anniversary Collection. A timeline in that box set establishes two parallel histories, dating the rise of apekind in the original timeline from 2050 to 2550.*

◆ As Caesar's declaration airs on the Internet, a priest views the footage on a laptop computer. Noise erupts outside as the rebellion reaches his temple, and he kneels before a crucifix, stunned that any animal but man could have "the divine spark" of intelligence. He seeks Christ's guidance, wondering if he should accept speaking apes as brothers. A gorilla crashes into the room, but rather than embrace peace, the priest grabs a cross and beats it to death, choosing a solution more befitting the Old Testament than the New. In its dying breath, the animal utters a single word, "mercy," but the man shows him none.

Revolution on the Planet of the Apes: "The Believer" (MR-c, unpublished)

NOTE: This tale, intended as a Revolution *back-up story, was written, penciled and lettered by Sam Agro, but was excluded from the miniseries due to concerns over religious overtones, as its conclusion featured the Lawgiver supplanting Christ. At presstime, however, it was slated to appear in issue #16 of Simian Scrolls magazine, with the author's permission. The use of a laptop in 1991 jibes well with the Internet, blogging and other technological innovations occuring earlier in the Apes mythos.*

◆ Caesar names MacDonald his liaison between humanity and apekind, and imprisons Breck in a cell.

Revolution on the Planet of the Apes #1: "Part One: The End of the World" (MR-c)

◆ The ape leader then renames the territory "Ape City."

Revolution on the Planet of the Apes #1: "Caesar's Journal" (MR-c)

NOVEMBER 11–23, 1991

◆ Armando's Old-Time Circus, slated to play a venue not far from Ape Management, fails to make its scheduled appointment. Without its founder and star performer, the circus presumably shuts down.

Conquest of the Planet of the Apes (MC-c)

NOTE: This information comes from Marvel's comic adaptation of the film.

PUBLISHER / STUDIO
AB . . . . ABC-TV
AC . . . .Adventure / Malibu Comics
AW . . . . Award Books
BB . . . . .Ballantine Books
BN . . . . Bantam Books
BW . . . . Brown Watson Books
CB . . . . CBS-TV
CV . . . . Chad Valley Sliderama
DH . . . . .Dark Horse Comics
ET . . . . Editorial Mo.Pa.Sa.
FX . . . . 20th Century Fox
GK . . . .Gold Key / Western Comics
HE . . . HarperEntertainment Books
HM . . Harry K. McWilliams Assoc.
MC . . . . .Marvel Comics
MR . . . Mr. Comics / Metallic Rose
NB . . . . NBC-TV
PR . . . . .Power Records
SB . . . . Signet Books
TP . . . . Topps
UB . . . . Ubisoft

MEDIUM
a . . . . animated series
b . . . . .book-and-record set
c . . . . .comic book or strip
d . . . . trading card
e . . . . e-comic
f . . . . .theatrical film
k . . . . .storybook
m . . . . .magazine article
n . . . . .novel or novelization
p . . . . promotional newspaper
r . . . . .recorded audio fiction
s . . . . short story
t . . . . television series
u . . . . .unfilmed script or story
v . . . . video game
x . . . . .Blu-Ray exclusive
y . . . . .young adult novel

◆ Kolp transfers his operations to a secure facility: a secret underground bunker housing Project Churchdoor (the code name for the Alpha-Omega Bomb). There, Kolp assembles a counter-insurgency commando unit to free Breck from Caesar's army.

Revolution on the Planet of the Apes #4: "Part Four: Truth and Consequences" (MR-c)

◆ The press scrambles to reach Caesar, who—enjoying the title's irony—grants an interview to *People News Monthly*. He confirms being the apeonauts' heir, and the New York tabloid covers his story in an issue titled "Hail Caesar!" However, Nora Rhodes, the president's media undersecretary, orders editor-in-chief Ivan Livingstone to bury the story before it hits stands, denouncing the rebellion as a hoax. Citing national security, she seizes the print run and demands the reporter, Karen Carroll, turn over all materials. Carroll resists, as Webcasts are already carrying the news, but her publisher, Arthur Bergen, fears the administration's wrath. She "buries" a copy in a titanium wall safe, vowing to get the news out. Livingstone warns her not to throw her future away, but she knows they might not have a future if no one reads it.

Revolution on the Planet of the Apes #2: "People News" (MR-c)

NOTE: *This tale was previewed online at http://www.mrcomics.ca/freestory.html, but is no longer available at that site. The preview was entitled "People in the News," but the print issue's contents page lists it as "People News." Carroll's first name and Bergen's full name appear only in the comic's script.*

◆ Caesar's ape dynasty initially spans the ten city blocks housing Ape Management, but other U.S. cities soon face similar rebellions. The government tries to negotiate peace but Caesar refuses, prompting the *Daily News* to report, "Caesar Says No to Negotiations."

Revolution on the Planet of the Apes #1: "Part One: The End of the World" (MR-c)

◆ The day after the rebellion, pirate blogger Chris Leung watches Internet footage of the riot until the news feed is terminated for violating the Media Act. An approved broadcast of Nora Rhodes assures viewers the "minor ape disturbance" in the area dubbed the Exclusion Zone is "well in hand." His father dismisses the Caesar rumors as a hoax, until an ape drives a truck through their wall, bringing the rebellion to the Leung kitchen. Chris is knocked unconscious as the rest of his family is slaughtered.

Revolution on the Planet of the Apes #1: "Part One: The End of the World" (MR-c)

◆ History later records the Leung family as the first humans to die on the so-called Night of Fires.

Revolution on the Planet of the Apes #5: "If You Missed Issue 1" (MR-c)

NOTE: *But apparently not for long, given how quickly records of this era become lost to all but the ruling apes.*

◆ Caesar awakens in a panic that night after dreaming of Earth's destruction, and takes comfort in Lisa's arms. She cannot respond, but he promises to teach her to speak, knowing his mental abilities will soon make that a reality.

Revolution on the Planet of the Apes #1: "Part One: The End of the World" (MR-c)

◆ The apes christen the day following the Night of Fires as the Day of Freedom.

Revolution on the Planet of the Apes #5: "Ape Shall Not Kill Ape" (MR-c)

◆ The morning of his second day in power, hoping to bring order to the primitive apes before his empire collapses in chaos, Caesar establishes the Ultimate Law: "Ape shall never kill ape."

Revolution on the Planet of the Apes #1: "Part One: The End of the World" (MR-c)

◆ Similar rebellions mount in Newark, St. Paul, Bakersfield and other cities. Nora Rhodes assures Trundy the situation is contained, but Reich predicts the apes will win. Meanwhile, at Area 51, Aldo refuses to work and is sent to Dr. Constantine for punishment. Aldo overpowers his guards, beating them and the scientist to a bloody pulp while screaming a word he heard humans say many times: "No!"

Revolution on the Planet of the Apes #1: "Part One: The End of the World" (MR-c)

NOTE: Despite prior utterances of that same word by Lisa (in Conquest of the Planet of the Apes*) and Mandemus (in Ty Templeton's aborted* Empire on the Planet of the Apes *miniseries), the Sacred Scrolls will later record Aldo as the first primitive ape to speak.*

◆ Three days after founding Ape City, Caesar begins recording a journal. He keeps human captives alive to prevent the military from bombing the city, but no reprisal occurs. Some apes refuse to wear clothes, particularly orangutans, while others don the outfits of their oppressors; Caesar demands only that they be civilized. The once-gentle gorillas fight for territory, tribes and females, having grown aggressive after years under human rule. Fearing the Planet of the Apes will not last a week, he writes that his people must build their own civilization, founded on morality, purpose and life. Thus, he becomes the first Lawgiver.

Revolution on the Planet of the Apes #1: "Caesar's Journal" (MR-c)

◆ Aldo frees his fellow Area 51 apes, who slaughter their trainers and steal military jets. In the Exclusion Zone, Caesar watches the devastation from a high perch with Lisa, worried about the future he has created. He wishes he could tell his parents he survived, as well as beg their forgiveness.

Revolution on the Planet of the Apes #2: "Part Two: Lines of Communication" (MR-c)

◆ That night (day six post-revolution), Caesar continues his journal, describing nightmares of future events involving unknown people and places. The pain of the shock table still throbs, but he resists his desire to kill Breck, knowing that would doom apekind. He wishes Armando were here to advise him.

Revolution on the Planet of the Apes #2: "Caesar's Journal" (MR-c)

◆ Dr. Bryce Evans, a geneticist and ex-fiancé of Nora Rhodes, shoots an ape servant with a tranquilizer dart and carries the simian off to his lab.

Revolution on the Planet of the Apes #2: "Part Two: Lines of Communication" (MR-c)

◆ Evans conducts experiments to find a plague that would kill specific primates, but not man. The genetic similarity between apes and humans, however, makes it difficult to obtain the desired results.

Revolution on the Planet of the Apes #3: "Part Three: Intelligent Design" (MR-c)

NOTE: It's possible Evans' plague could have led to the eventual elimination of all non-Caucasian races, implied in the first film (the apes of 3978 had never seen a Black man before Thomas Dodge). His plague may also have contributed to mankind's future loss of intelligence.

◆ On day eight of Ape City's existence, Caesar writes a journal entry recalling a dream that has not come true—namely, his grandchildren fighting in a global war with humans, destroying the moon in "an orgy of violence and madness." He writes of his vision that one of his future sons and daughter will die by violence. His waking world has surpassed his dreaming world, however, and he has stopped dreaming of the future, making him wonder if that will prevent the sky from catching fire.

Revolution on the Planet of the Apes #4: "Caesar's Journal" (MR-c)

PUBLISHER / STUDIO

AB . . . . ABC-TV
AC . . . . Adventure / Malibu Comics
AW . . . . Award Books
BB . . . . Ballantine Books
BN . . . . Bantam Books
BW . . . . Brown Watson Books
CB . . . . CBS-TV
CV . . . . Chad Valley Sliderama
DH . . . . Dark Horse Comics
ET . . . . Editorial Mo.Pa.Sa.
FX . . . . 20th Century Fox
GK . . . . Gold Key / Western Comics
HE . . . HarperEntertainment Books
HM . . Harry K. McWilliams Assoc.
MC . . . . Marvel Comics
MR . . . Mr. Comics / Metallic Rose
NB . . . . NBC-TV
PR . . . . Power Records
SB . . . . Signet Books
TP . . . . Topps
UB . . . . Ubisoft

MEDIUM

a . . . . animated series
b . . . . book-and-record set
c . . . . comic book or strip
d . . . . trading card
e . . . . e-comic
f . . . . theatrical film
k . . . . storybook
m . . . . magazine article
n . . . . novel or novelization
p . . . . promotional newspaper
r . . . . recorded audio fiction
s . . . . short story
t . . . . television series
u . . . . unfilmed script or story
v . . . . video game
x . . . . Blu-Ray exclusive
y . . . . young adult novel

◆ ISPs airing rebellion footage are shut down, as per the American Truth Act. Ape revolts crop up across America, and the military loses contact with several southwest bases. With the National Guard overseas, Trundy is unable to address the threat. Sparks suggests they target Caesar, but Trundy prefers to wait for news of Churchdoor. In Los Angeles, police try to contain rioting. A cop named Wooley kills several humans before Leung knocks him out. Nearby, an orangutan paints "Hale Cezar" on a wall while trying to speak the words. Caesar subjects Breck to electric shock, questioning him about Churchdoor. Sparks and Rhodes travel aboard Government Flight Dave 14 to meet with the ape leader, but two aircraft piloted by Aldo's troops fire a missile at the cabin. Decompression expels Sparks and the pilots into the void.

Revolution on the Planet of the Apes #2: "Part Two: Lines of Communication" (MR-c)

NOTE: Wooley is likely named after a character in George A. Romero's Dawn of the Dead, *in which a racist policeman named Wooley indiscriminately shoots dark-skinned people along with the zombies, prompting a fellow cop to shout, "Wooley's gone ape-shit, man!"*

◆ Grabbing a parachute, Rhodes jumps from the plane, landing unharmed in the war zone.

Revolution on the Planet of the Apes #3: "Part Three: Intelligent Design" (MR-c)

◆ With Sparks dead, Trundy names Norman Akins (chairman of the Joint Chiefs of Staff) as acting defense secretary. Akins advocates a direct strike on Caesar's followers, despite the danger to Churchdoor.

Revolution on the Planet of the Apes #4: "Part Four: Truth and Consequences" (MR-c)

◆ Fourteen days post-rebellion, Caesar records several memories in his journal, including the day he learned of Project Churchdoor. Realizing the project's significance, he understands why the government has not retaken the city—and why he must get his hands on the Alpha-Omega Bomb.

Revolution on the Planet of the Apes #3: "Caesar's Journal" (MR-c)

EARLY 1992

◆ Caesar tortures Breck for the location of the Churchdoor bunker, then orders him held for trial. Kolp and two commandos, Mendez and Alma, spy on them with infrared goggles, intent on killing Caesar and rescuing the governor. Dr. Evans opens a vial of plague, killing every ape in his lab but not himself. Leung, filming the war for his blog despite government attempts to stop his Webcast, finds Rhodes lying in the street. Caesar invites them both to witness Breck's trial. Reich, meanwhile, suggests enacting the Inferno Protocol, for the apes outnumber them and may have already found Churchdoor.

Revolution on the Planet of the Apes #3: "Part Three: Intelligent Design" (MR-c)

NOTE: If Alma is the same age as actress France Nuyen (who portrayed the character in Battle for the Planet of the Apes), *then she would be 16 years old at this point. A note in* Revolution #6 *places these events 30 hours before full-scale nuclear devastation.*

◆ MacDonald and several gorillas escort Breck to the former ape pit, now a courtroom. Caesar serves as prosecution, MacDonald as defense, with humanity as judge and jury via Leung's camera. Caesar charges Breck with conspiracy to murder the world, citing Churchdoor as proof. Desperate to silence him, Rhodes grabs the camera and calls the trial a terrorist hoax. Explosions rock the area as Kolp's commandos rush in. MacDonald pins Breck to the ground, but Kolp gains the upper hand, holding the ape revolutionary at gunpoint.

Revolution on the Planet of the Apes #3: "Part Three: Intelligent Design" (MR-c)

◆ Leung's Webcast dominates the news, prompting rock star Bob Boomer to delay a "Live Ape" simian-benefit concert. Leung smashes Kolp's nose, saving Caesar's life. MacDonald stops Caesar from killing Kolp, however, saying Armando would not approve.

Revolution on the Planet of the Apes #4: "Part Four: Truth and Consequences" (MR-c)

◆ Caesar's rebellion sparks similar revolts across North America, with other apes throwing off the yoke of human oppression. It isn't long before the continent is in the hands of the apes.

Planet of the Apes #22: "Quest for the Planet of the Apes, Part I—Seeds of Future Deaths" (MC-c)

◆ The influence of the ape rebellion spreads to Europe and Asia, beginning with Japan.

Online Posting from Ty Templeton

NOTE: This information was posted in the POTA Yahoo Group by Ty Templeton, author of Revolution on the Planet of the Apes.

◆ Apes overrun Beijing, and the Chinese government destroys the city with a 30-kiloton bomb, launched from an orbital platform. Reich pushes for the Inferno Protocol, but still Trundy refuses. Aldo aerial-bombs Washington, D.C. The carnage overwhelms Caesar, causing him to collapse. Kolp frees Breck, who heads for the Churchdoor bunker. Trundy recalls all overseas troops as Russia bombs St. Petersburg and Moscow to stop its own ape revolution.

Revolution on the Planet of the Apes #4: "Part Four: Truth and Consequences" (MR-c)

NOTE: A note *in* Revolution #6 *places these events 29 hours before full-scale nuclear devastation.*

◆ Fearing further rebellion, the surviving countries in Europe and other parts of the world grant freedom to their apes. In such areas, man and ape live together peacefully for many years.

Ape City #3: "Monkey Planet" (AC-c)

◆ Akins' local forces fall to the air gorillas, who storm the White House, looking for President Trundy. Eventually, the apes take over the War Room, slaying Akins and anyone else in sight.

Revolution on the Planet of the Apes #4: "Part Four: Truth and Consequences" (MR-c)

◆ Trundy barely escapes the slaughter, fleeing the White House via helicopter.

Revolution on the Planet of the Apes #6: "This is How Man's World Ends" (MR-c)

◆ Considering mankind's bleak future, Reich shoots himself in the head. Finally, in the Oval Office, Aldo kills Trundy's Secret Service men and assumes the president's chair, lighting a cigar in triumph.

Revolution on the Planet of the Apes #4: "Part Four: Truth and Consequences" (MR-c)

NOTE: Revolution #6 places these events 28 hours before full-scale nuclear devastation. Ty Templeton's original script, Combat on the Planet of the Apes *(alternate title:* War on the Planet of the Apes*), featured Thade from Tim Burton's* Planet of the Apes *remake. Fox approved the concept but changed its mind, and the story was rewritten. Originally, Thade would have taken over the White House, not Aldo. According to Templeton, Thade would have arrived on Earth 10 years after* Conquest, *to find Earth peacefully co-ruled by two governments (ape and human). Interrogated by humans, Thade would have escaped and urged Caesar to mount a full-scale war. Caesar's refusal would have created a schism, with the gorillas backing Thade, and the genetically enhanced apes of Semos' world would have been offshoots of those at Area 51. Caesar would have killed Thade, erecting the statue seen onscreen to mend the division, and Thade would have become the Lawgiver revered in the future, said to have written the "Beware the beast 'man'" passage. (Adventure Comics had identified that ape as Jacob, an orangutan.)*

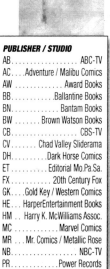

◆ Caesar's army arrives at the bunker too late to stop Breck from riding an elevator to a secure facility. Evans knocks MacDonald unconscious and frees Rhodes.

Revolution on the Planet of the Apes #4: "Part Four: Truth and Consequences" (MR-c)

NOTE: A note in Revolution #6 *places these events 26 hours before full-scale war.*

◆ His dream of ape freedom becoming a reality, Caesar writes a journal entry expressing his hope that as his fellow apes find their voice, they'll tell him about their own dreams.

Revolution on the Planet of the Apes #4: "Caesar's Journal" (MR-c)

◆ Police officer Tammy Taylor, the 23-year-old daughter of astronaut George Taylor, sees four men terrorizing a chimp mother and baby. She warns them away, but a man named Darryl hits her with a pipe. The men kill the baby, then are slain by a pack of angry gorillas. Tammy awakens to hear a woman crying for help; the grief-stricken mother chimp has stolen her infant son Tommy and climbed a nearby building. Tammy climbs after the animal, soothes her into handing over the baby and then kills her, finally becoming the "magnificent bastard" her mother had always called her father.

Revolution on the Planet of the Apes #4: "Paternal Instinct" (MR-c)

◆ MacDonald awakens to find Evans holding a gun to his head, but armed gorillas free him. Assuming control, MacDonald assures his fellow humans that Caesar is trying to save the world.

Revolution on the Planet of the Apes #5: "Part Five: Weapon of Choice" (MR-c)

NOTE: This issue is set three weeks post-revolution. A note in Revolution #6 *places these events 25 hours before nuclear devastation.*

◆ Trundy surveys the damage from his helicopter. Lacking sufficient fuel to reach a secure bunker at Mount Rushmore, he heads for Fort Liberty. Akins reports that Chinese nuclear missiles have destroyed satellite communications. Moments later, Aldo's gorillas fire missile-launchers at them. Caesar's forces erect a battering ram in the bunker. Half a mile belowground, Breck threatens to fire the Alpha-Omega Bomb if Caesar doesn't surrender. Breck tells Mendez to contact Trundy, but with satcom disrupted, nothing gets through.

Revolution on the Planet of the Apes #5: "Part Five: Weapon of Choice" (MR-c)

NOTE: A note in Revolution #6 *places these events 24 hours before full-scale nuclear devastation. According to author Ty Templeton, a cut scene would have occurred within Mount Rushmore—an homage to Marvel's "Terror on the Planet of the Apes," in which that story's heroes found the bunker's remains and a human corpse inside Lincoln's nose. Templeton says the cut scene would have revealed the body to have been Trundy's vice president, whom the Marvel series named Henry.*

◆ Rhodes uses Leung's camera to hack an ANN broadcast and warn Trundy of Breck's actions. The network cancels the transmission, but Leung hacks back in. Hearing the broadcast, several apes bomb Fort Liberty. Trundy arrives to find the island in flames, the Statue of Liberty in pieces, and tunes in just in time to hear Rhodes recommend he launch a thermonuclear strike at Caesar's territory.

Revolution on the Planet of the Apes #5: "Part Five: Weapon of Choice" (MR-c)

NOTE: The statue's head and torch will survive 2,000 years in their final resting place.

◆ One newspaper covering these events features the headline "Bombs Over New York."

El Planeta de Los Simios #3: "The Beach of Time" (ET-c)

◆ Aldo's gorillas arrive with a squad of fighter jets. Caesar sends the city's inhabitants to safety, but MacDonald stays to fight alongside him. Rhodes' warning spreads over the next 12 hours, causing China and Russia to drop "cleansing" tactical nukes on several European cities. Aldo's fighters level the bunker. Apes storm the launch bay, slaughtering Breck's troops. Kolp shoots MacDonald, who hits a trigger before dying, causing the bomb to leak radioactivity. Forced to save mankind by destroying civilization, Trundy initiates the Inferno Protocol, raining nuclear fire on the cities of North America. Caesar leads his people to the mountains, carrying MacDonald's body but leaving Kolp's soldiers behind.

Revolution on the Planet of the Apes #6: "Part Six: Survival of the Fittest" (MR-c)

NOTE: MacDonald's death is also mentioned in the novelization of Battle for the Planet of the Apes. *In an online posting at the POTA Yahoo Group, author Ty Templeton revealed that the Alpha-Omega Bomb seen in the first film is a next-generation version of Breck's prototype from* Revolution. *A timeline packaged with the* Planet of the Apes Widescreen 35th Anniversary Edition DVD *sets the nuclear war's start in December 1992, contradicting* Revolution's *placement earlier in the year.*

◆ As full-scale war begins, power is disrupted to a movie theater showing a James Bond film. The film remains on the reel, untouched for some 1,100 years.

El Planeta de Los Simios #1: "The Wandering Jew" (ET-c)

◆ Realizing they still love one another, Rhodes and Evans resume their former relationship.

Revolution on the Planet of the Apes #6: "Part Six: Survival of the Fittest" (MR-c)

◆ In the wake of the opening nuclear attack, chain reactions follow throughout the continent. Though spared a much-feared nuclear winter, North America becomes a barren wasteland.

Ape City #3: "Monkey Planet" (AC-c)

◆ In the course of the Great War, African and Chinese factions blow up two-thirds of the United States. After Washington D.C. is destroyed, President Trundy and his VP/chief advisor, Henry, seek shelter in a private refuge up Lincoln's nose at the Mount Rushmore bunker.

Planet of the Apes #14: "Terror on the Planet of the Apes, Phase 2 —
Up the Nose-Tube to Monkey-Trash" (MC-c)

NOTE: An unpublished Marvel tale entitled "Future History Chronicles VI: The Captive of the Canals" features descendants of former African nations isolated from apes and White humans, on whom they blame the destruction of civilization; apparently, they no longer recall Africa's part in the war.

◆ During the war, the noses of the other Mount Rushmore presidents are all destroyed, leaving three noseless faces on the once-proud national monument.

Planet of the Apes #13: "Terror on the Planet of the Apes, Phase 2 —
The Magick-Man's Last Gasp Purple Light Show" (MC-c)

◆ New York and San Francisco are obliterated in the war. Other cities remain partially intact, populated in some areas by "normal" humans, in others by irradiated mutants.

Battle for the Planet of the Apes (FX-f)

NOTE: The Planet of the Apes *TV series, Marvel UK's "Apeslayer" saga and the Adventure Comics line show other examples of cities inhabited by humans.*

◆ The Metropolitan Opera House in New York City survives the war intact.

Planeta de Los Simios #7: "The Circus" (ET-c)

PUBLISHER / STUDIO
AB . . . . ABC-TV
AC . . . . Adventure / Malibu Comics
AW . . . . Award Books
BB . . . . .Ballantine Books
BN . . . . Bantam Books
BW . . . . Brown Watson Books
CB . . . . CBS-TV
CV . . . . Chad Valley Sliderama
DH . . . . .Dark Horse Comics
ET . . . . Editorial Mo.Pa.Sa.
FX . . . . 20th Century Fox
GK . . . .Gold Key / Western Comics
HE . . . HarperEntertainment Books
HM . . Harry K. McWilliams Assoc.
MC . . . . Marvel Comics
MR . . . Mr. Comics / Metallic Rose
NB . . . . NBC-TV
PR . . . . .Power Records
SB . . . . Signet Books
TP . . . . .Topps
UB . . . . .Ubisoft

MEDIUM
a . . . . animated series
b . . . . .book-and-record set
c . . . . .comic book or strip
d . . . . trading card
e . . . . e-comic
f . . . . .theatrical film
k . . . . .storybook
m . . . . .magazine article
n . . . . .novel or novelization
p . . . . promotional newspaper
r . . . . .recorded audio fiction
s . . . . short story
t . . . . television series
u . . . . .unfilmed script or story
v . . . . video game
x . . . . .Blu-Ray exclusive
y . . . . .young adult novel

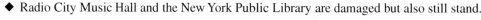

◆ Radio City Music Hall and the New York Public Library are damaged but also still stand.

Beneath the Planet of the Apes (FX-f)

◆ Wall Street and Times Square, however, are left in ruins.

Return to the Planet of the Apes episode #3: "The Unearthly Prophecy" (NB-a)

◆ Amazingly, the Liberty Bell of Philadelphia escapes destruction. In later years, the historical landmark will be revered as Ytrebil, Guardian of the Mountain and Protector of the Delphi.

Planet of the Apes—4 Exciting New Stories #1: "Mountain of the Delphi" (PR-r)

NOTE: "Ytrebil" is "liberty" spelled backwards, while "Delphi" is a shortened form of "Philadelphia."

◆ The war is swift and effective. Most major U.S. cities are leveled, though laser-defense ABM systems prevent the war from destroying all life.

Planet of the Apes #11: "Outlines of Tomorrow—A Chronology of the Planet of the Apes" (MC-m)

◆ One bubble-domed U.S. city survives the onslaught intact, its dome dented from the nuclear strike.

Planet of the Apes: "Journey to the Planet of the Apes" (MC-c, unpublished)

NOTE: This tale—originally titled "Return to the Planet of the Apes" but renamed, presumably, so as not to conflict with the cartoon series—was never released due to Marvel's decision to stop publishing Planet of the Apes *comics as of issue #29, in response to increased licensing fees. The above details come from a story outline and dialog breakdown provided by author Doug Moench.*

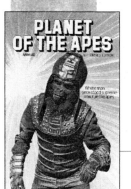

◆ The widespread nuclear war devastates Earth's surface. Human history does not record who started it, leaving future generations wondering if it was the work of a lone madman, international political pressure or a rival country taking advantage of the United States' governmental paralysis.

Planet of the Apes #11: "Outlines of Tomorrow—A Chronology of the Planet of the Apes" (MC-m)

◆ Somehow, Peru avoids destruction during the war and is still intact when the fighting ends. Those who live there believe U.S. apes must have caused the war.

Planet of the Apes (Authorised Edition) #3: "Flight From Terror" (BW-s)

◆ France and other parts of Europe also survive the war with their buildings intact.

Ape City #1: "Monkey Business" (AC-c)

◆ Some survivors theorize that an enemy power attacked while the United States was occupied with the ape problem, and that the U.S. government retaliated.

Planet of the Apes #22: "Quest for the Planet of the Apes, Part I—Seeds of Future Deaths" (MC-c)

◆ Another rumor claims the war began when a curious ape entered a Midwest nuclear power plant, accidentally triggering an explosion of enormous magnitude.

Ape City #3: "Monkey Planet" (AC-c)

◆ Still others suspect the *Psychedrome* aliens, the Keepers, may have launched the attack to punish humanity for defeating their planetary takeover plans a decade earlier.

Planet of the Apes #27: "Terror on the Planet of the Apes, Phase 2—Apes of Iron" (MC-c)

◆ The apes, meanwhile, know the truth: that mankind launched the war to retaliate for Caesar's rebellion, figuring if man could not rule the planet, he would ruin it for the apes.

The Forbidden Zone #1: "Part One—Forbidden Knowledge" (AC-c)

NOTE: This explanation is corroborated by Revolution on the Planet of the Apes.

◆ In time, this day will be deemed "the Destruction."

Planet of the Apes: "Hostage" (CB-u)

NOTE: This episode was never filmed, but the script is available online at Hunter's Planet of the Apes *Archive.*

◆ The East Coast Scientific Center sets up an automatic, repeating broadcast, inviting survivors to take refuge in its bomb shelter. The center is buried beneath rubble before anyone can use it, however, when a dam bursts, carrying in the ocean. Buried beneath a hill of sand on what will become known as the Beach of Time due to the many artifacts found there, the center repeats its broadcast for the next millennium.

El Planeta de Los Simios #3: "The Beach of Time" (ET-c)

◆ The apes eventually capture Breck, Alma, Mendez and other volatile humans, keeping them alive as a work detail. This reversal of fate infuriates the humans, who await the opportunity to seek revenge.

Planet of the Apes #22: "Quest for the Planet of the Apes, Part I—Seeds of Future Deaths" (MC-c)

NOTE: Revolution on the Planet of the Apes #6 implies Breck is crushed beneath the bomb, and that Alma and Mendez escape with Kolp. Breck's death is not explicitly stated, however, nor are the others named when Kolp evacuates. Since Marvel's "Quest" storyline, set two years later, has the trio prisoners of the apes, I assume all three to have survived and been captured with the other "volatile humans."

◆ Caesar leads his followers away from the city and into the provinces. There, he builds a new Ape City with help from human advisors, developing massive educational programs for the community. With the U.S. government breaking down entirely, Caesar faces little harassment in the provinces.

Planet of the Apes #11: "Outlines of Tomorrow—A Chronology of the Planet of the Apes" (MC-m)

NOTE: Marvel's "Quest for the Planet of the Apes" storyline in issue #22 makes it clear the human advisors' involvement in building Ape City was not voluntary.

◆ Caesar dreams of his people learning to speak, and his psychic abilities make his dreams a reality, beginning with Lisa. He soon stops dreaming events into existence and even starts forgetting his dreams, wondering if he has prevented the grim future he foresaw, or caused it. Elsewhere, Leung sits down to record his thoughts on paper, determined that humanity shall have its epitaph.

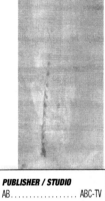

Revolution on the Planet of the Apes #6: "Part Six: Survival of the Fittest" (MR-c)

NOTE: The ending of Revolution *is ambiguous—Is it all just a parallel universe or alternate history?—and presents a potential continuity problem: Even if Caesar has forgotten his dreams, he'd still have his journals, not to mention Lisa's memories of what he's told her. As such, it's unclear why he's unaware of the future in* Battle for the Planet of the Apes. *Presumably, Mr. Comics had intended to address this question in the planned follow-up miniseries,* Empire on the Planet of the Apes.

◆ Aldo's power of speech evolves more quickly than other primitive apes' because of the genetic and biological experimentation he endured at Area 51.

Online Posting from Ty Templeton

NOTE: This information was posted in the POTA Yahoo Group by Revolution on the Planet of the Apes *author Ty Templeton.*

PUBLISHER / STUDIO
AB . . . . ABC-TV
AC . . . .Adventure / Malibu Comics
AW . . . . Award Books
BB . . . . .Ballantine Books
BN . . . . .Bantam Books
BW . . . . Brown Watson Books
CB . . . . CBS-TV
CV . . . . Chad Valley Sliderama
DH . . . . .Dark Horse Comics
ET . . . . Editorial Mo.Pa.Sa.
FX . . . . 20th Century Fox
GK . . . .Gold Key / Western Comics
HE . . . HarperEntertainment Books
HM . . Harry K. McWilliams Assoc.
MC . . . . .Marvel Comics
MR . . . Mr. Comics / Metallic Rose
NB . . . . NBC-TV
PR . . . . .Power Records
SB . . . . Signet Books
TP . . . . .Topps
UB . . . . .Ubisoft

MEDIUM
a . . . . animated series
b . . . . .book-and-record set
c . . . . .comic book or strip
d . . . . trading card
e . . . . e-comic
f . . . . .theatrical film
k . . . . .storybook
m . . . . .magazine article
n . . . . .novel or novelization
p . . . . promotional newspaper
r . . . . .recorded audio fiction
s . . . . short story
t . . . . television series
u . . . . .unfilmed script or story
v . . . . video game
x . . . . .Blu-Ray exclusive
y . . . . .young adult novel

◆ The apes deem their existence pre-Caesar as the Silent Times, many maintaining grudges over how they were treated during their enslavement.

Revolution on the Planet of the Apes #5: "Ape Shall Not Kill Ape" (MR-c)

◆ Caesar decrees the First Law: An ape may say "no" to a human, but a human may never say "no" to an ape. He also dictates that humans must live as vegetarians, and outlaws children's games based on war.

Battle for the Planet of the Apes (FX-f)

◆ The areas surrounding most major cities remain livable to a degree, but much of the United States is rendered vast irradiated deserts. The ape government prohibits its citizens from entering these areas, which Caesar declares Forbidden Zones.

Planet of the Apes #11: "Outlines of Tomorrow—A Chronology of the Planet of the Apes" (MC-m)

> NOTE: Other zones designated by the apes include the Rural Zone, the Blasted Zone, the Black Zone, the Forest Zone and the Danger Zone. It's interesting to note that following Caesar's rebellion, the U.S. government dubbed the city the Exclusion Zone—it's possible the apes, mimicking human nomenclature, continued this tradition when naming its territories.

◆ The fledgling ape society is not monetary-based. Instead, a ruling council provides every citizen a home at no cost, while a barter system makes other goods and services available.

Planet of the Apes #6: "Welcome to Ape City" (AC-c)

◆ As the apes gain control of the planet, Trundy tells his VP and only companion, Henry, that he wishes he could round them up and give them a good brainwashing in the *Psychedrome*. Ultimately, Trundy dies alone in his Mount Rushmore refuge, his remains undisturbed for nearly eighty years.

Planet of the Apes #14: "Terror on the Planet of the Apes, Phase 2— Up the Nose-Tube to Monkey-Trash" (MC-c)

◆ With the world lost to the apes, a group of humans attempts to wipe out apekind with a man-made plague, using Trojan horse-like tactics. The apes avert disaster, but a human is born who is destined to lead his people in revolt.

Planet of the Apes: "The Most Dangerous Animal" (AC-c, unpublished)

> NOTE: This story treatment was never scripted due to Adventure Comics losing the Planet of the Apes license. This synopsis was provided by author Charles Marshall. No further details are available, though Marshall says it would have involved time travel.

JANUARY 1992 TO 1993

◆ Aldo's anti-human hatred grows as the gorillas horribly mistreat Breck and other prisoners. Breck savors the trouble Caesar faces in building a society, convinced humans will one day have their revenge.

Planet of the Apes #22: "Quest for the Planet of the Apes, Part I—Seeds of Future Deaths" (MC-c)

EARLY TO MID 1992

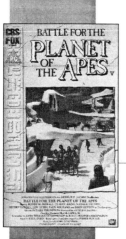

◆ Caesar and Lisa get married.

Battle for the Planet of the Apes (FX-f)

◆ After the war, the plague flares up once more, spreading among the remnants of humanity. As a result, many North American humans are rendered mute savages.

Planet of the Apes #17: "Countdown Zero—Part Four" (AC-c)

NOTE: It's possible (and, if so, ironic) that the plague's resurgence was caused by research Dr. Bryce Evans was conducting before the war (as seen in Revolution on the Planet of the Apes) *to find a virus that would kill all simians, but not affect humanity.*

◆ This time, the plague is quite virulent among humans, particularly in Europe—in fact, the species is nearly eliminated on that continent.

Ape City #1: "Monkey Business" (AC-c)

◆ Some blame the plague on the apes' rise and retaliate with violence. Most Europeans die from the plague; the few survivors become animal-like, robbed of speech capability and independent thought. In the end, human buildings in Europe still stand, electricity continues to flow and food and drink remain plentiful, but humanity's reign is completely over in that part of the world.

Ape City #3: "Monkey Planet" (AC-c)

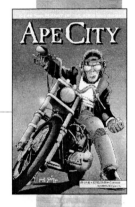

◆ Some pockets of sentient humans resist the plague in North America, including bands of irradiated mutants who take refuge in the rubble of major cities, while other healthy humans gather in tribes across the planet. Nonetheless, humanity's fall from the top of the evolutionary hill is complete.

Battle for the Planet of the Apes (FX-f)

◆ Many documents are lost in the war, destroying all records of the plague's origin.

Escape from the Planet of the Apes (FX-f)

◆ To avoid the post-nuclear horror and ape domination, a band of humans hides in dark caverns below the rubble of New York City. Carving out a subterranean home, which they dub the Below World, these humans call themselves the Underdwellers, and remain below the surface for two millennia.

Return to the Planet of the Apes episode #3: "The Unearthly Prophecy" (NB-a)

◆ Unbeknownst to the apes, the Below World—a vast network of caverns and caves filled with advanced technology—extends below Ape City.

Return to the Planet of the Apes episode #12: "Invasion of the Underdwellers" (NB-a)

◆ The Keepers, who crashed their *Psychedrome* starship during a failed planetary take-over a decade earlier, realize mankind is no longer a threat. Covertly brainwashing the minds of men and apes aboard their hidden ship, the aliens and their winged monkey-demon soldiers proceed as originally planned.

Planet of the Apes #20: "Terror on the Planet of the Apes, Phase 2—Society of the Psychedrome" (MC-c)

MID TO LATE 1992

◆ After a successful 16 months in space, Capt. James Norvell prepares his ship for a return to Earth. Having lost contact for the duration of the mission, he and his crew know nothing of the ape rebellion and nuclear war that wrecked the planet. Suddenly, the ship experiences a total systems failure.

Planet of the Apes #14: "Countdown Zero—Part One" (AC-c)

NOTE: Dayton Ward's timeline, published in The Planet of the Apes Chronicles, *dates these events in 2029. Since the astronauts know nothing of the ape revolution and nuclear war, however, and since they were only in space for 16 months, their voyage must take place concurrent with these events.*

PUBLISHER / STUDIO

AB . . . . ABC-TV
AC . . . .Adventure / Malibu Comics
AW . . . . Award Books
BB . . . . .Ballantine Books
BN . . . . Bantam Books
BW . . . . Brown Watson Books
CB . . . . CBS-TV
CV . . . . Chad Valley Sliderama
DH . . . . .Dark Horse Comics
ET . . . . Editorial Mo.Pa.Sa.
FX . . . . 20th Century Fox
GK . . . .Gold Key / Western Comics
HE . . HarperEntertainment Books
HM . . Harry K. McWilliams Assoc.
MC . . . . Marvel Comics
MR . . . Mr. Comics / Metallic Rose
NB. . . . . NBC-TV
PR . . . . .Power Records
SB . . . . Signet Books
TP . . . . Topps
UB . . . . .Ubisoft

MEDIUM

a . . . . animated series
b . . . . .book-and-record set
c . . . . .comic book or strip
d . . . . trading card
e . . . . e-comic
f . . . . .theatrical film
k . . . . .storybook
m . . . . .magazine article
n . . . . . .novel or novelization
p . . . . promotional newspaper
r . . . . .recorded audio fiction
s . . . . short story
t . . . . television series
u . . . . .unfilmed script or story
v . . . . video game
x . . . . .Blu-Ray exclusive
y . . . . .young adult novel

◆ His crew in grave danger, Norvell warns his fellow astronauts, August Anne Burrows and Lt. Ken Flip, to strap themselves in.

Planet of the Apes #9: "Countdown Five" (AC-c)

◆ The ship's descent is steep and fast. The stabilizer knocks out as the ship plummets back to Earth and the crew prepares for a crash landing.

Planet of the Apes #10: "Countdown Four" (AC-c)

◆ Norvell's ship crashes into the Mississippi River, dropping 300 feet below the surface. The captain tries to contact Control but gets no answer.

Planet of the Apes #11: "Countdown Three" (AC-c)

◆ The crew swims to the surface and boards an inflatable raft, stunned to find the lifeless, bombed-out ruins of what was once St. Louis, Missouri.

Planet of the Apes #12: "Countdown Two" (AC-c)

◆ The astronauts row to shore, and Burrows marks the spot in case they need supplies. Her sense of humor strained, she berates Flip for jokingly tossing his prosthetic limb at her.

Planet of the Apes #13: "Countdown One" (AC-c)

◆ Burrows begins a journal of her experiences. Their nerves frayed, the trio begins fighting over minutiae. They head east, dismayed by the devastation, and stunned to see apes walking upright, wearing clothes, and conversing—in Spanish. The apes give chase as the astronauts try to start an abandoned car. A distant drum scares the simians, enabling the humans to escape. Heading in the direction of the drum, they meet a tribe of gorillas. Their leader, a dangerous white-eyed ape called Zar, orders their capture.

Planet of the Apes #14: "Countdown Zero—Part One" (AC-c)

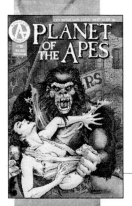

◆ After six days on the run, living off dehydrated food and boiled water, the astronauts find a Chevy pickup with keys in the ignition, but Norvell fails to climb aboard and is captured. Burrows rams the apes and rescues him, and they drive 200 miles before resting. Flip shows signs of snapping, so she eases his mind by having sex with him. Over the next two weeks, they encounter huge cracks in the road and Norvell gets food poisoning from a bad can of SpaghettiOs. Flip tries to resume his intimacy with Burrows, but she spurns his advances. As the men scavenge a K-Mart, she finds a library and reads a *Time* magazine article about the apes' status as replacement pets. Moments later, Zar's gang drops from the skylight.

Planet of the Apes #15: "Countdown Zero—Part Two" (AC-c)

◆ With Norvell's help, Burrows fights her way to the truck. Flip senses attraction between them and broods for three days. The truck dies, and they continue on foot until finding a Motel 6. Flip attempts intimacy once more, growing violent when she refuses. Norvell hits him, but Burrows says they must get along for survival's sake. They find a horse and name it Clementine, which they use to carry their belongings. Zar's apes shoot the horse, who gives them one last ride to safety, then collapses on Burrows' leg. Flip checks out an Acme grocery store with Norvell, fracturing the other man's skull with a shovel once inside the store.

Planet of the Apes #16: "Countdown Zero—Part Three" (AC-c)

◆ Zar's apes capture Burrows. When she awakens, he offers her tea and treats her with respect, saying he has come not to kill them, but to ask how evolution turned upside down. She tells him about the article, and though grateful, he orders her death. Norvell shoots Zar and most of his tribe, then dies in her arms. Burrows journeys east on foot, ignoring Flip. Realizing she's pregnant, she raids a Caldor department store for supplies, including a doll that says "Mama." Avoiding ape tribes for three weeks, she confronts Flip about his attempt to kill Norvell. He begs forgiveness, committing suicide when she refuses. In time, she reaches the shore of Long Island, where she seeks shelter in a cave to await the birth of her child.

Planet of the Apes #17: "Countdown Zero—Part Four" (AC-c)

NOTE: The cave and doll are implied to be those later excavated by Cornelius in the first Planet of the Apes *film.*

1992 TO 2020

◆ Arthur Vernon Kolp and his commandos eke out a scavenger existence in the irradiated ruins of a former city. Meanwhile, Caesar's community accepts survivors from other areas, and an ape/human society unfolds. Despite Caesar's ideals, humans become second-class citizens and ape cultural divisions develop. Aldo declares himself a general and begins training an army of gorillas. Residual radiation affects many humans and apes. The apes' plague-altered genes increase their already rapid intellectual development, while humans grow more docile from living among highly evolved apes easily able to kill them.

Planet of the Apes #11: "Outlines of Tomorrow—A Chronology of the Planet of the Apes" (MC-m)

NOTE: Marvel's timeline dates these events from 1992 to 2001, based on its 2001 placement for the fifth film; I've moved the end date to 2020. Marvel places the mutants in San Francisco, while Revolution on the Planet of the Apes *transfers the action to San Diego. Since early treatments for* Conquest of the Planet of the Apes *and* Battle for the Planet of the Apes *set both films on the East Coast, however, I've kept the location of Kolp's base vague.*

PUBLISHER / STUDIO
AB . . . . ABC-TV
AC . . . . Adventure / Malibu Comics
AW . . . . Award Books
BB . . . . .Ballantine Books
BN . . . . Bantam Books
BW . . . . Brown Watson Books
CB . . . . CBS-TV
CV . . . . Chad Valley Sliderama
DH . . . . .Dark Horse Comics
ET . . . . Editorial Mo.Pa.Sa.
FX . . . . 20th Century Fox
GK . . . .Gold Key / Western Comics
HE . . . HarperEntertainment Books
HM . . Harry K. McWilliams Assoc.
MC . . . . .Marvel Comics
MR . . . Mr. Comics / Metallic Rose
NB . . . . NBC-TV
PR . . . . .Power Records
SB . . . . Signet Books
TP . . . . Topps
UB . . . . Ubisoft

MEDIUM
a . . . . animated series
b . . . . .book-and-record set
c . . . . .comic book or strip
d . . . . trading card
e . . . . e-comic
f . . . . .theatrical film
k . . . . .storybook
m . . . . .magazine article
n . . . . .novel or novelization
p . . . . promotional newspaper
r . . . . .recorded audio fiction
s . . . . short story
t . . . . .television series
u . . . . .unfilmed script or story
v . . . . video game
x . . . . .Blu-Ray exclusive
y . . . . .young adult novel

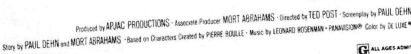

Part 5: From the Ashes
(1993 to 2020)

AFTER 1992

◆ The U.S. Air Force continues to function, though its members remain unaware of the ape rebellion and nuclear war that devastated the planet.

Planet of the Apes: Leo's Logbook—A Captain's Days in Captivity (HE-k)

◆ NASA also continues to operate, its officers similarly unaware of world events.

Return to the Planet of the Apes episode #1: "Flames of Doom" (NB-a)

NOTE: The unlikelihood that neither NASA nor USAF officers would know of the revolution illustrates why many fans ignore the Tim Burton film and the animated series.

◆ In Europe, as in North America, the Great Apes (chimps, orangutans and gorillas) attain intelligence. So do European baboons, though it's unclear if the same is true of North American baboons.

Ape City #1: "Monkey Business" (AC-c)

◆ In addition to the Great Apes, gibbons also gain sentience.

*Planet of the Apes #13: "Terror on the Planet of the Apes, Phase 2—
The Magick-Man's Last Gasp Purple Light Show" (MC-c)*

◆ Some mandrills achieve intelligence as well.

Urchak's Folly #3: "Chapter Three—The Savages" (AC-c)

NOTE: A mandrill also appears in Adventure Comics' Planet of the Apes Annual. A sketch created for Revolution on the Planet of the Apes (available online at http://www.mrcomics.ca/sketchbook.htm) features a drawing of a mandrill, with the question "Why are there no mandrills on the planet of the apes?" Apparently, the artist was unaware mandrills have, in fact, been utilized in the Apes universe.

◆ Bonobos also become sentient, some of whom reside in Ape City with the other Great Apes.

Revolution on the Planet of the Apes #5: "Ape Shall Not Kill Ape" (MR-c)

◆ Other members of the primate kingdom—baboons, Barbary apes (macaques), gibbons and lemurs—are resistant to accepting Ape City as the capital, settling instead in the outlying areas. Among the chimps, orangutans and gorillas, these other simians are considered "foreigners."

Return to the Planet of the Apes episode #8: "Screaming Wings" (BB-n)

*NOTE: This is revealed in the episode's novelization. Presumably, "foreigner"
status also applies to mandrills.*

◆ An air of aristocracy grows among the Great Apes, who consider themselves above monkeys and other primates. The word "monkey" becomes an offensive racial slur among the apes.

Escape from the Planet of the Apes (FX-f)

◆ Ape civilization rises from the ashes of mankind's fall, inheriting man's culture, language and clothing, as well as his strengths and weaknesses.

Revolution on the Planet of the Apes #6: "Part Six: Survival of the Fittest" (MR-c)

PUBLISHER / STUDIO	
AB	ABC-TV
AC	Adventure / Malibu Comics
AW	Award Books
BB	Ballantine Books
BN	Bantam Books
BW	Brown Watson Books
CB	CBS-TV
CV	Chad Valley Sliderama
DH	Dark Horse Comics
ET	Editorial Mo.Pa.Sa.
FX	20th Century Fox
GK	Gold Key / Western Comics
HE	HarperEntertainment Books
HM	Harry K. McWilliams Assoc.
MC	Marvel Comics
MR	Mr. Comics / Metallic Rose
NB	NBC-TV
PR	Power Records
SB	Signet Books
TP	Topps
UB	Ubisoft

MEDIUM	
a	animated series
b	book-and-record set
c	comic book or strip
d	trading card
e	e-comic
f	theatrical film
k	storybook
m	magazine article
n	novel or novelization
p	promotional newspaper
r	recorded audio fiction
s	short story
t	television series
u	unfilmed script or story
v	video game
x	Blu-Ray exclusive
y	young adult novel

◆ As such, the various ape factions mimic the human behavior they witnessed as slaves. In France, for instance, a gang of simian gangsters emerges, affecting the mannerisms and speech patterns of Chicago mobsters of the 1920s.

Ape City #1: "Monkey Business" (AC-c)

◆ Another European ape group models themselves after the Hell's Angels by donning leather, riding Harley Davidson motorcycles and calling themselves Hell's Apes.

Ape City #3: "Monkey Planet" (AC-c)

◆ A spiritual band of French baboons forms a martial arts cult—the Baboonjas, also known as Followers of the True Light. Their leader, a powerful sorcerer, can levitate objects and perform other mystical feats.

Ape City #1: "Monkey Business" (AC-c)

◆ Several ape cultures model themselves after the American Indians. One such group builds an isolated society a few miles outside Ape City. These mysterious, mystical apes call themselves the Lightfeet.

Planet of the Apes #6: "Welcome to Ape City" (AC-c)

◆ The Lightfeet live near a frontier town in which apes emulate old Western films, complete with outlaws, sheriffs and other accoutrements. A quartet of ape bounty hunters, the Ape Riders, police the area.

Planet of the Apes Annual—A Day on the Planet of the Apes: "High Noon" (AC-c)

◆ A Native American ape-human village forms in South Dakota. The peaceful tribe lives in cliffside adobe huts, guided by an orangutan shaman who uses psychedelic drugs to perform Rites of Divine Communion.

Planet of the Apes #19: "Terror on the Planet of the Apes, Phase 2—Demons of the Psychedrome" (MC-c)

◆ A third such simian tribe forms in Texas. This tribe, known as the Indiapes, keeps mute humans as slaves, its members raiding other villages for mates, food and supplies. During one such raid, a kidnapped female grows disgusted at her captor's mistreatment of humans. When she asks if the slaves can speak, the Indiape mocks a nearby human, entertained by the notion of a speaking man. She is not amused.

Indiape (AC-c, unpublished)

NOTE: Roland Mann, *author of Adventure's* Blood of the Apes, *conceived this story as a four-issue miniseries but never proposed it since the company opted to scale back its* Planet of the Apes *titles. Mann says his initial concept was never fleshed out, and that no specific date was included in his notes.*

◆ Several humans and apes move away from Ape City to form a peaceful seafaring civilization known as the River Society. The village resembles a Western frontier town, its citizens appropriately garbed.

Planet of the Apes #4: "Terror on the Planet of the Apes—Gunpowder Julius" (MC-c)

◆ A village outside Ape City is inhabited by a brutal band called the Nameless Apes.

Planet of the Apes #22: "Part Two—The Land of No Escape" (AC-c)

◆ In Kansas, along the former Route 80, a gorilla tribe evolves known as the Assisimians. Superstitious and primitive, the Assisimians are fierce, unrelenting warriors, ruled by a powerful chieftan.

Planet of the Apes #13: "Terror on the Planet of the Apes, Phase 2—The Magick-Man's Last Gasp Purple Light Show" (MC-c)

◆ In another isolated land, two rival mutant ape societies develop, known as Her Majesty's Cannibal Corps (who travel on giant mutant frogs) and the Industrialists.

Planet of the Apes #29: "Future History Chronicles V—To Race the Death-Winds" (MC-c)

◆ In an area known as the Sogan Desert, a simian population emerges known as the Ice Apes.

Return to the Planet of the Apes episode #1: "Flames of Doom" (NB-a)

◆ Bruce "Mac" MacDonald succeeds his brother as Caesar's trusted aide, representing Ape City's humans like Malcolm before him. Though loyal to Caesar, he resents the inequality among their species.

Battle for the Planet of the Apes (FX-f)

NOTE: Bruce's first name is revealed in Marvel's adaptation of the film. The comic makes no mention of his being Malcolm's brother—rather, they are said to be the same man, as Marvel used an early-draft script. Malcolm's first name is revealed in Revolution on the Planet of the Apes #4.

◆ Some of Ape City's humans feel MacDonald receives favored treatment from Caesar.

Battle for the Planet of the Apes (PR-c)

NOTE: This is revealed in the Power Records comic adaptation of the film.

◆ Religious zealots discover the journal of Dr. Lewis Dixon, revealing the fates of George Taylor, Cornelius and Zira. They christen it the *Book of Taylor*, revering the journal as a holy text and Taylor as their savior.

Urchak's Folly #3: "Chapter Three—The Savages" (AC-c)

◆ Calling themselves Taylorites, the zealots preach the *Book of Taylor*, promising Taylor will return to hold the world in his hands, offer salvation and create a new home for man and ape to live as equals.

Urchak's Folly #2: "Chapter Two—The Bridge" (AC-c)

◆ An ape village enslaves and tortures humans begging for food. When a human slays the local Lawgiver, the apes kill and consume the humans in a savage religious rite. Outside St. Patrick's Cathedral, human soldiers kill hundreds of starving apes seeking food. An ape lobs a grenade into the building, killing the human leader. Survivors of both camps, horribly mutated by nuclear radiation, form the New Order Born of Old Sins. Vowing to spread mutation to everyone on the planet, cleansing it of violent non-mutants, the New Order builds a vast cathedral-lined city-ship, the *Cathedraulus*, and leaves the Forbidden Zone.

Planet of the Apes #24: "Future History Chronicles IV—The Shadows of Haunted Cathedraulus" (MC-c)

NOTE: This sets the stage for the cathedral's significance in the films.

◆ A gypsy couple from the area once known as Greece travels the Atlantic Ocean (now called the All-antik Ocean) to live in North America. Traveling with them is their infant son, Saraband. After a long journey, the family joins the peaceful River Society.

Planet of the Apes #8: "Terror on the Planet of the Apes—The Planet Inheritors" (MC-c)

◆ A chimp uprising protests the oppressive gorillas, who have cowed the orangutans into submission. The outcome is unrecorded, though the gorillas dominate ape society for millennia. Some time later, on the so-called Night of Blood, gorilla swords run red, the streets lined with chimpanzee corpses.

Return to the Planet of the Apes episode #2: "Escape From Ape City" (BB-n)

NOTE: This is revealed in the novelization. Clearly, the "Ape shall never kill ape" law is not embraced by all.

◆ While North American apes and humans brave post-apocalyptic conditions, European apes maintain a life of peace and prosperity, since the plague has eliminated humanity on that continent.

Ape City #3: "Monkey Planet" (AC-c)

PUBLISHER / STUDIO
AB .... ABC-TV
AC ....Adventure / Malibu Comics
AW .... Award Books
BB ....Ballantine Books
BN .... Bantam Books
BW .... Brown Watson Books
CB .... CBS-TV
CV .... Chad Valley Sliderama
DH ....Dark Horse Comics
ET .... Editorial Mo.Pa.Sa.
FX .... 20th Century Fox
GK ....Gold Key / Western Comics
HE ... HarperEntertainment Books
HM .. Harry K. McWilliams Assoc.
MC ....Marvel Comics
MR ... Mr. Comics / Metallic Rose
NB .... NBC-TV
PR............ Power Records
SB.............. Signet Books
TP .... Topps
UB.................. Ubisoft

MEDIUM
a .... animated series
b ....book-and-record set
c .... .comic book or strip
d .... trading card
e .... e-comic
f ....theatrical film
k .... storybook
m ....magazine article
n ....novel or novelization
p .... promotional newspaper
r ....recorded audio fiction
s .... short story
t .... television series
u ....unfilmed script or story
v .... video game
x .... Blu-Ray exclusive
y ....young adult novel

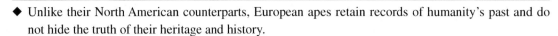

◆ Unlike their North American counterparts, European apes retain records of humanity's past and do not hide the truth of their heritage and history.

Ape City #2: "See No Evil, Hear No Evil, Speak No Evil" (AC-c)

◆ Without mankind to maintain Europe's power plants, however, they soon begin malfunctioning.

Ape City #1: "Monkey Business" (AC-c)

◆ Over time, the apes name many churches after Dr. Milo, reverently calling him "Milo the Pathfinder" for making Caesar's existence possible by bringing Zira and Cornelius into the past.

Revolution on the Planet of the Apes #6: "Catch a Falling Star" (MR-c)

NOTE: This is revealed in a dream, and thus might not have actually occurred.

◆ The Underdwellers build vast generators to provide heat and light in the Below World beneath New York City. They find a stone bust of astronaut Judy Franklin in the rubble, erected after the *Venturer* vanished in 1976, and create a prophecy that she will one day return to lead them back to the surface and re-take Earth. Since "USA" appears on the bust, they chant the name "Oosa" in their prayers.

Return to the Planet of the Apes episode #3: "The Unearthly Prophecy" (NB-a)

◆ Over the next 60 or so generations, the Underdwellers' eyes grow accustomed to living underground. As such, they find the light of the surface world uncomfortable.

Return to the Planet of the Apes episode #4: "Tunnel of Fear" (BB-n)

NOTE: This is revealed in the novelization.

◆ Other mutants emerge as well. A quintet of giant bodiless brains, floating in vast nutrient-globes, form a group consciousness (the Gestalt Mind, a.k.a. the Inheritors) in the caverns beneath an old city. Their leader is Be-One, with others similarly named: Be-Two, Be-Three, Be-Four, Be-Five and so on—each with a unique personality. Additional mutated brains are kept in frozen storage in case of damage.

Planet of the Apes #11: "Outlines of Tomorrow—A Chronology of the Planet of the Apes" (MC-m)

NOTE: It's unknown how these giant brains came to exist, but considering the various scientific experiments being conducted before the war, any explanation is possible.

◆ The Inheritors' ultimate goal is to wipe out all apes and non-mutant humans on the planet.

Planet of the Apes #3: "Terror on the Planet of the Apes—The Abomination Arena" (MC-c)

◆ Several human researchers survive the holocaust. Sequestering themselves in a basement lab beneath the New York Public Library, they repair their injuries with bionics and cybernetics, extending their lifespans and strength. Their minds grow deranged, causing them to pursue bizarre experiments. The Inheritors' mutant-drone soldiers encounter the crazed cyborgs, dubbing them the Makers for their propensity to build things. After a pitched battle, the Makers go into hiding to plot their revenge.

Planet of the Apes #27: "Terror on the Planet of the Apes, Phase 2—Apes of Iron" (MC-c)

◆ Many mutated humans go insane from radiation sickness. At the Ape Management complex, several of them find a band of dying apes trapped in a sub-basement with little food or water, having been cut off from Caesar's rebellion. The humans lock them in cages for 150 years, calling them "Funky Monkeys." The Children of the Forgotten Apes, as they call themselves, develop the ability to foresee the future. One such ape, the Knower, predicts Caesar's grandson Alexander will save them from this wretched existence.

Planet of the Apes #2: "The Monkey Planet—Escape" (AC-c)

◆ As a result of exposure to the radiation, an ape on a secret island is mutated to enormous proportions. Though intelligent, the giant ape is rendered an insane berserker from radiation sickness, appeased only through human sacrifice. Eventually, the mutant simian is relocated to Manhattan.

Planet of the Apes: [issue # and title unknown] (MC-c)

NOTE: This comic, outlined by Doug Moench but never written or illustrated, was intended as a back-up in the event that Marvel needed another story. This indicates Moench came up with the idea after Marvel ran the Apeslayer storyline, for it's reasonable to assume Marvel would have used it if it had been available, rather than hastily refitting its Killraven *series to fit the* Planet of the Apes *motif, as it did with* Apeslayer. *Moench says he conceived the tale as an homage to* King Kong, *but with an ironic reversal—the giant ape would have moved from civilization to primitive ruins, and New York would already have been destroyed when he arrived. Other* Kong *homages include Kygoor, from* Return to the Planet of the Apes; *Cong, seen in the* Adventure Comics *line; and Her Midgetsy, from an unpublished Moench story entitled "The Captive of the Canals." Moench recalls no further details of this story.*

◆ Several bizarre variants on humanity and apekind arise, including hybrids of the two species.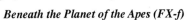

Beneath the Planet of the Apes (FX-f)

NOTE: Though never filmed or scripted, a scene was planned for the second film featuring a human/ape hybrid child. Makeup tests were created, but the idea never progressed beyond that point. A sixth film in the series, to have been written by Peter Jackson, would have featured such a hybrid. The comics have since validated the concept by introducing several hybrid creatures. This begs a disturbing question no author has yet addressed: Are these hybrids the result of radiation exposure...or is widespread interbreeding actually occurring between humans and simians? Both Marvel's "Terror on the Planet of the Apes" and Malibu's Blood of the Apes *feature ape-human romances, while* Urchak's Folly *features a gorilla keeping a human woman as his sexual slave, so such unions would not be without precedent.*

◆ One such hybrid, a race of timid, shaggy primates, makes its home in the Forbidden Zone.

Planet of the Apes #2: "Terror on the Planet of the Apes—Lick the Sky Crimson" (MC-c)

◆ Another hybrid, the Snow-Shamblers, evolves in the mountainous Northlands. These peaceful creatures seek only to love and nurture, but a nearby village of Viking-esque simians, the North Apes, mistakes them for a threat and wages war for years.

Planet of the Apes #26: "Terror on the Planet of the Apes, Phase 2—North Lands" (MC-c)

◆ A third human-ape hybrid, a Yeti-like species, evolves beyond the Forbidden Zone.

Planet of the Apes #5: "Evolution's Nightmare" (MC-c)

◆ Beyond the Forbidden Zone lives a tribe of aboriginal human-ape hybrids, known as the Mud People.

Urchak's Folly #3: "Chapter Three—The Savages" (AC-c)

◆ Many non-sentient creatures of the world undergo mutation as well.

Planet of the Apes #5: "Evolution's Nightmare" (MC-c)

◆ Rats in New York City's subway system grow human-sized, gain intelligence and enslave a blind sub-human species. The humans in a nearby tribe fear them, calling them the Monstrous Rodents.

El Planeta de Los Simios #2: "Depth" (ET-c)

PUBLISHER / STUDIO

AB . . . . ABC-TV
AC . . . . Adventure / Malibu Comics
AW . . . . Award Books
BB . . . . Ballantine Books
BN . . . . Bantam Books
BW . . . . . Brown Watson Books
CB . . . . CBS-TV
CV . . . . Chad Valley Sliderama
DH . . . . Dark Horse Comics
ET . . . . Editorial Mo.Pa.Sa.
FX . . . . 20th Century Fox
GK . . . . Gold Key / Western Comics
HE . . . HarperEntertainment Books
HM . . Harry K. McWilliams Assoc.
MC . . . . Marvel Comics
MR . . . Mr. Comics / Metallic Rose
NB . . . . NBC-TV
PR . . . . Power Records
SB . . . . Signet Books
TP . . . . Topps
UB . . . . Ubisoft

MEDIUM

a . . . . animated series
b . . . . book-and-record set
c . . . . .comic book or strip
d . . . . trading card
e . . . . e-comic
f . . . . .theatrical film
k . . . . .storybook
m . . . . .magazine article
n . . . . .novel or novelization
p . . . . promotional newspaper
r . . . . recorded audio fiction
s . . . . short story
t . . . . television series
u . . . . .unfilmed script or story
v . . . . video game
x . . . . .Blu-Ray exclusive
y . . . . .young adult novel

◆ Also mutated are alligators in New York City, which grow to enormous proportions.

Planet of the Apes #25: "The Sirens of 7ᵗʰ Avenue" (MC-c)

◆ Mutated lions inhabit the caves along the Forbidden Zone, their saliva emitting deadly mutative rays.

Planet of the Apes #4: "Terror on the Planet of the Apes—A Riverboat Named Simian" (MC-c)

◆ Giant river-slugs evolve in the rivers along the Forbidden Zone.

Planet of the Apes #6: "Terror on the Planet of the Apes—Malagueña Beyond a Zone Forbidden" (MC-c)

◆ Mutated horses also walk the deserted lands.

Planet of the Apes #13: "Terror on the Planet of the Apes, Phase 2—
The Magick-Man's Last Gasp Purple Light Show" (MC-c)

◆ Huge mutated crabs evolve near New York City, able to spit acid and with human-size claws.

Planet of the Apes #30: "Apeslayer Dies at Dawn" (MC-c)

◆ In old sewer systems near Ape City, giant spiders thrive.

Return to the Planet of the Apes episode #4: "Tunnel of Fear" (NB-a)

◆ In waters along the edge of the Forbidden Zone, giant carnivorous serpents evolve, which local human tribes call buh-hoy-yas.

Return to the Planet of the Apes episode #5: "Lagoon of Peril" (NB-a)

◆ The Forbidden Zone also becomes home to giant flying creatures known as snake-birds.

Return to the Planet of the Apes episode #10: "Attack from the Clouds" (NB-a)

◆ Giant mutant frogs evolve in an isolated land, used as mounts by a mutant ape society known as Her Majesty's Cannibal Corps.

Planet of the Apes #29: "Future History Chronicles V—To Race the Death-Winds" (MC-c)

◆ And on the strange island of Avedon, lizards mutate to the size of dragons.

Planet of the Apes #10: "Kingdom on an Island of the Apes—The Island Out of Time" (MC-c)

◆ Citizens of several African nations blame the apes and White humans for the devastation of the planet. Calling themselves Industrialists, they build Sexxtann, a 42-level hexagonal fortress with a vast canal system filled with giant newts, salamanders, frogs and other amphibians, forming a vicarium that provides amusement, transportation and sustenance. Shedding their former third-world status, these Africans make industry their way of life, further damaging the environment in the process.

Planet of the Apes: "Future History Chronicles VI—The Captive of the Canals" (MC-c, unpublished)

> NOTE: This story was never released due to Marvel's decision to stop publishing Planet of the Apes *comics as of issue #29, in response to increased licensing fees.* The above details come from a story outline provided by author Doug Moench. This *tale may have been Moench's response to the lack of dark-skinned humans in either* of the first two Apes *films.*

◆ Aldo accuses Caesar of preferring humans to apes, citing his friendship with MacDonald. Caesar rebuffs him for beating an old man, so Aldo sets fire to Caesar's home, blaming a human. When Caesar calls him a liar, Aldo challenges him to a quest: Each must journey to the human city and bring something back; whoever finds the "best thing" will rule. MacDonald urges him not to go, as does Lisa (who is pregnant), but Caesar feels compelled to accept. He brings back knowledge of what strife and peace each offer, while Aldo finds a stocked armory and tries to shoot Caesar. Meanwhile, Breck, Mendez, Alma and others revolt, knocking MacDonald unconscious. Though Caesar is the first to return to Ape City, Aldo awes the apes with his weapons. Breck's followers, however, seize Aldo's cart and take Lisa hostage.

Planet of the Apes #22: "Quest for the Planet of the Apes, Part I—Seeds of Future Deaths" (MC-c)

◆ Aldo and Caesar form a temporary truce. Mandemus knocks Lisa free, taking a bullet meant for Caesar. Lisa and a gorilla named Phineas carry the elderly ape to a healer. Caesar beats Breck to a pulp, but lets him return to the dead city, then heads home to find Aldo slaying humans. The gorilla claims rulership of Ape City, challenging Caesar to a fight. MacDonald and Mandemus urge Caesar to decline, knowing few will resist the gorillas. Caesar lures Aldo into a rope-trap, and Mandemus proclaims him the winner. The human compounds are dismantled and an era of cooperation begins. Mandemus suggests they destroy the guns, but Caesar says they'll be needed in the future, naming him Keeper of the Guns to ensure none are used for evil. Lisa wants to name the child Caesar Jr., but Caesar prefers the name Cornelius.

Planet of the Apes #22: "Quest for the Planet of the Apes, Part II—The Keeper of Future Death" (MC-c)

◆ Lisa miscarries her unborn child.

Conjecture

NOTE: "Quest" occurs two years after Conquest of the Planet of the Apes, *while* Battle for the Planet of the Apes *takes place at least 27 years later, as per Mandemus' dialog. If Lisa became pregnant for Cornelius in "Quest," he would have been 25 or more in* Battle. *The timeline in Marvel's issue #11 places Cornelius' birth in 1995, but that would imply Lisa remained pregnant for two years, so I am discarding both Marvel references and assuming she miscarried, got pregnant again years later and named that child Cornelius.* Revolution on the Planet of the Apes #5 *refers to Cornelius as "Caesar's first son," implying there were other births.*

◆ Breck dies shortly thereafter, likely from exposure to nuclear radiation.

Battle for the Planet of the Apes (FX-f)

NOTE: Kolp says the war killed the former governor, but Breck shows up in "Quest for the Planet of the Apes," two years post-war. This discrepancy is easily reconciled since Breck could have succumbed to radiation sickness after returning to the dead city.

BETWEEN 1993 AND 2020

◆ Arthur Vernon Kolp assumes the governorship, and Mendez and Alma rejoin his band of mutants. For a time, the fighting between humans and apes continues.

Battle for the Planet of the Apes (FX-f)

NOTE: Mendez and Alma escaped the stockade in Marvel's issue #22, "Quest for the Planet of the Apes." Given their allegiance to Kolp in Revolution on the Planet of the Apes and in the fifth film, it's logical to assume they met up with him after escaping.

PUBLISHER / STUDIO	
AB	ABC-TV
AC	Adventure / Malibu Comics
AW	Award Books
BB	Ballantine Books
BN	Bantam Books
BW	Brown Watson Books
CB	CBS-TV
CV	Chad Valley Sliderama
DH	Dark Horse Comics
ET	Editorial Mo.Pa.Sa.
FX	20th Century Fox
GK	Gold Key / Western Comics
HE	HarperEntertainment Books
HM	Harry K. McWilliams Assoc.
MC	Marvel Comics
MR	Mr. Comics / Metallic Rose
NB	NBC-TV
PR	Power Records
SB	Signet Books
TP	Topps
UB	Ubisoft

MEDIUM	
a	animated series
b	book-and-record set
c	comic book or strip
d	trading card
e	e-comic
f	theatrical film
k	storybook
m	magazine article
n	novel or novelization
p	promotional newspaper
r	recorded audio fiction
s	short story
t	television series
u	unfilmed script or story
v	video game
x	Blu-Ray exclusive
y	young adult novel

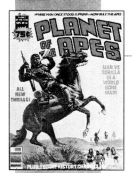

◆ Mendez is named chief lieutenant, serving as Kolp's trusted advisor and second-in-command.

Battle for the Planet of the Apes (MC-c)

NOTE: Mendez's title is provided in Marvel's comic adaptation of the film.

◆ Mandemus mentors a brilliant orangutan named Virgil, who absorbs all of the knowledge he can, happily expounding to any who will listen. In time, Virgil becomes a professor and serves as Caesar's aide. Caesar assigns Abe, a human teacher, to instruct apes how to read and write. The chimps and orangutans take to learning much more quickly than the gorillas, who prefer to follow Aldo's example and fight. The citizens of Ape City call Abe "Teacher," causing him at times to forget his own name. Humans and apes forge an uneasy peace in Ape City, though humans perform all menial tasks while apes enjoy the benefits.

Battle for the Planet of the Apes (FX-f)

1995

◆ The last atomic bomb falls, in upstate New York.

Planet of the Apes Revisited (FX-f, unfilmed)

NOTE: This information comes from an early treatment for the second film, written by Paul Dehn. The final version of the film was renamed Beneath the Planet of the Apes.

LATE 20ᵗʰ OR EARLY 21ˢᵗ CENTURY

◆ Future USAF *Oberon* crewman Lewisall Bledsoe is born in Buenos Aires.

Planet of the Apes: The Fall, Chapter 4 (HE-n)

◆ Future USAF *Oberon* crewman Norman Griswold is born in Muncie, Indiana.

Planet of the Apes: The Fall, Chapter 7 (HE-n)

◆ The U.S. government develops technology to wipe a criminal's personality.

Planet of the Apes: The Fall, Chapter 15 (HE-n)

NOTE: Reconciling this with the classic films' timeline is problematic, given the ape rebellion and subsequent nuclear war.

◆ Also developed is a neural connection training helmet, able to pump years' worth of knowledge directly into a brain in a matter of days. Though designed for humans, the device works on simian brains as well.

Planet of the Apes: Colony, Chapter 9 (HE-n)

NOTE: Reconciling this with the classic films is equally problematic.

1998

◆ Sandy, future Ape City doctor during Caesar's reign, is born.

Battle for the Planet of the Apes (FX-f)

NOTE: Since Sandy's age is unknown, I have based this figure on actress Heather Low's age (22) when the film (set in 2020) was produced.

2000

◆ Julie, future servant to Caesar's wife Lisa in Ape City, is born.

Battle for the Planet of the Apes (FX-f)

NOTE: Since Julie's age is unknown, I have based this figure on actress Colleen Camp's age (20) when the film (set in 2020) was produced.

BETWEEN 2000 AND 2009

◆ Leo Davidson, future pilot of the USAF *Oberon*, is born. Davidson has a sister and a younger brother. Also born during this period are fellow *Oberon* officers Hansen and Maria Cooper.

Planet of the Apes (FX-f)

NOTE: The film's script and young-adult novelization identify Davidson as being in his 20s in 2029 (actor Mark Wahlberg was 30 when the film hit theaters). The script mentions Davidson's siblings, and also specifies Hanson and Cooper as being around the same age.

EARLY 21st CENTURY

◆ A group of peace-loving apes, seeking freedom from oppression, relocates to the snowy mountain peaks north of Ape City to form a Tibet-like society, led by a wise ape called the High Lama, or Worthy One. The High-Mountain Apes worship a giant statue of Kygoor the Ice Ape—which comes alive to protect them when needed—and neither hate nor fear humans.

Return to the Planet of the Apes episode #6: "Terror on Ice Mountain" (BB-n)

NOTE: The novelization indicates the High-Mountain Apes moved to the mountains thousands of years before 3979, so I've placed their migration in the early 21st century.

◆ The daughter of former astronaut August Anne Burrows has a child of her own and names her Anne. The Burrows clan moves to Mexico and eventually leads a tribe of speaking humans.

Planet of the Apes #21: "Part One—The Terror Beneath" (AC-c)

◆ As a child, Molly Benavides attends a country carnival and rides a gravity well, a wooden contraption designed to propel children to the inside of a cylinder due to centrifugal force.

Planet of the Apes: The Fall, Chapter 3 (HE-n)

NOTE: Reconciling the following events with the classic films' timeline is problematic, given the ape rebellion and subsequent nuclear war.

◆ As a boy, Frank Barstow goes on several fishing trips with his uncle, whom he calls "Gramps." Too squeamish to bait his own hook, however, the youth feels ashamed when Gramps calls him a sissy.

Planet of the Apes: The Fall, Chapter 4 (HE-n)

◆ Future USAF *Oberon* crewman Norman Griswold attends the Space Force Academy, located near Pike's Peak in Colorado Springs.

Planet of the Apes: The Fall, Chapter 7 (HE-n)

PUBLISHER / STUDIO
AB . . . . ABC-TV
AC . . . .Adventure / Malibu Comics
AW . . . . Award Books
BB . . . . .Ballantine Books
BN . . . . Bantam Books
BW . . . . Brown Watson Books
CB . . . . CBS-TV
CV . . . . Chad Valley Sliderama
DH . . . . .Dark Horse Comics
ET . . . . Editorial Mo.Pa.Sa.
FX . . . . 20th Century Fox
GK . . . .Gold Key / Western Comics
HE . . . HarperEntertainment Books
HM . . Harry K. McWilliams Assoc.
MC . . . . Marvel Comics
MR . . . Mr. Comics / Metallic Rose
NB . . . . NBC-TV
PR . . . . .Power Records
SB . . . . Signet Books
TP . . . . Topps
UB . . . . Ubisoft

MEDIUM
a . . . . animated series
b . . . . .book-and-record set
c . . . . .comic book or strip
d . . . . trading card
e . . . . e-comic
f . . . . .theatrical film
k . . . . .storybook
m . . . . .magazine article
n . . . . .novel or novelization
p . . . . promotional newspaper
r . . . . .recorded audio fiction
s . . . . short story
t . . . . television series
u . . . . .unfilmed script or story
v . . . . video game
x . . . . .Blu-Ray exclusive
y . . . . .young adult novel

2008

◆ A conflict erupts between Ape City and Kolp's mutant community. Following this battle, peace is maintained for 12 years, during which time the mutants wonder if anyone else survived the war.

Battle for the Planet of the Apes (FX-f)

NOTE: The film's novelization incorrectly quotes this figure at nine years, not 12.

2009

◆ Alma becomes Governor Kolp's communications officer.

Battle for the Planet of the Apes (AW-n)

NOTE: Alma's title is established in the novelization and Marvel's comic adaptation.

2009 TO 2020

◆ Over the next 11 years and 3 months, Kolp and Alma develop a solid working relationship and, in time, a friendship. Alma develops romantic feelings for him, but he never seems to notice.

Battle for the Planet of the Apes (AW-n)

NOTE: This information appears in the film's novelization.

2010

◆ Lisa and Caesar have their first child—a boy, whom they name Cornelius to honor his father.

Battle for the Planet of the Apes (FX-f)

NOTE: The San Simian Sentinel, *a promotional newspaper distributed to moviegoers during the release of* Battle for the Planet of the Apes *(set in 2020), gives Cornelius' age as 10 at the time of that film.*

2019

◆ NASA turns Cape Kennedy into a space museum, moving its operations to California's Mojave Desert.

Return to the Planet of the Apes episode #9: "Trail to the Unknown" (NB-a)

NOTE: Cape Kennedy's closing occurs 60 years before Ron Brent's birth in 2079. The cartoons commit several snafus continuity-wise, and NASA's continued existence post-war is among them. Revolution on the Planet of the Apes *and Marvel's "Terror on the Planet of the Apes" indicate the government had secret bases at Mount Rushmore and Area 51, where the space program could still have operated—but why turn Cape Kennedy into a museum? Who'd visit it...the apes?*

2019 TO 2079

◆ At its new site in the Mojave Desert, NASA continues improving on the rocket fuels and capsule design of its space vehicles, enabling them to fly faster than previous models.

Return to the Planet of the Apes episode #9: "Trail to the Unknown" (NB-a)

◆ Aldo stops to help a human named Jake fix a wagon wheel and arrives late at school, where a man named Abe is teaching apes to write the Ultimate Law, "Ape shall never kill ape." Caesar's son Cornelius writes "Ape shall never kill Abe," but Aldo is less proficient, crumpling the boy's paper in humiliation. Abe yells "No," breaking the First Law, and the gorillas trash the school, chasing him through the village. Caesar intervenes, ordering the soldiers to clean up the mess, and wonders if his parents would have condoned killing evil in the name of good. Bruce "Mac" MacDonald tells him sealed tapes of his parents are stored in Ape Management's Archives Section beneath the dead city. Excited, Caesar vows to find them.

Battle for the Planet of the Apes (FX-f)

NOTE: Dating this film is difficult. Marvel's timeline (in issue #11) and Dayton Ward's (in The Planet of the Apes Chronicles*) both place it in 2001, but that figure does not jibe with dialog establishing peace between the mutants and apes for 12 years—in 1989, Caesar was still in the circus, and there were no mutants. Mandemus having been Caesar's armorer for 27 years also makes that date unworkable. A timeline packaged with the* Planet of the Apes *Widescreen 35th Anniversary Edition DVD dates this film in 2018, while another, in the* Planet of the Apes *40th Anniversary Collection Blu-Ray set, places it in June 2004. The novelization of* Battle *places it nine years post-*Conquest of the Planet of the Apes *(2000), while Marvel #22 has Mandemus named armorer in 1993, setting the film in 2020. I have chosen the latter date, as it makes the most sense. Why Caesar knows nothing of the future, however, having dreamed about it many times, written about it in his journal and told Lisa what he'd foreseen, is unclear.*

◆ Abe joins Mac and his mate Sandy (the village doctor) for a rabbit dinner. Mac tells them he plans to visit the city ruins with Caesar and Virgil, and they warn him to take weapons and a Geiger counter.

Battle for the Planet of the Apes (MC-c)

NOTE: This scene occurs in both the comic adaptation and novelization. In the comic, the teacher is sometimes named Ed. The novelization establishes MacDonald and Sandy as lovers.

◆ Caesar, Virgil and Mac obtain supplies from Mandemus, then cross the Forbidden Zone to the ruined city. Down in the archives, Caesar triggers an alarm. Wondering if he's come to re-take the city, Kolp orders his men to shoot the intruders, ending 12 years of peace. The trio view a tape of Cornelius and Zira discussing Earth's eventual destruction, and Virgil says the future can be changed with the right choices. Mutants ambush them disguised as dying refugees, but they escape. Mendez urges Kolp to let them go in peace, but Kolp dispatches scouts to find their village. Returning to Ape City, Caesar convenes a council meeting. He describes the diseased humans, warning that attack is likely. Mac, Abe, Jake and other humans attend the meeting at his request, enraging the gorillas.

Battle for the Planet of the Apes (FX-f)

NOTE: In Marvel's adaptation, based on an early-draft script, Breck commands the mutants, rather than Kolp.

◆ Radiation exposure causes Caesar to begin losing facial hair. Aldo uses this to his advantage, saying Caesar looks more human than ape.

Battle for the Planet of the Apes (MC-c)

NOTE: This occurs in an early-draft script, as well as in Marvel's comic adaptation.

◆ The gorillas storm out of the council meeting, refusing to attend with humans present.

Battle for the Planet of the Apes (FX-f)

PUBLISHER / STUDIO
AB . . . . ABC-TV
AC . . . . Adventure / Malibu Comics
AW . . . . Award Books
BB . . . . .Ballantine Books
BN . . . . Bantam Books
BW . . . . Brown Watson Books
CB . . . . CBS-TV
CV . . . . Chad Valley Sliderama
DH . . . . .Dark Horse Comics
ET . . . . Editorial Mo.Pa.Sa.
FX . . . . 20th Century Fox
GK . . . .Gold Key / Western Comics
HE . . . HarperEntertainment Books
HM . . Harry K. McWilliams Assoc.
MC . . . . Marvel Comics
MR . . . Mr. Comics / Metallic Rose
NB . . . . NBC-TV
PR . . . . .Power Records
SB . . . . Signet Books
TP . . . . Topps
UB . . . . .Ubisoft

MEDIUM
a . . . . animated series
b . . . . .book-and-record set
c . . . . .comic book or strip
d . . . . trading card
e . . . . e-comic
f . . . . .theatrical film
k . . . . .storybook
m . . . . .magazine article
n . . . . .novel or novelization
p . . . . promotional newspaper
r . . . . .recorded audio fiction
s . . . . short story
t . . . . television series
u . . . . .unfilmed script or story
v . . . . video game
x . . . . .Blu-Ray exclusive
y . . . . .young adult novel

◆ With the gorillas' seats vacated, Caesar formally invites the humans to join the council, urging man and ape to reason together and form a plan.

Battle for the Planet of the Apes (MC-c)

NOTE: This occurs in an early-draft script, as well as in Marvel's comic adaptation.

◆ Mendez urges Kolp not to renew the fighting, but when a scout learns of Caesar's war council, Kolp orders Alma to launch the Alpha-Omega Bomb if the apes win the coming battle.

Battle for the Planet of the Apes (FX-f)

NOTE: This and other scenes involving the bomb were filmed but cut from the final release. The scenes, restored on a Japanese laserdisc, were otherwise unavailable for many years until Fox finally released an extended edition of the film on DVD.

◆ Kolp notices Alma's beauty for the first time and kisses her.

Battle for the Planet of the Apes (AW-n)

NOTE: This scene occurs in the film's novelization.

◆ Lisa urges Caesar not to wage war, but he says the mutants are beyond reason. That night, Cornelius follows his pet squirrel Ricky into the woods and overhears Aldo plotting a coup. Spotting him in a tree, Aldo hacks off the branch, causing the child to fall. MacDonald later finds campfire ashes and the severed branch. Sandy tends to the boy, but his injuries are fatal and he dies in Caesar's arms. The mutant army crosses the Forbidden Zone, firing a charge at a pair of gorillas. One makes it back to warn Aldo, who declares martial law, corrals the humans, storms the armory and erects a barricade. The mutants reach the city; Kolp orders Sgt. York to alert Alma if they lose, then orders his troops to begin their invasion.

Battle for the Planet of the Apes (FX-f)

◆ The barrage decimates the city, burying Virgil in rubble and striking Caesar down. A student urges Virgil to take cover, but a missile hits the tree in which the youth hides. Grief-stricken, Virgil flees the battle.

Battle for the Planet of the Apes (MC-c)

NOTE: This scene occurs in Marvel's comic adaptation of the film.

◆ The mutant convoy finds a field of dead apes, but as Kolp prepares to kill Caesar, the apes spring to life, beating the mutants to death. As Kolp and others escape in a bus, gorillas storm the vehicle, shooting the mutants and chanting Aldo's name. Caesar frees the caged humans, but Aldo seizes control, ordering his troops to kill them all. Caesar stands before them, daring them to shoot. Virgil exposes Cornelius' murder, and the apes surround Aldo—even his own soldiers—chanting "Ape has killed ape!" Aldo panics and climbs a tree, brandishing a knife. Grabbing Aldo's wrist, Caesar throws the gorilla to the ground.

Battle for the Planet of the Apes (FX-f)

◆ Weakened by radiation, Caesar falls as well. Aldo's body cushions his fall, and he survives.

Battle for the Planet of the Apes (MC-c)

NOTE: This occurs in the comic adaptation and the novelization.

◆ MacDonald asks that his people be granted equality. Caesar insists man is too violent, but relents when Virgil reminds him of Aldo. York survives long enough to return to the city and signal Alma, but Mendez urges her not to activate the bomb, saying it must be respected and venerated—a reminder that humans can rise above ugliness. The rebuilding of Ape City commences, and the gorillas return the weapons to the armory. Mandemus asks that the installation be blown up, but Caesar knows that danger still lurks.

Battle for the Planet of the Apes (FX-f)

◆ Aldo survives the fall, earning the nickname "Aldo Apekiller." Banished from Ape City, he and his loyal gorillas spend their lives thereafter in nomadic wandering.

Planet of the Apes #11: "Warriors" (AC-c)

NOTE: Caesar's dialog in Battle for the Planet of the Apes *implies Aldo dies falling from the tree—a fate specifically stated in the novelization and Marvel's adaptation, as well as in a timeline packaged with the* Planet of the Apes Widescreen 35th Anniversary Edition DVD. *The Adventure Comics line, however, reveals otherwise. The fall is a rather short drop, so it's reasonable for Aldo to have survived.*

◆ In the spirit of equality among humans and apes, Caesar renames Ape·City "Our City."

Battle for the Planet of the Apes (AW-n)

NOTE: This information appears in the film's novelization.

◆ Mendez is named leader of the mutants, known thereafter as Mendez the First. Thus begins the Mendez Dynasty, spawning 26 generations of the House of Mendez over the next 2,000 years.

Planet of the Apes #11: "Outlines of Tomorrow—A Chronology of the Planet of the Apes" (MC-m)

◆ As the self-appointed Keepers of the Divine Bomb, the Mendez line and their followers exist only to protect and worship the Alpha-Omega device.

The Mutant News (HM-p)

AFTER 2020

◆ As human status in ape society erodes, the name "Ape City" is restored.

Conjecture

NOTE: The village is still known as Ape City in future stories—in fact, no other tale calls it Our City—so the new name must not last long (which makes sense, given the widespread anti-human sentiment).

◆ Aldo dies as a disgraced exile, but a gorilla cult, the Aldonites, carries on his anti-human militarism.

Planet of the Apes #11: "Warriors" (AC-c)

◆ Virgil records his memoirs, detailing the ape revolution and the actions of Caesar.

Revolution on the Planet of the Apes #6: "Catch a Falling Star" (MR-c)

◆ Virgil and his wife have a son, whom they name Jacob. Virgil jokes that Caesar is a fool, for only a fool would want to rule Ape City, but he actually respects him greatly. Unlike his father, however, Jacob distrusts all humans.

Planet of the Apes #1: "The Monkey Planet—Beneath" (AC-c)

PUBLISHER / STUDIO
AB . . . . ABC-TV
AC . . . .Adventure / Malibu Comics
AW . . . . Award Books
BB . . . . .Ballantine Books
BN . . . . Bantam Books
BW . . . . Brown Watson Books
CB . . . . CBS-TV
CV . . . . Chad Valley Sliderama
DH . . . . .Dark Horse Comics
ET . . . . Editorial Mo.Pa.Sa.
FX . . . . 20th Century Fox
GK . . . .Gold Key / Western Comics
HE . . . HarperEntertainment Books
HM . . Harry K. McWilliams Assoc.
MC . . . . Marvel Comics
MR . . . Mr. Comics / Metallic Rose
NB . . . . NBC-TV
PR . . . . .Power Records
SB . . . . Signet Books
TP . . . . .Topps
UB . . . . .Ubisoft

MEDIUM
a . . . . animated series
b . . . . .book-and-record set
c . . . . .comic book or strip
d . . . . trading card
e . . . . e-comic
f . . . . .theatrical film
k . . . . .storybook
m . . . . .magazine article
n . . . . .novel or novelization
p . . . . promotional newspaper
r . . . . .recorded audio fiction
s . . . . short story
t . . . . television series
u . . . . .unfilmed script or story
v . . . . video game
x . . . . .Blu-Ray exclusive
y . . . . .young adult novel

2020 TO 2040

◆ Ape City prospers with Caesar a benevolent ruler, but humanity's role in society erodes in time. The Forbidden Zones grow increasingly dangerous as animal and plant mutations abound. During this period, the mutants split into rival factions, led respectively by Mendez the First and Be-One of the Inheritors' Gestalt Mind.

Planet of the Apes #11: "Outlines of Tomorrow—A Chronology of the Planet of the Apes" (MC-m)

NOTE: Marvel's timeline dates these events from 2001 to 2040, based on its placement of the fifth film in 2001 rather than 2020. I have altered the beginning date to compensate for the discrepancy.

2020 TO 2320

◆ The Forbidden Zones expand, an irradiated desert isolating the land to the north. The mutants splinter into warring factions, including the Houses of Mendez and Kolp. The latter deem the Alpha-Omega Bomb a god, while the Mendez Dynasty comes to see it as a deadly evil. Meanwhile, a prosperous ape/human society emerges in the Primacy, a peaceful province to the south that avoids outside notice for 300 years.

The Forbidden Zone #1: "Part One—Forbidden Knowledge" (AC-c)

NOTE: It's somewhat surprising that the Mendez faction is the House that sees the bomb as a deadly evil, given that Mendez the First first urged his people to revere it, and that his descendant, Mendez XXVI, still does so in 3978.

◆ As the years pass, Mendez's people forget their origins, including the name "New York."

The Mutant News (HM-p)

◆ The mutants rename their home the Holy City.

The Forbidden Zone #2: "Part Two—Danger Zone" (AC-c)

c. 2020s OR 2030s

◆ Despite their ages, Lisa and Caesar have a daughter and at least one more son, names unknown.

Revolution on the Planet of the Apes #5: "Ape Shall Not Kill Ape" (MR-c)

NOTE: Marvel's timeline in Planet of the Apes #11 *denies any offspring after Cornelius. The Adventure Comics line, however, features a grandson, Alexander, even though Cornelius dies before fathering children of his own.* Revolution on the Planet of the Apes *backs up the existence of other heirs.*

Part 6: A New Hope
(2021 to 2069)

c. 2020s

◆ Leo Davidson takes his first flying lessons at a local airport, his home away from home until joining the U.S. Air Force. He earns a promotion to captain and becomes a pilot with the Space Division.

Planet of the Apes (HE-y)

NOTE: *This information comes from the film's young-adult novelization. The entries below, regarding Davidson, the Air Force, the* Oberon, Semos *and other concepts related to Tim Burton's film, do not jibe well with the events of the prior films and TV series, but are included here for posterity.*

◆ The U.S. Air Force launches the *Oberon*, a nuclear-powered orbital space research station, and chooses as its crew the military's most experienced fliers, scientists and astronauts. These include Lt. Col. Grace Alexander, chief medical officer and zoologist; Lt. Gen. Karl Vasich, flight chief and station commander; Specialist Hansen, a technician manning the exterior monitors; and Majors Frank Santos and Maria Cooper.

Planet of the Apes: Leo's Logbook—A Captain's Days in Captivity (HE-k)

◆ Also in the crew are computer technicians Frank Barstow and Norman Griswold, and Specialist 1st Class Molly Benavides. Adm. Aphasia "Phase" Klein is the executive officer and second-in-command.

Planet of the Apes: The Fall, Chapter 1 (HE-n)

◆ Lts. Cathy Mingo and Ken Kibo are among the station's crew as well.

Planet of the Apes: The Fall, Chapter 13 (HE-n)

◆ Other crewmembers include Mark Caprolione, Elizabeth Elwell and Kenneth Haugan.

Planet of the Apes (DH-c)

NOTE: *These names appear on a viewscreen in the comic adaptation of the film.*

◆ The *Oberon*'s high-tech computers can synthesize food from primal atomic building blocks, as well as laser-tailor uniforms and casual crew-wear.

Planet of the Apes: The Fall, Chapter 4 (HE-n)

◆ The station comes equipped with a medical chamber able to repair bodily damage and keep an injured person's organs running indefinitely.

Planet of the Apes: Colony, Chapter 1 (HE-n)

◆ The *Oberon* also contains a neural connection training helmet, able to pump data directly into a human or simian brain. Several years' worth of knowledge—math, history, medicine, genetics and so forth—can be thus downloaded in a matter of days.

Planet of the Apes: Colony, Chapter 9 (HE-n)

◆ Frustrated with frequent media attention to high soldier mortality rates, the U.S. Air Force begins training chimpanzees as frontline pod pilots—and, theoretically, for other duties as well.

Planet of the Apes: The Fall, Chapter 1 (HE-n)

PUBLISHER / STUDIO
AB . . . . ABC-TV
AC . . . . Adventure / Malibu Comics
AW . . . . Award Books
BB . . . . Ballantine Books
BN . . . . Bantam Books
BW . . . . . Brown Watson Books
CB . . . . CBS-TV
CV . . . . Chad Valley Sliderama
DH . . . . Dark Horse Comics
ET . . . . Editorial Mo.Pa.Sa.
FX . . . . 20th Century Fox
GK . . . . Gold Key / Western Comics
HE . . . HarperEntertainment Books
HM . . Harry K. McWilliams Assoc.
MC . . . . Marvel Comics
MR . . . Mr. Comics / Metallic Rose
NB . . . . NBC-TV
PR . . . . Power Records
SB . . . . Signet Books
TP . . . . Topps
UB . . . . Ubisoft

MEDIUM
a . . . . animated series
b . . . . book-and-record set
c . . . . comic book or strip
d . . . . trading card
e . . . . e-comic
f . . . . theatrical film
k . . . . storybook
m . . . . magazine article
n . . . . novel or novelization
p . . . . promotional newspaper
r . . . . recorded audio fiction
s . . . . short story
t . . . . television series
u . . . . unfilmed script or story
v . . . . video game
x . . . . Blu-Ray exclusive
y . . . . young adult novel

◆ For the program, scientists increase ape intelligence via gene splicing and chromosome enhancement.

Planet of the Apes (FX-f)

NOTE: This seems like a rather self-destructive move on the scientists' part, given the simian situation on Earth.

◆ The *Oberon* is selected as the testing ground for the training program.

Planet of the Apes: The Fall, Chapter 1 (HE-n)

EARLY 2027

◆ Leo Davidson is assigned to the *Oberon* to teach the genetically bred apes.

Planet of the Apes (FX-f)

EARLY 2027 TO 2029

◆ For two years, Leo Davidson oversees a flight simulator training program with several gorillas, as well as chimps Pericles, Alissa and Francis, and orangutans Doris and Cindy. During this time, Davidson is assigned no flying duties of his own, much to his annoyance.

Planet of the Apes (FX-f)

◆ Pericles' training culminates with his flying a pod once or twice per day. Despite his frustration over his own stalled career, Davidson takes a liking to his chimp protégé, who can operate the space vehicle with the same manual dexterity as a human commercial flier.

Planet of the Apes (DH-c)

NOTE: This information comes from the film's comic-book adaptation.

◆ Pericles possesses the intelligence of a five-year-old human, and his mate Aspasia is even smarter. When she becomes pregnant, Grace Alexander realizes the baby could turn out to be a genius.

Planet of the Apes: The Fall, Chapter 1 (HE-n)

◆ One particularly smart chimp in the pilot program is named Alcibiades.

Planet of the Apes: The Fall, Chapter 2 (HE-n)

◆ In addition to chimps, gorillas and orangutans, the *Oberon* carries several baboons.

Planet of the Apes #1: Force, Chapter 1 (HE-y)

◆ Bonobos are also among *Oberon*'s simian population.

Planet of the Apes: The Fall, Chapter 3 (HE-y)

NOTE: Bonobos also feature in the unpublished novel Rule, *which establishes Leeta as being a member of that species.*

◆ Several gibbons are aboard as well.

Planet of the Apes #3: Rule, Chapter 7 (HE-y, unpublished)

NOTE: No gibbons (or baboons, mentioned above) appear in the Tim Burton film on which these novels are based.

◆ Monkeys and dogs are also aboard the station.

Planet of the Apes #1: Force, Chapter 11 (HE-y)

♦ Aboard the *Oberon*, Davidson enjoys a romantic relationship with crewmember Molly Benavides.

Planet of the Apes: The Fall, Chapter 6 (HE-n)

MID TO LATE 2028

♦ Molly Benavides becomes pregnant with Leo Davidson's child.

Planet of the Apes: The Fall, Chapter 2 (HE-n)

NOTE: This date is based on a premature birth in February 2029.

♦ Davidson teaches Molly to fly a pod, though he never instructs her in hard-landing procedures since the vessels are primarily used for space-to-space missions, with landings required only in emergencies.

Planet of the Apes: The Fall, Chapter 9 (HE-n)

BEFORE FEBRUARY 2029

♦ *Oberon* officers Aphasia "Phase" Klein and Karl Vasich enjoy a romantic relationship.

Planet of the Apes: The Fall, Chapter 4 (HE-n)

NOTE: This novel spells Vasich's first name "Carl," but other sources use a "K."

♦ Klein foregoes marriage and family to focus on her career, knowing such attachments could handicap her pursuit of rank, honor and advancement.

Planet of the Apes: The Fall, Chapter 3 (HE-n)

♦ NASA maps out the surface of Mars.

Planet of the Apes: Leo's Logbook—A Captain's Days in Captivity (HE-k)

♦ The U.S. Air Force creates a device called the Messenger, enabling crew members to communicate remotely with a spaceship's computer.

Planet of the Apes (FX-f)

♦ An Air Force friend of Frank Barstow advises him never to let "the brass" know his name, for even if it looks good at first, nothing good can come of it in the end.

Planet of the Apes: The Fall, Chapter 6 (HE-n)

FEBRUARY 6, 2029

♦ Davidson records a log entry expressing frustration over being assigned chimp-training duties instead of actual piloting. He also chastises Grace Alexander for being too concerned with "control groups and repetitive test conditions" during the training, rather than with what matters most to a pilot: adaptability and thinking on one's feet.

Planet of the Apes (DH-c)

NOTE: This occurs in the comic-book adaptation of the film.

PUBLISHER / STUDIO	
AB	ABC-TV
AC	Adventure / Malibu Comics
AW	Award Books
BB	Ballantine Books
BN	Bantam Books
BW	Brown Watson Books
CB	CBS-TV
CV	Chad Valley Sliderama
DH	Dark Horse Comics
ET	Editorial Mo.Pa.Sa.
FX	20th Century Fox
GK	Gold Key / Western Comics
HE	HarperEntertainment Books
HM	Harry K. McWilliams Assoc.
MC	Marvel Comics
MR	Mr. Comics / Metallic Rose
NB	NBC-TV
PR	Power Records
SB	Signet Books
TP	Topps
UB	Ubisoft

MEDIUM	
a	animated series
b	book-and-record set
c	comic book or strip
d	trading card
e	e-comic
f	theatrical film
k	storybook
m	magazine article
n	novel or novelization
p	promotional newspaper
r	recorded audio fiction
s	short story
t	television series
u	unfilmed script or story
v	video game
x	Blu-Ray exclusive
y	young adult novel

FEBRUARY 7, 2029

◆ Leo Davidson's family and friends record a video postcard, which takes nearly a week to reach him.

Planet of the Apes (HE-y)

NOTE: The date is visible on the screen of Leo's video-mail.

FEBRUARY 14, 2029

◆ Hansen picks up radio transmissions from Earth's past, bounced back by an ion storm. Vasich sends Pericles to investigate in the *Alpha Pod*, but is pulled off course and disappears. Taking *Delta Pod* to find him, Davidson vanishes as well. Both pods are propelled to the year 5021, crashing on a two-moon planet on the far side of the anomaly, known as Ashlar.

Planet of the Apes (FX-f)

NOTE: The young-adult novelization sets the film a week after Davidson's e-mail was recorded, placing the start of the film on Valentine's Day. The name Ashlar appears in William Broyles' initial script for the film. The year 5021 is established in Dark Horse's comic adaptation.

◆ Davidson leaves behind a mother, sister, younger brother and uncle on Earth.

Planet of the Apes (HE-y)

◆ Molly Benavides reports three vectors into and out of the storm. Grace Alexander readies Alcibiades and two other chimp pilots to scan the cloud in additional pods.

Planet of the Apes: The Fall, Chapter 1 (HE-n)

◆ From the chimps' readings, Molly determines the anomaly to be a quantum time storm, which the pods could destabilize. The storm has a black hole at its core and exists in multiple dimensions and space-time layers; sentient, it senses the probes and shifts to minimize its discomfort, engulfing the station and pods.

Planet of the Apes: The Fall, Chapter 2 (HE-n)

◆ This causes a power surge that rocks the station, injuring Vasich and other crew members. The storm propels *Oberon* to the same planet, but it remains in the present, without a corresponding time jump.

Planet of the Apes (FX-f)

◆ The surge throws Molly across the bridge, but her fetus is uninjured. She and Barstow check *Oberon*'s scanners and find that the station is about to crash on the other planet.

Planet of the Apes: The Fall, Chapter 2 (HE-n)

◆ The apes panic, and Dr. Alexander and a technician, Norman Griswold, strap down Aspasia to protect her fetus. Stress pushes Molly into labor, and Klein delivers her baby boy, whom Molly names David.

Planet of the Apes: The Fall, Chapter 3 (HE-n)

NOTE: David's name is appropriate since he's the son of Leo Davidson ("David son"). It's unclear whether Alcibiades and the other two chimp pilots suvive the crash in their respective pods.

◆ The Great Nest—a species of rudimentally intelligent brachiopods ruled by a hive-mind queen called the Core—senses *Oberon*'s arrival on the alien world.

Planet of the Apes: The Fall, Chapter 3 (HE-n)

◆ In a distant valley on this strange world, lizards of varying shapes and sizes roam the land, from piranha-like water lizards to pterodactyl-esque flying lizards to huge dinosaurs. Sentient lizards rule the valley, using the dinosaurs as pack animals.

Planet of the Apes: Colony, Chapter 18 (HE-n)

◆ Also inhabiting the planet are giant glow worms and beetles, which feast on each other in a labyrinth of underground caverns. The beetles immobilize their prey hypnotically, then suck out their lifeforce.

Planet of the Apes #4: Extinction, Chapter 11 (HE-y, unpublished)

◆ Elsewhere lives a sentient humanoid race who are displeased by the Earthers' arrival, and by the apes' eventual assumption of the prime ecological niche.

Planet of the Apes #7 and beyond (DH-c, unpublished—titles unknown)

NOTE: Writers Ian Edginton and Dan Abnett offer this glimpse at their plans for Dark Horse's comic-book series based on the Tim Burton film, had the series continued past issue #6. Edginton describes his plans for these humanoids as experiencing a "parallel evolution" to Earth's mutant human population.

◆ Davidson returns from his journey through time and crashes *Alpha Pod* in Washington, D.C., at the steps of the Lincoln Memorial—which now honors Gen. Thade, a chimp military leader from the future alien world of Ashlar. Police surround him, and to his horror, the cops—and everyone else—are apes.

Planet of the Apes (FX-f)

NOTE: Ty Templeton, author of Revolution on the Planet of the Apes, *had intended, in his initial concept for that title, to explore how Thade changed Earth history. Fox, however, opted to keep the two* Apes *incarnations separate. Ian Edginton and Dan Abnett had also planned to reveal Thade's fate in an unpublished storyline for Dark Horse, which would have featured characters from Semos' world visiting Earth's past in the* Oberon*'s remaining pods, via the anomaly. Their plan had been that the Earth Davidson returned to was not the same Earth he left, but rather a parallel planet similar to that which Ulysse Mérou retuned at the end of Pierre Boulle's novel,* The Monkey Planet. *The Thade name, Edginton says, would have been a powerful ape dynasty on that Earth, much like the Kennedys or the Rothchilds.*

FEBRUARY 15-17, 2029

◆ Over the next three days, Klein assesses the *Oberon*'s losses: nearly half the crew dead or missing, many more incapacitated, leaving about 200 survivors.

Planet of the Apes: The Fall, Chapter 3 (HE-n)

◆ With the station's high-tech equipment decimated, food, clothing and medical care are very scarce.

Planet of the Apes: The Fall, Chapter 4 (HE-n)

FEBRUARY 17, 2029

◆ Vasich decides to launch all remaining pods and transmit a distress signal. When Klein says they need the pods' fuel to restart the reactor, he realizes she poses a threat to his authority.

Planet of the Apes: The Fall, Chapter 3 (HE-n)

PUBLISHER / STUDIO
AB . . . . ABC-TV
AC . . . .Adventure / Malibu Comics
AW . . . . Award Books
BB . . . . .Ballantine Books
BN . . . . Bantam Books
BW . . . . Brown Watson Books
CB . . . . CBS-TV
CV . . . . Chad Valley Sliderama
DH . . . . .Dark Horse Comics
ET . . . . Editorial Mo.Pa.Sa.
FX . . . . 20th Century Fox
GK . . . .Gold Key / Western Comics
HE . . . HarperEntertainment Books
HM . . Harry K. McWilliams Assoc.
MC . . . . .Marvel Comics
MR . . . Mr. Comics / Metallic Rose
NB . . . . NBC-TV
PR . . . . .Power Records
SB . . . . Signet Books
TP . . . . Topps
UB . . . . Ubisoft

MEDIUM
a . . . . animated series
b . . . . .book-and-record set
c . . . . .comic book or strip
d . . . . trading card
e . . . . e-comic
f . . . . .theatrical film
k . . . . .storybook
m . . . . .magazine article
n . . . . .novel or novelization
p . . . . promotional newspaper
r . . . . .recorded audio fiction
s . . . . short story
t . . . . .television series
u . . . . .unfilmed script or story
v . . . . video game
x . . . . .Blu-Ray exclusive
y . . . . .young adult novel

◆ Crew loyalties split aboard the ruined station—some support Klein's desire to colonize their new home, while others share Vasich's determination to return to Earth.

Planet of the Apes: The Fall, Chapter 4 (HE-n)

AFTER FEBRUARY 17, 2029

◆ Molly Benavides stays in Grace Alexander's lab, breast-feeding her incubating son while helping to repair the lab's animal diagnostic computers.

Planet of the Apes: The Fall, Chapter 4 (HE-n)

◆ In an effort to turn Grace's lab into a med center, and with main computers inoperable, Griswold and Molly code routines enabling the animal-lab comps to access *Oberon*'s human databases.

Planet of the Apes: The Fall, Chapter 5 (HE-n)

◆ Frank Barstow volunteers for scouting duty and is partnered with an engineer named Lewisall Bledsoe. As they map the landscape, Barstow finds a boulder covered in brachiopods. A gooey, acidic substance extends from the swarm to his right boot, and he feels "a billion eyes" watching him.

Planet of the Apes: The Fall, Chapter 4 (HE-n)

◆ The swarm dissolves Barstow's boot, forcing him to incinerate his foot. The pain makes him pass out, and hurts the Core of the Great Nest, which orders the surviving "appendages" in his body to multiply.

Planet of the Apes: The Fall, Chapter 5 (HE-n)

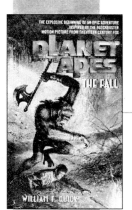

◆ Bledsoe brings Barstow back to the *Oberon*, where Grace gengineers him new toes.

Planet of the Apes: The Fall, Chapter 6 (HE-n)

◆ To eradicate the invaders, the Core commands digger drones to create four new swarms.

Planet of the Apes: The Fall, Chapter 10 (HE-n)

◆ Aspasia gives David a carrot, causing him to choke, then alerts Molly to the infant's distress. Grace removes the obstruction, saving his life.

Planet of the Apes: The Fall, Chapter 4 (HE-n)

◆ Grace recommends the crew begin reproducing for the sake of their species' survival. She and Molly also gengineer the apes to be smarter and breed faster, to help them build a civilization.

Planet of the Apes: The Fall, Chapter 5 (HE-n)

◆ The first to be gengineered is Aspasia's unborn fetus, whom Molly gives increased cranial capacity, an altered voicebox and a shortened sexual maturity time, hoping to keep her people from enslaving the apes. However, it also results in a skull too large to pass through a chimp's pelvis.

Planet of the Apes: The Fall, Chapter 6 (HE-n)

◆ This gengineering also enhances the fetus' senses, endowing him with limited psychic abilities.

Planet of the Apes: The Fall, Chapter 8 (HE-n)

◆ Aspasia dies in childbirth. Blaming herself, Molly names him Jonathan and raises him as her own.

Planet of the Apes: The Fall, Chapter 5 (HE-n)

◆ Grace and Klein notice the coding change but say nothing, curious about the effect a single super-intelligent chimp might have on the simian gene pool.

Planet of the Apes: The Fall, Chapter 12 (HE-n)

◆ Barstow returns to the site of his injury but fails to find the insects. Afraid none will believe him, he keeps the details private. Social barriers aboard the station break down as many officers begin wearing casual attire. Vasich accuses Klein of mutiny and says he intends to launch all five pods manned by ape pilots, leaving them in space until they detect a response or run out of fuel.

Planet of the Apes: The Fall, Chapter 6 (HE-n)

◆ Klein sends Griswold, Bledsoe and Mike McFerry on a hundred-mile hike to photograph the area using holographic ("holie") cameras. When they investigate the acidic bugs that attacked Barstow, thousands of brachiopods consume McFerry and Bledsoe. Griswold lasers his way to freedom and runs back to camp, his sanity shattered.

Planet of the Apes: The Fall, Chapter 7 (HE-n)

2029 TO 2033

◆ With rescue plans delayed by three damaged pods, Klein uses one pod's computers to replace the station's synthesizing machines and fabricate a shelter community, which the crew names New Hope. Grace adapts plants from the hydroponics bay to survive outside, while Vasich's people opt to remain aboard the station.

Planet of the Apes: The Fall, Chapter 8 (HE-n)

NOTE: Some 3,000 years in the future, in the unpublished novel Rule, the crew's savage descendants also name a city New Hope, unaware of the connection to their origins. It's unclear if this was the authors' plan or purely coicidenctal.

◆ With Griswold unable to care for himself, Barstow shares his living space (or "fab") with him.

Planet of the Apes: The Fall, Chapter 8 (HE-n)

◆ A crèche is established, and a guardian named Dorothy is assigned to watch Jonathan and David whenever Molly is on duty.

Planet of the Apes: The Fall, Chapter 9 (HE-n)

◆ Despite their different species, Jonathan and David grow up inseparably close.

Planet of the Apes: The Fall, Chapter 8 (HE-n)

◆ While David is the more intelligent of the two, Jonathan is stronger and faster. Rather than causing a rivalry between them, this draws the boys even closer.

Planet of the Apes: The Fall, Chapter 10 (HE-n)

◆ Barstow and Molly alter the gengineering program, hoping to reduce ape skull size and enable birthing. This lowers simian IQs a bit, but still allows for apes far smarter than Pericles.

Planet of the Apes: The Fall, Chapter 8 (HE-n)

◆ The chimps' limited psychic abilities remain after the second alteration to the program. Once more aware of the tampering, Grace fixes some mistakes but never lets on that she knows.

Planet of the Apes: The Fall, Chapter 12 (HE-n)

2030

◆ Angelina Piscopo, an inhabitant of the New Hope shelters, gives birth to a daughter and names her Kelsey ("Kels" for short).

Planet of the Apes: The Fall, Chapter 12 (HE-n)

PUBLISHER / STUDIO
AB	ABC-TV
AC	Adventure / Malibu Comics
AW	Award Books
BB	Ballantine Books
BN	Bantam Books
BW	Brown Watson Books
CB	CBS-TV
CV	Chad Valley Sliderama
DH	Dark Horse Comics
ET	Editorial Mo.Pa.Sa.
FX	20th Century Fox
GK	Gold Key / Western Comics
HE	HarperEntertainment Books
HM	Harry K. McWilliams Assoc.
MC	Marvel Comics
MR	Mr. Comics / Metallic Rose
NB	NBC-TV
PR	Power Records
SB	Signet Books
TP	Topps
UB	Ubisoft

MEDIUM
a	animated series
b	book-and-record set
c	comic book or strip
d	trading card
e	e-comic
f	theatrical film
k	storybook
m	magazine article
n	novel or novelization
p	promotional newspaper
r	recorded audio fiction
s	short story
t	television series
u	unfilmed script or story
v	video game
x	Blu-Ray exclusive
y	young adult novel

2030 TO 2043

◆ The human population of New Hope continues to grow. During this period, Angelina Piscopo delivers at least 11 more children.

Planet of the Apes: The Fall, Chapter 12 (HE-n)

2033

◆ Four years after the crash, Barstow takes Griswold back to the Great Nest. Terrified, Griswold vanishes in the night. To find him, Molly and Barstow steal a pod from the *Oberon* and begin searching the desert. Meanwhile, Jonathan awakens David in a panic, sensing danger to their mother.

Planet of the Apes: The Fall, Chapter 8 (HE-n)

◆ The Benavides brothers, age 4, sneak out to the desert. Jonathan, the ape, senses the Great Nest, which he dubs the Brax, and mentally forces them to leave Molly alone. She and Barstow find Griswold infested with Brax and incinerate him to end his misery. The insects surround them, combining to take scorpion-like forms.

Planet of the Apes: The Fall, Chapter 9 (HE-n)

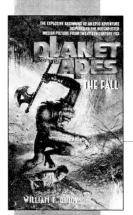

◆ Using the pod's torches, Molly roasts the brachiopods, then shows Klein and Vasich their scans. In agony, the Core of the Great Nest is helpless to stop the slaughter. Sensing Jonathan's mental influence, it sends another scorpion beast to kill the boys, but they force it to sting itself to death.

Planet of the Apes: The Fall, Chapter 10 (HE-n)

◆ A chimpanzee named Sophocles is born in New Hope.

Planet of the Apes: The Fall, Chapter 12 (HE-n)

2033 TO 2043

◆ New Hope's food synthesizers eventually give out.

Planet of the Apes: The Fall, Chapter 12 (HE-n)

◆ The community prospers, protected behind a massive fence. Vasich and Klein form a tentative truce, and Grace gengineers bees to pollinate food crops for both sides.

Planet of the Apes: The Fall, Chapter 11 (HE-n)

◆ Grace initiates a human breeding program, comprised of multiple sexual partners—as soon as one is old enough to mate—and artificial insemination. New Hope's human population rises from 102 to 650, most under the age of 14. As the firstborn human, David grows up a hero to other youths.

Planet of the Apes: The Fall, Chapter 12 (HE-n)

◆ Despite controlled breeding, the ape populace grows at a much faster rate than the humans.

Planet of the Apes: The Fall, Chapter 11 (HE-n)

◆ Because of Jonathan's unique simian genetics, however, he is barred from breeding.

Planet of the Apes: The Fall, Chapter 12 (HE-n)

◆ The humans of New Hope develop a society based on ancient Sparta and Athens, complete with Greek names for the apes. The true nature of the apes' role, however—slavery—is glossed over.

Planet of the Apes: The Fall, Chapter 15 (HE-n)

◆ Molly and Barstow forge a strong friendship that privately blossoms into something more, though her sons both wonder what she sees in the man.

Planet of the Apes: The Fall, Chapter 11 (HE-n)

◆ Molly realizes Barstow is ill and invites him to move into her family's unit so she can care for him.

Planet of the Apes: The Fall, Chapter 12 (HE-n)

◆ The first gengineered apes learn to speak, but not as well as Jonathan. David feels the simians are treated as second-class citizens, trained as soldiers subservient to humans.

Planet of the Apes: The Fall, Chapter 11 (HE-n)

◆ The human scientists categorize the Brax by size: single, swarm, cloud, blob and protonest.

Planet of the Apes: The Fall, Chapter 12 (HE-n)

◆ The city begins sending out scout-and-destroy patrols to burn the protonests, dubbing the teams the Brax Core. Jonathan leads one such team, and other apes revere him as the best of their breed.

Planet of the Apes: The Fall, Chapter 11 (HE-n)

NOTE: The term "Brax Core" is used to describe both the alien entity and the fighting force. It's possible the latter was intended to be called the Brax Corps.

◆ The head chimp in Jonathan's hunter-killer squad is named Thanatos.

Planet of the Apes: The Fall, Chapter 13 (HE-n)

2038

◆ Back on Earth, Caesar's wife Lisa dies.

Planet of the Apes #11: "Outlines of Tomorrow—A Chronology of the Planet of the Apes" (MC-m)

2039

◆ When Jonathan turns 10, his mother reveals why he cannot breed. Realizing their species will never be equals—and that humans see him as a threat—he begins relocating apes far from New Hope, at a rate of ten females to every male. Changing his name to Semos (an anagram of Moses), he organizes his people to build a great city, which he keeps secret even from his human family. He names that city New Hope as well, symbolizing simian domination over man. His goal: to destroy humanity once the Brax threat has been eliminated, and to strengthen his own race with his superintelligent seed.

Planet of the Apes: The Fall, Chapter 17 (HE-n)

◆ Eschewing human technology, Semos opts not to introduce electricity into his society.

Planet of the Apes: Colony, Chapter 1 (HE-n)

2039 TO 2048

◆ Semos' followers grow to a thousand by 2048. To maintain his own bloodline, Semos realizes he must eventually produce children, even though the mothers and children might die during childbirth.

Planet of the Apes: The Fall, Chapter 17 (HE-n)

◆ Semos falls in love and takes a wife, but refuses to mate, afraid to lose her during childbirth. Seeing other families raising children, however, she convinces him to take the risk.

Planet of the Apes: Colony, Chapter 1 (HE-n)

◆ As expected, his wife dies in childbirth, but their son survives, and Semos names him Thados. Upon learning why she died, Thados blames Semos (and himself) for her death.

Planet of the Apes: The Fall, Chapter 17 (HE-n)

◆ Semos takes two more wives. Despite the death of his first mate, he again risks fate for the sake of simian survival. Both die, but the children survive, and he lives with guilt for years to come.

Planet of the Apes: Colony, Chapter 1 (HE-n)

◆ Worried that Grace and Vasich might have him killed, Semos spends much of his time away from the city, assigning food tasters to check his meals—two of whom die from stomach cramps.

Planet of the Apes: The Fall, Chapter 17 (HE-n)

2040

◆ Back on Earth, Caesar dies at age 67, two years after Lisa. With no successors to his bloodline able to continue Caesar's dynasty, leadership of Ape City is turned over to a ruling council of apes and humans, led by a long line of respected orangutans with the title of Lawgiver.

Planet of the Apes #11: "Outlines of Tomorrow—A Chronology of the Planet of the Apes" (MC-m)

> NOTE: In the framing sequence of Battle for the Planet of the Apes, set in 2670, the Lawgiver says Caesar died 600 years prior, which is close enough to 2040 to jibe. Marvel's timeline claims Caesar died without heirs, but this discrepancy with Revolution on the Planet of the Apes and the Adventure Comics line (both of which indicate otherwise) can be reconciled by assuming his remaining children were too young to lead when he died. Despite his time at the Ape Management Breeding Annex in Conquest of the Planet of the Apes, no known children seem to have resulted from such matings.

◆ To protect simian society and ensure that the future remains unchanged, the future origin of Cornelius and Zira is officially denied by Ape City's ruling council, known only to a select few.

Planet of the Apes #6: "Welcome to Ape City" (AC-c)

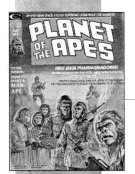

◆ A second Lawgiver, name unknown, succeeds Caesar in ruling Ape City. This Lawgiver is wise, honorable and sympathetic toward the plight of humanity.

Planet of the Apes #1: "Terror on the Planet of the Apes—The Lawgiver" (MC-c)

2041

◆ Back on Ashlar, 12-year-old David Benavides tells his mother of his wish to join Jonathan's scout-and-destroy patrol. When she refuses, he accuses her of devaluing his brother's life because he's an ape.

Planet of the Apes: The Fall, Chapter 11 (HE-n)

◆ The Core of the Great Nest instructs its appendages controlling Barstow to "kill the strongest."

Planet of the Apes: The Fall, Chapter 12 (HE-n)

◆ Barstow discreetly (and fatally) pushes Klein off a high ladder. Grieving her friend's death, Molly gives David permission to begin training.

Planet of the Apes: The Fall, Chapter 11 (HE-n)

2041 TO 2043

◆ The scout-and-destroy patrols are very successful, and for two years, no Brax are spotted within 20 miles of the *Oberon*. David commands his own hunter-killer squad, including a gorilla named Ajax and two chimps called Androcles and Sophocles. The Core of the Great Nest, unable to combat the fire, takes its swarms into hiding, devoting all of its energies to growing its numbers for an eventual retaliation.

Planet of the Apes: The Fall, Chapter 12 (HE-n)

2041 TO 2052

◆ Conditions between Earth's apes and humans worsen. Educational programs maintain the pretense of equality, but humans labor under an aura of inferiority, withdrawing from council participation to form their own community, separated by a river. The level of culture in Ape City, meanwhile, degenerates.

Planet of the Apes #11: "Outlines of Tomorrow—A Chronology of the Planet of the Apes" (MC-m)

◆ Recalling how a human war devastated the planet, the apes grow very wary of mankind.

Planet of the Apes #4: "The Monkey Planet—Battle" (AC-c)

◆ War erupts among the mutant factions of the Forbidden Zone. Be-One of the Gestalt Mind emerges victorious, with Mendez and his followers escaping into trans-national transport tubes to find a new home. They take with them the Alpha-Omega Bomb, which has gained a religious significance.

Planet of the Apes #11: "Outlines of Tomorrow—A Chronology of the Planet of the Apes" (MC-m)

> NOTE: This was Marvel's attempt to explain what it perceived as inconsistent settings for the first and fourth films—New York and California, respectively. Ty Templeton and Joe O'Brien, in their original concept for Revolution on the Planet of the Apes (titled, at the time, War on the Planet of the Apes), had intended a similar explanation. In that version, General Thade (from the Tim Burton remake) controlled the East Coast, while Caesar controlled the West. During a war between the two ape militaries, Templeton explains, a "wagon train" would have carried the bomb cross-country, in order to deal with Thade's more organized and militarized East Coast contingent. This idea, however, was dropped when Fox nixed the proposed Thade-Caesar crossover. Templeton has since realized he was in error regarding the later films' placement, not having seen the extended version of Battle for the Planet of the Apes, which strongly implies the film occurs in New York.

◆ Eventually, the House of Mendez relocates the Alpha-Omega Bomb to St. Patrick's Cathedral, where the doomsday missile supplants Christ's image at the altar as the center of church worship.

Beneath the Planet of the Apes (FX-f)

2043

◆ On Ashlar, Sophocles is allowed to begin breeding and produces two children.

Planet of the Apes: The Fall, Chapter 14 (HE-n)

◆ As 14-year-old David heads for training, his friend Kels—a year younger and of childbearing age—flirts with him openly, rousing his interest. Aboard *Oberon*, his mother and Grace Alexander deliver a chimp baby. The chimp mother senses "many eyes" watching them, and the Brax attack moments later.

Planet of the Apes: The Fall, Chapter 12 (HE-n)

PUBLISHER / STUDIO

AB	ABC-TV
AC	Adventure / Malibu Comics
AW	Award Books
BB	Ballantine Books
BN	Bantam Books
BW	Brown Watson Books
CB	CBS-TV
CV	Chad Valley Sliderama
DH	Dark Horse Comics
ET	Editorial Mo.Pa.Sa.
FX	20th Century Fox
GK	Gold Key / Western Comics
HE	HarperEntertainment Books
HM	Harry K. McWilliams Assoc.
MC	Marvel Comics
MR	Mr. Comics / Metallic Rose
NB	NBC-TV
PR	Power Records
SB	Signet Books
TP	Topps
UB	Ubisoft

MEDIUM

a	animated series
b	book-and-record set
c	comic book or strip
d	trading card
e	e-comic
f	theatrical film
k	storybook
m	magazine article
n	novel or novelization
p	promotional newspaper
r	recorded audio fiction
s	short story
t	television series
u	unfilmed script or story
v	video game
x	Blu-Ray exclusive
y	young adult novel

◆ The Brax breach the *Oberon*'s base, filling its lower levels with acidic goo. Millions of Brax tunnel through the dirt, leveling the fence and pouring out from cracks in the ground.

Planet of the Apes: The Fall, Chapter 13 (HE-n)

◆ Sophocles' mate and children are among those killed. Half the human population dies, and Grace loses an arm. Vasich admits the need to keep their species alive outweighs his desire to get back to Earth.

Planet of the Apes: The Fall, Chapter 14 (HE-n)

◆ Molly boards a pod and torches as many brachiopods as she can, saving her sons' lives. Unable to burn the bugs within the ship, Vasich and Ken Kibo use coolant to freeze them.

Planet of the Apes: The Fall, Chapter 13 (HE-n)

◆ Frank Barstow records a goodbye message for Molly, explaining how to find the Brax Core and destroy the nest. The hive-mind tries to make him destroy the *Oberon*, but he fights it. Jonathan finds him dead, bugs bursting from his abdomen. Vasich makes peace with Grace, combining their forces as a single colony, and Molly tells them about Barstow's message. David, meanwhile, loses his virginity to Kelsey.

Planet of the Apes: The Fall, Chapter 14 (HE-n)

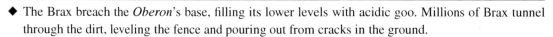

2043 TO 2047

◆ At Vasich's request, Grace compiles a colony history and message archive, to be transmitted into space on a repeating loop. During this period, the ape population in the fabs reaches about 3,000, a third of which receive military training. The apes remain a second-class race, sent to fight and die in the Brax Core to keep their population from dominating humanity.

Planet of the Apes: The Fall, Chapter 15 (HE-n)

2046

◆ In his secret ape community, Jonathan (Semos) marries his fourth wife, Aspasia, and fathers a son, Zaius. Unlike his previous mates, she survives childbirth and becomes mother to all of his children.

Planet of the Apes: The Fall, Chapter 17 (HE-n)

NOTE: *It's unclear if Aspasia is her real name, or if Semos so names her to honor his late mother, as he changed his own designation.*

2047

◆ Molly notices a rise in the female ape mortality rate (caused by Semos relocating them to his new city). Grace uses equine DNA from the station's animal database to gengineer horses for the Brax Core. David names his horse Silver, after an old *Lone Ranger* video, while Jonathan names his Lightning.

Planet of the Apes: The Fall, Chapter 15 (HE-n)

BEFORE 2048

◆ Grace gengineers several other Earth species as well, including monkeys and dogs.

Planet of the Apes #1: Force, Chapter 11 (HE-y)

NOTE: This is conjectural, based on the existence of such species on the planet 2,000 years in the future. It's unclear when she created them, but it must have been before Semos' massacre of humanity in 2048.

◆ Grace trains a gorilla named Helenos in the art of midwifery.

Planet of the Apes: Colony, Prologue (HE-n)

◆ Human scouts discover a distant valley inhabited by lizards of varying shapes and sizes, from piranha-like water lizards to pterodactyl-esque flying lizards to huge dinosaurs. Sentient lizards rule the area, using the dinosaurs as pack animals. The humans avoid the area, but never inform the apes of the danger, as a precautionary measure for the future.

Planet of the Apes: Colony, Chapter 18 (HE-n)

2048

◆ Grace Alexander engineers a virus to alter Brax DNA, rendering the insects sterile. Her hope is that infected Brax will spread the virus to other Cores, ultimately wiping out the Brax species.

Planet of the Apes: The Fall, Chapter 16 (HE-n)

◆ Grace discreetly makes sure the virus will affect apes as well, intending to infect them once the Brax are gone, thereby reducing simian intelligence so they'll be obedient servants.

Planet of the Apes: Colony, Chapter 2 (HE-n)

◆ When the time comes to infect the Brax, David and Jonathan assemble an army 1,500 apes strong. After a goodbye with their mother, the brothers, age 19, return to the site of first contact.

Planet of the Apes: The Fall, Chapter 15 (HE-n)

◆ Pregnant with David's child, Kelsey, disguised as an armored chimp, joins his squad to make sure her child doesn't lose him as he did his own father, Leo Davidson.

Planet of the Apes: The Fall, Chapter 18 (HE-n)

◆ Determined to keep the rising ape population in check, and hoping for a 90 percent death rate during the battle, Vasich takes steps to prevent the simians from summoning help.

Planet of the Apes: The Fall, Chapter 17 (HE-n)

◆ The hunter-killers eradicate the Great Nest, leaving only the Core. With Kelsey (still in ape disguise) guarding their rear, gorillas scorch the Brax queen, weakening it enough for David to deliver three virus-filled blowdarts. Finally, the Core dies in agony.

Planet of the Apes: The Fall, Chapter 16 (HE-n)

◆ Ninety percent of the ape military dies in battle. When the fighting is over, Semos brings David to his city and introduces his wife and sons. He reveals his plans for humanity, assuring David he intends only to destroy humans' high-tech weapons. David, however, realizes his brother plans to kill them all.

Planet of the Apes: The Fall, Chapter 17 (HE-n)

PUBLISHER / STUDIO
AB . . . . ABC-TV
AC . . . .Adventure / Malibu Comics
AW . . . . Award Books
BB . . . . .Ballantine Books
BN . . . . Bantam Books
BW . . . . Brown Watson Books
CB . . . . CBS-TV
CV . . . . Chad Valley Sliderama
DH . . . . .Dark Horse Comics
ET . . . . Editorial Mo.Pa.Sa.
FX . . . . 20th Century Fox
GK . . . .Gold Key / Western Comics
HE . . . HarperEntertainment Books
HM . . Harry K. McWilliams Assoc.
MC . . . . Marvel Comics
MR . . . Mr. Comics / Metallic Rose
NB . . . . NBC-TV
PR . . . . .Power Records
SB . . . . Signet Books
TP . . . . Topps
UB . . . . Ubisoft

MEDIUM
a . . . . animated series
b . . . . .book-and-record set
c . . . . .comic book or strip
d . . . . trading card
e . . . . e-comic
f . . . . .theatrical film
k . . . . .storybook
m . . . . .magazine article
n . . . . .novel or novelization
p . . . . promotional newspaper
r . . . . .recorded audio fiction
s . . . . short story
t . . . . .television series
u . . . . .unfilmed script or story
v . . . . video game
x . . . . .Blu-Ray exclusive
y . . . . .young adult novel

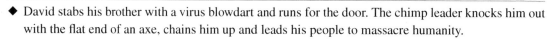

◆ David stabs his brother with a virus blowdart and runs for the door. The chimp leader knocks him out with the flat end of an axe, chains him up and leads his people to massacre humanity.

Planet of the Apes: The Fall, Chapter 18 (HE-n)

◆ The battle is over quickly, the apes slaughtering many of their former masters. Semos kills Karl Vasich, impaling him with a spear near his former captain's chair.

Planet of the Apes: Colony, Chapter 1 (HE-n)

> NOTE: Ian Edginton and Dan Abnett, in writing Dark Horse's Burton-based comic-book series, had intended to explore the origins of Semos and man's downfall on this planet. Their story would have diverged from The Fall and Colony, however, portraying humans and apes as equals. According to the writers, the Oberon crew would have left the station behind to explore the world, bringing their technology (including several pods) with them as they searched for a new home for both man and ape. Edginton had not been informed of the novels' existence until after the comics line began, but indicates he would still have pursued his original plans, even if he had known about them.

◆ Molly saves a few humans in a pod, but many are slaughtered. As apes burst into Grace Alexander's lab, she records one final message and broadcasts it into space, never knowing if anyone will hear it.

Planet of the Apes: The Fall, Chapter 18 (HE-n)

◆ Rather than killing her outright, however, Semos captures Grace alive.

Planet of the Apes: Colony, Chapter 1 (HE-n)

◆ Many humans escape into the jungle, but Semos lets his people think all have been killed, knowing the lie will give them hope for the future.

Planet of the Apes: Colony, Chapter 2 (HE-n)

◆ David awakens to find Kels killing two guards. Unlocking the chain, she leads him to his horse, Silver, and they ride out together into the jungle.

Planet of the Apes: The Fall, Chapter 18 (HE-n)

◆ Semos instructs his followers to leave everything from the *Oberon* behind, but some looting takes place as apes sneak out bottles of wine and other items to their new home.

Planet of the Apes: Colony, Chapter 8 (HE-n)

◆ Still, the fledgling ape society does retain some human concepts, including the metric system.

Planet of the Apes #2: Resistance, Chapter 15 (HE-y)

AFTER 2048

◆ Semos writes a set of Sacred Scrolls decrying mankind and providing the apes of his world with a set of laws. The 116th Scroll, known as *Discourses*, warns that apes should never kill their fellow apes.

Planet of the Apes—The Human War #1: "Part 1" (DH-c)

> NOTE: Semos' name is misspelled "Seimos" in this story. This set of Scrolls is separate from those later penned by the Lawgiver, back on Caesar's ape-controlled Earth.

◆ As on Earth, this tenet becomes Semos' people's most sacred law.

Planet of the Apes #1: Force, Chapter 9 (HE-y)

◆ Semos publicly rejects David and Molly Benavides, claiming they were never his family, though deep down he grieves their loss. He keeps Grace Alexander alive for years, trapped in the *Oberon*'s medical chamber. His hope: to glean knowledge of human technology to ensure his species' survival.

Planet of the Apes: Colony, Chapter 1 (HE-n)

◆ Molly tries to rescue her, but the doctor refuses to leave, determined to lead Semos to his own defeat.

Planet of the Apes: Colony, Chapter 18 (HE-n)

◆ The anti-Brax virus spreads to Semos' people, but instead of killing the apes, it causes bizarre gestational aberrations in several fetuses, altering their appearance. Semos learns about the virus while secretly recording everything Grace mutters in her solitude.

Planet of the Apes: Colony, Chapter 2 (HE-n)

NOTE: This would appear to be an explanation for the un-ape-like faces (some have described them as resembling Michael Jackson) of the female chimps in Tim Burton's Planet of the Apes *remake—virus-induced mutation.*

◆ Armed with this knowledge, Semos decides to split his people up into two colonies, hoping a change in location might reduce the disease's spread and give his people a better chance of survival.

Planet of the Apes: Colony, Chapter 17 (HE-n)

◆ Thus, Grace tricks Semos' people into invading lizard territory, hoping to bring about their slaughter.

Planet of the Apes: Colony, Chapter 18 (HE-n)

2052

◆ On Earth, a human named Jason and a chimp named Alexander, both residents of Ape City, are born in the same year. As they grow older, the duo forge a strong friendship despite their species' differences.

Planet of the Apes #11: "Outlines of Tomorrow—A Chronology of the Planet of the Apes" (MC-m)

NOTE: The youths' adventures are chronicled in Marvel's "Terror on the Planet of the Apes" saga, reprinted in part by Adventure Comics. This Alexander, of course, bears no known relation to the Oberon's *Grace Alexander.*

◆ Jason's parents are named Beth and David. Alex's parents' names are unrecorded.

Planet of the Apes #1: "Terror on the Planet of the Apes—The Lawgiver" (MC-c)

NOTE: This David, meanwhile, bears no relation to David Benavides.

2057

◆ An orangutan named Thaddeus, future attendant to Ape City's second Lawgiver, is born.

Planet of the Apes #23: "Terror on the Planet of the Apes, Phase 2—Messiah of Monkey-Demons" (MC-c)

BEFORE 2069

◆ Gen. Brutus, a power-hungry gorilla on Earth, rises through the ranks to become Ape City's peace officer under its second Lawgiver. Humanity's position in simian society, meanwhile, grows steadily worse.

Planet of the Apes #11: "Outlines of Tomorrow—A Chronology of the Planet of the Apes" (MC-m)

◆ Secretly, Brutus is also the leader of the Ape Supremacists—hooded gorilla racists who terrorize humans and hurt any simians who dare treat them as equals.

Planet of the Apes #1: "Terror on the Planet of the Apes—The Lawgiver" (MC-c)

2069

◆ In the Forbidden Zone, gorilla scouts discover the Caverns of the Inheritors, home to five giant brains suspended in glass nutrient-globes. The Inheritors (a.k.a. the Supreme Gestalt Commanders) are linked in a Gestalt Mind, backed by armies of cyborg mutant-drones. The giant brains are named Be-One, -Two, -Three, -Four and -Five, with replacement brains in storage, while the drones are named for letters of the alphabet (Mutant-Drone Ay [A], Bee [B], See [C] and so forth). Brutus forges an alliance with the Inheritors to take over Ape City, and his scouts are "persuaded" to forget what they saw.

Planet of the Apes #11: "Outlines of Tomorrow—A Chronology of the Planet of the Apes" (MC-m)

NOTE: The mutant-drones' cyborg nature is revealed in "Terror on the Planet of the Apes," in Marvel's Planet of the Apes #3.

◆ Unbeknownst to Brutus, the Inheritors have no respect for him or his kind. Rather, the Gestalt Mind plans to exterminate all apes and non-mutated humans once their "alliance" with his army no longer serves its purpose.

Planet of the Apes #4: "Terror on the Planet of the Apes—A Riverboat Named Simian" (MC-c)

BEFORE 2070

◆ Eccentric wayfarer Lightning Smith ("Lightsmith") and his mute gibbon companion Gilbert travel the Forbidden Zone seeking relics. Their goal: to restore civilization by promoting technology and progress. In South Dakota, they discover Mount Rushmore. Believing the monument to depict onerous criminals, Lightsmith dubs it the Last Mount Mug-Face and claims the well-stocked bunker up Lincoln's nose as his home. The Seal of the U.S. president hangs on the wall, the skeletal remains of President Arthur Trundy marking his refuge from the war in 1992. They find a recording in which Trundy discusses Caesar's rebellion with his chief advisor, Henry. Trundy comments that he'd like to brainwash all of the apes in the *Psychedrome*, and the wayfarers set out to find what they think must be a storehouse of artifacts (though it's really an alien spaceship) so Lightsmith can wash his brain clean of ignorance.

Planet of the Apes #14: "Terror on the Planet of the Apes, Phase 2— Up the Nose-Tube to Monkey-Trash" (MC-c)

NOTE: According to a Yahoo Groups posting by author Ty Templeton, a scene cut from Revolution on the Planet of the Apes #5 would have taken place inside the bunker as an homage to "Terror." The scene, he says, would have revealed the body to have been the vice president, not Trundy himself. Trundy is named in Revolution, but not in this storyline.

◆ Lightsmith discovers a rusty hypodermic needle and accidentally sticks himself. This causes him to get very ill, but he recovers. He also finds a stack of baseball cards, which he mistakes for portraits of great leaders of the past.

Planet of the Apes: "Terror on the Planet of the Apes, Phase 2—To Meet the Makers" (MC-c, unpublished)

NOTE: This story was never released due to Marvel's decision to stop publishing Planet of the Apes comics as of issue #29, in response to increased licensing fees. The above details come from an outline provided by Doug Moench.

LATE 21st CENTURY

◆ Back on Ashlar, New Hope's population grows to 5,000, so Semos builds a military to protect them.

Planet of the Apes: Colony, Prologue (HE-n)

◆ Leonidas, a chimp farmer, isolates his clan outside of New Hope to protect the virtue of Lykia—the daughter of his brother Leukippos and sister-in-law Dikte—from Zaius and other eager young males.

Planet of the Apes: Colony, Chapter 5 (HE-n)

◆ Over time, mutations result in several more unviable childbirths, killing the mothers.

Planet of the Apes: Colony, Prologue (HE-n)

◆ Semos and Aspasia have twin sons, Glyppos and Glaukos, and a daughter, Galateia. His relationship with his children is practically non-existent, however, as he spends weeks at a time aboard *Oberon*'s wreckage instead of showing them attention—and they resent him for it. Aspasia tries to hide her anguish, but she, too, resents his inattentiveness. Zaius, now nearly an adult, helps raise his younger siblings.

Planet of the Apes: Colony, Chapter 3 (HE-n)

◆ A chimp soldier named Hyllos marries Algaia, daughter of Aison.

Planet of the Apes: Colony, Chapter 11 (HE-n)

◆ Kallisto, the mate of Zaius' friend Archos, goes into labor, but her midwives, Helenos and Makaria, fail to stop her from dying. Her stillborn child has two heads—the tenth anomalous birth in a year.

Planet of the Apes: Colony, Prologue (HE-n)

◆ Semos takes Thados to the *Oberon*'s wreckage so he can reveal their true origins.

Planet of the Apes: Colony, Chapter 1 (HE-n)

◆ However, Semos neglects to inform Aspasia and Zaius beforehand, infuriating them.

Planet of the Apes: Colony, Chapter 3 (HE-n)

◆ Stripped bare, the *Oberon* is filled with human skeletons. Semos brings his son to the animal lab, where a scorched "**Caution: Live Animals**" sign now reads "Ca Li Ma." Amused, he dubs the station "Calima." Inside the lab is the ancient body of Grace Alexander, kept alive but in agony in a vat of goo.

Planet of the Apes: Colony, Chapter 1 (HE-n)

◆ Semos reveals his plans to build a second city and gives Thados a mission: to hunt down and kill the remaining humans, and to keep other apes (even Zaius) from learning that Semos let them escape.

Planet of the Apes: Colony, Chapter 14 (HE-n)

◆ Zaius, he says, will succeed Semos as ruler since he can produce children safely, creating an aristocracy of their bloodline to guide society for centuries.

Planet of the Apes: Colony, Chapter 2 (HE-n)

◆ Semos' plan: Thados will remain with the colony, take a wife and lead his people, while Zaius will learn about leadership from his brother, then return to New Hope to succeed Semos as its king.

Planet of the Apes: Colony, Chapter 9 (HE-n)

PUBLISHER / STUDIO
AB . . . . ABC-TV
AC . . . . Adventure / Malibu Comics
AW . . . . Award Books
BB . . . . .Ballantine Books
BN. . . . . Bantam Books
BW . . . . Brown Watson Books
CB. . . . . CBS-TV
CV . . . . Chad Valley Sliderama
DH. . . . . .Dark Horse Comics
ET . . . . Editorial Mo.Pa.Sa.
FX . . . . 20th Century Fox
GK . . . . Gold Key / Western Comics
HE . . . HarperEntertainment Books
HM . . Harry K. McWilliams Assoc.
MC . . . . .Marvel Comics
MR . . . Mr. Comics / Metallic Rose
NB. . . . . NBC-TV
PR . . . . .Power Records
SB. . . . . Signet Books
TP . . . . Topps
UB. . . . . Ubisoft

MEDIUM
a . . . . animated series
b . . . . .book-and-record set
c . . . . .comic book or strip
d . . . . trading card
e . . . . e-comic
f . . . . .theatrical film
k . . . . .storybook
m . . . . .magazine article
n . . . . .novel or novelization
p . . . . promotional newspaper
r . . . . .recorded audio fiction
s . . . . short story
t . . . . television series
u . . . . .unfilmed script or story
v . . . . video game
x . . . . .Blu-Ray exclusive
y . . . . .young adult novel

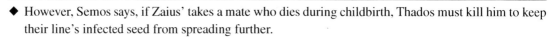

◆ However, Semos says, if Zaius' takes a mate who dies during childbirth, Thados must kill him to keep their line's infected seed from spreading further.

Planet of the Apes: Colony, Chapter 17 (HE-n)

◆ Semos rigs up the station's neural connection training helmet and pumps years' worth of knowledge into Thados' brain in a matter of days. Since some living humans retain such information, Semos believes their line must secretly protect it as well.

Planet of the Apes: Colony, Chapter 9 (HE-n)

◆ After a week's training, Thados comes to realize his father's plan is the right one.

Planet of the Apes: Colony, Chapter 2 (HE-n)

◆ Semos and Thados return to New Hope after three weeks aboard the *Oberon*.

Planet of the Apes: Colony, Chapter 3 (HE-n)

◆ Semos assembles his people in an amphitheater. Promising to find a way to stop the stillbirths, he proposes building a second city. Despite some protests, his followers support him.

Planet of the Apes: Colony, Chapter 4 (HE-n)

◆ Two weeks later, the brothers and a gorilla named Briarios lead more than 400 apes into the wilderness. Unaware of his father's intention that he one day return to succeed him as ruler, Zaius feels hurt when Semos is more emotional in his goodbye to Thados than to him.

Planet of the Apes: Colony, Chapter 4 (HE-n)

◆ Archos forces his way into the expedition at knifepoint. Thados refuses, but Zaius accepts him anyway. That night, Lykia tries to seduce Thados. Though attracted to her, he rebuffs her advances. Zaius tries to kill Thados so he can rule the colony with Lykia as his mate. Both survive, but are badly injured.

Planet of the Apes: Colony, Chapter 5 (HE-n)

◆ Lykia jumps Thados, thinking him the aggressor, then nurses Zaius back to health. Stricken with amnesia, Zaius has no idea he started the fight. Weeks later, Thados gives Zaius a choice: accepting his rule, or banishment. When Archos attacks Thados, Zaius submits to save his friend's life.

Planet of the Apes: Colony, Chapter 6 (HE-n)

◆ A month into the journey, the apes reach a swamp, which the carts cannot traverse. Leukippos suggests they build rafts. Archos tries to cross a shallow river, but his horse is attacked and consumed by a swarm of water lizards. He nearly drowns until Zaius rescues him and rushes him back to camp.

Planet of the Apes: Colony, Chapter 7 (HE-n)

◆ Leukippos' mate, Dikte, begins spying on his conversations with Thados, knowing her husband's memory is fading and that he might forget to tell her what they discussed.

Planet of the Apes: Colony, Chapter 16 (HE-n)

◆ Thados announces plans to share power with Zaius, knowing the council will back him if they disagree. He decides to cross the river, and Archos ties a bloody cloth to the saddle of his horse, Big Red. Drawn to the blood, the lizards swarm him, consuming the horse alive. They nearly eat Thados as well, though he climbs to safety. Passing out in agony, he awakens to find his genitals gone.

Planet of the Apes: Colony, Chapter 8 (HE-n)

◆ Zaius impregnates Lykia, and Thados grants his blessing to wed. The colonists build rafts to transport their belongings across the river. Leukippos suggests Thados step down, letting Zaius rule since he can continue Semos' bloodline. Thados pretends to agree, but murders him and feeds him to the water lizards.

Planet of the Apes: Colony, Chapter 9 (HE-n)

◆ Dikte witnesses the murder but tells no one, awaiting the right opportunity to reveal Thados' treachery.

Planet of the Apes: Colony, Chapter 15 (HE-n)

◆ Thados sends Zaius to scout for new colony sites. He asks Dikte to take Leukippos' place on the council and become his mate, knowing her support would prevent Zaius from gaining the upper hand. Despite his castration, she agrees to the arrangement to secure her own power base.

Planet of the Apes: Colony, Chapter 10 (HE-n)

◆ After a month, the apes fail to locate a suitable colony site. The brothers find a strange nest and a large bird scale. Their scouts come under attack, and a flying lizard mutilates Hyllos. Archos slays the creature, and a gorilla named Orthros rips its body apart.

Planet of the Apes: Colony, Chapter 11 (HE-n)

◆ Thados dissects the flying lizard and finds a wrought-iron arrowhead in its guts. He realizes humans made it, but tells no one. The apes build a colony and name it Cool Mountain, erecting a protective stockade fence. One night, a patrolling soldier named Teukros is eaten by a pack of flying lizards.

Planet of the Apes: Colony, Chapter 12 (HE-n)

◆ Dikte urges Thados to build her a home. He agrees, but worries they might need to relocate. Orthros and his lover Thaleia sneak off for a romantic interlude. Encountering five giant lizards, he realizes they're far more intelligent than anticipated. Thaleia escapes, but the lizards kill Orthros with a spear.

Planet of the Apes: Colony, Chapter 13 (HE-n)

◆ Zaius finds the ruins of an abandoned human village, along with evidence of smelted iron and gunpowder technologies. Thados reveals their father's secret—that several *Oberon* crew members escaped alive—and says Zaius must go back to New Hope and tell their father what they've found.

Planet of the Apes: Colony, Chapter 14 (HE-n)

◆ As Archos and a chimp named Laetron stand watch, a pack of giant lizards kill Zaius' squad. Only he and Archos (who loses a hand) survive. Other lizards, meanwhile, attack Thados' group. Realizing they can't win, Thados aborts the mission. The council disagrees, however, and Dikte exposes Leukippos' murder.

Planet of the Apes: Colony, Chapter 15 (HE-n)

◆ Thados denies the accusation. Zaius backs him up, and the colonists begin the trek back to New Hope. En route, the apes find a huge lizard's skull, its teeth larger than an ape's hand. They discover a valley containing a city filled with dinosaurs, which attack the caravan. Moments later, Lykia goes into labor.

Planet of the Apes: Colony, Chapter 16 (HE-n)

◆ Dinosaurs stampede the camp, ridden by smaller lizards. Briarios, Archos and many others fall in the attack. Lykia's son's head gets stuck during birth. The baby survives, but a crazed Dikte stabs Lykia to death to destroy the "demon seed." Zaius escapes with the child alive, and Thados tells him to climb on his shoulders. He runs across the river, braving water lizards so Zaius can survive to warn Semos. Before dying, Thados reveals the truth of their father's plans, begging Zaius' forgiveness.

Planet of the Apes: Colony, Chapter 17 (HE-n)

PUBLISHER / STUDIO
AB . . . . ABC-TV
AC . . . . Adventure / Malibu Comics
AW . . . . Award Books
BB . . . . Ballantine Books
BN . . . . Bantam Books
BW . . . . Brown Watson Books
CB . . . . CBS-TV
CV . . . . Chad Valley Sliderama
DH . . . . Dark Horse Comics
ET . . . . Editorial Mo.Pa.Sa.
FX . . . . 20th Century Fox
GK . . . . Gold Key / Western Comics
HE . . . HarperEntertainment Books
HM . . Harry K. McWilliams Assoc.
MC . . . . Marvel Comics
MR . . . Mr. Comics / Metallic Rose
NB . . . . NBC-TV
PR . . . . Power Records
SB . . . . Signet Books
TP . . . . Topps
UB . . . . Ubisoft

MEDIUM
a . . . . animated series
b . . . . book-and-record set
c . . . . comic book or strip
d . . . . trading card
e . . . . e-comic
f . . . . theatrical film
k . . . . storybook
m . . . . magazine article
n . . . . novel or novelization
p . . . . promotional newspaper
r . . . . recorded audio fiction
s . . . . short story
t . . . . television series
u . . . . unfilmed script or story
v . . . . video game
x . . . . Blu-Ray exclusive
y . . . . young adult novel

◆ Semos' human brother David and his mate, Kels, view the carnage from a distance as the surviving apes escape in wagons. Since the apes cannot defeat the lizards without human technology, David says, they'll either have to ask his people for assistance, or die—either way, humanity will regain the *Oberon*. Meanwhile, Grace Alexander finally dies in her medical chamber, a satisfied smile on her face.

Planet of the Apes: Colony, Chapter 18 (HE-n)

NOTE: According to novelist William T. Quick, additional novels were planned in this series beyond Colony, *though he had no specific plans in mind for how he'd continue the story, had the line not been canceled due to lack of sales.*

LATE 21ˢᵗ CENTURY AND BEYOND

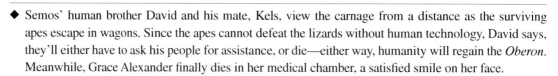

◆ Ashlar's simian population grows more advanced and warlike. Humans and apes alike eventually forget their Earth origins, and an ape religion evolves around Semos, believed to be divinely sent.

Planet of the Apes (FX-f)

◆ According to the scriptures of that religion, the Almighty raised Semos up from the dust and breathed life into him as the First Ape.

Planet of the Apes #1: Force, Chapter 2 (HE-y)

◆ Semos' betrayal of humanity fades from memory, with future apes awaiting his return to bring peace to his children. The First Ape's descendants bury all knowledge of simian subservience to man, hoping to prevent humanity from ever rising again, and refer to the era before his revolt as the Time Before Time.

Planet of the Apes (FX-f)

◆ Mankind on Semos' planet degenerates into several clans, including the light-haired Valley Clan (known as Teks) who grow and cook food, and sew leather into clothing; and the dark-haired Wildings, who grow nothing, wear animal furs like savages and eschew fire since it attracts ape attention.

Planet of the Apes #1: Force, Chapter 5 (HE-y)

◆ Many humans come to fear the apes' horses as flesh-eating monsters. This serves to further separate mankind from civilization.

Planet of the Apes (DH-c)

NOTE: This information appears in the comic adaptation of the film.

◆ In memory of Karl Vasich, the Wildings take his last name as the title of each tribal leader. Thereafter, all Wilding chieftans are known as Vasich.

Planet of the Apes #3: Rule, Chapter 2 (HE-y, unpublished)

◆ Hanuman the Wise, an orangutan on Ashlar, leads three tribes into the wilderness. Traveling for a year, he divides them into nine groups, sending each to conquer a separate distant land. His son Pharo builds the First City and takes a gorilla mate, who bears a son, Kine—who, in turn, founds a warrior band known as the Chimerae. Others inter-marry as well, enabling the Chimerae to incorporate each species' best attributes. Proud and arrogant, the warriors inbreed to keep their bloodline pure, causing future generations to grow deformed and disturbed, and to turn against those under their protection. All non-Chimerae abandon the First City, leaving the monstrous regiment behind. The jungle swallows up the city over time, and the Chimerae devolve into myth. Thus, inter-marrying between species becomes a taboo among civilized apekind, those of mixed ancestry deemed half-castes.

Planet of the Apes #3: "Old Gods, Part 3" (DH-c)

21ˢᵗ CENTURY TO 3978

◆ Earth's ape rulers set down the *Simian Book of Prophecy*, foretelling an invasion by grey-hooded creatures with glowing red eyes (the technologically advanced mutant human Underdwellers).

Return to the Planet of the Apes episode #12: "Invasion of the Underdwellers" (NB-a)

◆ The apes vow to destroy the Underdwellers, who long for the fulfillment of their own prophecy that a savior, Oosa, will lead them back to the surface and help retake the planet.

Return to the Planet of the Apes episode #3: "The Unearthly Prophecy" (NB-a)

NOTE: The conflict's origin is undated, but is said to have occurred long before the era of the animated series.

◆ Ape City's gorilla army emerges victorious from several wars, protecting the city from the Underdwellers in the Battle of the Bridges, and from the Ice Apes during a skirmish in the Sogan Desert.

Return to the Planet of the Apes episode #1: "Flames of Doom" (BB-n)

NOTE: This is revealed in the novelization.

◆ An artistic ape renaissance makes Earth's oppressive simian government nervous. A human revolt adds to the council's difficulties, as does the existence of a half-human, half-ape hybrid, sheltered by a group of liberal apes from the gorillas trying to hunt it down.

Planned Planet of the Apes Sequel (FX-f, unfilmed)

NOTE: In 1992, Peter Jackson had been invited to write (with partner Fran Walsh) and direct a sixth entry in the classic film series. Unlike Tim Burton's 2001 "re-imagining" and various other proposed remakes by Adam Rifkin, Terry Hayes and Sam Hamm, the Jackson-Walsh script would have followed Battle for the Planet of the Apes *and featured Roddy McDowall as a grey-haired chimp artist modeled after Leonardo da Vinci. However, this project never came to pass, due to a change in 20ᵗʰ Century Fox management, and to the writers' discomfort with Fox's decision to cast Arnold Schwarzenegger in the lead and hire James Cameron as producer. As documented in Brian Sibley's authorized biography,* Peter Jackson: A Film-Maker's Journey, *the duo opted to leave the project, knowing with such big names attached, Jackson would have had little control over the final product.*

◆ A legendary figure named Kerchak emerges in ape lore, known for his powerful claws and horns.

Return to the Planet of the Apes episode #3: "The Unearthly Prophecy" (BB-n)

NOTE: Kerchak is mentioned in the novelization of this and other episodes.

◆ A national holiday, Kerchak's Day, is named in this hero's honor.

Return to the Planet of the Apes episode #7: "River of Flames" (BB-n)

NOTE: This is revealed in the novelization.

◆ Other simian lore reveres an ape figure known as Great Guzo.

Return to the Planet of the Apes episode #6: "Terror on Ice Mountain" (BB-n)

NOTE: This is revealed in the novelization.

PUBLISHER / STUDIO
AB . . . . ABC-TV
AC . . . .Adventure / Malibu Comics
AW . . . . Award Books
BB . . . . .Ballantine Books
BN . . . . Bantam Books
BW . . . . Brown Watson Books
CB . . . . CBS-TV
CV . . . . Chad Valley Sliderama
DH . . . . .Dark Horse Comics
ET . . . . Editorial Mo.Pa.Sa.
FX . . . . 20th Century Fox
GK . . . .Gold Key / Western Comics
HE . . . HarperEntertainment Books
HM . . Harry K. McWilliams Assoc.
MC . . . . Marvel Comics
MR . . . Mr. Comics / Metallic Rose
NB . . . . NBC-TV
PR . . . . Power Records
SB . . . . Signet Books
TP . . . . Topps
UB . . . . Ubisoft

MEDIUM
a . . . . animated series
b . . . . .book-and-record set
c . . . . .comic book or strip
d . . . . trading card
e . . . . e-comic
f . . . . .theatrical film
k . . . . .storybook
m . . . . .magazine article
n . . . . .novel or novelization
p . . . . promotional newspaper
r . . . . .recorded audio fiction
s . . . . short story
t . . . . television series
u . . . . .unfilmed script or story
v . . . . video game
x . . . . .Blu-Ray exclusive
y . . . . young adult novel

◆ Apes experiment with hot air balloons, but the balloons always collapse at a certain height. As such, flight is deemed against the laws of nature.

__Return to the Planet of the Apes episode #6: "Terror on Ice Mountain" (NB-a)__

NOTE: This seems an odd thing for the apes to presume, given that birds and insects clearly are able to fly.

◆ Although orangutans remain the dominant ruling class of ape society, several ambitious gorilla rulers seize temporary control on numerous occasions over a two-millennia period.

__Return to the Planet of the Apes episode #8: "Screaming Wings" (BB-n)__

NOTE: This is revealed in the novelization.

Part 7: Age of Terror, Era of Adventure (2070 to 2199)

2070

◆ Gen. Brutus advises the Lawgiver to visit the Forbidden Zone and make peace with the Inheritors, intending to seize Ape City once the Gestalt Mind imprisons the elder orangutan.

> *Planet of the Apes #4: "Terror on the Planet of the Apes—Gunpowder Julius" (MC-c)*
>
> *NOTE: In an article printed in Marvel's* Planet of the Apes *#4, Chris Claremont places the "Terror" saga circa 3978 (the time of the first film), but all evidence indicates otherwise: Humans can speak, knowledge of mankind's past remains prevalent, the Lawgiver is only the second ape with that title and so forth. Marvel's own timeline in issue #11 sets the story in 2070, so I have adhered to that placement.*

◆ The Lawgiver, aware of the Inheritors' existence, recognizes Brutus' duplicity but still agrees to meet with them, hopeful of negotiating peace with the Gestalt Mind.

> *Planet of the Apes #11: "Terror on the Planet of the Apes—When the Lawgiver Returns" (MC-c)*

◆ Jason and his friend Alexander (a human and chimp, respectively, both age 18) leave school early to hear a speech given by the Lawgiver. The orangutan pushes for equality between both species, announcing that he'll be gone indefinitely. He leaves in charge a fellow orangutan named Xavier, whom many consider inept. Meanwhile, Ape Supremacists (hooded simian racists bent on scaring humans into submission) assault Alex's father for befriending humans, then burn Jason's parents, Beth and David, to death.

> *Planet of the Apes #1: "Terror on the Planet of the Apes—The Lawgiver" (MC-c)*

◆ Alex joins Jason on a quest to find the killers, and both are captured by Ape Supremacists. When Brutus' wife Zena discovers his involvement with the hate group, Brutus kills her, framing Jason for the crime. Mounting pressure from human-hating factions in Ape City forces Xavier to sentence Jason to death. Alex frees him from jail, and the two head for the Forbidden Zone to find the Lawgiver and clear Jason's name.

> *Planet of the Apes #1: "Terror on the Planet of the Apes—Fugitives on the Planet of the Apes" (MC-c)*

◆ A gorilla named Tyrinius almost spots Alex and Jason hiding in a tree, but they slip by. At Zena's funeral, presided over by the Minister of the Second Life, Brutus uses his wife's death to spread anti-human bigotry. Jason accuses Brutus of murder, and a guard shoots his shoulder with a crossbow. He and Alex attempt to lure Xavier to Brutus' camp, but the racist group slaughters Xavier's peace officers and pin these murders on the youths as well.

> *Planet of the Apes #2: "Terror on the Planet of the Apes—The Forbidden Zone of Forgotten Horrors" (MC-c)*

◆ Jason and Alex take refuge in the Forbidden Zone, where they encounter a mutated race of timid, shaggy, ape-human hybrid primates. A crane captures one creature and heads into a tunnel. Jason and Alex follow it to the Caverns of the Inheritors, where mutant humans use the beasts to build war machines. There, Alex and Jason find themselves trapped between mutant-drones and Ape Supremacists.

> *Planet of the Apes #2: "Terror on the Planet of the Apes—Lick the Sky Crimson" (MC-c)*

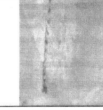

PUBLISHER / STUDIO

AB	ABC-TV
AC	Adventure / Malibu Comics
AW	Award Books
BB	Ballantine Books
BN	Bantam Books
BW	Brown Watson Books
CB	CBS-TV
CV	Chad Valley Sliderama
DH	Dark Horse Comics
ET	Editorial Mo.Pa.Sa.
FX	20th Century Fox
GK	Gold Key / Western Comics
HE	HarperEntertainment Books
HM	Harry K. McWilliams Assoc.
MC	Marvel Comics
MR	Mr. Comics / Metallic Rose
NB	NBC-TV
PR	Power Records
SB	Signet Books
TP	Topps
UB	Ubisoft

MEDIUM

a	animated series
b	book-and-record set
c	comic book or strip
d	trading card
e	e-comic
f	theatrical film
k	storybook
m	magazine article
n	novel or novelization
p	promotional newspaper
r	recorded audio fiction
s	short story
t	television series
u	unfilmed script or story
v	video game
x	Blu-Ray exclusive
y	young adult novel

◆ The duo trick the apes and mutants into fighting one another, then steal a mutant scorch-weapon and run outside, only to face more mutant drones. They steal a tram, but the drones lower a wall onto the tracks and take them to Gestalt Headquarters to face facilitation or execution.

Planet of the Apes #3: "Terror on the Planet of the Apes—Spawn of the Mutant-Pits" (MC-c)

◆ The Inheritors order Jason and Alex killed. Mutant-drones bring them to a cell with moving walls that push them into a great arena. The Supreme Gestalt Commanders watch as they combat giant beasts alongside one of Brutus' gorillas, First Lt. Warko, who helps them break free, liberate the Lawgiver and steal a sky-sled. Out in the Forbidden Zone, however, Warko captures them again at gunpoint.

Planet of the Apes #3: "Terror on the Planet of the Apes—The Abomination Arena" (MC-c)

◆ Jason throws the sky-sled into a nose-dive. Alex tries to wrestle the gun away, causing Warko to blast the controls, crashing the vehicle into an ancient Roy Rogers restaurant. Jason nearly kills Warko, but Alex and the Lawgiver stop him, and they head for Ape City. A mutated lion attacks, and Jason saves the Lawgiver from its deadly saliva. The Inheritors give Brutus the resources to stop the Lawgiver from reclaiming Ape City, intending eventually to betray him and exterminate both apekind and humanity.

Planet of the Apes #4: "Terror on the Planet of the Apes—A Riverboat Named Simian" (MC-c)

◆ The Lawgiver is pulled away by a river's current. Alex and Jason try to save him, and a shaggy, mute humanoid jumps in to help. The water carries them over a waterfall to the River Society, a frontier town of apes and humans led by a gorilla named Gunpowder Julius and his human friend, Steely Dan. They nickname the humanoid Shaggy. Mutant-Drone Ess shows Brutus a mountain passage around the water. A sentry warns Dan and Julius of the apes' approach, and they create a gunpowder-filled trench. The mutants' war machines fall into the trench, forcing Brutus' forces to retreat. A parting shot kills Shaggy.

Planet of the Apes #4: "Terror on the Planet of the Apes—Gunpowder Julius" (MC-c)

◆ Julius and Dan bring the fugitives to Ape City aboard their keelboat, the *Simian*. Giant river-slugs nearly kill them along the way. They meet a friendly ape/human nomad band in gypsy garb, led by an elderly simian called Mama Lena. Among them is a beautiful human woman named Malagueña. Her chimp lover, Grimaldi, reacts jealously to Jason, so Mama Lena orders them to resolve their disagreement in a fight to the death. Jason gains the upper hand. He hesitates to kill Grimaldi, but Brutus arrives with a mutant-drone army and finishes the job with a single shot. In Ape City, meanwhile, civil unrest erupts when Xavier fails to act after Ape Supremacists kill three more humans.

Planet of the Apes #6: "Terror on the Planet of the Apes—Malagueña Beyond a Zone Forbidden" (MC-c)

◆ Plagued by protests of anti-human persecution, Xavier seeks advice from Phaiton, an orangutan scribe, who says he should back his fellow apes. Ape Supremacists—including Xavier's personal guard, Zartor—crucify the temporary leader, sparking widespread human harassment. Fearing for the safety of his species, a human named Ivor leads others out of the hate-filled Ape City.

Planet of the Apes #11: "Terror on the Planet of the Apes—When the Lawgiver Returns" (MC-c)

◆ A gypsy named Saraband and his midget chimp companion, Trippo, help subdue Brutus' forces. Malagueña urges Jason to show mercy, and he lets the gorilla warrior live. Julius taunts Brutus into a fight, knocking him out, and Jason forces him to lead them to the Inheritors' caves. Saraband and Trippo come along for the ride as they steer the *Simian* to the giant brains' Mutant Pits, where they face more drones.

Planet of the Apes #8: "Terror on the Planet of the Apes—The Planet Inheritors" (MC-c)

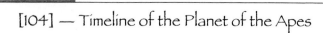

◆ Julius and Dan return to their village. The fugitives encounter Ivor's caravan en route to Ape City, and the Lawgiver convinces them not to leave. He shames the rioting masses into lowering their fists, but the violence resumes, with Alex and Jason taking opposite sides. The Lawgiver exposes Brutus' treachery, then is shot by an Ape Supremacist. Brutus is banished, but Jason considers the punishment insufficient. Denouncing the Lawgiver, he decks Alex and leaves Ape City to bring Brutus to justice himself.

Planet of the Apes #11: "Terror on the Planet of the Apes—When the Lawgiver Returns" (MC-c)

◆ Jason finds a map in Brutus' camp, highlighting a site in South Dakota. Alex and Malagueña are abducted by the Assisimians, a savage gorilla tribe in Kansas, led by Chieftan Maguanus. Jason meets Lightning Smith and Gilbert, wayfarers searching for the *Psychedrome*. They spy on the Assisimians and see Alex and Malagueña in bonds. Lightsmith plays a recording of Orson Wells' *War of the Worlds*, then dons an old Ku Klux Klan outfit (the original use for which he's oblivious) and amazes the apes with magic. He ignites fireworks and scares the tribe into releasing their captives, then drives them all to his home—up Abe Lincoln's nose at Mount Rushmore.

Planet of the Apes #13: "Terror on the Planet of the Apes, Phase 2—
The Magick-Man's Last Gasp Purple Light Show" (MC-c)

◆ Brutus offers the Inheritors a choice at gunpoint: their war machines, or their lives. At Mount Rushmore, Lightsmith shows the fugitives a recording of President Trundy discussing the *Psychedrome*. When the Assisimians arrive, Gilbert slingshots a warning up Lincoln's nose. Lightsmith pops out Lincoln's eyes as lookout holes, telling the others to lob grenades, don parachutes and jump to his Wonder Wagon. As they ride to safety, Jason spots Brutus' army, flanked by mutant-drones and war machines.

Planet of the Apes #14: "Terror on the Planet of the Apes, Phase 2—
Up the Nose-Tube to Monkey-Trash" (MC-c)

NOTE: *Trundy is not named in this story; rather, he is so identified in Mr. Comics'*
Revolution on the Planet of the Apes miniseries.

◆ Brutus interrogates Maguanas in his search for Jason. The fugitives, meanwhile, discover a cliffside village of apes and humans living like American Indians. An orangutan shaman shares psychedelic drugs with them, and Jason hallucinates Malagueña taking Alex as a lover, causing him to pummel his friend. The next morning, neither recalls the fight. Lightsmith trades a "magic talisman" (a 7-UP button) for tunnel access to the *Psychedrome*, and they blast the spaceship door with dynamite. Winged monkey-demons take the wayfarer to a Conditioning Center, where they brainwash him to be a submissive "good person."

Planet of the Apes #19: "Terror on the Planet of the Apes, Phase 2—Demons of the Psychedrome" (MC-c)

◆ Alex and Jason battle the flying monkeys, then travel a levitrough (a glassite tube) up to an artificial sun (or Lumenark). They enter the globe and find a multi-eyed alien called the Keeper of the Light, whom they force to take them to the catatonic Lightsmith.

Planet of the Apes #20: "Terror on the Planet of the Apes, Phase 2—Society of the Psychedrome" (MC-c)

◆ The alien's mate is known as the Keeper of the Liquid Sustenance.

Planet of the Apes #26: "Terror on the Planet of the Apes, Phase 2—North Lands" (MC-c)

◆ In a hidden lab beneath the New York Public Library, the Makers—deranged human scientists self-augmented with bionics—capture numerous gorillas to create an army of berserker cyborg apes, which they dub Gorilloids. The cyborgs resent their masters for turning them into machines, but are compelled by their programming to obey.

Planet of the Apes #27: "Terror on the Planet of the Apes, Phase 2—Apes of Iron" (MC-c)

PUBLISHER / STUDIO
AB . . . . ABC-TV
AC . . . .Adventure / Malibu Comics
AW . . . . Award Books
BB . . . . .Ballantine Books
BN . . . . Bantam Books
BW . . . . Brown Watson Books
CB . . . . CBS-TV
CV . . . . Chad Valley Sliderama
DH . . . . .Dark Horse Comics
ET . . . . Editorial Mo.Pa.Sa.
FX . . . . 20th Century Fox
GK . . . .Gold Key / Western Comics
HE . . . HarperEntertainment Books
HM . . Harry K. McWilliams Assoc.
MC . . . . Marvel Comics
MR . . . Mr. Comics / Metallic Rose
NB . . . . NBC-TV
PR . . . . .Power Records
SB . . . . Signet Books
TP . . . . Topps
UB . . . . .Ubisoft

MEDIUM
a . . . . animated series
b . . . . .book-and-record set
c . . . . .comic book or strip
d . . . . trading card
e . . . . e-comic
f . . . . .theatrical film
k . . . . .storybook
m . . . . .magazine article
n . . . . .novel or novelization
p . . . . promotional newspaper
r . . . . .recorded audio fiction
s . . . . short story
t . . . . television series
u . . . . .unfilmed script or story
v . . . . video game
x . . . . .Blu-Ray exclusive
y . . . . .young adult novel

◆ The Inheritors replace two damaged brain jars with new units, known as Be-Six and Be-Seven.

Planet of the Apes #23: "Terror on the Planet of the Apes, Phase 2—Messiah of Monkey-Demons" (MC-c)

◆ The fugitives fight their way to a railway filled with weapons of mass destruction. Mutant-drones destroy the nearby village. Brutus tortures Malagueña, ordering Warko to locate secret presidential documents regarding "Project: Last Ditch." Back in Ape City, as conditions worsen between humans and gorillas, two scribes (Heironymous and Centarius) find the Lawgiver near death.

Planet of the Apes #20: "Terror on the Planet of the Apes, Phase 2—Society of the Psychedrome" (MC-c)

◆ Thaddeus, an orangutan attendant, vows to find a cure said to exist in the Forbidden Zone. Brutus locates the *Psychedrome*'s weapons silo. Monkey-demons attack, enabling Jason's group to escape. To prevent Brutus from gaining nuclear technology, the Inheritors order a drone to set off the warheads. Maguanus attacks the mutant, detonating the bombs and leveling the mountain on the apes. Furious, Brutus kills the Assissimian. Alex and Jason, meanwhile, force the Keeper of the Light to lead them to safety via railcar.

Planet of the Apes #23: "Terror on the Planet of the Apes, Phase 2—Messiah of Monkey-Demons" (MC-c)

◆ The Assisimians rage over Maguanas' death, so Gunpowder Julius and Steely Dan stockpile weapons to protect the River Society. Meanwhile, a gorilla named Moravius is chosen to succeed Brutus as Ape City's peace officer.

Planet of the Apes #27: "Terror on the Planet of the Apes, Phase 2—Apes of Iron" (MC-c)

◆ Unlike most gorillas, Moravius sees apes and humans as equals.

Planet of the Apes #28: "Terror on the Planet of the Apes, Phase 2—Revolt of the Gorilloids" (MC-c)

◆ The railcar carries the fugitives to the Northlands, far from the *Psychedrome*. Lightsmith vanishes, and a trio of North-Apes—Eriko, Flarn and Jardo—accuse them of trespassing. When Malagueña bests Flarn in a sword fight, however, they accept the group as equals. Eriko claims Lightsmith was abducted by an ape-human hybrid race called Snow-Shamblers. In truth, the creatures are quite nurturing—one, Eet-Eet, frees Lightsmith from his brainwashing, then sacrifices her own life to save him when the North-Apes attack. Humbled, the North-Apes make peace with the primitives and give the fugitives a great vessel, the *Longship*, to return home. The alien, believed to be an Oracle promised in their religion, is left behind at their fjord, despite its objections.

Planet of the Apes #26: "Terror on the Planet of the Apes, Phase 2—North Lands" (MC-c)

◆ The Gorilloids capture Brutus' army, killing the horses and mutants, but he forges an alliance with them, promising to destroy the Makers if they help conquer Ape City. Julius and Dan meet up with the *Longship*, which follows the *Simian* to their compound. Assisimians storm the stockade, and Julius proposes to put aside their differences with combat. When he and Jason best the Assisimians' champions, the tribe agrees to a truce. The fugitives return to Ape City in time for Moravius' inauguration, moments before the Gorilloids launch an assault. The Makers, meanwhile, capture and cyborg Thaddeus.

Planet of the Apes #27: "Terror on the Planet of the Apes, Phase 2—Apes of Iron" (MC-c)

◆ Shells flatten the Lawgiver's lodge, killing Physician Zilenus; the Lawgiver, however, survives. Alex is reunited with his parents, and Jason broods angrily until Malagueña kisses him. Ape City's citizens ignite an oil slick. Programmed to fear flame, the cyborgs hold back until the fire is extinguished. Reveling in wanton destruction, the berzerkers ignore Brutus' orders, forcing him to destroy them with a war machine. Brutus and Warko are arrested, Lightsmith reclaims his Wonder Wagon and rebuilding begins. Nearby, Thaddeus reports the Gorilloids' failure to the Makers, who vow to kill every man and ape in the city.

Planet of the Apes #28: "Terror on the Planet of the Apes, Phase 2—Revolt of the Gorilloids" (MC-c)

> NOTE: "Terror on the Planet of the Apes" ends prematurely due to the comic's cancellation, leaving the characters' fates unknown. A comment in the letters page of issue #29 offers this hint of Marvel's plans: "Although 'Terror' has had its lighter moments, so long as Brutus and his ilk are abroad to loot and destroy and propagate their hate philosophies, tragedy will dog the heels of Jason and Alex. True, their saga has been a sad one so far, though we suspect our two protagonists will emerge from this adversity with a better understanding of their world and what really makes it tick." That said…

◆ The Makers signal Thaddeus to kill Lightsmith, who pokes the orangutan with a rusty hypodermic needle, making him ill. In Ape City, a human rabble-rouser tries to incite anti-ape hatred. His words resonate with Jason, who views his parents' burnt cabin and taunts Brutus in his cell. Lightsmith asks Alex's parents to care for Thaddeus as he and Alex warn Moravius about the Makers. The wayfarer reads a medical text claiming glycerin can heal heart ailments; retrieving nitro-glycerin from his wagon, he offers to cure the Lawgiver, mistaking the explosive for medication. The Makers attack in Volkswagen rickshaws, but the apes repel them using captured war machines. An explosion jars the Lawgiver awake as Smashore—a giant albino Gorilloid—levels the city. To their surprise, mutant-drones arrive to help fight the invaders. Smashore shoots the jail, freeing Brutus. Alex, Dan and Julius lure Smashore into a trap, burying him in an avalanche. The mutants then bring the Makers before the Inheritors, who warn Ape City that despite this brief alliance, they will eventually resume their own attack. Moravius tries to make peace with Jason, saying their species can be friends, and that both are capable of good and evil. Moments later, Alex's house catches fire. Before dying, Thaddeus says thugs in black hoods kidnapped the chimp's parents. Alex and Jason mount a rescue, stunned to find the thugs are human. Realizing how wrong he's been about everything, Jason tries to apologize to Brutus for his hatred—but the gorilla is gone.

Planet of the Apes: "Terror on the Planet of the Apes, Phase 2—To Meet the Makers" (MC-c, unpublished)

> NOTE: This "double-length special" was never released due to Marvel's decision to stop publishing Planet of the Apes comics as of issue #29, in response to increased licensing fees. The above details come from a story outline provided by author Doug Moench.

2070 TO 2220

◆ Ape and human cultures expand into the Forbidden Zones, taming wastelands to meet population needs, and growing increasingly isolated and bitter toward one another. Devolving due to the radiation, the humans grow ever more barbaric. A sudden, fierce strain develops out of the docility, heading the human and gorilla armies toward inevitable conflict. During this period, DNA from the House of Mendez's followers mixes with that of other local mutant bands, producing rudimentary psychokinesis and telepathy in New York's mutant population. Mendez's descendants continue to rule until 3979.

Planet of the Apes #11: "Outlines of Tomorrow—A Chronology of the Planet of the Apes" (MC-m)

PUBLISHER / STUDIO
AB . . . . ABC-TV
AC . . . . Adventure / Malibu Comics
AW . . . . Award Books
BB . . . . Ballantine Books
BN . . . . Bantam Books
BW . . . . Brown Watson Books
CB . . . . CBS-TV
CV . . . . Chad Valley Sliderama
DH . . . . Dark Horse Comics
ET . . . . Editorial Mo.Pa.Sa.
FX . . . . 20th Century Fox
GK . . . . Gold Key / Western Comics
HE . . . HarperEntertainment Books
HM . . Harry K. McWilliams Assoc.
MC . . . . Marvel Comics
MR . . . Mr. Comics / Metallic Rose
NB . . . . NBC-TV
PR . . . . Power Records
SB . . . . Signet Books
TP . . . . Topps
UB . . . . Ubisoft

MEDIUM
a . . . . animated series
b . . . . book-and-record set
c . . . . comic book or strip
d . . . . trading card
e . . . . e-comic
f . . . . theatrical film
k . . . . storybook
m . . . . magazine article
n . . . . novel or novelization
p . . . . promotional newspaper
r . . . . recorded audio fiction
s . . . . short story
t . . . . television series
u . . . . unfilmed script or story
v . . . . video game
x . . . . Blu-Ray exclusive
y . . . . young adult novel

MAY 2, 2079

◆ Future NASA astronaut Ronald "Ron" Brent is born.

Return to the Planet of the Apes episode #1: "Flames of Doom" (NB-a)

NOTE: If Brent was born a century after nuclear war leveled the cities of North America, how could he have been in NASA? We know, from Revolution on the Planet of the Apes *and Marvel's "Terror on the Planet of the Apes," that the U.S. government maintained secret locations in Mount Rushmore and Area 51, where they could have continued operating a space program...but wouldn't Brent have known about the future? Ubisoft's PC game and Tim Burton's film remake suffer similar continuity problems.*

AUGUST 6, 2081

◆ Bill Hudson, Jeff Allen and Judy Franklin—NASA astronauts aboard the spacecraft *Venturer*, which launched on an interstellar mission in 1976—read their ship's internal chronometer shortly after take-off. Due to time dilation, although it still seems like 1976 aboard ship, the chronometer reads 2081, proving correct Dr. Stanton's theory of time-thrust...though only the astronauts know it. Hudson transmits a message to NASA's Houston Spaceflight Center, and the *Venturer* vanishes in a strange energy distortion, propelled to the year 3979.

Return to the Planet of the Apes episode #1: "Flames of Doom" (NB-a)

NOTE: One would assume NASA would be unable to receive the message at this point, but given that future *astronaut Ronald Brent is only two years old at this point, anything is possible.*

c. 2090

Alexander ("Alex"), grandson of Caesar and Lisa, is born.

Planet of the Apes #1: "The Monkey Planet—Beneath" (AC-c)

NOTE: Alexander's existence contradicts the timeline in Marvel's issue #11 (which claims Caesar had no heirs after Cornelius), but is supported by Revolution on the Planet of the Apes, *which reveals he and Lisa produced other children. Alex's age is not provided, but this date seems sensible; his parents were obviously born before Lisa's death in 2038, and he appears middle-aged in the Adventure line, set in 2140. A setting of 2090 splits the century between those dates, allowing a half-century until his birth and another 50 years until the comics.*

BETWEEN 2090 AND 3000

◆ Fixer-Two, -Three and -Four, maintenance robots aboard the *Psychedrome*, finish repairing the damage to the crashed alien spacecraft caused by Brutus' mutant-drone army in 2070.

Planet of the Apes #26: "Terror on the Planet of the Apes, Phase 2—North Lands" (MC-c)

NOTE: The repairs, begun in 2070, are predicted to last 20 to 30 years. Whether the Psychedrome *aliens resume their attack upon completing repairs is unknown.*

c. 2090 TO 2110

◆ As the princely heir to Caesar's legacy and bloodline, Alexander enjoys an easy childhood.

Planet of the Apes #5: "Loss" (AC-c)

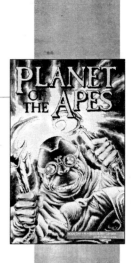

LATE 21st OR EARLY 22nd CENTURY

◆ Caesar's grandchildren are involved in a global war against humanity, destroying Earth's moon in "an orgy of violence and madness."

Revolution on the Planet of the Apes #4: "Caesar's Journal" (MR-c)

NOTE: Ty Templeton, in conceiving Revolution, *planted seeds for a future storyline following up on the idea presented in the original* Planet of the Apes, *that Earth had no moon in 3978. According to Templeton, he conceived the destruction as occurring a century or so after* Conquest of the Planet of the Apes. *Though he never worked out specifics, his notes included the detonation of an Alpha-Omega Bomb on a lunar colony.*

EARLY 22nd CENTURY

◆ Ronald Brent, like all NASA astronauts-in-training in this era, receives a medical education.

Return to the Planet of the Apes episode #11: "Mission of Mercy" (NB-a)

NOTE: This figure is based on his birth in 2079. That there even are astronauts-in-training in this era, however, makes little sense, given the state of the planet.

BEFORE 2109

◆ Despite events on Earth, the arts flourish as mankind continues to hold music dear. The classics become popular once more, while scientific advances in electronics free music of many restrictions. Eventually, a new type of music evolves, known as C-10, created entirely without the aid of a human musician.

Return to the Planet of the Apes episode #9: "Trail to the Unknown" (BB-n)

NOTE: This is revealed in the novelization. How any of this could happen following a nuclear war is anyone's guess.

AUGUST 6, 2109

◆ A NASA spaceship, commanded by Col. Ronald Brent, lifts off from the agency's launch site in California's Mojave Desert. Caught in a time-warp, Brent's ship is propelled in time to the early 3960s.

Return to the Planet of the Apes episode #9: "Trail to the Unknown" (NB-a)

NOTE: Judy Franklin says Brent launched more than 150 years after her mission, but the Venturer *vanished in 1976, 133 years before Brent's disappearance. In any case, Brent's launch date does not jibe with other* Planet of the Apes *lore, as the world has been devastated for over a century at this point.*

PUBLISHER / STUDIO
AB . . . . ABC-TV
AC . . . .Adventure / Malibu Comics
AW . . . . Award Books
BB . . . . .Ballantine Books
BN . . . . Bantam Books
BW . . . . Brown Watson Books
CB . . . . CBS-TV
CV . . . . Chad Valley Sliderama
DH . . . . .Dark Horse Comics
ET . . . . Editorial Mo.Pa.Sa.
FX . . . . 20th Century Fox
GK . . . .Gold Key / Western Comics
HE . . . HarperEntertainment Books
HM . . Harry K. McWilliams Assoc.
MC . . . . Marvel Comics
MR . . . Mr. Comics / Metallic Rose
NB . . . . NBC-TV
PR . . . . .Power Records
SB . . . . Signet Books
TP . . . . .Topps
UB . . . . .Ubisoft

MEDIUM
a . . . . animated series
b . . . . .book-and-record set
c . . . . .comic book or strip
d . . . . trading card
e . . . . e-comic
f . . . . .theatrical film
k . . . . .storybook
m . . . . .magazine article
n . . . . .novel or novelization
p . . . . promotional newspaper
r . . . . .recorded audio fiction
s . . . . short story
t . . . . television series
u . . . . .unfilmed script or story
v . . . . video game
x . . . . .Blu-Ray exclusive
y . . . . young adult novel

◆ Brent's ship is powered by a solar generator and comes equipped with a large volume of modular books and molecular music recordings.

Return to the Planet of the Apes episode #9: "Trail to the Unknown" (BB-n)

NOTE: This is revealed in the novelization.

BEFORE THE 2120s

◆ The spirit of the late General Aldo visits Ollo, a gorilla soldier and loyal Aldonite. The ghost tells Ollo to be strong, for the weak do not deserve to live. "You are my instrument," Aldo says, so Ollo kills his entire tribe and travels to Ape City. Working his way up to head of the military, he enlists many followers to the Aldonite cause.

Planet of the Apes #11: "Warriors" (AC-c)

◆ Ollo's right-hand ape is a fellow gorilla named Col. Noorev.

Blood of the Apes #1: "Part One" (AC-c)

◆ Ollo takes a mate in Ape City. She gives birth to a hugely-built mute, whom they name Grunt. Ollo considers his son's inability to speak, and his pacifistic ways, a disgrace to his family name, and shows him no love or respect.

Planet of the Apes #1: "The Monkey Planet—Beneath" (AC-c)

NOTE: No date is specified, but I assume it to have occurred after Ollo's arrival at Ape City since he slaughtered everyone in his former tribe.

EARLY TO MID 2100s

◆ A rotund, jolly oranguntan known as Travellin' Jack introduces a tradition mirroring the human concept of Christmas. Traveling the land in a horse-drawn cart, he collects items of interest so he can return each year to share them with the citizens of Ape City. After delivering his gifts, much like his human counterpart, Jack departs with a hearty "Ho! Ho! Ho!" Children and adults alike look forward to the annual visits of the simian Santa.

Planet of the Apes #8: "Here Comes Travellin' Jack" (AC-c)

2120 TO 2123

◆ Caesar's grandson Alexander leaves Ape City to explore the land. During his three-year absence, the plague that killed the dogs and cats, then nearly destroyed humanity, spreads once more. Many humans are rendered mute in this latest outbreak, their mental faculties destroyed. The plague kills elder apes and also spreads among rabbits, deer and cattle. Among the casualties are Alexander's parents.

Planet of the Apes #5: "Loss" (AC-c)

NOTE: The plague's resurgence is conjectural, intended to reconcile contradictory accounts of its origin and effects, which place the disease's spread in different eras. Rather than choose one over another, I accept all accounts as having occurred.

2123

◆ Alexander returns from abroad and learns of his parents' deaths. Despite a fear of failing to live up to their legacy, he assumes the leadership of Ape City and earns Ollo's immediate enmity. Alex's insecurity proves unfounded, however, as the masses embrace his rule.

Planet of the Apes #5: "Loss" (AC-c)

DECEMBER 4, 2125

◆ NASA launches the spaceship *Cassiopeia*. All communications cease after takeoff, and the ship is lost. The crew of four—Cmdr. Ulysses, Martinez, Romulus and Sophie—are placed in cryogenic sleep for the voyage's duration. Entering a time-warp, the ship is propelled forward to the year 3889.

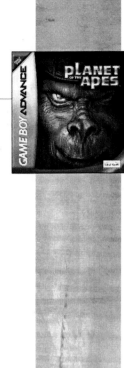

Planet of the Apes (UB-v)

> *NOTE: Ulysses is named for the main character of Pierre Boulle's original source novel,* The Monkey Planet. *This video game does not fit well into* Planet of the Apes *continuity, as NASA should no longer be operating at this point. Moreover, the nature of video games is such that events vary from one game session to the next. Thus, I am including only the game's premise for posterity, but not the specifics of gameplay.*

BEFORE 2139

◆ A female chimp named Coure is exiled from her village for rebuking an elder.

Planet of the Apes #3: "The Monkey Planet—Conquest" (AC-c)

2139

◆ Joshua, a chimp archeologist, saves a human dwarf named Max from villagers about to eat him. He meets Coure, and the two fall in love, adopting Max as a fond pet. Joshua later departs to study the ruined Statue of Liberty, never to return home. He is unaware Coure is pregnant when he leaves.

Planet of the Apes #3: "The Monkey Planet—Conquest" (AC-c)

BEFORE 2140

◆ An elderly orangutan named Zenir is named armorer of Ape City.

Planet of the Apes #1: "The Monkey Planet—Beneath" (AC-c)

◆ Dr. Moto, the city's sadistic chief scientist, is assigned to track the plague in various species.

Planet of the Apes #5: "Loss" (AC-c)

◆ The plague kills a large number of East Coast humans, rendering many survivors as mute savages. A few speaking, reasoning humans survive, but fear of reprisal forces them to keep their abilities a secret. Among them are a young woman and her son, Simon.

Planet of the Apes #1: "The Monkey Planet—Beneath" (AC-c)

> *NOTE: Promotional materials for the Adventure Comics line set this issue 100 years after Caesar's death, which Marvel's timeline in issue #11 places in 2040. Hence, I've set the series in 2140. Dayton Ward's timeline, published in* The Planet of the Apes Chronicles, *dates this series in 2080. The story's title, "The Monkey Planet"—also the title of Pierre Boulle's original source novel—does not appear in the issue, but rather in a trade paperback collection of the first four issues.*

◆ Max, Coure's pet dwarf human, falls into a trap and hurts his leg, causing a permanent scar.

Planet of the Apes #9: "Changes" (AC-c)

PUBLISHER / STUDIO

AB	ABC-TV
AC	Adventure / Malibu Comics
AW	Award Books
BB	Ballantine Books
BN	Bantam Books
BW	Brown Watson Books
CB	CBS-TV
CV	Chad Valley Sliderama
DH	Dark Horse Comics
ET	Editorial Mo.Pa.Sa.
FX	20th Century Fox
GK	Gold Key / Western Comics
HE	HarperEntertainment Books
HM	Harry K. McWilliams Assoc.
MC	Marvel Comics
MR	Mr. Comics / Metallic Rose
NB	NBC-TV
PR	Power Records
SB	Signet Books
TP	Topps
UB	Ubisoft

MEDIUM

a	animated series
b	book-and-record set
c	comic book or strip
d	trading card
e	e-comic
f	theatrical film
k	storybook
m	magazine article
n	novel or novelization
p	promotional newspaper
r	recorded audio fiction
s	short story
t	television series
u	unfilmed script or story
v	video game
x	Blu-Ray exclusive
y	young adult novel

◆ An ape named Shiloh trains to join the Lightfeet, a Navajo-esque tribe with the power of mind control. He learns self-healing techniques, and how to place others in a trance. Training with him is Northstar, an exceptional tracker unable to limit his anger. When Northstar kills unnecessarily, Lightfoot leader Zakula strips him of his name and heritage. Calling himself Dirty Hairy, Northstar begins a life of crime.

Planet of the Apes #20: "Cowboys and Simians" (AC-c)

◆ Mojo, an ape actor, reads about the Old West in ancient books. Fascinated, he forms a team of bounty hunters known as the Ape Riders. Riding with him are Shiloh of the Lightfeet; Deadeye, a quick-drawing ex-bandit; and the Monk, a renowned gambler and the group's physician.

Planet of the Apes Annual—A Day on the Planet of the Apes: "High Noon" (AC-c)

◆ Sgt.-Major Caspian, a soldier in Col. Urchak's gorilla regiment, encounters two humans quite unlike the local savage tribes he's used to meeting.

Urchak's Folly #1: "Chapter One—The Valley" (AC-c)

◆ The Knower, a mutated psychic among the Children of the Forgotten Apes, predicts Caesar's grandson Alexander will save them from enslavement beneath the Ape Management Complex.

Planet of the Apes #2: "The Monkey Planet—Escape" (AC-c)

◆ Dr. Benday, an orangutan scientist in France, experiments with genetics to create Cong, a gorilla several stories high with the mind of a child, who forms a bond with Benday's chimp assistant, Flannagan.

Ape City #2: "See No Evil, Hear No Evil, Speak No Evil" (AC-c)

◆ Benday also works to repair mankind's malfunctioning power plants.

Ape City #1: "Monkey Business" (AC-c)

◆ Benday's bodyguard, Blackjack, teaches Flannagan how to fire a weapon.

Ape City #2: "See No Evil, Hear No Evil, Speak No Evil" (AC-c)

◆ A French ape named Mongo, a musician and troublemaker, befriends Dinga, leader of a pack of Harley Davidson-riding simians called Hell's Apes.

Ape City #3: "Monkey Planet" (AC-c)

◆ Europe's ape civilization develops its own television shows, including *The Mating Game*, *Championship Wrestling With Gorilla Monsoon* and the talk-show *Gorillado*. Television stations include MTV (Monkey Television) and ABC (Ape Broadcasting Company).

Ape City #4: "Monkey See, Monkey Do" (AC-c)

2140

◆ Deetra, the mate of an ape military officer named Tonus, dies as both of their careers are taking off—killed by a human while working to integrate humanity into ape society. Hardened by her death, Tonus earns a reputation as a top assassin with a hatred of humans—and any apes who help them. Violating the apes' most sacred law ("Ape shall never kill ape"), he earns the nickname "Tonus the Butcher." Only Tonus' value to Ollo and Noorev in capturing traitorous apes allows him to sidestep the law with impunity.

Blood of the Apes #1: "Part One" (AC-c)

> NOTE: In an interview conducted as research for this book, author Roland Mann said he'd intended Blood of the Apes *to occur during the first film. However, this does not jibe with the mention of Ollo, which sets it in the same era as Adventure's comics, circa 2140. Mann himself agrees that this placement makes more sense. Dayton Ward's timeline, published in* The Planet of the Apes Chronicles, *dates this storyline in 2095.*

◆ Ollo learns of the Taylorites' existence, and of an ape smuggling ring supplying them with weapons and supplies. Determined to wipe out all speaking, reasoning humans, Ollo sends Tonus to Phis (once known as Memphis, Tenn.) to halt the Taylorites' operations.

Blood of the Apes #2: "Part Two" (AC-c)

◆ Ollo decides to execute Grunt for being a pacifist. Elsewhere in Ape City, Simon practices writing until his mother stops him, fearing for his safety. Ape soldiers later kill her. Alexander, meanwhile, decides to visit the Forbidden City to relive Caesar's journey and become a better leader. Alex's friend Jacob, son of Virgil, joins him. En route, they encounter Coure and Max, bound for the Forbidden City to find Joshua. The four travel to the ruins of the former Ape Management Complex, where Coure goes into labor as mutants close in on them. Back in Ape City, Ollo's Aldonites slay Zenir and use his weapons cache to imprison all humans and non-gorillas alike. Ollo renames the city Gorilla City, proclaiming himself its ruler.

Planet of the Apes #1: "The Monkey Planet—Beneath" (AC-c)

NOTE: *If Jacob is Virgil's son, that would make him rather old, given that Virgil was an adult in* Battle for the Planet of the Apes, *120 years before this issue.*

◆ Ollo orders Vonar, an Ape City sculptor, to build a great statue of Aldo.

Planet of the Apes #3: "The Monkey Planet—Conquest" (AC-c)

◆ Ollo's gorillas catch Simon reading Tolkein's *The Hobbit*. Grunt jumps to the boy's defense, scaring them off and motioning for the boy to read him the story. In the Forbidden City, Alex leads his group to safety. Crazed with radiation sickness, the mutants try to stop them from finding several caged simians, known as the Children of the Forgotten Apes—descendants of apes who tried to join Caesar's rebellion but were trapped in a sub-basement with little food or water. For 150 years, the mutants have kept them captive, torturing them and their progeny. The Forgotten Apes' leader is named Dunzell.

Planet of the Apes #2: "The Monkey Planet—Escape" (AC-c)

◆ Mutated from living in low-level radiation, some of the Forgotten Apes have developed psychic abilities, such as healing and prophecy.

Planet of the Apes #21: "Part One—The Terror Beneath" (AC-c)

◆ Alex frees the Children of the Forgotten Apes, who slay their human tormentors. He offers them refuge in Ape City, but they consider the ruins their home. Coure gives birth, then the group prepares for the return voyage. The Knower—a psychic ape who'd foreseen their arrival—says Ape City faces its darkest hour.

Planet of the Apes #2: "The Monkey Planet—Escape" (AC-c)

◆ Ollo orders all resistant apes shot, then gives Vonar three days to finish the Aldo statue. Alex finds Joshua's body and buries him near the Statue of Liberty, naming the baby after her mate. Jacob encounters Joshua's Aldonite murderers, who torment the orangutan until Simon and Grunt save his life. Dazed and disoriented, Jacob mistakes Simon for an ape. Upon learning what Ollo has done, Alex vows to liberate his people. Ollo orders Dr. Moto to torture and test humans until he can prove the plague's effects are permanent.

Planet of the Apes #3: "The Monkey Planet—Conquest" (AC-c)

◆ Ollo orders Moto to extract the tongues and vocal cords of Joshua's killers without anesthesia, then tells Capt. Pato to find Simon and Grunt. Simon teaches the mute Sign Language. The friends plan to re-take Ape City, but Jacob distrusts the human. Coure dispatches a gorilla guarding the prisoners, who rebel against their captors. As Simon frees the penned humans, Jacob burns his books, afraid of the danger they represent. Aldonites rush the armory, but Grunt knocks them unconscious. Ollo charges his son, who tosses him into a lake. Alex challenges Ollo to a knife-staff duel, slicing Ollo's face and banishing him from Ape City. Vonar later unveils his creation: a statue of Alex.

Planet of the Apes #4: "The Monkey Planet—Battle" (AC-c)

◆ A goofy pair of gorilla guards, JoJo and Frito, are assigned to protect the statue.

Planet of the Apes #6: "Welcome to Ape City" (AC-c)

◆ Ollo's Aldonite followers are banned as well. As word of Ollo's fall from grace spreads, many outsiders relocate to Ape City, hoping it will be a place of peace and harmony once more.

Planet of the Apes #6: "Welcome to Ape City" (AC-c)

◆ The spirit of Aldo reappears to Ollo, promising he will soon have the opportunity to avenge himself.

Planet of the Apes #11: "Warriors" (AC-c)

◆ Ollo forces all of his followers to disfigure their faces to match his own.

Ape Nation #1, Limited Edition: "Who's Who in Ape Nation" (AC-c)

◆ Alex shares a night of passion with Coure. He names Jacob his Defender of the Faith, grants Coure a seat on the council and invites Grunt to lead the army, but the mute declines. He tells Jacob to make Simon an honorary council member, but Jacob disobeys, unwilling to give a human such power. Unaware of Jacob's treachery, Simon resents being left out after planning Ape City's defense.

Planet of the Apes #5: "Loss" (AC-c)

NOTE: Dayton Ward's timeline, published in The Planet of the Apes Chronicles, *dates this storyline between 2080 and 2095.*

◆ Having lived in Ape City for a week, Coure realizes she has found a place she can call home.

Planet of the Apes #6: "Welcome to Ape City" (AC-c)

◆ The council arrests Moto, then drops all charges, deciding Ollo forced him to serve the Aldonites. Furious over the book-burning, Simon stabs Alexander. Doctors save the chimp's life, and Simon flees when Jacob and Grunt catch him trying again. On the run, he meets Capt. Doda, an Aldonite soldier. Doda invites him to meet with Ollo, saying their common enemy makes them allies. Meanwhile, Jacob adds a passage to the 29th Sacred Scroll, 6th Verse: *"Beware the beast 'man,' for he is the Devil's pawn. Alone among God's primates, he kills for sport or lust or greed. Yea, he will murder his brother to possess his brother's land. Let him not breed in great numbers, for he will make a desert of his home and yours. Shun him, drive him back into his jungle lair, for he is the harbinger of death."*

Planet of the Apes #5: "Loss" (AC-c)

NOTE: *Although Marvel's timeline in issue #11 indicates the Sacred Scrolls were penned in 2750, Jacob writes this revered passage more than 600 years prior. It's possible the scrolls were completed in 2750 after being written by various apes over the centuries. Ty Templeton's original concept for* Revolution on the Planet of the Apes, *titled* Combat on the Planet of the Apes, *would have established Gen. Thade (from Tim Burton's remake) as the Lawgiver who wrote the "Beware the beast 'man'" verse.*

◆ Grunt agrees to lead Ape City's new army. Unable to speak except with Sign Language, he communicates his intentions to his soldiers through physical means. Burying his pain over the betrayals of his father and Simon, Grunt sets about restoring the military's honor.

Planet of the Apes #6: "Welcome to Ape City" (AC-c)

◆ In time, Simon regrets his decision to join Doda, who treats him with contempt rather than as an ally.

Planet of the Apes #8: "Here Comes Travellin' Jack" (AC-c)

◆ The council calls Col. Urchak to account for his role in Ollo's coup. As a gesture of loyalty, Urchak brands his face to mirror Ollo's. Eager to see him leave Ape City, the council sends Urchak on a mission to carve out a road into the unknown. As word of the trip spreads, scientists and other curious apes volunteer to join the colonel in his exile, anxious to learn what lies west of the city. Urchak's punishment turns into a major expedition that lasts two years.

Urchak's Folly #2: "Chapter Two—The Bridge" (AC-c)

◆ Rox, a European gorilla warrior, is exiled from her village and travels to France to work as a bodyguard for her late father's dear friend, renowned orangutan scientist Dr. Benday.

Ape City #3: "Monkey Planet" (AC-c)

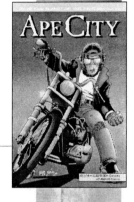

◆ Jacob orders the construction of an ape history museum.

Planet of the Apes #6: "Welcome to Ape City" (AC-c)

◆ In France, as chimp lounge-singer Mongo works a gig at Fats' Palace, a spacecraft arrives in orbit, carrying the Vindicators—Scab, Devon, Moriah, Jo Taylor, MX and π [*pi*]—an assassin team from 1990 sent to alter the future by killing as many apes as possible. Dr. Benday's assistant, Flannagan, boards the ship, steals a power crystal and takes it to Benday's lab. Baboonjas, a baboon martial arts cult led by the sorcerer Krak, sense the crystal's power and decide to steal it. Mongo meets Rox and travels with her to see Benday, who hires them as bodyguards. Chimp crime-boss Big Mal also learns of the crystal and tells an assistant, Weenie, to send the East Side Boys to steal it. After killing 57 apes, the Vindicators discover the crystal missing and track it to Benday's lab. As they burst into the lab, the Baboonjas and gangsters arrive as well.

Ape City #1: "Monkey Business" (AC-c)

NOTE: Dayton Ward's timeline, published in The Planet of the Apes Chronicles, *dates this storyline between 2080 and 2095.*

◆ To create a distraction, Benday blows an ultrasonic whistle, agitating Cong. The three invaders attack the giant gorilla, enabling Flannagan to lead the others to the spaceship. Jo Taylor bars their way, but Benday assures her their intentions are peaceful. Mongo retrieves the crystal from Benday's home, stopping to attend to Cong's wounds. When he doesn't return, Rox and Flannagan head out to find him. Seeing how the apes care for one another, Jo questions the righteousness of her mission. She asks Benday how the planet became ape-controlled, and he tells her the history of Caesar and the war.

Ape City #2: "See No Evil, Hear No Evil, Speak No Evil" (AC-c)

◆ Despite Jo's apparent change of heart, Flannagan doesn't trust her and hides aboard her spaceship.

Ape City #4: "Monkey See, Monkey Do" (AC-c)

◆ Mongo catches up with his friend Dinga and the Hell's Apes, then arrives at Benday's home, now a battleground. Scab launches napalm at the other factions, enabling MX and Devon to search for the crystal. Mongo steals a thug's clothes, but Big Mal sees through his "Rocco" disguise. Devon finds the crystal, which changes hands several times before Mongo grabs it while driving by on Dinga's motorcycle. However, Dinga mistakenly drives off a cliff.

Ape City #3: "Monkey Planet" (AC-c)

PUBLISHER / STUDIO
AB . . . . ABC-TV
AC . . . .Adventure / Malibu Comics
AW . . . . Award Books
BB . . . . .Ballantine Books
BN . . . . Bantam Books
BW . . . . Brown Watson Books
CB . . . . CBS-TV
CV . . . . Chad Valley Sliderama
DH . . . . .Dark Horse Comics
ET . . . . Editorial Mo.Pa.Sa.
FX . . . . 20th Century Fox
GK . . . .Gold Key / Western Comics
HE . . . HarperEntertainment Books
HM . . Harry K. McWilliams Assoc.
MC . . . . Marvel Comics
MR . . . Mr. Comics / Metallic Rose
NB . . . . NBC-TV
PR . . . . .Power Records
SB . . . . Signet Books
TP . . . . Topps
UB . . . . .Ubisoft

MEDIUM
a . . . . animated series
b . . . . .book-and-record set
c . . . . .comic book or strip
d . . . . trading card
e . . . . e-comic
f . . . . .theatrical film
k . . . . .storybook
m . . . . .magazine article
n . . . . .novel or novelization
p . . . . promotional newspaper
r . . . . .recorded audio fiction
s . . . . short story
t . . . . television series
u . . . . .unfilmed script or story
v . . . . video game
x . . . . .Blu-Ray exclusive
y . . . . .young adult novel

◆ Dinga jams the crystal into the bike's gas tank, enabling it to fly. The Hell's Apes force the Baboonjas and gangsters to retreat. Jo orders the Vindicators to drop their weapons—then betrays the apes once she has the crystal, intent on completing her mission. Flannagan, still hiding aboard her ship, pulls the gem free and throws the vessel into a dive. Cong catches it, frees Flannagan and discards the ship. MX pulls Jo from a lake, vowing to continue the fight. That night, Benday's team and the Hell's Apes celebrate at Fats' Palace, where Mongo wows the crowd with his rendition of "Born to Be Wild."

Ape City #4: "Monkey See, Monkey Do" (AC-c)

NOTE: It's unknown if the Vindicators resume their mission, or return to their own era.

◆ Henry, a young ape prince in line for the throne of England—a job he does not want—embarks on an adventure of discovery throughout former Europe. In the course of his travels, he witnesses a variety of ape cultures.

Henry the Ape (AC-c, unpublished)

NOTE: Roland Mann, author of Adventure's Blood of the Apes, *verbally proposed this working concept for a four-issue miniseries to creative director Tom K. Mason as well. Although Mason liked the idea, Mann never submitted anything in writing, nor fleshed out the story beyond a single paragraph, because Malibu opted to scale back its* Planet of the Apes *titles. Mann's notes contain no date for the tale, and he does not recall his intention; for lack of a better placement, I have set it following the* Ape City *miniseries, also set in Europe.*

◆ When an ape named Reador moves to Ape City, its citizens welcome the newcomer: Coure gives Reador a tour of the city; Vonar explains the city's origins and shows off his statue; Heston tells Reador about the Lightfeet and introduces Grunt; and Jacob takes Reador to see the new ape history museum, where Moto outlines plans to control human breeding to prevent the species from regaining dominancy. Reador is mugged in a bad part of town, but Alex intervenes. Reador then heads home to find a gathering of citizens waiting to offer their welcoming wishes.

Planet of the Apes #6: "Welcome to Ape City" (AC-c)

NOTE: This story served as the publisher's way of welcoming new "readers" to the title by providing an overview of the comic's cast. Thus, Reador's gender is unspecified. Heston, of course, is named for actor Charlton Heston.

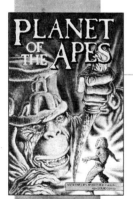

◆ Dr. Moto begins abducting humans and apes to conduct scientific experiments on their bodies.

Planet of the Apes #9: "Changes" (AC-c)

◆ Moto snatches Coure's pet dwarf Max. Dissecting his body for scientific research, Moto puts the man's head in a freezer, ignoring the guilt gnawing at him over his unethical work.

Planet of the Apes #7: "Survival of the Fittest" (AC-c)

◆ Alex, his spirit broken by recent events, grows cold and distant to everyone around him. To reduce his stress, Coure plans a two-day trip into the wilderness with Alex and baby Joshua.

Planet of the Apes #8: "Here Comes Travellin' Jack" (AC-c)

◆ An ornery orangutan named Roto begins picking fights in town, so Grunt challenges him to a brawl that lasts two days with no clear winner. Alex gives Jacob several scrolls to copy, including a record of Caesar's revolution, but Jacob buries the knowledge so future generations will never know the world was once ruled by humans. Alex and Coure venture into the wilderness and are robbed by bandits. An earthquake injures 50 citizens, killing the bandits and Freeta the Seamstress. Grunt and Roto rescue children from a damaged building, bonding in friendship. When Alex and Coure fail to return, scouts locate the bandits' bodies and Coure's jewels, and assume the couple to be dead. Jacob convenes the council to read Alex's last orders, naming Jacob his successor as administrator.

Planet of the Apes #7: "Survival of the Fittest" (AC-c)

◆ Saddened by Alex's and Coure's "deaths," Ape City's citizens eventually go about their lives.

Planet of the Apes #8: "Here Comes Travellin' Jack" (AC-c)

c. DECEMBER 25, 2140

◆ On what was once the humans' Christmas holiday, an ape child named Rayla hears jingle-bells as Travellin' Jack arrives with his horse-drawn cart full of gifts. The city rejoices, but Dr. Moto disapproves, thinking Jack a threat to security. Jack gives JoJo two fruitcakes to share with Frito, but JoJo eats both and claims Jack left him nothing. As Jack finishes his gift-giving and prepares to leave, a grateful child named Lara gives him a present in return. The jolly ape rides over the wilderness, dropping a box of coats, food and first-aid materials for Alex's family, who have fallen ill in the desert. As Coure opens the box, Jack heads for the hills with a hearty "Ho! Ho! Ho!" Meanwhile, hundreds of miles west, Doda and Simon arrive at Ollo's camp.

Planet of the Apes #8: "Here Comes Travellin' Jack" (AC-c)

NOTE: Why Jack neither rescues them, nor alerts others to where they are, is unclear.

2141

◆ Doda meets with Capt. Pato, who begins training Simon to fight in Ollo's name.

Planet of the Apes #10: "Return to the Forbidden City" (AC-c)

◆ Ollo allies with the Children of the Forgotten Apes, coercing Dunzell into waging war against a neighboring tribe, known as the Swamp-Apes.

Planet of the Apes #10: "Return to the Forbidden City" (AC-c)

◆ Col. Urchak makes camp west of the Forbidden Zone, in the rainforest-covered remains of a city. Heat, disease and the cruelty of Urchak's soldiers take their toll on his expedition.

Urchak's Folly #2: "Chapter Two — The Bridge" (AC-c)

◆ Urchak's team begins building a great bridge. Frequent raids by gorillas clearing out the area cause death and suffering to the Mud People, a tribe of aboriginal human-ape hybrids. Miranda, a Taylorite priestess, and her mandrill protector, Argo DiVencenzo, introduce the aborigines to the *Book of Taylor*, the journal of Dr. Lewis Dixon, revealing the time-lost fate of astronaut George Taylor. Prophecy foretells that Taylor will hold the world in his hands, offer salvation and create a new home where man and ape can live together in peace. The Mud People embrace the Taylorite teachings, making Miranda their beloved spiritual leader.

Urchak's Folly #3: "Chapter Three — The Savages" (AC-c)

NOTE: Argo DiVencenzo has the distinction of being one of the only apes ever said to have a first and last name.

PUBLISHER / STUDIO
AB . . . . ABC-TV
AC . . . .Adventure / Malibu Comics
AW . . . . Award Books
BB . . . . .Ballantine Books
BN . . . . Bantam Books
BW . . . . Brown Watson Books
CB . . . . CBS-TV
CV . . . . Chad Valley Sliderama
DH . . . . .Dark Horse Comics
ET . . . . Editorial Mo.Pa.Sa.
FX . . . . 20th Century Fox
GK . . . .Gold Key / Western Comics
HE . . . HarperEntertainment Books
HM . . Harry K. McWilliams Assoc.
MC . . . . Marvel Comics
MR . . . Mr. Comics / Metallic Rose
NB . . . . NBC-TV
PR . . . . .Power Records
SB . . . . Signet Books
TP . . . . Topps
UB . . . . Ubisoft

MEDIUM
a . . . . animated series
b . . . . .book-and-record set
c . . . . .comic book or strip
d . . . . trading card
e . . . . e-comic
f . . . . .theatrical film
k . . . . .storybook
m . . . . .magazine article
n . . . . .novel or novelization
p . . . . promotional newspaper
r . . . . .recorded audio fiction
s . . . . short story
t . . . . television series
u . . . . .unfilmed script or story
v . . . . video game
x . . . . .Blu-Ray exclusive
y . . . . .young adult novel

◆ A gorilla named Jeeta threatens to reveal Moto's unethical activities unless he earns a seat on the council, so Moto kills him and experiments on his body. A human is caught stealing vegetables, meanwhile, and Jacob sentences him to death. Heston protests such anti-human sanctions, but Jacob argues that mankind would rain down violence if he regained the capacity for thought. In the desert, Coure recalls a body with a leg scar in Moto's lab and realizes it was Max. Grunt rescues Coure and her son, but Alex, feverish and amnesiac, wanders away. A young ape named Xanda offers Alex food, and he dubs her Echo since she repeats everything he says. The two save a Swamp-Ape named Narobi from an alligator, and Narobi takes them to his village, where his tribe embrace Alex as a savior sent to protect them from invading gorillas.

Planet of the Apes #9: "Changes" (AC-c)

◆ Alexander leaves Echo in Narobi's care and leads a squad of Swamp-Apes to the Forbidden City. He spots Dunzell and the Children of the Forgotten Apes strategizing with Ollo, but does not remember them. Dunzell's forces surround Alex and bring him to Ollo, who delights at having his greatest enemy handed over to him.

Planet of the Apes #10: "Return to the Forbidden City" (AC-c)

◆ At Coure's request, Grunt takes Joshua to stay with Leta, a trustworthy human female. Jacob disagrees with her decision to leave an ape child with a human.

Planet of the Apes #11: "Warriors" (AC-c)

◆ Coure heads for Moto's lab to accuse him of murder, asking Grunt and Jacob to meet her there. Before she can present her evidence, however, the scientist hypnotizes her into forgetting it.

Planet of the Apes #10: "Return to the Forbidden City" (AC-c)

◆ Moto encases Max's body behind a brick wall to hide the evidence of his crimes.

Planet of the Apes #11: "Warriors" (AC-c)

◆ Simon grows tired of apes ordering him around and beats Pato with a tree branch. Knocking him off a cliff, Simon ignores the gorilla's pleas for assistance as he dangles over the edge.

Planet of the Apes #10: "Return to the Forbidden City" (AC-c)

◆ As Grunt and the Swamp-Apes search for Alex, Ollo clubs the latter unconscious and leaves him to drown in a stream. Dunzell finds Alex's body and uses a mutant healing touch to restore his vitality. The Swamp-Apes battle the ape mutants until Alex intervenes, urging both to avoid the mistakes of mankind. He then offers Ollo a hand in friendship, apologizing for banishing him. After a beat, the gorilla accepts the peace offering, and the two return to Ape City with Dunzell and Narobi.

Planet of the Apes #11: "Warriors" (AC-c)

◆ Heston provides firewood to a bar-owner named Dundee and receives an ale in payment. Roto then smashes a table and offers the wood as payment for his own drinks. Elsewhere, Alex and Coure decide to wed. To afford a gift, JoJo trades Frito's bed to Borno the Traveler for three rifles; the guns to Zinga the Wheeler for two wagon wheels; the wheels to Dugga the Digger for a shovel; the shovel to Looma the Weaver for blankets; the blankets to Gumba the Potter for a serving bowl; the bowl to Farmer Bob for a dozen apples; the fruit to Babo the Baker for a loaf of bread; and the bread to Vonar for a bottle of wine—which Frito breaks over his head. The bell-ringing ceremony is interrupted when Ollo attacks Joshua's caretaker, Wosha. Ollo then departs the city, leaving the infant on Coure's doorstep with a note saying he plans to return as a conqueror.

Planet of the Apes #12: "Bells" (AC-c)

NOTE: It has been 12 months since Alex and Coure first met.

◆ Alex and Coure formally adopt Echo as their child.

Ape Nation #4: "Pains" (AC-c)

NOTE: Herein, the couple refer to the child only as Echo, seemingly forgetting that her name is actually Xanda.

◆ Vonar trades a fake treasure map to Frito and JoJo for most of their belongings. Too dimwitted to realize they've been conned, they follow the map 50 miles outside Ape City. JoJo digs up the treasure since Frito "forgets" to bring a shovel. Buried underground are boxes of Hostess fruit pies, still fresh after a century. The apes gorge themselves on hundreds of pies, then pack up the remaining snacks and head home the next morning, hoping Vonar has another map they can trade for.

Planet of the Apes #13: "Frito & JoJo's X-cellent Adventure" (AC-c)

◆ In France, the strain of Cong's size endangers his health, so Dr. Benday experiments on mass reduction. Cong shrinks so small, however, that Benday must also shrink Mongo to find him. Before Benday can restore their size, two weasels escape Flannagan's grasp and nearly eat them. Flannagan attempts to shrink the animals but reverses the beam, growing them to enormous height. Rox rushes in to slay the beasts, and Benday restores Mongo, but the overheated lab equipment explodes, leaving Cong an inch tall. Benday places the gorilla in a small glass tank until he can figure out how to restore Cong's size.

Planet of the Apes #13: "Ape City: Honey, I Shrunk the Apes" (AC-c)

NOTE: It's unknown if Benday ever finds a way to reverse the shrinking.

◆ A chimpanzee traveler with wanderlust explores the great unknown beyond Ape City, fascinated with artifacts of the past. Losing his map in a stream, he relies on his sense of direction to get home, the knowledge that his loving mate and child await giving him the hope to keep trudging on.

Planet of the Apes Annual—A Day on the Planet of the Apes: "Morning Glory" (AC-c)

◆ In a frontier town, Sheriff Cody arrests an outlaw ape called Little Mo. The outlaw's kinsmen (Pa, Horse and Scumhound) stage a jailbreak. The bounty hunters known as the Ape Riders offer their assistance, and before long, the outlaws are locked up safely in Cody's jail.

Planet of the Apes Annual—A Day on the Planet of the Apes: "High Noon" (AC-c)

NOTE: Mo's kinsmen are named for characters in the classic Western series, Bonanza.

◆ Sent to obtain tar-pit samples, Frito and JoJo discover a fallout shelter stocked with food. The halfwit guards enjoy several dozen cans of beer, then brawl over whether the beverage tastes great or is less filling. Among their other finds: a *Playboy* centerfold (which makes Frito vomit) and a stereo boombox. The goofy gorillas eat and dance until nightfall, then return to Ape City, forgetting their assigned task. Sentenced to seven days outside the city without food or supplies, the buffoonish apes smile, knowing they'll be just fine.

Planet of the Apes Annual—A Day on the Planet of the Apes: "Afternoon Delight" (AC-c)

◆ An ape storyteller scares three children with a campfire story: *Two teenage chimps, Bobo and Jina, spend the night in an abandoned mansion reputed to be haunted. Bobo is afraid, but the thought of getting Jina alone counters his fears. An un-dead vampire mandrill is also in the house, who kills them both and feasts on their blood.* The ape kids are delighted and frightened, so the storyteller relates an even-more terrifying tale, about an ape who, on full-moon nights, turns into a human.

Planet of the Apes Annual—A Day on the Planet of the Apes: "Eternal Dusk" (AC-c)

NOTE: It's highly doubtful the tales can be taken as truthful.

◆ One night in France, Big Mal and Weenie stop by Fats' Palace. Mal tries to purchase the sexual services of a singer named Monique, but Fats defends her honor. The gangsters rough him up until Dinga's biker apes jump to Fats' defense, leaving the club in tatters.

Planet of the Apes Annual—A Day on the Planet of the Apes: "A Night at Fats' Palace—
An Ape City Tale" (AC-c)

◆ The road-weary chimpanzee traveler finally returns to Ape City, to find that his lonesome mate has lit a candle for every night he was away. Now he is home, and their reunion is joyous.

Planet of the Apes Annual—A Day on the Planet of the Apes: "Midnight Tears" (AC-c)

◆ Enjoying a day with his life-mate Keysha, Heston is nearly slain by a bear. Meanwhile, out in space, a Tenctonese officer named Caan tries to spend time with his mate but is interrupted when a meteor storm threatens their ship. Running for the bridge, Caan destroys the meteors and saves his people.

Ape Nation #1, Limited Edition: "Twice Upon a Time" (AC-c)

NOTE: This crossover tale between Planet of the Apes *and* Alien Nation *continues in 2150. Caan is named for James Caan, star of the* Alien Nation *theatrical film. The* Alien Nation *movies, TV series, spinoff novels and other comic books are not covered on this timeline.*

BEFORE 2142

◆ Col. Urchak orders the construction of a great bridge in the wilderness so he can cross a river and conquer all of North America.

Urchak's Folly #2: "Chapter Two—The Bridge" (AC-c)

◆ Urchak's ultimate goal: to prove himself superior to Caesar, Alexander and Ollo.

Urchak's Folly #1: "Chapter One—The Valley" (AC-c)

◆ Some of Urchak's underlings disagree with his plans. Two scientists, Drs. Titus and Morris, conspire with Claudius, the bridge's designer, and Sgt.-Major Caspian, an officer in Urchak's army, to demolish the bridge. Their plan: to force William (a captured mutant from the Forbidden Zone, his mouth stitched closed) to detonate himself and the bridge once they cross, so they can study the savage civilization to the west, free of the military's control.

Urchak's Folly #2: "Chapter Two—The Bridge" (AC-c)

◆ The apes find the remains of Elvis Presley's Graceland and convert it into a bar called Gracela Tavern.

Blood of the Apes #1: "Part One" (AC-c)

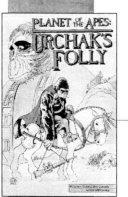

2142

◆ Miranda, the Taylorite priestess of the Mud People, enters Urchak's camp, hoping to make peace with the apes. Urchak ignores her overtures, however, making her his sexual slave for weeks until she escapes.

Urchak's Folly #2: "Chapter Two—The Bridge" (AC-c)

◆ Sebastian Thorne, a mute asylum patient transported through time by Dr. Foucault, evil proprietor of a 19th-century mental institution, arrives in Urchak's era, suffering from amnesia. Six Mud People ambush him in the rainforest, but Miranda spares his life. A squad of gorillas led by Capt. Renko nabs the priestess. Thorne kills Renko with a tree branch, but is captured and brought before Urchak. When he resists, Sgt. Chenko beats him. Urchak then orders Thorne crucified and makes Miranda his slave once more.

Urchak's Folly #1: "Chapter One — The Valley" (AC-c)

NOTE: *Dayton Ward's timeline, published in* The Planet of the Apes Chronicles, *dates this storyline between 2080 and 2095.*

◆ William telepathically warns Thorne that they're all about to die. The apes assign him to the bridge construction crew. Titus and Morris ask permission to search for herbs across the river. Chenko denies the request, but Caspian approves it, humiliating Chenko into hitting Caspian with an axe. Claudius, unwilling to sacrifice William, decides to destroy the bridge himself. Titus and Morris dash across the water, followed by Thorne and William. Claudius then pulls a grenade pin, reducing the bridge to timbers.

Urchak's Folly #2: "Chapter Two — The Bridge" (AC-c)

◆ Urchak executes and crucifies Caspian for his role in the conspiracy. Across the river, Taylorites surround Thorne's group. Miranda's mandrill protector, Argo DiVencenzo, shares with them the *Book of Taylor* and explains the prophecy of Taylor's resurrection. Hoping Miranda might be able to help him recover his missing past, Thorne helps Argo rescue the priestess. Crossing back to Urchak's camp, Thorne slips into the general's room to find Miranda lying naked on a bed. Urchak beats him near-fatally, jarring his blocked memory, then orders both humans executed. Knowing they'll die the next day, they enjoy a night of love-making in their cell.

Urchak's Folly #3: "Chapter Three — The Savages" (AC-c)

◆ The Taylorites attack at dawn, killing many apes and freeing Thorne and Miranda. Thorne shoots Chenko, and a massacre ensues as he and Miranda escape into the jungle. There, they locate the ruins of Foucault's Institute for Mental Incurables. Urchak follows, and Thorne tricks him into entering the time machine, propelling the ape back to the year 1900. Thorne and Miranda find the village in flames, the Taylorites in control. Chenko staggers into the clearing, killing Titus, and Argo fells the giant gorilla with an axe. Burying the dead, Thorne and Miranda head for the Forbidden Zone, inviting William to join them.

Urchak's Folly #4: "Chapter Four — The War" (AC-c)

NOTE: *The fates of Thorne, Miranda and William are unrecorded.*

◆ Tonus, a gorilla bounty hunter and firm protector of ape dominancy, visits Phis (the area once known as Memphis, Tenn.) to detain a chimp suspected of helping humans. Tonus delivers him dead to Col. Noorev, who chides him for killing a fellow ape. Across the Mizziphee (Mississippi) River, in a Taylorite colony, a woman named Myndith teaches human children how to read. Her partner, Luthor, says their ape contact has been caught — their second contact killed in the past three weeks. Frustrated, they push on with educating humanity.

Blood of the Apes #1: "Part One" (AC-c)

NOTE: *Tonus' claim that Ollo assigned him to Phis would seem to place this story before Ollo's exile in 2140, but issue #2 sets it after* Urchak's Folly, *which occurs two years beyond that point. I've placed* Blood of the Apes *directly after* Urchak's Folly, *assuming Ollo assigned Tonus to Phis before his exile.*

◆ Myndith's colleague Richard sends a fellow Taylorite named Marcus to steal weapons from the apes.

Blood of the Apes #2: "Part Two" (AC-c)

◆ Tonus gets drunk at Gracela Tavern, then stumbles outside and mistakes a female ape—Valia, an animal-rights activist favoring human-ape equality—for his lost love, Deetra.

Blood of the Apes #1: "Part One" (AC-c)

◆ Marcus is arrested for the weapons theft, setting off an alarm.

Blood of the Apes #2: "Part Two" (AC-c)

◆ Tonus rushes outside to investigate, stunned when Marcus speaks.

Blood of the Apes #1: "Part One" (AC-c)

◆ Myndith chastises Richard for sending Marcus on a fool's mission. She breaks Marcus out of jail, and many blame the ape activists. Valia meets with a human named Edward and an ape called R.E., who supply her with weapons for the Taylorites. Argo DiVencenzo warns them not to head north, for the Mud People will attack any apes they see. As they leave, Tonus apprehends her for arming humans.

Blood of the Apes #2: "Part Two" (AC-c)

◆ Gen. Stedal arrives from Ape City, sent to handle Noorev's human problem. Several Taylorites beat Tonus with a baseball bat, but Valia convinces Richard to spare the ape in an effort to make him see the light. Myndith ponders their leniency, hoping that showing such compassion to "the hardest of all apes" might make others see mankind's worth. As a gesture of peace, she rallies the Taylorites to march on Phis unarmed. After they leave him, Tonus locates a weapons cache and sights a human mother and her child in his rifle scope.

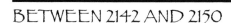

Blood of the Apes #3: "Part Three" (AC-c)

◆ Tonus lowers his weapon, however, letting the family live. En route to Phis, he encounters Noorev's army preparing to slaughter every human in the area. He protests, claiming the marchers pose no threat, and steals a horse to warn Valia, but the soldiers shoot them both. Stedal beats the bounty hunter for betraying apekind, and Valia intercedes, taking a bullet for Tonus, who admits his love for her before dying. Pulling off a mask to reveal her true identity—the human, Myndith—she admits she loves him as well, then dies in his arms.

Blood of the Apes #4: "Part Four" (AC-c)

BETWEEN 2142 AND 2150

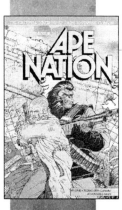

◆ Roto is jailed for a string of offenses.

Ape Nation #1: "Plans" (AC-c)

◆ Keysha, Heston's pregnant life-mate, dies from a prolonged illness, their unborn child dying with her. Heston learns to get on with his life but is never quite the same. Growing more serious with the passing years, he enlists in the ape military as a border guard.

Ape Nation #1, Limited Edition: "Twice Upon a Time" (AC-c)

NOTE: It's not clear when Keysha dies. I have chosen this gap in time since it takes place before the events of Ape Nation. However, there is room for debate.

◆ Alexander and Coure add a third child to their family: a sister to Joshua and Echo, named Zina. A couple of years later, they have a fourth, whom they call Milo.

Ape Nation #4: "Pains" (AC-c)

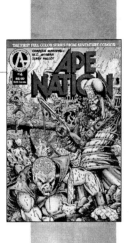

NOTE: The children's birth years are unspecified, but most likely occur before Ape Nation, *given their ages in the miniseries and in the monthly series thereafter.*

◆ Winnipeg of the Lightfeet dreams of an alien takeover of Ape City, including the time and place the alien spaceship will touch down.

Ape Nation #1: "Plans" (AC-c)

NOTE: This, of course, begs the question of why he did not prevent the events that follow.

◆ Simon befriends a wolf pup, which he names Dingo. Over time, Simon grows quite powerful, acquiring a legion of human followers and mounting frequent attacks on the apes.

Ape Nation #1, Limited Edition: "Twice Upon a Time" (AC-c)

NOTE: The pup's name changes during the course of the story, from Dingo to Lobo.

◆ This earns him the nickname Simon the Slaughterer.

Ape Nation #1: "Plans" (AC-c)

c. 2150

◆ A Tenctonese refugee ship commanded by Capt. Caan experiences equipment failure and breaks away from the rest of its fleet, headed for Earth to seek sanctuary from slavers.

Ape Nation #1, Limited Edition: "Who's Who in Ape Nation" (AC-c)

NOTE: Ape Nation, a crossover with the Alien Nation *franchise, marks the second of three thwarted alien takeovers of Earth. The first occurs in the 1980s, the third in 2200. The miniseries is undated, but is said to occur several years after Ollo's exile. Given Simon's age, as well as those of Alex's and Coure's children, it would appear ten or so years have passed since Simon's betrayal. Thus, I have set this tale circa 2150, though there is room for debate.*

◆ Sucked into a black hole, the Tenctonese ship is propelled through a space-time warp, to land beyond the Forbidden Zone in an alternate future. Caan's brother Danada stages a coup, imprisoning him.

Ape Nation #1: "Plans" (AC-c)

◆ Danada also imprisons his sisters, Pascha and Elysa.

Ape Nation #2: "Pasts" (AC-c)

◆ When ape soldiers spot the ship while hunting for Simon, the council promotes Heston to special officer and sends him to investigate. His team includes Packer, who carries all of his belongings at all times; Winnipeg of the Lightfeet; Roto, pardoned for his crimes in exchange for undertaking the mission; and Jacob's naïve nephew Bartholomew ("Bart"), a teen who volunteers so he can travel the world.

Ape Nation #1: "Plans" (AC-c)

◆ Some speculate that Heston agreed to take Bart just to irritate Jacob, with whom Heston does not get along. However, Heston never confirms or denies the validity of this rumor.

Ape Nation #1, Limited Edition: "Who's Who in Ape Nation" (AC-c)

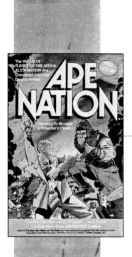

◆ Danada allies with Ollo and Simon, consolidating their forces into a single, massive army. Heston's group travels six weeks without incident before meeting the combined forces. Badly outnumbered, the five apes fall in battle, and Heston is taken aboard the alien ship, shackled and bleeding.

Ape Nation #1: "Plans" (AC-c)

◆ The combined forces storm the countryside. Elysa escapes her cell, freeing Caan and Heston. Simon stabs her with a knife, and the others pummel him to a pulp, then flee on horseback. Danada strikes Ollo for failing to capture them, earning the gorilla's hatred. Simon takes Dingo to find the prisoners, his partners conspiring to eliminate him from the troika. Caan and Heston, meanwhile, hide in a farmhouse. Caan drinks a bucket of sour milk, wanders off drunk and falls into a lake, just as Roto arrives on the scene.

Ape Nation #2: "Pasts" (AC-c)

◆ Roto tosses Caan at Simon. Tenctonese guards arrest them all, and Simon realizes Ollo and Danada betrayed him. To atone for his crimes, he helps the others fight the guards. The trio then rush to find Heston and stop the invasion. Heston discovers Elysa alive, only one heart pierced by the blade, and helps her thwart Danada's plans. Out in the woods, a boar chases Bart, causing him to fall from a tree; feeling useless, he returns to Ape City. Meanwhile, Danada orders his guards to assassinate Ollo.

Ape Nation #3: "Pawns" (AC-c)

◆ Heston and Elysa burst into Danada's quarters just as Ollo slays the alien. Escaping through a trash chute, they separate to foster dissent among their enemies. Before long, the aliens and apes turn on one another. Simon, Roto and Caan continue fighting despite impossible odds, until Bart returns with the Lightfeet and a battalion from Ape City, who quickly defeat the combined army. Ollo ultimately escapes on horseback, and Heston and Elysa settle down in the woods to "get wrecked" on fruit juice and sour milk.

Ape Nation #4: "Pains" (AC-c)

◆ The Lightfeet realize their culture's end is impending when eight of nine prophesied omens come true. Zakula, the tribe's leader, awaits the final omen—seven crows roosting together—so his people can battle a great evil.

Planet of the Apes #22: "Part Two—The Land of No Escape" (AC-c)

◆ Relaxing with Elysa, Heston recalls his life-mate Keysha and their unborn child. Elysa consoles him over their deaths, then leads him back to their camp.

Planet of the Apes #13: "Ape Nation—Drunken Interlude" (AC-c)

◆ Caan, Heston and Elysa free those imprisoned in Danada's coup—including Packer, who has absorbed Winnipeg's spirit into his own to save the other's life, and who decides to live with the Lightfeet tribe therein. Elysa and Caan give Heston a canteen of wine and a necklace, symbolizing the eternity of their friendship. Bidding farewell, the Tenctonese take to the stars as the simians return to Ape City, each changed by their mutual experiences.

Ape Nation #4: "Pains" (AC-c)

◆ Simon makes a home within the ruins of the Statue of Liberty, from which he spies on Ollo's activities.

Planet of the Apes #21: "Part One — The Terror Beneath" (AC-c)

NOTE: *Dayton Ward's timeline, published in* The Planet of the Apes Chronicles, *dates this storyline between 2080 and 2095.*

◆ For seven nights, a guilt-ridden Moto dreams of Max breaking through the wall to expose his evils. The scientist tries to bury himself in his work, but fails to assuage his anxiety. Elsewhere, Frito brings JoJo a cannon for them to guard the statue of Alexander, accidentally blowing up the monument in the process; horrified, he falls over a cliff. JoJo begs him not to die, promising a house, horses and bananas if he survives, and the mention of bananas revives him. Heston briefs Coure and Alex about the Tenctonese front, which they decide to withhold from the masses. That night, Milo has a nightmare of Ollo returning to kill them. Moto, meanwhile, hangs himself in his lab.

Planet of the Apes #18: "Gorillas in the Mist" (AC-c)

◆ An ex-Lightfoot once named Northstar (now called Dirty Hairy) abducts Princess Zo, daughter of King Louie, the orangutan leader of New Dodge. Louie asks the Ape Riders to find her, but four henchapes (Dolenz, Tork, Nesmith and Jones) stand in their way. Hairy shoots Shiloh, putting him in a brief coma, then kills Monk. Deadeye shoots three of the outlaws, forcing Jones to reveal Dirty Hairy's location. A former thespian, Mojo poses as Zakula to fool the fallen Lightfoot, but Hairy sees through his disguise. Shiloh kills the fallen Lightfoot, promising one day to offer his own life to atone for violating the Lightfoot code.

Planet of the Apes #20: "Cowboys and Simians" (AC-c)

NOTE: *Hairy's henchapes are, of course, named for the musical group The Monkees.*

◆ In the Forbidden City, a ragged group of human mutants holds a séance in the ruins of Ape Management, hoping to summon the spirit of Governor Arnold Jason Breck so he can save mankind. Breck's ghost destroys them, however, disgusted by their mutations and determined to rid the world of all non-humans.

Planet of the Apes #21: "Part One — The Terror Beneath" (AC-c)

◆ Shiloh of the Lightfeet senses an intense evil near the Forbidden Zone. Despite the odds against them, the Ape Riders head out to confront the source of his vision.

Planet of the Apes #22: "Part Two — The Land of No Escape" (AC-c)

◆ Roto arrests a speaking human named Anne (granddaughter of former astronaut August Anne Burrows), whom Jacob tortures to learn her tribe's location. In the Forbidden City, Breck kills the Children of the Forgotten Apes. Only Dunzell, absent at the time, survives—but after years of living in radiation, he is now dying. Cared for in Ape City's medical center, Dunzell whispers "seize her," then expires. Breck burns the Swamp-Apes' village, killing Narobi and Echo, then slays Ollo's troops as well, choking the general to death.

Planet of the Apes #21: "Part One — The Terror Beneath" (AC-c)

NOTE: *As if the ghosts of Breck and (two issues later) Caesar weren't unusual enough, this four-part story reveals that August Anne Burrows, last seen in issue #17—set in 1992—is still alive and leading a human colony in Mexico. At this point, she would be nearly 160 years old...must be the radiation.*

PUBLISHER / STUDIO
AB . . . . ABC-TV
AC . . . .Adventure / Malibu Comics
AW . . . . Award Books
BB . . . . .Ballantine Books
BN . . . . Bantam Books
BW . . . . Brown Watson Books
CB . . . . CBS-TV
CV . . . . Chad Valley Sliderama
DH . . . . .Dark Horse Comics
ET . . . . Editorial Mo.Pa.Sa.
FX . . . . 20th Century Fox
GK . . . .Gold Key / Western Comics
HE . . . HarperEntertainment Books
HM . . Harry K. McWilliams Assoc.
MC . . . . Marvel Comics
MR . . . Mr. Comics / Metallic Rose
NB . . . . NBC-TV
PR . . . . .Power Records
SB . . . . Signet Books
TP . . . . Topps
UB . . . . Ubisoft

MEDIUM
a . . . . animated series
b . . . . .book-and-record set
c . . . . .comic book or strip
d . . . . trading card
e . . . . e-comic
f . . . . .theatrical film
k . . . . .storybook
m . . . . .magazine article
n . . . . .novel or novelization
p . . . . promotional newspaper
r . . . . .recorded audio fiction
s . . . . short story
t . . . . television series
u . . . . .unfilmed script or story
v . . . . video game
x . . . . .Blu-Ray exclusive
y . . . . .young adult novel

◆ Jacob urges Alex to take the talking human issue seriously, saying Anne's existence endangers society. Anne tricks JoJo into giving her a knife, then locks him up with Frito and escapes. Elsewhere, a Lightfoot named Gayla spots seven crows roosting; recognizing the ninth omen, Zakula calls his people to battle, and Packer asks Heston to join them. Breck goes on to kill Travellin' Jack, the Ape Riders and the Nameless Apes, then meets a scavenging human tribe and promises to help them restore human dominance. They embrace him as a savior, and Simon offers Alex and Coure his assistance in the coming war.

Planet of the Apes #22: "Part Two—The Land of No Escape" (AC-c)

◆ Despite Jacob's objection, Alex accepts Simon's offer. Zakula "hears" Dunzell's final words in Heston's mind, realizes they refer to Caesar and instructs his tribe to summon Alexander so they can revitalize the First Lawgiver. As Ape City's council mounts a defense against Breck's rising numbers, Jacob accuses Simon of aiding the enemy, but Grunt forces Jacob to leave, forgiving his friend despite all he's done. Roto finds Anne, but instead of arresting her, he brings her to Dundee's to hear her story. And in the Lightfeet camp, a shimmering glow surrounds the tribe as Caesar's spirit returns from the afterworld.

Planet of the Apes #23: "Part Three—The Final Conquest" (AC-c)

NOTE: *Given the crying statue of Caesar in the year 2670, as seen in* Battle for the Planet of the Apes, *the First Lawgiver's return from the dead may not be so difficult a premise to accept.*

◆ Simon urges Roto and Grunt to help him overpower Breck's followers without bloodshed. Caesar fights Breck's spirit as others battle on the physical plane. Breck gains the upper hand, but Alex distracts him, offering to care for the humans if Breck ends the war. As Caesar engulfs Breck's spirit, the Lightfeet join minds to lend their power, sacrificing themselves to close the door to the spirit-world. Normalcy restored, Simon and Anne urge the council to bridge the species divide. Jacob resists, but ultimately agrees to give it a try. Alex decides the future lies not on the path of fear and racism, but in making the world a better place.

Planet of the Apes #24: "Part Four—Last Battle" (AC-c)

NOTE: *Sadly, like his grandfather Caesar, Alexander is rather naïve in his hope for a peaceful future.*

◆ Somehow, JoJo and Frito end up traveling through time.

Planet of the Apes: "Back from the Future" (AC-c, unpublished)

NOTE: *This story treatment was never scripted or published due to Adventure Comics losing the* Planet of the Apes *license. This brief synopsis was provided by author Charles Marshall. No further details are available.*

AFTER 2150

◆ The gorillas of Ape City—descendents of those worst persecuted during the so-called Silent Times—continue to harbor resentment toward mankind. Many wish to exterminate the species, but the chimpanzees prefer to live in peace with humanity.

Empire on the Planet of the Apes (MR-c, unpublished)

NOTE: *Details of this proposed sequel to* Revolution on the Planet of the Apes *were by authors Ty Templeton and Joe O'Brien.*

◆ Many gorillas, unable to accept men as equals, leave Ape City to form their own community in the hills. Convinced God would not want all apes to live together—or among humans—the self-exiled form the High Clans, also known as the Hill Tribes. Though they value Caesar's decree that "Ape shall not kill ape," the gorillas prefer the words of Jacob: "Beware the beast 'man.'"

Revolution on the Planet of the Apes #5: "Ape Shall Not Kill Ape" (MR-c)

NOTE: These events are said to occur at the time of Caesar, but "Terror on the Planet of the Apes" and Malibu's comics both feature gorillas in Ape City throughout the century following Caesar's death in 2040. What's more, the "Beware the beast" stanza wasn't written until 2140, as shown in Malibu's issue #5. Revolution co-author Ty Templeton, in discussing this point via e-mail, suggests the seeds of the gorilla-chimp conflict were planted during Caesar's time, but that the societal split occurred a century later, after 2150. It's unknown if gibbons, mandrills, baboons, macaques and lemurs (all featured in Apes *lore) choose to remain in Ape City, or to leave with the others.*

◆ A civil war erupts between these factions, lasting a century. Orangutans and bonobos inhabit both camps; as the smartest apes, the two species assume responsibility for the sciences and schooling.

Empire on the Planet of the Apes (MR-c, unpublished)

◆ Still, in an area known as the Valley, apes and humans do achieve a true peace.

Revolution on the Planet of the Apes #5: "Ape Shall Not Kill Ape" (MR-c)

◆ Eventually, the apes develop a monetary system, using "simian silver" pieces as currency.

Return to the Planet of the Apes episode #9: "Trail to the Unknown" (NB-a)

NOTE: This apparently replaces the barter system in use at the time of the Adventure comics line. The existence of a monetary system is supported by Cornelius' statement, in the first film, that he is up for a raise.

◆ This currency is measured in units called frailins and gridgens.

The Ape News (HM-p)

PUBLISHER / STUDIO

AB	ABC-TV
AC	Adventure / Malibu Comics
AW	Award Books
BB	Ballantine Books
BN	Bantam Books
BW	Brown Watson Books
CB	CBS-TV
CV	Chad Valley Sliderama
DH	Dark Horse Comics
ET	Editorial Mo.Pa.Sa.
FX	20th Century Fox
GK	Gold Key / Western Comics
HE	HarperEntertainment Books
HM	Harry K. McWilliams Assoc.
MC	Marvel Comics
MR	Mr. Comics / Metallic Rose
NB	NBC-TV
PR	Power Records
SB	Signet Books
TP	Topps
UB	Ubisoft

MEDIUM

a	animated series
b	book-and-record set
c	comic book or strip
d	trading card
e	e-comic
f	theatrical film
k	storybook
m	magazine article
n	novel or novelization
p	promotional newspaper
r	recorded audio fiction
s	short story
t	television series
u	unfilmed script or story
v	video game
x	Blu-Ray exclusive
y	young adult novel

Part 8: Upside-Down World (2200 to 3084)

c. 2200

◆ The Masters—simian aliens from Mars—invade Earth and enslave humans still living in the ruined cities. Human scientists, brainwashed to work for the aliens, act as a controlling force known as the Generals, with drone-tripod war machines decimating the planet beyond its war-torn state. Eventually, mankind rises up against the alien apes, but their victories are futile, for the alien hold on Earth remains strong.

Planet of the Apes #23: "Prologue: Future Imperfect" (MC-c)

> NOTE: This marks the third alien invasion of Earth, following others in the 1980s and 2150. Published in issues #23-30 of Marvel UK's Planet of the Apes *title, the story first ran in* Killraven, Marvel's War of the Worlds *spinoff. When the weekly format required additional stories beyond those from the U.S. run,* Killraven *was adapted to fit the* Apes *mythos. Several references to* Killraven *were overlooked, however, and continuity snafus abound. No date is provided, but centuries have passed since the ape revolt. The timeline in Marvel's issue #11 cites 2220 as "the last gasp of human aggressiveness," so I have placed the* Apeslayer *storyline in that era. There is room for debate (or, better, for ignoring the* Apeslayer *saga altogether, as it's quite possibly the most irreconcilable* Apes *spinoff to date).*

◆ Dr. Kempleton, a human scientist, is among those to serve the Martian simians. This arrangement allows him to continue conducting his ribonucleic acid (RNA) experiments.

Planet of the Apes #25: "The Sirens of 7ᵗʰ Avenue" (MC-c)

◆ The Masters capture and brainwash a rebel scientist named Raker, making him a tyrannical General and placing him in charge of gathering human youths for gladiator training. Despite the aliens' control, Raker secretly plots against them, searching for a youth with the potential to throw off their yoke of slavery.

Planet of the Apes #24: "The Birth of Apeslayer" (MC-c)

◆ Drone tripods level the remains of Manhattan, Boston and San Francisco. In Manhattan, Maureen Dozer tries to get her sons to safety, crossing the bridge to Welfare Island moments before the aliens destroy it. Several crazed mutants, hospitalized by a resistance group led by Dr. Ann Carver, escape and attack anyone in sight. Carver saves the Dozer family, hiding for 15 days until spotting an approaching helicopter.

Planet of the Apes #23: "Prologue: Future Imperfect" (MC-c)

◆ In the chopper is Gen. Raker, who orders a guard named Saunders to kill them all except for one of the boys, whom he senses has a special power that will one day enable him to defeat the simian aliens. He brings the child, Jonathan Dozer, before his masters, who commence the boy's gladiator training.

Planet of the Apes #24: "The Birth of Apeslayer" (MC-c)

PUBLISHER / STUDIO
AB . . . . ABC-TV
AC . . . . Adventure / Malibu Comics
AW . . . . Award Books
BB . . . . Ballantine Books
BN . . . . Bantam Books
BW . . . . Brown Watson Books
CB . . . . CBS-TV
CV . . . . Chad Valley Sliderama
DH . . . . Dark Horse Comics
ET . . . . Editorial Mo.Pa.Sa.
FX . . . . 20th Century Fox
GK . . . . Gold Key / Western Comics
HE . . . HarperEntertainment Books
HM . . Harry K. McWilliams Assoc.
MC . . . . Marvel Comics
MR . . . Mr. Comics / Metallic Rose
NB. . . . . NBC-TV
PR . . . . Power Records
SB . . . . Signet Books
TP . . . . Topps
UB . . . . Ubisoft

MEDIUM
a . . . . animated series
b . . . . book-and-record set
c . . . . comic book or strip
d . . . . trading card
e . . . . e-comic
f . . . . theatrical film
k . . . . storybook
m . . . . magazine article
n . . . . novel or novelization
p . . . . . . promotional newspaper
r . . . . recorded audio fiction
s . . . . short story
t . . . . television series
u . . . . unfilmed script or story
v . . . . video game
x . . . . Blu-Ray exclusive
y . . . . young adult novel

c. 2200 TO 2205

◆ Jonathan Dozer spends five years learning swordplay, karate, savate and wrestling, excelling in them all, under the tutelage of a cruel alien named Warlord. Having bested his opponents, Dozer earns the name "Apeslayer."

Planet of the Apes #24: "The Birth of Apeslayer" (MC-c)

NOTE: This span of time is an estimate, based on his appearance as a boy of 12 or 13 when abducted, and 17 or 18 after his training.

c. 2205

◆ Apeslayer eventually escapes the Martian simians, injuring Warlord in the process.

Planet of the Apes #24: "The Birth of Apeslayer" (MC-c)

◆ Warlord's face and arm are replaced with cybernetic implants, leaving him hungry for revenge.

Planet of the Apes #28: "Airport of Death" (MC-c)

c. 2205 TO 2206

◆ Apeslayer spends 12 months foraging in the ruins of Queens, eating whatever cats, dogs and rabbits he can find, and reading old books to revisit life before the invasion. He learns that the alien apes genetically breed human slaves as sirens to lure others to their doom. In Brooklyn Heights, he kills an alien molesting a human female, then escapes to Staten Island, where he meets a resistance cell called the Freemen.

Planet of the Apes #24: "The Birth of Apeslayer" (MC-c)

NOTE: As with the television series, the Apeslayer storyline features dogs centuries after their extinction.

c. 2206 TO 2212

◆ Apeslayer lives among the Freemen for six years, eventually becoming their leader.

Planet of the Apes #24: "The Birth of Apeslayer" (MC-c)

c. 2212

◆ The Freemen sneak aboard an ancient ferry bound for Manhattan to terrorize the former mayor, who has betrayed humanity for comfort and power. This infuriates the aliens and draws new members to the rebel cause. Apeslayer and a fellow rebel, Dagger, decide to breach Raker's defenses and kill the traitor.

Planet of the Apes #24: "The Birth of Apeslayer" (MC-c)

◆ The Freemen storm Grand Central Station. Defeating an alien named Scrapper, Apeslayer battles several mutant creatures bred by Raker. Making his way to the General's office, he fatally impales the man with a shard of machinery, breaking the aliens' hold over him. Raker thanks him for ending his nightmare.

Planet of the Apes #23: "Prologue: Future Imperfect" (MC-c)

◆ Raker tells Apeslayer he has a special power enabling him to defeat the simian Martians, and that he chose the boy for that very reason. The old scientist then dies, his dignity restored. As Apeslayer exits at 7th Avenue, a trio of sirens try to ensnare him with their alluring gaze.

Planet of the Apes #24: "The Birth of Apeslayer" (MC-c)

◆ Immune to siren song, Apeslayer kills attacking mutants with help from Freemen named Eagle and Mala. A war machine opens fire, and a mutated alligator tries to eat them. He tricks the two into colliding, and they escape to South Street Seaport. Another Freeman, Arrow, spots aliens unloading human slaves. Freeing the slaves, the rebels steal a ferry, topple a drone tripod and return to their Staten Island base. Viewing the attack from his lab, Dr. Kempleton informs the Masters of the damaged war machine.

Planet of the Apes #25: "The Sirens of 7th Avenue" (MC-c)

◆ Master Twelve orders a scout to investigate, and the pilot finds the abandoned ferry on fire. Kempleton's superiors recall him to New Jersey, assigning Skarlet, Queen of the Sirens, to kill the Freemen. Skarlet infiltrates the rebel base, entrances Arrow, Mala and others, and ensnares Apeslayer in a tripodal machine that takes him to Madison Square Garden. The overlords order Slasher, a cybernetic gladiator, to kill him, but Apeslayer breaks free of his bonds, kills Slasher and escapes with his fellow rebels.

Planet of the Apes #26: "Death in the Ape-Pit" (MC-c)

◆ Master Four and Warlord prepare a trap to capture Apeslayer at LaGuardia Airport, planting a weapons cache there to lure him in.

Planet of the Apes #28: "Airport of Death" (MC-c)

◆ Besieged by Martians, the Freemen hide in a museum until the aliens destroy it. Mala dislodges a hanging vessel to kill one simian, and Apeslayer impales another with a silver-star. They demand the location of the aliens' supply cache, and the dying ape sputters "LaGuardia." The Freemen load guns and armor from the museum into an abandoned truck, then head back to Staten Island.

Planet of the Apes #27: "The Museum of Terror" (MC-c)

◆ A drone tripod destroys the Verrazano Narrows Bridge, dropping Apeslayer and Mala in the water. The men topple the machine by loosening the sandstone upon which it rests, then swim ashore. They locate the airport weapons cache, but are quickly subdued and sentenced to fight in the Arena of Mutants.

Planet of the Apes #28: "Airport of Death" (MC-c)

◆ Apeslayer kills several mutant apes, including his final opponent (Kre-kor) and an elite force of soldiers. Warlord enters the arena, slams him with a metal arm and orders him prepped for surgery sans anesthesia. Sandra "San" Simian, a human molecular biologist running the aliens' Alteration Division, watches the games with Warlord, then betrays the Martians, summoning a mutant named Grok Zom to help her storm the prison and rescue the Freemen.

Planet of the Apes #29: "The Mutant Slayers" (MC-c)

◆ Bursting into the surgery ward to rescue Apeslayer, the Freemen engage Warlord's Red Canal Units. Grok Zom and Sandra lead the men to safety, but mutated animals in the ruins of Yankee Stadium try to eat them. Warlord arrives as Zom aids Apeslayer in fighting a giant acid-spitting crab. Aliens and Freemen stand by as their leaders face off. Apeslayer dissolves Warlord's arm in the crab's body fluids, warning that if he continues enslaving humanity, he'll receive no such mercy in the future. The Freemen escape through a subway tunnel, hoping one day to enjoy the stadium for its original purpose.

Planet of the Apes #30: "Apeslayer Dies at Dawn" (MC-c)

NOTE: *The fates of Apeslayer, San Simian, the Freemen and Warlord are unrecorded (mainly because this is not a storyline any* Planet of the Apes *author would wish to revisit). Given the Martians' absence in other tales, Apeslayer's victory seems likely.*

2220

◆ Gorilla and human armies fight a savage battle that litters the Forbidden Zone with corpses. Two soldiers survive: Jovan, a human, his legs shattered, and Solomon, an ape, his arms broken. Too injured to fight, they call a truce so both can survive. Jovan strides a sling atop Solomon's back, each compensating for the other's lost limbs. Together they cross the desert, battling mutated beasts and harsh weather. Caught in a lightning storm, they take refuge in a cave, where an ape-human hybrid named Mordecai offers shelter and healing salves. When they resume fighting, he binds their hands, urging them to resolve their differences peacefully, then evicting them when they persist. Seeing the body-strewn battlefield, they finally put aside their hatred and vow to end the war. Bands of mutant humans and mutant apes square off to protect their ridges of rubble, however, and Jovan and Solomon both die in the crossfire.

Planet of the Apes #5: "Evolution's Nightmare" (MC-c)

◆ This battle serves as a balancing point in history, where human devolvement most clearly coincides with ape evolution. It is also the last major gasp of human aggressiveness.

Planet of the Apes #11: "Outlines of Tomorrow—A Chronology of the Planet of the Apes" (MC-m)

2220 TO 2750

◆ The remaining sentient humans become a slave culture, tolerated but disrespected in gorilla-dominated ape society. Exploration flourishes, as populations expand in all directions. Land is tamed and cultivated with slave labor, outposts are established and contact is made with other surviving tribes. A few minor wars break out, sparked by gorilla aggressiveness, but peace otherwise reigns as energies are channeled into retaking the planet. The cultural heritage of Caesar's Ape City gains widespread popularity, with regional governments modeled after the Lawgiver/council mold. Still, some bands of renegade humans continue to harass ape outposts.

Planet of the Apes #11: "Outlines of Tomorrow—A Chronology of the Planet of the Apes" (MC-m)

LONG BEFORE 3085

◆ A tribe of reclusive humans, the Delphi, takes refuge within a mountain in Philadelphia's Forbidden Zone. In the ruins of Independence Hall, the Delphi worship the *Declaration of Independence*, awaiting the fulfillment of a prophecy that saviors shall descend from the sky and lead them to a promised land where all creatures live in harmony. A similar legend forms among the apes, who name this area the Mountain of the Delphi. Some ape scholars wonder if the Delphi might be a missing link between humans and apekind.

Planet of the Apes—4 Exciting New Stories #1: "Mountain of the Delphi" (PR-r)

NOTE: This placement is conjectural, as no specific date is provided—just that it happened centuries before the TV series, set in 3085.

c. 2260

◆ Dogen, future Lawgiver of the Primacy, is born.

The Forbidden Zone #1: "Part One—Forbidden Knowledge" (AC-c)

c. 2290

◆ In a peaceful ape-human community known as the Valley, Lawgiver Greybeard teaches Caesar's Ultimate Law—"Ape shall not kill ape"—to his students. An army of gorillas, chimps, orangutans and bonobos—descendants of those who left Ape City centuries past to protest humanity's place in society—storms the school, led by Augustus, Lawgiver of the Hill Tribes. Augustus preaches that Aldo and Caesar were divinely inspired to speech by God, and declares humans non-reasoning vermin, able to speak only as a trick of the Devil. To prove his claim, he unleashes a savage human from the hills, who brutally slays Greybeard. Shooting the savage, Augustus orders all humans stripped and cast out into the river, then introduces the students to a new Ultimate Law, set down by Jacob, son of Virgil: "Beware the beast 'man.'"

Revolution on the Planet of the Apes #5: "Ape Shall Not Kill Ape" (MR-c)

NOTE: No date is specified, just that this occurs three centuries after Caesar's rebellion. Jacob is not named in this story; rather, his role as the author of the "Beware the beast 'man'" speech is revealed in Malibu's issue #5.

SHORTLY AFTER 2290

◆ The bonobo species, too small and gentle to survive in ape society, dies out on Earth.

Empire on the Planet of the Apes (MR-c, unpublished)

NOTE: Details of this proposed sequel to Revolution on the Planet of the Apes *are provided courtesy of authors Ty Templeton and Joe O'Brien. According to Templeton, the extinction happens within a few generations of Caesar's rebellion. Since bonobos still exist in 2290, it must occur after that date. Bonobos continue to thrive on Ashlar, however, as evidenced in* Rule, *an unpublished spinoff novel to Tim Burton's re-imagined* Planet of the Apes *film.*

BEFORE 2320

◆ Ape City's high council issues a decree not to kill humans for sport since they are part of the natural wildlife. Some, however, such as Col. Arvo, continue hunting them despite the ruling. Gen. Brak, a silverback gorilla, learns of Arvo's defiance and is displeased.

The Forbidden Zone #1: "Part One—Forbidden Knowledge" (AC-c)

◆ The mutant population of New York City, now hideously scarred from radiation, begin wearing masks of "normal" human faces to hide their inner selves, and to project an aura of outer beauty. It is deemed a sacrilege to be seen in public without one's mask.

The Forbidden Zone #2: "Part Two—Danger Zone" (AC-c)

NOTE: It's unclear when this occurs, but since the mutants are using the masks in 2320, the tradition must have begun before then.

◆ Only during church service, in the ruins of what was once St. Patrick's Cathedral, do the mutants remove their facial coverings, revealing their inner selves to the Alpha-Omega Bomb they worship.

Beneath the Planet of the Apes (FX-f)

c. 2320

◆ Zoe, minister of science and leader of Ape City's ruling council, assigns a gorilla named Julius to lead an expedition to the Forbidden Zone to locate new farmlands. Excited by science and history rather than the military, Julius embraces the chance to practice archeology. Also in the expedition are four chimpanzees: Hector, Nero, Antony and Martin. Though they like Julius, they believe he only got the job through nepotism, since Avro is his father (and, ironically, ashamed that his son chose not to become a soldier).

The Forbidden Zone #3: "Part Three—Battle Zone" (AC-c)

NOTE: No date is specified, just that these events occur 300 years after the fifth film, set in 2020. Dayton Ward's timeline, published in The Planet of the Apes Chronicles, *dates these events in 2390.*

◆ In New York's St. Patrick's Cathedral, the House of Kolp defeats Mendez X in a clash for control of the mutants' Holy City. Kolp believes the Alpha-Omega Bomb a god, while Mendez considers it evil. Framed for murder, Mendez is exiled and wanders the desert for days before collapsing in the woods. Julius finds a gas station with restrooms for men, women and apes—a sign that apes and men once shared the world, with humans in charge—and sends Nero to inform the council. In the Primacy, Lawgiver Dozen (an orangutan) and Security Cmdr. Pell Shea (a human) visit the classroom of a teacher named Circe to educate her students about Primacy history. The two are suddenly called to a hospital, where Drs. Romulus and Titus treat Mendez X, found in a forest by a border scout. Watching these events in his mind, Kolp sends Gen. Jaekel to wipe out all life in the village.

The Forbidden Zone #1: "Part One—Forbidden Knowledge" (AC-c)

NOTE: That Mendez would consider the Alpha-Omega Bomb evil is surprising, given that his ancestor, Mendez the First, introduced the bomb worship in Battle for the Planet of the Apes, *and that the House of Mendez still favors the bomb in 3978, as seen in* Beneath the Planet of the Apes. *Why the Mendez line would go from deifying the bomb to thinking it evil, and then back to worship, is unknown.*

◆ Panicking upon seeing the ape doctors, Mendez creates an illusory sea of fire. When a terrified gorilla named Bock incites a riot, Shea orders Sgt. Garth to arrest him, then tries to calm the mutant, granting him Primacy citizenship. As Kolp's army marches to the Primacy, Jaekel tells his lieutenant, Conrad, to let the soldiers remove their life masks and keep cool, despite the sacrilege of doing so. In Ape City, Julius' report outrages Arvo, who rips up the scroll, calling it blasphemous.

The Forbidden Zone #2: "Part Two—Danger Zone" (AC-c)

◆ Though his methods are harsh, Arvo's intentions are noble. Having heard legends of humans enslaving the ape race, he fears what mankind might do if ever given the chance to do so again.

The Forbidden Zone #3: "Part Three—Battle Zone" (AC-c)

◆ Zoe tells Brak to let Arvo destroy the site, then to eliminate all witnesses. Brak's second, Durga, refuses to take part, but agrees not to stop them. Julius studies the gas station and finds a U.S. map behind a Cooky Cola machine. Fascinated to learn that the Forbidden Zone was once called New York, Julius sets out to locate more cities and stumbles upon Primacy's Outpost 12. Two guards—a human, Lt. Jasper, and an orangutan, Nebo—arrest him.

The Forbidden Zone #2: "Part Two—Danger Zone" (AC-c)

◆ Expeditions from Ape City, the Primacy and the Holy City converge on the Forbidden Zone, many dying in the resultant three-way battle. As Mendez X repels invaders using his illusory powers, Shea interrogates Julius. Arvo slays Antony, Hector and Martin, and orders two gorillas, Corp. Taak and Sgt. Orka, to destroy the ruins. Brak's army arrives to clean up the mess, but upon seeing talking humans through a telescope, he orders his soldiers to attack the Primacy—just as the mutants attack as well.

The Forbidden Zone #3: "Part Three—Battle Zone" (AC-c)

NOTE: One Primacy soldier is named MacDonald. It's possible, though not directly stated, that this MacDonald is a descendant of the films' Bruce and Malcolm MacDonald.

◆ Surveying the battlefield, Brak realizes humans and apes died fighting as brothers, and that his people need not fear the Primacy. Arvo's troops decimate the mutants and nearly kill Shea's troops, but Brak shoots the gorilla, ending the war. Dogen honors Shea, Mendez and Julius, hoping the hard-won peace will last. Kolp rejoices despite losing the battle, for the ape military has been weakened; what's more, Primacy poses no threat and the "stunted" mutants have been culled, allowing his people to evolve unfettered by genetic inferiority.

The Forbidden Zone #4: "Part Four—War Zone" (AC-c)

AFTER 2320

◆ The House of Mendez regains dominancy in the Holy City.

Beneath the Planet of the Apes (FX-f)

◆ In time, the reclusive human mutants lose all memory of the apes' existence.

The Mutant News (HM-p)

NOTE: Though undated, this must occur after the mutants' battle with the Primacy's simian population in Malibu's The Forbidden Zone.

◆ The Holy City's government ceases the practice of killing its enemies. Instead, the mutants begin using their advanced mental abilities to force their enemies to kill each other. The House of Mendez reverses its stance on the Alpha-Omega Bomb, affirming it as divinely sent.

Beneath the Planet of the Apes (FX-f)

NOTE: This is conjecture, intended to explain the oddity of Mendez's House viewing the bomb as evil in Malibu's The Forbidden Zone miniseries, despite his dynasty's onscreen worship of the bomb before and after that story.

2503

◆ A photo of an unbombed, futuristic-looking New York City is said to be from this era.

Planet of the Apes episode #1: "Escape from Tomorrow" (CB-t)

NOTE: The episode implies the photo was taken in 2503, but since the city was decimated 500 years earlier, I assume the book containing the photo must have been published before the war, with the photo merely an artistic interpretation of a possible future.

MID-2600s

◆ In caves along the shores of Long Island, early ape creatures inhabit New York's Forbidden Zone, existing in a state of primitive barbarism, unlike the more evolved apes of Ape City and elsewhere.

Planet of the Apes (FX-f)

PUBLISHER / STUDIO
AB . . . . ABC-TV
AC . . . .Adventure / Malibu Comics
AW . . . . Award Books
BB . . . . .Ballantine Books
BN . . . . Bantam Books
BW . . . . Brown Watson Books
CB . . . . CBS-TV
CV . . . . Chad Valley Sliderama
DH . . . . .Dark Horse Comics
ET . . . . Editorial Mo.Pa.Sa.
FX . . . . 20th Century Fox
GK . . . .Gold Key / Western Comics
HE . . . HarperEntertainment Books
HM . . Harry K. McWilliams Assoc.
MC . . . . Marvel Comics
MR . . .Mr. Comics / Metallic Rose
NB . . . . NBC-TV
PR . . . . .Power Records
SB . . . . Signet Books
TP . . . . Topps
UB . . . . Ubisoft

MEDIUM
a . . . . animated series
b . . . . .book-and-record set
c . . . . .comic book or strip
d . . . . trading card
e . . . . e-comic
f . . . . .theatrical film
k . . . . .storybook
m . . . . .magazine article
n . . . . .novel or novelization
p . . . . promotional newspaper
r . . . . .recorded audio fiction
s . . . . short story
t . . . . television series
u . . . . .unfilmed script or story
v . . . . video game
x . . . . .Blu-Ray exclusive
y . . . . .young adult novel

◆ One such family of primitive apes makes its home in a cave inhabited centuries earlier by former astronaut August Anne Burrows.

Planet of the Apes #17: "Countdown Zero—Part Four" (AC-c)

NOTE: This cave will later be excavated by Cornelius in the first film.

2670

◆ In one section of the United States, man and ape live together in a peaceful agrarian society. Religion teaches that God created beast and man so both might live in friendship, sharing dominion over a world of peace. The Lawgiver of this land reverently recounts the exploits of Zira, Cornelius and Caesar for the ape and human children of his era, so that both species might learn from the mistakes of the past. Playful brawling between the children, however, serves as an omen of darker times to come—as does a statue of Caesar, which is seen to cry tears.

Battle for the Planet of the Apes (FX-f)

MARCH 23, 2673

◆ *Liberty 1* astronaut Col. George Taylor records a message to ANSA before joining his crewmates in suspended animation. Though 700 years have passed on Earth, only six months have passed aboard ship due to the effects of relativity. The onboard chronometer reads July 14, 1972, while on Earth the date is March 23, 2673. Wondering if man is still cruel to his fellow man, Taylor signs off and enters a frozen slumber that lasts some 1,300 years.

Planet of the Apes (FX-f)

2750

◆ A human raid into a large ape population causes a public outcry of rage. The systematic destruction of the human outlaw bands is thus instituted, and the Lawgiver of the day writes the Sacred Scrolls, presenting a rather unflattering portrait of humanity.

Planet of the Apes #11: "Outlines of Tomorrow—A Chronology of the Planet of the Apes" (MC-m)

NOTE: The first film, set in 3978, places the writing of the Scrolls 1,200 years prior. Marvel's timeline, thus, indicates a date of 2750. Malibu's issue #5 reveals the "Beware the beast 'man'" verse to have been penned by Jacob in 2140, but this need not be seen as a contradiction, as the apes likely altered the dating of the scrolls to fit a revised ape history in which humans never ruled the planet.

◆ The Sacred Scrolls usher in a more ape-centric view of history, suppressing all knowledge of simian subjugation and urging apes to shun mankind. The Scrolls offer wisdom, religion and laws, claiming ape history began at this point in time. Only the ruling council's orangutan elders know the truth. Any ape questioning the wisdom or truth of the Scrolls can be charged with heresy and sentenced to up to two years' imprisonment.

Planet of the Apes (FX-f)

◆ The 13th Scroll states: *"And Proteus brought the upright beast into the garden and chained him to a tree, and the children made sport of him."* The 23rd Scroll, 9th Verse, warns: *"Beware the beast 'man,' for he is the Devil's pawn. Alone among God's primates, he kills for sport or lust or greed. Yea, he will murder his brother to possess his brother's land. Let him not breed in great numbers, for he will make a desert of his home and yours. Shun him, drive him back into his jungle lair, for he is the harbinger of death."*

Planet of the Apes (FX-f)

◆ The 19th Scroll, 27th Verse, reads: *"Wheresoever goest man, there with him goes ignorance, pestilence and destruction."*

Revolution on the Planet of the Apes: "The Believer" (MR-c, unpublished)

NOTE: This tale, intended as a back-up story for Revolution on the Planet of the Apes, *was written, penciled and lettered by Sam Agro, but was not published in that miniseries due to concerns over religious overtones, as its conclusion featured an image of the Lawgiver supplanting Christ. At presstime, however, it was slated to appear in issue #16 of* Simian Scrolls *magazine, with the author's permission.*

2750 TO 3085

◆ The Sacred Scrolls prove reactionary, reinstating isolationism. Growth slows, and the orangutan elders take ever more power from the gorillas until ruling completely. The loss of communication among population centers is slow at first, speeding up as the Forbidden Zones become unlivable due to poor conservation techniques. The radiation-blasted soil dies, deserts bloom and humankind grows docile. Cultural patterns in the isolated areas retain shards and snippets of others; thus, one area might have a Lawgiver, while another might operate differently. Ape City grows isolated after its incorporation into pan-American ape society.

Planet of the Apes #11: "Outlines of Tomorrow—A Chronology of the Planet of the Apes" (MC-m)

◆ Disgusted at the bigotry pervading ape society, a band of humans and apes departs for a distant island, which they name Avedon. Together, they build a civilization of honor and peace, based on depictions of the Middle Ages in ancient writings—complete with King Arthur and his Knights of the Round Table.

Planet of the Apes #10: "Kingdom on an Island of the Apes—The Island Out of Time" (MC-c)

◆ In the former western United States, a number of human settlements form, separated by wide distances, each governed by an ape prefect with a garrison of soldiers to maintain the peace.

Planet of the Apes episode #2: "The Gladiators" (CB-t)

◆ These settlements are overseen by the Supreme High Council, located in Central City, in an area once known as California.

Planet of the Apes episode #1: "Escape from Tomorrow" (CB-t)

◆ An ape creation myth develops in Central City. According to this myth, the first ape civilization arises from an age of inferior humans, in an area south of Philadelphia untouched by the Great War. After the apes abandon the area, a race of tree-dwelling humans—the Tree People—inhabit it in their wake. Driven by a fear of the apes, the Tree People build their homes high in the trees.

Planet of the Apes—4 Exciting New Stories #2: "Dawn of the Tree People" (PR-r)

NOTE: This would seem to contradict the first film's account of ape creation myth.

PUBLISHER / STUDIO
AB . . . . ABC-TV
AC . . . .Adventure / Malibu Comics
AW . . . . Award Books
BB . . . . .Ballantine Books
BN . . . . Bantam Books
BW . . . . Brown Watson Books
CB . . . . CBS-TV
CV . . . . Chad Valley Sliderama
DH . . . . .Dark Horse Comics
ET . . . . Editorial Mo.Pa.Sa.
FX . . . . 20th Century Fox
GK . . . .Gold Key / Western Comics
HE . . . HarperEntertainment Books
HM . . Harry K. McWilliams Assoc.
MC . . . . Marvel Comics
MR . . . Mr. Comics / Metallic Rose
NB . . . . NBC-TV
PR . . . . .Power Records
SB . . . . Signet Books
TP . . . . Topps
UB . . . . Ubisoft

MEDIUM
a . . . . animated series
b . . . . .book-and-record set
c . . . . .comic book or strip
d . . . . trading card
e . . . . e-comic
f . . . . .theatrical film
k . . . . .storybook
m . . . . .magazine article
n . . . . .novel or novelization
p . . . . promotional newspaper
r . . . . .recorded audio fiction
s . . . . short story
t . . . . television series
u . . . . .unfilmed script or story
v . . . . video game
x . . . . .Blu-Ray exclusive
y . . . . .young adult novel

EARLY TO MID 2900s

◆ Apes begin raiding the human village of Borak for slaves to work in the mines. The humans fight back, causing many deaths on both sides. A meeting is arranged, and the apes allow those of Borak to choose five slaves, twice each summer month, from among any healthy humans they can find. This enables those in Borak to avoid slavery by kidnapping passing humans—such as the Meadow People, a community of barbarians—to go in their place. The ape masters of several captured humans protest, hoping to get their servants back, but the local ape garrison commander never honors such requests.

Planet of the Apes episode #13: "The Liberator" (CB-t)

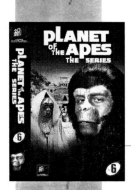

NOTE: *This is said to occur "a long time ago," but no date is provided. In the episode's script, Brun says it happened before his "father's father's father"—that is, three generations before his birth year of 3035, or roughly a century earlier. The Meadow People's status as barbarians is established in the script.*

BETWEEN 3016 AND 3025

◆ Farrow, a simple-minded human male from Chalo, is born.

Planet of the Apes episode #1: "Escape from Tomorrow" (CB-t)

NOTE: *Farrow is described as a young man in an early-draft episode synopsis included in the TV series writer's bible, reprinted in* Simian Scrolls *issue #12. In the episode's final script, Farrow is said to be in his 60s in 3085.*

BETWEEN 3026 AND 3028

◆ Barlow, future chimpanzee prefect of Kaymak, is born.

Planet of the Apes episode #2: "The Gladiators" (CB-t)

NOTE: *In the episode's script, Barlow is said to be in his late 50s in 3085.*

BETWEEN 3026 AND 3034

◆ Jasko, a human farmer in a simple community along the shore, is born.

Planet of the Apes episode #8: "The Deception" (CB-t)

NOTE: *The novelization of the episode reveals that Jasko is in his 50s in 3085.*

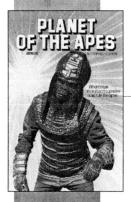

◆ John, a human known in his adult years as "the Prophet," is born.

Planet of the Apes (Authorized Edition) #3: "The Prophet" (BW-s)

NOTE: *John is said to be in his 50s in 3085.*

BETWEEN 3029 AND 3031

◆ Future Central City High Council leader Zaius, an orangutan, is born.

Planet of the Apes episode #1: "Escape from Tomorrow" (CB-t)

NOTE: *In the script, Zaius is said to be in his mid-50s in 3085. This is not the same Zaius as those seen in the first two films, the animated series or Tim Burton's remake.*

c. 3035

◆ Leuric, a human from the village of Chatka, is born.

Planet of the Apes episode #14: "Up Above the World So High" (CB-t)

NOTE: The episode's script names Leuric and says he is "fiftiesh" in 3085.

3035

◆ Miller, a human farmer from the village of Numay, is born.

Planet of the Apes episode #3: "The Trap" (CB-t)

NOTE: In the episode's script, Miller is said to be 50 in 3085.

◆ Brun, a human male and future Master of Borak, is born.

Planet of the Apes episode #13: "The Liberator" (CB-t)

NOTE: In the episode's script, Brun is said to be 50 in 3085.

BETWEEN 3036 AND 3038

◆ Tolar, a human and future gladiatorial champion of Kaymak, is born.

Planet of the Apes episode #2: "The Gladiators" (CB-t)

NOTE: In the episode's script, Tolar is said to be in his late 40s in 3085.

BETWEEN 3036 AND 3049

◆ Mary, a human farmer from the village of Numay, and future wife of Miller, is born.

Planet of the Apes episode #3: "The Trap" (CB-t)

NOTE: In the episode's script, Mary is said to be in her 40s in 3085.

◆ Talbert, a human male from the village of Trion, is born.

Planet of the Apes episode #12: "The Cure" (CB-t)

NOTE: In the episode's script, Talbert is said to be in his 40s in 3085.

3040

◆ Travin, future head human at a medical center outside Central City, is born.

Planet of the Apes episode #7: "The Surgeon" (CB-t)

NOTE: In the episode's script, Travin is said to be 45 in 3085.

3040s

◆ Urko, future chief of Central City security, is born. Aboro and Bulta, the gorilla's future academy-mates and long-time friends, are born around the same time.

Planet of the Apes episode #11: "The Tyrant" (CB-t)

NOTE: Since Urko's age is unknown, I am basing this figure on his having attended the academy 20 years before "The Tyrant," set in 3085. That would place his academy years circa 3065. If he were an ape in his late teens or early 20s at the time, that would place his birth sometime in the 3040s. (Actor Mark Lenard was 50 at the time that he portrayed Urko.) Since the trio attended school together, I assume them to be approximately the same age.

3045

◆ A human male named Martin, a future blacksmith, is born in the village of Venton.

Planet of the Apes episode #9: "The Horse Race" (CB-t)

NOTE: The episode's novelization establishes that Martin is 40 in 3085

BETWEEN 3050 AND 3060

◆ A human woman named Arn is born in or near the ruins of Oakland, Calif.

Planet of the Apes episode #5: "The Legacy" (CB-t)

NOTE: In the episode's script, Arn is said to be in her late 20s or early 30s in 3085.

c. 3055

◆ Clim, a human from the village of Borak, is born. His father is Porto, his mother's name unknown.

Planet of the Apes episode #13: "The Liberator" (CB-t)

NOTE: In the episode's script, Clim is said to be about 30 in 3085.

BETWEEN 3056 AND 3060

◆ Katrin, a human female and future member of the United Freedom Force (UFF), is born.

Planet of the Apes: "Hostage" (CB-u)

NOTE: This script was never filmed. Katrin is said to be in her late 20s in 3085.

BETWEEN 3056 AND 3064

◆ Delphia, daughter of a chimpanzee farmer named Telemon, is born in a village in northern Arizona.

Planet of the Apes: "A Fallen God" (CB-u)

NOTE: This script was never filmed. Delphia is said to be in her 20s in 3085.

BETWEEN 3059 AND 3061

◆ Galen, a chimpanzee and future fugitive of justice, is born.

Planet of the Apes episode #1: "Escape from Tomorrow" (CB-t)

NOTE: In the episode's script, Galen is said to be in his mid-20s in 3085.

◆ Galen's parents, Yalu and Ann, are a respected couple living in Central City.

Planet of the Apes episode #10: "The Interrogation" (CB-t)

◆ Augustus, Galen's third cousin on Ann's side, is born that same year. The two grow up close friends.

Planet of the Apes episode #11: "The Tyrant" (CB-t)

NOTE: Galen's specific relation to Augustus is revealed in the episode's novelization.

◆ The sound of running water from a small brook running behind Galen's Central City home is often a source of comfort to the young chimpanzee.

Planet of the Apes episode #13: "The Liberator" (CB-t)

LATE 3050s OR EARLY 3060s

◆ A human girl named Nebia is born to a slave family and forced to work on the Beach of Time, sorting out ancient relics mixed with the sand so the latter can be used for construction. A rebellious child, she often takes items home with her—a taboo punishable by death since the relics' very existence is deemed heresy. Her parents often protect her from heresy charges, but her defiant nature never fades.

El Planeta de Los Simios #3: "The Beach of Time" (ET-c)

NOTE: Nebia's age is not provided, but she appears to be in her 20s in 3086.

3060

◆ Miro, a human male from Borak, is born to the village leader, Brun.

Planet of the Apes episode #13: "The Liberator" (CB-t)

NOTE: In the script (in which he is named Trung), Miro is said to be 25 in 3085.

◆ Barlow, a chimpanzee in his mid 20s, becomes prefect of Kaymak, a human settlement north of former San Francisco. Searching for a way to control mankind's aggressive nature, Barlow initiates a series of gladiatorial battles—known as the Games—to keep his humans occupied, entertained and less likely to rebel.

Planet of the Apes episode #2: "The Gladiators" (CB-t)

3060s

◆ Janor, a human youth from the village of Hathor, often plays a game with his younger brother, Mikal, in which humans and apes live together as equals.

Planet of the Apes episode #11: "The Tyrant" (AW-n)

NOTE: This information appears in the novelization. The placement is conjectural, based on Mikal's appearance.

PUBLISHER / STUDIO
AB . . . . ABC-TV
AC . . . .Adventure / Malibu Comics
AW . . . . Award Books
BB . . . . .Ballantine Books
BN . . . . Bantam Books
BW . . . . Brown Watson Books
CB . . . . CBS-TV
CV . . . . Chad Valley Sliderama
DH . . . . .Dark Horse Comics
ET . . . . Editorial Mo.Pa.Sa.
FX . . . . 20th Century Fox
GK . . . .Gold Key / Western Comics
HE . . . HarperEntertainment Books
HM . . Harry K. McWilliams Assoc.
MC . . . . Marvel Comics
MR . . . Mr. Comics / Metallic Rose
NB . . . . NBC-TV
PR . . . . .Power Records
SB . . . . Signet Books
TP . . . . Topps
UB . . . . Ubisoft

MEDIUM
a . . . . animated series
b . . . . .book-and-record set
c . . . . .comic book or strip
d . . . . trading card
e . . . . e-comic
f . . . . .theatrical film
k . . . . .storybook
m . . . . .magazine article
n . . . . .novel or novelization
p . . . . promotional newspaper
r . . . . . .recorded audio fiction
s . . . . short story
t . . . . television series
u . . . . . . .unfilmed script or story
v . . . . video game
x . . . . .Blu-Ray exclusive
y . . . . .young adult novel

3063

◆ Dalton, a youth in the human settlement of Kaymak, is born. His father Tolar is a gladiator, his mother (name unknown) a pacifist. She dies young, forcing Tolar to bring him up alone. Dalton shares his mother's pacifistic beliefs, but Tolar is unable to accept that about his son and trains him as a gladiator anyway.

Planet of the Apes episode #2: "The Gladiators" (CB-t)

NOTE: In the episode's script, Dalton is said to be 22 in 3085.

◆ Arna, daughter of Travin, is born to a medical community on the outskirts of Central City.

Planet of the Apes episode #7: "The Surgeon" (CB-t)

NOTE: The novelization reveals her to be 18 in 3085.

c. 3065

◆ Urko attends the Central City military academy and befriends two fellow gorillas, Aboro and Bulta. The three young apes show promise as leaders, but Aboro is caught cheating, his reputation irreparably tainted.

Planet of the Apes episode #11: "The Tyrant" (CB-t)

c. 3065 TO 3085

◆ Despite Aboro's scandal, he, Urko and Bulta remain friends for the next two decades. Urko is named chief of Central City security, hiring Bulta as his assistant. Aboro rises only to the level of Hathor district chief, however, and though he pretends to accept his fate, he secretly covets his friends' success.

Planet of the Apes episode #11: "The Tyrant" (CB-t)

3066

◆ Talia, a human female from the village of Borak, is born.

Planet of the Apes episode #13: "The Liberator" (CB-t)

NOTE: In the episode's script, Talia is said to be 19 in 3085.

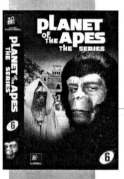

LATE 3060s

◆ A boy is born to a human named Travin and his wife, who work at a medical clinic on the outskirts of Central City.

Planet of the Apes episode #7: "The Surgeon" (CB-t)

NOTE: This is an approximate figure, given that we know the boy's age when he dies—16—but not the year in which his death occurs.

◆ As a young chimp, Galen sometimes hides in a secret gully to play hooky from school.

Planet of the Apes episode #7: "The Surgeon" (AW-n)

NOTE: This is revealed in the novelization, and in an earlier draft of the script.

3060s TO 3070s

◆ Polar and Zantes, chimpanzee farmers, marry and have three children. The oldest son is named Anto, the youngest son Remus. Between them in age is a daughter, Jillia.

Planet of the Apes episode #4: "The Good Seeds" (CB-t)

NOTE: The children's ages are not revealed, but the first-draft script reveals Jillia to be the middle child.

BETWEEN 3068 AND 3070

◆ Galen and his cousin Augustus, age 9, steal apples from a neighbor ape's farm.

Planet of the Apes episode #11: "The Tyrant" (CB-t)

NOTE: This assumes a birth-year for Galen between 3059 and 3061.

3069

◆ Gregor, son of a human blacksmith named Martin, is born in the village of Venton.

Planet of the Apes episode #9: "The Horse Race" (CB-t)

NOTE: The episode's novelization establishes that Gregor is 16 in 3085

BETWEEN 3069 AND 3072

◆ Dardon, the son of chimpanzee farmer Telemon, is born in a village in northern Arizona.

Planet of the Apes: "A Fallen God" (CB-u)

NOTE: This script was never filmed. Dardon is said to be a young teenager in 3085.

BETWEEN 3069 AND 3085

◆ As Gregor grows up in the village of Venton, the youth develops a passion for riding horses, knowing full well that humans are forbidden to do so.

Planet of the Apes episode #9: "The Horse Race" (CB-t)

3070

◆ A human girl, Lisa, is born to a farming couple named Miller and Mary, from the village of Numay.

Planet of the Apes episode #3: "The Trap" (CB-t)

NOTE: In the episode's script, Lisa is said to be 15 in 3085.

3072 OR 3073

◆ A human boy named Kraik is born in the ruins of Oakland, Calif. His parents die when he is young, leaving him an orphaned urchin, forced to survive by stealing food and selling secrets to the apes.

Planet of the Apes episode #5: "The Legacy" (CB-t)

NOTE: In the episode's script, Kraik is said to be 12 or 13 in 3085.

PUBLISHER / STUDIO
AB . . . . ABC-TV
AC . . . .Adventure / Malibu Comics
AW . . . . Award Books
BB . . . . .Ballantine Books
BN . . . . Bantam Books
BW . . . . Brown Watson Books
CB . . . . CBS-TV
CV . . . . Chad Valley Sliderama
DH . . . . .Dark Horse Comics
ET . . . . Editorial Mo.Pa.Sa.
FX . . . . 20th Century Fox
GK . . . .Gold Key / Western Comics
HE . . . HarperEntertainment Books
HM . . Harry K. McWilliams Assoc.
MC . . . . Marvel Comics
MR . . . Mr. Comics / Metallic Rose
NB . . . . NBC-TV
PR . . . . .Power Records
SB . . . . Signet Books
TP . . . . Topps
UB . . . . .Ubisoft

MEDIUM
a . . . . animated series
b . . . . .book-and-record set
c . . . . .comic book or strip
d . . . . trading card
e . . . . e-comic
f . . . . .theatrical film
k . . . . .storybook
m . . . . magazine article
n . . . . .novel or novelization
p . . . . promotional newspaper
r . . . . .recorded audio fiction
s . . . . short story
t . . . . television series
u . . . . .unfilmed script or story
v . . . . video game
x . . . . .Blu-Ray exclusive
y . . . . .young adult novel

3070s

◆ As Galen and his cousin Augustus grow through adolescence, Augustus often chides him for being impulsive, predicting it will one day get Galen into trouble. On at least one occasion—when Galen allows himself to be captured by a human farmer so his cousin could get away secretly—that impulsivity proves to be an asset.

Planet of the Apes episode #11: "The Tyrant" (AW-n)

NOTE: This is revealed in the episode's novelization.

BEFORE 3075

◆ A spaceship crashes near Central City. Four human survivors—Taylor, Thomas, LaFever and Bengsten—are captured, claiming to be from Earth's past. Councilor Zaius, leader of the High Council, and Urko, the city's chief of security, realize they have greater intelligence and abilities than local humans, as well as a greater sense of independence and freedom. Worried that their influence might spread, Urko kills the astronauts, which infuriates Zaius, who'd intended to interrogate them.

Planet of the Apes episode #1: "Escape from Tomorrow" (CB-t)

NOTE: The astronauts' names are noted in an early-draft script of the first episode, written by Rod Serling; the names Thomas and LaFever are holdovers from Serling's early-draft script from the first Planet of the Apes *film, in which George Taylor and John Landon were known, respectively, as John Thomas and Paul LaFever. It's unclear if this Taylor is related to George Taylor and his daughters, Jo and Tammy. The astronauts' arrival is undated, said to occur "more than ten years" before 3085.*

LATE 3070s TO EARLY 3080s

◆ Galen teaches an ethics class while working with the Free Speech Movement. Lora, daughter of Senator Sallus, attends as a freshman, along with two apes named Aro and Manus. The three students eventually join the United Freedom Force (UFF), an illegal organization promoting human-simian equality.

Planet of the Apes: "Hostage" (CB-u)

NOTE: This episode was never filmed, but the script is available online at Hunter's Planet of the Apes *Archive.*

c. 3070s TO 3085

◆ Lucian, a book-collecting chimp living in a simple home along the shore, shares his collection with his daughter Fauna. After she loses her sight, he reads them to her every night by the fire.

Planet of the Apes episode #8: "The Deception" (CB-t)

NOTE: This placement is conjectural, based on her appearance in 3085.

MID 3070s

◆ A human boy, Jick, is born to a farming couple named Miller and Mary, from the village of Numay.

Planet of the Apes episode #3: "The Trap" (CB-t)

NOTE: I have based Jick's age on his appearance as a young boy of 10 in 3085.

3080

◆ Anto, a young chimpanzee farmer, son of Polar and Zantes, decides to start his own farm.

Planet of the Apes episode #4: "The Good Seeds" (CB-t)

3080 TO 3085

◆ Since ape tradition dictates that a son coming of age must await the birth of a bull calf before starting his own farm, Anto begins the appropriate rituals to summon a bull calf. All new cows born to the farm are heifers, however, and are taken by the family's landlord. For five years Anto waits for a male birth, convinced the signs are against him.

Planet of the Apes episode #4: "The Good Seeds" (CB-t)

EARLY 3080s

◆ Drs. Kira and Leander, ape surgeons at a medical center on the outskirts of Central City, attempt blood transfusion. The test patient, a human boy of 16, is badly injured in a hunting accident. His father Travin allows the experiment, knowing he'd otherwise die. Travin's daughter Arna is chosen as a donor, but the doctors inadvertently kill the boy, unaware of the need to match blood types. Leander deems transfusion against the laws of nature, and the girl is branded as having evil blood, her name and status stripped. Only her father speaks to her therein, and he and the 11 other humans at the compound routinely beat her for any mistakes.

Planet of the Apes episode #7: "The Surgeon" (CB-t)

NOTE: The boy's death is said to occur "a few years" before 3085.

3081 OR 3082

◆ Galen enjoys time spent with his cousin and friend, Augustus, now a member of the Central City council. It is the last time the two will see each other for the next three or four years.

Planet of the Apes episode #11: "The Tyrant" (CB-t)

NOTE: This information appears in the script but not in the televised episode.

3083

◆ Farrow, a human from Chalo—a settlement 30 miles south of Central City—discovers an ancient bomb shelter and makes it his "secret cave." Within the shelter, he finds books and other artifacts from centuries past. Unable to read them, he uses the books to start fires, keeping one because he enjoys looking at its pictures.

Planet of the Apes episode #1: "Escape from Tomorrow" (CB-t)

NOTE: The script says Farrow found the bomb shelter two years before the episode, set in 3085.

◆ A human male is killed by ape soldiers. Devastated, his wife Katrin joins the United Freedom Force (UFF), an illegal organization promoting human/simian equality, so she can help end ape brutality.

Planet of the Apes: "Hostage" (CB-u)

NOTE: This episode was never filmed, but the script is available online at Hunter's Planet of the Apes Archive.

3084

◆ Telemon, a chimpanzee farmer, finds a radio transmitter buried on his farm in northern Arizona. Thinking it a holy relic, he cleans it up and brings it home, where he and his family worship the device as a "god-thing." Recognizing it to be the creation of an advanced intelligence—and fearful that the village's dogmatic religious leader, Syrinx, will deem the radio evil and take it from them—Telemon keeps it secret from others outside the family.

Planet of the Apes: "A Fallen God" (CB-u)

NOTE: This episode was never filmed, but the script is available online at Hunter's Planet of the Apes *Archive.*

◆ The council passes the Human Control Laws, which impose a strict curfew and prohibit humans from leaving their villages without a pass. This makes humanity even more placid. In response, the United Freedom Force (UFF) increases its activity. Though labeled a terrorist group, the UFF—consisting of apes and humans unhappy with societal inequities—usually sticks to non-violent protests, so the government takes a light hand in dealing with it. For eight months, Urko searches for the UFF headquarters, but to no avail.

Planet of the Apes: "Hostage" (CB-u)

NOTE: This episode was never filmed, but the script is available online at Hunter's Planet of the Apes *Archive.*

BEFORE 3085

◆ For an unspecified length of time, Galen lives in Nufort, a human-less village administered by an orangutan named Ponar. Galen's closest friend there is a chimpanzee named Shako. Another chimp, Naten, is not so fond of him.

Planet of the Apes (Authorized Edition) #1: "A Promise Kept" (BW-s)

◆ In the early part of the Ornan Period, several hundred humans are found dead of an unknown illness in the Rural Zone. Once known as malaria, the disease is named the Sleeping Sickness because it causes its victims to convulse horribly and die. For years, the entire sector remains barren.

Planet of the Apes episode #12: "The Cure" (CB-t)

NOTE: Dating these events is impossible. The episode, set in 3085, places them in the Ornan Period of ape history, but does not specify when that period occurs.

◆ A male orangutan named Doswa serves as leader of the Central City High Council, later remembered as one of Zaius' most admired predecessors.

Planet of the Apes episode #7: "The Surgeon" (CB-t)

◆ Lucian, a chimpanzee tired of seeing humans mistreated, forms a clandestine group sympathetic to man's plight. Befriending several humans, he secretly shares ape knowledge with them. This angers other apes, including his brother Sestus, a member of an anti-human hate group called the Dragoons.

Planet of the Apes episode #8: "The Deception" (CB-t)

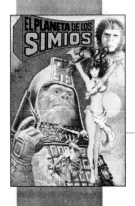

◆ The ruins of New York City become a safe haven for those hiding from Urko's forces. The security chief wishes he could destroy the city to stop fugitives and traitors from taking refuge there.

El Planeta de Los Simios #4: "Ultrasonic" (ET-c)

◆ A human armed with advanced technology is captured sneaking into Central City. Zaius orders his execution without learning his name, convinced he represents a danger to the status quo. Zaius finds grenades among the man's belongings and stores them in his office as a reminder of man's violence.

Planet of the Apes episode #1: "Escape from Tomorrow" (CB-t)

NOTE: *With the TV series' cancellation, this human's identity and the source of his advanced technology were never revealed.*

◆ A human couple named Arn and Tomar fall in love. Tomar, who works on a farm with his brother Derlin, dislikes how mankind is treated, and is arrested and executed for trying to convince others to rebel. The apes let Arn live, which Urko considers a mistake, believing the family of a rebel should always be killed to prevent the spread of poisonous ideas. After time spent in a stockade, she is set free. Unable to face the loneliness of farming without Tomar, she ends up a homeless scavenger in the ruins of Oakland, Calif.

Planet of the Apes episode #5: "The Legacy" (CB-t)

NOTE: *Arn's stockade time is established in the episode's script. The novelization spells the brother's name as "Durlin," but the DVD's subtitles use the spelling "Derlin."*

◆ Galen romances a female chimpanzee named Landa, the prefect of a peaceful artist's village.

Planet of the Apes—4 Exciting New Stories #3: "Battle of Two Worlds" (PR-r)

◆ Galen also meets Kira, a surgeon at a medical center on the outskirts of Central City. The two fall in love and eventually make plans to wed.

Planet of the Apes episode #7: "The Surgeon" (CB-t)

◆ A young chimp named Fauna and her lover spend time in a secret grotto whenever they can. When she loses her eyesight, however, he leaves her alone and heartbroken.

Planet of the Apes episode #8: "The Deception" (CB-t)

◆ Galen's cousin Augustus is promoted to prefect of Hathor. A decent and honest ape, he prides himself on the fairness and justice of his administration. One of his district chiefs (Aboro) becomes corrupt, however, damaging the legitimacy of Augustus' reign.

Planet of the Apes episode #11: "The Tyrant" (CB-t)

◆ Galen's father Yalu does an unspecified favor for Zaius, who owes him one in return.

Planet of the Apes episode #1: "Escape from Tomorrow" (CB-t)

◆ Ape scientists try to analyze the Blasted Zone, a barren, desolate stretch of irradiated countryside left over from the Destruction. Lingering radiation, however, causes their hair to fall out over the course of several weeks, and two of them die. The cause of death remains a mystery to the apes.

Planet of the Apes: "Hostage" (CB-u)

NOTE: *This episode was never filmed, but the script is available online at Hunter's* Planet of the Apes *Archive.*

◆ Security Chief Urko marries a female ape named Elta.

Planet of the Apes episode #3: "The Trap" (CB-t)

◆ Zantes, the wife of a chimpanzee named Polar, trains to be a nurse.

Planet of the Apes episode #4: "The Good Seeds" (CB-t)

◆ A disciplinary camp is established outside of Central City, where human workers who are unruly or disobey orders are sent for reconditioning.

Planet of the Apes, episode #7: "The Surgeon" (CB-t)

◆ Daku, aide-de-camp to District Chief Aboro of Hathor, hires Amhar, a human from the village of Loban, to murder an enemy. The crime is successful, and the gorilla employs Amhar's services several more times.

Planet of the Apes episode #11: "The Tyrant" (CB-t)

◆ A human named John finds 2,000-year-old library tapes that educate him about humanity's history before the nuclear war. Pretending to be a prophet from two millennia past, he uses this knowledge to bypass other humans' distrust of machines and offer them hope for the future.

Planet of the Apes (Authorized Edition) #3: "The Prophet" (BW-s)

◆ Prefect Kobal, an orangutan leader in a province near the former New York Metropolitan Opera House, turns the Met—the only building still standing in its vicinity, now called the Palace—into a fighting arena known as the Circus. Humans are horribly mistreated and forced to fight to earn food, with a grand prize of freedom promised to the winner of the Great Tournament. In reality, however, all winners are executed so Kobal can mate weaker humans and reduce the likelihood of rebellion.

Planeta de Los Simios #7: "The Circus" (ET-c)

◆ A brilliant gorilla named Sover is expulsed from the High Council and accepts a posting as the prefect of a small village, where he turns the human population into his personal labor force. There, he discovers an underground military base containing more than a dozen working rockets, built a thousand years earlier by humans. With permission from the council, he studies the rockets to figure out how to launch them.

El Planeta de Los Simios #7: "Rockets" (ET-c)

NOTE: This Spanish-language comic was published only in Argentina. Though the seventh issue in the series, "Rockets" is numbered "1" due to the publisher's name change from Editorial Mo.Pa.Sa. to Editorial Tynset S.A.

◆ Dr. Pandere, an ape expert in geothermal energy, puts forth a controversial theory on shifting continental plates. Dr. Zaius dismisses her findings as outlandish.

Planet of the Apes—4 Exciting New Stories #4: "Volcano" (PR-r)

◆ At a fishing village along the shore of what was once Pismo Beach or Malibu, Prefect Hurton struggles to keep up with frequent quota increases from his superior, Bandor. To keep overhead low, Hurton decides to eliminate elderly humans by tying them to a raft and sending them out to sea to be consumed by sharks.

Planet of the Apes episode #6: "Tomorrow's Tide" (CB-t)

◆ Harimon, an elderly orangutan and an expert in sound waves, is exiled from ape society for sorcery.

El Planeta de Los Simios #4: "Ultrasonic" (ET-c)

◆ The Ministry of Knowledge declares it a crime for any ape to read books deemed forbidden.

Planet of the Apes episode #8: "The Deception" (CB-t)

LATE 3084 OR EARLY 3085

◆ Leuric, a human from Chatka, begins designing a glider, hoping to be the first human to fly.

Planet of the Apes episode #14: "Up Above the World So High" (CB-t)

NOTE: This is undated, but Leuric says he's been working on the glider for months.

Part 9: Man, the Fugitive
(3085 to 3086)

MARCH 21, 3085

◆ ANSA spacecraft *Probe Six* nears its final destination. Crewed by three astronauts—Col. Alan J. Virdon, Major Peter J. Burke and a third nicknamed "Jonesy"—the ship was lost in a time warp while en route to Alpha Centauri in 1980. The ship's internal chronometer is damaged in flight and stops functioning on this date, Earth-time.

Planet of the Apes episode #1: "Escape from Tomorrow" (CB-t)

NOTE: The opening credits of the Planet of the Apes *TV series establish the series as beginning on June 14, but the chronometer reads March 21 after the crash. The damage to the chronometer, mentioned by Burke in the episode, provides a plausible way to reconcile this discrepancy. Virdon's rank can be found in an early-draft script of the pilot, written by Rod Serling. The name of the ship,* Probe Six, *comes from an unused script, entitled "A Fallen God." Jonsey's full name is unknown.*

EARLY 3085

◆ Lisa, a human teen from the village of Numay, ventures to the ruins of San Francisco and finds several ancient computer parts, which she takes home with her as mementos.

Planet of the Apes episode #3: "The Trap" (CB-t)

JUNE 14, 3085

◆ Near the village of Chalo, a dog chases a human named Farrow until a chimp child, Arno, intervenes. *Probe Six* crashes in the woods outside Chalo, and Arno runs to tell his father, Prefect Veska. Farrow finds Virdon and Burke unconscious (Jonesy is dead), and pulls the duo to safety. Veska orders Jonsey cremated to bury knowledge that humans could build such machines, then sends Lt. Turvo to alert the council. Virdon and Burke awaken in a bomb shelter. Farrow brings them food and heads out for clothing. As the astronauts scout the area, gorillas on horseback fire at them but they get away. Farrow shows them a book containing photos of New York, c. 2503, and they realize they've traveled to Earth's future. Meanwhile, Galen visits Zaius in Central City, hoping to become his assistant. Turvo arrives, delivering word of the fugitives to Ullman, Zaius' human servant. Urko wants to hunt down and kill the as-tro-nauts (as he pronounces it), but Zaius prefers them taken alive. Finally, Zaius offers Galen a job.

Planet of the Apes episode #1: "Escape from Tomorrow" (CB-t)

NOTE: The TV series seems to commit several continuity errors—living dogs after a plague killed all canines, humans speaking and so forth—but most can be explained away. The biggest snafu is a book showing an unbombed New York City some 500 years after it was leveled in a nuclear war. One can assume the book was published pre-war, the photos merely artistic interpretations of a possible future. In early drafts of this and several other episode scripts, Burke is named Ed Rowak or Stanley Kovak, Urko is called Ursus, and Central City is Simian City. Turvo's name is in the script and View-Master storybook adaptation. The Chad Valley Picture Show filmstrips (combining concepts from several episodes, along with the first film's courtroom scene, to create an alternate version of the astronauts' adventures) incorrectly date the ship's loss and future arrival in 2105 and 3975, respectively.

JUNE 15, 3085

◆ Farrow brings the astronauts to the crash site, telling a gorilla guard he saw humans in the woods. As the ape investigates, the men sneak aboard to find the ship gutted. Virdon locates a photo of his wife and son. Hearing a commotion, they exit the ship to find Farrow dead, with Urko, Galen and others surrounding them. Urko arrests them, and Galen retrieves the book. Confused by images of human cities and caged apes, he asks the astronauts about the photos but refuses to believe their claims that humans once ruled the planet.

Planet of the Apes episode #1: "Escape from Tomorrow" (CB-t)

NOTE: Farrow was originally intended to survive the episode, according to a synopsis included in the TV series writer's bible, reprinted in Simian Scrolls *issue #12.*

JUNE 16, 3085

◆ As the apes prepare a trial, Urko retrieves a grenade from Zaius' office. Zaius, Proto (an orangutan), Grundig (a chimp) and two others preside. Urko proclaims Virdon and Burke enemies of the state. Proto and Grundig ask for their beliefs about ape and human equality, deeming their answers heresy. Urko calls for their deaths, destroying the chamber door with the grenade to illustrate the danger they represent, but the council opts to keep them alive for study. Urko throws them in a cell, instructing a guard to kill them after dark. Galen tells Zaius the world would be a better place if no creature ruled another, but the orangutan calls his comments sacrilege.

Planet of the Apes episode #1: "Escape from Tomorrow" (CB-t)

NOTE: Proto and Grundig are named in the script.

◆ In Zaius' study, Galen notices a book on human anatomy, written by humans before mankind's fall.

Planet of the Apes episode #7: "The Surgeon" (CB-t)

◆ Virdon wonders who built the grenade, hoping they might have a computer able to read a magnetic disk containing the ship's telemetry data. He asks Galen to free them, but the chimp fears being charged with treason. That night, the guard leaves their cell door ajar. Realizing it's a trap, they risk heading outside. Galen sees the guard take aim and warns them, grabbing the gun. The weapon accidentally fires in the scuffle, killing the guard, and Urko arrests Galen for murder and possession of a heretical book.

Planet of the Apes episode #1: "Escape from Tomorrow" (CB-t)

JUNE 17, 3085

◆ Zaius refuses to pardon Galen, whose crimes carry a death sentence. Virdon and Burke await the elder in his home, grenade in hand. He admits to keeping mankind's past a secret to protect apes from making the same mistakes. Forcing him to take them to the jail, they overpower a guard, lock him up in a cell with Zaius and free Galen. Urko gives chase as the trio escape.

Planet of the Apes episode #1: "Escape from Tomorrow" (CB-t)

JUNE 18, 3085

◆ The fugitives hide for the night, visiting their ship in the morning to retrieve the computer disk. At the sound of horses, they run for the trees. Hearing an explosion in the distance, they assume the ship destroyed and walk away from the crash site, hoping one day to find a way home.

Planet of the Apes episode #1: "Escape from Tomorrow" (CB-t)

◆ Upon learning that the ship survived the explosion, the astronauts return to continue salvage efforts. Apes guarding the half-submerged vehicle attack, and more apes await inside. The captain, Pingor, takes them captive and orders the ship destroyed, then walks them to a village several hours distant. The duo break loose and run for the woods, where they meet Golli, a human woman from a jungle village. Her family are slaves, forced to plant and harvest for the apes. The guards find them, and a scuffle ensues; one ape dies, the other knocked unconscious. Golli leads them to a farm occupied by apes friendly to humans, then returns to her people. Following their trail, Galen reunites with his new friends across a river.

El Planeta de Los Simios #2: "New Life... on the Old Planet" (ET-c)

NOTE: In this Spanish-language comic, published only in Argentina, Virdon and Burke return to their ship, seemingly destroyed in the first episode. Since the destruction does not occur onscreen, it's possible the explosion heard in the background may not have been the ship's detonation, but rather something else entirely. It's a stretch...but it does explain the discrepancy.

◆ Dr. Kira, Galen's fiancée, learns that the ape she loves has become a criminal and traitor. Angry that he would choose to live with humans instead of her, she turns her back on him and moves on with her life. In time, she forms a friendship—and potentially more—with her hospital superior, Dr. Leander.

Planet of the Apes episode #7: "The Surgeon" (CB-t)

◆ Galen's parents, Ann and Yalu, are heartbroken at the news of their son's actions. Ann is more forgiving that her stubborn politician husband, who cannot fathom apes being friends with humans.

Planet of the Apes episode #10: "The Interrogation" (CB-t)

◆ Virdon, Burke and Galen visit the human settlements of Radec and Slonk while heading west toward the sea. In both villages, someone recognizes the fugitives and reports their location to Urko.

Planet of the Apes episode #2: "The Gladiators" (AW-n)

NOTE: This is revealed in the episode's novelization.

◆ The fugitives are spotted moving toward the sea, and Urko sends his lieutenant, Jason, to kill them. In a valley near Kaymak, the astronauts intervene in a brawl between a gladiator, Tolar, and his son Dalton—who surprise them by fighting back as a team. Prefect Barlow arrives to check on Dalton's training for the Games. Virdon runs for cover, dropping the disk, which Barlow pockets. Hoping to retrieve it, Galen visits Barlow posing as an archeologist. The astronauts are arrested for stealing horses. A gorilla named Morko guards Virdon, while Burke is forced to fight Tolar. When Tolar refuses to kill, a riot ensues and Barlow imposes a curfew. Galen and Burke ask Tolar to hide them. Though he refuses, Dalton offers to help. Jason considers having Barlow dismissed for letting them escape, but instead says to arrange their deaths in the Games. Dalton declines to fight and is arrested. Tolar frees him, but he and Jason kill each other. His career no longer endangered, Barlow gives Virdon the disk and agrees to end the Games. The fugitives invite Dalton to join them, but he remains in Kaymak to spread pacifism.

Planet of the Apes episode #2: "The Gladiators" (CB-t)

NOTE: Morko is named in the novelization, in which Barlow is called Irnar.

PUBLISHER / STUDIO
AB . . . . ABC-TV
AC . . . .Adventure / Malibu Comics
AW . . . . Award Books
BB . . . . .Ballantine Books
BN . . . . Bantam Books
BW . . . . Brown Watson Books
CB . . . . CBS-TV
CV . . . . Chad Valley Sliderama
DH . . . . .Dark Horse Comics
ET . . . . Editorial Mo.Pa.Sa.
FX . . . . 20th Century Fox
GK . . . Gold Key / Western Comics
HE . . . HarperEntertainment Books
HM . . Harry K. McWilliams Assoc.
MC . . . . Marvel Comics
MR . . . Mr. Comics / Metallic Rose
NB . . . . NBC-TV
PR . . . . .Power Records
SB . . . . Signet Books
TP . . . . Topps
UB . . . . Ubisoft

MEDIUM
a . . . . animated series
b . . . . .book-and-record set
c . . . . .comic book or strip
d . . . . trading card
e . . . . e-comic
f . . . . .theatrical film
k . . . . .storybook
m . . . . .magazine article
n . . . . .novel or novelization
p . . . . promotional newspaper
r . . . . .recorded audio fiction
s . . . . short story
t . . . . television series
u . . . . . . .unfilmed script or story
v . . . . video game
x . . . . .Blu-Ray exclusive
y . . . . .young adult novel

◆ Urko sets up camp outside of San Francisco. A signal operator spots the fugitives, who knock him out and signal false information to send the troops in the wrong direction. They visit Numay, a farm town that harbors fugitives, and stay with a farmer named Miller, his wife Mary and their children, Lisa and Jick. Noticing computer parts Lisa found in the city, they visit the ruins hoping to learn more. Urko questions the family, then heads for the city with three soldiers (Memo, Olam and Zako). An earthquake buries Urko and Burke in the Sutter Street subway station. Burke urges Urko not to kill him since they need each other to survive, but angers the ape by claiming the station proves humans once ruled the world. Urko nearly kills him in outrage until Burke "admits" apes built it, lying to appease the gorilla. Virdon and Galen find a cement slab covering the hole, and Zako agrees to free them if they help rescue Urko. Burke shows Urko how to build a ladder, while Virdon helps the others erect a fulcrum to lift the cement. Urko sees a poster of a caged gorilla at the San Francisco Zoo, and tries to kill Burke to suppress the truth. Burke shocks him with a solar-powered light, then ties him up for the others to pull out. Urko orders the fugitives executed, but Zako keeps his word and lets them depart. Seeing the poster on the ground, he quickly rips it up.

Planet of the Apes episode #3: "The Trap" (CB-t)

NOTE: The city's name, spelled "Numay" in the script, is misspelled "Numai" in the DVD subtitles.

◆ Running from gorillas, Galen is hurt falling down a hill. His friends carry him to the farm of chimpanzee couple Polar and Zantes, who leave them in the barn as they take Galen inside. Polar's oldest son, Anto, is outraged to find them sleeping near his cow; humans are considered bad luck, and he awaits the birth of a bull calf in order to start his own farm. Zantes, a nurse, tells Galen to stay off his feet, so Polar puts the men to work. The astronauts teach the family advanced farming methods, such as windmill power, irrigation and planting the best seeds to produce better crops. Remus, the youngest son, is amazed, but Anto refuses to trust them. The cow goes into labor, and Anto urges his father to send the men away, convinced they plan to eat it. Polar's daughter Jillia flirts with Galen, who pretends not to notice. A patrol gorilla named Lupuk spots the astronauts showering and alerts his superior, Barga, who rides out to arrest them, thinking them recently escaped slaves. The calf turns in utero, but Virdon turns it around, delivering twin bulls. The fugitives hide in a loft when Urko visits the farm. Realizing he was wrong about them, Anto claims it was him in the shower. He later names the bulls "Burke" and "Virdon" in their honor.

Planet of the Apes episode #4: "The Good Seeds" (CB-t)

NOTE: Lupuk and Barga are named in the novelization.

◆ The fugitives find an ancient computer in the ruins of the Oakland Science Institute. The machine emits a hologram of an elderly scientist, claiming the sum of human knowledge was stored in several vaults when war was imminent. The power falters, and as they search for materials to build a battery, gorillas spot them and they separate. Virdon is captured and imprisoned with Arn, a widower whose husband Tomar was killed as a rebel, and Kraik, a street urchin. Urko, meanwhile, tortures Virdon. Burke builds a battery and the hologram reveals a vault embedded in the Midtown Railway Station. Kraik, hired by apes to spy in exchange for food, asks about Virdon's friends, but Virdon changes the subject. He carves a wooden airplane for Kraik, which the boy takes without permission. When Virdon chastises him, he smashes the plane and informs the apes about the computer. Feeling guilty, he helps the astronaut rejoin his comrades. Zaius finds the computer, watches the hologram and orders the building destroyed. As the vault burns, the fugitives escort Arn and Kraik to the farm of Tomar's brother, Derlin. Arn adopts Kraik as her own child. Though in love with Virdon, she knows he must return to his family.

Planet of the Apes episode #5: "The Legacy" (CB-t)

NOTE: This episode was originally titled "Second Family."

◆ Urko plans a trip to an area known as the New Territory.

Planet of the Apes episode #7: "The Surgeon" (CB-t)

NOTE: The purpose of Urko's visit is unstated. It's possible he intends to inspect his troops in that region.

◆ At a fishing village along the shore near Pismo Beach or Malibu, Prefect Hurton begins exiling elderly humans to keep overload low. A man named Gahto, father of Soma, is the next slated to die. Tied to a raft, Gahto is set afloat at sea to be consumed by sharks.

Planet of the Apes episode #6: "Tomorrow's Tide" (CB-t)

◆ Drs. Kira and Leander, surgeons at a medical center on the outskirts of Central City, send a human orderly to disciplinary camp for disobeying orders. Kira wonders if they were too harsh, but Leander thinks the punishment appropriate since the human was acting unruly.

Planet of the Apes episode #7: "The Surgeon" (CB-t)

◆ The fugitives drag Gahto's raft ashore, but he tries to return to the water, saying the gods have willed him to die. Leaving Galen to watch him, they spy on the labor camp where Gahto worked. Captured and taken to see Hurton, they claim to be fishermen. The ape puts them to work so he can meet new quotas imposed by his superior, an old orangutan named Bandor. Posing as Zuma, a Central City official—and the astronauts' master—Galen visits the camp. Hurton orders them fed to the "gods of the sea" (sharks) for lying, but Galen slips them a knife, enabling them to kill the animal and earn their freedom. Guards spot Gahto's raft and search for the old man. Hurton puts the fugitives to work, refusing to release them to Galen until Bandor arrives. Galen sends Soma to retrieve Gahto, but her husband Romar runs after her and is shot. Bandor arrives the next day and rules in Hurton's favor. The fugitives build a net to catch fish, impressing Bandor with their large haul. Galen and Soma return with Gahto, claiming he built the net, and that Hurton let him live so he could teach others, thereby raising production and ending the need to kill the elderly. Bandor agrees to this arrangement, and the delighted but confused Hurton increases rations for all humans. The fugitives then escape by tricking the orangutan into letting them paddle out to sea.

Planet of the Apes episode #6: "Tomorrow's Tide" (CB-t)

NOTE: Galen's alias is spelled "Zooma" in the script, but "Zuma" in the DVD subtitles.

◆ When a gorilla shoots Virdon, Galen poses as a surgeon named Dr. Adrian so he can seek help from his ex-fiancée, Dr. Kira. The astronauts are housed in human quarters. Travin, the head human, tells them not to talk to the serving girl (his daughter), who has been stripped of her name (Prunella Alexandrina—"Arna" for short) for having evil blood. Kira's texts contain no data on human anatomy, so Galen offers to find one written by humans. Bluffing his way through a meeting with Dr. Leander, Galen takes Burke to Zaius' home and tells a guard, Chester, that the councilor has had a heart attack. They grab a 20th-century tome—*Principles of Surgery*, by Walter Mather—and fool the guards with a bust of Doswa on a stretcher. Burke explains how to transfuse blood, deemed impossible after Arna's blood killed her injured brother (due to incompatible blood types). Only two humans have AB-negative blood like Virdon. One, Lafer, refuses to donate, but Arna volunteers. Surgery commences, with Galen and Burke consulting techniques in Zaius' book. Leander accuses them of treason, but Galen holds him at knifepoint while Kira removes the bullet. Urko investigates the theft at Zaius' office, urging him to burn his ancient texts before they fall into the wrong hands. Leander protects Kira when Urko arrives, claiming the fugitives fled when Black Plague hit the area. Urko departs, Virdon recovers and Travin helps them escape, vowing to make it up to his daughter. Finally, Galen bids farewell to Kira, knowing she'll be safe and happy with Leander.

Planet of the Apes episode #7: "The Surgeon" (CB-t)

NOTE: Arna's full name appears in the novelization, and in an early draft of the script.

PUBLISHER / STUDIO
AB . . . . ABC-TV
AC . . . . Adventure / Malibu Comics
AW . . . . Award Books
BB . . . . Ballantine Books
BN . . . . Bantam Books
BW . . . . Brown Watson Books
CB . . . . CBS-TV
CV . . . . Chad Valley Sliderama
DH . . . . Dark Horse Comics
ET . . . . Editorial Mo.Pa.Sa.
FX . . . . 20th Century Fox
GK . . . . Gold Key / Western Comics
HE . . . HarperEntertainment Books
HM . . Harry K. McWilliams Assoc.
MC . . . . Marvel Comics
MR . . . Mr. Comics / Metallic Rose
NB . . . . NBC-TV
PR . . . . Power Records
SB . . . . Signet Books
TP . . . . Topps
UB . . . . Ubisoft

MEDIUM
a . . . . animated series
b . . . . book-and-record set
c . . . . comic book or strip
d . . . . trading card
e . . . . e-comic
f . . . . theatrical film
k . . . . storybook
m . . . . magazine article
n . . . . novel or novelization
p . . . . promotional newspaper
r . . . . recorded audio fiction
s . . . . short story
t . . . . television series
u . . . . unfilmed script or story
v . . . . video game
x . . . . Blu-Ray exclusive
y . . . . young adult novel

◆ Galen keeps the book of surgery when they leave.

*Telefilm #4: **Life, Liberty and Pursuit on the Planet of the Apes** (AB-t)*

NOTE: *Galen still has the book years later, in new footage filmed for this telefilm edited from several TV episodes.*

◆ The fugitives meet a human whose brother, a friendly farmer named Jasko, offers to provide them shelter and food to break up their travels.

***Planet of the Apes** episode #8: "The Deception" (AW-n)*

NOTE: *This is revealed in the episode's novelization.*

◆ Lucian, a chimp sympathetic to humans, angers a hate group called the Dragoons for sharing knowledge with humans. His brother Sestus (a Dragoon) and the group's leader, Zon (a police deputy), warn him to stop. Zon hits Lucian, causing him to crack his head on a rock and die, then bullies Sestus into claiming humans were the culprits. A chimp named Chilot and two gorillas, Macor and Krono (also Dragoons), want to punish all humans for the crime, but police chief Perdix demands it be handled within the law. The fugitives arrive at Jasko's home, and he feeds them and recounts recent events. The Dragoons later set the home aflame and drag Jasko to his death.

***Planet of the Apes** episode #8: "The Deception" (CB-t)*

NOTE: *Macor and Krono are named in the novelization.*

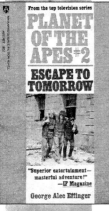

◆ Galen obtains directions to the home of Lucian's daughter Fauna from a neighboring ape farmer. Fauna shares the home with her uncle Sestus.

***Planet of the Apes** episode #8: "The Deception" (AW-n)*

NOTE: *This is revealed in the episode's novelization.*

◆ The fugitives visit Fauna posing as apes named Phoebus (Galen), Alar (Virdon) and Pargo (Burke), and are careful not to let on that two of them are human. When her uncle arrives, Burke claims the Ministry of Knowledge is pursuing them for reading forbidden books, and she hides them in a grotto at Sandy Point.

***Planet of the Apes** episode #8: "The Deception" (CB-t)*

NOTE: *In the novelization, Burke's alias is spelled "Pago." Why Fauna wouldn't be able to smell the difference between humans and apes is unclear.*

◆ The astronauts recognize the site as Hanson Point, where they relaxed after preflight indoctrination.

***Planet of the Apes** episode #8: "The Deception" (AW-n)*

NOTE: *This is revealed in the episode's novelization.*

◆ When Fauna asks to touch Burke's face, Galen offers his instead. She invites them to stay, promising food in the morning. After she leaves, they plot to infiltrate the Dragoons. Claiming humans stole his horse, Galen befriends Sestus, espousing anti-human sentiment. Virdon follows Krono to the Dragoon hideout, knocks him out, discovers a hood in his bag and heads for the grotto. Burke, meanwhile, keeps Fauna company. She asks about the books he's read, and he offers a retelling of *Robinson Crusoe*, but with ape characters.

***Planet of the Apes** episode #8: "The Deception" (CB-t)*

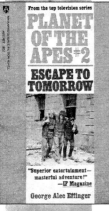

◆ Sestus informs Perdix and Zon that two humans stole Galen's horse, and the deputy promises to hunt them down. Perdix, determined to prevent more bloodshed, reminds Zon that they must stay within the bounds of the law, but Zon is unhappy about such a restriction.

Planet of the Apes episode #8: "The Deception" (AW-n)

NOTE: This is revealed in the episode's novelization.

◆ Urko transfers Barlow from Kaymak to the village of Venton. The chimp prefect resents the decision, and is unhappier still when he learns Urko has arranged a horse race in the province. If he loses—and Barlow knows all prefects lose against Urko—the price will be half his lands and his horses.

Planet of the Apes episode #9: "The Horse Race" (CB-t)

NOTE: This placement is approximate, based on Martin's reference to Barlow as "the new prefect." The script calls Kaymak "Alar," Virdon's alias in the previous episode.

◆ When word of the race circulates, a friend in the village of Regego warns Barlow that Urko is known to cheat, even when he's clearly ahead.

Planet of the Apes episode #9: "The Horse Race" (AW-n)

NOTE: This is revealed in the episode's novelization.

◆ The fugitives read about Lucian's pro-human activities in his diary and suspect murder. Fauna admits she loves Burke, and though he tries to let her down gently, he hurts her feelings. Feeling guilty, he tells her the Biblical story of Jacob, who pretended to be his brother Esau out of desperation. The astronauts try to bring Perdix to the Dragoons' meeting spot but grab a deputy instead, enabling Perdix to subdue them. The High Council of Dragoons indoctrinates Galen. Zon gives him a gun to kill Rico, a human shepherd, on their next raid. Galen tries to lure them to Sandy Point, but they prefer to wait until daybreak. He frees his friends from jail, and they bring Perdix to the caves to apprehend the Dragoons. Zon threatens to kill Perdix, but Sestus refuses to harm a fellow ape. Fauna falls into the sea, and Burke dives in to save her. She touches his face, recoiling at his skin. Sestus tells her Burke saved her life and reveals the truth of Lucian's death. Horrified, the Dragoons renounce Zon and disband. Perdix arrests his deputy, and Sestus invites the fugitives to stay on his farm, but they decline.

Planet of the Apes episode #8: "The Deception" (CB-t)

NOTE: According to Simian Scrolls issue #12, an early-draft episode outline in the TV series writer's bible identifies Sestus, not Zon, as Lucian's killer. Esau is the name of a main character in Dark Horse's comic-book spinoff of the Tim Burton film, while Jacob is an orangutan official in the Adventure comics line.

◆ In the village of Venton, a human male is spotted riding a horse—a crime carrying the death penalty. The youth (Gregor) evades capture, but ape soldiers keep an eye out in case he dares ride again.

Planet of the Apes episode #9: "The Horse Race" (CB-t)

◆ Galen's father Yalu is elected to the Central City Council.

Planet of the Apes episode #10: "The Interrogation" (CB-t)

NOTE: Galen's mom, Ann, says Yalu has just been elected to this position, so I have placed this event before the previous episode.

PUBLISHER / STUDIO
AB . . . . ABC-TV
AC . . . .Adventure / Malibu Comics
AW . . . . Award Books
BB. . . . . Ballantine Books
BN. . . . . Bantam Books
BW . . . . Brown Watson Books
CB . . . . CBS-TV
CV . . . . Chad Valley Sliderama
DH. . . . . .Dark Horse Comics
ET . . . . Editorial Mo.Pa.Sa.
FX . . . . 20th Century Fox
GK . . . .Gold Key / Western Comics
HE . . . HarperEntertainment Books
HM . . Harry K. McWilliams Assoc.
MC . . . . Marvel Comics
MR . . . Mr. Comics / Metallic Rose
NB. . . . . NBC-TV
PR . . . . .Power Records
SB. . . . . Signet Books
TP . . . . Topps
UB . . . . .Ubisoft

MEDIUM
a . . . . animated series
b . . . . .book-and-record set
c . . . . .comic book or strip
d . . . . trading card
e . . . . e-comic
f . . . . .theatrical film
k . . . . .storybook
m . . . . .magazine article
n . . . . .novel or novelization
p . . . . promotional newspaper
r . . . . .recorded audio fiction
s . . . . short story
t . . . . television series
u . . . . . . .unfilmed script or story
v . . . . video game
x . . . . .Blu-Ray exclusive
y . . . . .young adult novel

◆ Urko arranges a horse race between his champion rider, Kagon, and that of a village prefect. Given Urko's history of cheating, the prefect knows he'll lose everything. The price: half his land and horses. Urko's horse Tusan, however, throws a shoe and loses its first race.

Planet of the Apes episode #9: "The Horse Race" (CB-t)

NOTE: In the novelization, Urko's jockey is named "Kagan," but the DVD subtitles spell it "Kagon." The horse's name comes from the episode's novelization.

◆ Furious, Urko orders the blacksmith executed. Gorilla guards drag the man off to his death.

Planet of the Apes episode #9: "The Horse Race" (AW-n)

NOTE: This occurs in the episode's novelization.

◆ Two humans, Levis and Roras, help the fugitives. Word of their criminal assistance reaches the council, which opens an investigation into the matter.

Planet of the Apes episode #10: "The Interrogation" (CB-t)

NOTE: This is conjectural, based on Wanda's question regarding whether these two humans ever helped Burke and his friends.

◆ Martin, a Venton blacksmith, and his wife Seelah offer the fugitives food, and they work in his shop to repay his kindness. Urko's lieutenant, Zandar, orders Martin to shod Tusan for an upcoming race. Galen is bitten by a tiger scorpion, and with the nearest doctor five miles away, Martin's son Gregor rides out for an antidote. Gorillas arrive, seeking the human rider. Virdon tries to take the blame, but Gregor admits his crime and a soldier named Zilo arrests him to face execution. Galen asks Barlow for leniency, and the prefect offers a deal: the boy will go free if Virdon wins the race for him. Zaius allows Barlow to use a human jockey, but Virdon's horse, Woda, is untamed. Urko ups the stakes, betting all of Barlow's horses and land versus reassignment to Kaymak. Urko's soldiers create pitfalls to make sure Woda falls, so Galen and Burke even the odds. Martin offers to rig the race if Urko frees his son, and the gorilla agrees—but orders Zilo to shoot both Gregor and the human jockey, win or lose.

Planet of the Apes episode #9: "The Horse Race" (CB-t)

NOTE: In the novelization and script, the boy's name is spelled Greger and the village is called Venta, but DVD subtitles identify them as Gregor and Venton. The novelization calls Kaymak "Cela." Seelah appears in the script.

◆ Urko orders a soldier named Moro to rig a branch to knock the human jockey from his horse.

Planet of the Apes episode #9: "The Horse Race" (AW-n)

NOTE: This occurs in the episode's script and novelization, but not onscreen.

◆ Martin puts wedges in Woda's shoes, causing the horse to throw Virdon. Zilo sets traps for Woda, but Virdon manages to catch up with the other horse. Urko recognizes him and orders Zilo to fire, but Galen puts a scorpion on the soldier's shoulder, immobilizing him and enabling Virdon to win. Zilo frees Gregor, intending to shoot him, but Burke beats the ape senseless. Galen steals a wagon and joins the others outside town, sending the empty cart for Urko's apes to chase. Barlow leaves Venton, allowing Gregor and his family to come work for him in Kaymak.

Planet of the Apes episode #9: "The Horse Race" (CB-t)

◆ Gorillas capture Burke and take him to a secret base at Crystal Cavern. To discover who has aided him since his arrival, a chimp scientist named Wanda brainwashes him using an ancient human textbook. Galen and Virdon visit the chimp's parents, but Yalu denounces their friendship. A servant, Loomis, signals a gorilla squad's arrival, and Yalu hides the duo in a floor compartment while troops search their home. Galen and Virdon break into a local jail, but Burke isn't there. Wanda ties Burke to a spinning table and induces hallucinations. When he refuses to talk, Urko beats him badly. Burke's friends find records of the base in Urko's office, arriving in time to stop Dr. Malthus from lobotomizing him. Ann helps them get into the base, overpower the guards and free Burke, then hides them as Urko questions her and Yalu about the break-out. Before Galen leaves, Yalu expresses pride in his son. ●

Planet of the Apes episode #10: "The Interrogation" (CB-t)

NOTE: In the script, the Crystal Cavern is called the Hemisphere Building.

◆ Two human farmers, Janor and his younger brother Mikal, give refuge to the fugitives. Lt. Daku, aide-de-camp to District Chief Aboro, orders his driver, Hosson, to take all of the grain the farmers have shoveled. The gorillas head for the Darog farm, en route to a gold caravan at Hathor. Aboro, fancying himself the "Lord of the Apes," has been trading grain for gold to buy a promotion from Urko's corrupt assistant, Bulta. With Mikal's help, the astronauts trip Daku's horse, hijack the cart and retrieve the grain. Before passing out, Daku recognizes Mikal's shirt.

Planet of the Apes episode #11: "The Tyrant" (CB-t)

NOTE: The novelization names Hosson and reveals Aboro's nickname. The TV series writer's bible, excerpted in Simian Scrolls #12, *mentions a female version of Janor named "Jana," and has Aboro stealing pelts and plotting to kill Urko from the onset.*

◆ Burke and Virdon hide the wagon in a cave and recognize Jennings' Nose, a hill near Edwards Air Force Base that they, as cadets, jokingly named after their hook-nosed commanding officer. With Mikal's help, the astronauts distribute the grain to local human farmers.

Planet of the Apes episode #11: "The Tyrant" (AW-n)

NOTE: This is revealed in the episode's novelization.

◆ Mikal's acts inspire Janor to resist, but Aboro and Daku shoot both men and burn the barn, killing Mikal. Galen visits his cousin Augustus, Hathor's prefect, to report Aboro's crimes. Aboro arrives, however, bypassing a human servant, Gola, to deliver a scroll naming him prefect. Augustus is reassigned to the remote village of Dorvado, and Aboro assumes command. Urko, who attended the academy with Aboro and Bulta 20 years prior, makes a surprise visit during an inspection tour, to congratulate Aboro on his promotion. After the security chief leaves, Galen claims to be Zaius' crippled assistant, Octavio, and conspires with him to frame Urko so Aboro can replace him. Aboro prefers a more direct approach, however: hiring a human named Amhar to kill the gorilla, then having Daku kill Amhar. First, however, Aboro requests confirmation of Octavio's identity.

Planet of the Apes episode #11: "The Tyrant" (CB-t)

NOTE: Gola is named in the episode's script.

◆ The fugitives knock out a heliograph operator named Gorak and intercept the confirmation request. Using the device, they pose as Bron, the Supreme Council's acting secretary, and respond in the affirmative.

Planet of the Apes episode #11: "The Tyrant" (AW-n)

NOTE: This is revealed in the episode's novelization.

◆ The astronauts ambush Daku, then use Aboro's seal to create a false letter to Amhar. Galen sneaks into Urko's tent to warn him of Aboro's plot, but Urko disbelieves him, even upon reading the letter.

Planet of the Apes episode #11: "The Tyrant" (CB-t)

◆ Suspicious, Urko asks a guard, Kronak, if he's ever heard of Amhar. To his surprise, Kronak confirms the human to be a known hired killer.

Planet of the Apes episode #11: "The Tyrant" (AW-n)

NOTE: This is revealed in the episode's novelization.

◆ Burke and Virdon show up with weapons, but Urko knows they can't fire without alerting guards. They urge him to accompany them to Aboro's home so Burke can pose as Amhar and trick Aboro into admitting the crime. Despite his skepticism, Urko agrees to the ruse.

Planet of the Apes episode #11: "The Tyrant" (CB-t)

◆ Intent on killing Aboro, Janor hitches a ride to Hathor. Galen and Virdon spot him headed for Aboro's home and explain their plan, urging him not to resort to murder.

Planet of the Apes episode #11: "The Tyrant" (AW-n)

NOTE: This scene occurs in the episode's novelization.

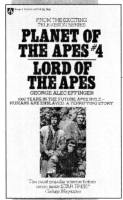

◆ Freed by a guard named Feena, Daku tells Aboro he failed to contact Amhar. Aboro sets an explosive, telling Daku to summon him before lighting the fuse. Urko arrives with Galen, and when Burke shows up claiming to be Amhar, Urko orders him arrested. Virdon discovers the bomb, leaving its fuse lit to fool Aboro. The prefect hears the fuse and runs for the door. Urko grabs a gun and stops him from leaving. Virdon enters holding the bomb, forcing the apes to lower their weapons so the fugitives can escape. Urko arrests Aboro for bribery, corruption and conduct unbecoming an ape, then returns to Central City to expose Bulta.

Planet of the Apes episode #11: "The Tyrant" (CB-t)

NOTE: Feena's scene appears in the script but not onscreen.

◆ The fugitives return to Janor's farm, where he thanks them for avenging Mikal's death. Knowing the council will restore Augustus as prefect, Galen hopes to stay and visit his cousin, but the approach of a gorilla patrol sends the trio on their way once more.

Planet of the Apes episode #11: "The Tyrant" (AW-n)

NOTE: This scene occurs in the episode's novelization.

◆ In Trion, a villager named Talbert and his daughter Amy offer the fugitives refuge. Amy falls in love with Virdon, reacting badly when he reveals his identity (an indiscretion that upsets Galen). A worker drops near a stagnant pond, twitching with the Shaking Sickness. The disease spreads, and Talbert is among its victims. Zaius quarantines Trion, assigning Dr. Zoran, the council's chief medical officer, to study the plague. A coal-carrier named Mason tells the fugitives about the disease. Recognizing malaria, they instruct the locals to burn the dead, but Zoran and his assistant, Inta, scoff at the idea—until an ape named Neesa dies as well. Zoran offers Virdon's diagnosis as his own, and though skeptical, Zaius lets him seek a cure. Virdon creates breathing masks, instructing villagers to drain the pond and extract quinine from a cinchona tree. Amy falls ill, and Zoran hears her muttering about a man from another time. A second ape, Kava, falls sick as well. The council gives Zoran another day to find a cure, after which Urko plans to burn the village. Virdon secretly gives Kava the medicine, and he recovers. Seeing the drug's success, Zaius orders Urko's troops to withdraw. Zoran intends to turn the fugitives in despite his gratitude, but keeps silent when they threaten to reveal their part in the cure.

Planet of the Apes episode #12: "The Cure" (CB-t)

NOTE: Neesa is named in the episode's script and novelization. In early drafts of the script, Amy was said to be age 12, then 14, reminding Virdon of his 14-year-old daughter back home. When his daughter was removed from the final draft, Amy's age was increased to make the bond a romantic one instead.

◆ Gorillas raid Borak for human slave miners. Brun, the "Master of Borak," offers two captured Meadow People, plus three of his own—Clim, Lorko and Arma. Clim runs off, and when Virdon saves his life, he lures the fugitives to his village as replacements. Brun's son Miro imprisons them all, refusing Galen's demands for their release. In the Valley of Stillness, Miro ties Clim to a cart to punish him. As Clim's mate Malana protests, the masked Brun asks the gods to pronounce sentence, and Clim dies without being touched. Miro conducts another hunt and brings back a Meadow Person. The barbarian cuts Miro, and Virdon stops the bleeding with a tourniquet. When Miro's mate Talia is chosen for the next allotment, he frees the astronauts, demanding they take her with them. Burke passes out upon entering the temple, and Virdon pulls him to safety, realizing the structure contains a poison gas spring. Using charcoal breathing filters, they find an ancient gas mask and several canisters—Brun has been making gas bombs to kill all apes. Galen accidentally starts a fire, and Brun dies in an explosion. As the new Master of Borak, Miro vows to end his people's slavery, make peace with the Meadow People and oppose ape oppression.

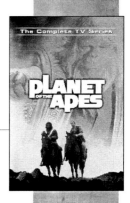

Planet of the Apes episode #13: "The Liberator" (CB-t)

NOTE: This episode was originally entitled "The Conqueror." The script names the Valley of Stillness and establishes the Meadow People as barbarians, while also calling Miro "Trung." Malana's protest occurs in the script, but not in the televised version.

◆ To protest a new curfew and anti-human regulations, the United Freedom Force (UFF)—a radical group promoting human-simian equality—kidnaps Lora, the daughter of Senator Sallus. The UFF, consisting of human and ape members, is run by two human extremists named Grayson and Kemmer.

Planet of the Apes: "Hostage" (CB-u)

NOTE: This unfilmed script is available online at Hunter's Planet of the Apes *Archive.*

◆ Leuric, a human inventor, builds a hang-glider but crashes it near Chatka. Virdon and Burke hide him from ape guards, urging him to stop flying before he gets caught. He refuses, but agrees to find a more concealed area. Burke borrows a hunk of lightning-formed glass in his lab to make a magnifying glass. A chimp scientist named Carsia suggests they examine the glider, and Zaius orders Cmdr. Konag to kill the pilot. The apes arrest Leuric, and Carsia provides a lab to continue his work. Posing as Protus, an archeologist, Galen seduces Carsia so he can monitor Leuric's work. The astronauts realize the glider was faulty and build their own. Setting Leuric's glider afire with the magnifying glass, Galen offers "servants" and materials to start anew. Carsia shows Galen a book of pro-chimp sentiments, saying their kind should rule the planet. Among her belongings is an ancient fragmentation cosmoline pack, with which she plans to bomb Urko's HQ and the council chambers, then lead a chimp revolution. Galen is captured trying to free Leuric, however, and the inventor is injured during the escape, so weapons instructor Robar forces Galen to fly with him. When they fly too far, the apes shoot down the glider, causing it to crash into the sea. The astronauts rescue them with a raft, and Galen suffers sea-sickness as they row to safety.

Planet of the Apes episode #14: "Up Above the World So High" (CB-t)

NOTE: The script names Chatka and reveals Robar's title; features several unfilmed scenes, included above; and has Virdon flying with Leuric. According to Simian Scrolls *issue #12, an early-draft episode outline in the TV series writer's bible revealed a wife for Leuric and had the astronauts shooting him down using a "javelin catapult."*

◆ The fugitives discover the secret base of the United Freedom Force (UFF). Apes raid the site moments later, forcing an evacuation, and Kemmer lobs a grenade as he leaves. Troops capture the fugitives and two UFF members—Aro (an ape) and Black (a human)—and Urko gives Galen and Virdon 48 hours to locate Lora. Sallus and his wife Clia visit Burke's cell. He suggests Lora might be freed if the council relaxed restrictions. Virdon and Galen traverse the Blasted Zone to the new UFF base—the former NASA Research Center HQ—to find Lora has joined the rebels. A woman named Katrin gives Virdon a tour, and romance stirs between them. The UFF sends the council Lora's bracelet and a ransom note demanding the abolition of the new laws, but Urko executes Black instead. Galen urges Lora to return home, but she fears the others' wrath. Furious over Black's execution, Kemmer and Grayson decide to kill Lora, causing a schism among the rebels. Katrin's supporters free the hostages, and Grayson tries to shoot Virdon using an ancient laser gun, but the weapon overloads, destroying half the building and killing both leaders. Lora returns to her parents and testifies on the fugitives' behalf, and Zaius lets them go. The rebels head out to form a peaceful human-simian society beyond the Blasted Zone, which Lora considers joining one day.

Planet of the Apes: "Hostage" (CB-u)

NOTE: This unfilmed episode script is available online at Hunter's Planet of the Apes *Archive. Apparently, Virdon has forgotten about his wife back home.*

◆ After years of hiding, an ethnic minority tribe of humans is convicted of resisting the apes. Facing extermination, some push for an accommodation with the apes, but others prefer either to go down fighting in a last glorious battle, scratch out a subsistence existence in a secret canyon or risk a trek to a better life beyond the Forbidden Zone. The latter poses many dangers, with no certainty such a "promised land" exists. The fugitives and Galen become involved with the tribe when they save a tribesman from summary execution by a gorilla patrol. The astronauts advocate finding the Forbidden Zone, despite Galen's superstitious fears of that area, and his belief that the tribe is dangerous. Ultimately, Galen overcomes his fears and leads the tribe through the wasteland.

Planet of the Apes: "The Trek" (CB-u)

NOTE: The humans' "ethnic minority" is unspecified. No scripts for this or the following three unfilmed episodes are available, though synopsis are included in the TV series writer's bible, reprinted in Simian Scrolls *issue #12.*

◆ A human named Odin is recognized while saving one of the astronauts. A gorilla prefect offers amnesty to anyone with information about the fugitives. The trio allow Odin to accept such amnesty once they've escaped, but fear it might be a trap. Galen visits the prefect and learns the offer is legitimate, and that the gorilla is investigating the disappearance of several prominent humans, who may have left to forge a rebellion. As such, the prefect forbids travel within his territory without passes. The fugitives discover an underground railroad for apes and humans seeking Shangri-La. They accompany the group to the contact point, then set out for the "promised land." Avoiding patrols, they reach the next railroad stop—Urko's trap to ensnare rebellious humans. Foiling the gorilla in charge of the stop, the passengers embark to build a better life, while the fugitives continue on their own quest.

Planet of the Apes: "Freedom Road" (CB-u)

◆ An old man locates a once-advanced human city and uses its technology to build a water-driven mill. The fugitives find the mill and hope whoever built it might help them find a way home. The old man is forced into slave labor, mining salt for the apes. A corrupt gorilla operates the mine, cheating the council and forcing extra work from his slaves by feeding them in proportion to productivity. The astronauts lose track of Galen while trying to free the man, and are themselves captured and enslaved. To free them, Galen assumes the guise of a government inspector, not realizing the corrupt leader would feel threatened by—and try to kill—an inspector. The astronauts convince the slaves not to compete for food, then escape and save Galen's life. The old man and the gorilla leader are killed in the process. Failing to learn the great civilization's whereabouts, the astronauts wonder if it really exists.

Planet of the Apes: "The Mine" (CB-u)

◆ A nasty gorilla in a highly productive village hazes a human field worker. Virdon defends him, inadvertently killing the ape. The commanding gorilla orders Virdon's execution, but Galen and Burke raise doubts about his guilt. The humans refuse to work if Virdon is unfairly punished, and the commander agrees to a trial. Virdon discovers that a human has been selling homebrewed whiskey to gorillas, whose drunken brutality caused the tragedy. Vowing to execute Virdon, the second-in-command contacts Urko, who gives him control of the village. Ignoring all evidence, he sentences Virdon to death, but Galen and Burke ply the guards with whiskey, rescue their friend and escape prior to Urko's arrival. Furious at losing his quarry, Urko blames the officer for the drunken guards' failure.

Planet of the Apes: "The Trial" (CB-u)

◆ Gorilla hunters mistake Burke and Virdon for Stern and Lang, escaped humans from a village north of Central City. The prefect realizes they're not from his settlement and interrogates them. Wary of their rebellious nature, he sends a messenger to summon Urko. The actual escapees encounter Galen and take him hostage. When they tell him of the slave-labor conditions in their village, he agrees to help stop the ruling gorillas' tyranny. Virdon and Burke overpower a guard and try to escape, but are quickly subdued outside the prison. The messenger returns with orders from Urko to deliver the astronauts. Galen, Stern and Lang destroy an armory, inspiring others to rebel. Galen frees his friends in the confusion, and when the outnumbered soldiers retreat, the humans head east to build their own mountain village. The astronauts decline their invitation to join them, knowing their path lies elsewhere.

Planet of the Apes (Authorized Edition) #1: "Journey Into Terror" (BW-c)

NOTE: Released in Britain, the following three hardcover annuals (or "authorised editions," as stated on their covers) contain a number of comic-strip and text stories.

◆ After several days unpursued, the fugitives arrive at Galen's old home, Nufort, a human-less village home to 30 or 40 apes. Galen visits his chimp friend Shako, and Ponar, the village's sympathetic orangutan leader. Zaius and Urko tour the village, and Ponar worries that a troublesome chimp named Naten might inform them of Galen's arrival. When Galen tries to talk to Zaius in private, the elder refuses to help him, though he pities the chimp and promises not to tell Urko—which Naten does. Urko declares martial law and orders soldiers to search each home, but Shako and others take up arms, enabling Galen to escape. Urko turns on Naten, who swears he saw Zaius talking to the fugitive, but the orangutan denies Naten's claims. Guards arrest Naten for lying, and Galen returns to his friends.

Planet of the Apes (Authorized Edition) #1: "A Promise Kept" (BW-s)

NOTE: Zaius' conspiratorial leniency toward Galen seems a bit out of character.

◆ When Virdon is injured in an earthquake, Galen visits Prefect Koro in a nearby village, claiming to be on a relic hunt for the council. An orangutan physician, Dr. Yasu, refuses to help Virdon, but a servant named Dane refers him to Jefferson, a human herbologist. Koro shows Galen old Beatles albums (which Galen erroneously deems an ancient game), and brings him to a quaint human ceremony: the worship of an ancient warplane. Astonished, Galen borrows a horse and informs the astronauts, who find the plane resting on a cliff. A mob of angry humans attacks, and the trio hide in the plane as gorillas subdue the mob, firing two rockets as a diversion. The rockets trigger a quake, dropping the plane—along with several apes and humans—over the cliff. The fugitives flee in the chaos.

Planet of the Apes (Authorized Edition) #1: "When the Earth Shakes" (BW-c)

◆ Pursued by apes, the fugitives hide among ancient city ruins. In an old shop, Galen finds signs of a recent fire and a store of food—proof they're not alone. When the occupant (a human named Creel) returns, he sees Galen and panics, afraid he might be searching for runaways. Reassured that they pose no threat, Creel says other runaways live in the city as well. Soldiers arrive, sending the humans scurrying. Among them are two men named Wheeler and Sinclair. Cooper, a frantic human, attacks Galen on sight, saying the apes have taken Sinclair and will return to flush them out. Taking to the sewers, the astronauts help the runaways drop brickwork on the apes, then pull Sinclair into a manhole. Thinking the town haunted, the apes ride off in fright, leaving the humans in peace.

Planet of the Apes (Authorized Edition) #1: "The Scavengers" (BW-s)

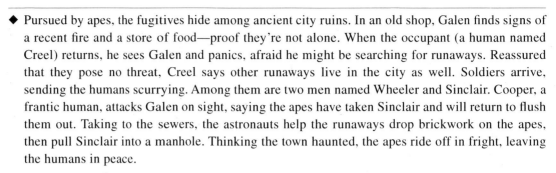

◆ Apes pursue the fugitives through a swamp. After a day of chasing, Urko arrives to direct operations. Clambering onto an earthen bank, they find a path through the bog but are captured by gorillas. Before dawn, they escape back to the bayou and use a tinder box to ignite marsh gas in a pool of water. The resultant explosion scares off all soldiers except Urko, who falls into the muck and is nearly sucked down to his death. The fugitives offer to save his life if he'll set them free. He accepts, warning that once the sun comes up, the hunt will resume.

Planet of the Apes (Authorized Edition) #1: "Swamped" (BW-s)

◆ Entering an earthquake zone, the fugitives meet a band of humans in the ruins of a futuristic city. One man, Green, shares his shelter. Virdon asks to see his people's holy place, and he takes them to a decrepit skyscraper. None dare enter, he says, since most fear the flashings and whirrings within. They enter and find a computer center powered by a miniature nuclear generator. Virdon hits a master switch, activating a light. A quake damages the generator, however, cutting power to the computer. Burke builds a wind generator, but before they can access the computer again, Green's people throw rocks through the windows, calling them sorcerers and blasphemers. Another quake threatens to level the building, and the fugitives barely get to safety before it crashes down around them.

Planet of the Apes (Authorized Edition) #2: "From Out of the Past" (BW-s)

◆ Stopping to rest, Galen falls through a hole. Virdon and Burke dive in after him when ape sentries arrive. Inside is a U.S. Army bioweapons storage bunker, used to store plagues for germ warfare. While one soldier stands guard, the other summons his superior, Cmdr. Griz. Determined to keep the contents out of ape hands, the fugitives search for a way to close the tanks, but Griz's troops enter the shelter before they can do so. The astronauts blow up a corridor, cutting off their pursuers. Griz mistakes a deadly germ sample for poison gas and releases it, killing himself and his troops. The fugitives destroy the corridor, escaping to the surface uninfected.

Planet of the Apes (Authorized Edition) #2: "Pit of Doom" (BW-c)

◆ Galen follows the scent of stewing fruit and comes face-to-face with Urko's troops. Urko forces him to lead them to his friends, but the astronauts see them coming and evade capture. Staying to the trees, they follow Urko's group to a nearby village, where Galen is escorted to the local prefect. Virdon lights a brush fire as a distraction, then Burke overpowers a guard and frees Galen. Avoiding the firelight, they make for the woods and escape into the night.

Planet of the Apes (Authorized Edition) #2: "The Captive" (BW-s)

◆ The trio visit the village of Zingu. Berga, the local headman, offers shelter, but Hemming, a human spy, informs Urko. The security chief releases his sister from mine labor as payment, then orders his troops to surround Zingu. Galen sprains his ankle in a fall, forcing his friends to leave him behind. Urko imprisons Berga for refusing to hand them over, then calls for Burke and Virdon to surrender, lest he kill the villagers. The duo turn themselves in, claiming Galen left to visit his sick mother. When Urko threatens to kill 20 female villagers, the men of Zingu rise up against him, freeing the fugitives, who liberate Berga. Guilt-ridden at causing so many deaths, they run when Zaius arrives. Zaius chastises Urko for sparking a rebellion, ordering him to produce the fugitives or face the council's wrath. The astronauts build a stretcher for Galen and continue on their way.

Planet of the Apes (Authorized Edition) #2: "Raiding Party" (BW-s)

◆ Pursued by gorillas, the fugitives reach the Pacific Ocean shore and hide in a cave down a steep slope. They hear the sounds of machinery and spot a small boat and a band of fishermen planning to sail west across the sea. Scouts capture Galen as a spy, and Virdon and Burke fight for his freedom. A schism forms between their leader, Werner, who trusts Galen, and Miller, who refuses to accept an ape. Werner invites the trio to sail with them. Miller protests but is more concerned with survival when the local prefect and his soldiers are seen nearby. The fugitives break free of Miller's hold, taking to the hills to lead the apes away and give the men time to set sail. Burying the gorillas in an avalanche, they return to the beach in time to watch Werner's men sail safely away.

Planet of the Apes (Authorized Edition) #2: "Ship of Fools" (BW-c)

◆ The fugitives see apes acting fearfully toward an old building. They meet a farmhand named Jess and claim to be on a secret mission to investigate the structure. Jess says villagers bring daily offerings to a spirit within, which lights up the edifice when pleased. Inside, the astronauts hear laughter as the light goes out, and pull back a curtain to find a man named Gulik creating a smoke bomb. Gulik admits he poses as a ghost so others will leave him alone. Jess accidentally exposes them by mentioning their mission to others. Apes rush to catch them, and Gulik helps stage a visitation to scare the soldiers. Bidding farewell, the trio urge the hermit to use his skills to help others.

Planet of the Apes (Authorized Edition) #2: "When the Ghosts Walk" (BW-s)

◆ Zaius launches an experiment in a remote village, recalling the prefect and all ape citizens to study how humans fare in isolation. Looking to seize control of the council, Urko makes a deal with a human named Cluf to kill Zaius. The fugitives encounter ape sentries guarding the town. Galen pretends to be studying human behavior, with Virdon and Burke as his servants. The apes let them pass but warn that the area is a protected zone. An old man invites them to stay at the prefect's house, but seems to be hiding something. They hear distant gunshots at night and discover that the shooter is not an ape, but Cluf. Realizing what he's up to, they subdue him and expose his assassination plans. Zaius tours the city unharmed, and Urko punishes Cluf for his failure.

Planet of the Apes (Authorized Edition) #2: "The Marksman" (BW-s)

◆ A gorilla named Jehan leads a revolt against Urko. Forewarned by spies, Urko ambushes Jehan's troops, then orders a hunt for the soldier, promising a hundred human slaves for his capture. An orangutan assistant named Oris reports the revolt to Zaius, who visits the battle scene. Jehan and a half-dozen supporters head for Skull Pass, where troops surround him. A stalemate ensues as Jehan's fighters hide among the rocks. Jehan challenges Urko to unarmed combat. He gains the upper hand and tries to kill Urko, but Zaius offers a conduct pass to the Outlands in exchange for Urko's life. Jehan accepts exile, and Zaius decides he could prove useful should Urko ever become too much trouble. As the orangutans return to Central City, Urko vows one day to take revenge on Zaius.

Planet of the Apes (Authorized Edition) #3: "Blow For Blow" (BW-c)

NOTE: This story is one of three from the third annual in which the fugitives make no appearance.

◆ Virdon and Burke attend a village meeting to hear a speech by an old man named John, also called the Prophet. He claims to be from an era when men ruled the world, urging others to strive for such greatness. The astronauts learn that he appeared a few months prior and lives outside the village, sometimes visiting to obtain food and give speeches. Gorillas demand John be handed over, and the fugitives slip out to warn him. In his cave, they learn the truth: John uses makeup and effects to achieve "immortality." Having studied millennium-old library tapes, he'd taken on the Prophet ruse to bypass the villagers' distrust of machines and offer hope for the future. The fugitives help the man rig a trap to bury the gorillas in the cave, giving him time to lead the villagers into the hills.

Planet of the Apes (Authorized Edition) #3: "The Prophet" (BW-s)

◆ The fugitives discover a prison camp for renegade humans. A ragged inmate named Ellis welcomes them, saying his people have been unable to escape the ape sentries surrounding the village and would gladly go with them if the newcomers had a plan. Finding a natural gas vent in the ground, Virdon and Burke teach the prisoners to build a hot air balloon to distract the apes, allowing time for escape. Only a few apes follow the balloon, so Burke rigs an explosion at the vent, luring the rest into ambush. Beating the gorillas to death, the renegades split up into small groups and scatter, while the fugitives continue on their way.

Planet of the Apes (Authorized Edition) #3: "Breakout" (BW-c)

◆ A gorilla squad pursues the trio to the ruins of an old city, where Burke falls upon catching his foot on a rock. Galen and Virdon help him hobble to an old apartment building to hide from the gorillas. Galen scouts the structure and finds a massive armory, which they realize must be one of Urko's secret arms dumps, in case the council tries to replace him. The fugitives blow up the building and shoot the few remaining gorillas, then steal horses to ride off before more gorilla soldiers can arrive.

Planet of the Apes (Authorized Edition) #3: "The Arsenal" (BW-s)

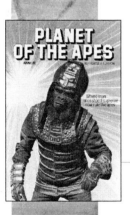

◆ Urko interrupts a council meeting, demanding additional troops to control the human population. Zaius rebuffs him, reminding Urko of his past failures. Zaius launches a plan to offer humans more freedom to quell their rebellious nature, but his assistant Oris doubts it will work. Narza, a gorilla prison camp commander, steals a draft of the plan as leverage for Urko to seize control. As Zaius leads an orangutan-chimp search party, Narza asks a scribe named Mardik to alter the documents, making it appear Zaius was freeing humans entirely. During a prison inspection, Zaius confronts Mardik, knowing no chimps serve on Narza's staff, and Mardik admits the forgery. Narza tries to kill Zaius, but Urko stops him and orders his soldiers arrested, then offers to drop the whole affair if Zaius agrees not to give humanity any concessions. To avoid being discredited by the fake plans, Zaius relents.

Planet of the Apes (Authorized Edition) #3: "Power Play" (BW-s)

NOTE: This story is one of three from the third annual in which the fugitives make no appearance. Ironically, it's one of the best stories set in the TV-series era.

◆ Burke and Virdon spot a spaceship propelled through time by the same anomaly that brought them here. Apes find the landing site before they do. The astronauts shoot the gorillas and free a female astronaut named Verina—a friend of Burke's who was still in the Space Academy when they vanished. Her vessel is mostly undamaged, but her two shipmates are dead. The astronauts set about fixing the ship, a fuel leak limiting them to only one passenger for the return trip. Verina suggests Virdon go, but as the lightest human, she has the greatest chance of surviving and rescuing them. She lifts off when additional gorillas arrive, scorching the pursuing apes and their horses in exhaust flames. Continuing on their journey, the trio hope she'll find a way to get them home again.

Planet of the Apes (Authorized Edition) #3: "From Out of the Sky" (BW-c)

NOTE: It's unknown if Verina rescues her fellow astronauts, but it's possible she does, as extra scenes of Galen filmed for an ABC-affiliate broadcast of the Planet of the Apes *telefilms (re-edited from several TV-series episodes) include the revelation that they eventually made it home to their own era.*

◆ Disgusted by gorilla cruelty, a chimp named Caria steals two fishing boats so she, her husband Menuas, their friend Jango and 20 other chimps can forge a new home south of Central City. They put ashore when their food and water run out, and are captured by armed humans, who take them to the P'ru province of the Empire of Merica-South. Having never trusted apes since the war that leveled most cities but left theirs intact, they plan to wipe out apekind and restore humanity to its former glory. Caria and Menuas find Jango dead in his cell, beaten to death for resisting interrogation—an accident, according to their overseer, Pensward, though they know better. Pensward questions them about Central City's military, but they have no information to offer. That night, the chimps force Pensward to take them to the boats. Before setting out to sea to find another home, Menuas claims the apes possess weapons of mass destruction, hoping that will forestall the planned invasion of Central City.

Planet of the Apes (Authorized Edition) #3: "Flight From Terror" (BW-s)

NOTE: This story is one of three from the third annual in which the fugitives make no appearance. It's unknown if the P'ru humans carry through with their plan to attack Central City.

◆ The fugitives visit Arizona and find a village where humans are mute. Syrinx, a dogmatic preacher ape, captures Burke and Virdon, saying the ape god sent him to rid the world of mankind. Galen claims the men as his own, but Syrinx makes him sell them to Telemon, a chimp farmer. Telemon and his children, Dardon and Delphia, worship a radio transmitter found in their field. As the astronauts study it, Telemon mistakes them for intruders and shoots Virdon. Burke jumps out a window, heads for the hills and meets a tribe of speaking humans led by Gorn, who plans to raid the village and rescue Burke's friend. Tending to Virdon's wound, Dardon names him Thura and treats him with kindness. Virdon asks Galen to get him tools to fix the radio, then tells the family he can speak. The apes are willing to help, but the eavesdropping preacher believes the men to be evil. Galen urges Burke to abort the raid, saying the farmers are peaceful, but Burke calls him a sellout. Syrinx tries to destroy the radio, but the farmer lets Virdon fix it, amazed when someone responds. Gorn's people storm the farm, destroy the radio, beat up Galen and kill Syrinx. Running off the invaders, the fugitives set out to find whoever answered the radio, vowing to return if they find a place where humans and apes can live in peace. As they leave, Dardon tries to fix the transmitter.

Planet of the Apes: "A Fallen God" (CB-u)

NOTE: This unfilmed episode script is available online at Hunter's Planet of the Apes Archive. Since it takes place in Arizona, I have placed it after all other episodes and spinoff stories set in California. The mute-human motif of the early films is in place here, even though the TV series features speaking humans. Apparently, the degeneration of humanity was not consistent throughout the country.

◆ The fugitives climb a snowy trail in the Rocky Mountains. A group of armed men surround them and march them through a village to stand before a trio of leaders, who order them imprisoned as spies. Two council members, Seth and Thorn, listen to their tale but decide to execute them at the Full Moon Festival, to boost village morale. Plans change when the apes capture a hunter named Liman and extract the village's location through torture. The astronauts teach Galen human guerrilla tactics so he can train Seth's people and earn their freedom. When the apes invade at dawn, the guerillas succeed in defeating them. Grateful, Seth lets the fugitives go free.

Planet of the Apes (Authorized Edition) #2: "Galen's Guerrillas" (BW-s)

NOTE: Since the Rocky Mountains run northeast of Arizona, I have set this story after "A Fallen God," attempting to map a straight line for the fugitives' adventures, from one coast to the other.

PUBLISHER / STUDIO
AB . . . . ABC-TV
AC . . . .Adventure / Malibu Comics
AW . . . . Award Books
BB . . . . .Ballantine Books
BN . . . . Bantam Books
BW . . . . Brown Watson Books
CB . . . . CBS-TV
CV . . . . Chad Valley Sliderama
DH . . . . .Dark Horse Comics
ET . . . . Editorial Mo.Pa.Sa.
FX . . . . 20th Century Fox
GK . . . .Gold Key / Western Comics
HE . . . HarperEntertainment Books
HM . . Harry K. McWilliams Assoc.
MC . . . . Marvel Comics
MR . . . Mr. Comics / Metallic Rose
NB . . . . NBC-TV
PR . . . . .Power Records
SB . . . . Signet Books
TP . . . . .Topps
UB . . . . .Ubisoft

MEDIUM
a . . . . animated series
b . . . . .book-and-record set
c . . . . .comic book or strip
d . . . . trading card
e . . . . e-comic
f . . . . .theatrical film
k . . . . .storybook
m . . . . .magazine article
n . . . . .novel or novelization
p . . . . promotional newspaper
r . . . . .recorded audio fiction
s . . . . short story
t . . . . television series
u . . . . . . .unfilmed script or story
v . . . . video game
x . . . . .Blu-Ray exclusive
y . . . . .young adult novel

◆ Virdon and Burke encounter a female astronaut from the past, as well as Toomak, a human slave boy from this era, and share several adventures with them.

Unproduced Planet of the Apes animated series (NB-a)

NOTE: An animated series was discussed in the 1980s, but never produced. Joe Ruby and Ken Spears, story editors for the live-action series, asked comics legend Jack Kirby to create a concept drawing. Reproduced in The Jack Kirby Collector, *and in* Simian Scrolls #6, *the drawing featured Virdon, Burke, a woman identified as "blonde companion of astronauts" and a "human slave boy" named Toomak. No further details are available.*

3085 TO 3086

◆ Galen, Burke and Virdon travel to the east coast, pursued cross-country by Urko's troops and Zaius.

Conjecture

NOTE: Seven Spanish-language comics, released only in Argentina, place the fugitives on the East Coast instead of the western setting of the TV series. The Power Records audio adventures make the same error. To reconcile, I postulate that the trio headed east to escape Urko and Zaius, who pursued them all the way. (That might explain the existence of a future Zaius, Urko and Galen in New York's Ape City.)

3086

◆ The *Blue Star*, a spaceship lost in the 1970s, crashes in an ape village beyond a mountainous desert, killing the crew on impact. The opportunistic prefect, Arpo, finds human skeletons within. To guard its secret, and to keep his subjects frightened and subdued, he deems the wreckage an object of worship.

El Planeta de Los Simios #5: "The Star Gods" (ET-c)

◆ Near the coast of Long Island, the fugitives hear Glenn Miller's "Moonlight Serenade." They find a hilltop villa, but trigger a trap and fall into a crevice. Apes haul them out and beat Virdon. In the villa, Galen meets Ahasuerus, a hermit granted solitude in return for playing loud music so the apes can lure humans as slaves. Recognizing the astronauts from Urko's alerts, the prefect imprisons them in an old theater and summons Urko. Dr. Kalia, a chimp veterinarian, empathizes with their plight and suggests they take her hostage and climb to the projection booth. As Urko's gorillas storm the theater, Virdon gets a generator running, scaring the apes with a James Bond film. The generator fails, and as they flee the balcony, Kalia gives her life to save them. Galen and Ahasuerus await outside with horses. Ahasuerus, they discover, is a 2,000-year-old cyborg, created in late-20th-century life-prolongation tests and named for the story of the Wandering Jew. He passes out from exhaustion, and when apes show up, the fugitives escape. Eventually he rises, condemned—like his namesake—to walk the Earth ad infinitum.

El Planeta de Los Simios #1: "The Wandering Jew" (ET-c)

◆ Ape slavers round up primitive humans until Virdon shoots one from a tower. The other apes panic, for the tower is considered taboo. The primitives crowd into the crumbling tower, pursued by Capt. Tormo's gorilla squad. The fugitives lead the slaves to a subway station, lit by mutated luminous fungus. Terrified that the gods are punishing them, the humans run back to the surface and are recaptured. One woman stays with the fugitives, saying her people fear the Monstrous Rodents living in the tunnels. The giant rats, mutated to human size, keep blind sub-humans as slaves. The sub-humans attack, but Virdon convinces them he's a friend. Stirred by ancient memories of atrophied language, the sub-humans slaughter their former masters. Tormo, touched that men would risk their lives to help an ape, sets them free, promising to protect the sub-humans, and to urge the council to end the hunts.

El Planeta de Los Simios #2: "Depth" (ET-c)

◆ At the Beach of Time, where human slaves sift artifacts so the sand can be used for construction, the fugitives save a woman named Nebia from being fed to sharks. She shows them a heat-powered radio, which plays a recorded broadcast inviting war survivors to meet at the East Coast Scientific Center. Virdon dismantles the radio to build a goniometric radiometer, but lacks certain parts. To gain them beach access, Galen poses as a slave-tamer, sent to punish them for disobeying the prefect of Niursee. Put to work in the sand, Virdon uncovers a magazine kiosk, but Prefect Seiko orders it burnt before he can search for parts. Their cover is blown when Niursee's prefect arrives, but Galen, called to rescue humans buried beneath a Coca-Cola billboard, fails to warn his friends. When Nebia returns to her people, Seiko orders her executed. Virdon finishes the radiometer and tracks the broadcast to the Hill of Sacrifices, where he discovers a buried bomb shelter. Using loudspeakers, he impersonates a god, demanding that Nebia be freed and that the sacrifices be halted. Seiko dies when a gas explosion topples the hill, burying the beach.

El Planeta de Los Simios #3: "The Beach of Time" (ET-c)

◆ The fugitives visit New York City with Harimon, an outcast orangutan deemed a sorcerer by other apes. A sonic blast crumbles a nearby building. Harimon, a sound waves expert, attributes this to a single low-frequency chord. In the mall, they find a radio station with equipment capable of such a blast. Harimon activates an amplifier, emitting a pulse that shakes the building, alerting Urko's troops. When Harimon refuses to leave his new toy, Virdon knocks him out and carries him to safety. Along the way, he spots a set of solar-powered portable transceivers. At the sight of Urko, Galen grabs Burke and jumps to another building, dropping the radio. Urko pursues them and nearly chokes Burke to death, but Galen intervenes. Though shot, Harimon completes the amplifier circuit before dying. Virdon barely makes it out as a deep ultrasonic blast brings down the building, scaring off the troops.

El Planeta de Los Simios #4: "Ultrasonic" (ET-c)

◆ Galen learns of a crashed spaceship in a valley beyond the desert, where Prefect Arpo enslaves both humans and apes for his workforce. Galen approaches the village temple's supreme priest, posing as a theology expert. Arpo suspects him of spying for Zaius until the chimp feigns interest in his "new ideas" regarding ape history. After a night in the stables, the astronauts accompany the apes to see what Arpo calls the Ship of the Gods—the *Blue Star*, a vessel from their era. Arpo forces Virdon to repair the craft, and to train him and his lieutenants, Craor and Gard, to fly it so they can attack Central City. Virdon sabotages his plan, neglecting to tell the apes to open the floodgates before firing. The apes launch the ship and try to shoot the astronauts, but the rocket fails to clear the floodgate and destroys the spaceship instead. Grateful, the village apes give them a cart and horses for the journey ahead.

El Planeta de Los Simios #5: "The Star Gods" (ET-c)

◆ A bear knocks Galen unconscious. Tromh, self-proclaimed Master of the Forests, shoots the beast with a crossbow. The bald albino orangutan invites the fugitives to his medieval castle, where he and Galen enjoy a lunch of wild boar, while the astronauts eat filth; when Burke complains, Varlo (Tromh's best manhunter) roughs him up. Tromh offers to buy Virdon and Burke for his next hunt. Galen declines, so he forces the chimp to act as prey alongside the humans. Given a half-hour to hide, they cross a drawbridge and split up to search for weapons in the forest. Burke retraces his steps to the bear and retrieves his knife; Virdon makes a sling from his jacket drawstrings and a piece of cloth; and Galen fashions a trap out of a tied-back branch. The hunt begins, and Burke kills Varlo with the knife, while Virdon takes out another ape. Grabbing the hunters' weapons, they help Galen fend off two others. Tromh arrives, armed with a sidearm, which he uses to cheat in the crossbow-only tournaments. Virdon distracts him and shoots him with a crossbow, and the fugitives ride off into the sunset.

El Planeta de Los Simios #5: "The Master of the Forests" (ET-c)

PUBLISHER / STUDIO
AB . . . . ABC-TV
AC . . . .Adventure / Malibu Comics
AW . . . . Award Books
BB. . . . . .Ballantine Books
BN. . . . . Bantam Books
BW . . . . Brown Watson Books
CB. . . . . CBS-TV
CV . . . . Chad Valley Sliderama
DH. . . . . .Dark Horse Comics
ET . . . . Editorial Mo.Pa.Sa.
FX. . . . . 20th Century Fox
GK . . . .Gold Key / Western Comics
HE . . . HarperEntertainment Books
HM . . Harry K. McWilliams Assoc.
MC . . . . Marvel Comics
MR . . . Mr. Comics / Metallic Rose
NB. . . . . NBC-TV
PR . . . . Power Records
SB. . . . . Signet Books
TP. . . . . Topps
UB. . . . . Ubisoft

MEDIUM
a . . . . animated series
b . . . . .book-and-record set
c . . . . .comic book or strip
d . . . . trading card
e . . . . e-comic
f . . . . .theatrical film
k . . . . .storybook
m . . . . .magazine article
n . . . . .novel or novelization
p . . . . promotional newspaper
r . . . . .recorded audio fiction
s . . . . short story
t . . . . television series
u . . . . . . .unfilmed script or story
v . . . . video game
x . . . . .Blu-Ray exclusive
y . . . . .young adult novel

◆ Kalus, Zaius' chief advisor, authorizes an experiment to pacify humans with drugs. The residents of Fandomville, isolated by a ravine, receive opium-laced wine as a gift from the "gods," to drain them of vitality. The experiment's administrator, Kenio, lures the fugitives to the village to see how his "zombies" will react to their dissenting nature. Observing the test, Urko prefers just to kill them. An elder offers the trio food and lodging, and they help carry river water to repay this kindness. Virdon convinces them to build a giant water wheel. Mill, daughter of a villager named Maia, falls off a cliff and nearly drowns, but Virdon saves her life. Maia gratefully gives him wine, and he detects the opium in it, urging the humans to reject the wine and rebel. Urko decides to kill them, shooting Kenio when the scientist tries to stop him. Gorillas storm the town, and the humans rise up to fight them. Virdon tosses Urko into the river, and the humans take refuge in the mountains. Maia asks Virdon to join them, but the memory of his family prevents him from accepting. Disgraced, Urko vows to hunt them as long as he lives.

El Planeta de Los Simios #6: "The Zombies" (ET-c)

NOTE: Urko, apparently, does not abide by Caesar's "ape shall not kill ape" mandate.
And yes, the village really is called Fandomville.

◆ An ape hunting party captures Burke. Virdon and Galen follow their jail wagon to the Metropolitan Opera House, now called the Palace. An ape overseer whips penned humans within, providing Burke and others with fighting sticks. Urko arrives to inspect Prefect Kobal's local police. Kobal explains that all humans must fight for food in the Circus. Burke is put in the arena with a young man and given kendo knives. Seeing Urko, he beats the boy badly so he can leave before being spotted. In the Great Tournament, pairs of humans fight for their freedom. Burke knocks out a guard and runs with Galen for an exit, inadvertently entering the arena. Virdon sneaks into the building and finds bells in the Met's sound room. Urko recognizes Burke, but the bells pierce the air, vibrating the masonry to pieces. Everyone runs for cover as the building collapses, and the fugitives sadly depart the fallen opera house.

Planeta de Los Simios #7: "The Circus" (ET-c)

NOTE: Although the seventh issue in the series, "Rockets" is numbered "1" due to the publisher's name change from Editorial Mo.Pa.Sa. to Editorial Tynset S.A.

◆ The fugitives visit a village subjugated by an elderly gorilla, Prefect Sover. A rocket blasts forth from the ground, startling the slaves, and the astronauts realize it might be their ticket home. Galen meets a human named Anitra, who says the town is built over an underground lab called Down Below, where she and others perform heavy labor. When her mate, Bilé, is arrested for riding a horse, she agrees to take the fugitives to Sover's lab, telling his guard, Keno, that the prefect has sent for them. The astronauts find a science lab with anti-atomic protection, along with a bunker containing more than a dozen rockets. Sover enters, offering to free Bilé and give them one of the rockets if the astronauts make the vessels fly. He betrays them, however, putting Bilé in a test rocket that explodes on launch. He then threatens to kill Anitra if they don't help him, but slays her anyway once they finish. Galen helps the men escape, and Burke beats the gorilla to death with a pole. Setting the rockets to explode, they run for cover as the detonations cause a quake that swallows the entire building.

El Planeta de Los Simios #7: "Rockets" (ET-c)

◆ A human hunter shoots apes at a school until Virdon, Burke and Galen risk death to stop him.

El Planeta de Los Simios: "The Killer" (ET-c, unpublished)

NOTE: This and the following four tales were never published due to the cancellation of the Spanish-language comic series. These synopsis are provided courtesy of author Jorge Claudio Morhain; the full details of these stories are unavailable.

◆ A human survivor, resistant to radiation, struggles to live in the ruins of New York City, which has grown decrepit from the passage of time.

El Planeta de Los Simios: "Cain" (ET-c, unpublished)

◆ Thomas Alva Edison arrives from the past in a time machine of his own design. Virdon and Burke try to use it to return to their own era, but it only returns Edison, stranding them in the future.

El Planeta de Los Simios: "Encounter with Edison" (ET-c, unpublished)

◆ A human village, mobilized by a brainwashing device, digs up a lost civilization in New York's John F. Kennedy Airport. As the astronauts flee, they see the Statue of Liberty, semi-buried in the sand.

El Planeta de Los Simios: "The Archeologist" (ET-c, unpublished)

◆ The fugitives are captured by a group of apes who have created a fanatical community.

El Planeta de Los Simios: "The Queen" (ET-c, unpublished)

◆ The fugitives are buried by falling boulders in Philadelphia's Forbidden Zone, where primitive humans—the Delphi—surround them. Within a nearby mountain lies Independence Hall, where the Delphi worship the *Declaration of Independence*, awaiting the fulfillment of a prophecy that saviors from the sky will lead them to a promised land. The astronauts reveal their origin to Tamarane, Guardian of the Delphi, who instructs Braylock, head of defense, not to harm them. Zaius sends an army to deal with the Delphi, fearful they might influence other humans. Tamarane brings the fugitives to a ruined cathedral, where he reads to his congregation from the *Declaration*. Braylock stages a coup, ushering Urko's troops into the hall. Shooting Braylock, Tamarane leads the fugitives to safety on the mountain top. There dwells Ytrebil, Guardian of the Mountain and Protector of the Delphi, prophesized to save them at their hour of greatest danger. A quake brings the mountain down, dropping Ytrebil—the Liberty Bell—on the apes. Urko's troops and the Delphi are all killed in the collapse.

Planet of the Apes—4 Exciting New Stories #1: "Mountain of the Delphi" (PR-r)

NOTE: The narration places "Mountain of the Delphi" in 3885. I have ignored that date in favor of the TV series' 3085 setting. "Ytrebil" is "liberty" spelled backwards.

◆ Moving south, the fugitives find an area untouched by war. Urko's troops approach, and the men become ensnared in quicksand. Magnum of the Tree People and his son Molan save the astronauts, then lead them to a treetop village. The reclusive Tree People fear Galen—particularly a man named Bronto, who thinks him Urko's spy. Magnum offers shelter for the night, convening a council meeting to decide their fate. Bronto demands Trial by the King, so Magnum forces Virdon to fight him in King's Lagoon, home of a giant alligator. Virdon wrestles the reptile into submission, pulling Bronto to safety and earning the respect of Molan's fiancée. The astronaut urges them to deal with the outside world and stop living in fear. Magnum accepts the challenge, and the Tree People rejoice.

Planet of the Apes—4 Exciting New Stories #2: "Dawn of the Tree People" (PR-r)

◆ Time-traveling Nazi-esque invaders attack a peaceful artist's village. An airship dispatches armored vehicles and troops to kill its human and ape inhabitants. The Nazi leader, Trang, plans to subjugate both species and repopulate the world with his kind. Prefect Landa, Galen's ex-lover, escapes into the woods and meets the fugitives. Her description of the ship reminds them of an experimental NASA craft of the 1970s. Zaius holds a council session to report a band of killer humans invading the planet. Despite unbalanced odds, Urko orders an attack. Landa and the astronauts examine the Nazis' tank tracks. A gorilla, Sgt. Blendo, spots the tracks and alerts Urko. The fugitives visit an armory ten miles distant and discover weapons and military vehicles. As apes battle the Nazis, Virdon and Burke take out the tanks with gas grenades. Trang shoots Landa and steals her horse, jumping to safety as Burke destroys his spaceship. After a romantic farewell with Galen, Landa returns to her village to begin rebuilding.

Planet of the Apes—4 Exciting New Stories #3: "Battle of Two Worlds" (PR-r)

◆ Dr. Pandere, an expert in geothermal energy, warns Zaius that an eruption of the volcanic crater at Mount Pralox is imminent. He agrees to evacuate but says the Pralox District is one of Urko's strongest support bases, inhabited almost exclusively by gorillas. His relationship with Urko has reached a breaking point, with clashes rising between gorillas and other apes. The citizens of Pralox think this a trick to divide and conquer. Urko plans a coup and sends his second-in-command, Capt. Soma, to Mount Pralox. Hidden in bushes, the astronauts watch as gorillas threaten to slay any apes attempting to leave. Stunned that they would dare break the most sacred law, Galen fears a civil war. Earthquakes rock the area, and the astronauts urge the citizens to evacuate. Soma recognizes the fugitives and orders their arrest, but the explosion of Mount Pralox rains lava down on everyone. Humans and apes barely make it out alive as the magma levels the entire city. Galen hopes his people will learn a lesson and stop fighting.

Planet of the Apes—4 Exciting New Stories #4: "Volcano" (PR-r)

AFTER 3086

◆ Virdon and Burke eventually locate a working computer in the ruins of a city and discover a way to return to space. They invite Galen to go with them, but he declines, knowing he'd be as out of place in their world, where apes are caged, as they were in his. Galen bids farewell to his friends and resumes his former life. Years later, he befriends another human time-traveler and shares his adventures involving the former fugitives, including his shock at seeing a spaceship for the first time, and what it was like being a fugitive on the run from Urko.

Telefilm #1: Back to the Planet of the Apes (AB-t)

NOTE: Ten episodes of the TV series were re-edited into five telefilms, which ABC affiliates aired with newly filmed framing footage starring Roddy McDowall as Galen, speaking to an unseen human time-traveler about his past adventures with Burke and Virdon. The revelation of the return to their own time is the most intriguing aspect of these scenes, though it does create a paradox—if they could warn humanity of the ape-controlled future, why would mankind still take apes as pets, allowing that future to unfold? How Galen avoids prison is unknown, as is the traveler's identity, and no date is specified as to when the new scenes occur. These scenes were excluded when the TV series was released on DVD, but can be viewed online at Kassidy Rae's Planet of the Apes: The Television Series Website.

◆ The time-traveler returns to Galen's hut the next day to hear more stories of Virdon and Burke. While entertaining the traveler with his stories, Galen begins putting together a doll-like toy.

Telefilm #2: Forgotten City on the Planet of the Apes (AB-t)

◆ Resuming his story-telling a day later, Galen recalls how difficult it was risking his life for his two human friends, and how they braved constant danger in their search for a computer, knowing all the while that Urko could find them at any moment. Meanwhile, Galen sews clothing for the doll.

Telefilm #3: Treachery and Greed on the Planet of the Apes (AB-t)

◆ The time-traveler visits Galen once again, and the chimp shares the book of human anatomy he stole from Zaius. Fascinated with the human body's complexity, Galen recounts Virdon's ordeal in the hospital after being shot by gorillas. As he does so, he plays with the tiny doll's hand.

Telefilm #4: Life, Liberty and Pursuit on the Planet of the Apes (AB-t)

◆ While painting the doll's head, Galen tells one last story to the time-traveler, recounting how his friends eventually found a computer and returned to their own era, while he remained in his. Finally, he applies the finishing touches to his toy—which consists of a windup chimpanzee and a clapping human doll.

Telefilm #5: Farewell to the Planet of the Apes (AB-t)

BETWEEN 3085 AND THE 3400s

◆ Deterioration caused by radiation exposure, combined with the demoralization of being subservient to apes, wipes the minds of most humans. Humanity is eventually expelled from many ape cities as unproductive, useless animals, forced to live wild in the forests.

Planet of the Apes #11: "Outlines of Tomorrow—A Chronology of the Planet of the Apes" (MC-m)

◆ Dark skin is largely bred out of the human gene pool, giving most humans a "tan Caucasian" look.

Escape from the Planet of the Apes (AW-n)

NOTE: The first two films contain no Black humans other than Thomas Dodge and some mutants, and the novelization of Escape from the Planet of the Apes *indicates the apes were amazed upon seeing the astronaut since they'd never met a dark-skinned human before. How all non-White races ceased to exist is unexplained, but this apparently happened after the TV series, since humans of color still lived during that period, and before the 3400s, when (in an unpublished Marvel tale by Doug Moench), dark-skinned humans were unheard of.*

BETWEEN 3085 AND 3978

◆ Apes re-discover the lost art of photography.

Planet of the Apes episode #5: "The Legacy" (CB-t)

NOTE: In the TV series, Zaius is amazed to see a photo of Virdon's family and wonders how humans created such images, implying photography was not in use by the apes in 3085. The first film, however, clearly shows the Hunt Club posing for photos with their trophies, indicating the lost art eventually re-emerged.

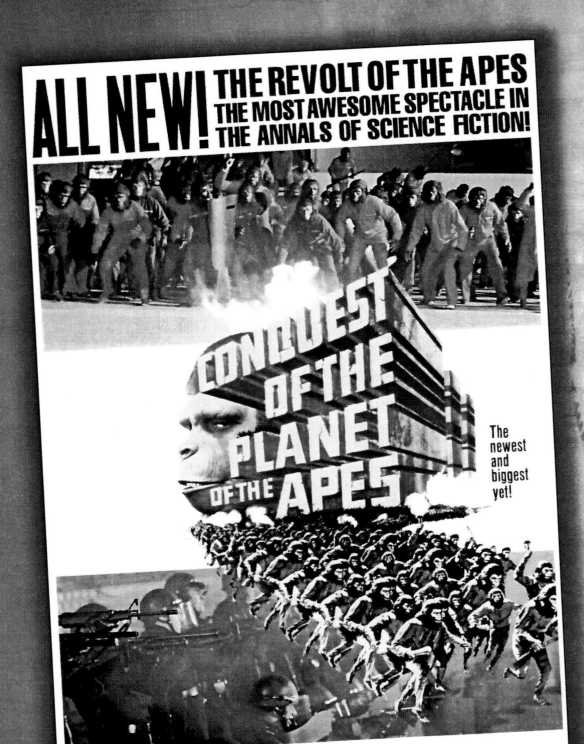

Part 10: Beginning of the End
(3087 to 3977)

BETWEEN THE 3100s AND 3979

◆ A maritime civilization develops, with great city-ships carrying apes and humans across the oceans. One particular city-ship, the *Dymaxion*, ruled by the orangutan Cmdr. Dymaxius, captures hundreds of human slaves to sell to other city-ships. A number of these humans, including a man named Alaric, his friend Starkor and his lover Reena, transfer to the *Hydromeda*, where they are treated horribly.

Planet of the Apes #15: "Future History Chronicles II—Dreamer in Emerald Silence" (MC-c)

> NOTE: Since "Future History Chronicles" is undated, I have chosen a time span far in the future, befitting the title. Dayton Ward's timeline, published in The Planet of the Apes Chronicles, dates this storyline between 3085 and 3925.

◆ Her Majesty's Cannibal Corps, ape environmentalists riding giant frogs, wages war on the Industrialists, citizens of former African nations who blame apes and White humans for the planet's nuclear devastation. The Cannibal Corps' leader, captured when her people try to stop the Industrialists from destroying the plants and trees, is subjected to genetic experimentation and radiation, causing her to grew to immense proportions, her mind greatly damaged in the process. Unable to remember her past, she recalls only a distorted form of her name: Her Midgitsy.

Planet of the Apes: "Future History Chronicles VI—The Captive of the Canals" (MC-c, unpublished)

> NOTE: This story was never released due to Marvel's decision to stop publishing Planet of the Apes comics as of issue #29. The above details come from a story outline provided by author Doug Moench. This tale may have been Moench's attempt to partially explain the lack of dark-skinned humans in either of the first two Apes films.

◆ Graymalkyn, a gorilla architect, serves aboard the city-ship *Chiropoda* with his friend Garshan, who transfers to the *Klarion*. Grimstark, an orangutan visionary, moors a dozen city-ships, including the *Klarion*, to form a massive island-ship called the *Federation*. His hope: that the merged crews will share knowledge, commerce, cultures and expenses. When others begin resenting him and his "demon-magic," however, he isolates himself in an ancient tower and lives out the rest of his life as a hermit. This earns him the nickname "Grimstark the Crazy One."

Planet of the Apes #17: "Future History Chronicles III—Graveyard of Lost Cities" (MC-c)

◆ Civil war erupts aboard *Hydromeda* when a gorilla named Barbarus leads a mutiny against the orangutan rulers. City Magistrate Argol splits the orangutans' power in half, giving Barbarus one territory. Humans take the gorillas' place as the lowest of society, and an area known as Demolition Row affords an uneasy truce for years. Councilor Lornus, an orangutan, is killed, and Argol's advisor Sage suggests he fortify palace defenses. This sudden defensive increase worries Barbarus, whose aide, First Lt. Swarthos, urges him to attack the orangutan's New Hydromeda territory. Lornus' assassin (Alaric) sneaks into the palace to kill Dymaxius during dinner, then returns to Old Hydromeda to poison its water and destroy supplies. The territories go to war, unaware a third party is fanning the fires of hatred. Alaric frees his friends from the ship's bowels. The humans fight their way to lifeboats, taking to the sea as the city-ship dies in flame. Many perish during the voyage to find land.

Planet of the Apes #12: "Future History Chronicles I—City of Nomads" (MC-c)

PUBLISHER / STUDIO
AB . . . . ABC-TV
AC . . . .Adventure / Malibu Comics
AW . . . . Award Books
BB . . . . .Ballantine Books
BN . . . . Bantam Books
BW . . . . Brown Watson Books
CB . . . . CBS-TV
CV . . . . Chad Valley Sliderama
DH . . . . .Dark Horse Comics
ET . . . . Editorial Mo.Pa.Sa.
FX . . . . 20th Century Fox
GK . . . .Gold Key / Western Comics
HE . . . HarperEntertainment Books
HM . . Harry K. McWilliams Assoc.
MC . . . . .Marvel Comics
MR . . . Mr. Comics / Metallic Rose
NB . . . . NBC-TV
PR . . . . .Power Records
SB . . . . Signet Books
TP . . . . .Topps
UB . . . . Ubisoft

MEDIUM
a . . . . animated series
b . . . . .book-and-record set
c . . . . .comic book or strip
d . . . . trading card
e . . . . e-comic
f . . . . .theatrical film
k . . . . .storybook
m . . . . .magazine article
n . . . . .novel or novelization
p . . . . promotional newspaper
r . . . . .recorded audio fiction
s . . . . short story
t . . . . television series
u . . . . .unfilmed script or story
v . . . . video game
x . . . . .Blu-Ray exclusive
y . . . . .young adult novel

◆ Alaric's people ally with a band of stranded apes, who agree to build the *Freedom Reaver*—a sailing ship smaller than *Hydromeda*, with a battering ram at its fore—in return for passage home. Construction lasts two years, under the guidance of Graymalkyn. Four city-ships approach, and when Starkor decides to ram them, Graymalkyn protests, causing a brawl that knocks Alaric overboard. When Starkor and Graymalkyn dive in after him, a creature swallows them and brings them to Dwelleron, the undersea palace of an orangutan named Ambrosia. Built inside a biomechanically bred mutation that organically sustains itself and its occupants, Dwelleron was designed so Ambrosia could destroy all city-ships and end the war. Ambrosia provides them with underwater gear, and the mutated creature's nerve-center exhales them into the sea. A giant squid kills Ambrosia's people, but the orangutan swims back to his palace, rescues Alaric's group and destroys *Dymaxion* with explosives. Alaric urges him to stop the killing, and Ambrosia relents, self-destructing Dwelleron. Zadnek, the new leader of the *Reaver*, prepares to ram the other ships, but Alaric orders him to halt further attacks while Graymalkyn is aboard.

Planet of the Apes #15: "Future History Chronicles II—Dreamer in Emerald Silence" (MC-c)

◆ Most of *Freedom Reaver*'s apes return to their homelands, but Graymalkyn and others remain aboard to help end human slavery. The *Reaver* docks with the *Federation* so Alaric can seek out Grimstark. A band of apes injure Starkor, and Garshan takes them to the Night-City, where a barkeep, Saxtur, directs them to Grimstark's tower. Grimstark mends Starkor's wound and shows them many marvels, including a flying machine of his design. His plan: to fly off, leaving the island-ship behind. Two drunk *Reaver* crewmen, believing Alaric weak, decide to sink the *Federation*. Reena kills the mutineers but the damage is done, and the panicked masses shoot Grimstark from the sky. Alaric's friends swim back to the *Reaver* as the broken portion of the *Federation* snaps off and sinks.

Planet of the Apes #17: "Future History Chronicles III—Graveyard of Lost Cities" (MC-c)

◆ The *Reaver* discovers the *Cathedraulus*, a radioactive city-ship containing many interconnected cathedrals. Alaric refuses to take Reena with him, and she ends their marriage when the argument becomes violent. Two corridors run the length of *Cathedraulus*; Graymalkyn takes one, Alaric and Starkor the other. Both meet slaves from their own species, each recounting massacres of their kind at the hands of the other. Masked beings—the New Order Born of Old Sins, mutated descendants of apes and humans altered in the war—await them at the tunnels' end, dragging hooded prisoners behind them. At the center of a garden is a nuclear missile, worshipped by the mutants. A priest prepares to sacrifice a slave—Alaric sees that it's Reena and realizes the prisoners are his crew. He and Graymalkyn jump to their rescue as Starkor topples the missile, crushing many beneath it. When the *Reaver* sinks in flame, Alaric's group has no choice but remain aboard *Cathedraulus*, where radiation has already begun to mutate them.

Planet of the Apes #24: "Future History Chronicles IV—The Shadows of Haunted Cathedraulus" (MC-c)

◆ Alaric sides with Graymalkyn in stopping Starkor from killing the mutant leader. Reena accuses him of preferring apes to their kind. A great balloon (the *Cloud Swarm*) ascends from the floor, and Graymalkyn and Starkor grab its ropes. Alaric shoots a crossbow line at the gondola, pulling Reena with him, then the four climb up and slaughter the mutants. The balloon enters the Death Mists, a black miasma of thunder and lightning. Waiting for the storm to pass, the companions put aside their anger. Three flying machines approach, ten times' the balloon's size, and set it afire. The gondola hits the ground, where Her Majesty's Cannibal Corps mistake them for the Industrialists. The ape mutants hang them by their feet above a kettle of boiling oil. Graymalkyn asks to join them as a ruse, but when the leader gives him a spear to kill his comrades, he up-ends the oil on their captors. Escaping, they find Sexxtann, a city on land with airships docked nearby. Alaric approaches in friendship, suggesting they settle down and live together in peace. Graymalkyn, however, has his doubts.

Planet of the Apes #29: "Future History Chronicles V—To Race the Death-Winds" (MC-c)

◆ Sexxtann, a 42-level hexagonal castle, is the Industrialists' home. An airship rescues Alaric's group, who have never seen dark-skinned humans before. Gondolas traverse a canal system filled with giant amphibians, forming a vicarium that provides amusement, transportation and sustenance. The Council for the Advancement of Sexxtann's Industry exiles them to a jungle at the fortress center. Forced to jump from an airship, the four fend off a giant salamander, then make camp. Lonely for the company of apes, Her Midgitsy snatches Graymalkyn during the night but does not hurt him. His friends attack, injuring the giant ape before he can stop them. Airships fire flamethrowers, starting a massive forest fire. Unable to flee, she lifts the others to safety. Her death throes topple the walls, shattering the vicarium, transforming the jungle into a lake and drowning Her Midgitsy.

Planet of the Apes: "Future History Chronicles VI — The Captive of the Canals" (MC-c, unpublished)

NOTE: The ultimate fates of Alaric, Reena, Starkor and Graymalkyn are unknown.

3400s TO 3978

◆ Encroaching Forbidden Zones usher in a new Dark Age. Progress slows to a halt in New York's Ape City, where human civilization is relegated to legend, then to nothing at all as the conservative orangutans conceal such knowledge, stifling the progressive chimpanzees. Late in this period, simians begin using humans as experimental animals and entertaining diversions for gorilla hunters. A certain instinctive survival pattern remains in the humans, but it is less than successful. Meanwhile, the Forbidden Zones' land masses begin shifting, with once-oceanic areas becoming endless miles of barren desert.

Planet of the Apes #11: "Outlines of Tomorrow — A Chronology of the Planet of the Apes" (MC-m)

◆ A large body of water outside of New York City dries up completely, replaced by a series of rocky valleys known to the apes as the Dead Lake.

Planet of the Apes (FX-f)

◆ The conservative ape government establishes the *Book of Simian Prophecy*, article 18 of which states that if ever talking humans are found, they must be exterminated immediately.

Return to the Planet of the Apes episode #1: "Flames of Doom" (NB-a)

◆ The orangutan Council of Elders knows the truth about man but guards the secret to protect society.

Planet of the Apes (FX-f)

◆ The apes create the *Book of Laws*, a set of governing mandates. Punishment for breaking these rules is harsh, handed out un-democratically by a small ruling body known as the Supreme Council.

Return to the Planet of the Apes episode #4: "Tunnel of Fear" (BB-n)

NOTE: This is revealed in the novelization.

◆ Both the *Book of Laws* and the *Book of Simian Prophecy* make it illegal to enter the Forbidden Temple of Mount Garr, after an unknown deadly factor kills most apes who remain inside for too long. Others who enter, however, are strangely cured of their illnesses. Radiation is the cause, though the apes do not understand the concept.

Return to the Planet of the Apes episode #6: "Terror on Ice Mountain" (BB-n)

NOTE: This is revealed in the novelization.

◆ The simian government eventually amends its *Book of Laws* to enable the Senate to override the High Council if necessary. However, this law is one the Senate never invokes.

Return to the Planet of the Apes episode #4: "Tunnel of Fear" (BB-n)

NOTE: This is revealed in the novelization.

PUBLISHER / STUDIO
AB . . . . ABC-TV
AC . . . .Adventure / Malibu Comics
AW . . . . Award Books
BB . . . . .Ballantine Books
BN . . . . Bantam Books
BW . . . . Brown Watson Books
CB . . . . CBS-TV
CV . . . . Chad Valley Sliderama
DH . . . . .Dark Horse Comics
ET . . . . Editorial Mo.Pa.Sa.
FX . . . . 20th Century Fox
GK . . . .Gold Key / Western Comics
HE . . . HarperEntertainment Books
HM . . Harry K. McWilliams Assoc.
MC . . . . Marvel Comics
MR . . . Mr. Comics / Metallic Rose
NB . . . . NBC-TV
PR . . . . .Power Records
SB . . . . Signet Books
TP . . . . Topps
UB . . . . Ubisoft

MEDIUM
a . . . . animated series
b . . . . .book-and-record set
c . . . . .comic book or strip
d . . . . trading card
e . . . . e-comic
f . . . . .theatrical film
k . . . . .storybook
m . . . . .magazine article
n . . . . .novel or novelization
p . . . . promotional newspaper
r . . . . .recorded audio fiction
s . . . . short story
t . . . . television series
u . . . . .unfilmed script or story
v . . . . video game
x . . . . .Blu-Ray exclusive
y . . . . .young adult novel

◆ The ape government also sets down the *Book of Military Procedure*, a set of rules dictating how and when the ape military may act. One article decrees that an officer must first obtain permission from the Council of Elders before deploying any amphibious operations.

Return to the Planet of the Apes episode #9: "Trail to the Unknown" (BB-n)

NOTE: This is revealed in the novelization.

◆ Talk of a democratic government replacing the "rule by Supreme Council" model spreads. One Council member, Elder Muvala, dismisses the notion by quipping, "There is absolutely no evidence that 100 stupid apes are smarter than several intelligent ones."

Return to the Planet of the Apes episode #5: "Lagoon of Peril" (BB-n)

NOTE: This is revealed in the novelization.

c. 3880s

◆ Surgora the Bold, one of ape history's greatest generals, attempts to cross the Forbidden Zone. Though his soldiers survive the trip through the desert, their vehicles are unable to climb the western mountains. With no way around the mountains, Surgora's forces keep heading north, looking for a pass—so far north that they find a land covered in ice—but still are unable to traverse the mountain range.

Return to the Planet of the Apes episode #4: "Tunnel of Fear" (BB-n)

NOTE: The novelization dates these events "almost a hundred years" before the series.

OCTOBER 18, 3889

◆ The *Cassiopeia*, a NASA spaceship lost in a time-warp in 2125, reappears in normal space and crashes in the Forbidden Zone. The computer awakens three of the four crewmembers—Ulysses (the commander), Romulus and Sophie—but the fourth, Martinez, is dead, her cryogenic unit having failed during the voyage. Romulus and Sophie are killed by apes, leaving Ulysses to fight for his survival alone.

Planet of the Apes (UB-v)

NOTE: This PC video game from UbiSoft does not fit seamlessly into Planet of the Apes *continuity—after all, how could NASA still be sending out ships after all this time, and how could the crews not know about the apes a century after Caesar's rebellion? What's more, the nature of video games is such that the sequence of events varies from game to game. Thus, I am only including the premise of the game on this timeline, not the specifics of gameplay—though, being a game, it should probably be ignored entirely.*

3911

◆ The wife of Augustus, the orangutan minister of science for Ape City's Supreme Council, has a son. They name him Zaius and agree that he will one day follow in his father's footsteps.

Planet of the Apes Special #1: "The Sins of the Father" (AC-c)

NOTE: Since Zaius' age is unknown, I have based this figure on actor Maurice Evans' age (67) when the film (set in 3978) was produced.

BEFORE THE EARLY 3900s

◆ Marriage between members of different ape species is forbidden. Any children born of such mixed pairings often face racial prejudice from both species.

Return to the Planet of the Apes episode #7: "River of Flames" (BB-n)

NOTE: This is revealed in the novelization. The passing of this decree is undated, though it must occur before Mungwort's birth, since his grandparents faced such a barrier to romance.

EARLY 3900s

◆ As a child, Zaius attends many sessions during his father's tenure on the council. Thus, he witnesses a number of debates between Gen. Kurda, hero of the Battle of Silkor, and Boniface, a leader in the field of humanoid anthropology.

Return to the Planet of the Apes episode #1: "Flames of Doom" (BB-n)

NOTE: This is revealed in the novelization.

◆ Truga, a male gorilla, elopes with a female chimp to the Wambo Province, to escape persecution for their forbidden cross-species love. Their grandson, Mungwort, later faces racial prejudice due to his resultant mixed heritage.

Return to the Planet of the Apes episode #7: "River of Flames" (BB-n)

NOTE: This is revealed in the novelization. Truga is named in the novelization of episode #2; his wife's name is unknown.

3920

◆ Ursus, a gorilla and future leader of Ape City's military, is born.

Beneath the Planet of the Apes (FX-f)

NOTE: Since Ursus' age is unknown, I have based this figure on actor James Gregory's age (59) when the film (set in 3979) was made.

3923

◆ Caspay, future inquisitor of New York City's human mutant population, is born.

Beneath the Planet of the Apes (FX-f)

NOTE: Since Caspay's age is unknown, I have based this figure on actor Jeff Corey's age (56) when the film (set in 3979) was made.

3928

◆ Honorius, an orangutan and future Ape City deputy minister of justice, is born.

Planet of the Apes (FX-f)

NOTE: Since Honorius' age is unknown, I have based this figure on actor James Daly's age (50) when the film (set in 3978) was made.

PUBLISHER / STUDIO
AB . . . . ABC-TV
AC . . . .Adventure / Malibu Comics
AW . . . . Award Books
BB . . . . Ballantine Books
BN . . . . Bantam Books
BW . . . . Brown Watson Books
CB . . . . CBS-TV
CV . . . . Chad Valley Sliderama
DH . . . . .Dark Horse Comics
ET . . . . Editorial Mo.Pa.Sa.
FX . . . . 20th Century Fox
GK . . . .Gold Key / Western Comics
HE . . . HarperEntertainment Books
HM . . Harry K. McWilliams Assoc.
MC . . . . Marvel Comics
MR . . . Mr. Comics / Metallic Rose
NB . . . . NBC-TV
PR . . . . .Power Records
SB . . . . Signet Books
TP . . . . Topps
UB . . . . Ubisoft

MEDIUM
a . . . . animated series
b . . . . .book-and-record set
c . . . . .comic book or strip
d . . . . trading card
e . . . . e-comic
f . . . . .theatrical film
k . . . . .storybook
m . . . . .magazine article
n . . . . .novel or novelization
p . . . . promotional newspaper
r . . . . .recorded audio fiction
s . . . . short story
t . . . . television series
u . . . . . . .unfilmed script or story
v . . . . video game
x . . . . .Blu-Ray exclusive
y . . . . .young adult novel

3932

◆ Zira, a chimpanzee and future scientist (and mother to Ape City founder Caesar), is born.

Planet of the Apes (FX-f)

NOTE: Since Zira's age is unknown, I have based this figure on actor Kim Hunter's age (46) when the film (set in 3978) was made.

◆ Zira's father, Pavel Fabian, is an associate of Zaius, the future minister of science.

Planet of the Apes Special #1: "The Sins of the Father" (AC-c)

NOTE: The Sins of the Father names Zira's father Pavel, but the novelization of Return to the Planet of the Apes episode #1 names him Fabian. To reconcile the discrepancy, I have combined the two.

◆ A much-respected member of ape society, Zira's father is widely considered a wise ape.

Return to the Planet of the Apes episode #1: "Flames of Doom" (BB-n)

NOTE: This is revealed in the novelization.

◆ Maximus, an orangutan and future Ape City commissioner for animal affairs, is born.

Planet of the Apes (FX-f)

NOTE: Since Maximus' age is unknown, I have based this figure on actor Woodrow Parfey's age (46) when the film (set in 3978) was made.

◆ Julius, a gorilla and future assistant at the Academy of Ape Sciences, is born.

Planet of the Apes (FX-f)

NOTE: Since Julius' age is unknown, I have based this figure on actor Buck Kartalian's age (46) when the film (set in 3978) was made.

3933

◆ Galen, future chimpanzee surgeon at Ape City's Academy of Ape Sciences, is born.

Planet of the Apes (FX-f)

NOTE: Since Dr. Galen's age is unknown, I have based this figure on actor Wright King's age (45) when the film (set in 3978) was made. This is a different Galen from the character appearing in the TV series; it's unknown if the two are related.

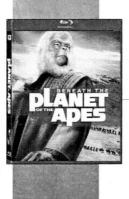

◆ Mendez XXVI, future leader of the New York City mutants, is born to the House of Mendez.

Beneath the Planet of the Apes (FX-f)

NOTE: Since Mendez's age is unknown, I have based this figure on actor Paul Richards' age (46) when the film (set in 3979) was made. It should be noted that 2,000 years (since the time of Mendez the First) would likely be insufficient for only 26 generations of Mendezes, unless each leader remained in power for an average of 77 years.

3938

◆ Cornelius, a chimpanzee and future scientist (and father to Caesar, founder of ape society), is born.

Planet of the Apes (FX-f)

NOTE: Since Cornelius' age is unknown, I have based this figure on actor Roddy McDowall's age (40) when the film was made.

♦ Cornelius' father, Trajan, is a wise and revered member of society, much like Trajan's father, Julian.

Return to the Planet of the Apes episode #1: "Flames of Doom" (BB-n)

NOTE: *This is revealed in the novelization.*

c. 3940s TO EARLY 3950s

♦ When Cornelius is a child, his father Trajan imparts to him sage advice: "Liberty means responsibility, and that is why most apes dread it." Neither know the quote was originally uttered by a human named George Bernard Shaw.

Return to the Planet of the Apes episode #1: "Flames of Doom" (BB-n)

NOTE: *This is revealed in the novelization.*

♦ Julian, Cornelius' grandfather, imparts a wise saying as well: "We have nothing to fear, but fear itself"—words first spoken by another human, Franklin D. Roosevelt. Cornelius' grandmother, Mokka, is equally wise: "Worry never robs tomorrow of its sorrow; it only robs today of its strength" (attributed to AJ Cronin, a human). His other grandmother, Steffa, often says, "It's always darkest before the dawn" (from the Jewish text, *Midrash Shocher Tov*).

Return to the Planet of the Apes episode #3: "The Unearthly Prophecy" (BB-n)

NOTE: *This is revealed in the novelization. It's unclear which grandparent—Mokka or Steffa—is the mother of Julian, and which is Cornelius' maternal grandmother.*

3947

♦ Adiposo, future inquisitor of New York City's human mutant population, is born.

Beneath the Planet of the Apes (FX-f)

NOTE: *Since Adiposo's age is unknown, I have based this figure on actor Victor Buono's age (32) when the film (set in 3979) was made. The character is identified as "Fat Man" in the film's credits; his actual name appears in* The Mutant News, *a promotional newspaper distributed to moviegoers during the film's release.*

♦ Ongaro, future inquisitor of New York City's human mutant population, is born.

Beneath the Planet of the Apes (FX-f)

NOTE: *Since Ongaro's age is unknown, I have based this figure on actor Don Pedro Colley's age (32) when the film (set in 3979) was made. The character is identified as "Negro" in the film's credits; his actual name appears in* The Mutant News, *a promotional newspaper distributed to moviegoers during the film's release.* Planet of the Apes Revisited *misspells his name "Ono Goro."*

♦ Milo, a chimpanzee and future genius scientist, is born.

Escape from the Planet of the Apes (FX-f)

NOTE: *Since Milo's age is unknown, I have based this figure on actor Sal Mineo's age (32) when the film was produced, given a 3979 launch date for Milo's time trip.*

3948

◆ Camille, daughter of Gen. Ignatius, Ape City's prefect of police, is killed. Minister of Science Augustus and his son, Zaius, determine that the killer was violent and smart. Ignatius believes his human slave responsible, but Augustus claims the killer was an ape and refuses to let him execute the man. Such blasphemy outrages many and confuses Zaius, as evidence indicates a human killer. Augustus sees Ignatius beating the slave and realizes the human must have killed Camille out of self-preservation. When the human confirms this theory, Augustus shoots both him and Ignatius, then claims the two died struggling for a weapon after Ignatius killed his own daughter. Ignatius is branded a heretic and a child-murderer. Zaius deems his father's actions unforgivable, so Augustus takes him to the Statue of Liberty and reveals man's true history. A speaking human, he says, would endanger society; though horrible, his actions preserved the greater good—a protection that will fall to Zaius when he succeeds him as minister of science.

Planet of the Apes Special #1: "The Sins of the Father" (AC-c)

NOTE: The original title, as per author Mike Valerio, was "Murder on the Planet of the Apes." Dayton Ward's timeline, published in The Planet of the Apes Chronicles—*which accepts* Beneath the Planet of the Apes' *3955 dating for the films—places this tale in 3925.*

BETWEEN 3948 AND 3978

◆ A venerable orangutan named Zao serves as leader of Ape City's Supreme Council. Following Zao's tenure, Dr. Zaius replaces him in the role. In his later years, other apes call him Old Zao.

Return to the Planet of the Apes episode #1: "Flames of Doom" (BB-n)

NOTE: This information appears in the episode's novelization.

◆ As leader of the Supreme Council, Zaius becomes privy to the top-secret personal writings of Caesar and Virgil, detailing the events surrounding Caesar's revolution two millennia prior. Most apes consider Caesar a myth by this time, but the orangutan elite know better. These accounts conflict with what is written in the Sacred Scrolls, particularly in regard to Aldo's place in history.

Revolution on the Planet of the Apes #6: "Catch a Falling Star" (MR-c)

3949

◆ Albina, future inquisitor of New York City's human mutant population, is born.

Beneath the Planet of the Apes (FX-f)

NOTE: Since Albina's age is unknown, I have based this figure on actress Natalie Trundy's age (30) when the film (set in 3979) was made. Her name appears in The Mutant News, *a promotional newspaper distributed during the film's release.*

NOVEMBER 23, 3955

◆ An ANSA space shuttle from 1973, containing John Christopher Brent and Donovan "Skipper" Maddox, nears its final destination after being hurled forward in time by the Hasslein Curve. Damage to the ship causes the external chronometer to stop functioning at 3955, freezing its reading at that year.

Beneath the Planet of the Apes (FX-f)

NOTE: This reconciles the films' inconsistent dating: in Planet of the Apes, *Taylor's chronometer reads 3978, whereas Brent's in* Beneath the Planet of the Apes *says 3955, an error compounded by later films. The November 23 date comes from a scene cut from* Escape from the Planet of the Apes, *showing the apeonauts aboard* Liberty 1. (In the first film, the date shown was November 25, 3978—23 years and two days later.)*

3956

◆ A human female is born to a mute tribe living near the New York City Forbidden Zone. As an adult, she will be called Nova, though she has no known name as a child since her people are mute.

The Ape (HM-p)

> NOTE: Nova's age in 3978 (22) is revealed in The Ape, *a promotional newspaper distributed to moviegoers during the release of* Planet of the Apes. *This jibes with actress Linda Harrison's age (23) at the time. The animated series creates a discrepancy involving Nova, in that it indicates that has been her name since childhood, even though George Taylor will first give her that name in 3978. (The cartoon also portrays Nova as able to produce speech.)*

3958

◆ Lucius, a chimpanzee and the nephew of scientist Dr. Zira, is born.

Planet of the Apes (FX-f)

> NOTE: Since Lucius' age is unknown, I have based this figure on actor Lou Wagner's age (20) when the film (set in 3978) was made.

EARLY 3960s

◆ A NASA spacecraft carrying astronaut Ronald "Ron" Brent crashes in the Forbidden Zone after being propelled in time from the year 2109. His leg broken, Brent nearly dies until a tribe of wandering humans finds him. The friendly primitives stay with him until he is well enough to travel. One of the tribe's children, Nova, grows quite fond of him, and he teaches her to say his name.

Return to the Planet of the Apes episode #9: "Trail to the Unknown" (NB-a)

> NOTE: The date of Brent's crash is unclear. He says only that he crashed 15-20 years before meeting the Venturer crew in 3979.

◆ Brent offers Nova his military dogtags, which she wears around her neck on into adulthood.

Return to the Planet of the Apes episode #1: "Flames of Doom" (NB-a)

> NOTE: Why she doesn't still have them in the first two films—when Taylor gives her his dogtags as well—is unclear... aside from the obvious explanation, that the cartoons don't fit the rest of the mythos, that is.

◆ Brent decides to travel with the humans wherever they're going, but a sandstorm separates him from the tribe. Unable to find them again, he returns to the wreckage of his ship and makes that his base of operations. Most of the ship is unsalvageable, though the self-destruct mechanism remains intact.

Return to the Planet of the Apes episode #9: "Trail to the Unknown" (NB-a)

EARLY 3960s TO 3979

◆ Ronald Brent spends the next 15 to 20 years alone in the desert, unsure of the passage of time. He makes many forays into the wilderness looking for the tribe, but fails to find them. His travels sometimes take him to New Valley, an area 25 miles south of the crash-site, where he fishes for food.

Return to the Planet of the Apes episode #9: "Trail to the Unknown" (NB-a)

PUBLISHER / STUDIO
AB.................. ABC-TV
AC....Adventure / Malibu Comics
AW .... Award Books
BB...........Ballantine Books
BN............. Bantam Books
BW .... Brown Watson Books
CB.................. CBS-TV
CV....... Chad Valley Sliderama
DH..........Dark Horse Comics
ET.......... Editorial Mo.Pa.Sa.
FX........... 20th Century Fox
GK....Gold Key / Western Comics
HE... HarperEntertainment Books
HM .. Harry K. McWilliams Assoc.
MC .... Marvel Comics
MR ... Mr. Comics / Metallic Rose
NB.................. NBC-TV
PR.............Power Records
SB.............. Signet Books
TP....................Topps
UB.................. Ubisoft

MEDIUM
a .... animated series
b ....book-and-record set
c ....comic book or strip
d .... trading card
e .... e-comic
f ....theatrical film
k ....storybook
m ....magazine article
n ....novel or novelization
p .... promotional newspaper
r ....recorded audio fiction
s .... short story
t .... television series
u ....unfilmed script or story
v .... video game
x ....Blu-Ray exclusive
y ....young adult novel

3960s OR 3970s

◆ Cornelius, a young chimp archeologist and psychologist, maps the southern and western edges of New York's Forbidden Zone. Some years later, he meets and falls in love with a veterinarian named Zira.

Return to the Planet of the Apes episode #4: "Tunnel of Fear" (BB-n)

NOTE: This information appears in the episode's novelization.

◆ Though attracted to Cornelius' eyes, Zira loves him most for his exceptional mind.

Return to the Planet of the Apes episode #13: "Battle of the Titans" (NB-a)

MID TO LATE 3900s

◆ An ambitious ape named Urko, the son, grandson and great-grandson of other military generals, attends the Simian Military Academy, determined to follow in his family's footsteps.

Return to the Planet of the Apes episode #9: "Trail to the Unknown" (BB-n)

NOTE: This information appears in the episode's novelization. The revelation that Urko hails from a long line of generals is intriguing, as it hints at kinship with the Urko from the television series—particularly since some of the spinoff stories from the TV series have Urko operating on the East Coast rather than the West.

3968 TO 3978

◆ Damage caused by humans scavenging for food among Ape City's crops increases by more than 400 percent over a ten-year period.

The Ape (HM-p)

MID 3970s

◆ Dr. Pleta, an ape scientist, attempts to build a lighter-than-air flying machine similar to a hot-air balloon. Unable to compensate for the weight of the stove needed to heat the air, he fails to make it fly. Though the Senate deems this conclusive proof that flight is impossible, Cornelius suspects an unknown design flaw might be overcome.

Return to the Planet of the Apes episode #6: "Terror on Ice Mountain" (BB-n)

NOTE: This information appears in the episode's novelization.

◆ Gen. Urko siphons funds for the construction and maintenance of a secret base in the Mulkalla Mountains, east of the Forbidden Zone and west of a series of caves inhabited by primitive humans. Over the next several years, Urko fills the base with artillery and equipment for an eventual governmental takeover. The orangutan elders learn of the base's existence, and the Senate discovers he has a Strategic Defense Headquarters where he trains troops, but the roughness of the nearby terrain and its proximity to the Forbidden Zone keeps either agency from investigating.

Return to the Planet of the Apes episode #8: "Screaming Wings" (BB-n)

NOTE: This information appears in the episode's novelization.

◆ The area surrounding the base—the Black Zone—is highly restricted. Word of clandestine activities here sometimes reaches the ears of ape society, though no one outside of Urko's officers may visit.

Return to the Planet of the Apes episode #8: "Screaming Wings" (NB-a)

BEFORE 3975

◆ Experiments by ape surgeon Dr. Cassius prove the human larynx capable of speech, but atrophied.

Planet of the Apes #10: "Kingdom on an Island of the Apes—The City" (MC-c)

3975

◆ Derek Zane, a naïve dreamer who built a time-machine in 1974, arrives in the year 3975, hoping to rescue George Taylor's lost *Liberty 1* crew. The crash demolishes his time machine, so he sets off across the globe to find the missing team. Sleeping in the wild, he awakens to find primitive humans watching him but is unable to elicit a response. Shots disturb the tranquility, scattering the mute humans and nearly killing Kane. The shooter, an eye-patched gorilla named Gen. Gorodon, is frustrated when Zane gets away—having spied the man's attempts to communicate, he'd hoped to impress his orangutan elder, Xirinius, by capturing a speaking human. He settles for Zane's knapsack and toolbox, then heads home with his chimp servant, Whelp. Zane follows, intent on retrieving his belongings.

Planet of the Apes #9: "Kingdom on an Island of the Apes—Arrival" (MC-c)

NOTE: When Marvel published this tale, it used the same 3975 date incorrectly attributed to the adaptations of the first two films. Although I have set the films in their proper years, I am keeping the 3975 setting for this story, as it adds to the tragedy of Zane's story that he arrived three years too early to find the Liberty 1. *Dayton Ward's timeline, published in* The Planet of the Apes Chronicles—*which accepts* Beneath the Planet of the Apes' *3955 dating for the first two films—places these events in that same year.*

◆ As gorillas prepare human slaves for target practice, Zane sneaks into Xirinius' home to retrieve his items. Gorodon enters with Xirinius, saying Cassius' research regarding the human larynx proves the council has lied regarding the species' intelligence. Xirinius accuses him of heresy, and of coveting his position as city administrator. Gorodon kills him, hoping to blame the talking human and become the first gorilla to serve as city administrator. Kane pulls a gun on him, however, and ties him up at the scene of the crime before escaping with the captured humans. With no hope of finding Taylor's crew, he builds a raft to carry him and a cache of gunpowder barrels to a distant island.

Planet of the Apes #10: "Kingdom on an Island of the Apes—The City" (MC-c)

◆ Disgraced following the murder, Gorodon is replaced by Gen. Zaynor. Bent on revenge, Gorodon takes 200 gorilla soldiers and sets out to track Zane down.

Planet of the Apes #21: "Beast on the Planet of the Apes" (MC-c)

◆ Sir Gawain, a gorilla in knight's armor, takes Zane to the Camelot court of a benevolent orangutan, King Arthur, on the island of Avedon. Gawain urges execution, but Zane claims to be a powerful wizard, and Arthur spares his life at the behest of the beautiful Lady Andrea. The island has been plagued by a dragon—a lizard mutated to enormous size—which Zane destroys with four bullets. Hailed as a hero, Zane is then consigned to a dungeon when Gawain challenges him to a duel. Andrea admits the medieval act is mere affectation, as their ancestors left mainland society to build a civilization of honor and peace, based on ancient writings. During the tournament, Zane wins without bloodshed by shining a flashlight in Gawain's eyes and lassoing him to the ground. Gawain tries to kill him and is banished, while Zane is knighted and begins a love affair with Andrea. On the mainland, Gorodon's troops build a raft to pursue Zane to his island paradise.

Planet of the Apes #10: "Kingdom on an Island of the Apes—The Island Out of Time" (MC-c)

◆ A talking human female is captured and delivered to Dr. Cassius and his assistant, Plexides, for study. Zaynor, however, petitions Magistrate Hastus to force them to give the human up for target practice.

Planet of the Apes #21: "Beast on the Planet of the Apes" (MC-c)

◆ Warned of Gorodon's attack, Zane instructs others to set up gunpowder traps and shoot fiery arrows at the gorillas. Two-thirds of Gorodon's troops die instantly, the rest slaughtered by Arthur's knights. Zane kills Gorodon with an axe, and later weds Andrea.

Planet of the Apes #10: "Kingdom on an Island of the Apes—Battle" (MC-c)

◆ Guilt-ridden over abandoning his search for *Liberty 1*, Zane returns to the shore on a steed called Gandalf. A chimp known as Robin Hood, impressed by his staff-dueling skill, offers to help with his quest. They steal clothing and a horse, pose Zane as Hood's slave and visit Cassius' lab, where Zane hears Plexides mention a talking human female. Zane recalls *Liberty 1*'s Maryann Stewart, but it's not her. As Cassius prepares to remove her larynx, Zane startles the doctor, and the woman slays him with a scalpel. Hood pulls her into hiding as guards capture Zane. Hastus orders him hanged, but Hood shoots the noose, catching him in a cart. Zaynor jumps onto the wagon but falls and is trampled by horses. Shot, the woman dies in Zane's arms. Blowing up the apes' armory, Zane rides out of town and buries her, etching "Hope" on her gravestone. Hood suggests they return to Avedon, but Zane is not yet ready to go back.

Planet of the Apes #21: "Beast on the Planet of the Apes" (MC-c)

3977

◆ Faron, a chimp scientist, discovers a bubble-domed, human-built city, now inhabited by apes. Branded a heretic, he is hunted down by gorillas. One soldier, Jurando, shoots him as he jumps over a waterfall. Primitive humans save his life, and he lives among them for months. Derek Zane meets the same tribe and befriends Faron, who tells him of the city. Soldiers arrest Faron and place him before a firing squad. Zane sets off homemade firecrackers to distract the apes, then frees Faron and rides with him to the city, hoping to find technology to build another time machine. A second time machine—*Chronos I*, built by NASA based on Zane's plans—arrives. Two "tempunauts," Mara Winston and Jackson Brock of the NASA Time Research Labs, disembark. Brock refuses to search for Zane, however, having volunteered only to profit from knowledge of the future. At the sight of the bleak desert, he tries to strand Mara in 3977 and travel to another era, but damage to *Chronos I* causes the device to explode, putting out one of his eyes. As she nurses him back to health, Jurando's gorilla squad captures them both.

Planet of the Apes: "Journey to the Planet of the Apes" (MC-c, unpublished)

NOTE: This tale—originally titled "Return to the Planet of the Apes" but renamed so as not to conflict with the cartoon—was never released due to Marvel's decision to stop publishing the comic as of issue #29. These details come from a story outline and dialog breakdown provided by author Doug Moench. With Marvel's film adaptations completed, the Zane storyline would have replaced them as the magazine's mainstay, with Faron and the tempunauts as regular characters. Although Zane says it has been a week since Hope's death in issue #21, this story takes place in 3977—two years later.

◆ Mara escapes her gorilla captors, encounters Zane and Faron, and begins traveling with the duo. Faron meets a female chimp in the domed city and falls in love. Eventually, Zane returns with his friends to Avedon, reuniting with Andrea, Gawain, Robin Hood and King Arthur. Brock, meanwhile, uses his 20th-century knowledge to lead a group of renegade gorillas, becoming a recurring nemesis to the others.

Planet of the Apes: [multiple issues, titles unknown] (MC-c, unpublished)

NOTE: Doug Moench's story breakdown for "Journey to the Planet of the Apes" concludes with notes to artist Val Mayerik and editor John David Warner, detailing future plans to craft a "movie sequel" spanning eight to 10 issues involving an ape culture similar to that from Pierre Boulle's novel The Monkey Planet. *Other multi-issue "sequels" would have followed, each starring Zane and his friends. The first of these would have been "Beyond the Planet of the Apes," outlined below. An art page for one issue of this unused storyline, created by Mayerik, was later repurposed as the cover to issue #117 of Marvel UK's* Planet of the Apes *run.*

◆ Zane, Mara and Faron blast off into space and battle a dangerous alien race before returning to 1977 Earth, but Zane soon feels like a misfit in his own era. Missing his future wife, Lady Andrea, Zane builds another time machine so he can return to 40th-century Avedon and be with her again.

Planet of the Apes: "Beyond the Planet of the Apes" [multiple issues] (MC-c, unpublished)

> NOTE: Moench's notes do not indicate the mechanism for space travel, though he describes this story arc as "John Chimper of Mars," a pun on Edgar Rice Burroughs' Mars novels. Zane's return to 3976, Moench says, would have occurred sometime around issue #60 or so, had the series run that long.

◆ Dr. Cornelius, a prominent chimp psychologist and archeologist, mounts an expedition to the Forbidden Zone with special permission from the National Academy of Science. His goal: to find ancient artifacts proving his theory that the ape evolved from a lower form of primate, possibly man.

Planet of the Apes (FX-f)

> NOTE: Dayton Ward's timeline, published in The Planet of the Apes Chronicles— which accepts Beneath the Planet of the Apes' 3955 dating for the first two films— places these events in 3954. A timeline packaged with the Planet of the Apes 40th Anniversary Collection sets them in 3953.

◆ Several chimp scientists join Cornelius' expedition, including his fiancée Zira, and Dr. Zaius goes along to contain any heretical information. Cornelius discovers a 1991 issue of *People News Monthly* with a cover photo of an ape, and estimates it to be 2,000 years old—older than the Sacred Scrolls. Before he can read it, Zaius grabs it and sees the title "Hail Caesar!" along with a blurb about the "King of the Apes" being the "fabled lost child of Cornelius and Zira." He denounces it as an abomination, a joke planted by a disgruntled student to discredit their work. Cornelius protests, but is reminded that his job security relies on Zaius' approval, that jobs of influence are a rare commodity and that he and Zira might one day have a family. Ripping up the magazine, Zaius leaves them alone. Recognizing a threat, Zira stops Cornelius from pursuing the matter further.

Revolution on the Planet of the Apes #2: "People News" (MR-c)

> NOTE: This tale was previewed online at http://www.mrcomics.ca/freestory.html, but is no longer available at that site. The preview was entitled "People in the News," but the print issue's contents page lists it as "People News."

◆ During several more trips to the desert, Cornelius discovers a cave containing evidence of a civilization older than the 12 recorded centuries of ape history. Zaius and the Academy dismiss his theories and work as heresy—punishable by death—and cancel his travel permit, saying he exceeded his orders.

Planet of the Apes (FX-f)

◆ Cornelius meets with Zaius to ask why his permit has been canceled. The orangutan says he wished to spare him "an exercise in futility," stating science must never supplant the spiritual truths of the Sacred Scrolls, and citing faith as the highest of all truths. To illustrate the point, Zaius quotes Verse 27 of the 19th Sacred Scroll, which states: "Wheresoever goest man, there with him goes ignorance, pestilence and destruction." He urges Cornelius to put this discovery out of his mind, to re-read his scriptures and to trust the Lawgiver's wisdom in all things.

Revolution on the Planet of the Apes: "The Believer" (MR-c, unpublished)

> NOTE: This tale, intended as a Revolution back-up story, was written, penciled and lettered by Sam Agro, but was cut due to concerns over religious overtones, as its conclusion featured the Lawgiver supplanting Jesus Christ. At presstime, it was slated to appear in issue #16 of Simian Scrolls magazine, with the author's permission.

◆ Scared of further damaging his career, Cornelius abandons this line of research for a year.

Planet of the Apes (FX-f)

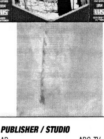

◆ Professors and other scholars at the Ape National Academy launch scientific experiments on humans to increase their knowledge of mankind's origin and evolution, and to dispel the heretical theory that ape descended from man.

The Ape (HM-p)

◆ A chimp architect named Viraga ("Vira" for short) grows furious when her husband Julius humiliates her by ridiculing her work in public—and not for the first time. Apologizing, he says he's grown cynical and bitter in his old age, unable to accept the cruelty ape society inflicts on humans. As he speaks, the young-at-heart chimp executes a series of acrobatic flips and jumps around the town square.

Planet of the Apes #30: [title unknown] (MC-c)

> NOTE: This tale, written for Marvel by Doug Moench, was unknown to fans until March 2006, when a page of original artwork was discovered for sale online. Little is known about the story, including its title or setting, though Moench (who himself does not recall any further details) confirms it was likely intended to appear in a 30th issue that was created but never saw print due to the series' sudden cancellation. The art page is credited to Philipino artist Sonny Trinidad, though Trinidad denies having produced any such illustrations.

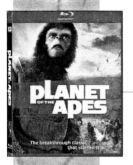

◆ The granddaughter of Dr. Zaius receives a human baby doll—but, naturally, not one that talks.

Planet of the Apes (FX-f)

◆ Human pelts become popular decorations in ape dens.

The Ape News (HM-p)

◆ The human mutants of New York City, led by Mendez XXVI, discover the apes' existence after a rock fault causes several simian soldiers to fall into the underground city. The apes are killed, their bodies destroyed immediately to protect the Holy City's inhabitants from potential alien diseases.

The Mutant News (HM-p)

◆ Pvt. Mungwort, a chimp-gorilla soldier frequently mocked for his mixed heritage, alienates Sgt. Brutar by refusing to torture a human prisoner, starting a garden for the troops to grow their own vegetables and assembling a party to attend a performance by a chimp dance group—as well as by preferring such TV shows as *Exploring Our World* and *Living with Grunt* over popular gorilla series like *Bloodsports* and *The Growler's Tales of Gorilla Force Ten*.

Return to the Planet of the Apes episode #7: "River of Flames" (BB-n)

> NOTE: This information appears in the episode's novelization. That the apes even have television, though, is a prime example of why the cartoons don't fit with the rest of the mythos. It's noteworthy that a character named Grunt features prominently in the Adventure Comics line.

◆ Zeat and Zeat, an ape weapons manufacturer, introduces the Rea Voom 88 hunting rifle. Meanwhile, a clothing designer called Zeeka's, located at 77 Simia Way, introduce its new "Long Look" robes.

The Ape (HM-p)

> NOTE: Given how little simian fashion ever seems to change, Zeeka's new robes can't be all that new.

◆ Zeeka's also operates a sauna for those looking to lose weight, touting the slogan "A trim ape is a happy ape." Other businesses include Lady L, an electrolysis provider promising to remove unwanted hair "for that young look"; and Zuuba Coats, providing "the *in* coat the *in* ape is in."

The Ape News (HM-p)

◆ A quota system is established to keep chimpanzees below orangutans on the social order, but is later abolished. Dr. Zira is among those who "make it" following the lifting of the quotas, and is given the resources needed to further her work in studying the cerebral functions of man in order to lay the foundation for scientific brain surgery.

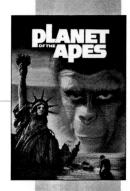

Planet of the Apes (FX-f)

NOTE: This information appears in an early draft of the film's script.

◆ Truga, father of Pvt. Mungwort, dies.

Return to the Planet of the Apes episode #2: "Escape From Ape City" (BB-n)

NOTE: This occurs only in the episode's novelization.

Part 11: Monkey Planet
(3978 to 3979)

3978

◆ Ape City's National Academy issues ten-year statistics showing that the damage caused by human food scavenging has increased by more than 400 percent. Famine becomes a vital concern as humans raid more and more of their crops. Zaius addresses a group of young simians at the academy, advocating the extermination of all humans. Reading to them from the Sacred Scrolls, he reminds them of the Lawgiver's warning to "beware the beast 'man,'" urging them to take part in ridding the planet of the species.

The Ape (HM-p)

◆ Sgt. Brutar is assigned to clean out a human nest. Mungwort rides around the perimeter of the battle while others handle the beasts. He claims to be checking for strays, but Brutar knows better—his chimp blood has made him a pacifist. Later, during bayonet practice, Mungwort gives a human a quick death rather than prolonging it, as orders dictate. Brutar is disgusted, knowing that neither Mungwort's deceased father nor his grandfather, Truga—gorillas, both—would ever have been so soft on humans.

Return to the Planet of the Apes episode #2: "Escape From Ape City" (BB-n)

NOTE: This occurs only in the episode's novelization.

◆ A simian filmmaker known as Citizen Naarthrok releases his highly successful theatrical film *An Ape for All Reasons*.

Return to the Planet of the Apes episode #2: "Escape From Ape City" (BB-n)

NOTE: This information appears in the episode's novelization.

◆ Marcus, chief of the Simian Secret Police, receives an intelligence report from the elite Gorilla Scouting Corps responsible for controlling the human bands roaming the remote, fertile lands north of Ape City. With human over-population—and pillaging of the rich corn fields along the Forbidden Zone—a growing problem, Marcus arranges for a gorilla squad to surround and capture them when they next come to feed. The primary purpose of the raid is to capture both male and female humans for scientific experiments.

The Ape (HM-p)

NOTE: In early drafts of the film's script, Marcus is named Mr. Digby.

◆ The gorillas involved in the raid are known colloquially as the Hunt Club.

Planet of the Apes (FX-f)

NOTE: This information is found in the film's script.

PUBLISHER / STUDIO

AB . . . . ABC-TV
AC . . . .Adventure / Malibu Comics
AW . . . . Award Books
BB . . . . .Ballantine Books
BN . . . . Bantam Books
BW . . . . . Brown Watson Books
CB . . . . CBS-TV
CV . . . . Chad Valley Sliderama
DH . . . . .Dark Horse Comics
ET . . . . Editorial Mo.Pa.Sa.
FX . . . . 20th Century Fox
GK . . . .Gold Key / Western Comics
HE . . . HarperEntertainment Books
HM . . Harry K. McWilliams Assoc.
MC . . . . Marvel Comics
MR . . . Mr. Comics / Metallic Rose
NB . . . . NBC-TV
PR . . . . .Power Records
SB . . . . Signet Books
TP . . . . Topps
UB . . . . Ubisoft

MEDIUM

a . . . . animated series
b . . . . .book-and-record set
c . . . . .comic book or strip
d . . . . trading card
e . . . . e-comic
f . . . . .theatrical film
k . . . . .storybook
m . . . . .magazine article
n . . . . .novel or novelization
p . . . . promotional newspaper
r . . . . .recorded audio fiction
s . . . . short story
t . . . . television series
u . . . . . . .unfilmed script or story
v . . . . video game
x . . . . .Blu-Ray exclusive
y . . . . young adult novel

NOVEMBER 25, 3978

◆ The *Liberty 1*—ANSA's first Interstellar Exploration spacecraft, commanded by Col. George Taylor—exits the Hasslein Curve into which it vanished in 1972, and begins falling back to Earth.

Planet of the Apes (FX-f)

NOTE: The first two films' placement has been hotly debated. Taylor's chronometer reads 3978, while Brent's says 3955 in Beneath the Planet of the Apes. *The three subsequent sequels uphold the latter placement (though Zira's comment in* Battle for the Planet of the Apes *is cut off, making it appear she says 3950), while Marvel's adaptation places it in 3975 and Marvel's timeline puts it in 3976. A timeline packaged with the* Planet of the Apes Widescreen 35th Anniversary Edition *DVD sets this film in 3978, while another, in the* Planet of the Apes 40th Anniversary Collection, *places it from November 3954 to January 3955. Dayton Ward's timeline, meanwhile, published in* The Planet of the Apes Chronicles, *accepts* Beneath's *3955 dating, while the* Beneath *novelization sets the first film 2,010 years after the ship's 1973 launch—or 3983. Marvel's Derek Zane storyline takes place in 3975, making a 3955 date for the Earth's destruction unworkable. And the animated series is set in 3979, also supporting a 3978 setting. Therefore, I assume Brent's chronometer malfunctioned, causing the discrepancy. The* Ape, *a mock newspaper released to promote the film, bears a date of March 1, 3978, but I've ignored that date since it does not jibe with other evidence.*

◆ At that moment, while overseeing an archeological dig, Dr. Zaius takes a nap and dreams of an alternate reality in which a more advanced ape society has suffered centuries of war with mutant humans: *Zaius visits Dr. Milo to tell him Taylor's spaceship—prophesized to bring doomsday to their world—was seen falling from the sky. Milo dismisses the Divinity of Taylor and Caesar as myth. Zaius shares millennia-old pages from Caesar's journals, describing how Milo, Zira and Cornelius traveled into the past. Caesar's existence is against God's Law, Zaius says; Aldo was supposed to lead the ape rebellion, not Caesar. To prevent the couple from giving birth in the past, Zaius has come to kill Milo. He stabs the young chimp, only to find the pages contain his own name, not Milo's.* Zaius awakens to find Cornelius and another chimp standing over him. Cornelius introduces the latest member of their expedition: Milo, a mechanically gifted engineer. As Zaius tries to recall where he's heard the name before, a bright light streaks across the sky. The apes think it a falling star, but it is really Taylor and the *Liberty 1*.

Revolution on the Planet of the Apes #6: "Catch a Falling Star" (MR-c)

◆ *Liberty 1* crashes near the Forbidden Zone's Dead Lake, an inland sea south of Long Island. Taylor, Thomas Dodge and John Landon awaken from their cryogenic slumber, but Maryann Stewart has died from an air leak in a cracked chamber. As the ship fills with water and sinks, the trio launch an escape raft and row to shore. Taylor checks provisions while Dodge scans the soil. A chrono-reading indicates they've travelled 2,000 years into the future. With no idea of which planet they're on, they head out to find food. As they do so, rainless lightning rocks the desert, with no moon visible in the luminescent sky.

Planet of the Apes (FX-f)

NOTE: Some fans have speculated that the lightning may be an illusion created by the mutated humans living in New York's irradiated ruins, intended to keep the astronauts from discovering their hidden community. This, however, is unstated on film.

LATE NOVEMBER 3978

◆ Several days into their trip, an exhausted Dodge discovers a plant in the desert, giving the astronauts hope of finding more life. Despite extreme exhaustion and thirst, they carry on.

Planet of the Apes (FX-f)

◆ At dawn, the Hunt Club, comprised of 50 gorilla guards, take up positions surrounding a large corn field skirting the eastern edge of the Forbidden Zone. Gorilla Scouting Corps intelligence indicates the presence of more than 100 humans feeding in the fields.

The Ape (HM-p)

◆ The rocky terrain leads to a ridge of scarecrow-like barriers, beyond which Taylor discovers trees and a waterfall, in an area known as Simia. Stripping off their uniforms, they run for the water, unaware of primitive humans stealing their belongings. They later find their clothes shredded, their equipment destroyed and the humans feasting on corn. A growl scares off the mute tribe, and the astronauts follow. The Hunt Club shoots many humans and nets others. Dodge is killed in the raid, and Taylor is shot in the throat, losing sight of Landon in the chaos.

Planet of the Apes (FX-f)

NOTE: Simia is named in The Ape, *a promotional newspaper distributed to moviegoers during the film's release.*

◆ Acting on the orders of Police Chief Marcus to show no mercy, the hunters shoot or club any humans who offer resistance or try to escape Simia into the Forbidden Zone.

The Ape (HM-p)

◆ The Hunt Club brings their human catch back to Ape City, posing for photos with their prizes.

Planet of the Apes (FX-f)

◆ The hunt is celebrated as being among the most successful in recent history. More than 30 humans are captured, many of them female and many viable candidates for scientific study. One female, a dark-haired beauty in vigorous health, is chosen for genetic experiments at the Academy of Ape Science.

The Ape (HM-p)

NOTE: The female, of course, is Nova.

◆ The hunters are intrigued by Dodge's dark skin color, having never seen a Black person before.

Escape from the Planet of the Apes (AW-n)

NOTE: This information is revealed in the film's novelization.

◆ Dodge's corpse is stuffed and put on display in the Great Hall of the Zaius Museum, his eyes replaced with glass replicas, as part of a re-creation of natural human habitats.

Beneath the Planet of the Apes (AW-n)

◆ Landon, meanwhile, is brought before Dr. Zaius, who discovers he can talk and immediately has him lobotomized so no one else will discover that speaking humans exist.

Planet of the Apes (FX-f)

NOTE: Zaius tells the tribunal that Landon received a skull fracture, necessitating emergency brain surgery, but later admits Taylor is not unique as a speaking human, adding, "There was the one you call Landon."

◆ Dr. Zira, a veterinarian laying the groundwork for simian brain surgery by studying humans, views the filthy conditions at the Academy of Ape Science. There, a surgeon colleague, Dr. Galen, tends to humans wounded in the hunt. Galen envies the preferential treatment she receives from the council.

Planet of the Apes (FX-f)

NOTE: The name of Zira's lab is revealed in The Ape, *a promotional newspaper distributed to moviegoers during the film's release. It's unknown whether this Galen is descended from the Galen in the* Planet of the Apes *television series.*

◆ Zira has three chimpanzee assistants, and an orangutan also helps her team from time to time as well.

Escape from the Planet of the Apes (AW-n)

NOTE: This information is revealed in the film's novelization.

◆ Taylor and other humans are caged separately. Unable to speak from his wound, he tries to communicate, much to Zira's delight, and the amusement of a gorilla named Julius. Naming him "Bright Eyes," Zira urges him to speak, but when he tries to grab her note pad, Julius beats him down. Zaius scorns Taylor's efforts as mimicry, cautioning Zira not to pursue heretical behavioral studies suggesting a link between ape and man.

Planet of the Apes (FX-f)

DECEMBER 3978

◆ Zira provides Taylor a mate—the dark-haired beauty caught in the hunt—but he shows little interest despite her obvious attraction to him. He scrawls "I can write" in the sand, but she wipes out the letters before the apes see them. Cornelius, meanwhile, plans another archeological dig, hoping to find more artifacts of the past. Zaius sees the remains of the letters and quickly erases them.

Planet of the Apes (FX-f)

◆ The price of bananas on the Simian Market rises by an unprecedented 17 percent. This spurs a rush of panicked buying among ape investors in anticipation of further rises.

The Ape (HM-p)

NOTE: This implies apes have a concept of financial market trading.

◆ Taylor grabs Zira's pad and writes, "My name is Taylor." She takes him home so he can tell them how he got here. When Cornelius disputes his claims, Taylor builds a paper airplane to prove flight possible. Zaius arrives with Dr. Maximus, commissioner for animal affairs, who orders Taylor returned to the lab. Zaius then destroys the plane, ordering Taylor gelded. Taylor tackles Julius and flees, pursued by Xirinius and other guards. He passes a gorilla funeral and frightens an ape child looking for a lavatory. The guards chase him into the Great Hall of the Zaius Museum, passing displays of stuffed humans—including Dodge. Dozens of apes stone Taylor so guards can capture him. Netted, he stuns them all by yelling for them to get their "stinking paws" off of him.

Planet of the Apes (FX-f)

NOTE: Marvel's comic adaptation names Xirinius and reveals that the child is looking for a bathroom. The Ape, a promotional newspaper distributed to moviegoers during the film's release, refers to the Great Hall of the Zaius Museum as the Simian Museum.

◆ The search for Taylor lasts 55 minutes. A dozen ape guards are injured in the incident, five of whom are detained for treatment at Ape Hospital. One injured ape dies, and the government awards the Simian Star—the highest decoration for ape valor—to several guards involved in Taylor's capture.

The Ape (HM-p)

◆ Over the next four weeks, neither Zira nor Cornelius visit Taylor. Left alone with his mate, he names her Nova and grows increasingly fond of her, wondering if she is capable of love.

Planet of the Apes (FX-f)

NOTE: The animated series, Return to the Planet of the Apes, *indicates Ronald Brent had already named her Nova when she was a child.*

JANUARY 3979

◆ Ape guards bring Taylor to the Ministry of Science, to stand before the High Tribunal of the National Academy. Zira and Cornelius serve as his defense, with Zaius, Maximus and the tribunal president sitting in judgment. Appearing for the State is Dr. Honorius, deputy minister of justice, who accuses Zira of working with Galen to alter Taylor's throat. To discredit Taylor, Zaius assembles all surviving humans from the hunt and says to identify his fellow talking humans. A lobotomized Landon is there, unable to speak. Furious, Taylor rushes at Zaius and is beaten senseless. When Zira insists Taylor represents proof of a missing link between their species, the council accuses the chimps of contempt, fallacious mischief and scientific heresy. Privately, Zaius later admits Landon was able to speak, and that he doesn't believe they were surgically altered. Demanding Taylor reveal where his tribe lives beyond the Forbidden Zone, he threatens to emasculate and lobotomize the man if he refuses.

Planet of the Apes (FX-f)

◆ Zaius orders John Landon terminated. Landon's body is stuffed for preservation in the museum alongside Dodge's, his eyes similarly replaced with glass replicas.

Beneath the Planet of the Apes (FX-f)

> NOTE: *Cornelius tells Brent that Taylor nearly ended up a museum specimen "like his two friends," which can only refer to Dodge and Landon since Stewart's body is still in the lake and half-decomposed.*

◆ Rumors spread through Ape City of an impending invasion by humans with ape-like intelligence. Zarka, chief government spokesman, provides an official denial, blaming the story's origin on apes unsatisfied with the current regime looking to create unease and unrest. Several ape intellectuals are not so easily swayed, however, particularly in light of reports of humans landing in an air vehicle.

The Ape (HM-p)

◆ Zira's nephew Lucius helps Taylor and Nova escape so Zira and Cornelius can sneak them to the Forbidden Zone to make a new home in the jungle. The Hunt Club tries to commandeer their wagon, but Lucius lies that the humans are rabid. Three days later, the group reach a beachside cave, where scaffolding marks Cornelius' former dig. Nova experiences nausea, and Zira discovers she's pregnant. Zaius arrives, but Taylor forces his guards away at gunpoint, offering Zaius a deal: If the couple prove their theories, Zaius will drop the charges. Cornelius displays a talking human doll and other artifacts, some more than 2,000 years old, but Zaius negates each finding with scripture. Hearing shots, Taylor forces Zaius to withdraw his troops. As Lucius fetches provisions and horses for the humans, Taylor demands Zaius keep his side of the bargain. In response, Zaius asks Cornelius to read the 29th Scroll, 6th Verse: *"Beware the beast 'man,' for he is the Devil's pawn. Alone among God's primates, he kills for sport or lust or greed. Yea, he will murder his brother to possess his brother's land. Let him not breed in great numbers, for he will make a desert of his home and yours. Shun him, drive him back into his jungle lair, for he is the harbinger of death."* Taylor invites Cornelius and Zira to join him, but they're confident they'll be exonerated. After he leaves, Zaius orders Xirinius to arrest them and Marcus to destroy the cave, in order to protect the future. Zira asks what Taylor will find, and Zaius replies, "His destiny."

Planet of the Apes (FX-f)

> NOTE: *Scenes involving Nova's pregnancy and the Hunt Club's attempt to commandeer the wagon were cut from the film. Adventure Comics' issue #17 line reveals the doll to have belonged to astronaut August Anne Burrows. The name Marcus appears in Marvel's comic adaptation, and also in* The Ape, *a promotional newspaper distributed to moviegoers during the film's release.*

PUBLISHER / STUDIO
AB . . . . ABC-TV
AC . . . . Adventure / Malibu Comics
AW . . . . Award Books
BB . . . . .Ballantine Books
BN . . . . Bantam Books
BW . . . . Brown Watson Books
CB . . . . CBS-TV
CV . . . . Chad Valley Sliderama
DH . . . . .Dark Horse Comics
ET . . . . Editorial Mo.Pa.Sa.
FX . . . . 20th Century Fox
GK . . . .Gold Key / Western Comics
HE . . . HarperEntertainment Books
HM . . Harry K. McWilliams Assoc.
MC . . . . Marvel Comics
MR . . . Mr. Comics / Metallic Rose
NB . . . . NBC-TV
PR . . . . .Power Records
SB . . . . Signet Books
TP . . . . Topps
UB . . . . Ubisoft

MEDIUM
a . . . . animated series
b . . . . .book-and-record set
c . . . . .comic book or strip
d . . . . trading card
e . . . . e-comic
f . . . . .theatrical film
k . . . . .storybook
m . . . . .magazine article
n . . . . .novel or novelization
p . . . . promotional newspaper
r . . . . .recorded audio fiction
s . . . . short story
t . . . . television series
u . . . . .unfilmed script or story
v . . . . video game
x . . . . .Blu-Ray exclusive
y . . . . .young adult novel

◆ The minister of housing issues a statement promising that a thousand new homes for gorillas, orangutans and chimpanzees will be built over the next five years.

The Ape (HM-p)

NOTE: Given the events of the second film, the minister's prediction is not likely to come to pass.

◆ Three days after Taylor leaves with Nova, Zaius recalls his father's warning from thirty years prior—that mankind is a dangerous animal—and finds his faith in that wisdom renewed.

Planet of the Apes Special #1: "The Sins of the Father" (AC-c)

◆ Riding along the beach with Nova, Taylor comes across the head and upper torso of the Statue of Liberty, dilapidated and half buried in the sand. Dropping to his knees in anguish, he realizes he's been home all along, and that mankind must finally have destroyed its own world in a nuclear war.

Planet of the Apes (FX-f)

◆ Profoundly affected by the plight of George Taylor, Lucius begins writing his own scrolls, recounting the story of Taylor's journey and what he found in the Forbidden Zone. The moral of the story, according to Lucius, is that "Whatever thinks can speak. And whatever speaks...can murder."

Beneath the Planet of the Apes (MC-c)

NOTE: This information comes from Marvel's comic book adaptation of the film, based on an introduction cut from the final script.

◆ Dr. Zaius calls a press conference, pleading for additional human bodies for experimentation. Humans' similar physical structure to that of the ape, he says, makes them an invaluable aid in the development and improvement of medical techniques.

The Ape News (HM-p)

◆ During this period, a USNSA astronaut named Ben (last name unknown), whose ship was thrown forward in time in the same manner as Taylor's, arrives searching for his lost comrades.

Planet of the Apes (UB-v)

NOTE: This video game is not easily added to a timeline—after all, which specific game session "happened?" What's more, it's unclear how USNSA relates either to NASA or ANSA. Thus, I am only including the game's premise, not the specifics of gameplay. Ben's ultimate fate is unknown, though it's unlikely pleasant since the Earth will be destroyed within months of his arrival. It's probably for the best—for readers, as well as for Ben—not to consider this game part of the greater story.

EARLY 3979

◆ An assassin, sent by the U.S. government to prevent Taylor from destroying Earth, arrives in a time-travel device, then sets out to hunt down and kill him. In the course of her mission, she must avoid being captured by apes.

Manhunt on the Planet of the Apes (AC-c, unpublished)

NOTE: Mike Valerio, author of Adventure's Sins of the Father, *proposed this second one-shot to creative director Tom K. Mason as well. However, Valerio says, the idea was deemed too reminiscent of* The Terminator *in terms of story, and the assassin (who presumably fails in her mission) was seen as too much like* Alien's *Ellen Ripley. It was also rejected due to several plot-logic problems.*

◆ Wandering the desert, Taylor and Nova find a small body of water and stop to quench their thirst. Taylor tries to teach Nova to speak their names, but to no avail, and places his dogtag around her neck as a gift. The couple travels the desert for a time, until a great wall of flame suddenly bars their approach to New York City. An earthquake and lightning ensue, throwing up a cavern wall to block their way. Suspicious of the reality of the situation, Taylor dismounts, telling Nova to find Zira if anything goes wrong. He then charges the wall and passes through it, vanishing before her eyes. In shock, Nova begins the long trek back through the desert.

Beneath the Planet of the Apes (FX-f)

> *NOTE: Marvel's comic adaptation places these events three days after Taylor finds the Statue of Liberty, with Brent meeting Nova two days later. However, it seems improbable that only five days pass between films, for a lot happens during that time—the trial and subsequent wedding of Zira and Cornelius, the loss of the gorilla scouts, Zira's entire pregnancy (the average chimpanzee gestational period is seven or eight months) and so forth. As such, it's possible the span of time between films could be greater than a week. Of course, that doesn't explain where Taylor hid his dogtag throughout the first film... and perhaps it's best that we not know.*

◆ Passing through the illusion, Taylor enters the ruins of New York City and makes his way to St. Patrick's Cathedral. Five mutant Inquisitors—Albina, Caspay, Ongaro, Adiposo and their leader, Mendez XXVI (a.k.a. Mendez the Divine and Invincible), a descendant of Mendez the First—torture him telepathically, accusing him of spying for the apes and pushing him to reveal the army's plans. Their weapons (traumatic hypnosis and visual/sonic deterrents) are illusory; as the Keepers of the Divine Bomb, they exist only to protect and worship it. Unable to get information from him, and convinced of his madness after he claims to be from another time, they lock him up in a cell.

The Mutant News (HM-p)

> *NOTE: Ongaro and Adiposo are identified as "Negro" and "Fat Man" in the film's credits; their names appear in* The Mutant News, *a promotional newspaper distributed to moviegoers during the release of* Beneath the Planet of the Apes. *The book* Planet of the Apes Revisited *misspells Ongaro's name as "Ono Goro." An early film treatment, also titled* Planet of the Apes Revisited, *identifies Caspay as a dwarf and gives him the title of minister of external affairs.*

◆ Pleading for clemency in the trial of Zira and Cornelius, Zaius arranges to have their charges dropped by making a deal: In exchange for their freedom and the privilege of learning the true history of humanity and apekind, they will agree to keep silent about their discoveries, and to support the council.

Beneath the Planet of the Apes (FX-f)

◆ As per this deal, Cornelius is granted access to secret scrolls few apes know about, which detail the history of how mankind once took apes as pets, then as servants, until an ape revolution and subsequent nuclear war ended human civilization.

Escape from the Planet of the Apes (FX-f)

> *NOTE: Apparently, these scrolls fail to mention that Caesar is his and Zira's son.*

◆ Zira and Cornelius marry. As a wedding gift, Zira's Uncle Hubert gives them a First Edition of the *Collected Works of William Apespeare*—a family heirloom that means a great deal to the chimp couple.

Return to the Planet of the Apes episode #12: "Invasion of the Underdwellers" (NB-a)

> *NOTE: Apparently, the validity of the maxim about an infinite number of monkeys hitting typewriter keys randomly for an infinite period of time and eventually typing the complete works of William Shakespeare may be more than just theoretical.*

PUBLISHER / STUDIO
AB . . . . ABC-TV
AC . . . .Adventure / Malibu Comics
AW . . . . Award Books
BB . . . . .Ballantine Books
BN . . . . Bantam Books
BW . . . . Brown Watson Books
CB . . . . CBS-TV
CV . . . . Chad Valley Sliderama
DH . . . . .Dark Horse Comics
ET . . . . Editorial Mo.Pa.Sa.
FX . . . . 20th Century Fox
GK . . . .Gold Key / Western Comics
HE . . . HarperEntertainment Books
HM . . Harry K. McWilliams Assoc.
MC . . . . .Marvel Comics
MR . . . Mr. Comics / Metallic Rose
NB . . . . NBC-TV
PR . . . . .Power Records
SB . . . . Signet Books
TP . . . . Topps
UB . . . . Ubisoft

MEDIUM
a . . . . animated series
b . . . . .book-and-record set
c . . . . .comic book or strip
d . . . . trading card
e . . . . e-comic
f . . . . theatrical film
k . . . . .storybook
m . . . . .magazine article
n . . . . .novel or novelization
p . . . . . . promotional newspaper
r . . . . .recorded audio fiction
s . . . . short story
t . . . . television series
u . . . . .unfilmed script or story
v . . . . video game
x . . . . .Blu-Ray exclusive
y . . . . .young adult novel

◆ Unfortunately, the couple are unable to take a honeymoon following the wedding.

Return to the Planet of the Apes episode #4: "Tunnel of Fear" (BB-n)

NOTE: This information appears in the episode's novelization.

◆ Cornelius and Zira are named directors of the Humanoid Behavioral Studies Laboratory.

Return to the Planet of the Apes episode #1: "Flames of Doom" (NB-a)

◆ Dr. Milo raises Taylor's damaged spaceship *Liberty 1* from the ocean floor, carting it to a secret area outside Ape City. There, despite the pretense of allying with Zaius, Cornelius and Zira aid him in studying the craft. Their hope: that the existence of a flying vehicle will convince the citizens of Ape City to escape the untruths holding back society.

Planet of the Apes #11: "Outlines of Tomorrow—A Chronology of the Planet of the Apes" (MC-m)

NOTE: Dayton Ward's timeline, published in The Planet of the Apes Chronicles*—which accepts* Beneath the Planet of the Apes' *3955 dating for the first two films—places these events in that same year. A timeline packaged with the* Planet of the Apes 40th Anniversary Collection *places these events in December 3954. Marvel's timeline and the third film both indicate the ship to be Taylor's, but that seems inconceivable—Milo would need to locate the waterlogged craft, raise it from the lake bottom, repair its damaged computers, refuel it, discern its operation and get it into orbit. Plus, the ship's chronometer reading does not match Taylor's (hence, the "3955 vs. 3978" debacle), and Stewart's corpse is missing. What's more, its design matches neither* Liberty 1 *nor Brent's ship—instead, it's similar to that used by Virdon and Burke in the TV series. The* Escape from the Planet of the Apes *novelization attempts to reconcile these discrepancies by establishing the craft as a separate vessel, found intact on the seacoast, with Milo learning to fly it by studying books and papers aboard ship. However, I've adhered to* Escape*'s claim (improbable though it may be) that it is, in fact,* Liberty 1.

◆ Milo reveals the spacecraft's existence, and his intention to make it fly, to Ape City authorities. Flight is deemed impossible, however, and his theories are dismissed. Though Zira and Cornelius agree to help him, they doubt him as well. Still, being an historian, Cornelius—having seen evidence that humans once had flying machines—knows his theories to be possible. Reading books and papers found aboard *Liberty 1*, Milo understands just enough of the ship's workings to discern how to make it spaceworthy.

Escape from the Planet of the Apes (AW-n)

NOTE: This information appears in the film's novelization.

◆ Ape society grows very advanced in a short span of time, as the apes build motorized vehicles, construct great buildings, utilize electricity, develop long-range communications and so forth.

Return to the Planet of the Apes episode #1: "Flames of Doom" (NB-a)

NOTE: The cause of such a sudden upsurge in technology is unknown—perhaps the apes found an ancient human city and relocated Ape City's population, then moved back to the country at a later date…I know, it's patently absurd. In truth, the series simply doesn't fit well with the films, no matter how hard one tries to make it jibe. Several sources place the animated series in 3810, based on the last date seen on the ship's chronometer. However, Hudson says they arrive in 3979, placing the show between the first two films…if it actually happened. The cartoon is a continuity nightmare, given the apes' advanced technology level and other factors, and is thus often ignored by fans.

◆ Zira discovers she is pregnant with Cornelius' child.

Escape from the Planet of the Apes (FX-f)

NOTE: It's possible Zira may have become pregnant before the first film, given her delivery of the baby in Escape from the Planet of the Apes. *She notes, in* Escape, *that she discovered her pregnancy before the war portrayed in* Beneath the Planet of the Apes.

◆ Gen. Urko, a gorilla, is named leader of the Ape City military.

Return to the Planet of the Apes episode #1: "Flames of Doom" (NB-a)

AUGUST 6, 3979

◆ The *Venturer*, an interstellar NASA spacecraft launched in 1976, splashes down in a lake near New York that resembles Deming, New Mexico, propelled forward in time by a spatial distortion. Aboard are three astronauts: Cmdr. Bill Hudson, Jeff Allen and Judy Franklin.

Return to the Planet of the Apes episode #1: "Flames of Doom" (NB-a)

NOTE: Hudson's rank is found in the novelization. Jeff Allen's name has been mistakenly listed as Jeff Carter in some online sources. The anomaly the Venturer *encounters is likely the Hasslein Curve. Franklin, in episode 7, says their home is 3,000 years in the past, but 1976 is only two millennia prior.*

◆ Among the apes, the lake is known as the Great Lagoon.

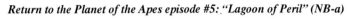

Return to the Planet of the Apes episode #5: "Lagoon of Peril" (NB-a)

NOTE: This body of water is apparently different than that in which the Liberty 1 *crashed, which the apes call the Dead Lake.*

◆ Urko convenes the Supreme Council of Elders of the Simian World to report on rumors that humans have learned to speak, and to request his army be dispatched to seek out and destroy all humans on the planet. Cornelius and Zira argue that they must study humans to learn more about simian origins.

Return to the Planet of the Apes episode #1: "Flames of Doom" (NB-a)

NOTE: The council's full title is revealed in the episode's novelization. It should be noted that humans in this series are called "humanoids," but I use the term "humans" instead since that's...well...what they are. "Humanoid" would imply they are a human-like species, separate from the humans of the planet Earth—which, clearly, they are not.

◆ The gorillas react in outrage at this suggestion, their behavior shocking many in attendance, including a venerable old orangutan council member named Zao.

Return to the Planet of the Apes episode #1: "Flames of Doom" (BB-n)

NOTE: This is revealed in the novelization.

◆ The *Venturer* crew takes a lifeboat to shore. With two days' rations in their survival packs, they head out into the desert to find food and water. An electrical storm begins and ends suddenly, without rain, and they decide to rest for the night.

Return to the Planet of the Apes episode #1: "Flames of Doom" (NB-a)

AUGUST 7, 3979

◆ The *Venturer* crew crosses the desert until collapsing in the sand. Judy Franklin gives Jeff Allen a ring, saying to deliver it to her sister Lily if she doesn't survive.

Return to the Planet of the Apes episode #1: "Flames of Doom" (NB-a)

PUBLISHER / STUDIO
AB . . . . ABC-TV
AC . . . .Adventure / Malibu Comics
AW . . . . Award Books
BB . . . . .Ballantine Books
BN . . . . Bantam Books
BW . . . . Brown Watson Books
CB . . . . CBS-TV
CV . . . . Chad Valley Sliderama
DH . . . . .Dark Horse Comics
ET . . . . Editorial Mo.Pa.Sa.
FX . . . . 20th Century Fox
GK . . . .Gold Key / Western Comics
HE . . . HarperEntertainment Books
HM . . Harry K. McWilliams Assoc.
MC . . . . Marvel Comics
MR . . . Mr. Comics / Metallic Rose
NB . . . . NBC-TV
PR . . . . .Power Records
SB . . . . Signet Books
TP . . . . Topps
UB . . . . .Ubisoft

MEDIUM
a . . . . animated series
b . . . . .book-and-record set
c . . . . .comic book or strip
d . . . . trading card
e . . . . e-comic
f . . . . .theatrical film
k . . . . .storybook
m . . . . .magazine article
n . . . . .novel or novelization
p . . . . . . promotional newspaper
r . . . . .recorded audio fiction
s . . . . short story
t . . . . television series
u . . . . . . .unfilmed script or story
v . . . . video game
x . . . . .Blu-Ray exclusive
y . . . . .young adult novel

◆ Below the surface, a band of mutant humans, the Underdwellers, recognize Franklin from an ancient NASA statue carved in her likeness, with the letters "USA" on its base. The statue has attained religious significance, as the Underdwellers have waited for their savior, "Oosa," to lead them back to the surface and retake the planet. Using their radiation-enhanced mental abilities, they create an illusion to draw her to them without revealing their whereabouts.

Return to the Planet of the Apes episode #3: "The Unearthly Prophecy" (NB-a)

NOTE: *Based on their manner, dress, motivation and surrounding, the Underdwellers would appear to be a separate mutant group from that living in the Holy City, as seen in* Beneath the Planet of the Apes.

◆ A sudden rockslide, the result of Underdweller illusion, nearly kills the astronauts, followed by spontaneous fire that burns their survival packs. An earthquake swallows Franklin. Seeking higher ground, Hudson and Allen see a mountain with ape faces carved into it—a monument known locally as Mount Apemore. Trudging on, the men befriend a band of primitive humans. Among them is Nova, who wears dog-tags around her neck from another NASA astronaut, Ronald Brent. Trumpets sound in the distance, and the primitives hide them as a convoy of ape-filled vehicles arrives. Urko and his aide-de-camp, Capt. Mulla, lead the charge as Tummo, Sgt. Rak and others use gas grenades to force the humans out of their caves. Allen and Nova get away by falling through a hole, but Hudson and the others are captured in wagons and taken to Ape City. There, Zaius tells Urko to let Cornelius and Zira have the six finest as lab specimens. Without his patronage, Zira fears, simian science would soon die of disinterest.

Return to the Planet of the Apes episode #1: "Flames of Doom" (NB-a)

NOTE: *Nova is drawn wearing two dog-tags; the first belongs to Ronald Brent, so the other could conceivably be Taylor's. Mulla, Tummo and Rak are named in the episode's novelization. Another novelization,* Return to the Planet of the Apes #3: Man, the Hunted Animal, *identifies the monument as Mount Apemore.*

3979, AFTER AUGUST 7

◆ Hudson awakens in a wagon cage with several primitives, who react in fear when he speaks. One claps a hand over his mouth so the apes won't hear. Urko and Mulla laugh at how easily they caught the humans, whom they've slated for war games. A parade heralds the return of Urko's army to Ape City, celebrating the largest catch of humans on record, with citizens and journalists lining the streets and rooftops.

Return to the Planet of the Apes episode #2: "Escape From Ape City" (NB-a)

◆ Cheerful ape children play a game of "Humanoids and Apes," amusing (or annoying) onlookers. Outside the Ape Senate Building, Sgt. Brutar regrets not being chosen to join Urko's hunt, while Pvt. Mungwort is content to remain behind. Brutar is disgusted, convinced he'll never make a soldier out of the pacifist Mungwort. Old Zao expresses distaste for the proceedings. Zaius agrees, but says the gorillas must be allowed to relieve their aggression. Warga, a gorilla soldier, requests the council fire cannons to honor the event, but Zao refuses. As Urko enters the scene, five chimp journalists—Zirko, Mikki, Ziora, Munko and Drik—prepare to record the big event.

Return to the Planet of the Apes episode #2: "Escape From Ape City" (BB-n)

NOTE: *This information appears in the episode's novelization.*

◆ Urko's warmongering disgusts Zira, but Cornelius says to mind her words. The hunt, Urko gloats, has bagged more humans than ever, and he scoffs at her notion that apes could learn from studying them. Zira sees Hudson in a cage and nicknames him "Bright Eyes." Urko refuses to give him to her, as he needs all of the humans for work details and war games. Zaius, however, splits up the humans among pet detail, labor detail and the animal replacement preserve. Zira runs a series of tests on Hudson, amazed at his high scores. Cornelius recommends operating on his brain center, causing the astronaut to burst out in protest. The couple stare in shock as he tells them who he is. A gorilla sentry overhears the exchange and reports it to the Council of Elders.

Return to the Planet of the Apes episode #2: "Escape From Ape City" (NB-a)

NOTE: Zira has apparently forgotten she already named Taylor "Bright Eyes"—and, in fact, that she and Cornelius even met Taylor. Their amazement at meeting sentient humans is yet another example of how the cartoons do not jibe well with the films.

◆ The Council debates what to do about the talking human. Zao urges them not to act hastily, and Zaius dreads the consequences of eliminating Urko's cannon fodder. Zuka, another councilor, questions whether Urko really needs the humans for his war games. Zaius suggests Urko may be close to rebelling, but others cite his loyalty to the Simian Nation. Removing the human work force could damage society, Zao argues. Ultimately, Zaius deems the risk worth taking if it protects society from talking humans.

Return to the Planet of the Apes episode #2: "Escape From Ape City" (BB-n)

NOTE: This information appears in the episode's novelization.

◆ Zaius reminds the council of the danger speaking humans represent, then sends the militia to Zira's lab to capture Hudson. As apes surround the building, Zira and Cornelius lead him to a ladder so he can escape via the roof. When Zaius enters the lab, the scientists pretend Hudson beat them and fled.

Return to the Planet of the Apes episode #2: "Escape From Ape City" (NB-a)

◆ A gorilla squad led by a soldier named Armic searches for Hudson, who sneaks past them across a cable. One ape, Warka, complains about the darkness. Inside, several journalists, including Tambor and Arro, question the scientists about the human's escape. Zaius is furious, knowing the future of their civilization depends on finding him. An ape sentry confronts Hudson, who knocks the guard onto his back, causing him to strike his head and die.

Return to the Planet of the Apes episode #2: "Escape From Ape City" (BB-n)

NOTE: This information appears in the episode's novelization.

◆ Hudson runs for cover, hiding in the shadows as search lights and alarms flood the city. Urko promises instant promotion to any trooper who finds him, and the streets fill with ambitious soldiers. A sentry spots Hudson hiding under a bridge, but he gets past the ape.

Return to the Planet of the Apes episode #2: "Escape From Ape City" (NB-a)

◆ A sergeant dispatches two groups, led by Zuira and Ranko, to head Hudson off by the lake. He sends another ape, Nutark, to summon Lake Patrol as backup, then orders Warka and Trebo to retrieve the sentry's body. Hudson, however, slips quietly into the lake and swims away.

Return to the Planet of the Apes episode #2: "Escape From Ape City" (BB-n)

NOTE: This information appears in the episode's novelization.

◆ In a nearby field, Allen and Nova hear rustling in the brush. Allen jumps what he thinks is a gorilla but turns out to be Hudson. Reunited, the astronauts and Nova get to safer ground.

Return to the Planet of the Apes episode #2: "Escape From Ape City" (NB-a)

PUBLISHER / STUDIO
AB . . . . ABC-TV
AC . . . .Adventure / Malibu Comics
AW . . . . Award Books
BB . . . . .Ballantine Books
BN . . . . Bantam Books
BW . . . . Brown Watson Books
CB . . . . CBS-TV
CV . . . . Chad Valley Sliderama
DH . . . . .Dark Horse Comics
ET . . . . .Editorial Mo.Pa.Sa.
FX . . . . 20th Century Fox
GK . . . .Gold Key / Western Comics
HE . . . HarperEntertainment Books
HM . . Harry K. McWilliams Assoc.
MC . . . . .Marvel Comics
MR . . . Mr. Comics / Metallic Rose
NB . . . . NBC-TV
PR . . . . .Power Records
SB . . . . Signet Books
TP . . . . Topps
UB . . . . .Ubisoft

MEDIUM
a . . . . animated series
b . . . . .book-and-record set
c . . . . .comic book or strip
d . . . . trading card
e . . . . e-comic
f . . . . .theatrical film
k . . . . .storybook
m . . . . .magazine article
n . . . . .novel or novelization
p . . . . promotional newspaper
r . . . . .recorded audio fiction
s . . . . short story
t . . . . television series
u . . . . .unfilmed script or story
v . . . . video game
x . . . . .Blu-Ray exclusive
y . . . . .young adult novel

◆ A forest fire in Bacra rages out of control, and a crop failure in Wambo Province causes further strife. The Council of Elders, therefore, releases an inspirational message titled "The Need for a United Apedom." In the small but growing simian film industry, meanwhile, Citizen Naarthrok announces his next project, *Zantar of the Humanoids*, based on a best-selling book about an ape raised by primitive humans who becomes the greatest of their tribe.

Return to the Planet of the Apes episode #2: "Escape From Ape City" (BB-n)

NOTE: This occurs in the novelization. Zantar is "Tarzan" spelled backwards.

◆ Zaius imposes a curfew on Ape City, ordering all non-essential personnel indoors. Zira wonders if they did the right thing in helping Hudson.

Return to the Planet of the Apes episode #2: "Escape From Ape City" (NB-a)

◆ Urko orders all forces to join the search for the astronaut, so Capt. Trimbo reassigns guards watching the caged humans, enabling Allen and Hudson to sneak into the jail without complications.

Return to the Planet of the Apes episode #2: "Escape From Ape City" (BB-n)

NOTE: This information appears in the episode's novelization.

◆ Hudson and Allen load all of the human prisoners onto a stolen truck, destroy all of the wagon cages and drive off in the night. Zaius is furious, blaming Urko for such ineptitude.

Return to the Planet of the Apes episode #2: "Escape From Ape City" (NB-a)

◆ Urko demotes Trimbo for letting the humans escape. Back at the cages, Hudson covers his face and arms with a primitive's furs to disguise himself as a gorilla driver.

Return to the Planet of the Apes episode #2: "Escape From Ape City" (BB-n)

NOTE: This information appears in the episode's novelization.

◆ Apes spot the stolen truck on the Boropark Mountain road. The astronauts push it onto the pass, barring their way. Worried about the primitives' safety, they decide to retrieve a laser drill from the *Venturer* and carve a defense perimeter out of nearby boulders. Unable to reach them, Urko vows to find the tribe.

Return to the Planet of the Apes episode #2: "Escape From Ape City" (NB-a)

◆ Urko leads a convoy into the Forbidden Zone to destroy the Underdwellers' cavern. His underlings fear his wrath, Nutark enduring the heat without comment, and Mulla following his orders word for word.

Return to the Planet of the Apes episode #3: "The Unearthly Prophecy" (BB-n)

NOTE: This information appears in the episode's novelization, which calls this tale "A Date With Judy," based on an early-draft episode script. Many Web sites and other resources have, thus, incorrectly identified "A Date With Judy" as the title of a "lost" 14th episode, when no such episode exists.

◆ Hudson and Allen search a 50-mile radius around the caves, finding no habitable areas. Mountains thrust from the ground, separating Urko and Hudson. A door in the sand opens near the astronauts, and they climb down. Grabbing a moving ladder, they enter a complex of caverns filled with energy-generating machinery—the Below World, home to the Underdwellers. A tunnel leads to the ruins of New York City, and they realize they're still on Earth. They follow two robed humans into a large computer room. The Underdwellers enter a cavern chanting "Oosa!" and Franklin is with them, similarly clad. The mutant leader, Krador, stuns them with eye beams, saying their ancestors took refuge underground when war ravaged the planet. Prophecy foretells that Franklin ("Oosa") will help them retake Earth from the apes. She enters, but appears to be in a trance.

Return to the Planet of the Apes episode #3: "The Unearthly Prophecy" (NB-a)

◆ Krador orders two Underdwellers, Zumor and Yathor, to escort the men to a forcefielded cell. Hudson wonders if their surroundings are illusory. Krador assures Franklin that her companions shall not stop her from fulfilling the prophecy, and the brainwashed astronauts agree.

Return to the Planet of the Apes episode #3: "The Unearthly Prophecy" (BB-n)

NOTE: This occurs in the novelization.

◆ Urko splits his team into three groups, led by Urko, Capt. Ramja and Major Sark. Franklin returns to her friends, saying she lied to fool Krador. Damaging a reflector dish, she disables the mutants' illusion generators, disabling power across the complex and freeing the astronauts—and revealing to Urko an entrance into the Below World. His defenses weakened, Krador uses the Chair of Power to repair the machinery and hide the entrance. The astronauts head back to the surface on a train car. Underdwellers try to stop them, but to no avail. Franklin grows weaker as Krador regains control of her mind, however, and as they reach the tunnel's end, she vanishes. Hudson and Allen climb back to the surface without her, wondering if they can get through to Nova's people to ask their help. ●

Return to the Planet of the Apes episode #3: "The Unearthly Prophecy" (NB-a)

NOTE: Ramja and Sark are named in the novelization.

◆ Allen and Hudson spot a group of apes preparing to attack the Underdwellers, and Hudson kills a soldier in self-defense. Allen suggests abandoning Nova's people, but Hudson points out that as a Black man sensitive to racial inequality, Allen isn't the type to dismiss people for being different. Urko, meanwhile, learns of his soldier's death and orders Capt. Mulla to find the humans responsible.

Return to the Planet of the Apes episode #4: "Tunnel of Fear" (BB-n)

NOTE: This is revealed in the novelization.

◆ Allen suggests moving the human colony to a safe place where they can fortify themselves. They decide to ask Cornelius and Zira for help. Hiding in a truck (whose driver is listening to a country song, "I'm Going Humanoid Over You"), the astronauts sneak into Ape City, steal a rowboat to cross a lake, jump overboard when a patrol boat passes and hide when troops approach the dock. The apes notice the boat, however, and mount a search party. The astronauts hide in a sewer, where a giant mutated spider captures them in its web. Hudson cuts them free with a piece of tin, and they run for cover. After a gorilla convoy passes, they crawl out of a manhole and head for the lab.

Return to the Planet of the Apes episode #4: "Tunnel of Fear" (NB-a)

◆ En route to the lab, the astronauts pass a movie theater showing the film *Zantar of the Humanoids*.

Return to the Planet of the Apes episode #4: "Tunnel of Fear" (BB-n)

NOTE: This is revealed in the novelization.

◆ Urko prepares to simultaneously storm the caves from the Forest Zone and other directions. Zira and Cornelius suggest the astronauts bring the primitives to an uncharted valley that is difficult to reach. Cornelius draws a map, saying two routes lead there—a mountain route patrolled by gorilla army units, and a river flowing beneath the mountains. When a gorilla desert patrol arrives, the men grab the map and paddle to safety on a river log. The current gets stronger, however, washing them over a waterfall. The river leads to the caves, where the tribe revives them, and Allen opts to return to the *Venturer*'s crash site to retrieve the ship's laser drill.

Return to the Planet of the Apes episode #4: "Tunnel of Fear" (NB-a)

◆ Julius, a chimp reporter for the Simian Broadcasting Company (SBC), hears rumors of a talking human, but government officials and the Supreme Council pressure him not to report the story.

Return to the Planet of the Apes episode #5: "Lagoon of Peril" (BB-n)

NOTE: This is revealed in the novelization.

◆ News spreads fast after a gorilla returns from the Forbidden Zone claiming to have seen a spaceship and sentient humans. The soldier is hospitalized, babbling about astronauts. The dawn edition of the *Ape City Tabloid* reports, "Intelligent Humanoids Invade Planet of the Apes."

Return to the Planet of the Apes episode #5: "Lagoon of Peril" (NB-a)

◆ Julius, the reporter, sees the *Tabloid* and regrets sitting on the news. A radio broadcast reports an unidentified flying object over the Forbidden Zone might have carried intelligent humans. The radio journalist compares the rumors to something out of the television series *Spokka the Space-Ape*.

Return to the Planet of the Apes episode #5: "Lagoon of Peril" (BB-n)

NOTE: This is revealed in the novelization.

◆ In the Simian Senate, an orangutan senator urges others to arm themselves, and to protect their families in case the rumor of sentient humans is true. Urko's solution: to destroy all humans first. The Lawgiver ends the debate, meeting with the Supreme Council to decide what to do.

Return to the Planet of the Apes episode #5: "Lagoon of Peril" (NB-a)

◆ Julius broadcasts an editorial questioning the wisdom of ushering in a new age of democracy, reporting that the Simian Nation is in an uproar over rumors of sentient humans from outer space. All are poised in anticipation of the answer to one question: Will this mean all-out war?

Return to the Planet of the Apes episode #5: "Lagoon of Peril" (BB-n)

NOTE: This is revealed in the novelization.

◆ Dick Hadley, of the Ape Broadcasting System (ABS), reports that observers foresee "dark days ahead." A mob of protestors bears out this prediction. Urko urges Zaius to act fast, so the council sends both apes to the Great Lagoon to investigate, authorizing full media coverage. Zira and Cornelius warn Hudson and Allen about the expedition, and they rush to the lagoon to blow up the ship before the apes can find it.

Return to the Planet of the Apes episode #5: "Lagoon of Peril" (NB-a)

◆ As the expedition traverses the Forbidden Zone, Mungwort bemoans his lot in life, always picked on and chosen for dangerous tasks. Pvt. Pooka, one of his only friends, sees something in the distance.

Return to the Planet of the Apes episode #5: "Lagoon of Peril" (BB-n)

NOTE: This is revealed in the novelization.

◆ In the Forbidden Zone, the astronauts and Nova encounter Underdweller illusions of fire and earthquakes, intended to keep them away. The same obstacles terrify the apes, who make camp for the night. A fire-emitting ape skull fills the sky, but vanishes when Zaius stands up to it. The apes survive a rockfall and additional flames, but ignore the illusions. Hudson and Allen leave Nova on the beach and row to the *Venturer*. Hudson swims to the entrance hatch and pries it open. Grabbing an oxygen mask, he retrieves the laser, then heads underwater again to destroy the capsule. As he swims back, a buh-hoy-ya (a giant mutated serpent) tries to eat him. Allen saves him, shooting the beast with the laser, then the duo erase their footprints and run for cover. The capsule explodes before the ape convoy hits the beach. Seeing the serpent but no ship, Zaius decides the soldier was in error and orders a retreat.

Return to the Planet of the Apes episode #5: "Lagoon of Peril" (NB-a)

◆ Hudson steals a truck from a gorilla named Zutta. Leaving the Forbidden Zone, he and Allen find Nova's tribe and abandon the vehicle, which Urko's troops locate miles from Zutta's corpse. They relax for a while in a watering hole, and Hudson teaches Nova to swim. He realizes he is falling in love with her, hoping one day to raise a family with her and help her people retake the planet.

Return to the Planet of the Apes episode #5: "Lagoon of Peril" (BB-n)

NOTE: This is revealed in the novelization.

◆ Back in Ape City, Zaius holds a press conference to dispel the rumors of spaceships and talking humans. Later, the *Ape City Bugle*'s headline reads, "Planet of the Apes Safe!"

Return to the Planet of the Apes episode #5: "Lagoon of Peril" (NB-a)

◆ Col. Boora sends a detachment of ape troops to investigate uncharted mountains at the extreme northern edge of Wambo province. Led by Capt. Jemmo, the soldiers don cold-weather gear and scout for humans.

Return to the Planet of the Apes episode #6: "Terror on Ice Mountain" (BB-n)

NOTE: This is revealed in the novelization.

◆ Cornelius digs up an ancient book titled *A Day at the Zoo*. Written by humans, with photos of caged apes and free humans, it proves man could once read and write. Urko demands to examine his lab for incriminating artifacts, but he and Zira refuse to let the gorilla in unless so ordered by the council. Cornelius suggests they destroy the book so Urko won't find it, but Zira knows it's too valuable. Cornelius has also found plans for a flying balloon. Ecstatic, he asks Hudson and Allen for help in building it. Cornelius and Hudson take a test flight to hide the book atop Mount Garr. The flight goes well until a storm crashes them on the snowy cliffs of an uncharted mountain west of their destination. As they fall from the gondola onto a snowy mountainside, a gorilla patrol guard spots them.

Return to the Planet of the Apes episode #6: "Terror on Ice Mountain" (NB-a)

◆ The patrol guard, Lt. Uka, contacts Jemmo, who locates the balloon with his binoculars, sends Uka and Corp. Tenzic to report to the council, and takes other soldiers to investigate.

Return to the Planet of the Apes episode #6: "Terror on Ice Mountain" (BB-n)

NOTE: This is revealed in the novelization.

◆ Passing an ice statue of a giant ape, Cornelius and Hudson collapse from the cold and awaken in a temple among fur-clad simians: the Ice Apes (or High-Mountain Apes), worshippers of Kygoor. Menluth, the High Lama (or Worthy One), is impressed at their friendship and agrees to fix the balloon after an impending pilgrimage. Menluth takes his visitors via cable car to meet their god. Jemmo's soldiers try to cut the cable, causing the statue to come alive and destroy them. Hudson gratefully asks the Worthy One to guard the book, which he places in a secret ice cave at the foot of Kygoor's statue. Kygoor lifts the balloon into the air, and the duo begin their journey home.

Return to the Planet of the Apes episode #6: "Terror on Ice Mountain" (NB-a)

NOTE: Menluth is named in the novelization. The High-Mountain Apes are named in episode #13.

◆ Zira and Cornelius stop at an old archeological dig site to pick up some pottery and bones before returning to Ape City, so as to stave off suspicion regarding their absence.

Return to the Planet of the Apes episode #7: "River of Flames" (BB-n)

NOTE: This is revealed in the novelization.

◆ Dr. Lykos, a chimp scientist, finds an intact fleet of P-40 World War II fighter planes, which Urko sees as a means to wiping out humanity and wresting power from Zaius. He assigns Lykos to restore the craft and discover how it works. An ape soldier, Wing Cmdr. Larko, trains to fly it, while other apes equip its torpedo chambers with nets for capturing humans on the ground.

Return to the Planet of the Apes episode #8: "Screaming Wings" (NB-a)

NOTE: It's unclear when this happens, but some time must pass for the apes to figure out how to fuel and fly the plane.

◆ When a lava river threatens the Below World, Krador projects a vision of Franklin to her friends, urging them to save the Underdwellers. Wary of tricks, they hide their laser and descend. Cornelius and Zira debate with Urko whether future funding should go to science or the military. Since Hudson has eluded the gorillas for months, Zaius suggests he might vote in Urko's favor were he to capture the man. The chimps question the wisdom of arming his enemy, but Zaius is more concerned with the danger Hudson represents to apekind. Krador tells the astronauts a volcano thought dormant has come to life; if the lava reaches their power supply, it will set up a chain reaction, destroying the planet. Their price for assistance is Franklin's freedom. Krador protests, but she promises to return.

Return to the Planet of the Apes episode #7: "River of Flames" (NB-a)

◆ Mungwort's woes continue as Brutar mocks his chimp accent. The pacifist watches his patrol—Dubark, Trommo and Kork gambling in secret; Corp. Morgo checking out a jeep engine; Theka and Pvt. Tritor trading jokes; Sturbo snoozing in the sun—and is reminded once more that he doesn't fit in.

Return to the Planet of the Apes episode #7: "River of Flames" (BB-n)

NOTE: This is revealed in the novelization.

◆ The astronauts ascend to the surface, but Mungwort finds the laser before they can retrieve it.

Return to the Planet of the Apes episode #7: "River of Flames" (NB-a)

NOTE: The novelization identifies Mungwort as the ape who finds the laser.

◆ Unfamiliar with the laser, Mungwort nearly kills his squad before Brutar can grab the gun. Brutar delivers it to Red Leader One, Urko's temporary Forbidden Zone command post.

Return to the Planet of the Apes episode #7: "River of Flames" (BB-n)

NOTE: This is revealed in the novelization.

◆ Urko studies the laser and realizes it must belong to Hudson.

Return to the Planet of the Apes episode #7: "River of Flames" (NB-a)

◆ The general meets with his officers to discuss the laser. Major Surga suggests a human might have built it. Col. Trafuna accuses him of heresy, but Urko realizes Surga is correct.

Return to the Planet of the Apes episode #7: "River of Flames" (BB-n)

NOTE: This is revealed in the novelization.

◆ As the meeting ends, Urko inadvertently knocks an energy cell loose from the laser. Hudson, meanwhile, decides to create a diversion so he and Allen can retrieve the weapon.

Return to the Planet of the Apes episode #7: "River of Flames" (NB-a)

◆ Sgt. Kukar assigns two soldiers, Wallo and Girk, to guard the pass so no humans can enter the Forbidden Zone. The guards discuss recent films they've seen, including *Doctor Hydo and Mister Jekkill*.

Return to the Planet of the Apes episode #7: "River of Flames" (BB-n)

NOTE: This is revealed in the novelization.

◆ Hudson interrupts Wallo and Girk's discussion of *The Apefather* so Allen can sneak into the camp, steal the laser from Capt. Wontor, create a rockslide and fire at the nearby rock wall.

Return to the Planet of the Apes episode #7: "River of Flames" (NB-a)

NOTE: *Wontor, Wallo and Girk are named in the novelization.*

◆ The blast kills several apes, including Girk. Urko, thinking Wontor fired the laser, tells Capt. Wimja to arrest the radio operator. He orders Mulla to form a column of soldiers to catch Hudson, then tells Trafuna to prepare to attack the caves. Allen, however, shoots both Wontor and Trafuna.

Return to the Planet of the Apes episode #7: "River of Flames" (BB-n)

NOTE: *This is revealed in the novelization.*

◆ The astronauts revisit the Below World and blast the side of a cavern, causing the lava to bypass the Underdwellers' power source. The laser's power drains, but howitzers finish the job when Urko orders the mountain fired upon. The resultant eruption kills many apes, destroying their vehicles and equipment. The Underdwellers free Franklin, promising their assistance if ever she requires it. The Senate holds Urko responsible for firing at an active volcano, agreeing to replace the lost equipment but granting future funding to science instead of the military.

Return to the Planet of the Apes episode #7: "River of Flames" (NB-a)

◆ Urko and Mulla return to their hidden Strategic Defense HQ stronghold in the Mulkalla Mountains, where they check on their latest secret weapon—the airplane fleet.

Return to the Planet of the Apes episode #7: "River of Flames" (BB-n)

NOTE: *This is revealed in the novelization.*

◆ The reunited astronauts return to Red Leader One and comb the sand until finding the laser's missing energy cell. After resting in the Forbidden Zone, they set out on a three-day journey back to the caves.

Return to the Planet of the Apes episode #7: "River of Flames" (NB-a)

◆ Crossing the Forbidden Zone, Allen and Hudson see Urko's army making camp. Larko's fighter plane zooms past, firing a net at human-shaped ground targets. Realizing the danger this poses to humanity, they vow to destroy or steal it. Urko announces the plane's existence, demanding Zaius give him control of the government, and invites all leaders and scientists to a demonstration at his Strategic Defense Headquarters. Zira and Cornelius provide the astronauts with a map of the Black Zone, the restricted area containing Urko's HQ. The men create a diversion by rolling a pile of gasoline tanks down a hill. As apes rush to contain the fire, the duo enter a hangar and discover Urko's fleet. Before they can act, however, a vehicle arrives carrying a load of primitive humans.

Return to the Planet of the Apes episode #8: "Screaming Wings" (NB-a)

◆ Cornelius reads a news article about a ballgame between the Ape City Marauders and the Kulak Killers, while Zira watches *The Unlikely Three*, a television series about a smart chimp detective, his gorilla sidekick and a juvenile orangutan named Plato, who roam Ape City solving crimes. *Apewitness News* begins, and newscaster Julius reports that Urko's military demo is imminent. Julius interviews the Marauders' coach, Durka, about his team's chances against the Wuwanni Blue Sox.

Return to the Planet of the Apes episode #8: "Screaming Wings" (BB-n)

NOTE: *This is revealed in the novelization.*

◆ In the morning, a band opens the event as a crowd awaits Urko's demonstration. Urko is full of himself, convinced his time has come. Cornelius and Zira are disgusted at such bravado.

Return to the Planet of the Apes episode #8: "Screaming Wings" (NB-a)

◆ En route to their seats, Cornelius and Zira meet fellow behavioral scientists, Drs. Galba and Vitellius.

Return to the Planet of the Apes episode #8: "Screaming Wings" (BB-n)

NOTE: This occurs in the novelization.

◆ Senator Demetrius and Old Zao suspect Urko of planning something evil. However, Franklin replaces Larko in the pilot seat, then buzzes the audience before flying off with the craft. Larko escapes his bonds and rushes to warn Urko. Humiliated, the general vows to start over—but without the original airplane, Lykos says, they cannot build more. Stealing a truck, the astronauts load the fearful humans aboard and drive them to safety.

Return to the Planet of the Apes episode #8: "Screaming Wings" (NB-a)

NOTE: Demetrius is named in the novelization.

◆ Urko orders several soldiers—Ranko, Zuira, Mulla, Surga, Tuka, Gurto and Kogora—to take action. Knowing his temper, they scramble to follow his command.

Return to the Planet of the Apes episode #8: "Screaming Wings" (BB-n)

NOTE: This is revealed in the novelization.

◆ Urko pursues the truck down Mulkalla Pass, but Franklin stops him with a net. Zaius orders an evaluation of Urko's competence. In the Forbidden Zone, meanwhile, the astronauts hide the stolen plane in a cave.

Return to the Planet of the Apes episode #8: "Screaming Wings" (NB-a)

NOTE: Mulkalla Pass is named in the novelization.

◆ Cornelius gives the astronauts a map of New Valley so Nova's people can be safe. The men teach the primitives to cut down trees and build four great rafts. Thinking Cornelius and Zira stole the plane, Zaius thanks them for saving civilization. Urko mounts a reconnaissance mission to the caves, while the rafts carry Nova's people downriver to their new home. Some become ill, but Hudson says they must keep traveling. As night falls, bats swarm the rafts. Leaving the jungle, they come to a high cliff and begin climbing. Urko vows to restore confidence in the military, promising a thousand pieces of simian silver to anyone who exposes the airplane thief.

Return to the Planet of the Apes episode #9: "Trail to the Unknown" (NB-a)

◆ Urko's troops prepare to ravage the caves and kill the humans, but the tribe is gone when they arrive.

Return to the Planet of the Apes episode #9: "Trail to the Unknown" (BB-n)

NOTE: This is revealed in the novelization.

◆ Seeing the cut trees, Urko orders his officers to send for rivercraft. The soldiers are reticent, for ape law demands they get permission from the council. The humans brave sandstorms and other hardships, then hide behind a mesa. In the morning, they find the remains of a crashed vehicle. Atop a hill stands Col. Ronald Brent, who offers to escort them to New Valley, 25 miles south of the crash-site. Allen suggests they take his ship's self-destruct device. Hudson tells Brent about the apes, whom he never encountered in the two decades since his crash. Arriving at New Valley, the men use the laser to cut building blocks out of boulders, to create a settlement of stone pueblos. Back in Ape City, the council questions Urko's ability to command. Zaius grants permission to find the elusive humans, warning him not to attack without a council mandate.

Return to the Planet of the Apes episode #9: "Trail to the Unknown" (NB-a)

◆ Urko and Mulla lead a military convoy into the Forbidden Zone. Mungwort, disgusted at the stupidity of his fellow officers, tries to nap away his annoyance.

Return to the Planet of the Apes episode #9: "Trail to the Unknown" (BB-n)

NOTE: *This is revealed in the novelization.*

◆ Lt. Samic informs Urko that scouts have picked up the humans' trail through the Southern Desert, an unexplored sector surrounding Dead Ape's Canyon. As the army converges on that spot, the humans take refuge in the adobe dwellings, pulling up ladders to deter invaders. The apes launch gas grenades, which bounce back to the convoy. Unable to reach the tribe, Urko returns to Ape City for proper weapons. With no defense against ape artillery, the astronauts use the self-destruct mechanism to destroy the land bridge. Their next move: to retrieve the airplane.

Return to the Planet of the Apes episode #9: "Trail to the Unknown" (NB-a)

NOTE: *Samic and Dead Ape's Canyon are named in the novelization.*

◆ As Nova's people domesticate a herd of horned cattle, a snake bird (a giant mutated flying creature) attacks. The panicked animals stampede and get stuck in a cave, so Allen uses the laser to cut a hole in the wall and feed them. Nova nearly dies in the stampede, but Brent pulls her to safety. Unable to reach the cattle, the snake-bird tries to eat the astronauts. In Ape City, the council votes to replace Urko if he fails. Franklin retrieves the plane in order to survey the pass, but Urko sees it flying overhead and dispatches his officers. She arrives at New Valley to find the panicked tribe under attack from the snake-bird. Clipping its wing, she forces the creature to fall into the river.

Return to the Planet of the Apes episode #10: "Attack from the Clouds" (NB-a)

◆ The astronauts fix the plane, then steal fuel from an ape aviation plant. Nova falls ill, and Brent diagnoses her with chronic acute infectious *streptococcalis*, which can be fatal if untreated. Franklin seeks Zira's help in finding a cure, hiding as two elderly apes solicit donations for the Gorilla Veterans' Relief Fund. Cornelius recognizes the disease as *inflamatus pneumococcal*, and creates a serum. The stolen truck overheats, forcing the astronauts to stop for water. Avoiding ape soldiers, they refuel the plane so Judy can rush the drug to New Valley. Despite stormy weather, she arrives in time to save Nova and inoculate the others. Hudson and Allen eventually return as well.

Return to the Planet of the Apes episode #11: "Mission of Mercy" (NB-a)

◆ Disguised as Underdwellers, Urko's troops stage a series of burglaries in order to convince the council to authorize an invasion of mutant territory. They steal valuable artwork from several museums, and a First Edition of the *Collected Works of William Apespeare*. Zira, Cornelius and the astronauts contact Krador, who denies involvement. Urko brings false witnesses before the council—Mrs. Thorto von Bruen, who claims an Underdweller robbed her home, and Capt. Graylor, a museum guard, who says hooded beings stole the *Apea Lisa*—then loads a barge with explosives to make the Ape City River flood the caves. Krador transports Franklin to the Great Cathedral and brings her friends to the Danger Zone—a line of tunnels beneath Ape City Graveyard, beyond which lies the Tomb of the Unknown Ape. Allen laser-cuts the wall, revealing the stolen objects and robes. Hypnotizing an ape to confess the crime, Krador projects Hudson's face to Cornelius' mirror so he can expose Urko, then transports the astronauts to the tunnel so they can send the barge in Urko's direction. Debris rains down on Urko's troops, and the Senate suspends the gorilla for three months.

Return to the Planet of the Apes episode #12: "Invasion of the Underdwellers" (NB-a)

PUBLISHER / STUDIO
AB . . . . ABC-TV
AC . . . . Adventure / Malibu Comics
AW . . . . Award Books
BB . . . . Ballantine Books
BN . . . . Bantam Books
BW . . . . Brown Watson Books
CB . . . . CBS-TV
CV . . . . . . Chad Valley Sliderama
DH . . . . Dark Horse Comics
ET . . . . Editorial Mo.Pa.Sa.
FX . . . . 20th Century Fox
GK . . . . Gold Key / Western Comics
HE . . . HarperEntertainment Books
HM . . Harry K. McWilliams Assoc.
MC . . . . Marvel Comics
MR . . . Mr. Comics / Metallic Rose
NB . . . . NBC-TV
PR . . . . Power Records
SB . . . . Signet Books
TP . . . . Topps
UB . . . . Ubisoft

MEDIUM
a . . . . animated series
b . . . . book-and-record set
c . . . . comic book or strip
d . . . . trading card
e . . . . e-comic
f . . . . theatrical film
k . . . . storybook
m . . . . magazine article
n . . . . novel or novelization
p . . . . promotional newspaper
r . . . . recorded audio fiction
s . . . . short story
t . . . . television series
u . . . . unfilmed script or story
v . . . . video game
x . . . . Blu-Ray exclusive
y . . . . young adult novel

♦ Placed in command, Col. Rotuk agrees to Urko's urging that he attack New Valley and exterminate mankind. The astronauts help Nova's tribe fortify the pueblos, then Cornelius and Hudson repair the hot-air balloon and revisit the High-Mountain Apes to retrieve *A Day at the Zoo*. The snake-bird attacks, but they lose the creature in the clouds. A gorilla spots them and alerts Rotuk. Franklin strafes the troops with the airplane, forcing a retreat. Nearly frozen, Hudson and Cornelius find Kygoor's temple, where the High Lama retrieves the book from beneath the statue. The snake-bird attacks their cable car, causing Kygoor to awaken and protect them. Eventually, the snake-bird flees in fear, and Cornelius and Hudson return to Ape City, hoping the book will help prove humanity's pre-ape civilization.

Return to the Planet of the Apes episode #13: "Battle of the Titans" (NB-a)

♦ With help from Nova's people, the *Venturer* crew formulate a plan to destroy the apes' ammunition dumps and airplane fuel tanks.

Return to the Planet of the Apes episode #14: [title unknown] (NB-u)

> *NOTE: This and the following two episodes were planned but neither scripted nor produced; a brief synopsis of each appears in* Planet of the Apes Revisited, *courtesy of director Doug Wildey. No further details are available.*

♦ A major battle ensues between the ape army and the fugitive humans and their allies.

Return to the Planet of the Apes episode #15: [title unknown] (NB-u)

♦ The battle concludes when New Valley's humans blow up the ammo dumps and fuel tanks, crippling the technology level of ape society and enabling the humans to build a community in the Forbidden Zone. Eventually, the leaders of both species agree to a truce.

Return to the Planet of the Apes episode #16: [title unknown] (NB-u)

♦ In the battle's aftermath, the apes abandon the city in favor of a simpler life. Disgraced, Urko is removed from power and replaced by Gen. Ursus. Peace between humans and apes, however, quickly crumbles.

Conjecture

> *NOTE: I offer this feeble attempt to explain the lack of technology in the second film, and to show the transition from Urko to Ursus. It doesn't really work...but what does? In truth, the only workable solution is to say the cartoons never happened.*

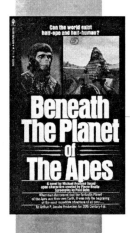

♦ Assuming command, Ursus—frustrated at Ape City's enclosure by the eastern sea and the desert on all other sides, and by humanity's infestation—decides to expand ape territory and exterminate the beasts.

Beneath the Planet of the Apes (BN-n)

> *NOTE: This information is revealed in the novelization.*

3979

♦ Rumors of speaking humans spread as Ape City grows awash in political undercurrents, despite Zaius' attempts to quash the ripples. Ursus believes the astronauts must hail from a tribe living beyond the Forbidden Zone. Powerful and charismatic, he is beyond even Zaius' control as he campaigns the council to let him build a massive army and wage all-out war on humanity.

Planet of the Apes #11: "Outlines of Tomorrow—A Chronology of the Planet of the Apes" (MC-m)

♦ Ursus sends 12 scouts to the Forbidden Zone. Eleven vanish, but a twelfth returns with tales of fire and earthquakes. The missing scouts are captured and interrogated by mutant humans living in the ruins of New York City, ruled by Mendez XXVI. The mutants try to control the gorillas' primitive minds but cannot hold the illusions for long. Urko petitions to invade the Forbidden Zone, and Zaius joins him.

Beneath the Planet of the Apes (FX-f)

◆ Ursus steps up his troops' training, and thousands of humans are captured for target practice. Since human and ape screams sound similar, the increased realism enhances the practice sessions. ●

The Ape News (HM-p)

NOTE: *As seen in* Beneath the Planet of the Apes, *mute humans cannot scream.*

◆ An ANSA shuttle crashes in the Forbidden Zone. Ship's medic John Christopher Brent survives, but his colleague, Donovan "Skipper" Maddox, is fatally wounded. Nova approaches on horseback, wearing Taylor's dogtag. She brings Brent to Ape City, where Ursus pushes for war at a Citizens' Council meeting. Zira refuses to applaud until Cornelius forces her, fearful of alienating the general. Zaius and Ursus debate the invasion during a steam bath at Zeeka's Simian Sauna. A gorilla shoots Brent in the arm, and Nova takes him to see Zira. Amazed to meet another talking human, she hides him when Zaius visits. Seeing Brent's bloody cloth, Zira pretends Cornelius hit her for showing disrespect. Zaius warns her against defying Ursus, asking them to put aside their convictions and guard science in his absence. Brent and Nova leave town, but a gorilla shoots their horse and cages them with other humans. Ursus claims them for target practice, but Zira unlocks the wagon door, enabling them to escape out on the road.

Beneath the Planet of the Apes (FX-f)

NOTE: *Brent's full name and medic status come from Marvel's adaptation. Marvel's timeline places* Beneath *in 3976, while the script sets it in 3975. An onscreen chronometer indicates 3955, as does Dayton Ward's timeline, published in* The Planet of the Apes Chronicles. *The Ape News* bears a date of March 1, 3955, whereas a timeline in the Planet of the Apes 40th Anniversary Collection *places it in February 3955. None of these dates jibe with the first film, said to occur in 3978. A timeline packaged with the* Planet of the Apes Widescreen 35th Anniversary Edition *DVD confirms the 3978 setting. This sequel underwent numerous incarnations, including a version in which Taylor featured throughout, rather than just in framing sequences, and a script by novelist Pierre Boulle entitled* Planet of the Men, *in which Taylor became a Messianic figure to Nova's people. The Ape News names Zeeka's Simian Sauna, and identifies Ape City as Apetown.*

◆ A deadly light leak forms in the extreme southwest fissure of the mutants' home beneath New York City, but the Holy City's leaders ignore the problem until two mutants die and several are injured. Faced with a public outcry over the leakage, Mendez XXVI sends a maintenance patrol to seal it.

The Mutant News (HM-p)

◆ Two days after Brent's departure, Zira and Cornelius return to *Liberty 1* to help Milo repair the shuttle's electrical and water damage. Donning spare spacesuits, they launch the vehicle and attain Earth orbit.

Planet of the Apes #11: "Outlines of Tomorrow—A Chronology of the Planet of the Apes" (MC-m)

NOTE: *How they could do this, given the apes' technology level, the short time span, and* Liberty 1*'s damage, is unknown. The 40th Anniversary Collection timeline indicates Zira and Cornelius were searching for Brent and Nova when they encountered Milo and the shuttle. Chris Shields' The Last Flight of the* Icarus *website proposes a third, undamaged spaceship, as does the* Escape from the Planet of the Apes *novelization, though* A Public Service Announcement From ANSA *would seem to negate the third-ship theory*

◆ Outside the city, Brent and Nova escape their cage and steal the wagon's horses. Dodging Capt. Odo's gorillas, they descend into a hidden cave, within which lies a subway tunnel containing 20th-century artifacts. A sign reading "Queensboro Plaza" reveals Brent is still on Earth—and in the town where he once lived. In Ape City, a minister prays for Ursus' army on the eve of war. The next morning, Ursus and Zaius assemble the troops. A group of chimp pacifists stage a peace demonstration, but the gorillas lift them out of the way and head into the Forbidden Zone.

Beneath the Planet of the Apes (FX-f)

NOTE: *Odo is named in Marvel and Gold Key's adaptations, and in the film's script.*

PUBLISHER / STUDIO
AB . . . . ABC-TV
AC . . . .Adventure / Malibu Comics
AW . . . . Award Books
BB . . . . .Ballantine Books
BN . . . . Bantam Books
BW . . . . . . Brown Watson Books
CB . . . . CBS-TV
CV . . . . Chad Valley Sliderama
DH . . . . .Dark Horse Comics
ET . . . . Editorial Mo.Pa.Sa.
FX . . . . 20th Century Fox
GK . . . .Gold Key / Western Comics
HE . . . HarperEntertainment Books
HM . . Harry K. McWilliams Assoc.
MC . . . . Marvel Comics
MR . . . Mr. Comics / Metallic Rose
NB . . . . NBC-TV
PR . . . . .Power Records
SB . . . . Signet Books
TP . . . . .Topps
UB . . . . Ubisoft

MEDIUM
a . . . . animated series
b . . . . .book-and-record set
c . . . . .comic book or strip
d . . . . trading card
e . . . . e-comic
f . . . . .theatrical film
k . . . . .storybook
m . . . . .magazine article
n . . . . .novel or novelization
p . . . . promotional newspaper
r . . . . .recorded audio fiction
s . . . . short story
t . . . . television series
u . . . . .unfilmed script or story
v . . . . video game
x . . . . .Blu-Ray exclusive
y . . . . .young adult novel

◆ Gorilla officers bring the picketers to a police station to be booked and paw-printed. Several are sent home pending further investigation, while others are detained for questioning. The Apes Civil Liberties Union (ACLU) takes up the protestors' cause.

The Ape News (HM-p)

◆ Brent explores the subway station. Following a high-pitched hum, he and Nova travel a tunnel that deposits them outside the ruined New York Public Library. Passing the New York Stock Exchange and Radio City Music Hall, they reach St. Patrick's Cathedral. Brent feels a strong compulsion to drown Nova in a fountain, forced upon him by the mutants. Fighting the urge, he enters the church to find a verger praying to an atomic missile—the Alpha-Omega Bomb. Guards bring him to a meeting hall near Grand Central Station's Lexington Ave. station, passing children singing "Ring Around the Neutron." The Keepers of the Divine Bomb—Albina, Caspay, Ongaro, Adiposo and their leader, Mendez XXVI—torture Brent telepathically, accusing him of spying for the apes. Finally, the mutant Inquisitors force him to violate Nova until he breaks down and tells them everything he knows of the apes' plans.

Beneath the Planet of the Apes (FX-f)

NOTE: Caspay and Albina are named in the film's novelization. Ongaro and Adiposo are identified as "Negro" and "Fat Man" in the credits, but their names appear in The Mutant News, *a promotional newspaper distributed during the film's release.* Planet of the Apes Revisited *misspells Ongaro's name as "Ono Goro." An early film treatment, also titled* Planet of the Apes Revisited, *identifies Caspay as a dwarf and gives him the title of minister of external affairs.* The Mutant News *dubs Mendez "Mendez the Divine and Invincible," and switches Albina's and Caspay's names in its photo captions. The "Ring Around the Neutron" scene was filmed but cut from the final version of the film.*

◆ As the mutants prepare for an imminent ape attack, General of Defense Ygli VII trains citizens in the use of such mental deterrents as brain torture and mind dissuasion. These defenses are expected to stop the apes at the boundaries of the Forbidden Zone.

The Mutant News (HM-p)

◆ A cryotube, hidden within the Statue of Liberty since 1991, activates. Janus, a clone of Cornelius created by a scientist of that era, emerges from the cryotube and sets out to activate a 20th-century device designed to prevent Earth's destruction. To that end, he places several nodes in a rough circle around the detonation site which, when activated, will form an energy field that will shunt the Alpha-Omega Bomb's energies into space.

Redemption of the Planet of the Apes (AC-c, unpublished)

NOTE: Lowell Cunningham, Men in Black *creator and author of Adventure's* The Forbidden Zone, *proposed this four-issue miniseries to creative director Tom K. Mason as well. However, Cunningham says, the idea was rejected for being too similar to the* Planet of the Apes *film remake then being considered, starring Arnold Schwarzenegger.*

◆ The mutants scare the army with illusions, but Zaius sees through them. Mendez calls a Public Thought Protection, sending all children indoors and all adults to the cathedral. Singing "Psalm of Mendez II," the mutants remove their masks, revealing their diseased flesh. Caspay and Ongaro take Brent to a cell. Unable to release him since he knows too much, Ongaro mentally forces him to fight Taylor to the death. Nova sees them and cries out Taylor's name, distracting the mutant long enough for the men to kill him. Brent tells Taylor about the missile, which the latter recognizes as the Alpha-Omega Bomb.

Beneath the Planet of the Apes (FX-f)

NOTE: The Psalm of Mendez II is named in the script and novelization.

◆ Outside the cathedral, Ursus encounters Caspay, Adiposo and the verger, and orders their execution.

Beneath the Planet of the Apes (BN-n)

NOTE: *This scene occurs in the novelization.*

◆ Brent and Taylor hide as an ape soldier, Xerxes, peers into the cell. Moments later, an ape kills Nova, devastating Taylor. Gorilla soldiers then decimate the Corridor of Busts, a hallways of stone statues honoring the 26 leaders of the House of Mendez.

Beneath the Planet of the Apes (FX-f)

NOTE: *Xerxes is named in Marvel's comic adaptation. The Corridor of Busts is named in the script and novelization.*

◆ Albina commits suicide, injecting a phial of poison. Zaius finds her corpse, disgusted when a gorilla guard bestially gropes her exposed human breast.

Beneath the Planet of the Apes (BN-n)

NOTE: *This scene occurs in the novelization.*

◆ Ape soldiers burst through the cathedral doors as Mendez arms the missile. Ursus' troops kill Mendez and pull the bomb down with ropes. The astronauts try to stop them, but Ursus shoots Taylor. Brent kills Ursus, then is himself slain. Shot down from a balcony, Taylor begs Zaius for help, then falls on the detonator when the orangutan rebuffs him, activating the bomb in one last defiant act.

Beneath the Planet of the Apes (FX-f)

◆ The device activated by Cornelius' clone, Janus, shunts the bomb's destructive energies away from the planet, enabling it to survive the missile's detonation.

Redemption of the Planet of the Apes (AC-c, unpublished)

◆ Shockwaves of tremendous energy cascade across the planet and out into space, striking the orbiting *Liberty 1*. From inside the shuttle, Milo, Zira and Cornelius witness a white, blinding light followed by a tornado-like effect as the planet's rim appears to melt.

Escape from the Planet of the Apes (FX-f)

NOTE: *According to writer Lowell Cunningham, the melting-rim effect seen by the apeonauts would actually have been the effects of Janus' device, rather than the planet's destruction, which would have been averted. This would enable the ship to be sent back to the past and also make the chimps think the Earth had been destroyed, thereby preserving the original timeline while also saving the planet.*

◆ The detonation causes a fold in the fabric of space-time, creating what will, in 1973, be known as a "Hasslein Curve" (named for Dr. Otto Hasslein). The fold is not technically a curve, however, so much as a recursive anomaly, folding back infinitely upon itself, from the future into the past and back again.

Revolution on the Planet of the Apes #3: "Hasslein's Notes" (MR-c)

NOTE: *Although the Hasslein Curve connects the years 1973 and 3978, its entry points are apparently not restricted to those years, as witnessed by the losses of the* Venturer *in 1976,* Probe Six *in 1980 and other time-lost spaceships. It's possible, though unstated, that Janus' device may have also played a part in creating the anomaly.*

◆ Due to this recursive anomaly, the *Liberty 1* and its simian occupants are thrown back in time to April 1973, resulting in a cycle of events that will culminate in the birth of the Planet of the Apes.

Escape from the Planet of the Apes (FX-f)

◆ Thus, *Liberty 1*'s return flight home causes its original journey into the future—a classic paradox.

Revolution on the Planet of the Apes #3: "Hasslein's Notes" (MR-c)

PUBLISHER / STUDIO

AB	ABC-TV
AC	Adventure / Malibu Comics
AW	Award Books
BB	Ballantine Books
BN	Bantam Books
BW	Brown Watson Books
CB	CBS-TV
CV	Chad Valley Sliderama
DH	Dark Horse Comics
ET	Editorial Mo.Pa.Sa.
FX	20th Century Fox
GK	Gold Key / Western Comics
HE	HarperEntertainment Books
HM	Harry K. McWilliams Assoc.
MC	Marvel Comics
MR	Mr. Comics / Metallic Rose
NB	NBC-TV
PR	Power Records
SB	Signet Books
TP	Topps
UB	Ubisoft

MEDIUM

a	animated series
b	book-and-record set
c	comic book or strip
d	trading card
e	e-comic
f	theatrical film
k	storybook
m	magazine article
n	novel or novelization
p	promotional newspaper
r	recorded audio fiction
s	short story
t	television series
u	unfilmed script or story
v	video game
x	Blu-Ray exclusive
y	young adult novel

Part 12: Stranger on a Strange World (After 3979)

AFTER 3979

◆ Despite extensive damage to the planet, Earth is not entirely decimated by the bomb's detonation. Small colonies of apes, including one in Australia, survive the blast. Simian civilization thus lives on, but is forever altered.

Untitled Comic (MR-c, unpublished)

> NOTE: Ty Templeton, in creating Revolution on the Planet of the Apes, *conceived several potential Apes comics, including this one, which he describes as "sort of an* Omega Man *with apes (to keep it all in the [Charlton] Heston zone)." This ties in nicely with Lowell Cunningham's unpublished story, "Redemption of the Planet of the Apes," which also reveals the planet to have survived the blast. (This notion, however, contradicts the ending of* Beneath the Planet of the Apes, *which explicitly states that the planet is dead.)*

◆ The explosion, however, does render humans extinct in the area once known as Texas. Mutated by radiation, a race of sentient tigers arises in that region and begins hunting apes as prey.

Sky Gods #2 (AC-c, unpublished)

> NOTE: Roland Mann, author of Adventure Comics' Blood of the Apes, *proposed this four-issue miniseries (alternately titled* Second Coming) *to creative director Tom K. Mason as well. Although Mason greenlit the proposal, it was ultimately scrapped before going to contract, when Malibu opted to scale back its* Planet of the Apes *offerings. No artist was assigned. It's unclear if Earth's humans became extinct in other parts of the world as well.*

c. 4000

◆ In Hitek, an ape city on Ashlar where humans and apes live together as equals, a deadly plague causes its victims' bodies to disintegrate. Unable to stop the disease, the citizens bury the dead in mass graves and the survivors abandon the city. In time, Hitek becomes a myth among Ashlar's ape population, as well as among local human tribes who sing children's songs about "spirits in the blood."

Planet of the Apes #1: Force, Chapter 11 (HE-y)

> NOTE: Most events beyond this point are from Tim Burton's "re-imagined" Planet of the Apes *film and its spinoff fiction. The name Ashlar appears in William Broyles' initial script for the Burton remake. Dating for these tales is based on Dark Horse's comic adaptation of the film, which sets it in the year 5021.*

◆ Written history on Ashlar officially begins. All knowledge of the 2,000 years since Semos' arrival, including Hitek's origins, is lost to time.

Planet of the Apes #1: Force, Chapter 2 (HE-y)

4171

◆ Ashlar's Ape City, also known as Derkein, is constructed at a time when apekind is not yet unified. During this period, Derkein faces a series of Raid Wars with apes from across the mountains.

Planet of the Apes #1: Force, Chapter 2 (HE-y)

NOTE: Derkein is named in an early draft of the film's script. An unpublished sequel to this novel—Rule, set in 5011—indicates the oldest known buildings in Ape City are only 400 years old at that time, contradicting this book's account of the city's origins.

c. 4620s

◆ Climate changes force the apes of Ashlar to abandon an early settlement and head east.

Planet of the Apes #3: Rule, Chapter 3 (HE-y, unpublished)

◆ This movement becomes known as the Eastward Migration. After heading east, the apes construct new buildings, with all records of previous civilizations lost over time.

Planet of the Apes #1: Force, Chapter 2 (HE-y)

c. 4620s TO 4720s

◆ No progress in ape society is recorded for approximately 100 years.

Planet of the Apes #1: Force, Chapter 2 (HE-y)

4924

◆ Zaius, a direct descendant of Semos, is born.

Planet of the Apes (FX-f)

NOTE: Since Zaius' age is unknown, I have based this figure on actor Charlton Heston's age (77) when the film (set in 5021) was produced. This Zaius is a separate individual from the various characters by that name on Earth.

4956

◆ Karubi, a human from the Tek tribe known as the Valley Clan, is born.

Planet of the Apes (FX-f)

NOTE: Since Karubi's age is unknown, I have based this figure on actor Kris Kristofferson's age (65) when the film (set in 5021) was produced.

MID 4900s

◆ Zaius' father reveals a secret known only to his family: that humans were once the apes' masters, and that the cause of their power—and downfall—was their reliance on guns and technology.

Planet of the Apes (FX-f)

NOTE: This date is an approximation, assuming Zaius was a young man at the time.

MID TO LATE 4900s

◆ A Wilding male (name unknown) and his daughter Sarai cross the mountains to join the Tek humans of the Valley Clan, who—unlike the savage Wildings—seek to develop technology for the betterment of humanity.

Planet of the Apes #1: Force, Chapter 5 (HE-y)

EARLY 4960s

◆ A human male named Luc—who will one day be known as Mad Luc—is born to the Valley Clan.

Planet of the Apes #1: Resistance, Chapter 1 (HE-y)

NOTE: Luc is said to be in his late 40s in 5010.

4961

◆ Sandar, a chimpanzee and future senator, is born.

Planet of the Apes (FX-f)

NOTE: Since Sandar's age is unknown, I have based this figure on actor David Warner's age (60) when the film (set in 5021) was produced.

LATE 4960s OR EARLY 4970s

◆ Bon, future human servant to the house of Senator Sandar, is born.

Planet of the Apes (FX-f)

NOTE: Since Bon's age is unknown, and since the age of actress Freda Foh Shen is unknown, I have estimated a range based on Shen's appearance when the film (set in 5021) was produced.

4970

◆ Krull, a silverback gorilla and future military officer, is born.

Planet of the Apes (FX-f)

NOTE: Since Krull's age is unknown, I have based this figure on actor Cary-Hiroyuki Tagawa's age (51) when the film (set in 5021) was produced.

4972

◆ Tival, future human servant to the house of Senator Sandar, is born.

Planet of the Apes (FX-f)

NOTE: Since Tival's age is unknown, I have based this figure on actor Erick Avari's age (49) when the film (set in 5021) was produced.

◆ Nado, an orangutan and future senator, is born.

Planet of the Apes (FX-f)

NOTE: Since Nado's age is unknown, I have based this figure on actor Glenn Shadix's age (49) when the film (set in 5021) was produced.

c. 4970s

◆ Sandar and Nado form a close friendship. The two future senators spend much of their youth climbing through the rain forests of Ape City.

Planet of the Apes (FX-f)

NOTE: This placement is an approximation, based on the characters' estimated ages.

4976

◆ Thade, a chimpanzee and future military leader, is born.

Planet of the Apes #2: Resistance (HE-y)

NOTE: On an enclosed trading card, Thade is said to be 34 in 5010, giving him a birth year of 4976 and making him 45 during the Planet of the Apes *remake, set in 5021 (actor Tim Roth was 40 at the time).*

LATE 4900s

◆ Sarai meets Karubi, and they eventually become mates. Sarai's father is named leader of the Valley Clan, and she succeeds him in the role. Many humans consider her line smarter than the apes.

Planet of the Apes #1: Force, Chapter 5 (HE-y)

NOTE: It's unclear when this occurs, but it must be before Daena's birth in 4997.

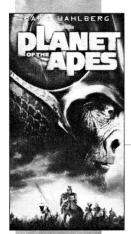

4987

◆ Limbo, an orangutan and future human slaver, is born.

Planet of the Apes (FX-f)

NOTE: Since Limbo's age is unknown, I have based this figure on actor Paul Giamatti's age (34) when the film (set in 5021) was produced.

4988

◆ Gunnar, a human from the Tek tribe known as the Valley Clan, is born.

Planet of the Apes (FX-f)

NOTE: Since Gunnar's age is unknown, I have based this figure on actor Evan Dexter Parke's age (33) when the film (set in 5021) was produced.

◆ Nova, a chimpanzee and future lover of Senator Nado, is born.

Planet of the Apes (FX-f)

NOTE: Since Nova's age is unknown, I have based this figure on actress Lisa Marie's age (34) when the film (set in 5021) was produced. Linda Harrison, who played a different Nova in the original Planet of the Apes, *has a cameo in this film—but not as Nova.*

4992

◆ Attar, a powerfully built gorilla, is born. An orphan, Attar is raised by harsh, disciplinary monks.

Planet of the Apes #1: Force (HE-y)

NOTE: On an enclosed trading card, Attar is said to be 17 in 5009, giving him a birth year of 4992 and making him 29 during the Planet of the Apes remake, set in 5021 (actor Michael Clarke Duncan was 44 at the time). Although Attar is said to be an orphan, the Planet of the Apes comic strip serialized in Dark Horse Extra issues #36-38 indicates his father to still be alive, and also gives Attar a brother, Tolan. This discrepancy remains unexplained.

4994

◆ Ari, daughter of chimpanzee Senator Sandar, is born.

Planet of the Apes #1: Force (HE-y)

NOTE: On an enclosed trading card, Ari is said to be 15 in 5009, giving her a birth year of 4994 and making her 27 during the Planet of the Apes remake, set in 5021 (actress Helena Bonham Carter was 35 at the time).

◆ Sandar's wife (name unknown) is an independent thinker—a trait Ari inherits.

Planet of the Apes #1: Force, Chapter 7 (HE-y)

c. 4990s

◆ Leeta, a chimpanzee and future friend of Ari, is born.

Planet of the Apes #1: Force (HE-y)

NOTE: Since the ages of Leeta and actress Eileen Weisinger are unknown, I have estimated her to be Ari's contemporary. Leeta is identified as a bonobo in the film's spinoff novels, though she appears to be the same chimpanzee species as Ari onscreen.

◆ The beautiful Leeta is the daughter of Senator Sandar's aide.

Planet of the Apes #3: Rule, Chapter 3 (HE-y, unpublished)

BETWEEN 4994 AND 5009

◆ Ari shows kindness to human slaves, offering strays food and shelter. Her parents indulge her, earning a reputation as human sympathizers. The young chimp frequently sneaks outside the city walls where none can find her, but as Sandar rises in politics, he urges her not to endanger their lives with her antics.

Planet of the Apes (FX-f)

◆ After Sandar's wife dies young, the senator raises Ari on his own.

Planet of the Apes #1: Force, Chapter 3 (HE-y)

PUBLISHER / STUDIO

AB . . . . ABC-TV
AC . . . . Adventure / Malibu Comics
AW . . . . Award Books
BB . . . . Ballantine Books
BN . . . . Bantam Books
BW . . . . Brown Watson Books
CB . . . . CBS-TV
CV . . . . Chad Valley Sliderama
DH . . . . Dark Horse Comics
ET . . . . Editorial Mo.Pa.Sa.
FX . . . . 20th Century Fox
GK . . . . Gold Key / Western Comics
HE . . . HarperEntertainment Books
HM . . Harry K. McWilliams Assoc.
MC . . . . Marvel Comics
MR . . . Mr. Comics / Metallic Rose
NB . . . . NBC-TV
PR . . . . Power Records
SB . . . . Signet Books
TP . . . . Topps
UB . . . . Ubisoft

MEDIUM

a . . . . animated series
b . . . . book-and-record set
c . . . . comic book or strip
d . . . . trading card
e . . . . e-comic
f . . . . theatrical film
k . . . . storybook
m . . . . magazine article
n . . . . novel or novelization
p . . . . promotional newspaper
r . . . . recorded audio fiction
s . . . . short story
t . . . . television series
u . . . . unfilmed script or story
v . . . . video game
x . . . . Blu-Ray exclusive
y . . . . young adult novel

4997

◆ A human girl named Daena is born to Karubi and Sarai, a Tek couple of the Valley Clan.

Planet of the Apes #1: Force, Chapter 5 (HE-y)

> *NOTE: Daena is said to be 12 in 5009, giving her a birth date of 4997 and making her 24 during the* Planet of the Apes *remake, set in 5021 (actress Estella Warren was 23 at the time). The novel* Resistance, *set in 5010, gives her age as 14, which I have discounted since it does not jibe mathematically.*

LATE 4990s TO EARLY 5000s

◆ Sandar's daughter Ari earns a reputation as a genius, able to form full sentences months before other ape children can speak a single word.

Planet of the Apes #1: Force, Chapter 3 (HE-y)

◆ In school, Ari is taught that apes are at the top of the food chain, followed by monkeys and so on, down to unintelligent species. Humans are considered a mistake, slightly smarter than dogs and unable to reason, though they can be taught to speak and perform simple tricks. Ari disagrees with such teachings.

Planet of the Apes #1: Force, Chapter 11 (HE-y)

◆ Young Attar grows up in the Temple of Semos' orphan wing. Though he questions the priests' teachings, and though some let power go to their heads, he does not see religion as entirely evil.

Planet of the Apes #1: Force, Chapter 1 (HE-y)

> *NOTE: Given that the* Planet of the Apes *comic strip serialized in* Dark Horse Extra *issues #36-38 indicates his father to still be alive, it's unknown why Attar would be raised in an orphanage.*

◆ The head of the orphanage is the city's spiritual pontifex, a chimpanzee named Timon.

Planet of the Apes #1: Force, Chapter 2 (HE-y)

◆ Timon sees in Attar the potential to be a great priest, though the gorilla believes Timon uses the orphans as slaves, forcing them to wait on him under the guise of discipline. When Attar leaves to join the military, Timon accuses him of turning away from Semos, predicting he'll amount to nothing outside the temple.

Planet of the Apes #1: Force, Chapter 6 (HE-y)

◆ One night, Ari uses her father's influence to sneak into the orphan ward. Attar attacks her, thinking her a burglar, but from their brief fight springs a strong friendship.

Planet of the Apes #1: Force, Chapter 1 (HE-y)

◆ Thade becomes the only chimpanzee to attain a position as a top commander in the Ape City army; the rest are all silverback gorillas.

Planet of the Apes #1: Force, Chapter 1 (HE-y)

◆ Sandar exposes corruption among Derkein's fruit traders, including an orangutan named Limbo, who steals fruit from local shopkeepers, sells it, then uses the money to buy his own booths and sell other fruit cheaply enough to put his competitors out of business. Falling on hard times, Limbo begins trading human slaves. He runs against Sandar for public office and insults the other's good name, but later supports Sandar's election to suit his own purposes. An enmity between the two continues for years.

Planet of the Apes #2: Resistance, Chapter 10 (HE-y)

◆ Among Limbo's rivals in the slave trade is an ape named Picatto, whom Limbo tries to discredit by claiming the other's humans have worms.

Planet of the Apes (DH-c)

NOTE: This information appears in the comic adaptation of the film.

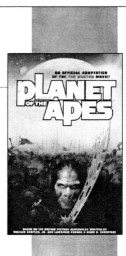

c. 5000

◆ A time-lost colony spaceship—launched in the 20th century to preserve humanity following the apeonauts' warning of Earth's destruction—exits the Hasslein Curve and crashes on what the crew believes to be a distant planet, but is actually Earth, in one-time New Orleans. A few survivors escape the wreckage before it explodes. The colonists bury their dead and inventory their equipment. One survivor, Nick, surveys the land and sees two creatures in the distance, astride horses. He and another man investigate while the rest prepare a permanent settlement, which they call Plymouth. Arrows fly past as a bipedal figure runs between them. One rider on horseback chases the figure, the other confronting the newcomers—who are stunned to see that he is a tiger, clad in American Indian-style garb.

Sky Gods #1 (AC-c, unpublished)

NOTE: Roland Mann, author of Adventure's Blood of the Apes, *proposed this four-issue miniseries (alternately titled* Second Coming) *to creative director Tom K. Mason as well. Although Mason greenlit the proposal, it was scrapped before going to contract, when Malibu opted to scale back its* Planet of the Apes *titles. The story is undated, but Mann says he conceived it as occurring a thousand years after* Beneath the Planet of the Apes, *or approximately the year 5000. His notes reveal he'd contemplated having the tigers run on all four legs rather than ride horses, and that he'd considered making them of extraterrestrial origin, though he opted to keep them Earth-born and mutated by radiation.*

◆ The men dive for cover as the tiger pulls back a bow to kill them. Unable to find them, the rider resumes the hunt, and Nick watches as the tigers ride off with a man-like figure slung over a horse. Stopping to rest, the men discover an ape with an arrow in his stomach, who begs for help, then passes out. Stunned to see a talking ape—as their ship left Earth to avoid that very thing—Nick brings him back to the human camp. There, tending to the ape's wounds, the colonists debate what to do next, and what planet they're on. The ape, Teryl, tells them they're on Earth. Detailing the war one millennium earlier, he says he'd assumed mankind extinct until seeing Nick. Nick and the other man offer to help him return to his people, but a tiger jumps them en route to the ape village.

Sky Gods #2 (AC-c, unpublished)

◆ The tiger tears Nick's companion apart, slashing Nick's chest. Apes surround them, ripping the tiger to pieces. Teryl tells them not to disturb the dead human, then quickly leads Nick away as the apes' enter a blood frenzy, consuming the tiger. They enter the apes' treetop camp, where Teryl's people are amazed to see a living human. Nick and Teryl return to the human colony to find it destroyed by tigers, though no one was killed since a guard was on watch. Teryl tells them to move downstream, away from the tigers, then returns with Nick to the ape tribe, hoping to ally their groups. A tiger shoots at them from below, following on horseback as Teryl swings from vine to vine, Nick holding onto him. Changing direction, Teryl catches the tiger off-guard and attacks, then Nick kills the creature with its own bow. Recovering from their wounds, the two decide to launch a surprise attack on the tigers.

Sky Gods #3 (AC-c, unpublished)

◆ Nick, Teryl and other apes locate the tiger encampment, which is lined with teepee-like tents. Sneaking into the chief's hut, they carry him to a nearby hill, followed by several tigers, and threaten to kill him if they don't leave the area. A bilingual member of one species translates their terms, to which the chief (fascinated by the newcomer) agrees. One tiger objects, however, insisting they are superior and must destroy both man and ape. This constitutes a formal challenge, and Teryl is forced to face him in battle. The ape wins, but spares his opponent. Accepting the loss, the tigers agree to move east and leave them alone. Before returning to his colony, Nick tells the apes that despite their species' past troubles, in this era it is man and ape versus tiger. They agree, and as a gesture of peace, Teryl and other apes volunteer to live in the human camp so each can learn about the other.

Sky Gods #4 (AC-c, unpublished)

5006

◆ Birn, a male Tek in the Valley Clan, is born.

Planet of the Apes (FX-f)

> NOTE: *The film's script cites Birn as being 15 in 5021, matching actor Luke Eberl's age when the movie was produced, for a birth year of 5006. But in the novel* Resistance, *set in 5010, he seems older than 4.* Rule, *an unpublished sequel to* Resistance, *rectifies the discrepancy by describing Birn as "a little boy."*

BEFORE 5009

◆ Snaks, the son of a gibbon weapons maker named Mel and his wife, shows no interest in his father's line of work, preferring instead to arrange flowers.

Planet of the Apes #3: Rule, Chapter 7 (HE-y, unpublished)

5009

◆ Reading the Sacred Scrolls during her final year of school, Ari notices gaps in recorded ape history and informs Sandar. Knowing his daughter's reputation as a genius, Sandar looks into the matter further.

Planet of the Apes #1: Force, Chapter 3 (HE-y)

> NOTE: *This book is said to occur 12 years prior to the Tim Burton film, thus setting it in 5009.*

◆ Attar attends a science class at Ape City's war academy, taught by Professor Nestor, a baboon instructor. Nestor urges him to apply himself, saying battles are won in the brain before the field. Attar receives a visit from his friend Ari, who has come to research history in the library for her father. A cadet named Gaddi harasses her for visiting during classes, but Attar protects her. She says her father's friend, General Krull, has called Attar the finest cadet in the academy, and that he'll soon see military action. This fills the young gorilla with pride.

Planet of the Apes #1: Force, Chapter 1 (HE-y)

◆ Attar and Ari hang from a chandelier to eavesdrop on a meeting between Sandar, Krull, Thade and Timon. Sandar asks to mount an expedition to Hitek to discover why 2,000 years' worth of ape history following Semos' arrival has been lost. Thade calls the mission dangerous, saying he's about to launch a campaign to exterminate humanity. As a compromise, they put the invasion on hold until after the Hitek quest.

Planet of the Apes #1: Force, Chapter 2 (HE-y)

◆ Attar's strength gives out, causing the lamp (and the two apes) to hit the floor. Ari assumes the blame, but Thade is furious at Attar, deeming it treason to spy on a private meeting. Sandar orders his daughter not to tell anyone what she's heard, denying her request to join the expedition.

Planet of the Apes #1: Force, Chapter 3 (HE-y)

◆ Rather than court-martial Attar, Krull assigns him as sanitation officer to Third Company, saying he'll make a fine officer if he lives down the humiliation. Attar reports in to a baboon supply officer, who refers him to a chimp baggage handler—or, rather, Ari posing as the baggage handler so she can join the expedition. Torn between duty and friendship, Attar chooses not to expose her.

Planet of the Apes #1: Force, Chapter 4 (HE-y)

◆ When the land of the Valley Clan grows short on food, clan leader Sarai, her husband Karubi and their 12-year-old daughter Daena cross the mountain to forage in the jungle. There, they meet a group of Wildings hunting apes. Because Sarai's ancestors were Wildings, they allow her people to look for food, but warn them to stay out of their way. In the distance, a war cry marks the arrival of an ape army.

Planet of the Apes #1: Force, Chapter 5 (HE-y)

◆ Sarai hopes to join her clan with other human tribes in the area. Although humans outnumber apes five to one, the simians' tree-climbing skills and superior weaponry make them impossible to defeat. Ultimately, she hopes to make peace with the apes, but Karubi and Daena do not share her optimism.

Planet of the Apes #1: Force, Chapter 10 (HE-y)

◆ En route to Hitek, Attar weathers taunts from soldiers named Maga and Kestos, while Timon gloats over his misfortune as he digs latrines. The Wildings attack, clubbing the priest unconscious. Attar protects Ari until the soldiers scare off the savage humans. Impressed with Attar's fighting skills, Krull gives him a sword and assigns him to guard Ari—whom he recognizes through her disguise.

Planet of the Apes #1: Force, Chapter 6 (HE-y)

◆ Krull informs Sandar of his daughter's presence. Furious, Sandar suggests she be sent home, but Krull says it would be too dangerous. Outside, Ari finds Attar wearing soldier's armor, proud in his new role.

Planet of the Apes #1: Force, Chapter 7 (HE-y)

◆ In Hitek, Ari and Attar sense someone watching them. Timon is dismayed to see the Temple of Semos in tatters, the remains of beds and rotten food untouched after a thousand years. As scribes rush to copy a damaged holy book, Maga and Kestos pick a fight with Attar, angry that he was rewarded despite missing most of the fight. Attar throws Maga at a crumbling wall, knocking him and Ari into a hole.

Planet of the Apes #1: Force, Chapter 8 (HE-y)

◆ Ari and Maga land in a burial pit filled with dozens of mummified ape corpses, buried alive. Krull lowers a rope, and Maga is treated for a head wound. Timon dismisses their find, as it violates the tenet that ape shall never kill ape. When a sentry reports a sighting of the human tribe, Krull cancels the expedition, and with the injured Maga on point, the group disembarks for Ape City.

Planet of the Apes #1: Force, Chapter 9 (HE-y)

◆ The Wildings kill Maga and leave him for others to find. In burying him, Kestos becomes covered in his blood. As they make camp for the night, Ari grows dizzy and short of breath. Kestos suddenly goes into convulsions and disintegrates in a bloody mess. The Wildings attack again, and Ari runs into the woods.

Planet of the Apes #1: Force, Chapter 10 (HE-y)

PUBLISHER / STUDIO
AB . . . . ABC-TV
AC . . . . Adventure / Malibu Comics
AW . . . . Award Books
BB . . . . .Ballantine Books
BN . . . . Bantam Books
BW . . . . Brown Watson Books
CB . . . . CBS-TV
CV . . . . Chad Valley Sliderama
DH . . . . .Dark Horse Comics
ET . . . . Editorial Mo.Pa.Sa.
FX . . . . 20th Century Fox
GK . . . .Gold Key / Western Comics
HE . . . HarperEntertainment Books
HM . . Harry K. McWilliams Assoc.
MC . . . . Marvel Comics
MR . . . Mr. Comics / Metallic Rose
NB . . . . NBC-TV
PR . . . . .Power Records
SB . . . . Signet Books
TP . . . . .Topps
UB . . . . Ubisoft

MEDIUM
a . . . . animated series
b . . . . .book-and-record set
c . . . . .comic book or strip
d . . . . trading card
e . . . . e-comic
f . . . . .theatrical film
k . . . . .storybook
m . . . . .magazine article
n . . . . .novel or novelization
p . . . . promotional newspaper
r . . . . .recorded audio fiction
s . . . . short story
t . . . . television series
u . . . . .unfilmed script or story
v . . . . video game
x . . . . .Blu-Ray exclusive
y . . . . .young adult novel

◆ Knocked unconscious, Ari awakens in the dark. She encounters Sarai, who notices her illness and gives her medication called meeda. Sarai explains her goal of interspecies peace, and offers to help her get home. Ari's recounting of Kestos' and Maga's deaths reminds Sarai of a children's song about "spirits in the blood." Horrified, Ari realizes the Hitek apes died of a plague—which they've contracted as well.

Planet of the Apes #1: Force, Chapter 11 (HE-y)

◆ Karubi hands Ari the holy book's remains. Ari is stunned to see an image of humans and apes living as equals. Sarai says she wants her daughter to grow up in a safer world, and that Ari will help make that happen. En route back to the ape camp, they find the body of an infected soldier. Others attack, chasing Sarai despite Ari's protests. The warriors then carry the infected soldier back to Ape City.

Planet of the Apes #1: Force, Chapter 12 (HE-y)

◆ Ari tells Sandar about the plague, but Thade and Timon reject the story since it violates gospel. When the injured ape dies in agony, Sandar sends Attar to offer the tribe blankets in exchange for medication. Timon decides to thwart their efforts and make sure no ape ever learns about Hitek. Thade agrees, adding the infected soldier's blanket to the pile so the humans will die of the plague.

Planet of the Apes #1: Force, Chapter 13 (HE-y)

◆ The Hitek expedition is quarantined in Sandar's house until the crisis has passed, but still the disease spreads among the citizens of Derkein.

Planet of the Apes #1: Force, Chapter 16 (HE-y)

◆ Ari notices a cut on Attar's arm, caused by Timon while blessing his mission. The gorilla departs to find Sarai's tribe, but Ari overhears Thade and Timon plotting and realizes Attar is in danger. The two leaders are unconcerned, for death in defense of apekind is a noble way to die.

Planet of the Apes #1: Force, Chapter 14 (HE-y)

◆ On horseback, Ari travels for hours before finding Sarai. She vows to help make peace if the humans help her find Attar. Karubi locates him lying weak in the woods. Sarai says they must climb a nearby mountain to the Cave of Paintings, the only place they can find the moss used to make meeda. Despite his illness, Attar decides to join them.

Planet of the Apes #1: Force, Chapter 15 (HE-y)

◆ Sandar asks Thade to help retrieve his daughter. Thade sends a soldier named Ronin to track her, secretly ordering him to kill Ari to prevent apekind from learning the truth. Meanwhile, the Wildings' scarred leader attacks Attar, who is too weak to fight back. Sarai and Ari step in, frightening the savages into the woods. With Attar unable to travel, Sarai stays with him and tells Ari how to reach the cave.

Planet of the Apes #1: Force, Chapter 16 (HE-y)

◆ Delusional and feverish, Attar sees visions of Timon, Krull, Thade and Semos expressing disappointment at his failures. Out in the woods, Ronin slays the scarred human, then prepares to kill Ari as well.

Planet of the Apes #1: Force, Chapter 17 (HE-y)

NOTE: Semos is said to be a gorilla in this book, when he was, in fact, a chimpanzee. This discrepancy can be explained by the disease affecting Attar's mental faculties.

◆ Attar dreams of Semos saying he created the plague in order to make apes stronger, and to bring humans and apes together—a goal he says Attar will one day help fulfill. Two demons attack Semos, and he somehow finds the strength to defeat them. As his delirium fades, he realizes he has just saved Sarai from two apes.

Planet of the Apes #1: Force, Chapter 18 (HE-y)

◆ Splattered with Attar's blood, the two soldiers contract the plague.

Planet of the Apes #1: Force, Chapter 20 (HE-y)

◆ Ronin chases Ari through the woods. She ambushes him and breaks his neck, but injures her knee in the process, making it difficult to walk.

Planet of the Apes #1: Force, Chapter 18 (HE-y)

◆ Ari follows Sarai's directions to the Cave of Paintings. Ignoring her fear of enclosed spaces, she crawls through a tiny opening and deep into the mountain, where she finds a vast chamber filled with cave paintings detailing centuries of ape and human history. Overwhelmed, she collects the healing moss.

Planet of the Apes #1: Force, Chapter 19 (HE-y)

◆ Sarai shows Ari how to brew meeda. The apes awaken, and Sarai threatens to dump the medicine if they try to arrest her. When they relent, she administers the cure.

Planet of the Apes #1: Force, Chapter 20 (HE-y)

◆ Despite a quarantine, the plague spreads in Derkein until Ari returns with the moss and cures the sick. Krull allows Attar to finish his Academy training. Attar submits a report describing his dreams, which Timon and Thade dismiss as human trickery. Thade compliments his performance, telling Attar to see him after graduation, then burns both the report and the remains of the holy book.

Planet of the Apes #1: Force, Chapter 21 (HE-y)

5009 TO 5010

◆ Several Wildings join the Valley Clan, looking to Sarai for leadership. Among them are a man named Vasich and his son Pak. Vasich urges her to move their group further from ape civilization, but she refuses, determined to make peace with the simians.

Planet of the Apes #2: Resistance, Chapter 3 (HE-y)

NOTE: Vasich—a title given to all Wilding leaders, according to Rule, *the unpublished third book in the series—is a reference to USAF Oberon officer Karl Vasich.*

◆ Thade is promoted to the rank of colonel.

Planet of the Apes #2: Resistance, Chapter 9 (HE-y)

◆ Thade and Timon decide to build a new Temple of Semos, and to teach human slaves to read and write so they can follow blueprints and construct the temple for them. To that end, they hire an orangutan slave trader named Limbo to capture and tame wild humans for the project. Attar, meanwhile, attains the rank of lieutenant. Over the next year, he and Ari rarely speak, as he spends most of his time trying to become the best soldier he can be.

Planet of the Apes #2: Resistance, Chapter 10 (HE-y)

5010

◆ Ari's aunts, who live on the other side of the jungle from Ape City, visit Sandar and Ari—the first time Ari has seen them since the death of their sister (her mother).

Planet of the Apes #3: Rule, Chapter 8 (HE-y, unpublished)

PUBLISHER / STUDIO	
AB	ABC-TV
AC	Adventure / Malibu Comics
AW	Award Books
BB	Ballantine Books
BN	Bantam Books
BW	Brown Watson Books
CB	CBS-TV
CV	Chad Valley Sliderama
DH	Dark Horse Comics
ET	Editorial Mo.Pa.Sa.
FX	20th Century Fox
GK	Gold Key / Western Comics
HE	HarperEntertainment Books
HM	Harry K. McWilliams Assoc.
MC	Marvel Comics
MR	Mr. Comics / Metallic Rose
NB	NBC-TV
PR	Power Records
SB	Signet Books
TP	Topps
UB	Ubisoft

MEDIUM	
a	animated series
b	book-and-record set
c	comic book or strip
d	trading card
e	e-comic
f	theatrical film
k	storybook
m	magazine article
n	novel or novelization
p	promotional newspaper
r	recorded audio fiction
s	short story
t	television series
u	unfilmed script or story
v	video game
x	Blu-Ray exclusive
y	young adult novel

◆ Daena, age 14, and her friends Birn and Pak (a Wilding) practice hunting by spying on Mad Luc, a late-40s human considered crazy for spending his time alone and performing such "magic" as flying kites. Armored apes suddenly charge into the clearing, abducting Luc.

Planet of the Apes #2: Resistance, Chapter 1 (HE-y)

> *NOTE: Since the characters refer to the Hitek incident as occurring a year earlier, I am setting this novel in 5010. The chronological setting is inconsistent, however—as with* Force, *the back cover places it 12 years before the film—but Daena is said to be 12 years old in* Force, *and 14 in* Resistance.

◆ Ganji, a baboon professor, teaches Luc to read so he can lead other humans in building the temple.

Planet of the Apes #2: Resistance, Chapter 14 (HE-y)

◆ The human children try to sneak out of the area without the apes noticing, but the sound of a snapping twig alerts them. The apes give chase, and Birn is captured. Thrusting a tree branch into an ape's face, Daena saves the young boy, and the trio escape into the forest.

Planet of the Apes #2: Resistance, Chapter 2 (HE-y)

◆ Daena's group returns to camp to tell Sarai and Karubi what happened. Relieved that they're safe, Sarai chastises them for wandering off alone. Blaming the incident on their clan's proximity to the apes, Vasich accuses Sarai of poor leadership and challenges her position as clan ruler.

Planet of the Apes #2: Resistance, Chapter 3 (HE-y)

◆ Sarai and Vasich undergo three tests. Vasich chooses tests of strength, relying on sheer musculature to beat her, but she outsmarts him on two trials and retains leadership. Humiliated, Vasich accepts her rule but warns the clan that Sarai will lead them to their deaths.

Planet of the Apes #2: Resistance, Chapter 4 (HE-y)

◆ The apes abduct an increasing number of humans, including Tarik, son of Suni. Several elders, such as Mellie and Ark, urge Sarai to relocate the tribe. Defending her mother's decision, Daena claims apes aren't as dangerous as most think, so Pak and Birn dare her to touch Ape City's walls. Though she succeeds, a column of soldiers exits the city gates, heading in the direction of the boys' hiding spot.

Planet of the Apes #2: Resistance, Chapter 5 (HE-y)

◆ Daena distracts the apes by calling out insults, giving Birn and Pak time to head for the forest. Pak is scooped up by the hunters, but Birn makes it to safety among the trees.

Planet of the Apes #2: Resistance, Chapter 6 (HE-y)

◆ Captured by apes, Daena is caged with other humans. A woman named Mai recognizes her tribe and says many of her people have been captured. Sarai, she asserts, keeps her tribe too close to Ape City.

Planet of the Apes #2: Resistance, Chapter 7 (HE-y)

◆ Sarai announces plans to head into the mountains and find a permanent home for the Valley Clan. Birn runs into the camp, revealing what happened to Pak and Daena. The news devastates Vasich, who blames Sarai for his son's capture. Sarai decides to visit Ape City and seek help from Ari.

Planet of the Apes #2: Resistance, Chapter 8 (HE-y)

◆ With Sarai gone, Karubi rules in her name, facing frequent opposition from Vasich.

Planet of the Apes #2: Resistance, Epilogue (HE-y)

◆ Ari brings a slave named El into her home to teach her to sew and groom. Determined to help humans create their own civilization, she tries to remain patient when the frightened girl makes mistakes. Thade, Timon and Krull visit, and Thade threatens violence when she stands up to his mocking.

Planet of the Apes #2: Resistance, Chapter 9 (HE-y)

◆ Ari tries to eavesdrop on their meeting again, but Attar stops her. He says a new temple is being built, and that human enslavement is rising. Curious, Ari visits Limbo, who shows off his operations, hoping to get in her father's good graces. In a room filled with filthy humans, she notices Sarai in one of the pens.

Planet of the Apes #2: Resistance, Chapter 10 (HE-y)

◆ Ari watches as humans are sorted into carts—Teks in one vehicle, Wildings in another—and follows them to the new temple's construction site. Slaves lift rock slabs into place, managed by an ape overseer armed with a whip. When one human fails to complete a task, he is crushed between two slabs, frightening the rest into working faster.

Planet of the Apes #2: Resistance, Chapter 11 (HE-y)

◆ Timon tells the Tek slaves on Sarai's cart that Semos has singled them out for education because they utilize more of their brains than most humans. To reinforce the penalty for failure, guards bring forth eight humans to be executed—and Daena is among them.

Planet of the Apes #2: Resistance, Chapter 12 (HE-y)

◆ Sarai pleads for Daena's life. Timon agrees to spare the girl if Sarai does the work of four. She tries to negotiate for the others' lives, but he has them executed to spite her. Daena and Sarai are penned in separate work crews, then the apes begin teaching them to read and write so they can follow blueprints.

Planet of the Apes #2: Resistance, Chapter 13 (HE-y)

◆ Sarai befriends a woman named Pica. Ganji tells Luc to teach the humans to read and write, threatening to kill them if he fails. After the baboon leaves, Pica and others accuse Luc of aiding the apes, but Sarai says Luc is following her orders to learn all he can so she can build a safe, new home for humankind. Mollified, they begin instruction.

Planet of the Apes #2: Resistance, Chapter 14 (HE-y)

◆ For three days, Luc educates the Teks in the metric system, pulleys, architecture and reading. Sarai learns all she can, then is paired with Luc, Daena and Pak to build the temple. Timon and Thade inspect the project. Attar is with them, but spurns Sarai's attempts at familiarity, saying Semos saved his life, not her.

Planet of the Apes #2: Resistance, Chapter 15 (HE-y)

◆ Ari visits the temple, amazed at the project's immensity. Thade and Timon belittle her pro-human stance, but she cites the temple as proof of human intelligence, saying others will agree once it is done. But she realizes the truth: Thade plans to kill them all. Ari sneaks into the worksite to warn them of the danger, and Luc forms an escape plan.

Planet of the Apes #2: Resistance, Chapter 16 (HE-y)

◆ Without revealing his plan to avoid exposure, Luc carves grooves into the stone blocks so that when all are set in place, they will form a tunnel invisible to those outside the structure.

Planet of the Apes #2: Resistance, Chapter 19 (HE-y)

PUBLISHER / STUDIO
AB . . . . ABC-TV
AC . . . .Adventure / Malibu Comics
AW . . . . Award Books
BB . . . . .Ballantine Books
BN . . . . Bantam Books
BW . . . . Brown Watson Books
CB . . . . CBS-TV
CV . . . . Chad Valley Sliderama
DH . . . . .Dark Horse Comics
ET . . . . Editorial Mo.Pa.Sa.
FX . . . . 20th Century Fox
GK . . . .Gold Key / Western Comics
HE . . . HarperEntertainment Books
HM . . Harry K. McWilliams Assoc.
MC . . . . Marvel Comics
MR . . . Mr. Comics / Metallic Rose
NB . . . . NBC-TV
PR . . . . .Power Records
SB . . . . Signet Books
TP . . . . .Topps
UB . . . . .Ubisoft

MEDIUM
a . . . . animated series
b . . . . .book-and-record set
c . . . . .comic book or strip
d . . . . trading card
e . . . . e-comic
f . . . . .theatrical film
k . . . . .storybook
m . . . . .magazine article
n . . . . .novel or novelization
p . . . . . . promotional newspaper
r . . . . .recorded audio fiction
s . . . . short story
t . . . . television series
u . . . . .unfilmed script or story
v . . . . video game
x . . . . .Blu-Ray exclusive
y . . . . young adult novel

◆ After temple construction is completed, Luc tries to escape but is captured and seemingly crushed between stone blocks. Thade then orders all humans sealed up in a room with no doors or windows.

Planet of the Apes #2: Resistance, Chapter 17 (HE-y)

◆ As the entombed humans panic in pitch blackness, Sarai calms them by having them call out their names. The stone behind her moves, and Luc, still alive, crawls into the space and ignites a torch.

Planet of the Apes #2: Resistance, Chapter 18 (HE-y)

◆ Luc explains how he survived, then shows them the tunnel he created. The humans crawl through to the temple's interior, surprising Attar. The gorilla lifts Sarai by the neck, but when she questions whether Semos would condone burying humans alive in his temple, he lets them go.

Planet of the Apes #2: Resistance, Chapter 19 (HE-y)

◆ Sarai guides her people outside. Ari shows them the underground water pipes she sometimes uses to sneak out of the city at night. Leading her people to safety, Sarai realizes she must move her clan far from Ape City.

Planet of the Apes #2: Resistance, Chapter 20 (HE-y)

◆ Returning to the Valley Clan, Sarai stops Vasich and Karubi from fighting. Many slaves, both Tek and Wilding, remain with her tribe, and those who return home inform their people that humanity will soon build its own city.

Planet of the Apes #2: Resistance, Epilogue (HE-y)

5010 TO 5011

◆ Sarai's people begin building the city in a fertile mountain valley. They name it New Hope.

Planet of the Apes #3: Rule, Chapter 1 (HE-y, unpublished)

> NOTE: Rule *was contracted and written by J.E. Bright, but never released due to low sales on the first two books. The following details come from the unpublished manuscript (the cover proof of which incorrectly lists John Whitman as the author). This book is said to occur a year after the temple escape. New Hope is also the name of the first city built by the* Oberon *crew (in the novel* The Fall) *3,000 years prior; Sarai is likely unaware of this connection to her tribe's origins.*

◆ A woman named Yatai becomes pregnant. Several boys are stricken with red fever. And an insect infestation damages some of the clan's fruit supplies.

Planet of the Apes #3: Rule, Chapter 2 (HE-y, unpublished)

◆ During this period, Attar avoids Ari. Though he regrets hurting her, he feels guilty over helping the humans escape, and vows to spend his life dedicated to the glory of Semos. Still, he watches Ari from afar, ready to protect her.

Planet of the Apes #3: Rule, Chapter 4 (HE-y, unpublished)

◆ Several tribes merge with the Valley Clan, forming the biggest, most stable human settlement in living memory—nearly 400 members. Pica's tribal leader is killed by apes, and her people pledge their loyalty to Sarai as well. Sarai assigns a council of advisors: Ark, in charge of information gathering; Vasich, security head; Pica, clan healer; Luc, lead architect; Toni, head of agriculture; the blacksmith Dornal, managing craftspeople; Karubi, peacekeeping; and Daena, construction head.

Planet of the Apes #3: Rule, Chapter 2 (HE-y, unpublished)

5011

◆ Despite her age, Daena oversees the building of a great wall to protect the city. Karlo, a former slave from the temple-building crew, helps manage the work. Pak supervises the construction of a monument, the Spire of Hope, for which a Wilding girl named Brona carves a stone top.

Planet of the Apes #3: Rule, Chapter 1 (HE-y, unpublished)

◆ Sarai convenes her council of advisors. Rosulo, leader of a human tribe decimated by the apes, allies with the clan, offering to teach them to weave cloth. Sarai announces plans to return to Ape City to seek peace. Daena offers to join her, jealous when Sarai takes Brona instead.

Planet of the Apes #3: Rule, Chapter 2 (HE-y, unpublished)

◆ Ari meets her friend Leeta for dinner. Leeta ignores the fawning of several cadets, preferring powerful males like Attar. A human boy saves a baby ape from being crushed, but is punished for attacking the child. Ari defends the boy, enraging onlookers. Sandar and Krull arrive with Timon and Thade, who chide her for siding with a human.

Planet of the Apes #3: Rule, Chapter 3 (HE-y, unpublished)

◆ Attar heads for the Temple of Semos, avoiding Thade and Timon. The pontifax sees him, however, and tells him to spy on Ari, then orders the human boy's execution. Attar disagrees but says nothing.

Planet of the Apes #3: Rule, Chapter 4 (HE-y, unpublished)

◆ Sarai and Brona travel for a week before reaching Derkein. Traversing the sewer, they sneak under the city wall, ascend to the surface and locate Ari at a public celebration. Ari leads them to her home to speak in private, but despite Ari's willingness to help, she still harbors false precepts about humanity.

Planet of the Apes #3: Rule, Chapter 5 (HE-y, unpublished)

◆ Ari hides the humans in her sunroom, and Brona gratefully makes her a sculpture. A servant named El runs away after being scolded, and Sarai advises her to handle the situation with respect. This elicits a better response from El, and Ari realizes this is how ape masters should always treat their humans.

Planet of the Apes #3: Rule, Chapter 6 (HE-y, unpublished)

◆ Attar conceives a design for an improved catapult, which a gibbon named Mel helps him create. Thade and Timon chastise him for neglecting his duties and remind him of the danger Ari's attitudes represent. Despite his dislike for Timon, he agrees that she must be stopped.

Planet of the Apes #3: Rule, Chapter 7 (HE-y, unpublished)

◆ After days spent hiding with Ari, Sarai begins to find the chimp's enthusiasm—and her tendency to see simians as superior, despite her claims of tolerance—grating. When Ari comments that humans could never build a city of their own, Sarai decides to take her to New Hope.

Planet of the Apes #3: Rule, Chapter 8 (HE-y, unpublished)

◆ Ari pretends to visit her aunts. Once on the road, Sarai takes the reigns and blindfolds Ari for security purposes. The chimp is stunned at the sight of the human city. Attar, having followed her, returns to Derkein to report the city's existence—and Ari's involvement—to his superiors.

Planet of the Apes #3: Rule, Chapter 9 (HE-y, unpublished)

◆ Karlo erects a great hall while Luc oversees the building of a gatehouse for a 25-foot wall with arrow slits and other protective measures. Sarai and Brona return home, where a feast is held to celebrate New Hope's completion.

Planet of the Apes #3: Rule, Chapter 10 (HE-y, unpublished)

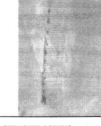

PUBLISHER / STUDIO
AB . . . . ABC-TV
AC . . . .Adventure / Malibu Comics
AW . . . . Award Books
BB . . . . .Ballantine Books
BN . . . . Bantam Books
BW . . . . Brown Watson Books
CB . . . . CBS-TV
CV . . . . Chad Valley Sliderama
DH . . . . .Dark Horse Comics
ET . . . . Editorial Mo.Pa.Sa.
FX . . . . 20th Century Fox
GK . . . .Gold Key / Western Comics
HE . . . HarperEntertainment Books
HM . . Harry K. McWilliams Assoc.
MC . . . . Marvel Comics
MR . . . Mr. Comics / Metallic Rose
NB . . . . NBC-TV
PR . . . . .Power Records
SB . . . . Signet Books
TP . . . . .Topps
UB . . . . Ubisoft

MEDIUM
a . . . . animated series
b . . . . .book-and-record set
c . . . . .comic book or strip
d . . . . trading card
e . . . . e-comic
f . . . . .theatrical film
k . . . . .storybook
m . . . . .magazine article
n . . . . .novel or novelization
p . . . . promotional newspaper
r . . . . .recorded audio fiction
s . . . . short story
t . . . . television series
u . . . . .unfilmed script or story
v . . . . video game
x . . . . .Blu-Ray exclusive
y . . . . .young adult novel

◆ Ari realizes New Hope proves ape precepts about humans erroneous. Leeta warns her to be careful, for the military is sure to destroy the city once Thade hears of it. Ari heads home to ask her father for help, but Attar accuses her of being a traitor, scoffing at her plea not to tell anyone about the human city.

Planet of the Apes #3: Rule, Chapter 11 (HE-y, unpublished)

◆ Learning of New Hope's existence, Thade vows to crush the city, but Krull is worried about potential military losses. Attar tells them about his catapult, suggesting they might use it to level the wall.

Planet of the Apes #3: Rule, Chapter 12 (HE-y, unpublished)

◆ Leeta warns Ari that soldiers have come to arrest her. Ari submits to the guards, who drag her through the streets amidst taunts of "human lover." Locked in a prison dungeon, Ari lies helpless as Timon and Thade plan an assault.

Planet of the Apes #3: Rule, Chapter 13 (HE-y, unpublished)

◆ Sarai congratulates Pak for building the Spire of Hope, then unveils Brona's statue to wild applause. To Daena's astonishment, the statue depicts her. She is their future, Sarai says, urging her to keep human-ape relations moving forward when Daena becomes ruler. Despite her doubts, Daena promises.

Planet of the Apes #3: Rule, Chapter 14 (HE-y, unpublished)

◆ Guided by Mel and Attar, a carpentry team builds three catapults. Meanwhile, as Thade drills his soldiers, Timon blesses the army, promising Semos will welcome into paradise those slain in battle.

Planet of the Apes #3: Rule, Chapter 15 (HE-y, unpublished)

◆ Leeta seduces a guard named Laran to help Ari escape her cell, then rides out with her friend to warn the New Hope humans of the impending attack.

Planet of the Apes #3: Rule, Chapter 16 (HE-y, unpublished)

◆ Gatehouse sentries bar Ari and Leeta from entering New Hope. A human boy named Colcol summons Sarai, and Ari tells her Thade's plan. Ari offers to fight alongside them, but Sarai says to attend to her own troubles so she can continue acting as a messenger of peace.

Planet of the Apes #3: Rule, Chapter 17 (HE-y, unpublished)

◆ The attack begins at dawn, and many apes die trying to pierce the fortified city. Viewing the bloodbath, Attar and Timon realize the humans must have known they were coming. Attar's first war leaves him disillusioned, unable to see the valor and heroism he'd expected. With resources exhausted, Thade orders the catapults fired.

Planet of the Apes #3: Rule, Chapter 18 (HE-y, unpublished)

◆ Daena drops rocks on the apes below, then helps Luc dump boiling oil on the troops. Two chimps make it to the ramparts, but Daena dispatches them. Suddenly, entire sections of the wall crumble, blasted by the catapults. As debris rains down on her, Daena and others run for cover.

Planet of the Apes #3: Rule, Chapter 19 (HE-y, unpublished)

◆ Ape soldiers storm New Hope, and Sarai's guards lead her to safety. Watching her city burn, Sarai calls a retreat. Thade corners her and Brona, however, recognizing Sarai from the temple. He orders the Great Hall set aflame, killing many humans hidden within, then executes both Brona and Sarai.

Planet of the Apes #3: Rule, Chapter 20 (HE-y, unpublished)

◆ Karubi stops Daena from attacking Thade, then leads her, Birn and Pak into the woods. An axe-wielding chimp attacks, and Karlo sacrifices his life to save theirs. The humans make their way to a waterfall, where Luc and others await. Luc shows them a tunnel he'd built through the mountain, and they escape.

Planet of the Apes #3: Rule, Chapter 21 (HE-y, unpublished)

◆ Thade congratulates Attar, promising to reward him when they return to Derkein. Even Timon now shows him respect. Basking in their praise, Attar leads a band of soldiers in leveling Brona's sculpture.

Planet of the Apes #3: Rule, Chapter 22 (HE-y, unpublished)

◆ The 20 survivors of the Valley Clan travel for days before resting, with Pica tending to the wounded. Karubi decides his people must now live like Wildings, for their survival outweighs the need for revenge. Daena, however, vows one day to make her mother's dream of freedom a reality.

Planet of the Apes #3: Rule, Chapter 23 (HE-y, unpublished)

◆ At Ari's trial, Thade suggests that Sarai must have brainwashed her, and Ari denounces the human to save her own life. The council stays her execution, sentencing her to a year's solitary confinement in her home. Locked in her room, Ari finds Brona's statue and holds out hope that their two species can one day live in peace.

Planet of the Apes #3: Rule, Epilogue (HE-y, unpublished)

5011 TO 5012

◆ Thade expends a good deal of time and military resources tracking Karubi's people through the jungle. This annoys Krull, who considers the effort wasted for such a small group of humans.

Planet of the Apes #4: Extinction, Chapter 8 (HE-y, unpublished)

NOTE: Author John Whitman submitted a chapter-by-chapter outline for Extinction. *Due to low sales on the first two volumes, however, it was never written, published or contracted. The following breakdown comes from the author's submitted outline.*

5012

◆ Nearly captured by apes, Karubi's people escape across a river. They pick up several stragglers, including Ethan, a cave painter. Seeing painting as useless, Daena takes a quick dislike to the young man.

Planet of the Apes #4: Extinction, Chapter 1 (HE-y, unpublished)

◆ Daena suggests they hide in the Cave of Paintings at the mountain's peaks, but Karubi and Ethan disagree since the caves are sacred. Suddenly, the apes discover a way across the river and attack.

Planet of the Apes #4: Extinction, Chapter 2 (HE-y, unpublished)

◆ With little choice, Karubi leads his people into the caves, and even Daena is impressed at the paintings' beauty. Seeing them, her father urges the tribe never to forget what humans are capable of doing.

Planet of the Apes #4: Extinction, Chapter 3 (HE-y, unpublished)

◆ When ape troops question the wisdom of pursuing a single band of humans, Thade backhands one soldier for such sentiments. Krull opts to cancel the search, but Thade orders Attar to fetch Ari.

Planet of the Apes #4: Extinction, Chapter 4 (HE-y, unpublished)

PUBLISHER / STUDIO
AB . . . . ABC-TV
AC . . . .Adventure / Malibu Comics
AW . . . . Award Books
BB . . . . .Ballantine Books
BN . . . . Bantam Books
BW . . . . . Brown Watson Books
CB . . . . CBS-TV
CV . . . . Chad Valley Sliderama
DH . . . . .Dark Horse Comics
ET . . . . Editorial Mo.Pa.Sa.
FX . . . . 20th Century Fox
GK . . . .Gold Key / Western Comics
HE . . . HarperEntertainment Books
HM . . Harry K. McWilliams Assoc.
MC . . . . Marvel Comics
MR . . . Mr. Comics / Metallic Rose
NB . . . . NBC-TV
PR . . . . Power Records
SB . . . . Signet Books
TP . . . . .Topps
UB . . . . .Ubisoft

MEDIUM
a . . . . animated series
b . . . . .book-and-record set
c . . . . .comic book or strip
d . . . . trading card
e . . . . e-comic
f . . . . .theatrical film
k . . . . .storybook
m . . . . .magazine article
n . . . . . . .novel or novelization
p . . . . . . promotional newspaper
r . . . . .recorded audio fiction
s . . . . short story
t . . . . television series
u . . . . . . .unfilmed script or story
v . . . . video game
x . . . . .Blu-Ray exclusive
y . . . . .young adult novel

◆ Despite his anger that Thade has brought an important civilian into a military scenario, Krull orders Ari to reveal what she knows about the humans' whereabouts.

Planet of the Apes #4: Extinction, Chapter 5 (HE-y, unpublished)

◆ Ethan views paintings of large beetle-like creatures. Spotting a small opening, they notice another tunnel up ahead. A moment later, water pours into the cave as the apes try to drown them.

Planet of the Apes #4: Extinction, Chapter 6 (HE-y, unpublished)

◆ Daena and Ethan urge their people into the new tunnel. Large luminescent worms burrow through the mountain, creating additional caves. Suddenly, a giant beetle moves toward them.

Planet of the Apes #4: Extinction, Chapter 7 (HE-y, unpublished)

◆ When Attar fails to locate the tribe, Thade sends a squad in to find them. This angers Krull, but Thade ignores his objection, knowing other apes will sympathize with humanity if he doesn't end the problem.

Planet of the Apes #4: Extinction, Chapter 8 (HE-y, unpublished)

◆ The beetle spots a glow worm and sucks out its insides. A pleasant smell accompanies the bug, and Daena and others are hypnotically drawn to it. One woman stands passively as the beetle consumes her lifeforce.

Planet of the Apes #4: Extinction, Chapter 9 (HE-y, unpublished)

◆ Karubi pulls his people away from the beetle, and they make camp in another cave. The light of their fire attracts more bugs, however, so Ethan stamps out the fire, plunging the tribe into darkness.

Planet of the Apes #4: Extinction, Chapter 10 (HE-y, unpublished)

◆ Daena falls into a lower tunnel and gets lost in deep catacombs, surrounded by glow worms feasting on a dead beetle. She lays down to cry and falls asleep, awakening when something moves above her.

Planet of the Apes #4: Extinction, Chapter 11 (HE-y, unpublished)

◆ Attar's squad encounters a giant beetle. More olfactorily attuned than humans, they succumb to its hypnotic scent. Attar grabs his soldiers and runs, but loses them in the darkness.

Planet of the Apes #4: Extinction, Chapter 12 (HE-y, unpublished)

◆ Attar finds Daena and lights a fire, attracting a beetle. With the hypnotized Attar her only way out, she kills the bug with his sword, attracting several glow worms, whose light draws more beetles. Daena and Attar are overwhelmed by the intoxicating smell as pincers pierce her sides.

Planet of the Apes #4: Extinction, Chapter 13 (HE-y, unpublished)

◆ Karubi's people save Daena and slay the beetle. She says not to kill Attar, and a deal is struck: If they protect him from the beetles and help locate his soldiers, he'll lead them to the exit and set them free.

Planet of the Apes #4: Extinction, Chapter 14 (HE-y, unpublished)

◆ This arrangement, Karubi asserts, proves humans and apes can live together, but Attar and Daena both disagree. Eventually, they find Attar's soldiers in the beetles' nest.

Planet of the Apes #4: Extinction, Chapter 15 (HE-y, unpublished)

◆ All but three soldiers have been consumed. The humans cover their faces with cloth and pull the survivors to safety.

Planet of the Apes #4: Extinction, Chapter 16 (HE-y, unpublished)

◆ Upholding his end of the bargain, Attar leads the tribe outside and instructs them to lure a beetle with torches. The creature causes panic in the ape camp, enabling the humans to escape. Before they leave, Attar tells Karubi he'll kill the man if ever they meet again.

Planet of the Apes #4: Extinction, Chapter 17 (HE-y, unpublished)

◆ The apes grow passive before the beetle, and Thade accuses them of weakness. Attar insists the scent is impossible to resist, so Thade walks up to the creature, waits for it to attack and slaps its mandibles, causing it to retreat in fear.

Planet of the Apes #4: Extinction, Chapter 18 (HE-y, unpublished)

◆ Thade orders the caves destroyed, eliminating the last remnant of human civilization. Daena weeps, but Karubi reassures her they must retain hope for the future.

Planet of the Apes #4: Extinction, Chapter 19 (HE-y, unpublished)

BETWEEN 5012 AND 5021

◆ Rising to the rank of captain, Attar becomes Krull's star pupil. Thade is named the military's top general and vows to wipe out the human species. Krull opposes the plan, however, and is stripped of rank. Attar replaces Krull and turns his back on his mentor, forging instead a bond with Thade that develops into a strong friendship. Disgraced, Krull accepts a position as chief servant of Senator Sandar's household.

Planet of the Apes (FX-f)

◆ Senator Nado, a portly orangutan, marries a string of female apes, but none of the marriages last.

Planet of the Apes (HE-n)

NOTE: This information appears in the film's novelization.

◆ Thade captures a blind psychic chimpanzee known as Oracle, who says she knows the truth of his family lineage. He imprisons her in the secret depths of Ape City so her gift of prophecy can serve only him. Her son is thus raised an orphan with no knowledge of her existence.

Planet of the Apes Collector's Comic (DH-c)

NOTE: This mini-comic was given out free at Toys'R'Us stores to publicize the film's theatrical release.

◆ When Attar's brother Tolan gets into trouble, Attar must save the other's life. Their father is displeased at Tolan's poor performance as a soldier.

Dark Horse Extra #38: "Planet of the Apes, Part 3" (DH-c)

NOTE: This three-part serialized story appeared in Dark Horse's anthology comic, Dark Horse Extra. Part 1 is available online at http://www.darkhorse.com/downloads. php?did=298. In the novel Force, Attar is said to be an orphan raised by monks. No mention is made of a brother in that book—and, as an orphan, Attar should have no living parents. This discrepancy remains unexplained.

◆ Attar and Tolan round up a pack of humans and make camp for the night. Many soldiers, including Tolan, are brutal to the prisoners to remind them of their place, but Attar sees capturing humans not in racist terms, but as a necessary task. An angry group of humans watches from nearby trees, waiting to avenge their slain tribesmen.

Dark Horse Extra #36: "Planet of the Apes, Part 1" (DH-c)

◆ The humans attack the soldiers, but the apes are experts at surprise raids and quickly gain the upper hand. Picking up a young girl trying to hurt him, Attar turns to find her father holding a knife to Tolan's neck. The man demands an exchange: the return of his daughter for the soldier's release.

Dark Horse Extra #37: "Planet of the Apes, Part 2" (DH-c)

◆ The human claims that his daughter was attempting to save her brother, who'd been taken captive by the apes. Impressed at her boldness—and disgusted at having to save his brother yet again—Attar frees the woman. Humiliated, Tolan grabs a spear and kills the man as he runs for the trees. Furious, Attar turns his back on his brother, asking if Tolan would venture into enemy ground to save *his* life, as the humans had done for their kin.

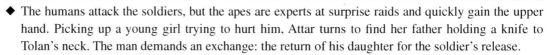

Dark Horse Extra #38: "Planet of the Apes, Part 3" (DH-c)

◆ Thade makes repeated romantic overtures to Ari, but she rebuffs him due to his attitude toward humans. Infatuated with her—and her father's Senate influence—he vows to win her affections. After being repeatedly jilted, however, he stops visiting Sandar's home for a time. Ari's friend Leeta thinks Ari's response a mistake, for Thade is a powerful ape who can provide her a privileged life.

Planet of the Apes (HE-n)

NOTE: This information appears in the film's novelization.

◆ Frustrated by Ari's rejection, Thade consoles himself by taking a half-gorilla, half-chimp courtesan as his lover. Unable to marry her because of her lower class, he keeps their relationship a secret, even when she bears his child. The courtesan devotes herself to him fully, receiving only empty promises in return.

Planet of the Apes—The Human War #1: "Part 1" (DH-c)

◆ Visiting Oracle's cell, Thade taunts her over the loss of her son. The blind psychic says his plan to destroy humanity is doomed, for the sky will be torn asunder and Semos shall return. The general dismisses the prophecy, knowing his fiercest soldier, Attar, leads his army. Oracle accuses him of corrupting the once-noble gorilla, predicting Ari and others will ultimately turn against him and fight for inter-species equality. Angered by such riddles, he mocks her prophecies, convinced he is destined to achieve greatness.

Planet of the Apes Collector's Comic (DH-c)

NOTE: This mini-comic was given out free at Toys'R'Us stores to publicize the film's theatrical release.

◆ The apes build cities encroaching on the humans' lands, and mankind has no choice but to raid the apes' orchards. Humans infest the provinces, breeding so quickly they soon outnumber the apes four to one. Some politicians propose sterilization, but the cost is too prohibitive, creating a welfare state that nearly bankrupts the government. Thade wants to dispose of them entirely, but with the Senate limiting his power and human-rights factions keeping a close eye on his activities, he finds it difficult to act. Still, his soldiers are able to kill the humans in large numbers with impunity, for though the Senators consider such actions extreme, they fear opposing Thade more.

Planet of the Apes (FX-f)

◆ Future senator Seneca breaks ape tradition as a child by learning to swim despite his species' aversion to water. His mother, therefore, nicknames the young chimp her "little sea monkey."

Planet of the Apes—The Human War #2: "Part 2" (DH-c)

c. 5021

◆ Senator Zaius grows ill with old age. Powerless to help him, and obsessed with the human overpopulation problem, Thade regrets his inability to visit his dying father as often as he'd like to.

Planet of the Apes (FX-f)

NOTE: It's unknown when, exactly, Zaius becomes ill, just that by 5021, he's dying.

LATE 5021

◆ Senator Nado vacations at his country house in the rain forest, enjoying the break from politics and spending much of his time sleeping. The elderly orangutan's latest wife—a high-maintenance young chimp named Nova—finds the trip boring and wishes they could go out instead.

Planet of the Apes (FX-f)

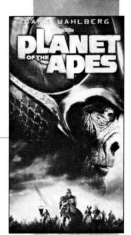

NOVEMBER 30, 5021

◆ Thrown through space-time by an ion storm, USAF *Oberon* pilot Capt. Leo Davidson crashes his shuttle, the *Delta Pod*, in a jungle lake. Karubi and Daena run by, followed by others in their tribe, including Gunnar and Birn. Gorilla and chimp soldiers herd Davidson and the tribe into a clearing, forcing them into wagons bound for Ape City. As the carts pass through Derkein en route to Limbo's pens, the tribe ignores Davidson's questions. Ape children throw stones at the humans until Ari forces them to stop.

Planet of the Apes (FX-f)

NOTE: The film's 5021 setting, established in Dark Horse's comic-book adaptation, contradicts a statement made by novelist William T. Quick in a Simian Scrolls *interview, indicating his* Apes *spinoff novels (set in the early 21st century) take place a thousand years before the movie. I have adhered to Dark Horse's dating since "onscreen" evidence would seem to outweigh information derived from an interview. The name "Derkein" comes from an early-draft film script, as well as Dark Horse's post-film comics.*

◆ A potential customer looks the new humans over but decides she can get a better deal from Picatto, one of Limbo's slaving competitors. Limbo warns her that Picatto's humans are low-quality.

Planet of the Apes (DH-c)

NOTE: This information appears in the film's comic adaptation.

◆ Thade brings his niece to Limbo's pens to purchase a human girl as a pet. As the slaver's menials brand the lot, Ari disrupts their work and opens the cage. Davidson holds the brand to her neck and begs for help. Soothing Limbo, she buys Davidson and Daena and puts them to work alongside Bon and Tival. Thade, Leeta, Attar, Nado and Nova join her family for dinner. Thade mocks Ari's pro-human sentiments, then follows her outside to soothe her anger. Two guards find the pod, and Thade kills them to keep it a secret. That night, Davidson escapes with Daena and Tival in tow, freeing Karubi, Birn, Gunnar and the little girl. The humans interrupt Nado and Nova's love-making, and startle many apes as they run through the city. Ari, Krull and Bon find them, and Davidson asks her help in getting out of the city. Ari relents, sending Bon home with the child. Attar tries to stop them, but Karubi rushes him, sacrificing himself so the rest can escape. Thade orders their capture but protects Ari by telling the Senate she was coerced. Ari tries to console Daena over her loss, but Daena rebuffs her, jealous of her attention to Davidson.

Planet of the Apes (FX-f)

NOVEMBER 31, 5021

◆ Davidson's group reaches the lake containing his pod. Like most apes, Ari fears the water, but Davidson and Daena dive in to retrieve a tool kit containing a laser gun, food and a Messenger communications device—which locates the *Oberon*, 36 hours distant, in Calima, the birth-place of ape civilization, located in the Forbidden Zone. Limbo tries to reclaim his property, but Birn jumps the slaver and Davidson fires the laser, dispersing his guards. As Gunnar manacles the orangutan, Krull destroys the laser so it can't be used again.

Planet of the Apes (FX-f)

DECEMBER 1, 5021

◆ Thade claims humans have kidnapped Ari, manipulating Sandar into declaring martial law. Zaius calls Thade to his death-bed, sharing their family secret that apes once served man. Before dying, he reveals an ancient human laser gun and urges his son to stop the humans from finding Calima. Davidson's team reaches a scarecrow-guarded path, blocked by an ape encampment. Attar assumes command of the camp, appalled at the lack of discipline. After dark, Davidson's group steal horses and set the apes' tents afire. Ari and Davidson are knocked from their horses, but he carries her across a lake to join the others. Outraged that the soldiers tried to kill him, Limbo changes loyalties.

Planet of the Apes (FX-f)

DECEMBER 2, 5021

◆ Davidson's group reaches Calima—the millennia-old wreckage of the *Oberon*, so named for a corroded sign reading "**Ca**ution: **Li**ve Ani**ma**ls." The ship is decimated, but its nuclear power source functions. Davidson finds database footage of an elderly Karl Vasich from millennia prior, issuing a mayday when the station crashed, then accesses a video of Grace Alexander regarding Semos' betrayal of mankind. Stunned, Ari realizes her people owe their existence to Davidson. Outside, hundreds of humans await, for word has spread that his friends are coming to save them. That night, Krull and Ari visit the ape camp. Ari offers herself to Thade in exchange for the humans' freedom, but he brands her like a human and casts her out to die with them.

Planet of the Apes (FX-f)

DECEMBER 3, 5021

◆ Davidson hides the tribe behind *Oberon*, intending to use its fuel tank as a weapon. Daena, Krull and Gunnar take the front line to lure in Thade's army. Birn tries to join them but falls off his horse. Saving his life, Davidson ignites the engine. The blast kills most apes, the tribe slaying the rest, but Gunnar and Tival die in battle. Ari saves Daena's life; upon seeing her brand, Daena apologizes for misjudging her. Attar kills Krull in hand-to-hand combat, then all fighting stops as *Alpha Pod* lands. Seeing Pericles, the apes think Semos has returned. Thade attacks Davidson, their fight taking them inside the station, where the general injures Pericles and steals a laser pistol. Ari and Attar enter as Davidson locks Thade in a compartment. Calling the Semos line traitors, Attar turns his back on his friend. Thade throws a fit of rage, laser shots ricocheting around the room. Attar organizes a mass burial for all fallen apes and humans, leaving the graves unmarked as a sign of unity. Limbo, meanwhile, launches a new career trading with humanity. Ari asks Davidson to stay with them, but he declines. Bidding farewell, he heads for space, leaving Pericles in Ari's care, then locates the ion storm and attempts to return home.

Planet of the Apes (FX-f)

DECEMBER 5021 TO EARLY 5022

◆ Calima is deemed off-limits to keep secret its revelations about the origins of human and simian life. Travel to the ruins is thus designated illegal.

Planet of the Apes—The Human War #2: "Part 2" (DH-c)

◆ Thade is publicly disgraced. Wary of his growing ambition, the Senate strips him of his rank and power, and he eventually vanishes without a trace. Attar, meanwhile, begins questioning his faith.

Planet of the Apes #7 and beyond (DH-c, unpublished—titles unknown)

NOTE: Writers Ian Edginton and Dan Abnett offer this glimpse at their plans had Dark Horse's comic based on the Tim Burton film continued past issue #6.

◆ Ari is arrested for treason. In exchange for Attar's surrender, she is freed and goes into hiding as well.

Planet of the Apes #1: "Old Gods, Part 1" (DH-c)

◆ Given Attar's past association with Thade and his newfound radical beliefs, the Senate permanently exiles him from Ape City, sending him to live as a prisoner on Shame Island.

Planet of the Apes #7 and beyond (DH-c, unpublished—titles unknown)

◆ There, Attar's prison guards—his former soldiers—treat him as badly as they would other criminals.

Planet of the Apes #1: "Old Gods, Part 1" (DH-c)

◆ Security on Shame Island is lax, and Attar knows he can escape at any time. But as an ape of honor, he accepts his punishment, knowing his sacrifice will save the lives of his friends.

Planet of the Apes #2: "Old Gods, Part 2" (DH-c)

◆ Attar's fall casts doubt on his family's honor, including his grandson, Cmdr. Kharim.

Planet of the Apes—The Human War #2: "Part 2" (DH-c)

NOTE: Presumably, Attar's brother Tolan and their father are dishonored as well, though this is never stated.

◆ Thade is officially pronounced dead. His half-chimp, half-gorilla courtesan keeps his belongings as mementos, unaware of their true significance for decades to come.

Planet of the Apes—The Human War #1: "Part 1" (DH-c)

5021 TO 5041

◆ Thade's love-child has a daughter, Shiva, who grows up to become a government minister.

Planet of the Apes—The Human War #1: "Part 1" (DH-c)

◆ Unmarried and without children, the cold-hearted Shiva has but one purpose in life: to succeed, and to make sure everyone else fails.

Planet of the Apes—The Human War #3: "Part 3" (DH-c)

◆ Ashlar faces two decades of civil war between the Insurrectionists—ape rebels advocating human integration, led by ex-senator Seneca and Esau, a bloodthirsty human—and the powerful ape regime, led by Kharim. Having faced violence and oppression his entire life, Esau is willing to die for freedom. Seneca comes from a privileged family, but believes society must change or face mutual extinction. Seneca's brother Fyn serves as a double-agent for the Insurrectionists, using his position as Shiva's personal assistant to monitor her military caravan's whereabouts.

Planet of the Apes—The Human War #1: "Part 1" (DH-c)

◆ Over time, Ari loses her dewey-eyed idealism and changes from a middle-class liberal animal activist to a full-fledged radical and heretic. Searching for the truth of simian origins, she promises to alert Attar, Daena and others at Calima once she finds it. Daena also matures during this time, losing some of her anger. She and Ari form a friendship, marked by sarcasm and sparring. Limbo, meanwhile, returns to a quiet life.

Planet of the Apes #7 and beyond (DH-c, unpublished—titles unknown)

BEFORE 5041

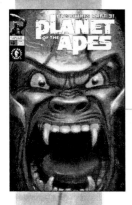

◆ Keyser, a skilled ape warrior, is cast out for professing a belief in tolerance for both apes and humans. Hiding behind armor and a mask, Keyser continues to fight for equality between the species.

Planet of the Apes #6: "Bloodlines, Part 3" (DH-c)

◆ In the enclave of Ultimar, a band of ape warriors mistreats their human slaves until the latter revolt and the streets run slick with blood. Slaves no more, they flee into the woods and call themselves the Forest Humans, living as nomads to avoid detection. The Ultimar vow to kill every human they meet, so the Forest Humans begin killing the apes. Keyser protects the Forest Humans, and is so fast that few ever see him coming, earning him a reputation as the Ghost in the Trees. The apes fear him, while the Forest Humans revere him as their guardian demon.

Planet of the Apes #4: "Bloodlines, Part 1" (DH-c)

5041

◆ Kharim lures the rebels to a fortress at Mikdoul so his cavalry can slaughter them. Facing Insurrectionist fire, his soldiers retreat. Esau revels in victory, but Seneca is appalled at the high body count.

Planet of the Apes—The Human War #1: "Part 1" (DH-c)

NOTE: *Issue #2 of Dark Horse's monthly title establishes 20 years' passage since Attar's imprisonment in 5021.*

◆ Trooper Bouel, a gorilla soldier, survives Esau's massacre. Witnessesing Fyn living among the rebels on good terms, the soldier returns to Derkein and tells Shiva what he's seen.

Planet of the Apes—The Human War #2: "Part 2" (DH-c)

NOTE: *Trooper Bouel is named for* Planet of the Apes *creator Pierre Boulle, author of* The Monkey Planet.

◆ Minister Rodi informs the Senate that the Insurrectionists are plundering their caravans, trade and commerce are floundering, food and grain prices are skyrocketing, and the rebels are well-armed. Shiva urges the Senate to exterminate all rebels, human and ape alike. Others agree, but the chairman prefers negotiation to genocide. Furious, Shiva vows to take over the government once the elderly ape dies. She shows Fyn a secret box belonging to her grandmother, Thade's courtesan, containing detailed drawings of the *Oberon*. Convinced these are the keys to changing the world, she assigns Fyn to an expedition to Calima.

Planet of the Apes—The Human War #1: "Part 1" (DH-c)

◆ The expedition visits munitions works at Ap'Jac. The rebels attack and surround them in a clearing.

Planet of the Apes—The Human War #2: "Part 2" (DH-c)

NOTE: *Ap'Jac is named for APJAC Productions, which produced all five classic* Planet of the Apes *films.*

◆ As troops slaughter the expedition, Seneca stops Esau from killing Fyn, exposing him as his brother.

Planet of the Apes—The Human War #1: "Part 1" (DH-c)

◆ Fyn tells them of Shiva's plans and half-caste status, then returns to Derkein claiming he was captured but escaped. Seneca swims to Shame Island, where Attar reveals the truth about Semos, their origins and Leo Davidson. Shiva visits Fyn at a Derkein hospital, dismissing his kidnapping story and letting Trooper Bouel torture him. Meanwhile, Seneca returns to the rebels, adamant that they must journey to Calima and reclaim their heritage.

Planet of the Apes—The Human War #2: "Part 2" (DH-c)

◆ Seneca leads his forces to the Forbidden Zone, to find Fyn's corpse stuffed in a scarecrow. Kharim's troops ambush the rebels, killing many, then head on to Calima. Seneca hears a trooper mock Fyn and slaughters every soldier. Aboard *Oberon*, Shiva tries to operate the reactor controls, but Esau and Seneca expose her half-caste status and family secret. Kharim betrays her, unwilling to watch her destroy others in her thirst for power. Shiva disengages the safety protocols, filling the station with light. Kharim kills her, then helps Seneca avoid a meltdown. He keeps the station a secret, blaming Shiva's death on the rebels, but refuses Seneca's hand of friendship, vowing one day to see the senator hang as a traitor.

Planet of the Apes—The Human War #3: "Part 3" (DH-c)

◆ When Kharim repeatedly catches the rebels off guard, they suspect an infiltrator. During one ambush, his forces capture Esau and Seneca. Attar's Shame Island guards, meanwhile, arrive three days late with food, which contains a note from Ari, asking for help. Building a raft, he dispatches his guards and rows to Derkein. Rodi orders the rebels' execution, but the masked executioner turns out to be Attar, who cuts their bindings, helping them escape.

Planet of the Apes #1: "Old Gods, Part 1" (DH-c)

NOTE: This three-part story was originally published untitled; the title comes from the trade paperback collection.

◆ Ape and human skulls line the road as the trio ride toward a township where humans happily serve ape masters. Few males between ages 15 and 50 are in evidence. Attar's group pretend to be farmers, and the prelate orangutan, Paracelcus, tells them his son was slain when ape killers decimated his town. Esau meets Crow, a woman whose family has been indentured to Paracelcus' for generations. Attar, deciding to help them, gives Esau a list of materials to obtain. That night, apes scale the walls with claw-like devices, slaying Paracelcus. Attar unleashes gunpowder grenades packed with nails, forcing the killers to retreat. Surveying the dead, Attar recognizes their foe as the Chimerae, a mythical band of deformed, deranged warriors, whom he calls "the best of us, and the worst."

Planet of the Apes #2: "Old Gods, Part 2" (DH-c)

◆ Attar's group mount a preemptive strike on the Chimerae as Crow gets her people to safety. Arrows rain down as they reach the warriors' First City, and though injured, Attar breaks his spear in truce. In response, Warlord Saghat agrees to hear their request. Attar asks him to leave the villagers in peace, but Saghat claims the town cleared his land and trees. Attar kills the warlord and demands the Chimerae swear fealty to him, but they attack en masse. Explosions rock the battle site as Crow fires explosive-tipped arrows, and the four seek refuge in the jungle.

Planet of the Apes #3: "Old Gods, Part 3" (DH-c)

WINTER 5041

◆ As snow falls, Esau's team seeks shelter from the Ultimar, a staunch band of human-haters.

Planet of the Apes #5: "Bloodlines, Part 2" (DH-c)

◆ The Ultimar, led by Lord Scarak, attack. Crow shoots the leader with an arrow, and a blurred figure enters the fray, killing many Ultimar soldiers; he is Keyser, "the Ghost in the Trees," a masked simian assassin feared by the Ultimar and dedicated to killing other apes. Decimating the Ultimar, Keyser turns his sword on Seneca, but Crow stops him. Surprised to see humans and apes fighting side by side, he takes them to meet the Forest Humans. Thinking Esau dead, they leave him behind, but he awakens and follows from a distance to the assassin's settlement.

Planet of the Apes #4: "Bloodlines, Part 1" (DH-c)

◆ The Forest Humans tie Attar and Seneca to posts in the snow. Tribal law, dictating that human shall never kill human, spares Crow and Esau. One human, Ewan, says he has no choice but to kill apes since they insist on hunting his kind. Crow points out that Keyser is an ape, but another human, Urlin, deems him a guardian demon sent to protect them. Ewan urges his tribesmen to execute the newcomers, while Urlin reminds his people that both species once lived together, until humans paid the price. The Ultimar attack before the execution can be carried out, and Keyser frees Seneca and Attar, knowing his people will need all the warriors they can get.

Planet of the Apes #5: "Bloodlines, Part 2" (DH-c)

◆ As Urlin leads the women and children to safety, the others face the Ultimar in a bloody battle. Touched at the sight of apes fighting alongside humans, Ewan dies by Scarak's hand. Esau charges the Ultimar leader, but Scarak knocks him to the ground and attacks Keyser. His sword severs the latter's blade, slashing through his armor and flesh, and he nearly kills Attar as well before Crow slays him with an arrow. The Ultimar flee for the hills, leaving Keyser mortally wounded. After burying the proud ape warrior, Attar's team continue on their quest.

Planet of the Apes #6: "Bloodlines, Part 3" (DH-c)

NOTE: *Since Dark Horse's* Apes *comic was canceled as of this issue, the fates of Esau, Seneca, Attar, Crow, Ari and Kharim were never revealed in print. That said...*

◆ Determined to restore his family honor, Kharim pursues the fugitives as they search for Ari. Attar's companions travel the planet, encountering other ape civilizations and discovering more about the origin of Semos. As news of Calima spreads among the populace, the regime grows ever more paranoid about the insurgency and turns to a martial leader—the disgraced Thade—to set things right. Seneca's group elicits help from Limbo and Daena, eventually finding Ari on a remote island in a community of human-friendly apes and the technologically advanced descendants of the *Oberon* crew. Kharim's forces siege the island, forcing Seneca and several others to escape in the station's remaining pods. This propels them through space-time, depositing them on Caesar's Earth.

Planet of the Apes #7 and beyond (DH-c, unpublished—titles unknown)

NOTE: *Writers Ian Edginton and Dan Abnett offer this glimpse at their plans for Dark Horse's Tim Burton-era comic series had the series continued past issue #6. When Dark Horse pulled the plug following the film's critical failure, the writers conceived a way of bridging this film with the classic five, hoping to relaunch the license in that reality. Such plans, however, were not approved.*

◆ Thade launches in a pod as well, and the spatial anomaly propels him into Earth's past. There, the general becomes an honored military icon among Earth's apes, supplanting the memory (and memorial) of Abraham Lincoln.

Planet of the Apes (FX-f)

NOTE: *Thade's trip to Earth is not explicitly stated, but can be inferred given the film's surprise ending, along with Dark Horse's unrealized plans, outlined above. The details of his launch are unrecorded.*

AFTER 5041

◆ A book of sketches of Thade, Attar, Ari, Daena, Shiva and others is discovered on the outskirts of the Forbidden Zone. Some attribute them to a human artist, but Secturus (Derkein's keeper of records) and other scholars dismiss the notion, convinced humans lack the dexterity and imagination to create such illustrations. Secturus archives the sketches nonetheless, deeming them the work of an ape.

Planet of the Apes Sketchbook (DH-e)

NOTE: This collection of sketches, intended to market Dark Horse Comics' Planet of the Apes series, is presented "in universe" and can be viewed online at http://www.darkhorse.com/downloads.php?did=297.

THE FAR DISTANT FUTURE

◆ A writer pens the tale of French astronaut Ulysse Mérou, who travels to Betelgeuse with a professor named Antelle and physician Arthur Levain. Due to time dilation, centuries pass on Earth during the characters' two-year journey. There, on a world they dub Soror, Mérou discovers a civilization where apes are the masters and humans live as primitives. Mérou befriends a chimp couple, Cornelius and Zira; earns the enmity of an orangutan, Dr. Zaius; and falls in love with a woman named Nova. When he uncovers evidence that humans once ruled the planet, some reject the find, while Zaius and others see this as a reason to exterminate humanity. Using Antelle's ship, Mérou returns home with Nova and their infant son, Sirius, to find that apes have taken over Earth as well. The novel ends with Mérou heading back to space to find a new home for his family, then recording his adventures on a roll of paper and leaving the manuscript floating in a bottle, which two vacationing apes, Jinn and Phyllis, discover and read. Though amused by the tale, they dismiss the concept of a speaking, reasoning human as ridiculous.

La planète des singes ("The Monkey Planet") (SB-n)

NOTE: Pierre Boulle's novel The Monkey Planet *was the basis for the* Planet of the Apes *screenplay by Michael Wilson and Rod Serling. Rather than break down its events, I am treating it as a fictional story told within the* Apes *mythos—a recounting of Taylor's adventures, but with his name and other details altered. How apes could travel the stars is unclear; clearly, they can't be from Earth, but they could be from Semos' world, Ashlar, far in the future. This novel was adapted as a Hungarian-language comic book titled* A Majmok Bolygája, *written and illustrated by Zórád Ernő. The comic, and an English translation, are available online at Hunter's* Planet of the Apes *Archive. An audio adaptation of the novel, presented as part of BBC Radio 4's* Book at Bedtime *series, was read by Michael Maloney. MP3 files of the adaptation are available at Hunter's site as well.*

I: Recommended Viewing/Reading Order

You've purchased the DVDs and all of the spinoff titles—so where do you begin? You could start with the films and both TV series, then move on to the comics and novels—Marvel first, then Malibu and so forth. Another option is to go chronologically. Presented below is a suggested viewing/reading order, separated by classic and re-imagined eras, and slightly modified to begin and end with Pierre Boulle's novel and the first two films, thus bringing the story full-circle. (See the Title Index on page 253 for further details.)

CLASSIC ERA

❑ *The Monkey Planet* (Pierre Boulle's source novel)
    –Plus adaptations: Hungarian comic book, BBC Radio 4 *Book at Bedtime* Audio

❑ *Planet of the Apes* (3978)
    –Plus adaptations: Marvel Comics #1-6, Power Records, 1975 British Annual, Manga

❑ *Beneath the Planet of the Apes* (3979—dialog mistakenly sets film in 3955)
    –Plus adaptations: Novelization, Gold Key Comics, Marvel Comics #7-11, Power Records

❑ *A Public Service Announcement From ANSA* (1972—included in 40th Anniversary
    Blu-Ray Collection)

❑ *Escape From the Planet of the Apes* (1973)
    –Plus adaptations: Novelization, Marvel Comics #12-16, Power Records

❑ *The Ape News* (promotional newspaper—1973, during *Escape*)

❑ "Hasslein's Notes" (1973, Mr. Comics—*Revolution on the Planet of the Apes* #3, during *Escape*)

❑ "Little Caesar" (1980s, Mr. Comics—*Revolution on the Planet of the Apes* #3)

❑ "For Human Rights" (1988, Mr. Comics—*Revolution on the Planet of the Apes* #1)

❑ *Conquest of the Planet of the Apes* (1991)
    –Plus adaptations: Novelization, Marvel Comics #17-21

❑ *Future News* (promotional newspaper—1991, during *Conquest*)

❑ "Quitting Time"—*Planet of the Apes* #19 (1991, Adventure Comics—during *Conquest*)

❑ "The Believer" (1991, Mr. Comics—after *Conquest*, cut from *Revolution* miniseries,
    published in *Simian Scrolls* #16)

❑ "People News" (1991, Mr. Comics—*Revolution on the Planet of the Apes* #2, first half of story)

❑ "The End of the World" (1992, Mr. Comics—*Revolution on the Planet of the Apes* #1)

❑ "Lines of Communication" (1992, Mr. Comics—*Revolution on the Planet of the Apes* #2)

❑ "Intelligent Design" (1992, Mr. Comics—*Revolution on the Planet of the Apes* #3)

❑ "Paternal Instinct" (1991, Mr. Comics—*Revolution on the Planet of the Apes* #4)

❑ "Caesar's Journal" (1991-2, Mr. Comics—*Revolution on the Planet of the Apes* #1-2 and #4-6)

❑ "Truth and Consequences" (1992, Mr. Comics—*Revolution on the Planet of the Apes* #4)

❑ "Weapon of Choice" (1992, Mr. Comics—*Revolution on the Planet of the Apes* #5)

❑ "Survival of the Fittest" (1992, Mr. Comics—*Revolution on the Planet of the Apes* #6)

❑ "Countdown Five"—*Planet of the Apes* #9 (1992, Adventure)

❑ "Countdown Four"—*Planet of the Apes* #10 (1992, Adventure)

❑ "Countdown Three"—*Planet of the Apes* #11 (1992, Adventure)

❑ "Countdown Two"—*Planet of the Apes* #12 (1992, Adventure)

❑ "Countdown One"—*Planet of the Apes* #13 (1992, Adventure)

❑ "Countdown Zero"—*Planet of the Apes* #14-17 (1992, Adventure)

❑ "Quest for the Planet of the Apes"—*Planet of the Apes* #22 (1993, Marvel Comics)

❑ *Battle for the Planet of the Apes* (2020)
   –Plus adaptations: Novelization, Marvel Comics #23-28, Power Records

❑ "Terror on the Planet of the Apes"—*Planet of the Apes* #1-4, 6, 8, 11, 13-14, 19-20,
   23 and 26-28 (2070, Marvel)

❑ "The Monkey Planet, Parts 1-4"—*Planet of the Apes* #1-4 (2140, Adventure)

❑ "Loss"—*Planet of the Apes* #5 (2140, Adventure)

❑ *Ape City* #1-4 (2140, Adventure)

❑ "Welcome to Ape City"—*Planet of the Apes* #6 (2140, Adventure)

❑ "Survival of the Fittest"—*Planet of the Apes* #7 (2140, Adventure)

❑ "Here Comes Travellin' Jack"—*Planet of the Apes* #8 (2140, Adventure)

❑ "Changes"—*Planet of the Apes* #9 (2141, Adventure)

❑ "Return to the Forbidden City"—*Planet of the Apes* #10 (2141, Adventure)

❑ "Warriors"—*Planet of the Apes* #11 (2141, Adventure)

❑ "Bells"—*Planet of the Apes* #12 (2141, Adventure)

❑ "Frito & JoJo's X-cellent Adventure"—*Planet of the Apes* #13 (2141, Adventure)

❑ *Ape City*: "Honey, I Shrunk the Apes"—*Planet of the Apes* #13 (2141, Adventure)

❑ *A Day on the Planet of the Apes* annual (2141, Adventure)

❑ *Urchak's Folly* #1-4 (2142, Adventure)

❑ *Blood of the Apes* #1-4 (2142, Adventure)

❑ "Twice Upon a Time"—*Ape Nation* Limited Edition #1 (between 2142 and 2150, Adventure)

❑ *Ape Nation* #1-3 (2150, Adventure)

❑ *Ape Nation*: "Drunken Interlude"—*Planet of the Apes* #13 (2150, Adventure)

❑ *Ape Nation* #4 (2150, Adventure)

❑ "Gorillas in the Mist"—*Planet of the Apes* #18 (2150, Adventure)

❑ "Cowboys and Simians"—*Planet of the Apes* #20 (2150, Adventure)

❑ "The Terror Beneath"—*Planet of the Apes* #21 (2150, Adventure)

❑ "The Land of No Escape"—*Planet of the Apes* #22 (2150, Adventure)

❑ "Final Conquest"—*Planet of the Apes* #23 (2150, Adventure)

❑ "Last Battle"—*Planet of the Apes* #24 (2150, Adventure)

❑ Apeslayer saga—*Planet of the Apes* #23-30 (c. 2200-2212, Marvel UK)

❑ "Evolution's Nightmare"—*Planet of the Apes* #5 (2220, Marvel)

❑ "Ape Shall Not Kill Ape" (2290, Mr. Comics—*Revolution on the Planet of the Apes* #5)

❑ *The Forbidden Zone* #1-4 (2320, Adventure)

❑ . *Planet of the Apes* TV Series, episodes #1-14 (3085)
    –Plus adaptations: Novelizations #1-4, Chad Valley Picture Show

❑ "Hostage"—*Planet of the Apes* TV Series (3085, unfilmed—script available online)

❑ *Planet of the Apes Authorized Edition* #1-3 (3085, Brown Watson Books)

❑ "A Fallen God"—*Planet of the Apes* TV Series (3085, unfilmed—script available online)

❑ *El Planeta de los Simios* #1-7 (3086—comics from Argentina, available online)

❑ *Planet of the Apes—4 Exciting New Adventures* (3086, Power Records, available online)

❑ *Planet of the Apes* telefilms, "old Galen" footage (post-3086, available online)

❑ "Future History Chronicles"—*Planet of the Apes* #12, 15, 17, 24 and 29 (between 3100s and
    3979, Marvel)

❑ *The Sins of the Father* one-shot (3948, Adventure)

❑ "Kingdom on an Island of Apes"—*Planet of the Apes* #9-10 (3975, Marvel)

❑ "Beast on the Planet of the Apes"—*Planet of the Apes* #21 (3975, Marvel)

❑ "People News" (3977, Mr. Comics—*Revolution on the Planet of the Apes* #2, second half of story)

❑ "Catch a Falling Star" (3978, Mr. Comics—*Revolution on the Planet of the Apes* #5)

❑ *Planet of the Apes* (3978)
    –Plus adaptations: Marvel Comics #1-6, Power Records, 1975 British Annual, Manga

❑ *The Ape* (promotional newspaper—3978, during *Planet of the Apes*)

❑ *Return to the Planet of the Apes*, episodes #1-13 (3979)
    –Plus adaptations: Novelizations #1-3

❑ *Beneath the Planet of the Apes* (3979—dialog mistakenly sets film in 3955)
    –Plus adaptations: Novelization, Gold Key Comics, Marvel Comics #7-11, Power Records

❑ *The Ape News/The Mutant News* (promotional newspaper—3979, during *Beneath*)

RE-IMAGINED ERA

❑ *Planet of the Apes* (2029—Tim Burton's film "re-imagining," opening sequence)

❑ *Planet of the Apes: The Fall* (2029-2048, HarperEntertainment)

❑ *Planet of the Apes: The Colony* (post-2048, HarperEntertainment)

❑ *Planet of the Apes* #1: *Force* (5009, HarperEntertainment)

❑ *Planet of the Apes* #2: *Resistance* (5010, HarperEntertainment)

❑ *Dark Horse Extra* #36-38: *Planet of the Apes* (pre-5021, Dark Horse Comics)

❑ *Planet of the Apes* Toys 'R' Us Collector's Comic (pre-5021, Dark Horse)

❑ *Planet of the Apes* (5021—Tim Burton's film "re-imagining," after opening sequence)
    –Plus adaptations: Novelization, Young-Adult Novelization, *Leo's Logbook*, Dark Horse Comics

❑ *Planet of the Apes: The Human War* (5041, Dark Horse)

❑ *Planet of the Apes: Old Gods* (5041, Dark Horse)

❑ *Planet of the Apes: Bloodlines* (5041, Dark Horse)

❑ *Planet of the Apes Sketchbook* (post-5041, Dark Horse—available online)

A TIM BURTON FILM

PLANET
OF THE APES

TWENTIETH CENTURY FOX PRESENTS A ZANUCK COMPANY PRODUCTION

A TIM BURTON FILM 'PLANET OF THE APES' MARK WAHLBERG TIM ROTH HELENA BONHAM CARTER

MICHAEL CLARKE DUNCAN KRIS KRISTOFFERSON ESTELLA WARREN PAUL GIAMATTI SPECIAL MAKE-UP EFFECTS RICK BAKER SPECIAL ANIMATION BY INDUSTRIAL LIGHT & MAGIC

MUSIC BY DANNY ELFMAN COSTUME DESIGNER COLLEEN ATWOOD FILM EDITOR CHRIS LEBENZON, A.C.E. PRODUCTION DESIGNER RICK HEINRICHS DIRECTOR OF PHOTOGRAPHY PHILIPPE ROUSSELOT, AFC/ASC EXECUTIVE PRODUCER RALPH WINTER

PRODUCED BY RICHARD D. ZANUCK BASED ON A NOVEL BY PIERRE BOULLE SCREENPLAY BY WILLIAM BROYLES, JR. AND LAWRENCE KONNER & MARK D. ROSENTHAL DIRECTED BY TIM BURTON

07·27·01   www.planetoftheapes.com

SOUNDTRACK AVAILABLE ON SONY CLASSICAL

II: A Brief History of Time Travel

In the *Planet of the Apes* universe, NASA, ANSA, the U.S. Air Force and other organizations have an amazingly poor track record when it comes to losing spaceships, shuttles, space stations and other spacecraft to time-warps or other unforeseen problems—and inventors creating time machines tend to face similar fates. A seemingly endless string of astronauts, scientists and military personnel have visited eras other than their own, making it difficult to track who departed when, the era to which each traveled and which time-travelers eventually made it home. With apologies to physicist Stephen Hawking, presented below is a brief history of time travel to help you navigate the Hasslein Curve. See the corresponding dates on the main timeline for further details.

SHORTLY AFTER 1871

◆ Asylum proprietor Dr. Foucault, determined to confirm Biblical creationism and disprove Darwin's evolutionary theory, builds a time machine and sends patient Sebastian Thorne to the year 2142—by which time Earth has become ape-controlled. Instead of Thorne, the machine later retrieves Col. Urchak, a silverback gorilla warrior.

BETWEEN 1877 AND 1931

◆ Thomas Edison builds a time machine and travels to the year 3085, where he meets time-lost astronauts Alan Virdon and Pete Burke. The machine later brings Edison home, stranding the others in the future.

LATE 1960s

◆ Dr. Otto Victor Hasslein theorizes a space-time tangent as a means of interstellar travel. His theories involve time, dimensional matrices and infinite regression, depicting the space-time continuum as a series of eight interlocking Möbius strips, made up of "curved time" and "alternative time-tracks." A spaceship, he postulates, could travel great distances at super-fast speeds, with time passing more slowly aboard ship than on Earth. To test this theory, Hasslein drives congressional funding to develop an experimental spacedrive. The theorized space-time tangent is later dubbed a Hasslein Curve in the scientist's honor.

1971

◆ The U.S. Congress approves Hasslein's spacedrive, and the Interstellar Exploration Program (IEP) is created to test it using the space shuttle *Liberty 1*. The president appoints ANSA astronaut George Taylor to spearhead the mission. Fellow astronauts John Landon, Thomas Dodge and Maryann Stewart are assigned to Taylor's team.

FEBRUARY 1972

◆ *Liberty 1* departs Cape Kennedy on a one-way trip to the Betelgeuse Star System, its crew in cryogenic sleep. The ship passes through a fold in space and is propelled to the year 3978. Hasslein's theory is thus proven true.

JULY 14, 1972

◆ George Taylor records a final message to ANSA before joining his crewmates in suspended animation. Due to the effects of time dilation, only six months have passed for Taylor, but on Earth, the date is March 23, 2673.

JULY 1972 TO EARLY 1974

◆ Inventor Derek Zane designs a time machine to retrieve the crew of the *Liberty 1*. Zane calls his invention the Time Displacement Module. The scientific community, however, ignores Zane's research.

NOVEMBER 1972

◆ Unable to reach Taylor, ANSA launches a second ship to find *Liberty 1*, crewed by Donovan "Skipper" Maddox and John Christopher Brent. This ship slips through the Hasslein Curve and is thrown forward to the year 3979.

AFTER 1972

◆ The USNSA sends a ship to locate Taylor's crew as well. This vessel, commanded by an astronaut named Ben, vanishes into a time-warp and is propelled to the year 3978.

APRIL OR MAY 1973

◆ *Liberty 1* splashes down off California's coast. Aboard the shuttle are three chimpanzee "apeonauts" from the future (Drs. Milo, Zira and Cornelius), thrown back in time following Earth's 3979 destruction at Taylor's hands.

AFTER JUNE 1973 .

◆ The U.S. government implements Operation: Hasslein, a shadow program dedicated to developing a time-travel device so an assassin can kill Taylor in the future before he can detonate the Alpha-Omega Bomb.

1974

◆ Derek Zane finishes building his time machine and presents it to Dr. Krigstein, a top-level NASA administrator. When Krigstein scoffs at his theories, Zane tests the machine on his own, propelling himself to the year 3975.

BEFORE 1976

◆ Scientist Dr. Stanton puts forth his controversial "time-thrust" theory. Similar to Hasslein's theory, Stanton's claims humans can propel themselves into the future if they travel fast enough.

AUGUST 6, 1976

◆ Three astronauts (Bill Hudson, Jeff Allen and Judy Franklin) embark on an interstellar mission to test the latest NASA spacecraft, the *Venturer*. Due to the ship's advanced speed, time moves more slowly than on Earth, proving Stanton's theory correct. Within minutes, the ship jumps to 2081, though ship time still reads 1976.

1977

◆ Investigating the disappearance of Derek Zane, Dr. Krigstein finds Zane's plans for the Temporal Displacement Module, which he deems revolutionary. NASA spends nine months building its own model, the *Chronos I*, to rescue the inventor. Two "tempunauts," Mara Winston and Jackson Brock, are chosen for the mission.

NOVEMBER 30, 1977

◆ The tempunauts board *Chronos I* at the NASA Time Research Labs on Long Island, New York, and vanish into the future, reappearing in 3977. Unable to broadcast radio signals through time, the duo are entirely on their own.

DECEMBER 1977

◆ Derek Zane returns from the future, along with Mara Winston and a chimp named Faron, but feels like a misfit in his own era. Missing his future wife, Andrea, he builds another time machine and returns to the 40th century.

1970s

◆ An ambitious Nazi named Trang steals an experimental NASA craft and travels to the year 3085 to subjugate Earth. The USAF spaceship *Blue Star* hits an electrical storm near Alpha Centauri and is propelled forward to the same year. Two months after *Blue Star*'s disappearance, ANSA launches *Probe Six*, assigning astronauts Alan J. Virdon, Peter J. Burke and "Jonesy" on a long-range reconnaissance mission to circumnavigate the Belt of Orion.

AUGUST 19, 1980

◆ *Probe Six* encounters radioactive turbulence near Alpha Centauri, causing a loss of ship control. Jonesy activates a homing device, redirecting *Probe Six* to Earth—and the ship is propelled to the year 3085, where it crashes. Jonesy dies on impact, but Virdon and Burke survive, eventually finding a way back to their own time.

AFTER AUGUST 1980

◆ Pete Burke's friend Verina and two other astronauts are assigned a mission for ANSA. Their vessel encounters an anomaly and is thrust forward to the year 3085. Eventually, Verina manages to return home.

MID TO LATE 1980s

◆ The United States launches a spaceship containing four astronauts: Taylor, Thomas, LaFever and Bengsten. Lost in a time warp, the ship reappears in the 3070s, where the crew is executed by a gorilla named Urko. Another spaceship is time-lost during this period as well, arriving sometime after 3086.

BEFORE 1990

◆ The U.S. government creates the top-secret Vindicator Project, intended to prevent apes from dominating Earth. A specialized flying vehicle, energized by a power crystal, is built to carry six covert operatives into the future.

1990

◆ Astronaut Jo Taylor (George Taylor's daughter) volunteers for the Vindicator Project, as does a man known as MX, and four convicted killers (Scab, Devon, Moriah and π [*pi*]) are offered amnesty for taking part as well. Their objective: to kill as many apes as possible, thereby giving humans a fighting chance to regain dominancy.

BEFORE 1991

◆ Heeding the apeonauts' warning regarding Earth's future destruction, mankind launches a colony ship carrying 40 females and 10 males into space in suspended animation, intending to preserve the species on another planet. The ship enters a Hasslein Curve, however, and is propelled to approximately 5000 A.D.

1991

◆ Astronauts James Norvell, August Anne Burrows and Ken Flip undertake the first U.S. manned orbit of Mars. Due to equipment malfunction, the team loses contact with Earth for the duration of their 18-month mission, and are thus unaware of Caesar's rebellion and the subsequent nuclear war.

MID TO LATE 1992

◆ Norvell's team prepares to return home. A systems failure crashes the ship in the Mississippi River, stranding the astronauts on ape-controlled Earth. Jealous of Norvell's relationship with Burrows, Flip kills him, then commits suicide. Burrows makes her way to a cave in the Forbidden Zone and leads a colony of human rebels.

FEBRUARY 14, 2029

◆ When USAF space station *Oberon* encounters an ion storm, a gengineered chimp pod pilot named Pericles is sent to investigate but vanishes in the anomaly. Pilot Leo Davidson goes after him and disappears as well. Both pods, and the *Oberon*, are propelled to the planet Ashlar—the station in the present day, the pods in the year 5021.

AFTER 2029

◆ A band of human and ape fugitives from the planet Ashlar arrive on Earth, having traversed a space-time anomaly in the *Oberon*'s remaining pods. General Thade, a ruthless military leader from Ashlar, arrives in another pod and becomes an honored military icon among Earth's apes. Davidson later returns home to find an ape-controlled Earth.

AUGUST 6, 2081

◆ The *Venturer* crew reads their ship's chronometer after take-off. Due to time dilation, it still seems like 1976 to them, but the clock reads 2081. The *Venturer* hits a strange energy distortion and jumps forward to the year 3979.

AUGUST 6, 2109

◆ A NASA spaceship commanded by Ronald Brent lifts off from California's Mojave Desert. Caught in a time-warp, the ship is transported to the early 3960s.

DECEMBER 4, 2125

◆ NASA launches the spaceship *Cassiopeia*, its crew of four (Ulysses, Martinez, Romulus and Sophie) in cryogenic sleep during the voyage. Entering a time-warp, the ship jumps ahead to the year 3889.

2140

◆ The Vindicator team arrives from the past. After killing 57 apes, the assassins discover their ship's power crystal missing, forcing them to abort their mission and instead focus on locating the crystal for the return voyage.

2142

◆ Asylum patient Sebastian Thorne arrives in an ape-controlled future and joins forces with a human religious sect, the Taylorites, to defeat a gorilla warrior known as Col. Urchak. Dr. Foucault tries to retrieve Thorne with his time machine, but the device pulls Urchak back instead, stranding the ape in the Victorian era.

2150

◆ A Tenctonese refugee ship experiences equipment failure and breaks away from the rest of its fleet headed for Earth to seek sanctuary [as seen in the *Alien Nation* TV series]. Sucked into a black hole, the ship enters a space-time warp, landing on the Planet of the Apes. Eventually, the ship lifts off again and returns to its own reality.

AFTER 2150

◆ Gorilla guards JoJo and Frito undertake a trip through time, the details of which remain unrecorded.

MARCH 23, 2673

◆ Astronaut George Taylor records a message to ANSA before joining his *Liberty 1* crewmates in suspended animation. Due to the effects of time dilation, it still seems like 1972 for Taylor, though 700 years have passed on Earth.

SHORTLY BEFORE 3075

◆ A 20th-century spaceship crashes near Central City. Gorillas capture four survivors (Taylor, Thomas, LaFever and Bengsten). Security Chief Urko realizes they have greater intelligence and abilities than local humans, as well as a greater sense of independence, and orders them killed so they cannot spread their influence.

MARCH 21, 3085

◆ ANSA spacecraft *Probe Six*, crewed by Col. Alan J. Virdon, Major Peter J. Burke and a man called Jonesy, nears its final destination. The ship's internal chronometer is damaged in flight and stops functioning on this date.

JUNE 14, 3085

◆ *Probe Six* crashes near the village of Chalo. Virdon and Burke survive, but Jonesy is killed on impact. Captured by apes, the astronauts befriend a chimp named Galen, who saves their lives and ends up a fellow fugitive.

3085, AFTER JUNE 18

◆ Verina, an ANSA astronaut and friend of Pete Burke, arrives via time-warp. Her vessel is mostly undamaged, but her shipmates both die en route. She, Burke and Virdon fix her ship, but a fuel leak allows only one occupant for the trip home. Verina returns to her own century, promising to come back for them if she can.

3086

◆ The *Blue Star*, launched in the 1970s, crashes in an ape village; the corrupt Prefect Arpo tries to repair the ship to conquer Central City, but Burke and Virdon rig it to explode when he fires its missiles. Thomas Edison arrives in a time machine that same year, returning to the past before the fugitives can use the device themselves. Trang, a 20th-century Nazi with a time-traveling airship full of armored vehicles, attempts to subjugate both ape and humankind.

AFTER 3086

◆ Virdon and Burke locate a working computer in the ruins of an ancient city and discover a way to return to space. Galen remains in his own era, knowing he'd be out of place in their human-led world. Years later, the chimp befriends another human time-traveler and relates his past adventures with the two astronauts.

OCTOBER 18, 3889

◆ The *Cassiopeia*, a NASA spaceship lost in a time-warp in 2125, crashes in the Forbidden Zone. The computer awakens three crewmembers—Ulysses, Romulus and Sophie—but a fourth, Martinez, dies during the voyage.

NOVEMBER 23, 3955

◆ An ANSA space shuttle containing John Brent and Donovan "Skipper" Maddox nears its final destination after entering the Hasslein Curve in 1973. Damage to the ship causes the external chronometer to stop functioning at 3955.

EARLY 3960s

◆ A NASA spacecraft, launched in 2109, crashes in the Forbidden Zone. Astronaut Ronald Brent nearly dies on impact, but a tribe of primitive humans saves his life.

3975

◆ Inventor Derek Zane arrives from the year 1974, using a time-machine he built in an effort to rescue the lost *Liberty 1* crew. The crash demolishes the device, stranding Zane in the future.

3977

◆ *Chronos 1*, a NASA-built time machine based on Zane's plans, shows up to rescue the inventor. Damaged on impact, the device explodes, leaving its "tempunaut" occupants, Mara Winston and Jackson Brock, unable to return home. Mara meets Zane and his chimp friend Faron, and the trio locate another way to return to the past.

NOVEMBER 25, 3978

◆ The *Liberty 1*, an ANSA shuttle lost in 1972, crashes in the Forbidden Zone's Dead Lake. Astronauts George Taylor, John Landon and Thomas Dodge make it to shore, but Maryann Stewart dies during the voyage following an air leak from a cracked cryogenic chamber. Dodge and Landon are later killed by apes, leaving Taylor the last survivor.

LATE 3978

◆ An astronaut named Ben, sent by USNSA to rescue the *Liberty 1* crew, is stranded in this era as well.

AUGUST 6, 3979

◆ The *Venturer*, an interstellar NASA spacecraft launched in 1976, splashes down in a lake near New York. Its three occupants (Bill Hudson, Jeff Allen and Judy Franklin) all survive the crash.

MID TO LATE 3979

◆ Three chimp scientists (Milo, Zira and Cornelius) repair the *Liberty 1* and get the vessel into orbit. Meanwhile, Brent's and Maddox's shuttle crashes in the desert, fatally wounding Maddox. Brent survives, only to die shortly before the Alpha-Omega Bomb's detonation. An assassin from the past attempts (and presumably fails) to kill Taylor before he can detonate the bomb. The explosion causes a fold in space-time, creating the Hasslein Curve that throws *Liberty 1* back to 1973—paradoxically spawning the very anomaly that carried it here in the first place.

5000

◆ A time-lost colony spaceship—launched in the 20th century to preserve humanity following the apeonauts' warning of Earth's destruction—crash-lands on what the crew believes to be a distant planet, but is actually Earth, in one-time New Orleans. There, the survivors must ally with the apes against a mutated race of sentient tigers.

NOVEMBER 30, 5021

◆ Thrown through space-time by an ion storm surrounding a black hole, USAF *Oberon* pilot Leo Davidson crashes his one-man shuttle, the *Delta Pod*, on the planet Ashlar. The shuttle is decimated on impact.

DECEMBER 3, 5021

◆ Pericles, Davidson's chimp pilot protégé aboard the *Oberon*, arrives in the *Alpha Pod*, which the human pilot then uses to get home again. Davidson leaves Pericles in the care of an Ashlar chimp named Ari.

WINTER 5041

◆ A band of human and simian fugitives encounter descendants of the *Oberon* crew on Ashlar. The military tries to capture them, but the rebels escape in the station's remaining pods, carried to Earth by the ion storm. General Thade, a ruthless military leader, follows in another pod and becomes an honored military icon among Earth's apes.

III: TITLE INDEX
Preserving the Sacred Scrolls

The following movies, television series and other tales were exhaustively mined while creating this timeline:

THEATRICAL FILMS (20th Century Fox Film Corp.)

PRODUCED

TITLE	YEAR	WRITER(S)	DIRECTOR
Planet of the Apes	1968	Michael Wilson, Rod Serling & John T. Kelly (early draft by Charles Eastman)	Franklin J. Schaffner
Beneath the Planet of the Apes (early title: Planet of the Apes Revisited)	1970	Paul Dehn & Mort Abrahams	Ted Post
Escape from the Planet of the Apes (early title: The Secret of the Planet of the Apes)	1971	Paul Dehn	Don Taylor
Conquest of the Planet of the Apes [1]	1972	Paul Dehn	J. Lee Thompson
Battle for the Planet of the Apes [2] (early titles: Epic of the Planet of the Apes, Colonization of the Planet of the Apes)	1973	Paul Dehn, John William Corrington & Joyce Hooper Corrington	J. Lee Thompson
Planet of the Apes (early title: The Visitor)	2001	William Broyles Jr., Lawrence Konner & Mark Rosenthal	Tim Burton

UNPRODUCED

TITLE	YEAR	WRITER(S)	DIRECTOR
Planet of the Men	1970	Pierre Boulle	(unknown)
Planet of the Apes	1992	Peter Jackson & Fran Walsh	Peter Jackson
Return of the Apes	1996	Terry Hayes	Philip Noyce
Return to the Planet of the Apes	1998	Adam Rifkin; story by Cassian Elwes and Adam Rifkin	Adam Rifkin
Planet of the Apes	1998	Sam Hamm	Chris Columbus
Planet of the Apes	1998	(unknown)	James Cameron

ANNOUNCED

TITLE	YEAR	WRITER(S)	DIRECTOR
Genesis: Apes (early title: Planet of the Apes: Genesis)	2009 or later	Rick Jaffa & Amanda Silver	Scott Frank

NOTE: *Eastman partially rewrote Serling's screenplay for the first film; this draft was discarded but later reprinted in* The Legend of the Planet of the Apes. *Kelly's contribution was noted in* Planet of the Apes as American Myth. *Pierre Boulle wrote a script for the second film entitled* Planet of the Men, *which was rejected. Jackson's intended film, as documented in* Peter Jackson: A Film-Maker's Journey, *would have been a sequel to the Roddy McDowall films, while Hayes, Rifkin and Hamm would have rebooted the series. The Hayes and Hamm projects would have involved Oliver Stone as executive producer and Arnold Schwarzenegger as lead actor. Several of these unused scripts are available online. In 1998, Coming Attractions posted a sequel outline reported to have been Cameron's, but this is believed to have been a hoax.* Planet of the Apes: Genesis *was first announced in August 2008 at ProductionWeekly.com, to be directed by Scott Frank and produced by Richard Zanuk and Ralph Winter; the title was later changed, as revealed at Chud.com, to* Genesis: Apes. *The film will be a remake of* Conquest of the Planet of the Apes, *revealing the story of Caesar's rebellion, but set in the modern day.*

[1] An alternate, "unrated" cut of *Conquest of the Planet of the Apes*, containing 12 minutes of new footage, was released on Blu-Ray in 2008.

[2] An extended cut of *Battle of the Planet of the Apes*, containing 10 minutes of new footage, was released on DVD in 2006, and previously on a Japanese laserdisc.

TELEVISION SERIES: *PLANET OF THE APES*

WEEKLY EPISODES (20th Century Fox Television / CBS-TV)

EPISODE	AIRDATE	WRITER(S)	DIRECTOR
1. "Escape from Tomorrow"	Sept. 13, 1974	Art Wallace; early drafts by Rod Serling	Don Weis
2. "The Gladiators"	Sept. 20, 1974	Art Wallace	Don McDougall
3. "The Trap"	Sept. 27, 1974	Edward J. Lakso	Arnold Laven
4. "The Good Seeds"	Oct. 4, 1974	Robert W. Lenski	Don Weis
5. "The Legacy" (early title: "Second Family")	Oct. 11, 1974	Robert Hamner	Bernard McEveety
6. "Tomorrow's Tide"	Oct. 21, 1974	Robert W. Lenski	Don McDougall
7. "The Surgeon"	Oct. 28, 1974	Barry Oringer	Arnold Laven
8. "The Deception"	Nov. 1, 1974	Anthony Lawrence, Joe Ruby & Ken Spears	Don McDougall
9. "The Horse Race"	Nov. 8, 1974	David P. Lewis & Booker Bradshaw	Jack Starrett
10. "The Interrogation"	Nov. 15, 1974	Richard Collins	Alf Kjellin
11. "The Tyrant"	Nov. 22, 1974	William Black	Ralph Senensky
12. "The Cure"	Nov. 29, 1974	Edward J. Lakso	Bernard McEveety
13. "The Liberator" (early title: "The Conqueror")	N/A	Howard Dimsdale	Arnold Laven
14. "Up Above the World So High"	Dec. 6, 1974	Arthur Browne, Jr. & Shimon Wincelberg	John Meredyth Lucas

UNPRODUCED

EPISODE	AIRDATE	WRITER	DIRECTOR
"Episode One"	N/A	Rod Serling	N/A
"Episode Two"	N/A	Rod Serling	N/A
"Hostage"	N/A	Stephen Kandel	N/A
"A Fallen God"	N/A	Anthony Lawrence	N/A
"The Trek"	N/A	Jim Byrnes	N/A
"Freedom Road"	N/A	Arthur Rowe	N/A
"The Mine"	N/A	Paul Savage	N/A
"The Trial"	N/A	Edward J. Lasko	N/A

TELEFILMS (20th Century Fox Television / ABC-TV)

TELEFILM	SYNDICATED	EPISODES RE-EDITED
Back to the Planet of the Apes (early title: *The New Planet of the Apes*)	Nov. 1980	"Escape from Tomorrow" & "The Trap"
The Forgotten City of the Planet of the Apes	Nov. 1980	"The Gladiators" & "The Legacy"
Treachery and Greed on the Planet of the Apes	Nov. 1980	"The Horse Race" & "The Tyrant"
Life, Liberty and Pursuit on the Planet of the Apes	Nov. 1980	"The Surgeon" & "The Interrogation"
Farewell to the Planet of the Apes	Nov. 1980	"Tomorrow's Tide" & "Up Above The World So High"

NOTE: *"The Liberator" never aired in the United States during the series' initial run, though it did run in Europe and was eventually syndicated on Sci-Fi Channel and other networks in the 1990s. The scripts to "Hostage" and "A Fallen God" are available online at Hunter Goatley's* Planet of the Apes *Archive; synopsis of the other four unfilmed episodes were included in the series bible, reprinted in* Simian Scrolls *issue #12. Rod Serling wrote two pilot scripts ("Episode One" and "Episode Two") that greatly differed from the aired versions. Ten episodes were re-edited into telefilms, with newly produced framing sequences featuring Roddy McDowall as Galen. These framing sequences were not included on the TV series' DVD release, but can be viewed online at Kassidy Rae's* Planet of the Apes: The Television Series *website. An animated version of this series was briefly discussed in the 1980s but never produced; a concept drawing by artist Jack Kirby, reproduced in* The Jack Kirby Collector *and later in* Simian Scrolls #6, *shows that it would have featured Virdon and Burke, along with a female "blonde companion of astronauts" and Toomak, a "human slave boy."*

ANIMATED SERIES: RETURN TO THE PLANET OF THE APES

WEEKLY EPISODES
(20th Century Fox Television / NBC-TV, DePatie-Freleng Enterprises)

EPISODE	AIRDATE	WRITER(S)	DIRECTOR
1. "Flames of Doom"	Sept. 6, 1975	Larry Spiegel	Doug Wildey
2. "Escape from Ape City"	Sept. 13, 1975	Larry Spiegel	Doug Wildey
3. "The Unearthly Prophecy" (early title: "A Date With Judy")	Oct. 4, 1975	Jack Kaplan & John Barnett	Doug Wildey
4. "Tunnel of Fear"	Sept. 27, 1975	Larry Spiegel	Doug Wildey
5. "Lagoon of Peril"	Sept. 20, 1975	J.C. Strong	Doug Wildey
6. "Terror on Ice Mountain"	Nov. 22, 1975	Bruce Shelly	Doug Wildey
7. "River of Flames"	Nov. 29, 1975	Jack Kaplan & John Barnett	Doug Wildey
8. "Screaming Wings"	Oct. 11, 1975	Jack Kaplan & John Barnett	Doug Wildey
9. "Trail to the Unknown"	Oct. 18, 1975	Larry Spiegel	Doug Wildey
10. "Attack from the Clouds"	Oct. 25, 1975	Larry Spiegel	Doug Wildey
11. "Mission of Mercy"	Nov. 1, 1975	Larry Spiegel	Doug Wildey
12. "Invasion of the Underdwellers"	Nov. 8, 1975	J.C. Strong	Doug Wildey
13. "Battle of the Titans"	Nov. 15, 1975	Bruce Shelly	Doug Wildey

UNPRODUCED

EPISODE	AIRDATE	WRITER(S)	DIRECTOR
14. *(title unknown)*	N/A	*(unknown)*	Doug Wildey
15. *(title unknown)*	N/A	*(unknown)*	Doug Wildey
16. *(title unknown)*	N/A	*(unknown)*	Doug Wildey

NOTE: The episodes were aired on television out of their proper order. Planet of the Apes Revisited *mentions the unfilmed entries, which Wildey conceived but never scripted. Some sources, such as* Planet of the Apes: An Unofficial Companion, *have erroneously cited "A Date With Judy" as an unfilmed episode, due to William Rostler's use of an early-draft title for "The Unearthly Prophecy" in that episode's novelization.*

SHORT FILM

BLU-RAY EXCLUSIVE (20th Century Fox)

TITLE	DATE	WRITER	DIRECTOR
A Public Service Announcement From ANSA	2008	*(unknown)*	*(unknown)*

NOTE: This six-minute "fake documentary," detailing the history of ANSA and Liberty 1, *is included in high-definition (HD) on the individual Blu-Ray release of* Planet of the Apes, *as well as in the* Planet of the Apes 40th Anniversary Collection. *No writer or director credits are provided for the production.*

NOVELIZATIONS

CLASSIC FILMS

TITLE	AUTHOR	YEAR	FILM ADAPTED	PUBLISHER
Beneath the Planet of the Apes	Michael Avallone	1970	Beneath the Planet of the Apes	Bantam Books
Escape from the Planet of the Apes	Jerry Pournelle	1973	Escape from the Planet of the Apes	Award Books
Conquest of the Planet of the Apes	John Jakes	1974	Conquest of the Planet of the Apes	Award Books
Battle for the Planet of the Apes	David Gerrold	1973	Battle for the Planet of the Apes	Award Books

LIVE-ACTION TV SERIES

TITLE	AUTHOR	YEAR	EPISODES ADAPTED	PUBLISHER
Planet of the Apes #1: Man the Fugitive	George Alec Effinger	1974	"The Cure" & "The Good Seeds"	Award Books
Planet of the Apes #2: Escape to Tomorrow	George Alec Effinger	1974	"The Surgeon" & "The Deception"	Award Books
Planet of the Apes #3: Journey Into Terror	George Alec Effinger	1974	"The Legacy" & "The Horse Race"	Award Books
Planet of the Apes #4: Lord of the Apes	George Alec Effinger	1974	"The Tyrant" & "The Gladiators"	Award Books

ANIMATED TV SERIES

TITLE	AUTHOR	YEAR	EPISODES ADAPTED	PUBLISHER
Return to the Planet of the Apes #1: Visions from Nowhere	William Rostler (as William Arrow)	1976	"Flames of Doom," "Escape from Ape City" & "The Unearthly Prophecy"	Ballantine Books
Return to the Planet of the Apes #2: Escape from Terror Lagoon	Donald J. Pfeil (as William Arrow)	1976	"Tunnel of Fear," "Lagoon of Peril" & "Terror on Ice Mountain"	Ballantine Books
Return to the Planet of the Apes #3: Man, the Hunted Animal	William Rostler (as William Arrow)	1976	"River of Flames," "Screaming Wings" & "Trail to the Unknown"	Ballantine Books

TIM BURTON'S "RE-IMAGINED" FILM

TITLE	AUTHOR	YEAR	FILM ADAPTED	PUBLISHER
Planet of the Apes	William T. Quick	2001	Planet of the Apes	HarperEntertainment
Planet of the Apes (young adult)	John Whitman	2001	Planet of the Apes	HarperEntertainment
Leo's Logbook: A Captain's Days in Captivity	Benjamin Athens	2001	Planet of the Apes	HarperEntertainment

NOTE: According to Films Into Books, Keith Laumer was first hired to novelize Beneath; Avallone was offered the job when Laumer backed out.

COMIC BOOKS (Marvel Comics)

U.S. MONTHLY SERIES: ORIGINAL STORIES

ISSUE/DATE	TITLE	WRITER(S)	ARTIST(S)
1. Aug. 1974	"Terror on the Planet of the Apes: The Lawgiver / Fugitives on the Planet of the Apes"	Doug Moench & Gerry Conway	Mike Ploog
2. Oct. 1974	"Terror on the Planet of the Apes: The Forbidden Zone of Forgotten Horrors / Lick the Sky Crimson"	Doug Moench	Mike Ploog
3. Dec. 1974	"Terror on the Planet of the Apes: Spawn of the Mutant Pits / The Abomination Arena"	Doug Moench	Mike Ploog & Frank Chiaramonte
4. Jan. 1975	"Terror on the Planet of the Apes: A Riverboat Named *Simian* / Gunpowder Julius"	Doug Moench	Mike Ploog & Frank Chiaramonte
5. Feb. 1975	"Evolution's Nightmare"	Doug Moench	Ed Hannigan & Jim Mooney
6. Mar. 1975	"Terror on the Planet of the Apes: Malagueña Beyond a Zone Forbidden"	Doug Moench	Mike Ploog
8. May 1975	"Terror on the Planet of the Apes: The Planet Inheritors"	Doug Moench	Mike Ploog
9. Jun. 1975	"Kingdom on an Island of Apes: The Trip / Arrival"	Doug Moench	Rico Rival
10. Jul. 1975	"Kingdom on an Island of Apes: The City / The Island Out of Time / Battle"	Doug Moench	Rico Rival
11. Aug. 1975	"Terror on the Planet of the Apes: When the Lawgiver Returns"	Doug Moench	Mike Ploog
12. Sep. 1975	"Future History Chronicles I: City of Nomads"	Doug Moench	Tom Sutton
13. Oct. 1975	"Terror on the Planet of the Apes, Phase 2: The Magick-Man's Last Gasp Purple Light Show"	Doug Moench	Mike Ploog
14. Nov. 1975	"Terror on the Planet of the Apes, Phase 2: Up the Nose-Tube to Monkey-Trash"	Doug Moench	Mike Ploog
15. Dec. 1975	"Future History Chronicles II: Dreamer in Emerald Silence"	Doug Moench	Tom Sutton
17. Feb. 1976	"Future History Chronicles III: Graveyard of Lost Cities"	Doug Moench	Tom Sutton
19. Apr. 1976	"Terror on the Planet of the Apes, Phase 2: Demons of the *Psychedrome*"	Doug Moench	Mike Ploog & Tom Sutton
20. May 1976	"Terror on the Planet of the Apes, Phase 2: Society of the *Psychedrome*"	Doug Moench	Tom Sutton
21. Jun. 1976	"Beast on the Planet of the Apes"	Doug Moench	Herb Trimpe, Dan Adkins & Sal Trapani
22. Jul. 1976	"Quest for the Planet of the Apes: Seeds of Future Deaths / The Keeper of Future Death"	Doug Moench	Rico Rival & Alfredo Alcala
23. Aug. 1976	"Terror on the Planet of the Apes, Phase 2: Messiah of Monkey Demons"	Doug Moench	Tom Sutton
24. Sept. 1976	"Future History Chronicles IV: The Shadows of Haunted Cathedraulus"	Doug Moench	Tom Sutton
26. Nov. 1976	"Terror on the Planet of the Apes, Phase 2: North Lands"	Doug Moench	Herb Trimpe, Virgilio Redondo & Rudy Mesina
27. Dec. 1976	"Terror on the Planet of the Apes, Phase 2: Apes of Iron"	Doug Moench	Herb Trimpe
28. Jan. 1977	"Terror on the Planet of the Apes, Phase 2: Revolt of the Gorilliods"	Doug Moench	Herb Trimpe & Virgilio Redondo
29. Feb. 1977	"Future History Chronicles V: To Race the Death-Winds"	Doug Moench	Tom Sutton

U.S. MONTHLY SERIES: FILM ADAPTATIONS

ISSUES / FILM	WRITER	ARTIST(S)
Planet of the Apes Issue 1—Chapter 1: Untitled Issue 2—Chapter 2: "World of Captive Humans" Issue 3—Chapter 3: "Manhunt" Issue 4—Chapter 4: "Trial" Issue 5—Chapter 5: "Into the Forbidden Zone" Issue 6—Chapter 6: "The Secret"	Doug Moench	George Tuska & Mike Esposito
Beneath the Planet of the Apes Issue 7—Chapter 1: Untitled / Chapter 2: "Enslaved" Issue 8—Chapter 3: "The Warhead Messiah" Issue 9—Chapter 4: "The Horror Inquisition" Issue 10—Chapter 5: "The Children of the Bomb" Issue 11—Chapter 6: "The Hell of Holocaust"	Doug Moench	Alfredo Alcala
Escape from the Planet of the Apes Issue 12—Chapter 1: "Upward to the Earth" Issue 13—Chapter 2: "Strangers in a Stranger Land" Issue 14—Chapter 3: "Trouble in Paradise Lost" Issue 15—Chapter 4: "In the Cradle of a Father's Sins" Issue 16—Chapter 5: "When the Calliope Cries Death"/ Chapter 6: "But Who Shall Inherit the Meek?"	Doug Moench	Rico Rival
Conquest of the Planet of the Apes Issue 17—Chapter 1: "Slaves" Issue 18—Chapter 2: "Rites of Bondage"/ Chapter 3: "To Serve the Slayer" Issue 19—Chapter 4: "The Savage is King" Issue 20—Chapter 5: "Army of Slaves" Issue 21—Chapter 6: "Hail Caesar! Hail the King!"	Doug Moench	Alfredo Alcala
Battle for the Planet of the Apes Issue 23—Chapter 1: "The Weapons Shop of Paradise" Issue 24—Chapter 2: "The Doomsday Spawn" Issue 25—Chapter 3: "A Tale of Mutant Hate"/ Chapter 4: "The War Machines" Issue 26—Chapter 5: "Assault on Paradise" Issue 27—Chapter 6: "Conquest of Blood" Issue 28—Chapter 7: "Tremor of Doom"	Doug Moench	Vicente Alcazar, Sonny Trinidad, Alfredo Alcala, Yong Montano, Dino Castrillo, Virgilio Redondo, Michele Brand & Marshall Rogers

U.K. WEEKLY SERIES: APESLAYER STORYLINE

ISSUE/DATE	TITLE	WRITER(S)	ARTISTS
23. Mar. 29, 1975	"Prologue: Future Imperfect"	Gerry Conway & Roy Thomas	Neal Adams & Frank Monte
24. Apr. 5, 1975	"The Birth of Apeslayer"	Gerry Conway & Roy Thomas	Howard Chaykin & Frank Monte
25. Apr. 12, 1975	"The Sirens of 7th Avenue"	Gerry Conway	Howard Chaykin & Frank McLaughlin
26. Apr. 19, 1975	"Death in the Ape-Pit"	Gerry Conway	Howard Chaykin & Frank McLaughlin
27. Apr. 26, 1975	"The Museum of Terror"	Marv Wolfman	Herb Trimpe & Frank Giacoia
28. May 3, 1975	"Airport of Death"	Marv Wolfman	Herb Trimpe & Frank Giacoia
29. May 10, 1975	"The Mutant Slayers"	Don McGregor	Herb Trimpe & Yolande Pijcke
30. May 17, 1975	"Apeslayer Dies at Dawn"	*(writer uncredited)*	*(artist uncredited)*

UNPUBLISHED

ISSUE/DATE	TITLE	WRITER	ARTIST
N/A	"Future History Chronicles VI: The Captive of the Canals"	Doug Moench	Tom Sutton (assigned)
N/A	"Terror on the Planet of the Apes, Phase 2: To Meet the Makers"	Doug Moench	Herb Trimpe (assigned)
N/A	(title unknown—story of a chimp couple, Viraga and Julius)	Doug Moench	Sonny Trinidad (assigned) [1]
N/A	(title unknown—King Kong homage)	Doug Moench	(no artist assigned)
N/A (conceived to span 8-10 issues)	"Journey to the Planet of the Apes" (early title: "Return to the Planet of the Apes")	Doug Moench	Val Mayerik (assigned) [2]
N/A (conceived to span multiple issues)	"Beyond the Planet of the Apes"	Doug Moench	(no artist assigned)

NOTE: Issues #7, 16, 18 and 25 contained no original stories—only movie adaptations. Issues #1-4 of "Terror on the Planet of the Apes" were reprinted in 1991 by Malibu Graphics as a four-issue miniseries. Malibu also reprinted Marvel's first three film adaptations. In addition, Marvel colorized and reprinted the first two film adaptations as an 11-issue series entitled Adventures on the Planet of the Apes. The Apeslayer storyline, adapted from Marvel's Killraven series, appeared in Marvel UK's weekly Planet of the Apes comic—all other U.K. issues reprinted material already published in the U.S. version, though some stories contained additional pages or individual panels not included in the U.S. versions. Details of Doug Moench's unpublished storylines were provided by the author himself.

[1] Moench no longer has a copy of the Viraga script, and does not recall the story's title. Although Trinidad's name appears on a surviving page of unpublished artwork, his son, Norman Trinidad, maintains that his father did not illustrate it.

[2] A page of Mayerik's artwork may have been repurposed as the cover for issue #117 of Marvel's UK Planet of the Apes series.

COMIC BOOK (Gold Key / Western Publishing)

FILM ADAPTATION: *BENEATH THE PLANET OF THE APES*

PUBLICATION	WRITER / ARTIST	YEAR
Beneath the Planet of the Apes	(unknown)	1970

NOTE: As was common when this adaptation was published, no creator credits were provided.

MANGA COMICS

FILM ADAPTATIONS: *SARU NO WAKUSEI* ("PLANET OF MONKEYS")

PUBLICATION	WRITER / ARTIST	YEAR
Bouken Ou Bessatsu	Jôji Enami	April 1968
Tengoku Zôkan	Minoru Kuroda	1970s

NOTE: These adaptations of the first film were released only in Japan, and never in English. The Kuroda publication date is unknown.

SPANISH-LANGUAGE COMIC BOOKS
(Editorial Mo.Pa.Sa. / Editorial Tynset S.A)

MONTHLY SERIES: *EL PLANETA DE LOS SIMIOS*

ISSUE/DATE	TITLE	WRITER(S)	ARTIST(S)
1. 1977	"The Wandering Jew"	Jorge Claudio Morhain	Sergio Alejandro Mulko
2. 1977	"New Life…on the Old Planet"	Jorge Claudio Morhain	Sergio Alejandro Mulko
	"Depth"	Jorge Claudio Morhain	Sergio Alejandro Mulko
3. 1977	"The Beach of Time"	Jorge Claudio Morhain	Sergio Alejandro Mulko
4. 1977	"Ultrasonic"	Jorge Claudio Morhain	Sergio Alejandro Mulko
5. 1977	"The Star Gods"	Ricardo Barreiro	T. Toledo
	"The Master of the Forests"	Ricardo Barreiro	T. Toledo
6. 1977	"The Zombies"	Jorge Claudio Morhain	Sergio Alejandro Mulko
7. 1977	"The Circus"	Jorge Claudio Morhain	Sergio Alejandro Mulko
	"Rockets"	Jorge Claudio Morhain	Sergio Alejandro Mulko

UNPUBLISHED

ISSUE/DATE	TITLE	WRITER	ARTIST
N/A	"The Killer"	Jorge Claudio Morhain	*(no artist assigned)*
N/A	"Cain"	Jorge Claudio Morhain	*(no artist assigned)*
N/A	"Encounter with Edison"	Jorge Claudio Morhain	*(no artist assigned)*
N/A	"The Archeologist"	Jorge Claudio Morhain	*(no artist assigned)*
N/A	"The Queen"	Jorge Claudio Morhain	*(no artist assigned)*

NOTE: This series, based on the TV show, was published only in Argentina. Fan-produced English translations can be found at Kassidy Rae's Planet of the Apes: The Television Series Website. *The seventh issue was numbered "1" on the cover because the company, in an effort to avoid legal problems, changed its name to Editorial Tynset S.A. Details of Morhain's unpublished storylines were provided by the author himself.*

BRITISH HARDCOVER ANNUALS (Brown Watson Books)

PLANET OF THE APES (AUTHORISED EDITION)

1975 ANNUAL	1976 ANNUAL	1977 ANNUAL
Short story: *Planet of the Apes* (film adaptation)	Short story: "Galen's Guerrillas"	Comic strip: "Blow for Blow"
Comic strip: "Journey Into Terror"	Short story: "From Out of the Past"	Short story: "The Prophet"
Short story: "A Promise Kept"	Comic strip: "Pit of Doom"	Comic strip: "Breakout"
Comic strip: "When the Earth Shakes"	Short story: "The Captive"	Short story: "The Arrival"
Short story: "The Scavengers"	Short story: "Raiding Party"	Short story: "Power Play"
Short story: "Swamped"	Comic strip: "Ship of Fools"	Comic strip: "From Out of the Sky"

NOTE: No writer or artist credits are available for the above tales, though John Bolton and Oli Frey are known to have been among the artists involved.

COMIC BOOKS (Adventure Comics / Malibu Graphics)

	MONTHLY SERIES: *PLANET OF THE APES*		
ISSUE/DATE	**TITLE**	**WRITER**	**ARTIST(S)**
1. Apr. 1990	"The Monkey Planet: Beneath"	Charles Marshall	Kent Burles & Barb Kaalberg
2. Jun. 1990	"The Monkey Planet: Escape"	Charles Marshall	Kent Burles & Barb Kaalberg
3. Jul. 1990	"The Monkey Planet: Conquest"	Charles Marshall	Kent Burles & Barb Kaalberg
4. Aug. 1990	"The Monkey Planet: Battle"	Charles Marshall	Kent Burles & Barb Kaalberg
5. Sep. 1990	"Loss"	Charles Marshall	Kent Burles & Barb Kaalberg
6. Oct. 1990	"Welcome to Ape City"	Charles Marshall	Kent Burles & Barb Kaalberg
7. Nov. 1990	"Survival of the Fittest"	Charles Marshall	Kent Burles & Barb Kaalberg
8. Dec. 1990	"Here Comes Travellin' Jack"	Charles Marshall	Kent Burles & Barb Kaalberg
9. Jan. 1991	"Changes"	Charles Marshall	Kent Burles & Barb Kaalberg
	"Countdown Five"	Charles Marshall	Kent Burles & Barb Kaalberg
10. Mar, 1991	"Return to the Forbidden City"	Charles Marshall	Kent Burles & Barb Kaalberg
	"Countdown Four"	Charles Marshall	Kent Burles & Barb Kaalberg
11. Apr. 1991	"Warriors"	Charles Marshall	Kent Burles & Barb Kaalberg
	"Countdown Three"	Charles Marshall	Kent Burles & Barb Kaalberg
12. May 1991	"Bells"	Charles Marshall	M.C. Wyman & Terry Pallot
	"Countdown Two"	Charles Marshall	M.C. Wyman & Terry Pallot
13. Jun. 1991	"Frito & JoJo's X-cellent Adventure"	Charles Marshall	M.C. Wyman & Terry Pallot
	Ape City: "Honey, I Shrunk the Apes"	Charles Marshall	M.C. Wyman & Terry Pallot
	Ape Nation: "Drunken Interlude"	Charles Marshall	M.C. Wyman & Terry Pallot
	"Countdown One"	Charles Marshall	M.C. Wyman & Terry Pallot
14. Jul. 1991	"Countdown Zero: Part 1"	Charles Marshall	M.C. Wyman & Terry Pallot
15. Aug. 1991	"Countdown Zero: Part 2"	Charles Marshall	M.C. Wyman & Terry Pallot
16. Sep. 1991	"Countdown Zero: Part 3"	Charles Marshall	M.C. Wyman & Terry Pallot
17. Oct. 1991	"Countdown Zero: Part 4"	Charles Marshall	M.C. Wyman & Terry Pallot
18. Nov. 1991	"Gorillas in the Mist"	Charles Marshall	M.C. Wyman & Terry Pallot
19. Dec. 1991	"Quitting Time"	Charles Marshall	M.C. Wyman & Terry Pallot
20. Jan. 1992	"Cowboys and Simians"	Charles Marshall	M.C. Wyman & Terry Pallot
21. Feb. 1992	"Part 1: The Terror Beneath"	Charles Marshall	M.C. Wyman & Peter Murphy
22. Mar. 1992	"Part 2: The Land of No Escape"	Charles Marshall	M.C. Wyman & Peter Murphy
23. May 1992	"Part 3: Final Conquest"	Charles Marshall	M.C. Wyman & Peter Murphy
24. Jul. 1992	"Part 4: Last Battle"	Charles Marshall	Craig Taillefer

COMIC BOOKS (Adventure Comics / Malibu Graphics, cont.)

MINISERIES: *APE CITY*

ISSUE/DATE	TITLE	WRITER	ARTIST(S)
1. Aug. 1990	"Monkey Business"	Charles Marshall	M.C. Wyman, Marvin Perry Mann & Steve Miller
2. Sep. 1990	"See No Evil, Hear No Evil, Speak No Evil"	Charles Marshall	M.C. Wyman, Marvin Perry Mann & Steve Miller
3. Oct. 1990	"Monkey Planet"	Charles Marshall	M.C. Wyman, Marvin Perry Mann & Steve Miller
4. Nov. 1990	"Monkey See, Monkey Do"	Charles Marshall	M.C. Wyman, Marvin Perry Mann & Steve Miller

MINISERIES: *URCHAK'S FOLLY*

ISSUE/DATE	TITLE	WRITER	ARTIST(S)
1. Jan. 1991	"Chapter 1: The Valley"	Gary Chaloner	Gary Chaloner & Dillon Naylor
2. Feb. 1991	"Chapter 2: The Bridge"	Gary Chaloner	Gary Chaloner, Dillon Naylor & Greg Gates
3. Mar. 1991	"Chapter 3: The Savages"	Gary Chaloner	Gary Chaloner, Dillon Naylor & Greg Gates
4. Apr. 1991	"Chapter 4: The War"	Gary Chaloner	Gary Chaloner, Dillon Naylor & Greg Gates

MINISERIES: *APE NATION* (an *Alien Nation* crossover)

ISSUE/DATE	TITLE	WRITER	ARTIST(S)
1. Feb. 1991	"Plans"	Charles Marshall	M.C. Wyman & Terry Pallot
1. Feb. 1991 (Limited Collector's Edition)	"Twice Upon a Time"	Charles Marshall	M.C. Wyman & Terry Pallot
2. Apr. 1991	"Pasts"	Charles Marshall	M.C. Wyman & Terry Pallot
3. May. 1991	"Pawns"	Charles Marshall	M.C. Wyman & Terry Pallot
4. Jun. 1991	"Pains"	Charles Marshall	M.C. Wyman & Terry Pallot

MINISERIES: *BLOOD OF THE APES*

ISSUE/DATE	TITLE	WRITER	ARTIST(S)
1. Nov. 1991	Chapters 1 to 3	Roland Mann	Darren Goodhart & Bruce McCorkindale
2. Dec. 1991	Chapters 4 to 6	Roland Mann	Darren Goodhart & Bruce McCorkindale
3. Jan. 1992	Chapters 7 to 9	Roland Mann	Darren Goodhart & Bruce McCorkindale
4. Feb. 1992	Chapters 10 to 12	Roland Mann	Darren Goodhart & Bruce McCorkindale

ANNUAL: *A DAY ON THE PLANET OF THE APES*

ISSUE/DATE	TITLE	WRITER	ARTIST(S)
1. Dec. 1991	"Morning Glory"	Charles Marshall	James Tucker & Greg Cravens
	"High Noon"	Charles Marshall	James Tucker & Greg Cravens
	"Afternoon Delight"	Charles Marshall	James Tucker & Greg Cravens
	"Eternal Dusk"	Charles Marshall	James Tucker & Greg Cravens
	"A Night at Fats' Palace: An *Ape City* Tale"	Charles Marshall	James Tucker & Greg Cravens
	"Midnight Tears"	Charles Marshall	James Tucker & Greg Cravens

ONE-SHOT: *THE SINS OF THE FATHER*

ISSUE/DATE	TITLE	WRITER	ARTIST
1. Mar. 1992	"The Sins of the Father" (early title: "Murder on the Planet of the Apes")	Mike Valerio	Mitch Byrd

MINISERIES: *THE FORBIDDEN ZONE*

ISSUE/DATE	TITLE	WRITER	ARTIST
1. Dec. 1992	"Forbidden Knowledge"	Lowell Cunningham	Leonard Kirk
2. Jan. 1993	"Danger Zone"	Lowell Cunningham	Leonard Kirk
3. Feb. 1993	"Battle Zone"	Lowell Cunningham	Leonard Kirk
4. Mar. 1993	"War Zone"	Lowell Cunningham	Leonard Kirk

UNPUBLISHED

ISSUE/DATE	TITLE	WRITER	ARTIST(S)
N/A	*Back from the Future*	Charles Marshall	*(no artist assigned)*
N/A	*The Most Dangerous Animal*	Charles Marshall	*(no artist assigned)*
N/A	*Manhunt on the Planet of the Apes*	Mike Valerio	*(no artist assigned)*
N/A	*Sky Gods* (early title *Second Coming*)	Roland Mann	*(no artist assigned)*
N/A	*Henry the Ape*	Roland Mann	*(no artist assigned)*
N/A	*Indiape*	Roland Mann	*(no artist assigned)*
N/A	*Redemption of the Planet of the Apes*	Lowell Cunningham	*(no artist assigned)*

NOTE: *Monthly issues #1-4 were collected in trade-paperback format, under the title* Planet of the Apes: The Monkey Planet; *individually, the issues did not contain the "Monkey Planet" title. Adventure also offered reprint collections of Marvel's first three film adaptations, as well as reprints of the first four issues of Marvel's "Terror on the Planet of the Apes" storyline. Details of the unpublished storylines were provided by the authors themselves.*

MINISERIES: *REVOLUTION ON THE PLANET OF THE APES*

ISSUE/DATE	TITLE	WRITER(S)	ARTIST(S)
1. Dec. 2005	*Revolution*, Part 1: "The End of the World"	Ty Templeton & Joe O'Brien	Salgood Sam
	"Caesar's Journal"	Ty Templeton	Bernie Mireault
	"For Human Rights"	Ty Templeton	Attila Adorjany (as "Attila")
2. Jan. 2006	*Revolution*, Part 2: "Lines of Communication"	Ty Templeton & Joe O'Brien	Salgood Sam
	"Caesar's Journal"	Ty Templeton	Bernie Mireault
	"People News" (early title: "People in the News")	Ty Templeton	Gabriel Morrissetts & Bernie Mireault
3. Mar. 2006	*Revolution*, Part 3: "Intelligent Design"	Ty Templeton & Joe O'Brien	Tom Fowler
	"Hasslein's Notes"	Joe O'Brien	(no art)
	"Little Caesar" (early title: "Armando's Marvelous Menagerie Circus")	Ty Templeton	Salgood Sam
4. May 2006	*Revolution*, Part 4: "Truth and Consequences"	Ty Templeton & Joe O'Brien	Salgood Sam
	"Caesar's Journal"	Ty Templeton	Bernie Mireault
	"Paternal Instinct"	Sam Agro & Ty Templeton	Sam Agro
5. Jul. 2006	*Revolution*, Part 5: "Weapon of Choice"	Ty Templeton & Joe O'Brien	Salgood Sam
	"Caesar's Journal"	Ty Templeton	Bernie Mireault
	"Ape Shall Not Kill Ape"	Ty Templeton	Kent Burles & Bernie Mireault
6. Aug. 2006	*Revolution*, Part 6: "Survival of the Fittest"	Ty Templeton & Joe O'Brien	Salgood Sam
	"Catch a Falling Star"	Ty Templeton	Steve Molnar

UNPUBLISHED

ISSUE/DATE	TITLE	WRITER(S)	ARTIST(S)
N/A	*Combat on the Planet of the Apes / War on the Planet of the Apes*	Ty Templeton & Joe O'Brien	Richard Pace
N/A	*Empire on the Planet of the Apes*	Ty Templeton & Joe O'Brien	*(no artist assigned)*
N/A	*(title unknown—story of moon's destruction)*	Ty Templeton	*(no artist assigned)*
N/A	*(title unknown—story of Australian apes)*	Ty Templeton	*(no artist assigned)*
N/A	"The Believer"	Sam Agro	Sam Agro

NOTE: Revolution on the Planet of the Apes *was originally to have been titled either* Combat on the Planet of the Apes *or* War on the Planet of the Apes, *and would have featured both Thade, from the Tim Burton film, and Caesar, from the originals. Artist Richard Pace created a poster for the series, as well as some interior art pages utilizing Thade as a character, but when Fox opted to keep the two incarnations separate, Thade's involvement (and, thus, Pace's artwork) was removed from the final product. Templeton's three other unpublished stories were slated to appear in* Empire on the Planet of the Apes, *a proposed followup miniseries, but were canceled due to low sales on* Revolution. *"The Believer," written as a back-up story for* Revolution, *was written, penciled and lettered by Agro, but did not run due to concerns over religious overtones—at presstime, however, it was slated to appear in issue #16 of* Simian Scrolls *magazine, with the author's permission. Templeton's name was listed as co-writer for that tale, though the story and art, according to Templeton, were Agro's creation. "People News" was originally released as a free online preview, entitled "People in the News." Details of the unpublished storylines were provided by the authors. "Little Caesar" was originally previewed in issue #1 of Mr. Comics' Big Max, under the title "Armando's Marvelous Menagerie Circus."*

COMIC BOOKS (Dark Horse Comics)

FILM ADAPTATION: *PLANET OF THE APES*

YEAR	TITLE	WRITER	ARTIST(S)
May 2001	*Planet of the Apes*	Scott Allie	Davide Fabbri, Christian Dalla Vecchia & Christopher Ivy

TOYS 'R' US COLLECTOR'S COMIC: *PLANET OF THE APES*

YEAR	TITLE	WRITER	ARTIST
Jul. 2001	*Planet of the Apes*	Phil Amara	Pop Mhan

SERIALIZED COMIC STRIPS: *DARK HORSE EXTRA*

ISSUE/DATE	TITLE	WRITER	ARTIST(S)
36. Apr. 2001	*Planet of the Apes*, Part 1	Scott Allie	Eric Powell & Dan Jackson
37. May. 2001	*Planet of the Apes*, Part 2	Scott Allie	Eric Powell & Dan Jackson
38. Jun. 2001	*Planet of the Apes*, Part 3	Scott Allie	Eric Powell & Dan Jackson

MINISERIES: *THE HUMAN WAR*

ISSUE/DATE	TITLE	WRITER	ARTISTS
1. Jun. 2001	Part 1	Ian Edginton	Paco Medina & Juan Vlasco
2. Jul. 2001	Part 2	Ian Edginton	Paco Medina & Juan Vlasco
3. Aug. 2001	Part 3	Ian Edginton	Adrian Sibar, Christopher Ivy & Norman Lee

MONTHLY SERIES: *PLANET OF THE APES*

ISSUE/DATE	TITLE	WRITER	ARTISTS
1. Sep. 2001	"Old Gods, Part 1"	Ian Edginton	Adrian Sibar & Norman Lee
2. Oct. 2001	"Old Gods, Part 2"	Ian Edginton	Paco Medina & Juan Vlasco
3. Nov. 2001	"Old Gods, Part 3"	Ian Edginton	Adrian Sibar & Norman Lee
4. Dec. 2001	"Bloodlines, Part 1"	Dan Abnett	Sanford Greene, Pop Mhan & Norman Lee
5. Jan. 2002	"Bloodlines, Part 2"	Dan Abnett	Adrian Sibar & Norman Lee
6. Feb. 2002	"Bloodlines, Part 3"	Dan Abnett	Paco Medina & Juan Vlasco

UNPUBLISHED

ISSUE/DATE	TITLE	WRITERS	ARTISTS
7. (and beyond)	*(titles unknown)*	Dan Abnett & Ian Edginton	*(no artist assigned)*

E-COMIC: *PLANET OF THE APES SKETCHBOOK*

ONLINE DATE	URL	ARTISTS
2001	http://www.darkhorse.com/downloads.php?did=297	Paco Medina, J. Scott Campbell & Davide Fabri

NOTE: Dark Horse's run was based on Tim Burton's film "re-imagining." Details of the unpublished storylines were provided by the authors.

FILMSTRIP COMICS (Chad Valley Picture Show)

PLANET OF THE APES SLIDERAMA PROJECTOR

CHAPTER	TITLE	CHAPTER	TITLE	CHAPTER	TITLE
529a	"Crashland"	534b	"The Curse"	540a	"Break Out"
529b	"Capture"	535a	"Malaria"	540b	"Alan Slips Up"
530a	"Escape"	535b	"The Cure"	541a	"Condemned"
530b	"The Cave"	536a	"Chased"	541b	"Surgery"
531a	"The Book"	536b	"The Fall"	542a	"Burke Returns"
531b	"Time Span"	537a	"Trapped"	542b	"The Skycraft"
532a	"Slaves"	537b	"Unearthed"	543a	"Airborne"
532b	"Urko"	538a	"Parted"	543b	"Fly Away"
533a	"Fishermen"	538b	"Enslaved"	544a	"Forbidden Zone"
533b	"Big Catch"	539a	"Unchained"	544b	"Three Alone"
534a	"The Raft"	539b	"The Trial"		

NOTE: These illustrated strips, released in 1975 (and only in the United Kingdom), provided a retelling of several TV-series episodes combined with the first film's courtroom scene, in a set similar to the Give-a-Show Projector sets sold in the United States. The set contained 16 filmstrips with two chapters apiece. The complete set of strips is available online at www.beegeesfever.com/posting/picture_show/planet_apes/, and fan-remastered versions can be found at Yahoo's Planet of the Apes *Discussion Group. The writers and illustrators for these strips are unknown.*

FRENCH SOURCE NOVEL (Signet Books)

TITLE	YEAR	WRITER
La planète des singes (English translation: *The Monkey Planet*)	1963	Pierre Boulle

NOTE: Boulle's novel, originally published in French, appeared abridged in Saga *and* Bizarre Mystery *magazines. An audio adaptation of the novel, presented as part of BBC Radio 4's* Book at Bedtime *series, was read by Michael Maloney. Hunter Goatley's* Planet of the Apes *Archive offers MP3 files of the adaptation for downloading.*

HUNGARIAN COMIC ADAPTATION (Publisher Unknown)

TITLE	YEAR	WRITER/ARTIST
A Majmok Bolygója (English translation: *The Monkey Planet*)	1981	Zórád Ernö

NOTE: A Hungarian publisher produced this comic-book adaptation of Boulle's novel in 1981. Scans of the comic, along with a fan-made English translation, can be found at Hunter Goatley's Planet of the Apes *Archive. No publisher information is indicated in the comic.*

AUDIO RECORDINGS (Power Records / Peter Pan)

FILM ADAPTATIONS (Book-and-Record Sets)

FILM	CREATORS	YEAR
Planet of the Apes	Arvid Knudsen and Assoc.	1974
Beneath the Planet of the Apes	Arvid Knudsen and Assoc.	1974
Escape from the Planet of the Apes	Arvid Knudsen and Assoc.	1974
Battle for the Planet of the Apes	Arvid Knudsen and Assoc.	1974

ORIGINAL TV-SERIES-ERA STORIES (Audio Only)

FILM	CREATORS	YEAR
"Mountain of the Delphi"	(unknown)	1974
"Dawn of the Tree People"	(unknown)	1974
"Battle of Two Worlds"	(unknown)	1974
"Volcano"	(unknown)	1974

NOTE: The film adaptations were collected as Planet of the Apes: 4 Exciting Stories (Conquest of the Planet of the Apes was not adapted). The four original tales were first released as individual LPs, then collected in a single volume, Planet of the Apes: 4 Exciting New Stories. All are available online at Hunter Goatley's Planet of the Apes Archive.

BURTON-FILM NOVELS (HarperEntertainment)

YOUNG-ADULT-LEVEL PREQUEL NOVELS

YEAR	TITLE	AUTHOR
2002	#1 Force	John Whitman
2002	#2 Resistance	John Whitman
(unpublished)	#3 Rule	J.E. Bright
(unpublished)	#4 Extinction	John Whitman

ADULT-LEVEL PREQUEL NOVELS

YEAR	TITLE	AUTHOR
2002	The Fall	William T. Quick
2003	Colony	William T. Quick

NOTE: These original novels were based on the film "re-imagining" directed by Tim Burton. Two additional young-adult novels were intended, but never published. J.E. Bright completed a manuscript for Rule (though John Whitman's name erroneously appears on a cover proof), while Whitman wrote only an outline for Extinction.

PROMOTIONAL NEWSPAPERS (Harry K. McWilliams Assoc.)

TITLE	YEAR	FILM PROMOTED
The Ape	1968	Planet of the Apes
The Ape News / The Mutant News	1970	Beneath the Planet of the Apes
The Ape News	1971	Escape from the Planet of the Apes
Future News	1972	Conquest of the Planet of the Apes
San Simian Sentinel	1973	Battle for the Planet of the Apes

NOTE: These mock heralds, available for download at the POTA Media Archive, were distributed to promote the films' releases, presenting in-universe facts as news. The Beneath newspaper was two-sided. The herald for Battle for the Planet of the Apes contained promotional materials only, and was not presented in-universe like the others.

ADDITIONAL RESOURCES

— *Simian Scrolls* Magazine (ed.: David Ballard, Dean Preston, John Roche, et. al., e-mail john@johnroche6.wanadoo.co.uk)

— *Planet of the Apes* Final Production Information Guide

— *Planet of the Apes* TV Series Writer's Bible

— *Planet of the Apes* Initial Concept Pages

— *Behind the Planet of the Apes* (Documentary, available on DVD and Blu-Ray)

— *Planet of the Apes: 40-Year Evolution* (Lee Pfeiffer and Dave Worrall, Cinema Retro, packaged with Blu-Ray box set)

— *Planet of the Apes Revisited* (Joe Russo, Larry Landsman and Edward Gross)

— *The Legend of the Planet of the Apes* (Brian Pendreigh)

— *Planet of the Apes as American Myth: Race, Politics and Popular Culture* (Eric Greene)

— *Planet of the Apes: An Unofficial Companion* (David Hofstede)

— *The Jack Kirby Collector* (ed.: John Morrow)

— *Peter Jackson: A Film-Maker's Journey* (Brian Sibley)

— *Films Into Books* (Randall D. Lawson)

— *Diaries of Hollywood: A Brazilian on the Planet of the Apes* (Luiz Saulo Adami)

— *The Only Good Human Is a Dead Human* (Luiz Saulo Adami)

OTHER *PLANET OF THE APES* TIMELINES

— "Outlines of Tomorrow—A Chronology of the *Planet of the Apes*" (Jim Whitmore, Marvel #11)

— "The *Planet of the Apes*—A Chronological History" (Dayton Ward, in Paul A. Woods' *The Planet of the Apes Chronicles*)

— *Planet of the Apes* Timeline (20th Century Fox, Widescreen 35th Anniversary Edition DVD)

— *Planet of the Apes* Timeline (Peter Ventrella and Gavin Howell, 40th Anniversary Collection)

RECOMMENDED WEBSITES

— Hunter Goatley's *Planet of the Apes* Archive (pota.goatley.com)

— Kassidy Rae's *Planet of the Apes*: The TV Series Website (potatv.kassidyrae.com)

— Chris Shields' Last Flight of the *Icarus* (www.goingfaster.com/icarus)

— *Planet of the Apes* Media Archive (www.potamediaarchive.com)

— Yahoo Group: POTA—A Community of *Planet of the Apes* Fans (movies.groups.yahoo.com/group/pota)

— Yahoo Group: POTA Discussion Group (movies.groups.yahoo.com/group/potadg)

— Friends and Fugitives: A Loving Tribute (www.netcomuk.co.uk/~pdownes/potatv/potatv.html)

— BrokenSea Audio Productions' *Planet of the Apes* Audio Drama, by Bill Hollweg (www.brokensea.com/planetoftheapes)

— The *Planet of the Apes* Fan Collective (www.potacollective.com)

— Terry Hoknes' International *Planet of the Apes* Fan Club / *Ape Chronicles* Magazine (www.hoknes.com/apes.htm)

— The Forbidden Zone (theforbidden-zone.com)

— Forum of the Apes (forumoftheapes.yuku.com)

— Apemania (www.apemania.com)

IV: Cover Gallery

The following gallery should aid you in your search for *Planet of the Apes* lore. A list of titles and credits begins on page 253, and a reading/viewing order appears on page 241.

— French Source Novel —

The Monkey Planet
(a.k.a. *Planet of the Apes*)

The Monkey Planet
(a.k.a. *Planet of the Apes*)

The Monkey Planet
(a.k.a. *Planet of the Apes*)

The Monkey Planet
(a.k.a. *Planet of the Apes*)

The Monkey Planet
(a.k.a. *Planet of the Apes*)

The Monkey Planet
(a.k.a. *Planet of the Apes*)

The Monkey Planet
(a.k.a. *Planet of the Apes*)

The Monkey Planet
(a.k.a. *Planet of the Apes*)

The Monkey Planet
(a.k.a. *Planet of the Apes*)

The Monkey Planet
(a.k.a. *Planet of the Apes*)

The Monkey Planet
(a.k.a. *Planet of the Apes*)

The Monkey Planet
(a.k.a. *Planet of the Apes*)

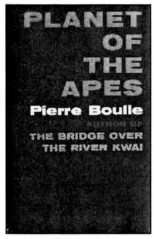

The Monkey Planet
(a.k.a. *Planet of the Apes*)

The Monkey Planet
(a.k.a. *Planet of the Apes*)

The Monkey Planet
(a.k.a. *Planet of the Apes*)

The Monkey Planet
(a.k.a. *Planet of the Apes*)

— Film Novelizations —

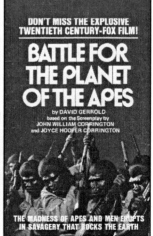

Beneath the Planet of the Apes Novelization

Escape from the Planet of the Apes Novelization

Conquest of the Planet of the Apes Novelization

Battle for the Planet of the Apes Novelization

**Planet of the Apes Remake
Young-Adult Novelization**

**Planet of the Apes Remake
Novelization**

**Leo's Logbook: A Captain's
Days in Captivity (Storybook)**

— TV Series Novelizations —

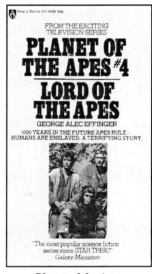

**Planet of the Apes
TV Series Novelization #1**

**Planet of the Apes
TV Series Novelization #2**

**Planet of the Apes
TV Series Novelization #3**

**Planet of the Apes
TV Series Novelization #4**

**Return to the Planet of the
Apes Novelization #1**

**Return to the Planet of the
Apes Novelization #2**

**Return to the Planet of the
Apes Novelization #3**

— VHS Releases —

Planet of the Apes
U.S. VHS Release

Planet of the Apes
U.K. VHS Release

Beneath the Planet of the Apes **U.S. VHS Release**

Beneath the Planet of the Apes **U.K. VHS Release**

Escape from the Planet of the Apes **U.S. VHS Release**

Escape from the Planet of the Apes **U.K. VHS Release**

Conquest of the Planet of the Apes **U.S. VHS Release**

Conquest of the Planet of the Apes **U.K. VHS Release**

Battle for the Planet of the Apes
U.S. VHS Release

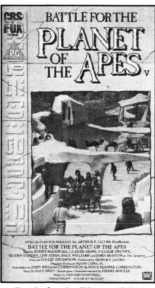

Battle for the Planet of the Apes **U.K. VHS Release**

Planet of the Apes Collection **VHS Box Set**

Planet of the Apes **Remake VHS Release**

Planet of the Apes
TV Series Australian
VHS Release Vol. 1

Planet of the Apes
TV Series Australian
VHS Release Vol. 2

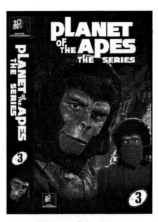

Planet of the Apes
TV Series Australian
VHS Release Vol. 3

Planet of the Apes
TV Series Australian
VHS Release Vol. 4

Planet of the Apes
TV Series Australian
VHS Release Vol. 5

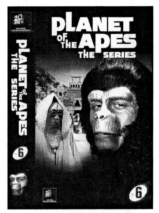

Planet of the Apes
TV Series Australian
VHS Release Vol. 6

— DVD Releases —

Planet of the Apes
DVD Release

Planet of the Apes
35th Anniversary Widescreen
Edition DVD Release

Planet of the Apes
DVD Release

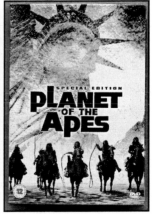

Planet of the Apes
British Special Edition
DVD Release

*Beneath the Planet
of the Apes* **DVD Release**

*Beneath the Planet
of the Apes* **DVD Release**

*Escape from the Planet
of the Apes* **DVD Release**

*Escape from the Planet
of the Apes* **DVD Release**

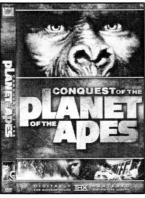
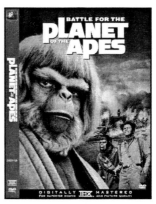

*Conquest of the Planet
of the Apes* **DVD Release**

*Conquest of the Planet
of the Apes* **DVD Release**

*Battle for the Planet
of the Apes* **DVD Release**

*Battle for the Planet
of the Apes* **DVD Release**

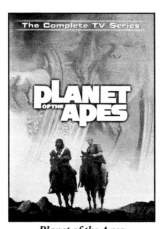

Planet of the Apes
TV Series DVD Release

*Return to the Planet
of the Apes* **DVD Release**

Planet of the Apes **Remake
DVD Release**

Planet of the Apes **Remake
DVD Release**

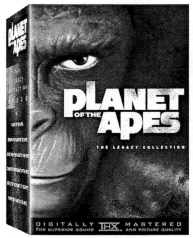

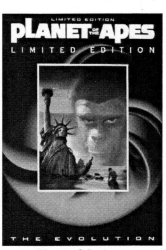

Planet of the Apes:
The Legacy Collection
DVD Box Set

Planet of the Apes:
The Evolution
DVD Box Set

Planet of the Apes:
The Ultimate DVD Collection

— Blu-Ray Releases —

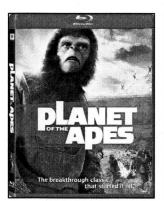

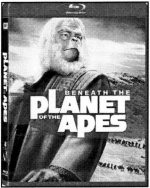

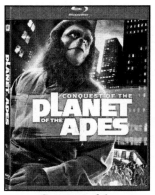

Planet of the Apes
Blu-Ray Release

Beneath the
Planet of the Apes
Blu-Ray Release

Escape from the
Planet of the Apes
Blu-Ray Release

Conquest of the
Planet of the Apes
Blu-Ray Release

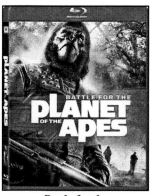

Battle for the
Planet of the Apes
Blu-Ray Release

Planet of the Apes Remake
Blu-Ray Release

Planet of the Apes 40th Anniversary Collection
Blu-Ray Box Set

— Power Records —

Planet of the Apes
Book and Record Set

Beneath the Planet
of the Apes
Book and Record Set

Escape from the Planet
of the Apes
Book and Record Set

Battle for the Planet
of the Apes
Book and Record Set

Battle of Two Worlds
Little LP Audio Adventure

Mountain of the Delphi
Little LP Audio Adventure

Dawn of the Tree People
Little LP Audio Adventure

Planet of the Apes
Little LP Back Cover

Planet of the Apes:
4 Exciting Stories
(Front Cover)

Planet of the Apes:
4 Exciting Stories
(Back Cover)

Planet of the Apes:
4 Exciting New Stories
(Front Cover)

Planet of the Apes:
4 Exciting New Stories
(Back Cover)

— Promotional Newspapers —

The Ape (Distributed at
Planet of the Apes Showings)

The Ape News (Distributed at
Beneath the Planet of the Apes
Showings—Front Cover)

The Mutant News (Distributed
at *Beneath the Planet of the Apes*
Showings—Back Cover)

The Ape News (Distributed at
*Escape from the Planet
of the Apes* Showings)

Future News (Distributed at
*Conquest of the Planet
of the Apes* Showings)

San Simian Sentinel
(Distributed at *Battle for the
Planet of the Apes* Showings)

— Hardcover British Annuals —

*Planet of the Apes
Authorised Edition* (1975)

*Planet of the Apes
Authorised Edition* (1976)

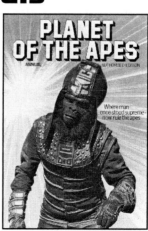

*Planet of the Apes
Authorised Edition* (1977)

— Marvel Comics (U.S.) —

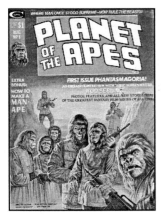

Planet of the Apes
Monthly Issue #1

Planet of the Apes
Monthly Issue #2

Planet of the Apes
Monthly Issue #3

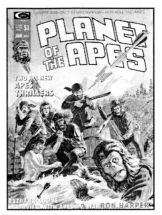

Planet of the Apes
Monthly Issue #4

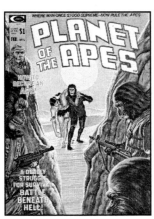

Planet of the Apes
Monthly Issue #5

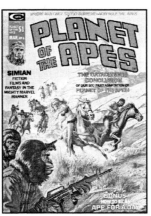

Planet of the Apes
Monthly Issue #6

Planet of the Apes
Monthly Issue #7

Planet of the Apes
Monthly Issue #8

Planet of the Apes
Monthly Issue #9

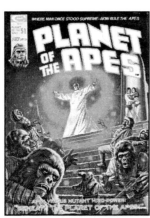

Planet of the Apes
Monthly Issue #10

Planet of the Apes
Monthly Issue #11

Planet of the Apes
Monthly Issue #12

Planet of the Apes
Monthly Issue #13

Planet of the Apes
Monthly Issue #14

Planet of the Apes
Monthly Issue #15

Planet of the Apes
Monthly Issue #16

Planet of the Apes
Monthly Issue #17

Planet of the Apes
Monthly Issue #18

Planet of the Apes
Monthly Issue #19

Planet of the Apes
Monthly Issue #20

Planet of the Apes
Monthly Issue #21

Planet of the Apes
Monthly Issue #22

Planet of the Apes
Monthly Issue #23

Planet of the Apes
Monthly Issue #24

Planet of the Apes
Monthly Issue #25

Planet of the Apes
Monthly Issue #26

Planet of the Apes
Monthly Issue #27

Planet of the Apes
Monthly Issue #28

Planet of the Apes
Monthly Issue #29

Adventures on the Planet of the Apes Issue #1

Adventures on the Planet of the Apes Issue #2

Adventures on the Planet of the Apes Issue #3

Adventures on the Planet of the Apes Issue #4

Adventures on the Planet of the Apes Issue #5

Adventures on the Planet of the Apes Issue #6

Adventures on the Planet of the Apes Issue #7

Adventures on the Planet of the Apes Issue #8

Adventures on the Planet of the Apes Issue #9

Adventures on the Planet of the Apes Issue #10

Adventures on the Planet of the Apes Issue #11

— Marvel Comics (U.K.) —

Planet of the Apes Weekly Issue #1

Planet of the Apes Weekly Issue #2

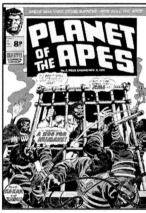

Planet of the Apes Weekly Issue #3

Planet of the Apes Weekly Issue #4

Planet of the Apes Weekly Issue #5

Planet of the Apes Weekly Issue #6

Planet of the Apes Weekly Issue #7

Planet of the Apes Weekly Issue #8

Planet of the Apes
Weekly Issue #9

Planet of the Apes
Weekly Issue #10

Planet of the Apes
Weekly Issue #11

Planet of the Apes
Weekly Issue #12

Planet of the Apes
Weekly Issue #13

Planet of the Apes
Weekly Issue #14

Planet of the Apes
Weekly Issue #15

Planet of the Apes
Weekly Issue #16

Planet of the Apes
Weekly Issue #17

Planet of the Apes
Weekly Issue #18

Planet of the Apes
Weekly Issue #19

Planet of the Apes
Weekly Issue #20

Planet of the Apes
Weekly Issue #21

Planet of the Apes
Weekly Issue #22

Planet of the Apes
Weekly Issue #23

Planet of the Apes
Weekly Issue #24

Planet of the Apes
Weekly Issue #25

Planet of the Apes
Weekly Issue #26

Planet of the Apes
Weekly Issue #27

Planet of the Apes
Weekly Issue #28

Planet of the Apes
Weekly Issue #29

Planet of the Apes
Weekly Issue #30

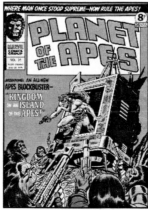

Planet of the Apes
Weekly Issue #31

Planet of the Apes
Weekly Issue #32

Planet of the Apes
Weekly Issue #33

Planet of the Apes
Weekly Issue #34

Planet of the Apes
Weekly Issue #35

Planet of the Apes
Weekly Issue #36

Planet of the Apes
Weekly Issue #37

Planet of the Apes
Weekly Issue #38

Planet of the Apes
Weekly Issue #39

Planet of the Apes
Weekly Issue #40

Planet of the Apes
Weekly Issue #41

Planet of the Apes
Weekly Issue #42

Planet of the Apes
Weekly Issue #43

Planet of the Apes
Weekly Issue #44

Planet of the Apes
Weekly Issue #45

Planet of the Apes
Weekly Issue #46

Planet of the Apes
Weekly Issue #47

Planet of the Apes
Weekly Issue #48

Planet of the Apes
Weekly Issue #49

Planet of the Apes
Weekly Issue #50

Planet of the Apes
Weekly Issue #51

Planet of the Apes
Weekly Issue #52

Planet of the Apes
Weekly Issue #53

Planet of the Apes
Weekly Issue #54

Planet of the Apes
Weekly Issue #55

Planet of the Apes
Weekly Issue #56

**Planet of the Apes
Weekly Issue #57**

**Planet of the Apes
Weekly Issue #58**

**Planet of the Apes
Weekly Issue #59**

**Planet of the Apes
Weekly Issue #60**

**Planet of the Apes
Weekly Issue #61**

**Planet of the Apes
Weekly Issue #62**

**Planet of the Apes
Weekly Issue #63**

**Planet of the Apes
Weekly Issue #64**

**Planet of the Apes
Weekly Issue #65**

**Planet of the Apes
Weekly Issue #66**

**Planet of the Apes
Weekly Issue #67**

**Planet of the Apes
Weekly Issue #68**

**Planet of the Apes
Weekly Issue #69**

**Planet of the Apes
Weekly Issue #70**

**Planet of the Apes
Weekly Issue #71**

**Planet of the Apes
Weekly Issue #72**

**Planet of the Apes
Weekly Issue #73**

**Planet of the Apes
Weekly Issue #74**

**Planet of the Apes
Weekly Issue #75**

**Planet of the Apes
Weekly Issue #76**

**Planet of the Apes
Weekly Issue #77**

**Planet of the Apes
Weekly Issue #78**

**Planet of the Apes
Weekly Issue #79**

**Planet of the Apes
Weekly Issue #80**

Planet of the Apes
Weekly Issue #81

Planet of the Apes
Weekly Issue #82

Planet of the Apes
Weekly Issue #83

Planet of the Apes
Weekly Issue #84

Planet of the Apes
Weekly Issue #85

Planet of the Apes
Weekly Issue #86

Planet of the Apes
Weekly Issue #87

Planet of the Apes
and Dracula Lives
Weekly Issue #88

Planet of the Apes
and Dracula Lives
Weekly Issue #89

Planet of the Apes
and Dracula Lives
Weekly Issue #90

Planet of the Apes
and Dracula Lives
Weekly Issue #91

Planet of the Apes
and Dracula Lives
Weekly Issue #92

***Planet of the Apes
and Dracula Lives***
Weekly Issue #93

***Planet of the Apes
and Dracula Lives***
Weekly Issue #94

***Planet of the Apes
and Dracula Lives***
Weekly Issue #95

***Planet of the Apes
and Dracula Lives***
Weekly Issue #96

***Planet of the Apes
and Dracula Lives***
Weekly Issue #97

***Planet of the Apes
and Dracula Lives***
Weekly Issue #98

***Planet of the Apes
and Dracula Lives***
Weekly Issue #99

***Planet of the Apes
and Dracula Lives***
Weekly Issue #100

***Planet of the Apes
and Dracula Lives***
Weekly Issue #101

***Planet of the Apes
and Dracula Lives***
Weekly Issue #102

***Planet of the Apes
and Dracula Lives***
Weekly Issue #103

***Planet of the Apes
and Dracula Lives***
Weekly Issue #104

*Planet of the Apes
and Dracula Lives*
Weekly Issue #105

*Planet of the Apes
and Dracula Lives*
Weekly Issue #106

*Planet of the Apes
and Dracula Lives*
Weekly Issue #107

*Planet of the Apes
and Dracula Lives*
Weekly Issue #108

*Planet of the Apes
and Dracula Lives*
Weekly Issue #109

*Planet of the Apes
and Dracula Lives*
Weekly Issue #110

*Planet of the Apes
and Dracula Lives*
Weekly Issue #111

*Planet of the Apes
and Dracula Lives*
Weekly Issue #112

*Planet of the Apes
and Dracula Lives*
Weekly Issue #113

*Planet of the Apes
and Dracula Lives*
Weekly Issue #114

*Planet of the Apes
and Dracula Lives*
Weekly Issue #115

*Planet of the Apes
and Dracula Lives*
Weekly Issue #116

***Planet of the Apes
and Dracula Lives***
Weekly Issue #117

***Planet of the Apes
and Dracula Lives***
Weekly Issue #118

***Planet of the Apes
and Dracula Lives***
Weekly Issue #119

***Planet of the Apes
and Dracula Lives***
Weekly Issue #120

***Planet of the Apes
and Dracula Lives***
Weekly Issue #121

***Planet of the Apes
and Dracula Lives***
Weekly Issue #122

***Planet of the Apes
and Dracula Lives***
Weekly Issue #123

The Mighty World of Marvel
Weekly Issue #231

The Mighty World of Marvel
Weekly Issue #232

The Mighty World of Marvel
Weekly Issue #233

The Mighty World of Marvel
Weekly Issue #234

The Mighty World of Marvel
Weekly Issue #235

The Mighty World of Marvel
Weekly Issue #236

The Mighty World of Marvel
Weekly Issue #237

The Mighty World of Marvel
Weekly Issue #238

The Mighty World of Marvel
Weekly Issue #239

The Mighty World of Marvel
Weekly Issue #240

The Mighty World of Marvel
Weekly Issue #241

The Mighty World of Marvel
Weekly Issue #242

The Mighty World of Marvel
Weekly Issue #243

The Mighty World of Marvel
Weekly Issue #244

The Mighty World of Marvel
Weekly Issue #245

The Mighty World of Marvel
Weekly Issue #246

— Malibu Graphics/Adventure Comics —

**Planet of the Apes
Issue #1**

**Planet of the Apes
Issue #1 (With Slipcover)**

**Planet of the Apes Issue #1
Limited Collector's Edition**

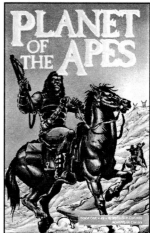

**Planet of the Apes
Issue #2**

**Planet of the Apes
Issue #3**

**Planet of the Apes
Issue #4**

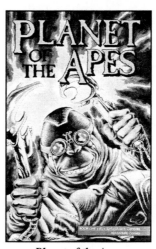

**Planet of the Apes
Issue #5**

**Planet of the Apes
Issue #6**

**Planet of the Apes
Issue #7**

**Planet of the Apes
Issue #8**

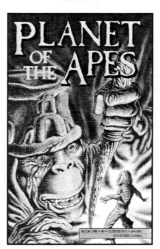

**Planet of the Apes
Issue #9**

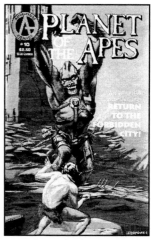

**Planet of the Apes
Issue #10**

Planet of the Apes
Issue #11

Planet of the Apes
Issue #12

Planet of the Apes
Issue #13

Planet of the Apes
Issue #14

Planet of the Apes
Issue #15

Planet of the Apes
Issue #16

Planet of the Apes
Issue #17

Planet of the Apes
Issue #18

Planet of the Apes
Issue #19

Planet of the Apes
Issue #20

Planet of the Apes
Issue #21

Planet of the Apes
Issue #22

Planet of the Apes
Issue #23

Planet of the Apes
Issue #24

*Planet of the Apes:
The Monkey Planet*
(Collects Issues #1-4)

Planet of the Apes
(Collects Marvel's
Film Adaptation)

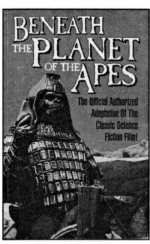

Beneath the Planet of the Apes
(Collects Marvel's
Film Adaptation)

*Escape from the Planet of the
Apes* (Collects Marvel's
Film Adaptation)

Unpublished *Ape Nation*
Cover (Used in Solicitation)

Ape Nation Issue #1
Limited Collector's Edition
(*Alien Nation* Crossover)

Ape Nation Issue #1
(*Alien Nation* Crossover)

Ape Nation Issue #2
(*Alien Nation* Crossover)

Ape Nation Issue #3
(*Alien Nation* Crossover)

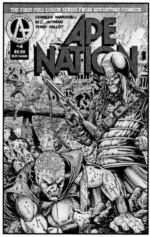

Ape Nation Issue #4
(*Alien Nation* Crossover)

Ape City Issue #1

Ape City Issue #2

Ape City Issue #3

Ape City Issue #4

*Terror on the Planet
of the Apes* Issue #1
(Reprints Marvel Issue #1)

*Terror on the Planet
of the Apes* Issue #2
(Reprints Marvel Issue #2)

*Terror on the Planet
of the Apes* Issue #3
(Reprints Marvel Issue #3)

*Terror on the Planet
of the Apes* Issue #4
(Reprints Marvel Issue #4)

Urchak's Folly Issue #1

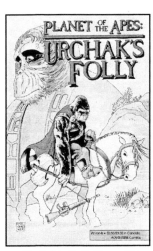

Urchak's Folly Issue #2

Urchak's Folly Issue #3

Urchak's Folly Issue #4

Blood of the Apes Issue #1

Blood of the Apes Issue #2

Blood of the Apes Issue #3

Blood of the Apes Issue #4

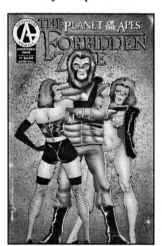
The Forbidden Zone Issue #1

The Forbidden Zone Issue #2

The Forbidden Zone Issue #3

The Forbidden Zone Issue #4

Planet of the Apes Annual:
A Day on the
Planet of the Apes

The Sins of the Father

— Misc. Comics —

Beneath the Planet of the Apes
Comic Book Adaptation
(Gold Key Comics)

The Monkey Planet
Comic Book Adaptation
(Published in Hungary)

— Dark Horse Comics —

Planet of the Apes
Film Adaptation (Remake)

Planet of the Apes
Film Adaptation (Remake)

Planet of the Apes Sketchbook
(Online at www.dhorse.com)

Planet of the Apes
Toys 'R' Us Collector's Comic

Planet of the Apes Serialized Strip
(*Dark Horse Extra* Issues #36-38)

Planet of the Apes:
The Human War
(Collects Miniseries #1-3)

Planet of the Apes:
Old Gods
(Collects Issues #1-3)

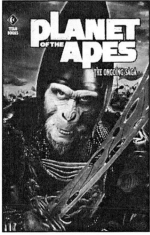

Planet of the Apes:
The Ongoing Saga
(Collects Issues #1-3)

Planet of the Apes:
Bloodlines
(Collects Issues #4-6)

The Human War
Issue #1

The Human War
Issue #1

The Human War
Issue #1

The Human War
Issue #2

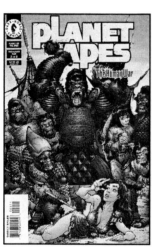

The Human War
Issue #2

The Human War
Issue #2

The Human War
Issue #2

The Human War
Issue #3

The Human War
Issue #3

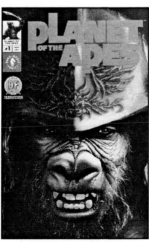

Planet of the Apes
Monthly Issue #1

Planet of the Apes
Monthly Issue #1

Planet of the Apes
Monthly Issue #1

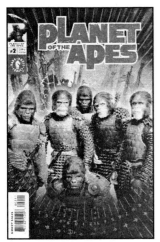

Planet of the Apes
Monthly Issue #2

Planet of the Apes
Monthly Issue #2

Planet of the Apes
Monthly Issue #3

Planet of the Apes
Monthly Issue #3

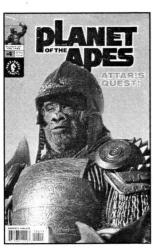

Planet of the Apes
Monthly Issue #4

Planet of the Apes
Monthly Issue #4

Planet of the Apes
Monthly Issue #5

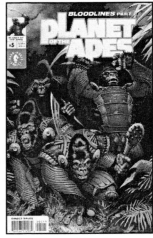

Planet of the Apes
Monthly Issue #5

Planet of the Apes
Monthly Issue #6

Planet of the Apes
Monthly Issue #6

Planet of the Apes
Monthly Issue #6

— Editorial Mo.Pa.Sa. —

Published in Spanish, and released only in Argentina.

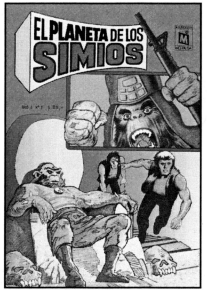

El Planeta de los Simios Issue #1

El Planeta de los Simios Issue #2

El Planeta de los Simios Issue #3

El Planeta de los Simios
Issue #4

El Planeta de los Simios
Issue #5

El Planeta de los Simios
Issue #6

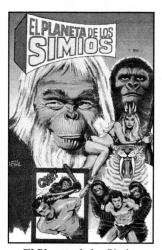

El Planeta de los Simios
Issue #7 (Numbered
on Cover as #1)

— Video Games —

**Windows PC
(Ubisoft)**

**Game Boy Advance
(Ubisoft/Torus Games)**

**Game Boy Color
(Ubisoft/Torus Games)**

**PlayStation 1
(Ubisoft/Visiware)**

— Metallic Rose/Mr. Comics —

*Revolution on the
Planet of the Apes* Issue #1

*Revolution on the
Planet of the Apes* Issue #2

*Revolution on the
Planet of the Apes* Issue #3

*Revolution on the
Planet of the Apes* Issue #4

*Revolution on the
Planet of the Apes* Issue #5

*Revolution on the
Planet of the Apes* Issue #6

— Manga Editions —

Bouken Ou Bessatsu

Tengoku Zôkan

— Filmstrips —

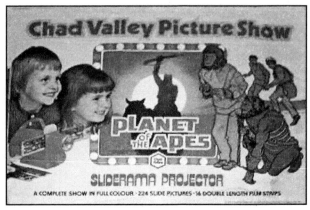

Chad Valley Picture Show
Planet of the Apes Sliderama Projector

— About the Author —

Rich Handley has authored three licensed *Star Wars* fiction titles ("Lady Luck," in Dark Horse Comics' *Star Wars Tales* #3, with Darko Macan; "Lando Calrissian: Idiot's Array" on starwars.com; and "Crimson Bounty," in West End Games' *Star Wars Adventure Journal* #14, with Charlene Newcomb), as well as the story "Grateful, the Dead" in the horror anthology *Breaking Boundaries*. Rich has penned numerous articles for official Lucasfilm publications, including *Star Wars Insider*, *Star Wars Galaxy Collector*, *Star Wars Gamer*, *Star Wars Fact Files* and starwars.com. He served as a writer for *Star Trek Communicator* for several years, and has written for a number of other genre magazines and websites as well, such as *Cinefantastique*, Cinescape.com (now known as Mania. com), *Dungeon/Polyhedron*, *Toons: The Animation Magazine*, *Star Trek Magazine*, *Sci-Fi Invasion!* and *Simian Scrolls*, a British *Planet of the Apes* fanzine. On the flipside of the desk, Rich provided editorial assistance on Realm Press' *Battlestar Galactica* comics, and he has edited and written for a variety of trade publications and newspapers over the past decade. Currently, Rich is a member of the editorial team at *RFID Journal*. This book originated as a website known as The Hasslein Curve.